Lis Leigh was born in Hampstead, and was educated at the North London Collegiate, and Somerville College, Oxford, where she read French and Italian. She worked for five years with the BBC, before going freelance as a producer/director. Her writing career began with the *Sunday Times* and her first novel, *Greed*, was published by Bantam Books in 1992.

Lis Leigh lives in West London.

Also by Lis Leigh

GREED

ENVY

Lis Leigh

BANTAM BOOKS

TORONTO • NEW YORK • LONDON • SYDNEY • AUCKLAND

ENVY

*In this work of fiction, the characters, places
and events are the product of the author's imagination or
they are used entirely fictitiously.*

A BANTAM BOOK: 0 553 02783 3

Simultaneously published in Great Britain by Bantam Press,
a division of Transworld Publishers Ltd

PRINTING HISTORY
Bantam Press edition published 1993
Bantam Books edition published 1993

This book is set in 10/11pt Plantin by
County Typesetters, Margate, Kent

Bantam Books are published by Transworld Publishers Ltd,
61–63 Uxbridge Road, Ealing, London W5 5SA,
in Australia by Transworld Publishers (Australia) Pty Ltd,
15–25 Helles Avenue, Moorebank, NSW 2170,
and in New Zealand by Transworld Publishers (NZ) Ltd,
3 William Pickering Drive, Albany, Auckland.

Printed and bound in Great Britain by
Cox & Wyman Ltd, Reading, Berks.

Dedicated to the memory of Maria Callas

Acknowledgements

First of all, my warmest thanks to the soprano Vivian Tierney and the former tenor, now agent, David Bartleet who gave me generous help at all stages of *Envy*.

I'm also grateful to the many people involved in opera production who gave me their time, in spite of busy schedules. In particular, Jeremy Isaacs and Julio Trebilcock at Covent Garden; Sally Burgess, Kristine Ciesinksi, Keith Cooper, Joseph Evans, Catherine Pope, David Pountney and Phillip Turner at the English National Opera; Girolamo Arrigo, artistic director of Palermo Opera House; Graziella Sciutti, former leading soprano and teacher of singing at the Royal College of Music; Gita Denise, singing teacher; Dr Jonathan Miller, in his role as opera producer; Mel Cooper, writer on opera; Leon Lovett, conductor and opera producer; Jeremy Coleman who manages opera spectacles; Graham Kaye and Kate Hardy, editor and assistant editor of *Opera Now*.

Chapter One

Gloria Wagner could see nothing wrong with staying in a convent even if you weren't a Catholic. It was cheap, they didn't serve bacon for breakfast and her daughter was unlikely to bump into the wrong kind of boy. Friends of hers who'd done Marla's Travel Italian Culture Break (Milan, Florence and Rome in seven days) all said the same. 'Be careful, Gloria. It's not like England.' She suspected they were right.

She jumped with remarkable agility onto a rickety stool, given that she was forty-five, hated exercise, was short-sighted, suffered from tight skirts and was addicted to unsuitable footwear. She reached up and placed the distasteful object back on the rusty nail where it belonged.

'It's crooked.'

Her daughter Anastasia pushed back the coarse sheet and sat up against the iron bars of the bedhead. She took in a great breath of the musty air, with its aroma of unwaxed wood and cracked horsehair plaster, and expelled it with feeling. 'Drunken Jesus meek and mild, Comfort me a little child.'

Gloria hopped off the stool and glared at her daughter. At twenty-two, Anastasia was tall, like her father; she didn't need to stand on a stool. Gloria had asked her to put the thing back on the wall, and Anastasia had said she would and hadn't and was now being cheeky.

'Shush. They might hear.'

'So what? No one speaks English.'

'Suppose they recognize the tune? They might think you're a Catholic. Next thing, they'll make you go to confession and eat those biscuits.'

'I wouldn't mind being a Catholic. Except incense is bad for the throat.'

'Always wanting to be what you're not. I don't know how Larry puts up with it.' Gloria threw her arms outwards in a gesture of despair, and sat down to fulfil the next step in her morning ritual. The bare scrubbed wooden table was covered in pots, jars and other devilish accessories including a folding mirror. When she had transferred some of their contents onto her face, she pondered the stack of lipsticks, selected one in bright pink and drew a shape roughly approximating to her mouth. 'Time you got up. Don't you be late, darling.'

'I know what the time is.' Anastasia continued to watch her mother as she sucked in her lips, rubbed the upper lip against the lower, and grimaced into the mirror. 'That's crooked, too.'

'What do you want? Perfection? I'm only going shopping. There's a boutique in the Galleria with a sale on. Maybe I'll find you a decent skirt.'

'I don't need another skirt.'

Gloria rubbed a smudge from her cheek, smoothed down her blouse, and gave her face a final check. Although her departure seemed imminent, she showed no signs of leaving. 'I can't think why they put that thing on the wall. Who needs to look at a man on a cross all day? It's sick and it's pagan. But nicely done. Are you taking a shower?'

'I might. Does the New Testament send you to hell if you have a bath?'

'How would I know about the New Testament? Ask the nuns. And don't forget to put on a robe.'

Anastasia let out a middle register 'Huh!' which she hoped sounded derisive. 'Why? The only man around here is the Holy Spirit.'

'Stasi, in this life, you never know. A girl on her own has to be prepared for anything.'

'In a convent?'

'There might be something they can't cope with,

10

something wrong with the plumbing. Or the electrics.'

'I'll let you know if there's a rapist around.'

'Stasi! You think that's a joke?'

'You wouldn't know one if you saw one.'

'What a daughter!' Gloria squirted some perfume of doubtful origin behind her ears, on her wrists, and between the swelling of her wire-caged breasts until the air was weighed down with the smell of rotting roses and stale musk. Anastasia winced and drew the sheet up over her mouth.

'Mum? Can I ask you something?'

'Long as it's quick.'

'I've decided. I'm not going to marry Larry Cohen. So do you mind not going on about him?' She could read her mother's thoughts as easily as she could sight-read a music score.

'Who said anything about Larry Cohen?'

Anastasia pulled the sheet over her head. You needed time (and silence, if you could get it) to creep slowly into your character. Today Anastasia Wagner from Muswell Hill would become a pagan priestess. Observe the nuns. Study the crucifix hanging off-centre on the bare wall. Devotion to an object which is not an object. Devoted like a nun. Calm-faced, cool peachy skin, unmarked by bitterness, serene like Sister Livia cutting up bread with pensive deliberation or sweeping the refectory with slow rhythmic movements like a reaper in the cornfield.

'Stasi? Anything the matter?'

There was a grunt from under the sheet.

'You sure? You're not sick? You're not nervous? No need to be nervous. Just do your best.'

Today, she would come face to face with her idol, the one they all talked about with such reverence. She had been accepted by Amelia Busconi, the greatest singing teacher in Italy, who had known every one who mattered – Callas, Tebaldi, Di Stefano, Von Karajan, Visconti, Zeffirelli. She had been asked to prepare 'Casta diva' from Bellini's *Norma*, showcase of bel canto, those long notes you had to pour out like a nightingale. Today had better be wonderful. Come on, honey voice. They said that in Italy. *Voce di miele.* Honey voice.

'It takes time.' Gloria was, as usual, following her own train of thought which she assumed was communicated by osmosis.

'What does, Mum?'

'Falling in love. Believe me. I know. You'll find out one day. And please God you'll learn to recognize what's good for you.'

'He isn't called Larry Cohen.'

'I thought we weren't talking about Larry. Always saying one thing and doing another. Impossible girl.'

Stasi couldn't help thinking about him, since there was no other boy to think about. He was the only person outside the family who knew her well enough (they had been going together for four years) to give her clues about her identity. At twenty-two, you were meant to know who you were. Maybe that took time, too. Larry Cohen had told her she was different, that's why he loved her, not just because she was bright and beautiful. She didn't believe that. When pressed to say what annoyed him about her, he said she could be a bit moody and intense but he didn't mind. Did that mean she didn't smile enough?

'I'm off now. Don't be late. And don't put on too much make-up. Oh, and don't fidget with your hands when you're singing. That's all I have to say.'

'Just go and do your shopping.'

'Don't you tell me what to do.' Gloria paused by the door and gave a glowing smile. 'Now you're not to worry. You'll be wonderful, darling.'

Stasi listened, lying motionless in bed, as the wooden latch clicked shut and her mother's high heels echoed down the stone corridor with purposeful clacks, as though she was catching up on a late order.

Had she forgotten anything? Would she come back? Stasi waited a few more minutes before she opened the window and looked down from on high at the snaking stage below. Across the narrow street, boxed in by the ponderous dark grey buildings of Milan, there were shouts, piercing horns, motorbikes edging past the delivery lorries, old ladies waddling along with oversized bags laden with faggots of bread sticks. And the girls, stepping out with heads held high, skirts swinging below tight little jackets, glancing at the polished young men who acknowledged them briefly as they continued their easy, purposeful strides towards the commercial centre of the city. Her audience.

She took in the early spring air, a pungent mix of petrol fumes, garlic, coffee and a hint of disinfectant released by the van which brushed its way along the gutters cleansing the debris from the small shops whose wares were being set out on the pavement.

A cascade of vowels escaped her throat as she careered up and down the scale, ee-o, ee-o, ee-o, ee-o, flexing her singer's muscles. Relief! Her voice was still there. Every morning, she was surprised. Perhaps God would punish her, and she would open her mouth to silence. The constant fear renewed itself each day, that her mysterious talent would be gone, like a spring which is trickling and bubbling one day, gone the next, suddenly extinguished by the heat of summer. Then who would she be? Yet another hopeful north London girl looking for a house and a husband. Or, worst of all, running a salt-beef sandwich bar in Muswell Hill like her mum.

Every time she sensed the notes pouring out which she would never hear as others heard them, and the rhythmic reverberation in her chest, she was happy. I, Anastasia Wagner, am a singer.

'Here I am!' she sang to the street below, but the unorchestrated bursts of streetsound, merging and detaching themselves in violent competition, were too loud for the passers-by to hear.

Shut the window when you leave. She would shut the window before she left. Make the bed. No. Do it when I get back. Anastasia sat down on the crumpled sheets, half

13

expecting a nun to put her head round the door and ask why she hadn't had breakfast. She hated warm porridge and cold bread, no butter, no jam, thick black coffee weakened with cold milk, but she hated the reproach more.

'Signorina Anastasia. Please. You must have breakfast. Otherwise how can you sing?'

But today there was no knock. Perhaps they had given her up as a lost cause. She had heard them whispering at supper, the charcoal grey-serged nuns with faces smooth and rosy as newly fruited crab-apples who thought she could not understand their language.

'How old, the English girl?'

'Eighteen perhaps?'

'She seems young for her age.'

'But a beautiful face. A little sad, maybe.'

They're lying, she thought. Or they have no standard of beauty. It must be because I don't take half an hour to cover my face like the Italian girls do, bravura performances even to go shopping, grinning at everybody.

'*Amo. Amas. Amat. Amamus. Amatis. Amant.*'

The high-voiced chorus from the convent schoolroom was sounding down the corridor as Anastasia headed for the shower room. Ilove-youlove-heloves. Then followed the halting solo. *Amo. Amas. Amat.* Stasi held up her hair and shuddered under the fierce spray of cold water splashing over her goose-pimpled body onto the stone floor. She would mortify her flesh in deference to the nuns. And today she needed to be glacier cold. For her part. Once dressed, she crept as quietly as she could up the creaking wooden stairs to the tiny music room.

Even though it meant a detour, she took the trundling trolley bus to the Piazza del Duomo and walked along the Galleria Vittorio Emanuele to the Piazza della Scala. She paused to look briefly at the outside of the Teatro alla Scala. It seemed far grander and more beautiful than Covent Garden even though Gloria's guide book, written for British cognoscenti who were snooty about architecture, sneered at its insignificance. Behind that darkened window, she suspected, was one of the star dressing rooms. If the cast was in rehearsal, she might hear a great singer easing into her voice.

A caped policeman approached and eyed her indulgently. 'You waiting for someone, signorina?'

'My boyfriend,' she snapped.

'He shouldn't keep a beautiful young lady waiting.'

Anastasia scowled, buttoned up her coat tight round her neck and changed to a brisker pace. She resented the carabiniere's assumption that she would be drawn into conversation, although she had been in Milan long enough, a week, to realize that anything in Italy could be excused in the name of love. *Amo. Amas. Amat.* Even the nuns. *L'amore. L'amore.* Blasted out in grating sharpness from a million inadequate speakers.

She walked up Via Manzoni towards Signora Busconi's apartment in Via delle Stelle, neck stretched, head tilted so she could look over the heads of the passers-by, taking care to avoid the eyes of those who were her equal in height. She had been taught never to look at anyone she didn't know. Her legs felt out of control. Sometimes her stride was firm, sometimes she fell into the small steps she had cultivated to match Gloria's pace. This was the first time she had walked the streets of Milan without her mother at her side. Gloria, who was five inches shorter than Anastasia, walked as though she had been born and bred into high heels, the way some people were born and bred into money. The worst thing Stasi could imagine was that when she was old, forty say, she would be a carbon copy of her mother.

Via delle Stelle, number six. Street of the Stars. A lucky street, so it should be a lucky day. Stasi avoided looking at number thirteen and was elated when a wiry-furred, skinny black cat ran in front of her. Even if you weren't meant to believe in omens, you noticed. She was wearing blue for optimism, a dark blue pleated skirt and a pale

15

blue silk shirt which Gloria had insisted on ironing for her – how could you trust a nun with silk?

'Anastasia Wagner.'

'Third floor,' replied the intercom in accented English, emphasizing the explosive 'th'. The heavy wooden door buzzed open, giving way to a marble entrance hall, on one side a heavy, gilded mirror, on the other a portrait of a woman in a négligé sitting at a dressing table staring at her wan face in the mirror. Stasi smiled, proud of having recognized Amelita Galli-Curci, prima donna from Milan, legendary Violetta in *La Traviata*.

Signora Busconi, seated behind a gilt-edged walnut table in a high-backed, elaborately carved chair, rose majestically to greet her. She was typically Italian, just as Stasi would have imagined her, with jet black hair pulled tightly away from her broad, well-shaped forehead, a strong nose, and a generous mouth. Like Sophia Loren, when she wasn't smiling, she looked intensely serious, almost severe, her head poised over a high-necked blouse fastened with a cameo brooch.

She clasped Stasi's hand, studying her face, then her figure, then her face again. Pupils from abroad came on the recommendation of the few teachers she respected and trusted, and would be preceded by a tape and a photograph.

'Your picture does not do you justice. Do sit over there.'

Stasi joined four girls, sitting bolt upright in a row. One was Japanese. Another one could be English. Two looked Spanish or Italian. Coffee was brought in by an elderly grey-haired woman who disappeared once she had placed the tray gingerly down on the desk.

One girl got up and started pouring out the coffee. 'How do you like it?' The voice was Australian. 'Cream, milk or straight?'

'I am expecting another one.' Signora Busconi held up a sheet of paper in front of her. Her hands were wrinkled. They seemed older than her handsome, broad-boned face. 'Carla is not here. No matter. We will continue.'

They sat on delicate needlepointed chairs with cabriole legs balancing the tiny china cups on their knees, dwarfed by the imposing room. Stasi was overwhelmed by the splendour; it was like having a private invitation to a duke's palace. She had never seen such a massive chandelier, its glass shading from pink to purple; the pillared red fireplace looked like marble, and the silvery bronze brocade curtains tied back in great swathes gleamed like silk. A small Biedermayer grand piano stood in the corner, in front of a flowered tapestry. The antiques must have cost a fortune. There were huge dark oil paintings in heavy gold frames, Wagnerian landscapes and portraits of Amelia Busconi at the height of her powers in various theatrical poses.

One of the cups was rattling on its saucer, betraying a shaking hand. However fine your voice, if you were unable to control your nerves you would never perform on stage. Anastasia's pulse was speeding but she remained still. Her sense of awe at being in the presence of the great teacher had, for the moment, quelled her anxiety.

Signora Busconi went over to the piano, played a chord and sang an arpeggio which swelled in volume and tailed away to a whisper.

'Now, ladies. Can you tell me in which key I was singing?'

'B major,' replied Anastasia instantly.

'I'd say A.' The Australian.

'Other suggestions?'

The other girls looked at one another, not daring or unable to reply.

'It is not necessary to have perfect pitch, but it is helpful. Now you can all sing. As I did it. Keiko, you begin. One . . . two . . . three . . .'

Anastasia listened intently to each voice. Might there be someone better than she? As yet, it was difficult to tell. Until now she had had no fear about excelling. In the small world of the music school where she had studied for four years, they would not forget her. She alone in her year had

17

given a professional concert recital, had received prizes, a scholarship to go to Italy. The other students were sick of hearing her name, then came to accept that she was outstanding, that she possessed a rare ability which would lift her far above them, that they must be proud of her. Now that she was in Milan, she would have to make an impression all over again. And the best singers in the world still came to Italy to study.

There was a call for Maestra Busconi. The maid put her head round the door and whispered. Carla Livorno would be late. Her fiancé was ill and she had to see him, but she couldn't possibly miss her lesson. Anastasia was unable to catch the dialect, but she recognized the name. Could Carla Livorno possibly be related to the legendary opera conductor Paolo Livorno?

The Tangenziale encircling Milan was crowded, even in the afternoon, the vapours emitted by determined drivers blasting into Carla's face as she headed north-east towards Bergamo. She drew up her scarf over her mouth. Everything was bad for the throat, especially the virulent fumes from the ring road, but she drove with the roof down, tipping her head back to receive the rush of wind streaming over her. Pursing her lips as she sucked at a mentholated lozenge, she breathed shallow and imagined the pure air of the mountains. There would not be time to stroll along the shore of Lake Iseo, as she often did to escape the dryness of Milan. Still, opera singers had to withstand the dust of the stage; she was toughening up her larynx for her debut. Pa had decided she was virtually ready. About time. All those lessons were getting tedious.

Carla turned off the autostrada before Bergamo, speeding along a winding country road until she reached the small village of Roccagrande. As her red Alfa Romeo veered round the square, past the tables set outside the café, the old men looked up and sucked in their lips, nodding ominously to one another as she disappeared down the private road which led to the Villa degli Spiriti.

After a couple of kilometres, Carla suddenly halted in front of the great wrought iron gates embellished with two gilded crests, one on either side. As she grappled with the unwieldy locks which bent her carefully manicured nails, she cursed, then glanced at the villa in front of her. With the spring sun firing the faded rooftiles, the stark rectangular outline looked more pleasing. What a difference it would make if the outside was painted in a cheerful colour, even a few rose-beds would make it more homey, she thought, as she drove up the cyprus-lined drive. After all, you could still tell it was sixteenth century and inspired by Palladio; it wasn't as though she wanted to tear it down and build something else. He might agree to new locks on the gate.

He would be up again now, having read *Le Monde* – Italian newspapers were too insular, he complained – attended to his correspondence, supervised the restoration of some minor detail – there was always something in the villa or its grounds which he needed to restore – taken a light lunch in company with a young Englishman from Finarte or Christie's in Via Borgogna, finished his siesta, had his massage and shower and changed his shirt. The window would be open. He would be listening for her footsteps.

The Marchese Maurizio Gerolamo Pietro della Robbia had reduced his staff to three, but done nothing to change a routine which had been developed and perfected several years before Carla was born. At six o'clock precisely the butler-come-secretary would serve Invergillen whisky with iced water, and stuffed olives in a silver bowl. Such a pronounced regimen made it easier. Unlike many Italians, including Carla, he understood about time. She could come to him for an hour, and an hour it would be – he would not expect her to forgo her singing lesson.

They would converse in Italian. Carla would use the intimate 'tu' even though his late wife would never have dreamed of doing so. When she lapsed into English, or rather American, her second language, he winced. The marchese spoke precisely articulated English which he had learned at Harrow, but it bore no relation to this uncouth reminder of the debasement of Shakespeare. The American invasion of language, he felt, was more wounding in the long term to European civilization than their clumsy military attempts to bring democracy to the ungovernable or their passionate devotion to computers.

From an upper window, whose shape was almost hidden by the half-drawn thick tapestry curtains hanging in equal folds, he watched her as she leapt lightly up the steps like one of his Burmese cats, each movement of her body melting into the next, and he longed for her as he longed for everything beautiful. Sometimes he had disturbing thoughts. He dreamed of keeping her locked up in his favourite mirrored salon, so that he could possess her beauty and see it reflected in a thousand facets. Whenever he passed the portrait of his wife, he asked her forgiveness. Had she survived the sudden assault of cancer, she would have been over sixty by now. He had been spared the tragedy of watching her decline into the unseemly withering of age.

'My treasure. How is my little songbird?'

Carla leaned back on the cushions of the chaise-longue, and he grasped one of her heels, then the other, slowly edging off the tight-fitting boots. He kissed her black-stockinged feet, the Caravaggio feet he adored.

'Always Verdi, Verdi, Verdi. But guess what? It's Bellini this time. *Norma*. I'm taking a new class. Pa thinks my repertoire needs extending. I ought to go through the blasted piece before I leave.'

'Really? Of course, if you feel it's necessary.' There was a hint of disappointment in his voice. 'You work so hard, my darling.'

'Never mind. There isn't time and it won't make any difference.'

'Are you sure?'

Carla swung her legs round and curled up beside him,

resting her head in his lap. 'As long as you give me a little help, darling. My throat is so dry.'

He bent his head down, and kissed her without parting his mouth, his lips soft and cool as a cherry on a bed of ice.

'You must make sure I don't sound like your yawling cats. I need you for my *bella voce, Mauro mio*.'

Carla stroked his chiselled beard, and glanced at her watch. She was always aware of time, even if she ignored its demands. Then she slid to the floor, and he kissed her hands, drawing them down his body, waiting for her to release the small buttons, holding his breath as the opening grew a little wider, a little wider.

Would it? Would it not? Would his anticipation fire his desire? How long should he wait before acknowledging the humiliation of failure? With closed eyes, he abandoned himself to Carla's touch. And then his thin aristocratic lips parted and he smiled.

If she only knew the gratitude he felt, that she was able to arouse the exquisite stirring of lust, bring back memories of the heated blood of youth, memories of agility as the smooth member swelled, enlarged, lifted its head to mock the rest of his flesh, subsiding into wrinkled folds over his belly and his neck, stretching taut over his wasting limbs. He prayed the hardness would remain, as her tongue nuzzled down its length. Control. If only control had remained to him. 'No. No. Disgraceful! Damn!'

'You are such a man, my darling.'

Carla's mouth and chin were wet, as though she had been glazed with the uncooked white of an egg, and he gently wiped them dry.

'Was there enough for you? You are not disappointed?'

'How could I be? It is the most precious gift for a singer. The best lubrication in the world.'

'One day when we are married I will do it properly.'

'Then it will be wasted. Think of my voice!' Carla went over to a mirror, dusted powder over her face and fluffed up her flattened curls.

'Stay a little.'

'My darling, you know I want to. But I will be late. I'm late now. Signora Busconi will be cross and give me bad marks.'

'I want you to choose what you would like in your room. There is to be a sale at the Villa Frescobaldi next week. Perhaps there will be something to your liking.'

'We'll go together, then.'

'I was thinking, if it suits you, that July might be an appropriate month.'

'July?'

'For the wedding. Does that leave enough time for the preparations? I don't know how much time one needs for such things. I leave it to you, I am in your hands. Only tell me when it suits you.'

'Let's talk about it later. I must rush.'

The marchese embraced Carla, then drew back, his hands on her shoulders. 'Sweet girl, you are quite sure? I don't want you to feel that I am forcing anything. But sometimes I fear.'

'Fear? What is there to fear?'

'That you will change your mind.'

'What a ridiculous idea. You should know me better.'

Anastasia was mid-stream, the arpeggio notes flowing out liquid and pure, just as she wanted them, when there was a strident buzz from outside the door, and she stopped abruptly. 'Again,' barked Signora Busconi. 'A performer must ignore everything.'

The phrase was repeated, but she stopped again, flexing her shoulders, bending down from the waist, trying to shake out the constricting muscles. 'It's not right. I can't help it. I can't sing if I'm tense.'

Her fellow pupils glanced at one another as though to say 'One of those': the temperamental ones who took up time in class. There was an uneasy silence, and then a determined rap on the door followed by a sing-song voice: '*C'è una signorina la giù.*'

"Falla entrare.' Signora Busconi smoothed down her silky, pale cream skirt and returned to her desk. 'Carla has decided to come,' she said, smiling indulgently. Anastasia noticed her perfectly even teeth, the soft mobile face which could adapt itself to the pertness of a servant girl or the hauteur of a queen with equal ease.

What an entrance! A flurried appearance like Marilyn Monroe arriving late on the set, a pleading look, begging for love and forgiveness. The long sable coat open, a silk scarf draped perfectly round her neck, a lemon-yellow dress contoured tightly to her figure, fine suede boots hugging her legs, and a large crocodile bag. How could this newcomer have arrived so unforgettably, if immodestly, on the first day of class, wearing clothes which came straight from this season's collections which Stasi had ogled in all their inaccessible glory along the Via Montenapoleone where even the air was perfumed with Armani? As Carla tripped into the room, tossing her curls back, makeup perfectly applied, Anastasia was convinced that every detail had been worked on for days. She had come in as though greeting her crowd of admirers at the stage door. Stasi could not ignore her; she would try not to hate her. Perhaps her voice would let her down.

'*Scusi, scusi, Signora Busconi. La prego di scusarmi. Questa mattina, una cosa terribile, non posso dirLe . . .*' She draped her coat across a chair and sat with crossed legs and an expression of disconsolate sorrow on her impossibly pretty face. At least Stasi was taller than she was.

'This is Carla Livorno, ladies. Next time, she will arrive on time.'

'*Ma certo, certo.*'

'Carla, in this class we speak English. We have Anastasia from England, Grace from Australia, Keiko from Japan, and Maria and Sofia from Italy.'

Carla turned to the girls and responded with a wide friendly smile and a heavy New York accent. 'Hey, that's great. Pleased to meet you all. But we sing in Italian, OK?'

Signora Busconi nodded regally.

Anastasia shut herself off in her own world, seeing neither the heavily curtained room nor the animated gestures of Signora Busconi, nor the faces of the other girls alongside her. Eyes closed, she listened to Carla. A good voice, but she had neither Stasi's strength nor her own peculiar character. Good, like the others. Relieved, Anastasia could concentrate on herself. No one else mattered.

The vocal exercises were over, and a lean, bespectacled man with a mop of red hair came quietly into the room, briefly acknowledged Signora Busconi and sat at the grand piano, his small, marble-white hands modestly clasped on his lap. The accompanist needed no music. He could no sooner have forgotten the lilting support of 'Casta diva' from Bellini's *Norma* than the face of his own mother.

'Casta diva', the classic bel canto aria, represented one of the ultimate tests of young sopranos. They all sang it, Grace, Keiko, Maria and Sofia, but Keiko was the best so far. A Japanese Norma? It was hard for Anastasia not to be critical, not to analyse each note, wondering whether her way was better or inferior. For several minutes, she had forgotten Carla, then she noticed her turning up her wrist to examine a tiny bejewelled watch. Everyone was so still, even this small movement had a dramatic impact.

'Carla will sing for us now.'

Carla looked up, opened wide her questioning eyes, which Stasi noticed were softly greenish, the colour of a weeping willow tree on a misty morning. As a singer, you watched mouths, throats, not eyes. With Carla, you watched every feature. Stasi's gaze was riveted to her face, her delicate ears emphasized by a cluster of tiny emeralds, her round-hipped, graceful full-breasted figure, as she moved to the space between Signora Busconi's desk and the row of singers.

She was hardly note perfect. She used too much portamento, trailing one note towards another, the vulgar signal of the exhibitionist, but Signora Busconi ignored it, to Stasi's surprise. Any good teacher should have stopped her. Was Signora Busconi as good as they said?

'Listen, Carla. Norma is a Druid priestess who has betrayed her calling. Not only has she given body and soul to a man and borne him two children, but this man is a Roman. The enemy of her people. She has betrayed her country, her divinity and herself. She is praying to the goddess of chastity. Yet you sing her like La Cicciolina who takes a new lover every week.'

Grace gave a throaty laugh, Keiko looked puzzled, and the others were apparently unaware of the Italian call-girl turned representative of the people who was more familiar than the constantly changing prime ministers.

'I want purity, simplicity and passion. Try again. The opening bar.'

Carla began again, deciding to clasp her hands in front of her instead of describing random balletic patterns around her head. Signora Busconi listened with rapt concentration, a wrinkled trace on her smooth forehead. Halfway through she gestured to the accompanist to stop.

'I know. I know, signora. More work. I promise. But this part, it's so hard. It's not my kind of role. I mean, no kidding, I'm not a dramatic coloratura.'

'You are certainly dramatic, *figlia mia*. Come. Let's try again.'

They all laughed, and Carla took what Stasi would have interpreted as an insult with a toss of the head and an expression of comic regret. The tension began to dissipate.

Later, as they sat drinking *limonata* in the bar on the corner, they heard that Carla's father was a conductor, her sister becoming known as a pianist, her grandfather a composer, related to Rossini. Just luck.

'How come the American accent?' asked Grace.

'Ma comes from New York. Italian origin with a voice like a cab driver. Boy, was she some mezzo when she was young.'

Carla regarded her heritage with indifference. Although she had grown up in the privileged protection of the musical aristocracy, she did not believe that it would make a turkey into a skylark. 'You got talent, you work. That's what counts.' Already she was acting as leader of the group, everyone allowing her to talk first.

Stasi was sure that Carla already disliked her. She was talking to the others, but had asked her nothing. By now, Stasi had grown used to the glances of admiration mixed with envy. Anyone would have felt a pang of resentment. When it was her turn to sing, Signora Busconi had listened without interruption, whispering almost to herself, 'Brava. Bravissima.' Afterwards Carla had clapped, and the others had joined in. Students never clapped one another. Was Carla mocking her? Even if it had been sincere, Stasi would have been embarrassed. She did not want acknowledgement until she was ready to sing on stage.

'Your family musical?'

Stasi was staring through the steamy glass windows of the bar, where the sudden spring shower was beginning to stream down in rivulets.

'Anastasia, right?' Carla leaned across the table, and lightly tapped her hand.

'Me?'

'With a voice like yours, I guess you don't care. We're all wildly jealous.'

'I sang the end too loud. I should have made it more piano.'

'Who's complaining? Don't you worry. We're all friends. All that stuff about singers hating one another is a load of crap. If people want to invent stories about us, fantastic. In Italy there's room for you and me and all of us. That's what's so great.' Carla waved at the waiter who was shuffling through his bills, daring anyone to disturb him. *'Eh! Ancora sei limonate!'*

'By the way, I'm Stasi. Except on my passport.'

'When your name's up top on La Scala posters, believe me you'll be Anastasia. Wish I had a name that long. And Wagner! You come from a German family? Don't tell me you're related?'

'Wag-ner. Not Varg-ner. No connection. Absolutely none. I'm not related to anyone.'

'Best way to be.'

At first, Anastasia found herself wishing that she had a fur coat trailing from her chair onto the floor, one fine leather purse for coins, another for credit cards, another for notes and enough confidence for the entire Wagner family. But by the time they said goodbye, shaking hands formally and embracing one another on the cheek in the Italian fashion, she had thrown off her distrust and begun to feel easy in Carla's company, even laughing at her frank exuberance. Carla made you feel that you could jump through a plate-glass window and emerge unharmed.

She loved her teacher. She would make friends. Soon, her mother would go back to England. The sun was warming her back as she looked up into the cloudless sky, wondering whether she would walk in the gardens of the Villa Reale or revisit the Brera gallery. Then she became aware of a bright red open-topped Alfa Romeo which had slowed down and was drawing up beside her, cars honking and hooting on all sides.

'Stasi!'

It took her a second to recognize Carla, dark glasses masking most of her face, showing only a delicate nose, a small, determined chin and freshly glossed lips. As she jumped out (she could have stayed in the car) she showed a length of black-stockinged leg which took hands off horns and silenced the noise.

'Where you going?'

'I was thinking maybe I'd visit the Villa Reale.'

'Give you a lift.'

It was out of Carla's way, and she was already late for an appointment, but she could boast of her new friend. English, from London, so natural, unaffected, shy, the kind who flung on the first thing in her wardrobe and still looked ravishing. She would describe her meticulously, filling out her portrait with a few extra details culled from her study of profiles in British *Vogue*, as she sipped Earl

Grey tea in the Piazza Signoria. Stasi did not know that even without a Barbour jacket and a tweed skirt she was about to become an object of veneration and awe to the smart young Milanese.

'Staying in a convent? You're a Catholic? You mean, they have Catholics in England?'

Stasi was wondering where Carla had learned to veer round corners and manoeuvre through the narrow backstreets of Milan whilst talking, observing, waving occasionally to someone she knew, and fast-footing the clutch and accelerator in high-heeled boots. 'Of course we have Catholics. But I'm not. Mum thinks it's good for discipline.'

'Come on. Good for keeping boys out of your pants! You must get one of these.' Carla took one hand off the steering wheel and pointed a long manicured finger which was encircled by a platinum ring made conspicuous by a glinting stone of hefty size.

'I don't seem to be the kind who attracts jewellery. Not that I mind.' She could feel an embarrassed blush on her cheeks. Larry Cohen had wanted to buy her an engagement ring, but she had refused. 'I don't get it from boys I like, anyhow.'

'Boys don't give diamonds. We'd better find you a real guy. You fancy Italian men?'

Anastasia laughed. 'Never met any.'

'I met an Englishman once. He was cute, but he didn't kiss me till the fifth date. Is that smart over there?' The car stopped abruptly. 'The villa's in there. Have fun.'

'I hope you won't be too late, Carla. Thanks a million.'

'Be good to the nuns!' Carla gave her a farewell embrace, throwing an arm round her neck, an abandoned kiss on both cheeks, warm lips pressed against hers. And she hardly knew her.

Chapter Two

Gloria Wagner was packing. With every major addition to the suitcase, she summoned Stasi to jump up and down to reduce the swelling, then she kneeled down to peer at the metal catches. The recent additions to the Wagner heritage included chipped china shepherdesses and small cracked pots and jars she was convinced were Meissen or Delft, if only the identity mark hadn't been rubbed off. There was no more room for the remaining gourmet luxuries, which would have to be crammed into a series of plastic bags. She was preparing to cross the Channel like a fleeing refugee who might have to last out a world war, or at least a period of prolonged famine.

'Why all this tissue paper? You can iron everything when you get home.'

'If the train crashes, you think I want them to find Mrs Wagner's suitcase not packed nicely? I'm always saying, if you do something, do it properly.'

'Trains don't crash, Mum.'

'Listen. In Italy, everything crashes. Even trains. Who knows, the ferry might sink.'

There was a moral pall hanging over the room. It had nothing to do with the crooked crucifix, which Gloria had finally taken for granted as she took for granted the mezuzah hanging over her front door. The intense atmosphere weighed on Stasi's stomach as though she had given in and had a second bowlful of Gloria's matzo balls. Family arrivals and departures were invested with a heart-searching seriousness normally associated with weddings and funerals.

'Don't forget this.' She started to wrap a silver-framed

29

photograph in what remained of the tissue paper.

'I'm not taking it. I want you to have it while I'm gone. Here. Take it. You must have a picture of your father.'

'Suppose I lost it or it got broken? You'd never talk to me again. Mum, take it home.'

Then came the moment Stasi had anticipated.

'Every time I look at it, he looks different. I can almost hear him talking. Sam had such a wonderful way of putting things, he should have been a rabbi instead of writing for the *Financial Times*. He made you feel a better person. And I never met another journalist who made you feel a better person. You can't imagine how proud he'd have been. He adored you, Anastasia. If only . . . I know I mustn't.' Gloria sniffed as she unpacked one bag and transferred its contents to another. 'You can keep these toilet rolls. I won't need them.'

'Mum, don't get upset. You've been brilliant. For God's sake. If you hadn't made me practise, I wouldn't be here.'

'And you can keep the Fly-Go,' Gloria added. Then she sniffed again. 'All I've ever been is second best. You think I don't know how you miss your father?'

'I hardly remember him.'

'No one should have to be father and mother on their own. In my women's group they said you could. Don't you believe it. Women aren't cut out for it, being on their own. Gloria Wagner. Can't even change a plug without looking up how to do it. I should have had an education.'

'You can cook.'

'Everyone can cook. Mind you eat well. Lots of salads and fish, only well-cooked meat. Not too many sweets. You want me to send you something? When you're working hard, you forget. It's no trouble.'

Stasi watched her face brighten and knew she was unable to say no. 'Some chopped liver.'

'And maybe some strudel. Yes?'

The last bags were sellotaped together and there was still an hour before the taxi would arrive to take Gloria to the station. She never went by air. How could she, when Sam Wagner had died in a plane crash?

'Come over here and sit on the bed. You think the taxi will be on time? I want to have a talk.' Gloria opened her imitation Gucci Gladstone bag and pulled out a small, flat box, gift-wrapped with a ribbon rosette, which she placed tantalizingly on her lap. She pushed back Stasi's long hair behind her ears and examined her face. 'You don't need make-up. All that hair, I can't see you.'

'You keep saying that.'

'And you keep ignoring me.'

'I listen.'

'What good is that? I can see you how you look, you can't. Just because all those Italian girls plaster themselves.'

'You wear it.'

'I'm a widow, darling. I'm entitled. And anyway, I've got lines.'

'What you mean is, the boys might think I'm an easy lay. I'm not a child any more. I can look after myself. And what's so wrong with going to bed with someone? You did, when you were young. Before you met Dad, you had tons of boyfriends. And slept with them all.'

'And where did that get me? In bed with cystitis, that got me.'

'You had a good time.'

'When you're young, you think fooling around and not being bored is having a good time. Anything rather than work. I should have gone to university, like Sam. Making salt-beef sandwiches isn't a career.'

'Mum, please don't start.'

'You made me lose my train of thought.'

Now there was less than an hour to go. Go. Go. Go. Gloria's departure was operatic, one long, interminable death scene. It reminded Stasi of Massenet's *Werther*. After he had shot himself – for impossible love, why else? – the poor tenor had to go on singing for half an hour before he could leave for another world.

31

'I'm talking. You listening? I believe in you. All you've got to do is your best. I won't grieve if you don't get to the top. Sometimes the third in class has a better life. You can always be a singing teacher, it's a good career.'

Stasi got up from the bed and stood by the window, biting her lip.

'Did I say anything wrong? All right, I won't speak. Have it your own way. But don't do anything stupid. And write. Even a postcard. It's time I said goodbye to the nuns. Give me a hand.' As Gloria jumped to her feet, the beribboned package fell to the floor. 'This is for you, darling. For when I'm gone. Some spare tights. For best, sixty denier. You might need them.'

She embraced her daughter, and they both staggered down the stone steps. Gloria hugged the nuns she met in her path, giving each a packet of bonbons, Sister Teresa and Sister Angelica and Sister Maria, exhorting them to keep an eye on her precious girl. With hands clasped, they nodded with smiling eyes even though they did not understand one word.

'Have you got the seasickness pills?'

Gloria put her head out of the taxi window. 'In my bag.'

The taxi driver pulled away, but she continued waving and blowing kisses, only withdrawing her arm from the window when they turned the corner.

The room looked as though it was ready for the next occupant. Now it was almost bare, nothing of the Wagners visible except for Stasi's battered felt childhood rabbit with grubby pink threadbare ears, sitting on her pillow, some scores on the wooden table by her bed, and the reminder of her father, trapped in a silver frame like a faded wedding carnation.

There was a green sea (it must have been blue once) up to his knees, Gloria's arm was round his waist, and he was holding up a child over her head, like a flying fish. They were both laughing. Stasi was three. However often she had looked at his face, it told her nothing. She could recall his stubbly chin, long hair smelling of scented tobacco, and being held up miles in the air, looking at the ground far below her.

She slid the photograph out of its frame, now it was hers to guard, and turned it over. Gloria's familiar, rounded writing. 'Sam, Me and Stasi. Bognor Regis. Happiness.'

At that moment, Stasi promised herself never to be nostalgic, never to rest her hopes on one man, never to listen to her mother. She would be whatever she felt herself to be, however repugnant – and never would she allow herself to answer an advertisement for a singing teacher.

For the first time in her life, she would be able to walk down the street without saying where she was going, to meet whomsoever took her fancy, to go out without an umbrella, to put on her best shoes just to buy some stamps, to eat a chocolate bar whenever she felt like it, to put on yesterday's underwear, to throw her clothes on the floor, to leave her hair unkempt, to play her opera tapes at full blast, to leave the basin dirty, to lie in bed past nine o'clock . . .

When Stasi had mentally ticked off the obvious benefits of freedom, she remembered that the most important had been left until last. Now, at last, she could look straight into the eyes of strangers. She might even jump into bed with a wildly desirable man and leave before morning. Right this minute, she would take herself off to the poky little bar opposite the convent where entry had been forbidden ('You can see a mile off there's no hygiene. You want to get poisoned?'). As she crossed the road, weaving carelessly through the traffic, she was already rehearsing her order. A plate of shrimps, please. And then a toasted ham sandwich. And a sugary bun with custard inside.

In class that day, her shoulders were free, her larynx obeyed her, the notes which had slipped out of control fell into place. There were times when it was like that, and times when, however hard you practised, you still made the same mistakes. Young singers were unpredictable. It was impossible to tell which one was favoured by Signora

Busconi. Grace was standing by the piano, in a long, baggy cardigan, singing staccato notes up and down the scale.

'Oh ah oh ah oh ah oh ah.'

'Lighter, lighter.'

Grace stopped and folded her arms. 'If I do it like that, no one will hear me.'

They were all listening.

'Lightness is not smallness. There is a difference.'

'Usually I can hear Grace down the street,' said Carla.

'That's only because you're late.'

Signora Busconi clapped her hands. 'Who's going to sing the Cimarosa?'

It was like being in school, when you knew the answer but didn't put your hand up. Signora Busconi glanced at Stasi, nodded at her and then pointed to Keiko.

'You'd like to?'

Suddenly Carla got up from the floor. She said it made her feel more relaxed than sitting on a chair. 'Listen, maestra. I've been slogging my guts out with this goddamned piece. I've got to leave early. Couldn't I do it now, please?'

Keiko looked down and folded her hands in her lap, and Maria whispered to Sofia, *'Com'è maleducata!'*

'Shall I go down the street and listen?' said Grace, with a grin.

Signora Busconi looked from one to the other. 'Keiko first. Then Carla. Then Sofia and Maria.' She smiled at Stasi. 'Today, Anastasia, you will listen.'

She made a few comments to Keiko. Everything she did was well-paced, the phrases well-turned. Stasi could see her, in a few years' time, singing *Madam Butterfly*. They would like her, she would never do anything ugly, but would they hurl flowers on the stage? That was the moment Stasi dreamed of, when flowers rained down and you stood there clasping great bouquets. When you knew they loved you.

It was different with Carla. With a girl like that, anything could happen. Signora Busconi was giving her a hard time, telling her not to be lazy, to work her diaphragm. When she had finished vocalizing, Carla undid the buttons of her jacket and pushed it back with a sigh of relief. 'It's too tight. Mind if I sing like this?'

'Like the camisole,' remarked Grace, eyeing the delicate black lace which showed the outline of Carla's nipples.

Signora Busconi made no comment, but gestured to her pianist and Carla began to attack 'Perdonate, signor mio'. Before she had finished, she had collapsed into giggles. 'I couldn't make the high one. Sorry, sorry.'

'My dear, you are not racing in the Palio at Siena. Too fast, too fast. When you go to jump, you must be steady. And keep the rhythm, you are making too much rubato. Listen.' She sang a few notes, crystal clear.

'I get it. I get it. But those high ones are killers.'

'Sometimes I wonder if maybe you would be happier singing mezzo. Perhaps we are pushing too much.'

Carla stopped buttoning up her jacket, her mouth dropping open. 'Please, signora. I sing soprano. I'm a soprano. Ma's the mezzo. Was mezzo till she stopped singing. Can I go now?'

After she had left, Stasi began to regret her absence. However much the class grumbled behind her back about her timekeeping, she made everyone sit bolt upright, in case they might be taken by surprise or made to seem a fool. Signora Busconi took Stasi's arm and waited until they were alone. 'You were cross? Because you didn't sing today?'

'A little.'

'Then you should say, Anastasia. In Italy, it's allowed.'

'It would have been selfish, signora.'

She gave Stasi a warm smile, then shrugged. 'Like Keiko, you must be a little more *egoista*. Would you like to have private lessons with me? Sometimes we must fight, and I don't think you will do this in front of the others.'

Stasi looked down at her scuffed shoes and wondered how she could avoid seeming ungrateful. Little remained of her scholarship money after she had paid for half-board at the convent and the teaching fees. If it hadn't been for Uncle Monty's 'pocket money for extras' she would have been poorer than the nuns. 'Of course I'd like private lessons, signora. It would be fantastic. But . . .'

'But what?'

'I can't. I can't ask my family for more money.'

'Come with me. We'll talk. And I'll cook you something.'

Stasi followed her into a small kitchen with spotless, bare surfaces, as though no activity took place there. The only time she had seen Gloria's kitchen at home in such a pristine state was just before the annual visit of the VAT man.

'Maria hates me cooking,' Signora Busconi remarked as she pulled a bag of onions from the fridge. 'Tomorrow she'll spend an hour washing down the kitchen.'

Before she began to peel and chop the vegetables, she reached for a perfectly pressed white apron. It was then that Stasi realized that some people had maids, not cleaners, an idea she had never considered.

'Now I will cry,' said Signora Busconi, dividing an onion into neat sections. Then she stopped, reached for a tea-towel and dabbed her eyes. 'Are my eyes black like a boxer's?'

Stasi grinned and shook her head.

'I do this now, only now. Once I was too vain. Before my husband came home, I used to remake my face, change my clothes. Imagine! We had a cook then. I didn't even know how to cook pasta.'

'What was he like, your husband?' asked Stasi tentatively, watching her tossing the pile of neatly chopped onion into a pan of sizzling oil.

'Very serious, very strict and very noble. For a politician in Italy, that is a disaster. He was killed when he was only forty-eight. I couldn't sing any longer.' Catching sight of Stasi's look of horror, she quickly continued, 'But that love will never go. And he is still remembered. And I have my wonderful pupils. What about you, Anastasia? Do you have a special young man?'

Stasi made a rueful face. 'Only in my head. He'd have to be a saint to put up with me. Anyway, I'm not ready yet. Too much to do.'

Dipping her finger quickly in the bubbling liquid, Signora Busconi licked it, and wiped it down her apron. 'Do you know what is best for the beautiful voice, apart from my bolognese sauce? To make love. Then the throat opens out, the eyes sparkle, your movements are graceful. *Bellissima*.'

She left the sauce simmering, sending out a warm aroma of garlic and herbs, and led Stasi into a small dining room where a lace-covered table was already laid for two. When she had lit the candles, she began to pour out some dark red wine from a decanter into a glass goblet.

'Just a little,' began Stasi, but she went on pouring.

'You don't like wine? This is a good one.'

'Oh, yes I do, but we don't have it at home, hardly ever. Mum makes one bottle last for months.'

They raised their glasses.

'I will toast your first performance on an Italian stage,' said Signora Busconi.

Stasi gulped, and quickly put down her glass. 'You think I'm ready? God, the very idea. Suppose I was awful?'

Her shoulders suddenly went tense, but Signora Busconi ignored it. English girls all had this problem, in her experience, and she put it down to the cold climate and the unfortunate gloomy temperament with which they were afflicted. Sun and wine, she thought, were better remedies than the curious medicines they stuffed down their throats.

'Tell me, have you sung the part of Micaela in England?'

'Oh, yes,' replied Stasi. 'At opera school, that is. I know most of it.'

'My friend Sandro Passattella, a very well-esteemed producer, telephoned today. His Micaela has just cancelled, and he is looking for someone urgently. Soon he will begin rehearsing *Carmen*, a summer production in Fiesole. Would you like me to put forward your name? If we work hard together and prepare well, there might be a chance.'

Stasi took a deep breath, and clasped her hands together. Already she could see her first entrance. 'When can we start? Which day should I come? Tomorrow? But I'll still come to class?'

'Yes, yes. Let me go and find my diary.'

Stasi did not remember finishing her meal, or draining her wineglass. She was summoning up the part. Now she could change her interpretation, and make Micaela less like a well-behaved English miss, more like a passionate, religious girl from a Spanish village. Why did a virgin have to be prim, she wondered? When she was preparing to leave, Signora Busconi came up to her and held out her coat, which she had forgotten.

'We will do a marvellous audition for Maestro Passattella. But don't be disappointed if he turns you down. It will have nothing to do with your singing.'

'You mean, if he doesn't fancy me?' Stasi replied, looking hurt. 'I wish I had fair hair and blue eyes. Then I'd be in with a chance.'

'Nonsense, my dear. But this is Italy. There are always political considerations, even with Bizet.'

'Signora?'

'Amelia, please,' she said, as she buttoned up Stasi's coat.

'Amelia,' Stasi began, hesitantly. 'Will you ask Carla to audition as well?'

Signora Busconi smiled, as though she had guessed all along what was in her mind. 'I did think about it.' Then she laughed as she saw Stasi's sombre face. 'But I thought you would be better. Come, you must sleep.'

Stasi was reluctant to leave, but after an affectionate hug Amelia pushed her gently into the hallway.

It was hard to enter the spirit of Cio-Cio-San, which

Signora Busconi had given the class to study. Grace was grumpy, having decided that she would never attempt the role, and Keiko giggled when she had to show everyone how to walk like a Japanese girl. Maria and Sofia insisted on swaying their hips, and the class dissolved in helpless laughter when Carla said the only way to do the part was to stick a coin in your arse and keep it there.

'You were very quiet today,' commented Carla to Stasi, as they sat at their usual café.

'I can't get into *Madam Butterfly* yet,' said Stasi, who had seen a book on Spain she could not afford, but would read little by little in a bookshop near the Brera. She would only tell Carla, she decided, if she was successful in her audition. 'Anyway, I'm probably too tall. You'd be far better as Cio-Cio-San.'

'Me?' Carla hooted. 'I'd have sent the American guy packing and sued for maintenance.'

'You going for modern opera?' enquired Grace. 'I know I am. Even if it does restrict the options.'

'I'm going for versatile,' said Carla. 'How about you, Stasi?'

'I'll go for whatever I can get.'

Carla dropped Stasi back at the convent, and apologized for leaving her.

'I'd ask you back, but Ma and Pa have got some boring Polish composer and his wife staying. You OK?'

'Fine. Really.'

Carla put her hand on her shoulder. 'You should leave this place. Maybe I could find a family who'd take you in. Signora Busconi doesn't realize what it's like being on your own. She thinks life is just for singing. Tell you what, let's see a movie next week.'

As Stasi closed the convent door behind her, she thought it was the best place she could be. The echoing corridors, the measured footsteps of the nuns, took her away from the present and enabled her to enter into the simple life of a country girl who would spend her day making lace, washing clothes in the stream, going to the market with her mother, dreaming of her handsome soldier, praying each night for God's blessing. She watched the nuns making the sign of the cross. She would do that in Act Three, when she was hiding by the rock. Even in one aria, she would make Micaela live.

Hurrying up to the small music room with the ancient, untuned piano, Stasi shut herself away, practising until she was summoned to supper by a timid knock. When young, Amelia had told her, she sang for eight hours a day. Stasi, too, wanted to immerse herself as she had done, dedicating every possible moment to her art. Every morning, she awoke, her heart thumping with elation. She knew her voice was becoming more controlled, and Amelia was introducing her to a range of colours she never knew she possessed, teaching her the mysterious, languishing hollow sound which only Italians seemed to produce. And she was learning to hold back her power in the top notes, to make a pianissimo pure as dewbeads . . . Anastasia Wagner, her name in the programme . . . Although she was preparing herself for failure, she occasionally allowed herself the luxury of imagining the cries of 'Brava, brava'. They might even throw flowers onto the stage.

The maestro arrived at a day's notice, earlier than expected. Couldn't he wait until she was ready? Signora Busconi laughed; no one told Maestro Passattella when to come. He was in Milan, he could see her. There had just been time to find a long flowery dress in the market. Even if it resembled a nightdress and lacked the essential frills, if she took her hair down, and wore only a touch of lipstick, she could be taken for Micaela. A country girl, coming into town. Even for an audition, you had to look the part. Stasi covered her face in walnut-brown make-up and examined the effect. Lucky she wasn't blonde. She could almost pass for Spanish, she decided, although the only Spanish girl she had seen was in Gloria's glass cabinet, a painted plaster flamenco dancer in a red flounced dress.

A chubby man with a black moustache, round bright eyes and gleaming black hair touching the collar of his dark blue velvet jacket fervently kissed her hand. (Signora Busconi had told him about the young soprano, *dotissima*, an English girl from London. Really so much talent? He would judge for himself. Only this one from all Signora Busconi's gifted students? Only one? *Va bene.*)

'*Molto piacere.*'

'This is Signorina Anastasia Wagner.'

'A beautiful name. You are related to the great Richard?'

Stasi smiled. He had noticed her dress, that was obvious, and she liked the way he spoke English, with a touch of comic arrogance, like a Mozart servant putting on airs. 'Not as far as I know.'

'She will sing "Je dis que rien ne m'épouvante" from Act Three,' announced Signora Busconi.

'She sings in French? Good. I hope she will not have the accent of her prime ministers, like the last English girl I heard.'

As Stasi went over with her teacher to the piano, he sat himself down directly in her eye-line. As she began the aria, she looked past, to avoid him ('I said that nothing could scare me . . .'), then, gaining in confidence ('I'm frightened, all alone . . .'), she turned towards him. There was a slight smile of appreciation on his alert face. Then suddenly, without warning, he put up his hand. '*Basta.*'

Stasi, bewildered and shaken, did not move. Signora Busconi rose from the piano, Sandro Passattella kissed her hand and walked hurriedly towards the door.

'We will talk outside,' he said in Italian to Signora Busconi.

She was not good enough. Stasi wanted to run after him, fall at his knees, tell me, tell me, what didn't you like, what did you expect? Didn't I look right? Was my voice disappointing? I'll do it again, just wait, wait, I know I can please you. As she sat down, her legs were trembling, she could feel her racing pulse, she was overtaken by the panic of failure. 'I, Anastasia Wagner, am a singer,' she repeated to herself, and, oh, she was about to cry again. Couldn't help it. Everyone in the Wagner family cried, even when watching television. Curses. She could not prevent the hinted tears conjured up for the fictional Micaela moistening her eyes, escaping down her cheeks. What he had heard was good, she knew it was. Not perfect, but good. It suited her voice. Perhaps she should have sung it in Italian instead of French.

What right had he to behave like that? He was either arrogant or stupid. Walking out without saying goodbye. Stupid, self-important dolt, who had heard of him anyway? Everyone in Italy thought they were somebody. Even the man who sold doughnuts on the street corner said he was the great-great-grandson of Garibaldi. What did it matter? Why sing in Italy? There was England, France, Germany, even America. No one need know she'd failed her first audition, except Signora Busconi.

Stasi heard the sound of flowery compliments outside in the hall, and then a thud as the heavy door closed. Maestro Passattella would be hurrying off to hear a few bars from another hapless victim. Signora Busconi must have been taken in by his flattery, for she came into the room looking delighted.

'I was so proud of you,' she said, as she went over to the piano and closed the score.

'It doesn't matter. I know it's wrong to say it. I feel terrible. All that work.' A tear began to steal down Stasi's cheek, and she leaned over the back of a chair, covering her face with her hair. 'I'll go,' she sniffed, without moving. Then she straightened herself and turned to Signora Busconi angrily. 'Why did he have to do that? It's so humiliating. If he didn't like my singing, or didn't think I was right, why didn't he say so at the end instead of stopping me? What did I do wrong? Is it because I don't look right?'

'What an idea! Come here, Anastasia.' She went over to a chaise-longue and removed the shawl Stasi wore when rehearsing. 'Sit down here for a moment.'

Stasi obeyed reluctantly, as though she was about to hear a bad school report.

'Will you accept Maestro Passattella's offer? Will you sing in *Carmen* next month?'

'Are you serious? He wants me?'

'He says he'll try you out. This is unusual for Sandro. Mostly, he chooses Italian girls.'

'I . . .' Stasi's voice tailed away. She was caught in a rush of emotion, struggling to believe what she had heard. Anastasia Wagner was about to become a professional singer. It would no longer be enough to criticize herself, to listen to her teacher's opinion. Even if she only sang once, the critics would write about her, the audience would discuss her performance, they would compare her to others. If she failed, if they damned her performance, would she ever be able to sing again?

'Do you think I should accept?' Stasi said doubtfully.

'For your first part, this is ideal. The tessitura is right for your voice. This aria seems so simple, but I have seen many singers who can't achieve the range. You can do this, a rare thing.'

Stasi regained her composure and thought back to what she had sung. Unlike a painter, a singer left no trace, only in the memory. What did Maestro Passattella remember? 'I didn't float the top B natural properly. It wasn't right. Do you think he noticed? Do you really think I'll be good enough?'

'In performance, even better. We'll work some more on focusing the pianissimo, and even smoother legato. And we'll loosen up those shoulders!'

Maria came in with a tray bearing the now familiar silver English teapot and a plate of strawberry tarts. Without hesitating, Stasi took one and pushed it into her mouth, crunching through the strawberries into the soft, custardy cream beneath. She was about to take another one, then hesitated. 'Why did Maestro Passattella walk out? Does he always do that?'

Signora Busconi gave an indulgent smile, as though she would forgive him anything. 'There was no need to hear more,' she said firmly. 'He is a busy man.'

'Well, I think he's a rude pig. Don't worry, I won't tell him.'

As she hugged Stasi and kissed her on both cheeks, Signora Busconi whispered, 'You can teach him English manners.'

As soon as she had returned to the convent, Stasi's first thought was to telephone Gloria. It was little more than two weeks since her mother had left, but Stasi had already forgotten why she had been so relieved at her departure. Distance had transformed her into the essence of all-caring, all-knowing motherhood, glowing with unworldly kindness, tolerance and self-sacrifice, like the gaudy blue-eyed, blue-robed Virgin whose painting beamed down as though to say 'Eat! Eat!' to the expectant girls seated at the refectory table in the dining room.

Stasi wasn't to know that at the moment she chose to telephone, her mother was in the middle of writing an essay on 'What T.S. Eliot means to us today' for her evening class on Expressing Yourself Creatively and Raymond was arguing out loud with the referee in a football match on Sky television. 'It's the phone. You get it,' said Gloria, dotting an i for the third time. Raymond stretched out an arm towards the onyx machine, expecting a strident greeting from Lally Reuben or someone similar.

'Stasi. Where are you?'

'Who is it? Stasi? My daughter? Turn the set down, let me talk,' shouted Gloria, and she jumped up, spilling coffee over her opening paragraph in her excitement. 'Darling,' she cried, snatching the receiver from Raymond. 'Anything wrong? I got your card. Two weeks ago, mind. Are you well?'

'I've got a job, Mum.'

'Now she tells me. What kind of a job?'

'Singing in *Carmen*.'

Gloria put her hand over the mouthpiece. 'Raymond, she's starring in *Carmen*.'

'Great,' he replied, without taking his eyes from the screen. 'But I thought *Carmen* was mezzo.'

Gloria ignored him, and sat on her knees in front of the phone as though receiving a blessing, holding the receiver with both hands. 'I always knew it. I'm so thrilled, darling, so young and a triumph already. Now I want to know everything about it. You never say anything on your postcards. You got coins?'

'Just a few. I heard today. Did an audition for a famous Italian producer, only a few bars, and whumph! I had the part. He must have seen hundreds of singers.'

'Wonderful. I'm so happy. La Scala, is it?'

'Fiesole, outside Florence. A Roman arena with over two thousand seats.'

Gloria reflected. She wasn't familiar with arenas. 'Is that big?'

'Huge.'

'They'll put your name in the programme?'

'Yes, yes.'

'And write about it in the papers?'

'I expect so.'

'Then we're coming. All of us in the front row. And I'll get Lally to do the salt-beef. I forgot, when is it?'

'Next month. Mum, it's not big money. Else I'd send you the train-fare.'

'Who's talking about money? Just you wait till Uncle Monty hears about this. Starring in *Carmen* already, what a coup.'

'Mum, one more coin.'

'I'll talk fast then. You well?'

'Very well.'

'Eating properly? Getting your sleep?'

'Yes.'

'And don't fall in love, not till I come over and see if I like him.'

The time remaining from Stasi's last coin was ebbing

away in a series of beeps. Gloria just had time to shout a frantic 'Write, darling' before their communication ended. Stasi could imagine her mother straight away dialling Monty's number, then telling the whole of Muswell Hill that she was singing *Carmen* at La Scala.

The days passed into weeks. When she wasn't practising with Signora Busconi, Stasi was content to spend nearly all her time closeted in the tiny room at the convent, learning her part, or lying on her bed listening to her tapes until she knew every note of Bizet's *Carmen*. This would be her life. Arriving in strange cities. Working. Resting. Occasionally wandering the streets or seeing the sights. She began to love its simplicity. I, Anastasia Wagner, am a singer. It was only disturbed when Carla almost crashed into her outside Signora Busconi's apartment block.

'Hi! Where've you been hanging out, Stasi? What you been up to?' Carla's curls were caught back in a band. She was in tennis whites, in the briefest of tailored shorts, honey-gold skin, carrying her racket over her shoulder. 'There's been so much on, Stasi, but we must see that movie. Listen, I've found the most gorgeous tennis coach. Fancy sharing him? You play tennis?'

'Just about. But I can't take on anything, not now. I'm having extra singing lessons.'

'Christ, Stasi. What on earth for? You're way better than the rest of us.'

Stasi wondered whether it would be fairer to tell her. But the contract hadn't yet been signed, and it was bad luck to boast about success.

'It's just, well, there's a part I'm after,' she said, as casually as she could. Carla swung the racket to her side, and gave a friendly grin.

'Come on. You've got an audition at La Scala. I should have guessed.'

'Hardly.' Stasi smiled back. 'It's only a summer production of *Carmen*. I'm singing Micaela.'

'Not with dear old Sandro in Fiesole? You'll have a

great time. That's fantastic. You must have made some impression; he never goes for English girls. Time for a quick coffee?'

Glancing up at Signora Busconi's flat, Stasi shook her head. She would ask Carla later about Sandro Passattella. She might have guessed the Livornos would know him.

'Hey, Stasi, I nearly forgot. My birthday. You must come. Ma and Pa will be away so we're having a surprise party. Next Friday. Nothing formal, everything wild. Twenty-four. Isn't it just dreadful?' She scribbled her address on the back of Stasi's music score, then kissed her hastily on both cheeks and started a high-stepping jog down the street, her curls fanning behind her.

What time did parties begin in Milan? What exactly was a 'surprise party'? Back in her room at the convent Stasi examined the only evening garments she possessed, which the vendeuse in Gloria's favourite boutique in Muswell Hill, ten per cent off to special customers, had described ecstatically as 'the little ensemble which will take you anywhere'. The black taffeta skirt and white lace blouse had made their debut over three years ago in her first public recital, for the North London Friends of Music Society, held in a youth club in Golders Green. How did you make black taffeta and white lace into something sexy, outrageous and show-stopping?

When it came to practical matters, a mother like Gloria was indispensable. She had once thrown together a party dress in one afternoon, with just a remnant of curtain material. Making something out of nothing was the Wagner forte, the mysterious ability to turn one thing into another with the minimum of expenditure – a scullery into a kitchen, a scrubby back yard into a patio, a shed into a conservatory, a dressing gown into an evening coat.

Since Stasi had not inherited her talent, the most she could do was roll up the sleeves of the blouse and undo more buttons than would be seemly in Muswell Hill, but that left the skirt. She was about to slash it heedlessly from ankle-length to mid-thigh, when the voice of common sense ('Are you crazy?') reminded her that she would need a long rehearsal skirt.

The English girl arrived on foot and shivering – the evenings were still cold – in front of the swoopingly curved, marble-fronted thirties block near Piazza San Babila which concealed the Appartamento Livorno. Stasi fought her way through a chattering crowd with either short legs and long furs or long legs and short furs, bearing bottles of champagne and spangled boxes of various sizes, accompanied by overcoated escorts with close-cut hair and faces still tanned by the winter mountain sun.

'*Tanti auguri*,' they cried, edging past the struggling maid, invisible under a piling avalanche of coats. There was Carla, you couldn't miss her, a diamante ribbon across her brow, and a string of flashing crystal balls trailing from her ears. They criss-crossed round Stasi, ignoring her as she tried to search for a space, jolting, touching her hips, crushing her breasts, knocking her shoulders without acknowledging her presence. She suddenly loathed the intimate, crude physicality of Italy, which she had at first admired and envied. In a surge of movement she found herself driven towards Carla.

'Stasi! You made it!'

'Happy birthday!'

Carla took her arm and guided her towards a corner of the L-shaped room. She shouted, raising her voice against the thudding music. 'You still with the sisters of mercy? Because tonight you must stay here. Anyone who leaves before dawn pays a penalty. *Eh, Eduardo, basta*, come over here. Meet my friend.'

Stasi was pinned against the wall, forcing a smile as she watched the throng over Carla's head. Eduardo, whoever he might be, did not appear and the sea of guests closed round Carla, obscuring her from view as she wriggled forward into the mass of bodies.

The powerful perfumes, competing with each other in

strident waves, began to nauseate her, and she could only catch a few words of the speedy Milanese slang. She had to escape. She'd always been bad at parties. More gesticulating guests. Her senses were dulled, her head throbbing, and she pushed open one door after another in an attempt to find sanctuary. And then, at the end of the corridor, she found a room as spacious as the first she had entered.

Carla's music room. It was more overwhelming than the soaring arches of the Duomo – an eight-foot concert grand, a smaller practice piano, scores lining the walls, one of which had a large screen built into it, a recording control desk, speakers, a synthesizer, ornate music stands, marble busts in every corner, Verdi, Puccini, Toscanini, signed photographs, to my dearest, with admiration, unforgettable memories. Who was that? Von Karajan. And that? Kiri Te Kanawa. And those? Joan Sutherland with Luciano Pavarotti. Jessye Norman. All personal. All known to the Livornos. Carla outside La Scala, a long evening coat, how beautiful, with it must be her father or perhaps her grandfather, an old but fiercely upright, distinguished-looking man with a sculpted beard.

Even if Stasi became a fabled diva, how could she ever compete with this? Carla had only to open her mouth. She was going to be great. It was inevitable. While still in the womb, she would have heard the music of the angels. Her mother would have been sitting in a box in La Scala. They would all have been waiting for the next prodigy. A royal line.

Stasi drew in her breath, admiring, incredulous, resentful, then admiring again. A piece of music was open on the piano. She ran over and knew immediately from the pattern of notes what it was. 'Je dis que rien ne m'épouvante.' Micaela's aria from *Carmen*, covered in pencil marks, exclamation marks, underlinings. Why hadn't she mentioned it? That she was up for the same part? The notes, Stasi felt, belonged to her. Carla had stolen them, the familiar patterns were defaced in heavy, child-like scribbles as though she was venting her anger on

49

Bizet. She must have auditioned in this grand music room, and Maestro Passattella wouldn't have stopped her half-way through. All the same, he had turned her down. Carla Livorno, Paolo's daughter, rejected. No wonder she was silent; she would hardly confess to failure. No one talked about failures, in case they clung to you like moulting fur. How could she have done it, behind Signora Busconi's back? That must have made her feel even more ashamed.

Stasi pulled out the gilded piano stool and opened the lid of the concert grand. Then she gently pressed down a chord, and listened as the luscious, full-bodied sound reverberated round the room. Frightened of announcing her presence, she drew her hands away, gazing at the polished black wood, gleaming like patent leather. One day, she would have a piano this size, with ivory keys. As she slowly closed the lid, Stasi smiled, suddenly remembering the look of pleasure on Carla's face when she told her she was singing Micaela. There was no hint of resentment, nothing had changed. Why was she getting so upset? It wasn't as though Carla had stolen the man she loved, like Carmen. People failed auditions. So what? Something else always came along. Carla Livorno waiting months for a phone call? What could be more unlikely?

Stasi was so absorbed in forcing herself to be sensible that she failed to hear the door opening or the soft steps of a visitor.

'Excuse me. Do you mind if I come in? It's getting so noisy.'

Stasi glanced at the tall young man, hair the colour of a palomino pony softly hanging over his pale olive face, shoes mirror-polished, open-neck shirt, a sweater over one shoulder, standing with every intention of entering. He was irresistibly attractive, even-featured, pristine as though he had just steam-cleaned every pore, aware in a well-bred way that everything about him was in order.

'I'm Carla's brother. Eduardo. Are you English?'

The same American accent. She stretched out her hand. 'Anastasia. How did you know?'

He laughed, pleased at her surprise. 'When they go into a room, Italian girls head straight for the mirror. I saw you looking at the piano. Lovely tone, I'm told, but I wouldn't know. Do you play?'

'Sometimes.'

Stasi did not mind his easy familiarity. Through the open door, she became aware of laughter and music. Now that someone had sought her out, she could be part of it.

'You look uncomfortable, perched on that stool. Why don't you sit over here?' said Eduardo, moving towards a black leather settee at the side of the room. Stasi gathered up her taffeta skirt and sat down beside him, crossing her legs.

'Carla keeps on about you. I had to meet this amazing singer. Maybe she thought you'd convert me to opera.'

'Really?'

'Crazy, my sister.' The Livorno eyes. Misty green, long-lashed, golden olive skin. 'There had to be one Livorno who's tone deaf. That's me. I have a company exporting wine. You like wine?'

Stasi decided she would like anything he liked, for this evening at least, and watched him go over to a corner chest. He brought her a bottle and displayed its finely written label.

'You know this one? A Barbera di Roccagrimalda. It's very special. For you.'

He was talking, but Stasi only half-listened, distracted by his eyes looking into hers, watching him intently as he uncorked the bottle with a sweeping flourish. The kind of man you dreamed about on a hot summer night, silky-haired, rugged and fine-featured at the same time, the kind you never met in England. All his movements were graceful, without being effeminate. She had never seen anyone so beautiful. Or if she had, he would have looked right past her.

'Slowly, slowly. You must drink this the way you make love.'

Stasi giggled and put both her hands round the ample, thin-stemmed glass.

'Someone as sweet as you must always have the best.'

'Eduardo, you mustn't flatter me. Otherwise I won't believe anything you say. You don't know me.'

'I want to. You won't believe this, Anastasia, but mostly I say little to girls. With you, it's different. I feel I could say anything.'

He was so earnest, so appealing. And so sincere, saying nice things without showing off. (How different from Larry Cohen, who could only say 'You look pretty' even when she didn't.) Stasi overcame her hesitation and allowed Eduardo to rest his hand on hers. It was shocking, to feel the strong, firm fingers of a man caressing her own. Thoughts of love and desire had been buried, channelled into Micaela, denied in the discipline of life in the classroom and the convent. Suddenly all she wanted was to touch his smooth skin, to kiss his lips, to feel his hands stroking down her hips, to give way to desire, just this one evening to celebrate her achievement.

The door suddenly opened and Stasi pulled away her hand.

'Come to the kitchen. We have a feast!' Carla blew a kiss and ran out.

'When our parents are away, Carla makes a huge pot of pasta. Ma and Pa hate it.'

'Don't they mind? You having a party without them?'

Eduardo looked surprised. 'But that's why they went away. So we could have fun. Are you hungry?'

'Maybe later.'

'Come. Have a look round. Come and see my studio. Then we'll eat.'

She admired the framed maps of the wine-producing regions of Italy, pancake-sized medals displaying his expertise as a master of wine, small abstract paintings with dancing colours, everything polished, magazines stacked neatly, a room which did not jar, nor inspire. A spiral staircase led to a small gallery which jutted out into the room.

'Is there someone special waiting for you in England? A jealous fiancé?'

'There was,' she replied. 'But it's over now.' Then she looked up and gave a hesitant smile. 'Is that where you sleep?'

He stared at her for a moment, as though seeking her approval, and then he came close to her and put his arms round her waist. As she ran her fingers through her hair and leaned her head back, she thought of Carmen advertising her wares to Don José. They had hardly spoken and she could feel his hips pressing against hers. The moment he touched her, she felt her desire changing into passion. This was the beginning of love; at last she had discovered it. Hadn't Gloria told her she'd know when it happened? You meet someone, and you know immediately, from that special look in the eyes, that he's meant for you. And you know he feels the same. The wine was strong. She felt limp and languid, as though she had fallen asleep in the bath. How sophisticated she was, how well she manoeuvred her long skirt, lifting it above her knees, tripping a little unsteadily up the close wooden steps. Would he follow her?

She could lie right across the bed and there was still space. She had never seen such an expanse, low and inviting, covered by an exquisite fabric she was unable to identify, cushions to match, and a soft white light coming from the floor whose source was hidden. Tastefully modern, all harmony, all distinction.

She heard a click. He must be locking the door in case someone entered. Stasi lay back and closed her eyes. For the first time in her life, she would be undressed by a man whose physical beauty she was unable to fault, who would be unspoilt by thick hairs on his chest, or short legs, or fumbling, sweaty fingers like Larry Cohen's. How could she possibly resist him? Carla Livorno's brother. A brief, secret entry into the Livorno family. Perhaps she would know what it felt like to be one of them.

She felt his weight on the bed, his hand slipped under

the lace blouse, onto her breast, then stroked her nipples gently with his palm, hardly touching them.

'I want to know all about you,' he whispered into her ear. 'Everything. Not just your body. I am a man who falls in love, Anastasia. I don't do this with every girl. I knew you were special, the moment I saw you.'

He could have any girl he wished. Tonight, Stasi did not consider whether he had had one or twenty, whether he had rehearsed his lines in countless bedrooms. She was the only one and she was waiting. The light dimmed. Her skin was vibrant. He was still beside her, and then she felt his fingers running down her face, his tongue caressing her mouth, gently, hesitantly. Exquisite, tender waiting, the difference between love and lust. He was right: it was wrong to hurry, even though she longed to strip off her clothes, to have his naked weight crushing her onto the bed. But he was still beside her, his sweet warm breath kissing her skin.

He drew back the covers inviting her to slip inside the bed, and then he replaced them, tracing the line of her body through the soft sheets, stroking between her legs.

Che bello. Non ho mai visto un corpo così bello.

His voice was warm. She didn't listen to his words. They washed over her; she sensed only his tenderness. Did he know that she was on fire, holding herself back? How long would it be? Was she doing it right? Was she meant to say something in reply? Should she move or not? What did he expect? Were Italian girls different? Did they have rules about making love which she had yet to learn? Would he expect her to be a virgin? Larry Cohen didn't count. She was almost a virgin.

'I want you so much,' Stasi murmured as he slipped off her clothes. And then he kissed her with frenzy, all over her pale English body until she could wait no longer, taking his arms and pulling him across her, panting, heedless of anything except the strength of her desire, until she gasped with the sudden shock of his penetration.

'Do I hurt, darling?'

'No, no. Don't stop.'

At first she gave herself to him, lying limp as he pounded into her, and then she urged him on, thrusting her hips, taking up his rhythm, until they both cried out together. She thought she heard him say '*Ti amo*'. Yes, he had said it twice.

'Are you happy now, my *bella* Anastasia?'

'I've never been so happy.'

Eduardo Livorno, clasping her in his arms, his chin resting on her head. Her first real orgasm, but she couldn't tell him. It had been so intense, she could not imagine it happening again. They lay in silence for a while, her head on his chest, both breathing in unison. Then Stasi suddenly sat up.

'Eduardo, would Carla mind if she knew?'

'Why should she? Carla doesn't care about love. It bores her. We're very different. But she likes you. Admires you, Anastasia.'

'Is her fiancé here?'

'She asked him, but he detests pop music. And pasta! So now she can enjoy herself. The marchese wants her to lead her own life.'

'A marchese!'

'In Italy, that is nothing special. But we must talk about you. You are a girl who will marry a prince.'

'I've got better things to do. I might have a baby when I've sung *Tosca*.' Stasi swung her legs down onto the floor and started to pick up her clothes.

'You have a lovely body. Will you let me see you again?'

'I won't be in Milan much longer.'

'Anastasia, we have to meet, to be alone, talk, do crazy things together. May I hear you sing?'

'I'd love it. But I thought you didn't like music.'

'The musician, I like. You can teach me.'

'Eduardo, can we eat something? I'm starving!'

'A hungry girl must be obeyed.' As he buttoned up her blouse he said, 'One day you will make a beautiful baby.'

After she had thrust forkfuls of spaghetti into her

mouth, and some hunks of country bread, she took advantage of the crowded kitchen and slipped away. They had agreed to meet again; he had asked her to call him at work. She had nothing to say to the strangers around her. There was still time, if she found a taxi, to arrive at the convent before it was locked.

'Eduardo? You up?' Carla shouted as she pushed open his door. 'Put on the light.'

'I'm asleep,' he moaned, groping for the switch. She unsteadily ascended the steps, barefoot and holding up a long diaphanous shift.

'I'm twenty-four. Three years past twenty-one. Still, it was one hell of a party. Wasn't it? How many girls had you had by twenty-four? Come on. Tell Carla.'

'You're drunk. Go away. And you're sitting on my feet.'

'That better?'

Eduardo turned over.

'She's crazy about you.'

'Who is?'

'Was she a good fuck?'

Eduardo immediately sat bolt upright.

'Did she like your studio, or did she prefer what was in it? I saw her in the kitchen. She ate a bowlful of pasta. And those eyes. Shiny as marbles. I can always tell. Come on, do you like her?'

'I gave her some wine. That's all.'

'Nothing wrong with a good fuck.'

'Carla, clear off. Go and talk to the cactus.'

'I bet she's got a fantastic body. English girls who dress badly always do. They like hiding what they've got.'

'Or go clear up. Anything.'

'Eduardo?'

'What now?'

'Did she look around the music room?'

'How should I know.'

'Damn. I left my vocal score on the piano. You didn't tell her Sandro's letting me do Micaela, did you?'

'Why should I? I never know what you're doing. What or who is Micaela?'

'*Carmen*, dummy. The one I'm singing in Fiesole, remember? But she's second cast.'

'Anastasia? Then I'll have to come along.'

'Anyway. You keep quiet. Nearer the time, I'll say something. If I tell her now, she might kick up stink and make him change his mind.'

'What are you going on about?'

'Never mind. It's OK. Go to sleep.'

'She's a great girl. I want to see her again.'

'Far too good for you, darling. Good night. Don't forget to wake up in the morning.'

As he buried his head in the pillow, Eduardo could hear her tra-laing something vaguely Spanish down the corridor.

The first occasion had been so momentous, if Eduardo had asked her to marry him, she would have agreed there and then. He had arranged it so casually, would she like to go to La Scala, or would she like to go somewhere she had never been? Even though he yawned through *Die Meistersinger*, and looked at his watch, Stasi refused to be deterred as she strained forward to take in every note. This time, she could be like the fur-clad opera-goers of Milan, sitting in the stalls as though they owned every seat. She, like them, could see every shifting expression on the singers' faces, instead of viewing from a dizzy distance. She did not mind that she looked like a music student. She was their equal, more than their equal. Eduardo had to be the most beautiful young man in Milan, Paolo Livorno's son, attracting envious glances from those overdressed women with their bloated escorts. And even if he failed to respond to Wagner, what did it matter? He listened to her with such attention, she knew he would eventually succumb to the beauty of music.

The second date was a disappointment. Stasi had hoped they might see a film, eat out, tell one another their secrets; she might even confess that she had never loved

Larry Cohen. In the event they spent the evening with his friends. The men talked of nothing but wine-growing, comparing vintages with the obsession of opera-buffs assessing singers, and the girls ignored her after she failed to pass the shopping test.

'If only we could be alone,' she said to him. The car windows were steamed up with unconsummated love. Eduardo had parked in a backstreet round the corner from the convent.

'Come back with me. No one will be around. Carla's out with some guy.'

'She might come in. What about your parents?'

'You should get an apartment. All the girls I know in Milan have their own places, except my sisters. They like living at home. Ma says they'll never be liberated.'

'Why do you live at home, then?'

'Pa's away so much, Ma needs a man around the place. Help her keep Carla in order.' Drawing her towards him, he leaned over and kissed her again. 'Anastasia, I'm going crazy for you. I'm not like an Englishman. Sometimes I lose control. We must make love. This is bad for me, bad for you. Come with me. In our house, everyone does as they like. No one minds. You know Mick Jagger? You like him? You know this one? "Let's spend the night together"? I have the disc. Listen.' Eduardo started his car, and roared off.

In class next day, Stasi couldn't concentrate. Signora Busconi asked her if anything was the matter, she looked so pale. It was like being ill, the feverish exhaustion after a night of love. She had left Eduardo early in the morning, and had taken a tram going in the wrong direction. For once, she refused to sing.

By the evening, she was longing to hear his voice, some gentle words of concern to show that he still adored her. Then she began to fear that everything had happened too quickly. Hadn't Gloria told her it had taken two years before she realized she loved Sam? They never showed the slow blossoming of love in opera, or the mundane details which halted its progress, only the long emotional agony once it had happened. It would be ridiculous to cry out 'Why have you deserted me?' even though those were the words which came to her. Besides, you couldn't say that kind of thing over the phone. After a sleepless night and a silent breakfast, Stasi walked over to the bar opposite and called Eduardo's office. His secretary asked her which company she was from, and then told her he was unavailable.

There was nothing like the misery, the wretchedness of silence. Taking a deep breath, and reminding herself that she must make the enquiry sound relaxed and cheerful, Stasi dialled Carla's number. She sounded as though she had just woken up.

'Eduardo? No, he hasn't been around. Let me think – Christ, it's so early – some wine auction, I guess. You and he having a good time?'

'You know?'

'Why ever not, Stasi? We don't hide things, not in our family. You like him?'

'A lot.'

'He's coming out to the villa on the weekend. Why don't you come along?'

'I'd love to, but he hasn't asked me.'

'No problem. Eduardo's so hopeless. He must have forgotten, but I know he wants you to come. Sunday lunch, OK? Anyhow, it's time you met Maurizio.'

Eduardo was so surprised and pleased to see her, Stasi immediately forgave him. He thought he'd told her that he was going to a wine promotion in England. Suddenly everything seemed funny. Stasi collapsed into giggles as they argued about who should drive, which car they should take.

'Come on, you two. I'll decide. Let's go in the red one.'

'I'll drive that heap, then,' said Eduardo. 'Carla drives like an old lady. Hey, why don't you drive, Stasi?'

'I can't.'

59

Carla put her arms round Stasi's neck. 'Of course my friend doesn't drive. Didn't you know, Eduardo? It's very chic in London not to. That right, Stasi?'

Stasi sat in the front, admiring Eduardo who manoeuvred the Alfa with one hand on the wheel, another resting on her knee. Carla was singing away in the back, some scurrilous dialect song about a randy miller. There was hardly a moment when they weren't laughing. They headed north, and left the motorway down an unsigned road.

It took a couple of minutes for Carla to open the wrought iron gates guarding the della Robbia estate. Before she had time to lock them behind her, Eduardo roared through and screeched to a halt some distance away.

'Mean son of a bitch,' screamed Carla, as she ran to catch up with them. 'Now get out and I'll show you how to drive.' She pushed him playfully aside, and Eduardo climbed into the back seat. Carla swathed herself in a silk scarf, sat bolt upright and slowly moved off in first gear down the pock-marked road.

'This is how the marchesa drives,' she announced. 'Maurizio thinks this is going real fast. You get used to it. Country living, folks.'

'This slow? You're not married yet,' said Eduardo teasingly.

'I'm practising. I'm good at practising,' replied Carla, slipping into second gear.

The villa in the distance was long, only two storeys high, with regularly spaced, tall windows, a tiled roof and six great curving arches. It stood starkly against the sky. There were no columns, no statues striking attitudes on the façade, nothing to rival the palaces and churches of Milan. Even the row of uneven cypresses lining the road echoed its austerity. It was only when they came near that Stasi noticed the massive stone statue of a woman in a long folded tunic holding out a sword which pointed down the drive.

'Is it how you imagined?' asked Eduardo.

Stasi wrinkled her nose. 'Not exactly.'

'It's one of the best examples of a sixteenth-century rural villa. Isn't it great? A friend of mine has one out at Robecco, but that's much later. Far too extravagant for my taste.'

'I wish I knew about architecture.'

'You can ask Maurizio. He'll talk about it all day, Stasi.'

The car stopped, and Carla leaped out. 'Eduardo, he doesn't like my idea for a conservatory. Says it isn't authentic. He says that to every goddamned thing I suggest. Never mind. His father put in electricity. Boy, that must have rocked the family.'

An old butler opened the heavy wooden door as they approached and greeted them formally.

'The marchese is expecting you in the dining room. He has selected some wines for your approval, Signor Livorno.'

'Great,' said Carla to Stasi. 'We can get sloshed and they can spit it out.'

When Stasi first saw the marchese, she looked away in embarrassment. Instead of the slightly older version of Eduardo she had expected, she was staring into the wrinkled eyes of an old man, with a carefully trimmed beard like her Latin teacher at school, and he should have retired years ago.

'Do you appreciate wine, Miss Wagner?'

A long, dark table, seventeenth century, made of chestnut wood Eduardo told her, was covered in an array of glasses. A row of bottles was arranged behind them.

'Here we have some Grignolino, there's a Barbaresco, and a Barolo. Conscientious growers, Eduardo. See what you think.' His voice was surprisingly deep, coming from that thin mouth.

'I had some fine Barolo, just the other day,' Stasi said, smiling at Eduardo.

'I'm teaching her.' He showed her how to cup her hands round the glass, and sniff the rising fumes, swirling the liquid.

Carla poured herself out a glass of dark red wine, and threw it back. 'That's OK. What are we having for lunch, Maurizio darling?'

Maurizio licked his wine-stained lips, dabbed at his beard with a silk cloth and held up a glass towards the window. 'Wild boar, I believe.'

'Tell you what, you two can carry on. We'll be in the *cortile*. Roberto can bring us some champagne. Come on, Stasi, let's get some sun.'

Stasi followed her through the back of the house, over a terrace, and down some steps into a formal, sunken garden. They sat by a gargoyle which was splashing a small stream of water intermittently into a pool.

'With any luck, Roberto will get some decent stuff. That old boy knows everything in the cellar.' Carla stretched out on the wall of the fountain, kicked off her shoes, unbuttoned the front of her dress, closed her eyes and welcomed the sun. As she lay there, Stasi wondered if Carla would dare behave with such abandon when she became the Marchesa della Robbia.

'He's very impressive,' she began weakly.

'I think he looks like Verdi with that cute little beard, don't you?'

'A little thinner in the face. Yes, you're right,' said Stasi politely. She was unable to take her eyes from Carla's breasts, hanging opulently without a bra, the nipples just exposed. Then she imagined Maurizio in a tight cravat, ogling her at a distance like the men in *Déjeuner sur l'herbe*. 'Are you really going to marry him?'

'Sure. Why not?'

'Is it because he's so rich?'

Carla rolled over on her side and laughed. 'I know guys ten times richer. And I've seen better villas.'

'So you're really in love? I didn't think it could happen. Not with someone that . . .'

'That old, you mean?'

Flushing with embarrassment, Stasi was unable to continue.

'Don't worry, Stasi. Everyone thinks that, but they don't say it. To me, it's quite normal. I've got used to the idea. Even if he won't be able to get it up five times a night, there are compensations. You've no idea the books he reads. He's got a fantastic mind. Ma thinks he's a god come down from Olympus.'

'She doesn't have to marry him,' retorted Stasi. 'I didn't think it was possible. I'm sorry.'

'To marry an old guy? Girls do it all the time.'

'No, no. To fall in love with one. I couldn't imagine it.'

'Really?' Carla gave a giggle and sat up, lifted her skirt, and plunged her feet into the cool water of the fountain. 'Here comes Roberto.'

Without looking at either of them, the aged servant put down a tray with a bucket of champagne and two glasses on the edge of the fountain, and shuffled away towards the villa. Stasi took a glass and handed one to Carla.

'I do respect Eduardo,' began Stasi, dreamily. 'Even if he isn't that keen on music.'

'Listen, Stasi. You mustn't get too serious.'

For a moment, Carla reminded her of Gloria. Don't get too serious. Perhaps Carla's mother, too, had issued dire warnings in such a tone. 'Serious about what?' she said defensively.

'My brother. Has he said anything about Maria-Teresa?'

Stasi's eyes opened wide in alarm. 'What are you saying? That he's got someone else? Please tell me. I want to know.'

Stasi had lowered her eyes, and was staring wretchedly into her glass. Sometimes she looked as though she'd been born in a convent and never left it.

'Don't take it so hard, Stasi. Eduardo always has girls around. Pa lets him do as he wants, always has. *Figlio di pappa*, like all his friends.'

Stasi took a gulp of champagne and hoped it would bring oblivion, but the rapid intake of bubbles had the opposite effect. Her eyes watered, and she felt Carla's hand slapping her on the back. When she had retrieved her breath, she took the plunge. 'Have your parents said anything? Have I done something wrong?'

Carla grinned. 'Only drunk the champagne too fast. Here, have some more.'

When she had filled their glasses, they both sat splashing their feet in the pool.

'Ma believes in family planning. We can all do what we like as long as we leave the important decisions to her. She's decided that when Eduardo's thirty, he'll be marrying Maria-Teresa, a dippy-hippy bubblebrain whose daddy's in with Raoul Gardini.'

The name meant nothing to Stasi. Doubtless another friend of the Livornos, a famous musician she should have known. 'I suppose he's important.'

'He likes good wine,' replied Carla. 'And he's one of the richest men in Italy.'

By this time, Stasi had decided that there were advantages in being poor. Even if Larry Cohen had been a Rothschild, she would still have turned him down. 'I'm not interested in getting married. Anyway, why should I marry an Italian?'

'Fine if you find the right kind. It took Ma twenty years to realize she hadn't. Every time Pa goes away on a gig, he just can't resist. He's had every soprano and fiddle player from here to Sydney. She thinks I don't know.' Carla put her hand over her eyes, as though the sun was becoming too strong.

'Is Maurizio part of the family plan?' asked Stasi, as she dried her feet on Carla's scarf. Then she heard Eduardo shouting from the upstairs balcony of the villa, summoning them to lunch. At the sound of his voice, tears began to well up and drip down her cheeks. 'I like him so much,' she sobbed.

Carla took her hand and led her towards the villa. 'When you're a big star, you'll just remember some Italian guy who was good in bed. Bet you forget his name.'

'How do you know if he's good in bed?'

'Jesus, Stasi. He's Italian!'

Stasi forced a smile and tossed back her hair. 'I've known better.'

Over lunch, Stasi ate wild boar for the first time (better than bacon, she decided, and more sinful; she'd tell Gloria they'd had chicken) and was given a lecture by the marchese on the restoration of Windsor Castle. As she was sitting next to Eduardo, there was no need to meet his eye. She would save the confrontation until they were alone.

When she returned to the convent, she shed a few tears into her pillow to mourn her lost love. Once she had left Milan, and begun the rehearsals for *Carmen*, the pain would go away. It was obvious why it had happened. Didn't they all say that you got taken over by your part? Like Micaela, she had fallen in love with the wrong man. Carla had been right to tell her. How could she go out with someone who couldn't distinguish Bach from Bizet? Who wouldn't know whether she was singing well or badly?

Shortly before she left for Florence, Stasi accepted Eduardo's invitation to have dinner. They had little to say to one another, and she decided that there was no need for a confrontation. When he kept asking her what had happened, didn't she like him any more, she said she had to concentrate on her voice. 'And I'm missing England,' she added, to soften the blow. He couldn't understand. *Strana ragazza.*

Chapter Three

There was no need to write to Uncle Monty. Stasi could now pay for her extra lessons. The owner of the Hip Hop Bar in the Galleria Vittorio Emanuele was a former opera singer, a friend of Amelia Busconi's. It was better than selling programmes at La Scala, and she didn't sack Stasi for getting confused over the noughts on the bill. Sometimes she sat down with famous singers from La Scala, delighted to find that their waitress was an opera fan. Signora Busconi approved, for one day Stasi would sing Susanna in *The Marriage of Figaro*, and, recalling the experience of sore feet, carrying trays of rattling cups, being summoned from all parts of the room at once, she would understand what it meant to be a servant.

'Is that what you did, when you sang Susanna?' Stasi asked.

'I was not expected to act. Now everything has changed.'

One night, just as Stasi was clearing the tables, preparing to leave the bar, she saw a figure frantically waving outside the glass door. The sign had been turned from 'Aperto' to 'Chiuso'. Could it be Carla? She hardly recognized her. When she let her in, Stasi realized that her face was without make-up, she was wearing a drab, dark brown coat, and her tempestuous mane of curls was screwed back under a beret.

'Stasi, I had to see you. Are you all right?'

'Fine. The tips are good. But what's happened? You look terrible.'

'Get me a drink.'

Carla flung herself onto a banquette, and put her

elbows on the table, covering her face with her hands. At that moment, if Carla had asked for everything she possessed, little though it was, Stasi would have given it to her. Her face, unlike Stasi's own, was unsuited to sadness. Carla's natural expression was always alert, on the edge of a smile, as though anticipating some indefinable pleasure. Now she looked lost, hurt, shattered.

'Stasi. Something unspeakable has happened and I can't do anything about it. If you never talk to me again, I'll be miserable, but I won't blame you.'

Stasi went over to the manager who was cleaning up the bar and whispered in his ear. Carla Livorno! Daughter of Paolo Livorno, the great conductor? He ran round to the other side of the bar and reached for a bottle of champagne from the fridge.

'Tell her, a present from the Hip Hop Bar. And we hope she will come again.'

As he uncorked the champagne, Carla leaned towards Stasi, talking breathlessly. 'Pa was conducting in Turin, and he has dinner with this creep Passattella. A friend, so-called. Chat, chat. Pa asks him about the next production. *Carmen.* How's that for an exciting idea? Anyhow, Pa's polite, he asks him about the designer he's chosen, the set, the conductor, the cast, blah, blah. He says he's trying out an interesting new soprano for Micaela, an English girl.'

'My part?'

'Pa doesn't know we're friends. No reason to. I'm amazed he remembers *my* name. So he says to Passattella, "As a matter of interest, Carla should be just about ready to take on Micaela." The guy goes crazy. "Why didn't anyone tell me? Carla Livorno, of course I want her. I'll release the other girl. Pay her off." No one even thought to ask me. Isn't he a skunk?'

'Oh, God. When was this? When did it happen?'

'Wait. Pa comes home and I flip. Look, if I was good enough, Signora Busconi would have put me up for it. I won't do it. Then he gives me a lecture. I scream. I tell him we're friends. Then your friendship must be tested, he says. Your career comes first. Fuck my career, I say. See what I mean? If I wasn't called Livorno, we'd be sitting here having a good time like we always do.'

Stasi slumped over the table. Why should Carla know how much it mattered to her, or see that the Wagner tears were starting to flow? 'What about my contract? It's in writing. He can't do this.'

Then she felt Carla's arm round her neck. 'Contracts mean nothing. In Italy, the bastards do exactly as they please. Politicians, lawyers, artists, the whole fucking lot. I did everything I could. I said I'd only sing the role if I shared it with you. Otherwise he'd never see me in Florence again, not even if he got down on his knees and offered me twice his piddling fee. The bastard agreed. He had to.'

'Did you audition for him?'

Carla looked surprised. 'Oh, I sang through a coupla things.'

'When? When?'

'Stasi, how can I remember?'

This was not the time, Carla decided, to inform Stasi of the casting practice of opera houses. With so few decent roles, and so many good sopranos clamouring for parts, no one minded sharing, especially at the beginning. There was little point in telling her that it was a common arrangement, not when she was taking it so personally.

'I felt so awful. How could I tell you? When we were all having a great time, you, me and Eduardo? You mean so much to both of us. You're one of the family.'

Carla lowered her head. Neither spoke for a minute. Then Carla haltingly broke the silence. 'In Milan, having a name like Livorno is a curse. Like Brando in Hollywood. Sometimes I think I should call myself something different.'

'You're crazy!'

'Everyone expects you to have talent. Look, Stasi. In my family, if you don't have talent you're nothing. Zilch. They still hope I'll be the next Maria Callas. Work hard,

Carla, you'll get there. Fat chance, who are they kidding? Who wants to follow Callas anyhow? Catch me fucking up my life like she did. I don't mind just being OK, going out there and doing a good job, singing the right notes. What's wrong with that, for Chrissake?'

'Nothing.'

'That's not ambitious enough for Pa and Ma. If I don't compare with Callas, then I'll be the next best thing. The wife of a rich marchese. Ma and Pa set the whole thing up.'

Stasi's mouth dropped open. She was appalled. 'I thought you loved him.'

'At least I admire him.' Carla looked round despondently. 'You're far better than I am. Everyone knows that. And you really care. It just doesn't matter that much to me. I might even give up being a singer and do something else if it doesn't work out.' She pushed away her glass, and took up her coat. Stasi put it round her shoulders.

'Don't worry, Carla. I'll get over it.'

'I was praying you'd say that. You're a real friend. It's no great shakes working with a hack like Passattella. No one important comes to see *Carmen*, anyhow. We'll all have a good time in Florence and fuck it.'

Carla's car was still parked straddled across the pavement outside. As she jumped into the driver's seat, she made a face into the driving mirror. 'Jesus! I look a fright. Like Dracula in the morning.' With a few strokes, she brushed on eyeshadow, lips, blushing cheeks. 'I'll take you home.'

The convent door was locked. Sister Anna eventually answered Stasi's plea to open it. With the door ajar, she peered suspiciously into the dimly lit street.

'Do excuse us. We didn't realize it was so late.' Carla held out her hand in greeting. 'Carla Livorno. It was my fault, sister. We were having a cup of coffee together.'

Carla embraced Stasi and thanked her loudly in Italian for being such a wonderful friend. Sister Anna smiled. It was obvious that she came from a good family, such an educated accent, not speaking that awful dialect. She was always glad when English girls found suitable Italian girlfriends. Too often, they clung to one other without making an effort and refused to speak Italian. Being from a good family, Signorina Livorno would have had the advantages of a good Catholic upbringing, something Signorina Anastasia appeared, sadly, to lack.

Stasi removed her shoes, ran down the stone corridor to her room and flung herself onto the bed. She hated Italy, she decided. Lies and rudeness and tricks and machinations. No one went on like that in England. They wouldn't stand for it. How could she work with Passattella? She should have told Carla to sing the measly role – if that's what she wanted – and cleared off. Starting her career with a compromise, not bloody likely. Perhaps she really was selfish and difficult and demanding and impossible. Yes, Mum. So? You always want everything your way.

If nobody important saw her, what did it matter? She prayed that Carla would develop an illness, nothing too severe, a touch of laryngitis would do. On the opening night. Then she told God she didn't mean it.

Signora Busconi had invited Stasi to supper. They were sitting in her small dining room at a daintily set out, lace-covered table, but Stasi's usual appetite had deserted her. With an effort, she took a little soup and put down her spoon.

'How can I say nothing? After what he's done? I'll tell him I'm pulling out. Just a short letter. Dear maestro, in the circumstances . . .'

'No. I don't think that's the way.'

'It's honest. It's how I feel and what I want to do.'

Signora Busconi shook her head. Anastasia sounded determined but reasonable, and at least she was talking calmly.

'Why on earth did Maestro Passattella agree? Couldn't he be decent enough to tell me? Carla should never . . .'

Signora Busconi sighed. 'Carla is my pupil, too. But you know many famous singers have taken over in a production. It isn't so terrible.'

'You know I should have sung first.'

'Yes, I know. I've seen it happen before, Anastasia. We must learn to take these things.'

'Why?'

'She is, after all, sharing with you. You can learn. From Maestro Passattella. Even from Carla.'

'How can I learn from her? She's totally different.'

'You watch other people, and then you find your way.'

'Do you think my way will be better?'

Signora Busconi gave a gentle laugh. 'Let us say, I hope so.' It was the nearest she would ever get to voicing what she felt. She never criticized one of her absent pupils. 'I'm glad you're no longer angry. Keep your fire for the role. Agreed? If you feel your anger rising up, you can phone me. With hate, creation is impossible.'

'It will be so strange. Having someone else tell me what to do.'

'Ah. Sandro won't be too demanding,' she said enigmatically. 'But be careful of his hands.'

Stasi left the Via delle Stelle clutching a yellowing copy of *Carmen* signed by Mary Garden, the famous Scottish soprano who had last sung the role in 1932. Signora Busconi had no need to lavish her with praise, to make wild predictions about her future, to give her any more advice. She had given away to the English signorina one of her most treasured possessions.

For most of the train journey, Stasi was in a deep sleep, having stayed awake all the previous night, feverish with anticipation, until she heard the first early morning prayers reverberating down the corridor. Now someone was tugging at her arm, and she became aware of a cacophonous roar.

'*Signorina, signorina. Eccoci arrivati. Siamo a Firenze.*'

Stasi opened her eyes with a start. A sturdy woman was

71

bending over her, pulling down her case. Leaping to her feet, Stasi stammered out her thanks, jumped down from the train and began to charge through the milling passengers. She would have to take a taxi to the rehearsal room, the only address she had in Florence. Carla, who had been there for a week, had promised to find her somewhere to stay when she arrived. The disorderly crowd surging round the taxi rank had no intention of giving way. Eventually, Stasi forced herself in front of an arguing family, and threw herself into a taxi before anyone could stop her. The rehearsal would have started by now. They would think she was arriving late on purpose.

The taxi stopped abruptly outside an undistinguished concrete building in Via Magenta. Checking the address once more, Stasi grabbed her case, pushed open the glass door and was directed down a long corridor. She could hear a pianist pounding out the overture of *Carmen*. They had begun. Even though at first Stasi would only be sitting in on rehearsals to observe, she felt as nervous as when she had first auditioned. Would she be able to hide how she felt, that he had deceived and insulted her? Would he make it clear to all the cast that Signorina Wagner was just the replacement for the girl he really wanted?

Maestro Passattella had his back to her as he confronted a group of male singers, the soldiers who opened Act One. They were holding their scores; didn't they know their parts? Only Carla waved and blew a kiss as Stasi crept in and sat at the back of the room. Sitting next to Passattella was the harassed, elderly music director with frizzled Toscanini hair who clung to his baton like a circus artist to his trapeze, unaware that his rigid beat was being ignored by the pianist. After a few bars, the chorus managed to come together, and shouted out their achievement in a happy crescendo.

'Enough! Enough!' shouted Maestro Passattella, clapping his hands. 'You start soft and on the beat. Together! You are soldiers, Madonna Santa, soldiers are always together!'

'Not French ones,' came a barely audible voice.

'Silence! Is everyone ready now? May we begin?'

'Whenever you like. Some of us know our words,' remarked Assunta Melati, the well-seasoned mezzo-soprano in dark glasses and a flowing, flowered dress gathered under her ballooning breasts. 'This will be my three hundred and thirty-first performance.'

'Dearest Assunta, I know you're good at sums.'

She gave him a disapproving glance, knowing that he was referring to her contract.

'Subtract three hundred and thirty and think of it as the first time,' continued Passattella amiably.

Guido, the tenor playing Don José, whispered in Carla's ear. 'Poor thing. She's never had a first time. She's been trying to lose it for over thirty years, so I hear. Without success.'

Apart from Carla, the only person who appeared to notice Stasi was a man with carefully cut black sideburns and commanding eyes, sitting at the side. Rico looked up from the *Gazzetta dello Sport* and winked. Here was a new arrival to admire his tight blue bulging Levis and pink shirt covered in cavorting, cape-waving bullfighters. Baritones could rarely display the brooding sexuality commandeered by tenors, but *Carmen* was a glorious exception. Rico's Escamillo would steal the show. Didn't everyone say that he was the double of Rudolph Valentino? In profile there was a distinct resemblance. They had the same nose. Without the dashing bullfighter Escamillo what would be left of Mérimée's story? A low-ranking soldier falls for a common gypsy girl. Who would have cared? What a part. No need to even try. He'd upstage that fat Carmen the moment he appeared. Passattella might get to Act Two, his first entry, before lunch. He'd better hang around.

Singers liked working with Passattella. He didn't waste time faffing about with interpretation. You either knew your part or you didn't, and if you didn't all you'd get next time was a cover job with an opera house in some hick

73

place like Lecce or Catania where, if someone suddenly dropped out, they didn't give a damn if you read your part onstage. As likely as not, the audience would sing along with you.

Leaning forward to catch every note of Carla's first big aria, Stasi winced. All the careful coaching about French accent, the French line – how could she?

'Stop, if you please.' Passattella rose from his chair and moved in front of Carla. 'Darling. This interpretation is interesting, but for me, rather too controversial. More suitable to that cowboy, Morrison. If you wish to appear on Signor Berlusconi's TV strip show, tell me now.'

Carla tossed her head. Director's games. 'I wouldn't mind. Strip-opera. Fantastic idea.'

He allowed the giggles to die down. No harm in cultivating a relaxed atmosphere during rehearsals. He'd tighten the screws later on. 'Now. As you aren't singing Carmen, may we have Micaela, please? Will you let me hear a simple peasant girl? Pure, innocent, devoted – and a virgin?'

Rico put down his paper. Things were livening up.

'A simple peasant girl is just the kind who wouldn't be a virgin,' commented Guido acidly. He loathed *paesani*, they reminded him of stale sweat, mosquitoes and the smell of dung. 'Anyway, one's hardly likely to meet such people.'

'I've met hundreds. You want me to introduce you?'

Guido threw him a look of contempt which he had been practising for years. 'You think I'd pick at your leftovers, Rico?'

Passattella gestured to the music director. 'Come. We continue.'

'Maestro, I have to go in fifteen minutes,' announced Assunta Melati grandly. 'For my massage. He is the best man in Florence, booked up for months, and he's agreed to see me today.'

Sucking in his breath, Passattella oozed with understanding. 'My dear, in reception there is a telephone. You will go now and tell this genius to make another appointment. After rehearsals. For a great artist, he will do this.'

'Thank you, maestro.'

It was only the beginning. Everyone, Stasi supposed, had to start by observing in respectful silence. Even Maria Callas must have sat through rehearsals raging inside. The rehearsal room clock jerked on to the midday position, the pianist finished a phrase on his own, and the singers immediately deserted their music stands, rapidly took up their belongings, and prepared to leave for the next act. Lunch.

Passattella at last acknowledged Stasi's presence and approached her. 'Miss Anastasia? Welcome to Florence. I wasn't expecting you so soon. If you wish, you may come later in the week. Sebastiano, our music coach, will take you through your part. I'll hear you sing later. You are staying in a comfortable place?'

Stasi stiffened, and prepared a polite reply. 'I haven't had time to find anywhere, yet. But I'm not bothered. As long as it's clean.'

'Hah. You think all Italians are dirty and smell of garlic?' He chucked her under the chin. 'You British have strange ideas. We are not offended, my dear. We have Leonardo, Michelangelo, Puccini and Verdi, after all!'

The singers started to leave. Carla came running up to her. 'Stasi! You've arrived! Couldn't remember which day you were coming. Isn't this crazy? I have a lunch date but I'll see you later. We must hit town together. Ciao.'

Within seconds, Carla was gone, followed by Rico, strolling after her, smoothing down his hair. When Stasi got outside, she saw no one from the cast. There was just a large, black chauffeur-driven car parked on the pavement. The door was open and Maestro Passattella was stepping inside. She could see the outline of a girl with straight, shoulder-length blond hair, shrouded in a large floppy black straw hat and dark glasses, looking expectantly out of the back window.

'Always a different one.' Guido was standing beside her as the car pulled away. 'See those curtains at the back? Watch.' The view through the rear window was slowly obliterated. 'By the time he gets to Settignano, he'll have screwed her twice. Then they'll have a picnic in a field. He never changes the routine. No imagination, dear Passattella. Would you like a bite to eat? They haven't introduced us. Guido De Santis.'

'Stasi Wagner.'

'You a friend of someone in the cast?'

'No. I'm singing Micaela after Carla.'

'So you're the English girl.'

'Yes.'

'Wonderful. I love everything English. How.Do.You. Do.' Guido pulled in his chin and pushed back his shoulders. 'Do you think I look English? A little? I have sung in Covent Garden.'

'Congratulations, Guido.'

'Just a small role. But they noticed me. You know a shop called Austin Reed? I bought this jacket there. Very exclusive, very English gentleman.'

Over a pizza and a beer, Stasi changed her opinion of Guido. At first, she had responded with bored tolerance, listening politely to his self-congratulatory stories, his descriptions of working with people she had never heard of.

'What do you think of the new girl? Carla Livorno? Her first role, apparently. I hate working with beginners.'

Stasi looked away.

'Bet she's kicking herself she isn't a mezzo. Should have been cast as Carmen with that body. But we needn't feel sorry. With her name, she can go anywhere. Great smile. I don't know why she went off with that idiot. A football for a brain. Not that I care.'

Stasi swallowed hard. 'We have the same teacher. She sings well, doesn't she?'

'Not bad. Don't think much of her choice for lunch, though. She'll soon realize that Rico goes for anything with blond hair and big tits. Just wait till he starts trying to upstage her; she'll drop him soon enough. Stupid bastard!' He pushed away his plate. 'They can't make pizzas in Florence.' Guido extracted a couple of cloves of garlic from his pocket, and began to peel them. Then he pushed them both into his mouth, and began to chew them reflectively.

'You could order something else,' suggested Stasi, puzzled at his desperate act.

'For the voice, you must have ten raw cloves a day. Don't they teach you this in England? Here, have one of mine. You know, I never have problems with my larynx. Or my heart. Or my manhood. Go on, take it.'

'I'll eat it later,' said Stasi tactfully, putting the clove under her plate, covering her revulsion with a smile.

'Your first *Carmen*?'

'Yes.'

'Don't worry about it. This production has been going the rounds for ten years. I've done it in Bologna, Venice, Trieste, Argentina, Stockholm – you name it. The set's been renovated more times than La Melati's face. Which hotel are you in, Stasi?'

'I'm . . . staying with friends,' she replied doubtfully.

'Well, I'm at the Majestic. You must come over some time and use the gym. I'm sure I could get you in.'

'Thank you. Very kind of you.'

'Coffee?'

Guido was not inclined to expound more of his philosophy and Stasi was relieved when he headed off for a quick swim and work-out before the afternoon rehearsal. She wandered slowly along the Lungarno, soaking up the dry midday heat reflected off the ochre, red-tiled buildings lining the river, enchanted by the harmonious arches of Santa Trinità and Ponte Vecchio which straddled the wide, sun-drenched river. Then she turned right down a side street, assessing the buildings which had 'Affittasi camere' in the window, wondering if Florence was as expensive as it looked.

At the end of rehearsal, Carla promised to show her the real Florence. Much more sophisticated than Milan, she told her. The party scene is cool, the guys aren't jerks like the Milanese. They buy you Häagen-Dazs ice-cream sodas and whisky sours and don't go ape-shit if they miss out on the barber's. While she was elaborating on the clubs, the bars, the bright spots of Florence, Stasi lost her concentration.

'What's up?'

'I hope it gets better.'

'Life? What's wrong with it?'

'The production. Not you, I mean. It's like a pub when they've called time. Everyone drinking up because they have to.'

'Isn't Rico a gas? So uncool. He kills me.'

'Suppose it turns out to be a stinker?'

'*Carmen*? Why are we doing it? For a boring summer festival, Stasi. Tourist fodder. Looks good in the brochures. People that matter will be either on a surfboard or a yacht, not fucking around pointing their cameras at the Fiesole hills. And Passattella's a jerk. Ignore him. Anyhow, this beats Milan any day. Let's go eat.'

She was always on the move, drinking in everything around her, constantly distracted, pulling Stasi along to look in shop windows, exploring the backstreets, look at this, look at that. Wow!

'Carla. Time I found somewhere to stay.'

'Why didn't you say, silly goof? I was going to ask you to stay with me, but it's a bit far out. You'd need a car. Why don't you try the Hotel Regency? There's loads of English stay there. Ma's favourite place.'

Stasi was taken aback. Hadn't she realized by now? 'Something simple will do fine. I don't need anything luxurious. Really.'

'For Chrissake, Stasi. Are you still hard up for cash?' She sounded amazed.

'You could say.'

Carla stopped dead in the middle of the pavement. 'Here, you pretend you've got money. Even if you're poor. *Bella figura.* You go down Montenapoleone and take out a mortgage on a dress. Everyone knows it's the same dress, but you keep it looking good, stick on different jewellery. Then you change down indoors.'

Stasi was unconvinced by Carla's acquaintance with poverty. 'Have you ever had to count up lire coins?'

She laughed. 'Only for parking meters.'

'I need to know when we get paid. Any idea?'

'When my agent arrives with a Beretta.'

'Seriously.'

'One beautiful day!'

They had reached the Piazza della Signoria, coming to life in the washed-out light of early evening. The Palazzo Vecchio was as solidly assertive and threatening as the Tower of London, Stasi decided. She could picture Tosca hurling herself from the battlements casting a chilly shadow in the square.

A group of young men paused in front of them. 'Get those tits! Come with us, girls.'

Carla screwed up her face and gave a penetrating screech. 'Fascist louts!'

Her challenge was met by one of the sauntering group. 'Viva Mussolini!'

Stasi froze. Swastikas on graves. 'Fascists? In Florence? Aren't you scared?'

'Means nothing,' Carla said. 'They could have shouted out long live the dolphins. Here you can be green and fascist and catholic and social democrat all at the same time. Beliefs have designer labels. Mix and match. In one moment, out the next.'

'Teach me some insults.'

Carla laughed. 'Any time. You got all day?'

The only place for champagne cocktails was Harry's Bar, a discreet presence in Lungo Vespucci. Its high-ceilinged, gilded grandeur housed a collection of people who would have been at home in any of the world's capitals. Two Russians were loudly debating at the bar, Italians, French and Germans switched effortlessly from one language to another as they relayed the success of their financial or amatory transactions. An elderly woman with a stretched, lifted face caked in cosmetics, dressed entirely in black, swept in cradling two coiffeured Bedlington terriers, followed by a wide-shouldered young man dressed, for some reason of vanity, in a pink hunting jacket and white breeches. The only attention they attracted was from the barman, who signalled to a waiter.

Carla noticed Stasi staring at the strange couple. 'La Contessa Nera with her house-boy. She's the best known alcoholic in Florence. Don't sit anywhere near her. She'll bore you for hours. Had a bit part in a Fellini film once and never got over it.'

She lost count of the number of people who smiled, lifted a languid hand, sent over another tray of champagne, or in some way acknowledged Carla's presence. She was at home in their company, even though she did not know all their names. And there was Rico, the only one who was pretending to ignore her, giving himself away by a quick sideways glance, standing at the bar, one leg crossed round the other. When Carla was looking the other way, Stasi saw him looking in their direction, weighing up the appropriate moment to announce his presence.

'Well, if it isn't our very own sexpot Micaela,' he said, coming forward as though he had just noticed her. 'And the English miss?'

'Stasi.'

'Here.' He put down half a bottle of champagne on their table, and Carla flicked back a curl with studied insolence.

'Have you been here long, Rico?'

'Hours and hours. But I knew you'd come.'

'Only because we were passing.'

'I booked a table at the Enoteca. For two. Will you join me?'

'I might.' Carla gave Rico a brief, seductive smile, then turned away to face Stasi. 'We must find you somewhere good to stay. Come on, let's go. I know where we can try.'

In less than an hour, Carla had led her to the place she would have chosen herself, a spacious, wooden-floored roof-top room with Scandinavian furnishings in clear blue and yellow, opening out onto a small terrace overlooking the river Arno. While Carla went downstairs to find out the rates from the owner, a dreamy-eyed Swedish sculptress, Stasi was lost in admiration. The perfect place. Someone would like it, a student with wealthy parents, ideal for a painter. She would distance herself from her desires and store them up for a distant day. After years of training by Gloria, she was an expert at storing up unaffordable memories.

'You like it?'

'Fantastic.'

Carla opened the window. 'Great view. You'd be happy here?'

'I would be, but . . .'

'Just as well. I've rented it for a month. We'll move your things right away.'

'Is it very expensive?'

'About the price of dinner for two at the Enoteca. Don't worry.'

'You might have to wait till I get paid.'

Carla found a terrace at the back, with trailing flowers spilling from terracotta pots. She would ask for a table so they could breakfast there *all'aria aperta*. They could lie naked in the sun – you could have a tan for *Carmen* – no one would see them. Perfect, perfect. Stasi took her arm and pulled her inside.

'Of course it's perfect. But I don't know if I can . . .'

'We'll share it.'

'But you've got somewhere to stay.'

'I don't have to go back to my place every night. It's a

81

heck of a drive. So occasionally I can stay here. There's a spare bed. Any objection?'

''Course not.'

'I know what would be nice. A piano. It'll have to be small to get up those stairs. And a stereo.'

Carla opened the shutters and the sun came flooding through the windows, lighting up the textures of the thick woven cotton, the rugs, and the grainy, toffee-coloured wood. Then she contemplated the contents of the room as though she was about to transform them into something more magnificent. For a moment she was still, serenely beautiful. Was this her true face, which she revealed in the absence of men?

Stasi wanted to take her into her arms, to hug her, to show her that the cold English girl was possessed of feeling, but something held her back. The demonstrative bestowing of emotion had been devalued by the Wagner family, and their constant stroking, caressing and touching had left her with a horror of physical contact. She could not even bring herself to say thank you, thank you for saving me from some cheap, dreary pensione.

Then Carla ran over to her, threw her arms round her neck and pressed her lips against hers, but Stasi instantly drew back.

'I'm not contagious, Stasi! You allergic to lipstick? Let me wipe it away.' She took out a silk handkerchief and playfully dabbed off the scarlet.

'You surprised me. That's all.'

'Oh, Italians,' Carla said mockingly. 'We're so physical.'

'And I'm so English and reserved. You should have asked me first. Always ask first.'

'Please, would you mind awfully, Anastasia. OK? English enough?'

'Too familiar, Carla. You can shake hands with me.'

'Hands are boring. Unless they're kissed. Do you like having your fingers sucked?'

'Kids do that.'

'So I'm a kid.'

'Can I be serious?'

'Sure.'

'Thanks. For finding me this place.'

Carla was waiting, expecting her to continue.

'I hope we'll still be friends after *Carmen*.'

'Why ever not? I won't be any different. Will you? Unless you meet some guy who really turns you on . . .'

'Not interested.' Stasi was thinking of the three she'd noticed. Passattella. Guido and Rico. 'I don't want someone around who puts me off and starts bugging me all the time.' She grinned. 'Or turns out to be engaged.'

'Do you like me, Stasi?'

Now Carla was looking at her differently, like a man alone with his lover for the first time, seeing only her body, waiting. Stasi wanted to move away, to leave the room. She did not want to confront the unknown. She was both fascinated and invaded by fear.

'You mean, do I like girls? Physically?'

'There's no difference. You live through your body, all singers do. And yours is beautiful. Even though you hide it. Come here. Let me touch you.'

'No, no.'

'What's wrong? You put off by my tits? I don't mind you telling me. We can still be close, Stasi?'

Her tongue was locked. How could she express the vast ocean of difference between their culture, upbringing, tradition, even the way they articulated words? 'Listen. I don't understand what you want from me. It's something quite strange. If someone touches me, it's an invasion.'

'Someone you don't know?'

'Someone I do know. They're the only ones who count.'

Carla jumped onto one of the beds, and sat cross-legged, flexing her feet. 'When you make yourself come, what do you think about?'

'You don't have to shock me, Carla. All right. You did, but there's no need to carry on. I want to go now. Tell the woman downstairs I've changed my mind. It won't work out. I'm not a lesbian.'

'Do I look like a dyke? Come on. You think it's a sin and you're not even a Catholic. Everyone is bisexual, they just don't admit it.'

'I'm not.' Was that true? She had no way of knowing, had never given it a moment's thought. It was hard enough discovering where your voice lay, whether you should sing soprano or mezzo, without having to decide whether you preferred men or girls or both. 'Does your fiancé know?'

'Why take it so seriously? I'm hardly going to rape you. If that's what you're afraid of. Jesus! Hasn't a girl ever touched you before? Does anyone touch anyone in England?' She edged herself off the bed, approached Stasi from behind, and ran her hands down her back, down her buttocks. 'You've got an arse to die for.'

'The Wagner arse.'

They both laughed then. It was only when the hands crept round to her hips, and felt through her cotton skirt to the forbidden zone, that Stasi gasped, whether through revulsion or shock she could not tell.

'I'm much better at it than a man. Long, dreamy, drawn out pleasure. Wouldn't you like it? With all my fingers? Just the right place. Just the right touch. You ever known a guy with the right touch? Gently, gently. One after another. Like this?'

One hand swiftly lifted her skirt, the other wormed its way under her pants, past the throbbing lips to the point of desire, leaving a trail of dampness. A current surged through Stasi's body, and then she gave a start as though she had been stung by a hornet. With her back to the door, she allowed Carla's lips to rest on hers, and even opened her mouth slightly, enough to receive her fluttering tongue. After a few moments, she gradually pushed her away.

'Come on, Carla. Let's do my move.'

The rehearsal schedule for *Carmen* moved on, but as the days passed, there was little change nor any development that Stasi could observe. The singers had brought their predetermined characters along with their extensive luggage. Assunta had insisted on bringing her own Carmen costume which, she said, always brought her luck. The tiered and sequinned stiffened flounces which descended from the proximity of her waist were more reminiscent of a Blackpool Latin American trophy dance than Bizet's Spain, but comment was not only unnecessary, it was life-threatening. No dress, no Carmen. No Carmen, no show.

Acts One, Two and Three succeeded one another with repetitious similarity, the only difference being that Assunta was persuaded to sing in full voice for the final run-through. 'She's saving herself for the thousandth performance,' remarked Guido within earshot.

Stasi began to forget that this tedious production was destined for an audience. There was now nothing she could learn from the mechanical rehearsals, but she arrived sometimes when she was not needed. She found herself looking at the schedule to find out when Carla was singing. But it was not for her voice, it was for the pleasure of watching her, of basking in her brightness, her grace. She had no desire to explore Florence, except in her presence.

'You can stay with me whenever you like,' Carla had said early on, but no arrangement had been made. When she mentioned it again, she made no reference to her previous invitation. 'You must come out and see the villa. Belongs to a friend of Ma's. On one of our days off. Why not?'

Stasi wanted her to be there, in her room, just once. She might then discover if it was possible to remain friends, to sleep in separate beds, to breakfast together on the terrace, without touching, to kiss her on the cheek without being reminded of the sexual advances which she had accepted, which disturbed her, and whose consequences she had not yet understood. It was the duty of the artist to understand everything, she told herself. She often lay awake wondering if the attraction she felt had anything to do with love. Was it a wish to explore the boundaries of sex? Or was it simply that Carla represented everything she wanted to be?

On several occasions, when Stasi lay alone naked on her bed, half covering herself modestly with a sheet, attempting a siesta in the overbearing heat of the afternoon, she was convinced that she could smell the musky residue of Carla's perfume, as though she had recently passed through the room.

The Passattella *Carmen* would soon be ready for scrutiny. Judgement day was approaching.

'There's only one music critic who counts,' said Carla. 'Stefano Montini. If he comes, forget it. He hates everything. But he's a sweetie. Just been at it too long.'

No one else had any qualms about the success of the production. Maestro Passattella occasionally gave notes, often left his cast in the hands of the music director. He had said what he had to say. Sometimes he sat at the back, with a distant smile on his face as though he was perpetually thinking of lazy summers, Bacchic suppers in vine-covered courtyards and sprawling post-coital nakedness. The only event which interrupted his equilibrium was the arrival of Assunta's entourage, which he insisted on calling 'the cortège'. The stage manager was commanded to set chairs in the rehearsal room for Assunta's aged mother, her brother, her secretary, her cousin (also her manager) and a pudgy, sullen teenage girl who bore a striking resemblance to Assunta, but whom she introduced as her adopted daughter. A bony, red-bowed, nervous Yorkshire terrier was placed on a silk cushion and yapped when she started to sing, but no one appeared to mind.

By now, Stasi knew every pause, every move, almost every breath taken by the cast, and could notice better than Passattella when a bored member of the chorus tried an unexpected piece of business, like pinching the nearest bottom during the scene in Pastia's inn. The Spain of Bizet was moving little by little towards the Italy of the

Commedia dell'Arte. Signora Busconi would have thrown up her hands in horror. It was inevitable, Stasi supposed, that there should be some kind of confrontation. If you were asked to do something absolutely ridiculous, there was only one thing to do. Change it. She might be a beginner, but she knew when something felt wrong. For the first run-through for the scenes with Micaela, held especially for her, Stasi knew what she would do. And she wouldn't lose her temper.

Maestro Passattella waited until her first scene was over to give his rebuke in front of the whole cast.

'My dear Signorina Vag-ner. No relation of the great Richard, my friends. You have been coming to rehearsals, very good. You sing very well, sincerely. I mean that. The music, good. But please. If we spend two weeks working out moves for the singers, I do not expect you to change everything.'

'I wasn't changing for the sake of it, maestro. But there is no reason for Micaela to go leaping round the stage, jumping down steps and flinging herself about. It doesn't feel right. I can't do it. I'm sorry. I just can't.'

'Can't? Or won't, my dear? Here in Italy, we believe that singers should respect the wishes of the director. And we expect them to act.'

'You call running around like a demented frog acting? It doesn't suit the character. Micaela isn't Carmen, she's a quiet girl, thoughtful, placid . . .'

'Oh, my God. Patience, patience.'

The soldiers in the cast broke ranks and were soon passing round peppermints and bottles of Fanta. Passattella took Stasi by the arm and led her to a corner of the room.

'I know this is your first time. Let me explain, my dear. You may have noticed, the opera is called *Carmen*. This Carmen, who sings very well, moves hardly at all. Occasionally, yes, she walks from one part of the stage to the other. So. We make a contrast with Micaela. Micaela is a young girl, not mature like Carmen. So it's logical. She moves like a young girl. On the go, all the time, like my daughters, like all young girls. For the first time, we make her a real person. Believe me, trust me. Now do what I say.'

'But the music goes against it, maestro.'

'That is your opinion, Anastasia. Now. Can we have it my way, please?'

They began Act One. Stasi made her entrance, began to sing, then suddenly stopped.

'I can't do it. I've tried. Maybe it's right for Carla, but it isn't for me.'

'Ah. Now I understand. I knew it. Two sopranos singing the same role. Fatal. I thought you'd be grateful for the opportunity. But as you are not, I think you should return to Milan. Or to the rain in England if you prefer. Carla can stay for the whole run. You realize this rehearsal was for you? I will not allow such a waste of time.' He rose from his chair, and announced, 'Rehearsal break.'

This was the opportunity Assunta had been waiting for. After consuming half a bottle of mineral water, and dismissing her attendants for the afternoon, she sailed off to the ladies' cloakroom to remove her corset. Here she found Stasi staring in the mirror, grim-faced, wiping off the black smears round her eyes.

'Thank heavens. Do excuse me, dear, I was nearly fainting.' She pulled the long rehearsal dress over her head and it dropped to the floor in a bedraggled heap, revealing a pink boned structure which had left red weals on her rib-cage. 'Unhook me, quickly. It's too much to bear.'

Stasi struggled with the metal fastenings and the swollen breasts reared out of their prison and gravitated towards the faint indentation marking Assunta's waist.

'What a mood! The maestro must have quarrelled with that ghastly wife of his. Usually he's like a piece of pie. I hope he doesn't call us back today.'

'I've just fucked up.'

''Course you didn't. We all know it's silly. Having Micaela dancing around like a firecracker. Well done, my dear. It's time someone stood up to him apart from me.'

'What will happen now? Does that mean I'm fired? Do you think I'm mad?'

'It took me ten years to make him appreciate my artistic integrity. Stick to your guns, my dear. Those of us who have a voice don't need to prance around like chorus girls. She's bound to burn herself out in a couple of years. Carla Livorno! Of course, if it wasn't for her father. Come with me. You need something to calm you down.'

Over a glass of Fernet Branca, a concoction resembling syrup of figs whose effect, Assunta assured Stasi, was miraculous, she volunteered another gem from her repertoire. 'Take my advice, dear. Be nice. Say you've thought about it. Do it his way. But on the night, well, that's a different matter. It's surprising what happens, when you're overcome by nerves. Don't you think? After all, he can't hold up a candle to the great Luchino Visconti.'

'You worked with Visconti?'

Assunta pushed an array of glittering bangles up her arm and looked into the distance, tilting her chin up with pride. 'Indeed I did. Once. That, my dear, is greatness. He told me I had the voice of an angel.' She winked at Stasi. 'I may not have the voice of an angel any more. But I've lasted. And I've got a vineyard in Tuscany, an apartment in Rome worth ten times what I paid for it – and twelve fur coats. Not bad, eh?'

Better than a rented room (paid for by Carla) in a pensione. Stasi wondered what she was worth. Nothing, because she owned nothing. The Italians, she had noticed by now, liked putting a value on everything, even their voices.

'I don't want to own anything.'

Stasi's remark was met with a guffaw from Assunta. 'Darling, you can't be a diva and hitch-hike on the autostrada. But if you want to return to England and sing in a church choir, who am I to object?' Assunta peered at her tiny gold watch and reached forward for Stasi's hand. 'Come. We'll be late. The maestro will be in a good mood by now. So you tell him you've had the benefit of reflection. Yes?'

Stasi stayed seated, unwilling to reach a decision. How could she compose an uncompromising apology? Ever since she could remember, she had refused to apologize, preferring to endure standing alone outside the classroom in the school corridor or her mother's sulking silence. Since she only admitted her faults when she recognized them herself, even to say 'I'm sorry' seemed like a betrayal. The more she reflected, the more impossible it became.

Assunta gave a heave until she was upright. 'Now we'll find the maestro. I'll explain to him first. I'll say they do things differently in England.'

'I can't do it, Assunta.'

'Stupid nonsense. Of course you can. Anyway, if you don't, the word will spread fast. Oh, the English soprano. Trouble. Impossible to work with.'

'There are other producers.'

Assunta gave Stasi a pitying look, and then peered at the bill. 'So you don't mind if La Livorno makes her solo debut as Micaela?'

The words came out in a rush, only half coherent. Stasi's cheeks flushed angry red, and she was unable to look Signor Passattella in the face, hoping he was unable to detect her counterfeit apology. To her relief, he accepted it, led her back to the cast, wreathed in smiles, announced that all differences had been resolved and barked out at the pianist: 'From 242. Ready. And . . .'

Stasi thought Carla might have come to see her, even out of curiosity, but she stayed away. One day, seeing her standing outside the rehearsal room waiting for Rico, she went up to her.

'I'd like your opinion, Carla.'

She laughed. 'I like surprises. I'll see you on your first night.'

'Will you still be here?'

'Oh, yes, I expect so.' When Rico appeared, and they went off together, she shouted over her shoulder, 'You must come to the villa. Soon!'

Stasi was puzzled. Why did Carla wish to spend so much time in the company of a man she despised? Once she had remarked within earshot that he was just another dumb singer who confused brain power with cock power. 'Not for you,' Gloria would have said, and he did look unsuitable, the kind of man to be found loitering at the exit of a car-wash, who would suggestively wipe the suds from your windscreen, taking longer than was necessary. Once she saw them kissing goodbye openly, in the Lungarno, a few doors from his house. He was pulling her hips tight against his, she was leaning her head back, and Stasi felt revulsion. Or was it jealousy?

The cast moved up one morning to the hills of Fiesole, and Stasi saw the bare stone symmetry of the Roman amphitheatre for the first time.

'At last. Fresh air. Fresher air.' Assunta sniffed and expanded her chest as Stasi took in the sweep of countryside where the olive trees gave way to the dark candle shape of cypresses punctuating the hazy blue distance. Then she ran down to the bare stage, looking up at the stepped stone semicircle where the audience would sit.

'I bet the acoustics are great here,' she shouted to Assunta, who was picking her way gingerly down the gangway.

'Even better with a microphone, I find.'

'Surely not?'

'This audience wouldn't know the difference.'

'How wonderful to perform like the Romans, on a bare space. It's so beautiful. Who needs a set?'

'I wouldn't tell the designer, dear.'

By the time of the afternoon rehearsal call, the bare space had been transformed with a blood-red cloth, a huge silhouette of a black bull and a tangle of scaffolding supporting a wooden platform. The stage hands were hammering vigorously as Signor Passattella made the first appraisal of his work of art, a frown on his face, one hand resting on his lips as though restraining himself from a stream of invective.

'Stasi!' Carla came running towards her. 'I was hoping you'd come. Will you be here on the first night? My fiancé's decided to make it. Do you know, I'm nervous? God, it's gone on for ever.'

'Of course I'll come. Did you think I wouldn't?'

'You're fantastic. Where have you been? How's everything? How's it going? I hear Passattella thinks the world of you. I must change. Jesus Christ! That set's made for alpine climbers. See you.'

When she was not needed, Carla sat by Stasi, pointing out the obstacles, commenting, laughing. There was always something to laugh at when a rehearsal moved to the stage. Assunta was doing her best to dominate the chorus of soldiers and gypsies in Pastia's inn, shifting her weight as little as possible, performing miracles with her arms, flicking her fingers, fluttering her fan, flashing her eyes, leaning back seductively on a bench.

'Ah-eeee.'

The bench slowly tipped backwards. Assunta struggled to keep her balance, then thudded to the ground with raised legs and a flurry of flounces. Rico ran over, took her hands, then gripped her arms and struggled to get her upright. With the help of two of the chorus, she was on her feet.

'My God! Are you hurt?'

Passattella tried to sound solicitous, but his voice shook. Could she, would she, sue for negligence?

'I don't need a doctor, if that's what you mean,' replied Assunta sharply, checking her thighs. 'But you could do with a decent carpenter, maestro. Fix the bloody thing to the ground.'

'Excellent suggestion. It will be done.'

'Let us continue. If I faint, you will know that the pain is unbearable.'

With a gesture to the stage manager, Passattella shouted, 'Find a doctor immediately. And get an ambulance.'

'Stop fussing. A doctor? Do you think I'm an invalid? I continued performing during an earthquake in Palermo. Remember? Get going. I haven't got all night.'

Limping through Acts Two and Three, Assunta Melati received a standing ovation from the chorus and stage-crew which brought tears to her eyes. It was twenty years since that had happened.

As she drove herself and Stasi back to Florence, Carla said little. She seemed angry.

'You didn't have to drop me off, Carla. There's a bus.'

'We're too good for this crap.'

'It's a start, I suppose.' Stasi sounded so miserable that Carla laughed.

'We're like a couple of grannies at a funeral. Cheer up. After all, this is our first break.'

'Yours, you mean.'

'Why are you in a bad mood? Have I done something? Tell me.'

'We don't meet any more.'

'Oh, Stasi, I know. But Rico is getting serious. It's a real drag but I can't be mean to him. Anyway, I thought you were having a good time with Guido.'

'I don't understand you.'

'We're friends. It's not as though we're lovers. I didn't think you were interested.'

When Carla dropped her off, she gave Stasi a formal peck on both cheeks.

Chapter Four

'Why didn't you bring the car up here? Or tell me to bring hiking boots? Even in the army, they didn't send us out in this heat.'

Rico was examining every inch of the dry ground, placing each foot with care to avoid the rocky stones littering the hillside path.

'And it's meant to be my rest day.' He stopped, gave a dry cough and covered his mouth. 'All this dust. I should have brought my mask. You just want to torture my throat.'

'I'm not interested in your throat, darling.'

'Why don't we sit down? Then you can admire the view. What was wrong with the villa? We could have been plunging into a pool or sitting out on the terrace sipping iced lemon instead of busting our legs around Fiesole.'

Carla gave his bottom a playful shove. 'Come on.'

'At the Villa San Michele they have a pool, darling. Let's go there. It's downhill all the way.'

'What's the point? It doesn't work underwater. And I only swim in the sea.'

'We don't need to swim.' Rico began to quicken his pace. He could see a spreading tree inviting shade in a distant field. 'How about over there, Carla, my treasure?' he said, pointing.

It was early for lunch, but Carla decided to cut the day short. Rico's charm and attentiveness were fading as quickly as his stamina, and he was walking anxiously, stopping every now and again as though terrified that a rabid dog would attack them from behind a wall. The indoor type. He was only at home in a bar, she thought, giving him a contemptuous glance. She expected men to be equally at ease in a bar, in a bedroom, on the ocean or in the country. As she was herself.

'There'll be trouble tomorrow. Be prepared, Carla. Passattella's first nights are always a disaster.'

'That'll be fun.' Carla pulled a rug from her basket and spread it under the tree.

'How many performances are we in for? Thank God I'm off to Buenos Aires after this.'

Without looking round to see if she was observed, Carla stripped off her T-shirt, but as Rico lunged for her bare breasts she grasped his hands and replaced them by his side. 'Lunch first, sweetheart.'

'I'm not hungry.' Rico was breathing heavily, his eyes fixed on her golden skin and delicate nipples, wondering whether to release her from those tight-zipped white jeans as she emptied her basket and spread out an array of cold meats, cheeses, olives and tomatoes in front of him.

'I can't resist you, Carla. You make me forget everything. How can you do this to me? We shouldn't be doing this. I mustn't. I promised my wife that this time, no temptation. She even lit a candle for me.'

'Silly but touching,' said Carla as she sliced a mound of fresh mozzarella. 'Even Passattella wouldn't fire you for that. You're not doing anything wrong, Rico. It's your day off.'

'But I have and I will and I will again. My children, think of my children.'

'Fine.' Carla leaned her back against his, watching an old man pulling along a couple of scraggy goats in the distance. If he had seen them, he would have stopped and stared. And Rico would probably have hit him, believing his honour was at stake. A spray of tomato pips landed on her shoulder and began to dribble down her breast.

'Messy boy.'

'Allow me,' he said gallantly, but she pushed him away and slipped a sliver of cheese in his mouth, holding her fingers inside as he bit. Roused beyond endurance, Rico pulled her on top of him.

'It's too hot.'

'I am a passionate man, Carla *mia*,' he said into her ear. 'Do you do this with other men?'

'Have I looked at anyone else?'

'Not Guido?'

'Guido? He only cares about his pectorals.'

'Passattella?'

'Poor old thing. They must have dug him up in the Roman arena.'

'And what about your fiancé. He's older than you, isn't he?'

'The marchese? My kind old man? He's like my father.'

'You desire only me, then?'

'Only you. How can I sing without my Rico?' Carla wriggled down his body, pulled at his belt and released the buckle. 'Give me my elixir, darling,' she said, as she forced his rearing cock out of the tight opening.

'Oh, Carla. Don't. You mustn't. Ah. Not that. I promised. Now I must take confession. I haven't time to see a priest. Stop. It's a sin. Madonna!'

His cries of outrage changed to soft moans and then to an anguished cry as she spread her lips and the jet of sperm pulsed into her mouth. She swallowed little by little, allowing the lubricating liquid to trickle down her throat. There was nothing to beat it.

Rico looked down at her proudly. Only prostitutes did that, and she did it better. How she must love him.

'I'll think of you all the way to Buenos Aires, my darling. What are you doing next? Why don't you fly out? No, it's crazy of me to suggest that.'

'I might.'

He would tell the priest (if he could find one in Florence, a heathen city) about her smile. Father, you cannot imagine. The smile of a loving girl. Such innocence. Is it a sin? Such a sin?

'Will I see you after the first night?' he asked eagerly.

'Perhaps. My family are coming. Pa, Ma, Eduardo, Beatrice. It'll bore me to tears. I suppose they'll want to go somewhere afterwards. If only I could lie with you, dearest Rico.'

'And your fiancé. I suppose he'll come.'

'I suppose he will.'

'My wife, too. Worse luck. Why do we live in a prison? We were born to be free, my treasure.'

Carla nestled on his chest, entwining her legs around his. Soon, Rico grew hard again and longed to hurl himself inside her.

'No. We must go now.'

'Carla, Carla. One last time, before we meet in Buenos Aires.'

'No.'

'You don't mean it. You don't love me.'

She kissed him, jumped to her feet and pulled on her crumpled shirt. 'You'll tire yourself out. And blame me!'

'My beloved gypsy girl. I will do anything you ask. We must sing together. Always.' He took her by the hand, gazing at the sky as though expecting the end credits to come drifting down with a crescendo of violins.

The food was wrapped, only the flattened grass betraying their presence. Her mission accomplished, Carla slung the basket over her shoulder and began to sing Carmen's habanera as she strolled jauntily across the field towards the path.

The day before a first performance was like the day before you went into hospital for an operation, wondering if you would ever come round from the anaesthetic. Stasi was thinking of what Carla must be going through. She would need support, which was why she had chosen this moment to ask Stasi out to her villa. You needed people to distract you. Most of all you needed someone who was calm and understanding. A friend, rather than a lover.

From the terrace, she saw the red Alfa Romeo speed down the Lungarno, then lurch to a halt outside her building. A piercing hoot-hoot announced Carla's arrival. Stasi waved from the window and ran downstairs.

'Hi, Stasi. You don't mind having a quiet evening? I'll have to take it easy before tomorrow. Will I be glad when Act Three's out of the way.'

Unusually for Carla, her white jeans were stained, her shirt creased – she looked so much more attractive, Stasi thought, out of those flawless, perfectly accessorized designer clothes. She had barely settled in the passenger seat when Carla revved the idling engine and took off. As she pulled out at an abrupt right angle to overtake, Stasi tensed, gasped and closed her eyes.

'That surprised the guy in the Porsche. You OK? I'm much better than Eduardo and Ma drives even faster.'

'My mum would scream to get out.'

'Is she coming over to see you?'

'I can't stop her.'

'Shame I won't get to meet your ma. Soon as I've finished, I've got to go off to our place by the sea.'

'You won't see me then?'

'Stasi, I'd love to but I just can't stay on. In Italy, every summer you're a slave to the family. Like Christmas is for you. That right?'

Stasi nodded. It was not worth explaining that the Wagners ignored the festival of Christmas but had turkey and mince-pies. And she wouldn't show her disappointment. Why did she expect Carla to come to her first night? She had heard her sing, after all.

'How about your fiancé? Does he get on with your family?'

'Maurizio? Oh, he wouldn't dream of coming. I couldn't bear it either.'

'I suppose it's not much fun. Are you allowed to sleep with him?'

Carla laughed. 'My parents wouldn't mind if I slept with the dog as long as his pedigree was right.'

'Will they be staying at your villa?'

'Jesus, no! It's only small.' Carla interpreted Stasi's silence as disapproval, and added reassuringly, 'But it's very cute. It's got a pool. My sister Beatrice has shown up with her boyfriend, Julian Lieberman. She's nuts over him. One of those Englishmen I can't stand. The snob spiffy accent kind. Calls himself an investment analyst. Whatever it means, he's loaded. Not my type.' Carla grinned at Stasi, who was glancing at the speedometer less and less. 'Maybe he's your type.'

'Are you putting him on offer, then?'

'Personally I wouldn't fuck him. Even if my sister was keen on the idea. At least they both like music. She plays. He listens. Apart from that, he seems to ignore her pretty well.'

'I'd love to hear her.'

'Beatrice? She'll be practising all day. Some guy asked her once, "Do you like Shostakovich?" "I've never had it," she said. Everything Russian is vodka to her. Thick, like so many fantastic performers.'

Stasi looked puzzled, then wondered if Carla would say the same about her. That English singer. A real thicko. 'How can you be so stupid?' Even her mum thought that. Did having a voice take the energy away from the brain cells?

'I mean, she really is dumb. Lovely but dumb. Only someone real dumb could be crazy about Lieberman.'

The small villa, set in its own grounds a few kilometres from Settignano, had six bedrooms, a music room, a tennis court, an egg-shaped swimming pool and a terrace garden peopled with leering stone satyrs and well-hung Bacchic hunters. It was not pretty and creeper-clad, as country houses were meant to be, nor was it imposing, like Maurizio's villa, but Stasi didn't care. When the maid assigned her a bedroom, all to herself, looking over the terrace, she felt light-headed with happiness, like Violetta in *La Traviata*, at peace in the country.

She sprawled over the bed, attempted to read a short story by Pirandello, and soon became drowsy, lulled by the unaccustomed luxury of lavender-scented pillows, linen sheets and a thick, yielding mattress.

She slept longer than she intended. When she pulled

back the shutters and the mosquito guard against the window, she was surprised to find that it was dark. She could smell something mouthwatering. Wood-smoke permeating olive oil, the fragrance of fresh herbs. The terrace garden below her was now patchily lit by flares stuck randomly in flower-beds. Bright orange flames, blowing in all directions, were struggling to escape from a large rock-hewn barbecue, and someone, a man she hadn't met, was encouraging them with an ancient pair of leather bellows. Dark figures were stationed around him. She stood for a while, watching with intense happiness before pulling on a figure-hugging lycra dress. Not Galleria chic but it might look it in the dark.

'Here. Have some *anguilla marinata*.' Carla appeared out of the gloom, bright as a firefly, in a long silk caftan covered in the vivid colours of Pucci jungle flowers. She handed Stasi a burnt offering balanced on a slender stick.

'What is it?' she asked suspiciously.

'Eel, a local speciality. Come on, Stasi.' She pushed it in her mouth, and Stasi closed her eyes. 'We give it to old men to make them sexy. Good?'

'I think so.'

'Julian! Come over here. Meet Stasi.'

'In a second,' he shouted. 'I'm getting the fire to steak temperature.'

The fire sizzled and smoke billowed round the bays and oleanders.

'Oh. I know he'll set fire to the lavender. It's so dry. Do stop him, Carla.'

'Calm down. I'm sure he's dying to show his prowess with a fire extinguisher.'

'Have we got one?'

'Sure. In my car.'

A small figure leaped down from the stepped flower-beds and stood next to Carla. She was roughly the same height, but like a distant copy far removed from the original which had retained the outline of full breasts, high

100

buttocks and long legs, but fudged on the delicate details of the face and darkened the hair. She looked much younger than Carla.

'Beatrice, this is my dear friend Stasi Wagner.'

'Hi. Say, you're not related, are you?'

'Absolutely not.'

'I guess Wagner's a very common name. Is this your first time in Italy?'

Stasi was aware of the long, cool, supple fingers clasped weakly round hers, and it took a moment before she realized that Beatrice was unaware of the insult. Her high-pitched voice reminded Stasi of a Barbie doll programmed with set phrases for meeting over cocktails. Beatrice didn't wait for a reply, but ran off and took up a position close enough to observe the fire, but far enough away to avoid the flying sparks.

Carla had draped herself on a low wall, and was sipping a mint julep concocted by Julian from a recipe given in a yellowing copy of *The Perfect Hostess* circa 1930 which he had found in his bedroom.

'You know that movie, *White Keys*, about the drug scam in Florida? With Meryl Streep playing piano in a mob hotel?'

'Should I?'

'Not really. It's just Beatricé dubbed the piano. Went to Hollywood. Imagine, she was asked to play for Warren Beatty at some private party. She told him she didn't find Americans sexy. Can you believe? Still, she's a sweet kid. Too good for Lieberman. Hey, here's Eduardo.'

She had omitted to mention that her brother was staying. Eduardo gave Stasi a kiss on the cheek, and looked at her with a mixture of pleasure and embarrassment.

'You remember my friend, surely?' said Carla over her shoulder, as she left to assess the cooking.

'I hoped you'd come. Are you well?'

'Wonderful.'

'Fantastic tan, you have.'

A languid arm was placed round Eduardo's neck. It belonged to a wispy girl who looked out of place and time, wearing the freshly laundered Italian version of the hippy look, all beads and layered ethnic cottons, Afro hair, ankle bangles and dusty bare feet. She registered her disgust as Julian arrived with a tray of black-seared steaks, Carla in his wake.

'Isn't there anything else? You know Maria-Teresa doesn't eat meat.'

Carla shrugged and gestured towards the kitchen. 'Ask the maid. I told her to get some vegetables.'

Stasi saw them going off hand in hand through the French windows and felt a pang of jealousy. She would have preferred not to have met the girl he would marry. 'She's sweet. Why did you say she was dippy?'

Carla laughed. 'What I meant was, she's boring enough for Eduardo.'

'Don't be so mean. Eduardo's different from you, that's all.'

'We always insult one another like crazy. Doesn't mean anything. All that family closeness, ugh, it's far too Italian for the Livornos. We adore each other really but we'd rather stay cool. You know, like the English.' She reached out for a hunk of meat, wrapped it in a paper serviette and plunged it into her mouth. 'Julian. This is Stasi. You can call her Anastasia.'

'My hands are greasy. Pleased to meet you, Stasi.'

He looked the perfect model for a Harry's Bar man. With his athletic body, broad shoulders, erect bearing, immobile but good-looking face (only his nose seemed smaller than his clean-cut features deserved) and glossy dark hair cut severely short, he reminded her of the cavalry officers she had once seen trotting down St John's Wood high street on their way to Regent's Park. English upper class, tight-lipped and unapproachable, the kind who made you feel that Jew was a dirty word not to be mentioned in front of the servants. She couldn't imagine how you started a conversation. It was clear that

Carla disliked him and it appeared to be mutual.

'You may be a bummer on the tennis court, Julian, but you're a hot shot at steak.'

He pretended to be faintly irritated, then smiled. 'Thank you for the compliment, Carla.'

'We need red meat, us singers. And so do you. Otherwise you'd be fagged out balling my sister night and day.'

'No need to parade your sexual deprivation, Carla dear. Didn't your singer – my apologies, his name escapes me – come up to scratch?'

'I don't screw singers. Only men.'

As the conversation gathered momentum, Stasi struggled to catch the drift of the staccato idioms. She had to concentrate on the strange language, switching from American English to Italian and back mid-phrase, producing a confusing babble. If her only contribution to the conversation had been a description of going once as a child to see Aunt Lizzie singing at the Pink Cat in West Hartlepool, she had made them laugh. What if they did think she was just another air-head chant-ooze, as Carla would say. Perhaps she was. Or perhaps she just thought slowly.

'The chef's taking a break,' said Julian, strolling towards them. 'Does anyone fancy a dip?'

'No one cleaned the pool. It's filthy. Why doesn't anyone clean it?'

'One hasn't the staff. We have the same problem in England, Beatrice.'

'Just like in America. When I was in Hollywood . . .'

'Yes, we have heard about your trip to Hollywood. Several times.' Julian turned towards Stasi. 'Why don't you sit beside me? The Livornos have had enough airtime. I want to hear about Miss Wagner.'

Stasi liked the way he gave a slight smile while his eyes laughed.

'Well, Stasi, tell me something I don't know about Carmen,' he began.

'She's fat and she hardly moves but she's a great singer.'

'I said tell me something new. How did you prepare for Micaela, for example?'

Julian listened attentively while Stasi recalled her first interpretation of the part, how she had changed with Signora Busconi, so different from her English teachers. The discipline of the Italian school of singing was a revelation. She was discovering a new range of dynamics, improving her legato line, so important with a part like Micaela. Could he imagine how frightening it would be? Singing in front of an Italian audience who took all these things for granted?

'I've heard some dreadful singing in Italy, Stasi. If Amelia Busconi has accepted you as her pupil, that's enough. You shouldn't be afraid.'

He began to compare performances of *Carmen* he had seen, records he had heard, wondering why Bizet's earlier opera, *The Pearl Fishers*, was so rarely played.

'Do you sing yourself?' asked Stasi, marvelling at the understanding he showed.

'No,' he replied, without a trace of regret. 'I bank. I listen and I talk. Isn't that enough for a man who lacks any artistic talent?'

Stasi leaned back and examined his open face, which had a slight, well-fed chubbiness round the cheeks she found attractive. And what a relief, to hear the gentle, English self-mockery she had missed for so long.

'And I travel,' Julian added.

At her insistence, he described some of his wilder forays into the unknown. He was only interested in exploring for a purpose, hoping to bring some small benefit to the dwellers in the jungle, the desert. There was so much to achieve in the five years before he reached forty, when he hoped to retire. Stasi suspected that his modest accounts concealed the heat of passionately held ideals and convictions.

'What do you want to do most?' she enquired.

'Make Britain the home of opera. Doesn't that sound

pompous? But I mean to do it. Then you won't have to waste your talent on singing for these heathens.'

'Don't you like Italy?'

'Some of it isn't bad,' he replied, looking briefly towards Beatrice, who was attempting to feed a stray cat. She wondered what he was doing with such a young girl, whose range of expression seemed limited to either petulance or boredom.

'Have you been hearing about the secret life of Saint Julian?' said Carla, coming towards them bearing a basket of fruit. 'Where are we now? Up the Amazon or leading a convoy through the Bosnian mountains? Or was it bringing caviar to dying AIDS patients in San Francisco for their Last Supper?'

She put down the basket, and bit into a peach. Julian said nothing. The sound of the Grateful Dead wafted out from the house. Forgetting where she was and that her face was lit by a nearby flare, Stasi stretched out her arms and yawned into the night, anticipating the soft luxury of her bed. Carla, catching her yawn, gave a sympathetic laugh.

'Jesus, this is meant to be my early night.' She put her arm round Stasi. 'You tired, Stasi? Me, too. Sleep as long as you like. I will. Follow me. I've something for you.'

As Carla kissed Eduardo and Beatrice good night, Stasi hurried into the house. Carla caught her up on the stairs.

'Come to my room. It's so ghastly you've just got to see it.'

'Tomorrow, Carla.'

'I won't even kiss you good night. Christ, Stasi. I've got to sing in that fucking arena tomorrow!'

The first thing Stasi noticed about Carla's room was an absurdly large oil painting, a parody of Rubens with grotesquely abundant nudes flinging themselves in abandoned postures amongst Roman ruins. Then she saw the four-poster bed, with drapes of discordant floral silk held in place by oversized tassels, raised on a carpeted platform.

105

'Isn't it wild? The marriage boudoir. Typical of Ma's friends. No taste,' remarked Carla, as she opened the wardrobe door. Then she threw a shimmering grey dress onto the bed. 'You might need this. For tomorrow. It's Romeo Gigli. If you don't like it, I'll find another. Only I figured it was your colour. I thought it was mine when I bought it, but it makes me look like uncooked pastry. It's long on me, should fit. Try it and see.'

Stasi held it against her. She had no intention of getting undressed. 'It's a bit grand for me, Carla. I mean, it's very kind but it's not as though I'm going anywhere amazing.'

'No? Now you are.' Pushing a gold embossed card into her hand, Carla translated the curling script. '"Emily and Paolo Livorno and Marchese Maurizio della Robbia request the pleasure of your company at the Pitti Palace on June 7th at midnight to celebrate the debut of their daughter Carla as Micaela in Bizet's *Carmen*, a Sandro Passattella production for the people of Florence." I was going to give you a surprise and ask you tomorrow, then I thought what the hell. You'd probably like an invitation card for a memento. You will come? It'll be friends mainly. We could hardly invite the whole cast.'

'The Pitti Palace? Unbelievable!' Stasi's doubts melted away as she rushed over to Carla and briefly hugged her. She did not mind when Carla kissed her hair, kissed her cheek and wished her beautiful dreams. 'They're going to love you tomorrow, Carla.'

Carla laughed nonchalantly, as though it was a foregone conclusion. 'You have to say *merda*.'

'*Merda*?'

'It means shit. How you say good luck. Mustn't tempt the gods.'

'I know about that!'

The following morning, when Stasi came down searching for breakfast, the villa was deserted and silent except for the clattering of the maid on the kitchen tiles. She went outside, and heard the soft pop of tennis balls in the

106

distance. Heading off over the terrace towards the court, she saw Julian jumping high into the air, to lob a ball past Eduardo. They stood facing each other for a second, then Julian came forward and shook hands across the net.

'You're off form, my dear Eduardo. I should never have won.'

Stasi ran over, calling out to ask them if they had seen Carla.

'They've left, the girls,' said Julian. 'God knows where. Where do girls go?'

'How do I get back to Florence?'

'You haven't a car? Never mind. Hang on for a while. I'll probably be able to drop you off later.'

The terrace was slowly baking as the sun soared higher in the sky, and a sprinkler hose was swishing rhythmically, drenching the flowers and making the reds and pinks even more vivid. Stasi had become a stranger. She could not understand why she, a guest and friend, had been abandoned. Out of sight, out of mind. Perhaps they would return soon. Now that Carla was gone, the villa seemed lifeless. Stasi longed to get away, to be alone on her rooftop.

'Is there an autobus, to go to Florence?' she asked the maid who was swabbing down the floor. When she realized Stasi was seriously planning to go on a bus, a public bus, the maid took her by the hand and pointed to a bend in the road below.

'Round the corner. The *fermata*. You must wait a long time.'

Stasi packed away what little she had, but left the grey dress hanging in the wardrobe. At the last minute, she pulled it out, and pressed it up against her. The fine material was impregnated with Carla's perfume; she must have worn it once. It didn't matter – on the contrary. She folded it carefully and pushed it into her bag.

Only the front row of the Roman arena in which Stasi was seated was empty. She had watched the dress rehearsals from there with the covers, young singers who dreamed of being called in to replace Assunta, Guido or Rico if they were unable to appear. Now everything seemed unfamiliar, the presence of the public changed the dimensions, everything looked smaller. The semicircle of stone seating, now covered in flat cushions, was seething with people who sat down, then stood up again, calling out to friends and acquaintances, pulling children to order, changing places with others, climbing over obstacles, balancing picnic baskets on their knees, complaining, gossiping.

When the lights begin to dim, a shining crowd of latecomers made a dramatic entrance, and Stasi heard the whispers of recognition from the audience. As they settled themselves around her, they all shook hands with a massive man whose large head was crowned by a thick mane of grey hair. His partner, wrapped in a long pleated cloak, was a tall woman with piled-up rich gold tresses kept in place by a diamond clip gleaming in the darkness. Maestro Passattella waited until they were seated, and took his place beside them, followed by Beatrice, Julian Lieberman, Eduardo and Maria-Teresa. Finding himself next to Stasi, Julian kissed her hand and whispered, 'You look ravishing.' Farther along the row, Maestro Passattella was loudly announcing himself to be unworthy of the honour paid to him by Emily and Paolo, who had travelled especially from Milan for the occasion.

A stooped man with a lined face and gold-rimmed glasses sat down next to Stasi, put both hands on his gold-topped cane and nodded an acknowledgement. The conductor had been waiting for the front seats to be filled, which represented a major part of his future career, before he could quell the restless audience. Now he raised his baton, the scratch orchestra charged full pelt into the overture, and the soldiers made their way along the scaffolded ramparts.

'How did they get up there?'

'Shh, Beatrice.'

Eduardo tilted his head back as though he had just

nosed a superb sample of Barolo. They were all chatting, fidgeting at the unaccustomed discomfort of stone seats, except the man next to Stasi who sat scribbling on a small pad in the darkness. They were waiting for Carla's entrance.

'*Bellissima, nostra Carla.*'

She did look ravishing, pale blue muslin dress, a coquettish straw hat, ribbons trailing and curling down her back, like a little summergirl from the album of Lewis Carroll, so young, sweet, eager. No wonder the soldiers wanted her to stay. But Stasi was listening to her voice as though for the first time. A little unsteady, a little thin, a Gilbert and Sullivan voice. Hardly a Bizet voice. How would she cope with her great aria in Act Three? Stasi felt the warmth of illicit pleasure which she would confess to no one. She knew she could sing Carla off the stage.

She leaned forward to catch every nuance, her hand cupping her chin, apparently listening more intently than any of the shifting, whispering audience. Her thoughts belied the calm concentration expressed in her face, and brought a flush to her cheeks. I should be there. She has no right. Perhaps I should have tried to persuade Passattella. Look, I'm better. Why should she be hogging the stage? She's not worth it. Musical comedy, perhaps. Call that singing? '*Un baiser pour son fils.*' A kiss for her son? More like a fuck for her lover.

As the long duet with Don José ended, and Carla leaped into his arms, the audience roared with approval. Brava, brava. *Bellissima.* Passattella responded to the smiling faces of Pappa and Mamma Livorno by turning in their direction and kissing his lips with his thumb and finger.

The production went rumbling on, like the beribboned horse and cart in which Assunta sat regally propped. This Carmen was no gypsy peasant with dancing feet, she was a gaudy nightclub queen. Occasionally, she flicked a pair of castanets to remind the audience of her origins, or thrust forward her huge breasts as a gesture to sexuality. But she could sing.

The front row again grew restive and began to chatter. Passattella appeared not to take offence, but after Act Two Stasi could bear it no longer, and pushed through the crowd to find an unoccupied seat further back. She thought of leaving the arena. The torture was seeping into her, turning into rage, and she longed to silence the waves of applause for Carla still resounding in her head, longed for something to happen, her voice to crack, a rainstorm to appear from nowhere, someone in the audience to have a heart attack, anything, anything to remove Carla from the stage so that she could step in, still the fidgety audience and take them to her heart.

Twenty minutes before Carla would appear again. The orchestra had come into their own and were blasting out the menace. This was Passattella's hallmark, swashbuckling action. Escamillo and Don José were whipping out swords and clashing the blades together, drawing out the duel, shouting, grunting, whilst the conductor vainly raised his arms to continue with the finale. Escamillo, in skin-tight breeches, walked slowly round Carmen who was transfixed in a Statue of Liberty pose. Carla prepared for her entrance, and climbed up behind the set.

As she descended to her position, she could feel the welcome warmth of the spotlight, bathing her in light, a white star above the gypsy camp. Assunta looked up and waited. The second spotlight, which she was expecting, had been painstakingly rehearsed to follow her stately progress by Giuseppe, the chief gaffer who knew every trick in the book. It failed to appear. Assunta's derisive dismissal of Don José, *va t'en*, get out, get lost, came on cue, as Bizet intended. What he did not intend was that the high moment of drama should be performed in a chiaroscuro darkness, with only Micaela clearly visible on the stage, luminous in her pale dress like cherry blossom on a summer evening.

'*Luce!*' shouted an irate opera-buff. '*Luce, perbacco.*' Some of the audience sitting further back let out piercing whistles. 'Put a sock in it,' came a voice.

Carla walked blissfully downstage, still bathed in her white pool of light, having decided to deliver her appeal to Don José ('Come back with me, come back with me') from a better position. Instead of gazing raptly at her lover, she would look directly into the myriad eyes of the audience.

What was she doing? Stasi could hardly believe it. Changing the plotted moves? Walking downstage made nonsense of the whole scene. Ignoring Passattella's instructions, obscuring the chorus, carefully drilled for hours with comic business round the campfire? She'd get thrown out of the company. Surely she must know the rules. Only prima donnas were allowed to misbehave.

Was that the intention? Could this be Carla's way of showing her contempt for Passattella, her indifference towards the production? Was she clearing the way for Stasi to take over? Knowing she was better? The more she thought, the more she imagined Carla to be capable of just such a crazy, bold, impulsive, generous gesture of friendship.

Assunta had not played Carmen three hundred and thirty-one times for nothing. She could tell the difference between a missed cue and a well-timed bribe. Giuseppe with the follow-spot must have succumbed, damn him. A new piece of business, in character naturally, wouldn't come amiss. Daughter of Satan, Don José called her. She wandered amongst the chorus and whispered in the ear of a brigand.

Carla began her last, testing aria, begging Guido to come home with her. 'Moi, je viens te chercher.' She would wait, just before she had that high E flat. Now. Assunta took aim. Good shot! She was entitled to laugh, Carmen was always laughing. Ha ha ha! An orange missile caught Guido on the side of the face and bounced onto the floor of the stage. He gave a cry of astonished pain and clutched his cheeks. And who wouldn't be silenced by that?

'My God, my God. What is she doing?' Passattella hid his face, unable to watch, his stomach churning. Did he have a war on his hands? The orchestra continued without Carla. After a few bars she recovered, and as Guido led her away she was hissing bitch, bitch, bitch which echoed round the arena above the tremulos of the orchestra. By the time Don Escamillo appeared with the song of the toreador, the audience had erupted in gales of laughter and manic applause.

It would soon be over. Passattella was torn between giving vent to his rage, or taking a pill. He took a pill, praying that the shame was over. With relief, he watched Guido plunge the collapsible dagger into Assunta's back. She was relishing every moment of her twitching expiry. Catastrophe. He stiffened his neck and drew in his chin like a general who has just seen his battalion wiped out.

Then he heard roars from the audience as the cast returned to take their bows. Heathens. Disgraceful. A catastrophe. *Madonna santa*, he would have to re-cast. Assunta assumed the flamenco pose of defiance, and rattled her castanets. Carla sauntered forward from the opposite side of the stage and blew kisses. Again, the audience roared and whistled, as though applauding a favourite horse which had come in last. The performance was a resounding success.

Maestro Passattella was in a familiar situation. First nights were rarely a tribute to his artistic judgement. He had rehearsed his explanation, and would take the earliest opportunity to talk about his next production. The surroundings were conducive to dignity. The Mumm champagne served in the awesome surroundings of the Blue Room of the Pitti Palace was restoring his equilibrium.

'My dear maestro. Utterly memorable. Utterly. And that is quite an accomplishment, to produce a memorable *Carmen*.'

'You are too kind, my dear Paolo. In view of the technical disasters. Still, it would hardly be a first night without technical disasters.'

'The audience was ecstatic. You heard them. Audiences don't lie.'

Passattella came closer to Professor Paolo Livorno and gave his prepared speech sotto voce, as though it came from the depths of his soul. 'Your daughter Carla was charming, spell-binding, magnificent. Utterly magnificent. I will tell the director of La Scala to keep an eye on her. In my opinion, you have a pearl.'

'Too kind. Every pearl needs a setting, but I appreciate the compliment. Talking of pearls, here comes my wife.'

'She was a bad girl, our Carla.' Signora Emily Harriet Johnson-Livorno projected her twangy Italian for several yards, but Passattella barely took in what she was saying, riveted by a cleavage which exposed her breasts perilously near to the nipple and plunged down to her waist. Her virulent, clinging fuchsia dress was spattered in twinkling glass studs which could only have emanated from a boutique in Beverly Hills.

'N-n-nerves, dear lady.' He controlled a slight stutter. 'Just nerves.'

'Huh. Don't give me that! Think I don't know what the little minx was up to? Where is she anyhow?'

Stasi entered with Julian and Beatrice, and looked round for Carla, wondering whether she could bring herself to bring out the rhapsodic expressions of praise which would be expected.

'There's someone I have to see. Forgive me,' said Julian. They both watched him approach a tall man with a cavernous bony face, powerful nose and thin lips.

'He comes from London. I expect you know him,' remarked Beatrice, in a childish, unmodulated treble which communicated both confidence and naïveté. 'When he came round to lunch once, I didn't understand a word he said.' Beatrice looked mournfully into the distance, as though she had decided that melancholy was becoming. Or perhaps she was just practising English cool. Stasi wondered who could have chosen the sack-like khaki-coloured dress which was hanging limply by two shoestring

113

straps from her bare shoulders. Perhaps she wanted to distance herself from Carla. 'What did you think of my sister?'

'Very good,' said Stasi hastily. 'Though I'm not sure it's quite her part.'

'I wouldn't know. Singing's beyond me. I prefer piano. Ma says you should never judge the first night, but I don't see why. I only get one chance to get it right.' She sounded as if life was perpetually unfair, as if she wanted constant protection from the outside world, which could have been the reason for Julian's attraction.

'Pianos don't seize up or get colds,' said Stasi.

Beatrice responded to her smile with a minimal change of expression, and since she appeared unwilling to talk further Stasi began to wander off towards Emily and Paolo who were surrounded by a small circle of people, some of whom Stasi recognized from Carla's party.

'We haven't met,' said Emily, stretching out her hand. 'I'm Emily Livorno. You must be Carla's friend.' She gave a woman to woman grin. 'I recognize the grey dress. Far better on you. Stasi. Is that right? Short for Anastasia?' She came close up to Stasi in the way that Americans prefer to greet strangers. 'Carla says you have a great voice. At least she can recognize it in others. Paolo, *momento, caro*.'

The great mane of grey hair turned to reveal a sensitively lined face with forbidding dark eyes which looked straight into hers.

'Anastasia, Carla's English friend.'

He gave a slight bow, and gestured to his companion, who was leaning on a gold-topped cane. 'Stefano Montini, the only music critic who counts. Because he is honest.'

Emily made a face, hoping that his review would discreetly pass over her daughter's unfortunate debut.

'Did you know that Stasi is taking over Micaela after Carla? Maestro Passattella is very impressed with her.'

'Indeed? Then I might be persuaded to take a second look.'

As the men turned away to continue their conversation, Emily clasped Stasi's hand and drew her aside. 'I'm so sorry we won't be in Florence long enough to see you, my dear. But from what the maestro was saying, you might be getting a bigger part in his next production. Don't say a word. Not even to Carla.'

Stasi tried to edge away, but Emily was clasping her hand too firmly, as though she was a child about to cross the road, and she was unable to move. 'I'm sure that isn't true. He thinks I'm difficult to work with. I'm hoping to get a small part at La Scala. I wouldn't mind that.'

'Who wouldn't? I sang there a coupla times. Bit stuffy, to my mind. Do you know anyone there?'

'Not yet,' Stasi replied, at last disengaging her hand.

'Never mind,' said Emily comfortingly. 'I'm sure your agent knows the score.'

'I don't have one. Why does everyone need an agent? I don't want someone creeping around me and telling me what roles to take and not to take, and how I should do my hair. No thank you.' A moment later, Stasi regretted that she had aired her views so strongly, but Emily seemed to be impressed.

'You're a spunky kid! Good luck. Can I give you a word of advice?'

'Of course.'

'See that man over there?' Emily said, stretching out a bejewelled hand in the direction of the tall visitor from London.

'The one standing next to Julian?'

'Yeh. Can't you just tell he's British? That suit, hanging off him like a hobo. Sir Miles Mackenzie. Do you recognize him? He's over here staying at the Excelsior. Go over and introduce yourself. Or I will, if you're shy. You the shy type?'

'I don't know who he is,' answered Stasi, beginning to feel as though Emily would happily take her over as an addition to the Livorno tribe.

'My God, Anastasia. He's only going to revolutionize

the whole opera scene in England. You must have heard of the new opera house in London they've been building all this time?'

'Yes, of course. But it's no good talking to him now. He won't have heard of me.'

'Go and say hi. He's lining up the talent, Stasi. Why else would he be seeing some crummy production in the tourist season? These guys, if they're good – and he is – put themselves about. And you, you're British. Home-grown talent, new talent. Get in there.'

'If I've got what it takes, he'll be leaving me a note at the stage door. What do I say? Hey, I'm great?'

'And why not? If you are, as Carla says.'

'I'd hate myself. I can't do it.'

Emily shrugged. 'Being British used to work, thinking self-promotion is shit. Nowadays, it ain't going to change the world. Think about it.'

Emily's attention was diverted by the arrival of Carla in a large velvet hat, sequinned jacket and tight toreador pants, followed by Maurizio who stood motionless and ill at ease whilst her friends yelled out their congratulations and covered her with kisses. Mumbling an excuse, Stasi moved away, seeking out a part of the room which was minus Livornos. Money, contacts, agents, family. Without the whole portfolio of support, how was she going to manage? As yet, there was nothing to cling to, nobody except sweet Amelia Busconi who had written her a warm letter, wishing her good luck. She began to long for the production to be over, to be free of this seductive girl whose voice rang in her ears, whose face appeared in the empty air, whose mother wanted to manipulate her career. She began to feel that until she had exorcised the Livorno presence, the Livorno absence, she would never be able to sing again.

Thanks to Stefano Montini, the musical world of Florence had been alerted to the presence of Sir Miles Mackenzie. His diary was full for the day he had allotted himself. The first meeting would take place over a demure breakfast brought up to the sitting room of his suite at the Excelsior Hotel, and he was looking forward to having a serious discussion with Paolo Livorno. His flamboyant style would draw the crowds for his opening production at the Opera Palace, and you needed flamboyance for *Aida*.

Although the arrangement had been made with his daughter, he hardly expected her to arrive in his place. There would be no question of considering her for any role, not for a few years at least. He was fast becoming familiar with the devious tactics employed by singers, especially sopranos, and this one was no exception. She had obviously prepared herself for some fruitful outcome arising from the casting couch.

Carla Livorno apologized profusely. Unfortunately, her father had been unable to come. He had been called back to Milan to discuss a big recording project and sent his deepest regrets.

'I hear that you will only be singing for six performances.' His eyes seemed to be accusing, or perhaps that was his habitual expression.

'I just couldn't stay on for longer. How can you sing if you're not happy? I know I shouldn't say, but the cast is unbearable. Maestro Passattella is sweet, but he can't keep discipline. So sad. I really didn't want to break my contract.'

'Or have you received a more tempting offer, Miss Livorno?'

'You think I'd be tempted?'

Sir Miles was staring at his highly polished, overly heavy brogues, as though deliberately absenting his mind from the baroque fantasies which might have intruded. 'I was talking to that excellent music critic, Stefano Montini. He mentioned that an English girl's taking your place. Wagner the name?'

Carla nodded.

'Any point in seeing her?'

'I wouldn't know. They say she's not exactly reliable,

117

but you know what gossip is. A good voice, so I hear. Nervous. I hardly know her. We had coffee together a few times. Quiet type but she seems a nice kid.'

'Naturally the Opera Palace would like to open the door to new British talent. But, unlike some of my critics, I see no reason for not pursuing an internationalist policy.'

'I absolutely agree.'

'Opera has always travelled; it is an itinerant art. If I restricted myself to a diet of Britten and Tippett and worthy British singers who've graduated from church choirs in the provinces, how many seats would I fill?'

Carla crossed and uncrossed her legs contemplatively. 'That's just what Pa says. He conducts everywhere, not just in Italy, even though they keep begging him to go under contract. You know what I'd really like to sing one day?'

Sir Miles leaned forward a fraction. '*Salomé*, perhaps?'

Carla was unaware of his irony. 'Marie in *Wozzeck*. Real pumping sexuality. And fantastic music, too, wild. I can relate to that.'

'Yes, yes.' He looked away, then spoke as though addressing himself. 'Perhaps in a few years the public will be ready for it. My mission is to lead them gently on from "Nessun dorma", step by step. No one has seriously addressed the issue of giving the public what it wants. Despite the cynics, I still regard myself as their servant.'

'Oh, Sir Miles, I couldn't see you as a servant.'

'Figuratively. I approach my task with humility.' For the first time, his craggy face softened into a smile. 'At present, I am looking for elephants.'

'You've cast Aida then?'

'I have someone in mind.'

This attractive creature, overdressed in that ridiculous Italian fashion, might even be intelligent. She was exhibiting a sketchy but convincing enough knowledge of the parlous state of British opera, and she soon obtained his assurance that he would be charmed to see her if she should be passing through London. Sir Miles bit into a croissant, barely scattering a crumb, and sipped his espresso. There was something both attractive and repellent about her boldness – she appeared to have inherited the American characteristics of her mother, for there was little to remind him of her dark-featured, pensive Italian father. Americans might lack subtlety, but their energy, their naked ambition, had an extraordinary, revitalizing effect. They made you believe that anything was possible.

The large fleshy hand which shook hers, grasping it as though she was drowning, felt unexpectedly hot. A small vein in his forehead was throbbing. It was just possible Sir Miles Mackenzie was concealing an erection, but it was difficult to tell in the swathe of grey baggy trouser which so effectively masked his shape from the waist downwards. He had not mentioned her singing, which Carla found strange, but she realized that the British were not inclined to say things more than once. Hadn't he already said, at the party, how much he had enjoyed her performance? And he had sweetly ignored the fact that Assunta Melati had thrown an orange at the tenor and spoilt her best moment.

'I'll be in London come fall. My agent's fixed up some auditions. Welsh National Opera, Scottish, Covent Garden.'

Sir Miles rose to indicate that his attention would now be called elsewhere. 'Let's have a chat in London. Give my secretary a call when you arrive. I'll be planning the second season by then.'

Carla left the Excelsior just as optimistic as when she had arrived, waited for her car to be brought round, and headed off for the hills. If she had stayed, a couple of hours later she might have bumped into one of her houseguests who had arrived for a confidential meeting. Barely recognizable in a dark formal suit and carrying a briefcase, Julian Lieberman strode through the doors of the hotel. By now, Sir Miles should have received enough information from the City to finally convince him that he should be accepted as a member of the board.

Chapter Five

Since Gloria refused to fly, brother Monty and son Raymond shared the driving, helped by sister Lizzie in the back seat. It had taken two days, with a lost passport and several rows, but it was worth it. How could they miss a double celebration, Stasi's birthday on one day and her debut in *Carmen* the next?

They'd never have done that in England, not in a small two star hotel. The owners of the Albergo Sorriso had invited all the Wagners into their own living quarters and even followed Gloria's instructions for the birthday menu: smoked salmon (brought from England), *bistecca alla fiorentina* (their idea of English roast beef), *patate fritte* (same as chips), foreign vegetables (she could give them a try). And a surprise pudding, *zuccotto*, the gooey Florentine speciality, a kind of trifle. Twenty-three candles on top? Of course, signora. A bottle of wine? All right, one glass of something fizzy.

Stasi was suffering from a family overdose, and the realization that she was twenty-three.

'What do you mean you're going? Already? You haven't had a second helping. Come on, have some of mine.'

'Mum, really, I'm tired.'

'Anything wrong?'

'Leave her alone.'

'She can rest all day tomorrow. Aren't we tired? After driving all that way?'

'So who was driving? The chauffeur?'

'Monty, you did a wonderful job. You drive almost as well as Sam. Remember when he drove us all up to Scotland? What a holiday.'

'Stasi's tired, Mum.'

'All right, Raymond. I can see she's tired. We're all tired. A cup of cappuccino, yes everybody?'

'I've got to go. It's been such a super birthday. Fantastic seeing you, I never expected it. Such a wonderful surprise, Mum.'

She had said that half a dozen times already. Once, even twice, would have made little impression.

'And tomorrow?'

'Tomorrow I'm saving my voice.'

Aunt Lizzie, peroxided hair, recently applied lipstick spilling round her mouth, extracted a menthol cigarette from her overburdened handbag. 'She's right. I wish I'd saved mine. It was touring with that band killed it off. The Pink Cat in West Hartlepool, that was the worst. Remember that, Gloria? The drinking! Never seen anything like it. If I had my time again, I would never sing in front of drunks. And I'd sing classical. You're lucky to be singing classical, Stasi. I'm glad you listened to me, Gloria.'

'You think I'd have my daughter schlepping round the country with a dance band? Or screaming into a microphone with a Nazi shaven pop group shouting four letter words? It was never on the cards, Lizzie. You think Sam would have entertained the idea? Never.'

'Long as you're at the top, Gloria, you sing anything. Then what happens? They forget you. Mind you, as long as you're happy and make a living . . .'

'Do you have to argue?'

'Who's arguing? Just thinking things out. Life isn't black and white, Gloria.'

Stasi's exasperation was rising to temper point. 'I'm going. Good night.'

'The coffee's coming.'

'For crying out loud, Gloria. The girl's exhausted. Say good night.'

'If she wants to, of course she can go. Am I stopping her? A macaroon! And I didn't even ask for it. Here.'

Gloria stretched out a plate of almond biscuits towards Stasi.

'No thanks, Mum.'

'But you like them. Go on, helps the digestion.'

'Do you want me to be fat?'

'Fat? Fat? Who says you're fat? You're too skinny, that's your trouble, too skinny for a tall girl. Everyone wanting to be thin. And most of the world starving.'

'You can't get parts if you're fat today, Mum. I told you that.'

'Who says? So Pavarotti doesn't get parts? And look at Dame Kiri Whatsit, at least a size sixteen. She doesn't get parts?'

'They're older than me.'

'So suddenly age matters? Long as you've got the voice and a bit of make-up, who cares about age? Twenty-three and you're worrying about age already.'

'I'm not talking about that.'

'So what are you talking about?'

'What I was trying to say, Mum – oh, forget it.'

'Gloria, I'm getting Stasi a cab.'

'So soon? Doesn't your mother get a birthday kiss?'

Uncle Monty the peacemaker took Stasi by the arm and directed her towards the hotel lobby. 'Gloria gets overexcited going abroad. She'll calm down after a few museums. You look pale. You nervous?'

'Please. Don't you start.'

'Of course you're not. You forget all about us and just do your best. Whatever happens, we believe in you, Stasi.'

'It's not as though I'm singing in La Scala.'

'So?' He pressed a wadge of lira notes into her hands. 'Treat yourself from me.'

Stasi flung off her clothes and climbed into bed, without washing her face or cleaning her teeth. Anger and exhaustion would, she hoped, settle into sleep, but as soon as she had rid herself of the sound of her mother's voice (an Israeli voice, she often thought, vocal chords tough as leather boots from a pioneer kibbutz, fit for shouting across deserts and taking on the world in combat) the ignoble fear which was never mentioned began to take over. The fear of performance.

How could you banish the prickling thoughts which mounted inevitably into an avalanche of blank terror, the escalating panic engulfing the mind, distorting reactions, sweeping them up into mounds of apprehension, sizzling along the blood-vessels like a lit fuse? The gentle click of the alarm clock began to be drowned by the pumping beat of Stasi's heart, louder and louder, throbbing against her wrists, her head, constricting her throat, driving out her breath, creeping down her legs, her arms, numbing them in a tingling paralysis. The room became blacker and blacker, she was falling down a dark mineshaft lit by the dancing, shimmering lines of blank terror. Longing to put on the light, she dared not reach out for the switch. Now her body had caught fire, she was being consumed, her heart would give way, this was the end.

'I, Anastasia Wagner, am a singer.'

The rhythm of her thumping heart grew more frantic. The blood-vessels would soon burst, the machine would give out, she would be discovered lying in bed, lifeless, with an expression of terror constricting her face, like the close-up smudged photographs of murder victims daily plastered over Italian newspapers. Her rabbit, what had happened to Rabbit?

Stasi groped frantically down the mattress, failing to find the reassuring worn felt childhood toy, and then she leaned over and ran her hands over the floor, under the bed. Rabbit had disappeared. Mummy, I've lost Rabbit. Mummy, Mummy.

'I, Anastasia Wagner, am a singer.'

She thought it, then she whispered it, then she attempted to speak the words out loud. No voice. Nothing. Turn over. Relax. Start counting. Breathe deeply. For a few seconds, she became unconscious, long enough to have the recurring dream, the dream where she stood on stage in front of an audience of expectant thousands, cued by the conductor, breath gathered, mouth open. And silence. Followed by whistles, catcalls, hisses, boos, ferocious undirected missiles hurtling across the auditorium until, crumpling in slow motion, waiting to hit the boards of the stage, she awoke.

Stasi leaped out of bed and put on every light in the room. She was shivering, though it was not cold, her teeth chattered. Frozen, but still alive. She felt her pulse. Pumping, racing. Would she die young like Daddy, ending up in a silver frame kissed and touched by grieving mother? Would she ever reach the great age of thirty? Even if she was unable to sing, she wanted to live a few more years. Just a few, God, she prayed, don't let me die at twenty-three, not in my twenties. Let me live a little while longer.

There was Rabbit, fallen down by her slippers. God had answered. She would reach thirty. Suddenly life was an exciting prospect. Seven years. You could accomplish anything in seven years.

It was simply a *crisi di nervi*. In Britain, she would have been on the psychiatrist's couch, but Italians understood about these things, the times when the human mechanism ran amok. It happened to everyone. Especially women. *Camomilla, camomilla*. Did Gudrun have any? Stasi ran downstairs to the kitchen, without realizing she had regained the use of her limbs. It was there, the little daisy packet, amongst the rose-hip and lime tisanes, and the bottles of vitamins. Too much coffee at dinner, that's what it was. Carla was always drinking coffee. Born without nerves, Carla Livorno. Why think of her? She was gone. The audience would be waiting for the Micaela of Anastasia Wagner.

She had just fallen asleep, after those long hours which left her wrung out with exhaustion, when she was woken by a pounding on the door.

'Stasi! Stasi! Darling, you all right? I had to come, you looked so awful yesterday.'

The shutters rattled back and let in a stream of glaring sunbeams.

'Lovely day. You want a cup of tea? I've brought some Lipton's. Maybe I'll teach the Italians to make tea. Kitchen downstairs, is it? Gudrun, what a nice landlady, I told her I was your mother, she said I looked like your sister. How much you paying? Lovely room, nicely decorated, colours a bit bright for my taste. Sam wouldn't have yellow in the house. But then she's Swedish, you said. Oh and look, a little piano. Extra is it? Wake up, Stasi. It's past ten o'clock.'

Stasi turned over in her bed to face Gloria and kept her eyes shut. 'Please go away, Mum. I'm sleeping. Leave me alone.'

'Sleeping so late? When you left us so early? Not that I minded, you should get your rest. Sam always slept late on Sundays. Is this lunch or breakfast, I used to say to him. Remember? Let me make you a cup of tea. No good sleeping all day. Eight hours is all you need. Aren't I right?'

Was it going to be a storm in a mug or a teacup, a tiny droplet of anger, a torrent of rage or lip-buttoned silence? Gloria was staying put.

'I don't want you here.'

'You need looking after.'

'I don't.'

'You're pale. Of course you do. What's the point of a family if you aren't looked after? Now I'm here. Couple of days I'll be gone.'

'Good.'

'All this way, I've come. Stasi, one day you'll under-stand what it is to be a mother. Just you wait. See how you feel.' Gloria perched herself on the end of Stasi's bed, having reached the stage where resentment had mellowed into philosophy. 'A daughter never leaves the womb. Never. Now a son is different, not that I don't love Raymond, you understand. As long as I live, I'll always feel what you feel, I can't help it. It's nature, Stasi. A

125

mother wants to protect, she wouldn't be a mother if she didn't. Sam could never understand that, and he was a very understanding man.'

'Mum, I'm twenty-three. My friend Pat is having a baby, and she's younger than me. Her mother doesn't go on like you do.'

'Always comparing. Anyway, she's a shiksa. They're not the same.'

'You mean they grow up. How can you be so racist?'

'Because we're different.'

'No one thinks like that any more. Why should we have the monopoly on warmth and love and caring and family feeling? I can't bear it. Can't you take it for granted just for a day? What's so fucking special about being Jewish?'

'We don't swear, Anastasia. Or drink. And no one has a homosexual in the family. That's what's special.'

'Big deal.'

Gloria sighed. 'You'll never understand. Last night, I was so excited I didn't sleep. You're the first Wagner who's going to do something with life. Be somebody. And you won't let me share it. You're . . .'

'Mean and selfish. OK, Mum. For Christ's sake, go off to a gallery or something.'

'I haven't come here to look at pictures. I've come to see you. Or isn't that what mothers are meant to do? Is it so unnatural? All these weeks you've been away.'

'If you don't go, I'll scream and then I won't be able to sing.'

Gloria ignored Stasi, walked over to the window, promenaded round the room, wiped her finger over the dressing table and examined it with satisfaction. 'She keeps it clean, that Swedish lady. Uncle Monty is taking us all out after the show. Such a wonderful man. It's meant to be a secret. Don't say I said.'

Was there such a thing as matricide? At that moment, Stasi was wondering. She drove me crazy, your honour. Is that a reason to throw your widowed mother out of the window? Don't people kill because someone drives them crazy? Thou shalt not kill. God must have been thinking of mothers. She jumped out of bed, went over to the piano, struck a chord and started singing up and down the scale at first softly, then louder, louder until the room throbbed.

'I know when I'm not wanted!' shouted Gloria as she walked defiantly through the door.

Carla had sat here, in this chair still adjusted for her height, in the communal dressing room, in front of this mirror, all those cards of good wishes hanging from a ribbon on either side, flowers heaped up on the floor. This performance would be momentous to Stasi, but to no one else. She quickly tore open a small pile of cards, some from the cast, the stage hands, a king-sized Bugs Bunny from the Wagners covered in kisses, one from Signora Busconi, one from Stefano Montini. Had Carla forgotten? With a sigh of relief, Stasi picked up a small postcard which had fallen to the floor. A view of Florence with neat writing.

'Darling Stasi, give 'em hell. See you in London. Big kiss from us all. Carla, Eduardo, Beatrice, Paolo and Emily.'

She could not tell who had written it. It looked like a man's hand. Eduardo's probably. The card would have come from Carla, she was always buying up postcards. In spite of the marks of affection in front of her, Stasi felt abandoned. That was the worst part about singing in a foreign country, you couldn't be reassured by reminders from friends you had known for years.

Stasi subsided into gloom. She had the preoccupied, inturned expression of someone about to go on stage. Her dresser, Maria, laced up the back of the layered blue muslin costume which had been made for her, although the original had been designed for Carla, the little lace collar, lace cuffs. And that ridiculously large straw hat tied under her chin. It was like stepping into a dead woman's clothes. Except Carla wasn't dead. Stasi shivered. You weren't allowed to think of death in the theatre, even in the abstract.

'Cold, love? It's always cold when the sun goes down. Here, put this shawl on.'

Stasi looked pleadingly into the warm brown eyes of the stocky woman who was adjusting her dress.

'I can't help it. Nerves again. Oh, Maria, is everyone like this?' Stasi grasped her throat. 'I'm going to throw up. Supposing I'm sick on stage? I can't do it, I can't go on. How long have I got? What time is it?'

She glanced round and saw Assunta calmly painting blood-red strokes down her protruding finger nails. Did she have something in mind? A surprise? Something to test the new girl? Assunta finished a nail with a flourish and smiled, stretching her cupid's bow so that it resembled a letter box.

'That dress is much better on you. Some girls can wear period costume.' Another nail was begun. 'And some can't,' she added. 'Have you heard?'

Stasi jumped. 'Heard what?'

'Who'll be here tonight. That American producer who did *Don Giovanni* in a spaceship. Hah! Nothing like being controversial, is there? He'll be yawning his head off tonight. Fancy setting *Carmen* in Spain. How quaint and old-fashioned. Can't think why he's coming.'

Assunta gave her wig of curls a vigorous toss and stuck in another red ribbon. 'Good, this one stays on. Give me old-fashioned any day. They don't make wigs like they used to. This is my new one, not the same even though they swore it was human hair. Asian rubbish. Ten minutes to go. After tonight, it'll be my three hundred and thirty-eighth. Makes you think.'

She gave her eyelashes an extra go of the curling tongs, turned her head from side to side in the mirror, flicked her earrings and then fixed her sweepingly lined Cleopatra eyes on Stasi. 'You look ravishing. Come here, dear.' Stasi walked hesitantly over, her newly plaited pigtails swinging heavily against her neck, and Assunta placed something round her throat.

'For you. It always brings me good luck. Never fails.'

When Stasi looked up into the mirror, she saw a tiny silver crucifix. 'Assunta! You're so sweet. But I can't wear it, it's yours.'

She chuckled, and gave a dismissive wave of her hand. 'Don't worry. I don't need luck any more.'

'I'm not a Catholic.'

'Micaela wasn't a good Catholic? Wear it, dear. Good for the nerves.'

They were clapping the conductor. The first A major chord came crashing down to silence the chattering audience. Stasi was waiting behind the set, her face clasped in her hands, listening to the trills gather momentum, counting off the bars before she had to move, the soldiers' chorus, strange people, strange people, the cue for her entrance. She was unable to move, frozen, rooted in terror. Then she was aware of a warm hand firmly gripping her arm, propelling her towards the stage, giving her a final push until she found herself walking onstage, like a hesitant robot. The lounging soldiers were looking her up and down, insolently assessing her face and body. Now she was Micaela, in love with the wrong man.

From his seat at the end of the front row, Maestro Passattella grimaced and clenched his hands. What was she doing, standing still like that? Move, move, he muttered under his breath. Damned English girl, stubborn arrogant bitch. How many times had he told her? A burst of applause from the back of the arena erupted at the end of Stasi and Guido's duet – Guido's claque of scruffy students doing what he paid them to do. But, he had to admit, this time it was deserved. The English girl's purity of tone and strength of voice was, well, quite good for an English girl. If she learned to take direction, she might do well.

Assunta was singing a little flat. Would anyone notice?

He sighed and sat sideways on his seat so that he could observe the audience from the corner of his eye. What a surprise! Stefano Montini had come a second time even when he'd already written his usual ignorant, crass, paltry review. Sitting next to that American. Mor-ri-son. The kind who turned Mozart into a Madonna pornshow, debauched Verdi, spat on Puccini. Even looked as though he'd just swung from his saddle. Tall, good-looking bastard. How dare he? This was Fiesole, not Texas. He'd keep an eye on him, chat him up. If he was on the prowl to poach his best singers, he'd send this cowboy back to chasing cattle.

The maestro returned his concentration to the stage, his mood pleasantly revived by a gentle hand which was stroking his palm. Charming Alessandra. Why did he think of that name? Hadn't seen her for months, she'd gone to Turin. Dina resembled her, physically. He responded by slipping his other hand under her thigh. As though she needed rousing! What a girl! Could come just by having his tongue stuck down her ear.

Bravo. By Act Three, Giuseppe, at last, had aimed the follow-spot in the right place. Bravo. Even Assunta was acting. Card scene. Always got that right. Death in the cards. Now the English girl. On cue, good. Climbing round the scaffolding. Sings and moves, that one. When the mood takes her.

Had she sung the right notes? Were the high ones sure? All Stasi could remember was singing into silence, the lights in her eyes obliterating the dim faces of the audience who she sensed were still, unlike the rustle of shifting bodies and sporadic conversation she had heard earlier. Alone and afraid. It was easy to sing these words, as though they had been written for her alone. She felt ethereal, transported, exalted with that almost religious rapture sometimes experienced by singers which they can never summon at will. The high notes were as clear as summer stars. Carmen is dangerous, she is beautiful, but I won't be afraid. The timbre of Stasi's voice lightened. Her

130

appeal to God to protect her came from the depths, softly surfacing whilst the orchestra tailed away below her.

There was silence, then a sudden roar like waves crashing over pebbles, the stamping of feet, they were standing up, shouting, *brava inglesina, bravissima, bis, bis,* hundreds of clapping hands, frantic moth-wing movements, the audience vibrating through her. Stasi bowed her head and opened her arms, blinking away the tears of surprise and ecstasy in her eyes. Then she saw the conductor point his baton. Escamillo strutted onstage. The audience gradually subsided into attention.

'My daughter's famous!' Gloria blurted out, sobbing as she pushed her way past Assunta's entourage in the dressing room. Aunt Lizzie was sniffing, Raymond was grinning as though he'd won Musician of the Year and Uncle Monty stood like a bemused father who had just witnessed his wife give birth.

'Your name, your name in the programme!' Aunt Lizzie stuttered. 'Wagner, it says here. Printed in black and white. Wagner.'

'Great singing, Stasi. They could do with a decent violin section, though.'

'All right, Raymond.'

Gloria was watching Stasi sponging down her face. 'Shame to take it off. Lovely make-up.' She had now calmed down enough to observe her surroundings, and the bouquets of flowers piled up on the floor. 'Look, Stasi. What arrangements! You seen who they're from? Maybe there's some from a nice rich admirer.'

'Mum. Let me get changed.'

'Sam always bought me flowers, always a sweet-smelling bouquet, freesias, I love freesias. Every week. He knew I liked freesias.'

Stasi retired behind a screen to get dressed, and when she emerged Maestro Passattella was introducing himself to the family, kissing Gloria's hand, congratulating Uncle Monty, who he assumed was her father. He did not perform these duties, Stasi observed, with the same enthusiasm he had shown for the Livornos, nor was he wearing evening dress with medals tonight, as he had done for Carla's debut.

'My darling, you were magnificent.'

If she appeared disappointed, it was because she wanted to hear one thing only; that she had sung better than Carla.

'But there are one or two things I need to say. For the next performance, a few adjustments. Nothing serious. We must speak privately.'

'Did you really mean what you said? You're not just saying it?'

'Believe me, I always say what I mean.' Passattella took her hand, kissed it, and gestured to Stasi to follow him.

'Forgive me,' he said to the family. 'We won't be long. You are going somewhere to dine?'

'Uncle Monty has found a wonderful little place in Florence that's open late,' Gloria began.

'Write down the address. I will take Signorina Anastasia there myself.'

Stasi walked in a trance to the car park, cradling bouquets of flowers in her arms, hearing nothing but the music of *Carmen*, the rapture of the audience. There were two people waiting by Passattella's black Mercedes as they approached, but she barely took them in. One was leaning against the highly polished door, a pale girl with straw-bleached hair drawn back from her perfect, oval face, wearing a short fitted flame silk coat unbuttoned to her waist, a dog collar of sparkling stones gripped round her long, slender neck. She was strikingly beautiful. The man was asking her something, his back turned. Passattella hurried towards them, but Stasi stood at a distance, not yet ready to meet strangers.

'Anastasia. Come over here,' he called out.

The man turned round. She would remember that turn, the moment when she looked into his face for the first time, a moving image which froze in an instant to become a memory which she would recall again and again after that first meeting, which must have lasted five minutes at most. Although the flat, blanket illumination of the car park gave the appearance of clarity, she did not remember his features clearly. It was his presence which remained, something about him which entered her soul. There was a fractional moment of recognition when he came closer, shook her hand and scrutinized her face, as though piecing together the image he had taken from the stage, relating it to what he saw in front of him. She remembered him as having dark hair. The photograph she found later in a magazine proved it to be light brown streaked blond with the Italian sun. His eyes were light in colour. Grey or blue? She was unsure, knew only that they were searching intently for something deep within herself. He made her feel afraid, as though that look had penetrated something which she wished to keep secret.

'This is Dina. And Dominic Morrison, the opera producer who will soon take my place.'

'I doubt it, maestro. I was very impressed. Are you in a hurry, Miss Wagner? Can I say why?'

She must not be disheartened. There were few singers he would talk to in this way, but he felt she would understand. He had analysed her voice, knew she was nervous, told her to guard the transition between her upper and middle register, told her when she had pushed too hard. A shower of gold in a pot was how he described her. One day the pot would shatter, and the gold would flow out in an iridiscent stream, if only she would allow it.

'Your beauty is made for the stage,' he said. 'No one will ever forget you. You have begun the climb to Mount Olympus. Take it step by step and you will arrive. I promise you.'

His voice was firm and full-bodied, as though he was used to projecting in large spaces, on platforms, whilst still retaining the intimacy of conversation. Unlike the Italians to whom she was becoming accustomed, he seemed to be addressing her directly, disdaining the lightly tossed off expressions of praise and affection which skittered over

133

the surface like bright butterflies flower-hopping under blue skies. He spoke deliberately, sometimes pausing as though to find an exact expression, but no one interrupted him, not Passattella, not even his stunning girlfriend. Perhaps she was his wife. A man like this deserved no less. He was American, which meant he would have a grand house in Hollywood with pillars like the ones in Bishop's Avenue.

There were fragments which remained with her, and would always remain, even though she knew he would take off with his blond beauty and she was unlikely to see him again. He would never know that she had found the person she was seeking, that she had felt the irrational certainty of love. It was nothing like her first meeting with Eduardo. If he had asked her to leave with him, she would have gone just as she was, without baggage, without a change of clothes, abandoning her family, Passattella, her joyful attic room. She would have tossed aside all the careful planning of her career to be with this man. She had no idea why.

He smiled, took her hand again, held it. 'You'll never need luck, Anastasia. Just the right influences. I hope we meet again.' Then he handed her a card. 'If you need some advice, give me a call.'

Did he feel the same? Was he being polite? Did he want to work with her? Or was she too young and gauche for him to consider? She decided to seek him out, wherever he might be.

'Come, get in the car, Anastasia. Give me the flowers. I'll put them in the back. I'll see you two in Harry's Bar later. Order some champagne on my account. *Arrivederci.*'

Stasi handed him the bouquets, and Maestro Passattella laid them out one by one on the back seat.

'I can't think who sent all those.'

'The cast always give flowers to someone they like. It's our tradition. And Stefano Montini will have spread the word around. He was praising you to the skies, and he never praises anyone.'

As he found room for the last bouquet on the floor behind her, Passattella glanced at the elegant packaging and froze. Who had sent this?

'You're happy with everybody? You like my singers?'

'Of course. They've all been so kind, even Assunta. I was crazy to be so nervous. But I couldn't help it. Did you notice? I'm sorry to have let you down. I forgot things, didn't know what I was doing. It just happened. Yesterday I was fine . . .'

'Darling, the first time, everyone has nerves. We expect it. One singer I had last season, she told me she was so petrified, she wet her knickers. Now she sings on television, all over the world. Beautifully. If she is still nervous, you will never see it.' Passattella was foraging around in the pocket of the door. 'Do me a favour. I can't find my gloves. Perhaps they're in the boot. It's open. Could you have a look?'

Stasi got out of the car and walked round to the back. While she was searching amongst piles of papers and scores, Passattella took the bouquet he had put on the floor, quietly opened the door a little, and placed it underneath the car.

When they drove off, she would not notice it. Luckily he was observant, used to retaining the tiniest gesture, the position of a prop, the hanging of a drape, the transient look of pain on a singer's face might jeopardize a performance. He had no wish for Anastasia Wagner to have bad memories of her debut. One day, when he was retired, he would proudly say that he, Maestro Alessandro Passattella, had been the first to discern her extraordinary quality, that the world famous diva had taken her first steps on stage under his direction.

She must have offended someone, even unwittingly. Singers were like animals. Sometimes they took against one another for no apparent reason, but there was no need to go this far, no need to emulate the tactics of the *onorevole società*. This wasn't Sicily, after all. She would not know, he would tell no one, that someone had sent

Anastasia Wagner white chrysanthemums on her opening night, the spiky reminders of death reserved for funeral wreaths. Rico, perhaps? He had once substituted a rubber snake for Tosca's dagger when Tosca was being played by an English soprano. His grandfather had been a prisoner of war in England. No point in saying anything.

'I can't find your gloves, maestro.' Stasi settled herself in the front seat.

'Never mind. They must be at home.' He started the car, and surged forward. 'What did you think of young Dominic?'

'Who?'

'The American you met. Dominic Morrison.'

'Very, very . . . a serious person, I thought.'

'I hope that doesn't mean you're taking him seriously. Do you know his work?'

'Assunta told me he'd done *Don Giovanni* in a space-ship.'

'Only an American could do that. But of course he has worked mostly in the theatre. In New York and Los Angeles, so he says. Another theatre director who thinks he can direct opera. A charlatan, my dear. Learn to recognize them; we have many in Italy. He has found out that the quickest way to get ladies into bed is to discuss their singing. Or their photographs. Or their movies. Or whatever it is they do. He has a knack of making it sound plausible. As though the last thing on his mind is producing, forgive me, his American cock.'

Passattella laughed, took one hand off the wheel and glanced at Stasi. 'He will ask you to audition for him, in some convenient but modest hotel, at an innocuous time. Morning coffee, for example. He will ask you politely which aria you have chosen. Since he is not yet as well paid as he is well known, he will be able to afford neither a suite nor a piano. You will sing in the small space between the basin and the bed to the accompaniment of one of those wretched rehearsal tapes. Then he will ask you to move a little more . . . dramatically. Then, ah, then. You will find yourself rehearsing in the supine position. I need say no more.'

He put his hand back on the steering wheel. 'I've also heard that he employs the same technique with tenors.'

'Thank you for telling me, maestro.' Her dreams cascaded to the ground, mud-spattered.

'Sandro. Call me Sandro, please. We're friends, no?' He patted her knee, and left his hand resting on her thigh. Stasi tensed her shoulders.

'I mustn't be too late.'

Couldn't she be the one to pull this unhappy man from debauchery? He must be unhappy. Wasn't Don Giovanni weighed down by restless misery behind his cavalier mask? People could change; Dominic Morrison could change.

'Don't worry. I'll get you back to Florence. It's on the way. We'll just stop for a quick drink in Settignano. Do you know Settignano?'

She was taller, but that was not the point. Stasi never regarded herself as vulnerable, not in this land where only the younger, steak-fed, wealthier men reached above her shoulders. Settignano here we come. So Guido was right and Maestro Sandro Passattella was taking her on the milk run. He had removed his hand from her thigh and slipped a tape into the car cassette. A syrupy voice crooned, '*Ti voglio, ti voglio per sempre.*' I want you for ever.

'Your tape has stretched. It sounds dreadful,' Stasi remarked in the matter-of-fact voice she adopted to tell Gloria that she had a hole in her tights. She pressed the stop button. 'Maybe you should find a different one.'

'You never listen to popular music?'

'I dance to it sometimes.'

'I too. Have a look for something else which pleases you.'

For the rest of the journey, Stravinsky's *Rite of Spring* inhibited conversation until they drove up in front of an old country house which seemed inappropriate for the Settignano Country Club. Stasi was searching for husky golfers and sweating men in jogging suits, or at least someone with a tennis racket, but she was disappointed. Passattella led her past the wood-panelled entrance and down a corridor into a small 'retiring room' which contained an unexpectedly flamboyant marble fireplace supported by two bare-breasted amazons with serpentine hair, a long, leather-covered couch and two straight-backed armchairs.

'No need to be so formal, Anastasia. Come and sit here.'

Carla, she supposed, might have sat here before her, drawing up her skirt as she sat down, crossing one leg over the other high up on her thigh, inviting intimacy yet suggesting uncertainty as to the outcome. Stasi knew the Soprano's Rough Guide to securing a role (didn't all young singers?) but she was unable or unwilling to summon up the vocabulary of seduction which she had observed in others. Did she want to work with Passattella again anyway? And if she did, would she have put herself at the starting line by reapplying her lipstick, dabbing perfume on her wrists, arranging her long hair provocatively to one side, stretching out her legs to allow her skirt to ride up and gazing with mute admiration into Sandro's chubby face? Why ever not? I couldn't do that, she heard herself replying to Carla's mocking question. Just couldn't. *Strana ragazza*.

She allowed the maestro – 'Sandro, *per carità*' – to take her hand, keeping her legs closely parallel, examining the carpeted floor as he began his speech. Like a father, he wanted to guide her, he had so much to teach her, they would work together, he sensed they had much to give one another, they would create a fusion of talent (hers) and experience (his).

'My next production will be at Verona. Very very important, a new one. *Turandot*. You would be the best Liù I can imagine. And I won't ask you to run and jump, I promise. In a few years, you will be playing the title role.'

'Do you mean that?'

'Of course. Why do you always ask me that, Anastasia?

138

Strange girl. *Strana ragazza*. Don't you trust me? Do you imagine I'm pretending to offer you a part as an excuse to possess you? Really! I am not producing a Broadway musical, my dear.'

'Can I ask you something?'

'Of course.'

'Did you ask Carla Livorno first?'

Passattella gave a great guffaw and put his arm on Stasi's shoulder. 'The jealousy between singers is like the froth on a cappuccino. When you drink, it disappears.'

'But did you? Tell me.'

'Always such direct questions.'

'Why does everyone have to be so devious? I can take it. If you think she is better than me, why don't you say so?'

'You will be a diva, my dear.'

'Why do you say that?'

'Anastasia, you have the ability to create drama from the everyday and the commonplace. That is a great talent. You, my beauty, are raging inside because I haven't confessed that you looked superb, that you sang beautifully, that your interpretation was better than the one I suggested. You want me to go down on my knees. If only, if only I had chosen *la bella* Anastasia, if only I had put her first. My God. You think it is that simple?'

'I just want your opinion.'

'We will see. Well, are we going to work together?'

'Even though I'm so difficult?'

'All women are difficult. They believe their sex has the monopoly on insecurity. How do you think I feel when this upstart, talentless Morrison gets more attention in the international press than I do? And I have been producing for twenty years, I grew up with Verdi and Puccini throbbing in my ears, I have worked with Domingo, Carreras, Sutherland, as a student I worshipped La Divina, Maria Callas. Not one disaster. And now they are saying that opera needs to be redefined. Redefined? You know what that means? Hiring sopranos who will bare their buttocks.

Does Tosca have to throw off her clothes to gain our attention? My God!'

And if she did? There was only one person who would play Tosca. Carla Livorno would hardly need to audition.

'Who's singing Turandot?'

'She is not blond, does not have a famous daddy, and is called Eva Marton. Are you satisfied, my dear? Come, I must take you back to your impatient family. You can tell them you will be returning to Italy.'

'If I do.'

'You will.'

'Then I want to stay in a very expensive hotel and have a costume designed specially for me. Will I have that?'

'Anything, anything. Except for the red Alfa sports car. Mine is better, don't you think? Shall we go?' He led her back past reception, his arm linked through hers.

The car was creeping slowly through the meandering lanes of Settignano, and she was barely aware that they had turned off the narrow road and had come to a halt beneath the shadow of a clump of cypresses, obscuring the light of the full moon. Suddenly he turned off the engine, his lips close to her ear.

'Anastasia, you are like fire. I want to see you naked, with your beautiful pale English skin. I want to shower you with caresses, not with words. I won't touch you, I won't touch you. You have the legs of Diana, the mouth of Aphrodite, the voice of Gabriel.' He took her hand, ran it down the soft texture of his silk shirt, and pressed it against his cock. 'I won't touch you. You feel? The desire of a man who honours you. What is more beautiful?'

While Stasi was considering what she should say (Carla would have said the right thing, tactful, firm, allowing him to think she admired him), in a deft movement he leaned over her, lifted up her skirt and pressed his face against her tightly clenched thighs.

'I won't touch you, I won't touch you,' he murmured, as she leaned up against the door. Then he replaced her skirt, and pulled her neck towards him. 'Just one kiss.'

'Don't. You're being silly.'

'You're afraid. There's no need. I won't touch you. Listen. You must learn about love. I am controlling myself. I want you to be naked, to worship you, to, how do you say in English, I want to . . .'

'Fuck.'

'No, no, not this terrible word. Ah, what a language, which cannot express the tenderness of love. Anastasia, I want to lick, to suck, down there, so you will tremble with pleasure. Let me show you the Italian way.'

'Maestro!' Stasi pushed him back into his seat. 'I'm not the right girl for you. I'm in love. When English girls are in love, they can't fuck anyone else. You're embarrassing me, Sandro.'

'You don't find me attractive?'

'That has nothing to do with it.'

'It is possible. I am a grown man. I understand these things.' He jammed the key into the ignition. 'Who is this man?'

Stasi hesitated. 'It doesn't matter who it is. You're angry. You look as though you're going to hit the conductor.'

Passattella laughed, opened the driver's compartment, retrieved a pair of white cotton gloves, and drew them slowly over his hands. 'You have the address of this place in Firenze?'

'Do you hate me now?'

'Of course not. My dearest Anastasia, every man has to do these things. If not, who could be a man? There is always another girl. But between us, there is something more special. Yes? We are artists. Maybe it's better this way. No complications. Now I am no longer hard, we can be friends.'

He kissed her gently on the lips, then turned the car back onto the moonlit road and hurried off towards Florence.

★　　★　　★

A small trattoria in Florence had been turned by the onslaught of the Wagners into a den of iniquity. Tonight, they were going on the razzle, just as their ancestors would have done when they'd reached the Promised Land. They were only breaking one of the lesser commandments which Blessed be He had doubtless omitted as surplus to requirements. The survival instinct, honed and strengthened over thousands of years, made an edict from on high unnecesssary. Thou Shalt Not Drink was an unwritten rule. Was it the race memory of drunken Cossacks raping their women, hurling babies at the wall, slitting open the stomachs of their men, smashing their modest ghetto homes to fragments? Or the fear of having to flee at a moment's notice with all the belongings you could carry, when your legs would not support you, your eyes could not distinguish the enemy in the shadows? Was it the shame of pissing drunkenly on the floor when the Gestapo seized you by the throat? The Jews of the Diaspora would sooner have their bloodstream charged with cholesterol than the polluted shame of alcohol.

Maestro Passattella pushed open the net-covered doors of the small neighbourhood restaurant, where a hand-written board in the window announced, 'Menù Turistica. Cheap Tourist Menu.' He accompanied Stasi to the one long table still littered with plates and breadcrumbs, and empty bottles of wine standing up like accusing witnesses. There was no one there except Raymond, Uncle Monty, Aunt Lizzie and Gloria, and the two waiters, father and son, sleeves rolled up, whipping off paper cloths, pushing in the wooden chairs noisily, throwing clattering cutlery in a heap on trays, ignoring them with surly restraint. *Questi inglesi, bevono, bevono, ubriaconi, ubriaconi.*

Gloria was singing 'Auld Lang Syne' in chorus with Lizzie. They were both standing on chairs, holding hands and kicking up their legs. Mortified, Stasi ignored the whooping cries greeting their arrival and pulled Maestro Passattella back towards the entrance, banging the door shut behind her.

'They're never like this at home. I wish they'd stayed in England. I wish they'd never come. I hate them. God how I hate them. How could they let me down like this? You must think I'm a peasant. Now you know. You've seen it. You've seen where I come from.' She bowed her head, covered it with her hands and let the tears of humiliation begin to flow.

'Gently, gently, Anastasia.' He lifted up her chin so that she would look at him. 'Now listen before I go. Carreras' mother was a hairdresser, Bergonzi's father a cheese-maker, Van Dam's father a carpenter, Pavarotti's a baker. Most of our best singers come from the people. You should be proud.' For the last time, the maestro kissed her hand. 'Work hard. And remember, even if your body is as good as your voice, which sadly I will never discover, there is never a need to take off your clothes. And have one drink with your family. Always be generous with those who love you. Soon we can start studying *Turandot*. *Arrivederci*.'

She stood watching him as he strode away, walking with dignity towards his car. You have everything, she thought, except the dangerous ability of the truly talented. And I am looking for danger.

Inside the restaurant, Uncle Monty was throwing fifty thousand lira notes onto a plate. They were about to leave.

'Oh, darling. What you've missed. We've had such a wonderful time.'

'What an evening.'

'What a laugh.'

'They even found me a German beer.'

'My legs, my legs.'

'Has anyone seen it? My handbag?'

They squashed themselves into a taxi, limbs sprawling, talking, interrupting, joking, laughing, hugging one another. Suddenly Gloria remembered. 'Stasi darling. All that wine. Gone to my head. You thought I hadn't saved you anything, thought you'd go starving to bed. Not my Stasi. No one saw, I promise. Here. Take it, take it.'

Stasi opened the layers of paper napkins to reveal a sodden mass which she eventually distinguished as a piece of veal, some fried potatoes, beans, a bread roll and a mess of chocolate. Gloria peered at her trophy, as Stasi burst into hysterical laughter.

'Who did this? Who squashed it? That waiter! The *schweinhund*!' Aunt Lizzie leaned forward and tapped Gloria's knee. 'I must tell you something. How stupid can you be? I sat on it. Honestly, I didn't mean to, but you left it on my chair and I got up and . . .'

'Never mind. It'll taste the same.'

'Such a wonderful evening.'

There would be a family photograph, taken the day after in the Piazza Signoria, below the giant, brutish, bearded marble Neptune. Stasi in the middle, smirking, Gloria to one side, smiling with her mouth wide open, tiny Aunt Lizzie to the other, in a large straw hat, blinking, Uncle Monty and Raymond behind, arms crossed on their chests, serious and manly. On the back of the photograph, Gloria would write: After Stasi's First Performance in *Carmen*. Happiness. Florence.

Chapter Six

Sir Miles Mackenzie had, at long last, succeeded in creating his Palace of Opera in the historic heart of London. It had begun at a chance meeting on the golf course at Gleneagles with Sven Larsen. He, too, had seen that film about a man who was obsessed with creating an opera house in the jungle. Fitzcarraldo. Apparently it was a true story and had greatly impressed Sir Miles as a parable of the ordinary man who breaks the bounds of his ordinariness to achieve an impossible dream. In the pursuit of an ideal anybody could become a hero, mark his life with one, undeniable achievement. A secretary could become a prima ballerina, a postman could become an opera singer. It was within these people that the untapped wellsprings of genius lay, he was convinced.

The son of a Scottish Presbyterian minister and a Welsh schoolteacher, Sir Miles Mackenzie attracted both loyalty and respect. His stooped bearing (he was six foot two) and his slight stutter were more reminiscent of a retired academic than an administrative leader, but these draw-backs distanced him from the dangerous inroads of intimacy. As a former executive of the BBC, his battles had ended in compromise, and he was unlikely to be remembered for imposing his personal stamp on the cultural life of Britain. No one wrote you into history for reorganizing the current affairs department and giving a larger budget for natural history programmes. He longed to achieve something for which he would be remembered.

Sven Larsen, a Swedish industrialist with investments in various privatized British companies, lived in Stockholm with a leading opera singer. Although a success in the Royal Opera House in Stockholm, the Royal Opera House in London had consistently turned her down. So strong was Larsen's indignation, he was prepared to create a showcase for her talent in Britain. Was it for love of his wife, or because he felt a bitter slight to his homeland? Sir Miles could not decide, but Sven Larsen shared his enthusiasm for taking opera to the underprivileged masses, his passionate belief in the accessibility of art.

Soon after that first meeting, Sven Larsen's wife had died tragically in a road accident, but he had insisted that Sir Miles brought the project to completion. Five years later, the great pinnacles soaring from the roof of the Opera Palace had become a landmark by the river, close to Tower Hill. The glass and steel structure was topped by the jagged peaks of a crown like a paper hat worn at a children's party, with coloured lights cascading down, changing from one rainbow colour to another. The huge stage was centrally placed, like an egg-shaped arena, with seating for three thousand spreading round on three sides. There were no boxes, no bars exclusively for the privileged; it was open to all.

The foyer was designed as a miniature pleasure park, a gathering place for families, with fast-food stalls, the Words and Music bookshop, computer games, the Opera Palace lottery stand, the Palace pub with home-brewed ale, the Aria wine bar, a dress hire boutique, booths where you could be photographed standing next to cutouts of opera stars, and even a crèche for the tots. Moving escalators would carry the new audiences up to the top of the arena from where they could look down on the mysterious world of opera.

Sir Miles had been criticized at every turn, but he had stood firm, and refused to give in to despair. As director of the Opera Palace, he had only attracted sufficient funds for his first production, but once successfully launched, he believed, wealthy music lovers and industrial sponsors would rally round to support his venture. His critics would soon moderate their contempt for the 'punk pimple', an unfortunate description coined by one of the architects favoured by Prince Charles.

The Opera Palace was within days of throwing open its doors. Sir Miles felt apprehensive, and it had little to do with the faulty operation of the lifts and the fluctuating air conditioning. His unease stemmed from a decision he had taken against the advice of the board, which had sided with the newly appointed artistic director, Malcolm Fuerstein. Only Julian Lieberman, his financial director, had endorsed his policy, but Lieberman was one of those rare men who appreciated the turbulent confluence between profit and art.

Sir Miles owed much to Lieberman, for at the last minute, just when he had despaired of backing from the stony ground of British investment, he had come to the rescue. His business corporation DCCI (Julian jokingly referred to it as the Domination and Control Corporation International) had put forward a financial package of forward investment which would carry the Opera Palace for an initial five years. For Lieberman, too, the Opera Palace was more than a project. Right at the beginning, he had told Sir Miles that, although he had established his financial base on the back of companies in liquidation, he had come to loathe his carrion role. In the Opera Palace he saw the possibility of making reparation, of creating something from the wreckage of destruction, of planting the seeds of a flowering tree in the mud-flats of collapsed enterprise.

No one seemed to know about Lieberman in the City, but Sir Miles knew instinctively that he had been right in appointing him to the board. Unlike most of the young candidates he had interviewed, he didn't appear to have set his sights on occupying the seat of the man who had employed him. And he loved opera, with the passionate devotion usually accorded to golf or yachting by men of his class and background. If he had so chosen, he could have had an outstanding political career. Certainly he would have outshone Andrew Broughton, the unhelpful Minister for the Arts, who had only obtained the post, in Sir Miles's opinion, because he happened to know something about early Victorian art and was promoting low-budget touring companies as a solution to the lustreless, underfunded cultural climate of Britain.

Creating a new opera house would take time, a fact Malcolm Fuerstein failed to appreciate. World-class singers needed to be developed; they did not spring fully fledged from the provincial backwaters of the British Isles. How could they? Had Graham Greene and Evelyn Waugh (two of his favourite writers) become the mouthpiece of a generation through reading Enid Blyton? Only Julian got the point. With the best will in the world, what British singers could carry a multi-million pound production of *Aida*?

Sir Miles listened carefully to the objections which followed his comments, taking notes as always. With great reluctance, he felt unable to accept their suggestions.

'The fact that Ruggiero Gasparini is Italian is irrelevant,' argued Sir Miles. 'Even that he is a singer. He could just as well play football. He is a popular phenomenon. To open with him means two things. One, that we have the power and muscle of La Scala or the Met., where he regularly sings. Two, that we have the interest of a wide public at heart. If we don't achieve popular success from the outset, we might as well put on Pergolesi at Buxton. I know that Gasparini would not be your first choice for the Palace *Aida*. But he would be the choice of all those who will make our opening season a sell-out. And I want all these people to return. Otherwise we will have failed.'

After a few more late-night meetings, the decision was taken. Ruggiero Gasparini would be booked, whatever the price. He agreed to give four performances.

Everyone knew the moment of Ruggiero Gasparini's triumphal entry, for it would be the first time this world-renowned tenor had ever sung in Britain. His entourage spilled down the steps of his private jet, from a distinguished elderly man to a host of tiny children whom everyone presumed to have sprung from the prolific seed of the Gasparinis. By the next day, everyone also knew of Ruggiero's fondness for Liquorice Allsorts, a British delicacy he had taken to his heart ever since he had first visited his uncle's Italian restaurant in Streatham as a *piccolo bambino*.

Of course he had always loved England. Why hadn't he sung before? Ruggiero flung his arms into the air. 'You tell me,' he said, beaming a million dollar smile, only twice as great as his fee for singing Rhadames. His public soon knew that Harrods had been closed for an hour while he visited the Food Hall, that he had bought fifty giant packets of crisps, and had been disappointed to find that they were unable to supply the famous Yorkshire pudding.

Four limousines began their slow journey from the Dorchester Hotel, where Ruggiero had created 'Little Italy' within minutes of arriving, towards the acceptable landmarks of London. At appropriate points, Ruggiero eased his huge bulk out of the back seat, took a few steps and posed against Buckingham Palace, the Houses of Parliament and the Tower of London, joking to the photographers – 'The Queen is waiting in there to see me' – and accepting boxes of Liquorice Allsorts from small children. Outside the Opera Palace, a battery of television crews and photographers had been waiting for several hours.

It was hard for the Livornos, spending all day in the limousine behind Ruggiero's. No one came up to them or thrust cameras in their faces or even asked who they were. Carla was growing impatient.

'Why don't they photograph us?' she asked Emily.

'This is England, darling.'

'I know that. If Pa had been with us, they would have done.'

'Never mind. He'll be back from Germany next week.'

The trip to London had been suggested to Emily by

Ruggiero. He knew that her husband was constantly away. Emily was determined that Carla's marriage would be different from hers, and she was relieved that Maurizio was constantly making comparisons with Italy, longing to be home again. He preferred to voyage in his imagination. The rise in adultery, Emily was convinced, was due to the expansion of air-travel. Most men, arriving in a foreign country, immediately felt the need to prove their virility. (Not that Paolo would have succumbed, for he was a musician. Dr Mainz, her analyst, had explained the intricate and misunderstood relationship between artistic expression and sexual sublimation.)

When it came to the group photograph, Carla waited for the moment to escape through the great bronze and glass doors behind her. They had shuffled her to the back, with one of Ruggiero's objectionable nieces. Maurizio had gone back to the Halcyon Hotel with his usual *mal di stomaco*. Sir Miles had shaken her hand, Julian hardly seemed to notice her. Emily just had no idea, and Carla couldn't tell her how galling it was to be met with those blank 'she's nobody' looks from the photographers, knowing that in just a few years all those lenses should be pointing towards her, begging her to smile in their direction. The way things were going, there was no chance.

'Carla, darling, I'll be frank. You haven't got what it takes. And I should know.'

Emily really knew how to put the knife in. She always pretended she knew what was best, but she couldn't take her daughter's success, not when her own singing days were past. The Opera Palace could give Carla the opportunity she craved, away from Milan, away from Italy, away from Emily. All she needed was to meet Sir Miles Mackenzie again to renew his interest. And besides, it was easy, she suspected, to make an impression in England.

The moment she set foot on the enormous stage, Carla wanted to make it hers. She gazed round at the ranks of purple seating spreading out on three sides, dwarfed by clusters of fronds and palm trees, and silvery pyramids, while the lighting around her changed from warm orange to pale yellow to moonlit silver. She was imagining herself with deep-tanned Ethiopian skin and a black wig, a vast audience roaring its approval at her first entrance. Who in England had the grace, the sexiness, the power, the allure to play Aida? No one, otherwise they wouldn't have imported that black girl from Chicago. They had the voices, like Stasi Wagner, but they were all dead from the tits down. What England needed was Carla Livorno.

Julian Lieberman found her standing in a pool of light by a pillar, acknowledging the admiration of the stage-crew.

'Hello, Carla. You're looking splendid, as ever. Isn't this the best set you've ever seen? Come on, Emily's waiting. We're all meeting later in some ghastly pasta joint on the fringes of civilization. I couldn't convert the great man to San Lorenzo's. Ruggiero has rushed off to Kensington Palace to have a royal tea. Apparently the Queen's sister is a fan.'

Carla looked unimpressed, and looked up at the sounding boards suspended from the glass roof.

'What are the acoustics like?'

'Don't worry. Ruggiero will be heard in every corner.'

'I wasn't thinking of him. What a place! I'd rather sing here than La Scala any day.'

They began to climb the steps leading from the sunken arena.

'How's the dear fiancé?'

'Oh, he's fine.'

'I had a long letter from Beatrice. She refused to believe me when I told her they'd adore Mozart in Tokyo. Her concert tour seems to be going frightfully well. Aren't you pleased?'

'Julian, listen to me. The only way I'm going to make it is to leave Italy. Ma and Pa refuse to take me seriously. Can you imagine what it's like? It's all I care about. I'm a singer, for Christ's sake. Passattella has asked me to do

151

Micaela again in Piacenza. I know it's only because he wants to keep on the right side of Pa. I told him to fuck off. Ma was furious.'

'What do you want me to do?'

'Help me make it on my own. Help me make it in England.'

'Let's talk about it later.'

'No, now.'

'You might change your mind when you're the Marchesa della Robbia.'

There had been many before her, begging him to intercede, pretty young girls with charming, wan smiles, and the small rounded breasts and narrow hips he preferred, suddenly becoming obsessed with their careers when they found out that he was on the board. After they had bared their bodies, they began to bare their souls, as though the brief act of penetration entitled them to push home this illusory advantage. Carla, to her credit, at least had the courtesy to ask him directly.

'I have no influence with Sir Miles. I'd love to help you, but, as they say, it's not in my gift.'

'Don't give me that bullshit,' she cried. 'You got him the finance, didn't you?'

Julian smiled. 'You are well-informed.'

'Ma told me. I didn't sneak it out. I'll bet you could do something if you wanted to.'

'Such as? Get you the lead in *Aida* at three days' notice?'

'Don't be crazy. I just want a start.'

'In the chorus?'

'Well, a small part.'

'Unfortunately, I can't. Our policy is to fill all but the star roles with British singers. It is, after all, the first new British opera house. That's why we're in business.'

'That's why Ruggiero was booked, I suppose. He's as British as my arse.'

'We needed a star turn to put us on the map. But we've got some interesting British talent lined up for our next effort.'

Julian still managed to irritate her. She could never stop herself rising to the lofty way he put her down.

'Know something? I always knew you never liked me, Julian. I'd rather you said, Carla Livorno, get lost. But you haven't got the guts. You'd rather invent some crap about British singers. Good singers are good singers. Think I don't know that?'

'My dearest Carla, I've never even heard you. I've no reason to lie. I'm telling it, as the Americans say, how it is.'

'If you wanted to, you could help.'

'Nobody will risk taking an unknown singer. How could I put your name forward if no one has heard of you? The daughter of Paolo Livorno? Who's Paolo Livorno? Hardly anyone here is even aware he's one of our greatest conductors.'

'All I need is someone to handle my publicity. Look at Ruggiero. No one knew who he was a couple of days ago.'

'You could always try seducing Sir Miles.'

'That's real tacky. I always audition with my clothes on, by the way.'

Julian smiled. 'You do misunderstand me, Carla. Just like your delightful sister Beatrice.'

'OK. So I'm a brain-dead bimbo. I get the message. Give me a couple of years, and I'll pack every seat in the place.'

Julian took in the determined face, the owl-like eyes staring into his, the plunging line of her cashmere sweater, and began to revise his opinion. There was something about her to which he responded, even if he was indifferent to the blatant sexuality she took pains to promote on every occasion. They did share a passion, although they had never engaged in lengthy discussions about opera. And he liked her spirit, the way she answered back as though she had a knife between her teeth.

'I've a friend who might help. Ever heard of the Maison Blanche in Paris?'

'Of course. Everyone has.'

'Saffron is looking for premises in London. She wants to open up here.'

'I didn't know you knew Saffron.'

Anyone who scanned the society columns with Carla's thoroughness would have noticed that particular English face. It looked as though it had been washed in dew, eyes the colour of wild harebells, flawless, wholesome skin. But for the bobbed, fine hair settling neatly round her long neck, she could have changed places with one of the simpering favourites of the artist Romney. Saffron, however, was never pictured against the background of cultivated parkland, and was rarely seen in daylight. She was usually described as 'the well-known English hostess and party-giver'. Those seen entering or leaving La Maison Blanche, her tightly exclusive Parisian club, would need no further proof of their 'standing'.

Carla instantly dropped her belligerent tone. It had been easy to dismiss Julian as yet another of the good-looking, affable, rich hangers-on passing through Milan on business who frequented the Livorno household. He had never mentioned his friendship with Saffron. Her sister Beatrice would go crazy if she knew there was someone else.

'OK. I'm sorry, Julian. I'm in a strange country, and I'm acting like I was in Italy. You think Saffron could put me in the right places?'

'That's up to Saffron. Maybe a little spot at the club. She has rather good singers appearing from time to time. Jazz, popular classics, that kind of thing, I believe. It might get you on the scene here.'

'Maybe to begin with. I'm a versatile performer.'

Julian smiled. 'I'm sure you are, Carla.'

'But that doesn't mean I'm not serious. Still, I wouldn't mind.'

'Better than auditioning for the Welsh National Opera, I would have thought. Saffron's coming over to stay at my place sometime soon. I'll get you to meet her.'

'Fantastic.'

'Such a super girl. I think you two might hit it off. I suspect your interests are the same.'

Carla threw her arms round Julian and kissed his cheek. 'I'll call you from Milan. Deep down, you're an OK guy, Julian. Now come and be nice to Mamma.'

Ruggiero Gasparini had been indisposed for two days, refusing interviews, refusing to speak on the phone. Three times a day, his Italian doctor issued a communiqué. The press knew, the world knew, that he was fasting, drinking nothing but carrot juice. They also knew that in the room next to his suite, his buxom young wife Livia (number four in the Gasparini succession, his three divorces having made him the most expensive singer in the world), his acupuncturist, dietician, herbalist, masseuse and laryngologist were debating a treatment schedule which would resurrect the ailing singer and return him to his audience.

Thomas Campton-Fausey, the fresh-faced press officer, rapped lightly on the mahogany door of Sir Miles's office, even though it was half open.

'Ah, Thomas. Any hope?'

'Signor Gasparini has just eaten a softly boiled egg, Sir Miles,' he announced breathlessly.

'Do I take it that means an improvement?'

'Two boiled eggs might mean an improvement. A huge bowl of spaghetti with meatballs would make me more optimistic. Oh yes. Another thing. One of the elephants has diarrhoea.'

Sir Miles stroked his chin and forced a smile. 'I hope the cover is in good health.'

'He's waiting at the Royal Garden Hotel.'

'The elephant, Thomas, the elephant.'

'Of course. It's not a disaster. If we drop one elephant, the trainer says he can bring over a couple more camels for the same price. Or extra horses.'

'The public loves to see camels. Yes, camels. As long as they don't dribble and spit. Keep me posted.'

'Of course, Sir Miles.'

It was a quarter past ten. At six o'clock, the royal party would be arriving. Sir Miles clasped his long, bony hands together on the bare top of his maple desk, where only a leather folder embossed M.G.H.M. interrupted the shining expanse. He silently offered a short prayer.

'Dear Lord. Let him sing. Just let him sing tonight.'

There had just been time to take in some quick shopping, and Emily felt the rush of adrenalin she always felt after spending more than ten thousand dollars. They had done their best for Ruggiero, who loved everyone to look good. The fuchsia Chanel suit was cheaper than in Paris, and Carla's flirty Dolce e Gabbiano was adorable. Even Maurizio had made a purchase, a dozen shirts from Savile Row.

'I hope they won't throw us out,' remarked Emily to Maurizio, as she pressed the button of the penthouse suite of the Dorchester Hotel.

'Very unlikely, Signora Livorno. I have a visiting card which I use on such occasions.'

A figure, head shrouded in a voluminous towel like a courtroom criminal hiding from the press, was enthroned in a cavernous armchair. Bare red feet were resting in a large copper stockpot containing unpasteurized milk (apparently, copper and milk were both dilatory and restorative), provided through the ingenuity of room service. Arranged within striking distance of the sculptural folds of the seated figure were tables laden with oranges, grapes, crystallized fruits, cold pasta salads of various colours, French loaves, cheeses, bowls of bonbons, bottles of mineral water placed in buckets of ice and flagons of country wine. A series of crystal glass dishes piled high with Liquorice Allsorts occupied the foreground of each table.

The figure threw off the towel which was hanging from his head to his lap, revealing a large bowl which released puffs of eucalyptus steam.

'*Amici miei! Che piacere!*'

'Ruggiero!'

Ruggiero gave Maurizio a manly embrace as he leaned down cautiously to touch his heavy, steam-lacquered jowl. Emily allowed her fingers to be kissed, and Carla received a smack on the lips.

'My fiancé, you remember. Maurizio della Robbia.'

'Eh!' Ruggiero stretched out a hairy arm and winked. 'You leave her to me in your will. Come! Time for lunch.' Clapping his hands, he bellowed from his chair, 'Lunch, lunch, lunch, *tutti*.'

As though adding some veracity to a folksy village scene, a line of children of differing heights came bounding into the room, ignoring the visitors, crowding round the tables of food. There were always visitors, family, friends, children, never strangers, and they never saw him when he was alone, practising behind locked doors in his music room. Ruggiero Gasparini lived amongst his retinue like a beaming, Falstaffian feudal lord.

'Everyone takes what he wants.'

Still enshrined in his armchair, Ruggiero accepted a laden tray from Livia, and aimed forkfuls of pasta into his cavernous mouth, sweeping off the tomato smears with a grand gesture after each mouthful.

'We're so relieved to see you better, Ruggiero. Those dreadful reports in the paper,' Emily said, as she passed a plate of pasta to the marchese who was leaning against the window, vainly comparing the view to one painted centuries before by Canaletto, which he knew by heart. Carla draped herself elegantly on an embroidered stool.

'Better? Every day I'm better. All the critics say so except for the lousy sonofabitch ignoramus from *The Times*.'

'Darling,' remonstrated Livia. 'Don't get excited.'

'Me, excited?' he roared. 'I am the calmest man you ever met.' He tore a lettuce leaf apart, grimaced and tossed it back on the plate. 'English salad. I give to the chickens.'

'I hope you're off that egg diet,' continued Emily.

'You've got to be careful with eggs. My doctor advises one a week.'

'Never eat them, dear lady. Sometimes I like to throw them.' He chuckled, dabbed his chin again, took a sip of mineral water, and his expression turned to menace. 'Now. I tell you the truth. You listen to this. I arrive in England. Totally totally prepared. You know me?'

'Indeed, my friend.'

'When do I make a mistake in rehearsal?' His eyebrows rose, his eyes narrowed in anger.

'Never. Paolo always says it's a dream to work with you,' gushed Emily, filling in the beat set aside for comment.

'So. I arrive in England. I give half an hour to this other sonofabitch English ignoramus who calls himself a producer. I go on stage, I tell him what I will do. I show him my costume, my Rhadames costume. And then! And then!' There was a short splutter. His wife rushed to his side, fearing it might explode into a cough, but he waved her away. 'You know what? This impudent castrato suggests some things for my performance. He asks me sing "Celeste Aida" on my knees. On. My. Knees. I laugh. Are you serious? It will be so effective, he says in his shrivelled, constipated turd of a voice. Effective? Do you sing on your knees in England? I am so sorry. They did not tell me this. Then he asks me to make movements on the stage. For no reason. Listen, young puppy, I say. If I want to go for a walk, you know where I go? Hyde Park.'

The whole room laughed, the children giggled, until Ruggiero raised his hand for silence.

'"Come," I say. "We rehearse." I tell the conductor where to start, I show him my tempi. The orchestra, I must tell you, is not bad. Everyone is happy. The black girl who is Aida, she is not bad. They have other scenes to do, naturally, so I start to go. The head of costume, she comes. Excuse me, Mr Gasparini. Could I have a fitting? A fitting of what? My costume? I have my costume. And you will see, it fits.'

Waiting for the titters to die down, Ruggiero pressed another forkful into his mouth.

'Mr Producer comes to look for me, like a mouse hunting for cheese, pitta patta pitta patta down the corridor. He has told the Director of the Opera House – the name of this stupid man?'

'Sir Miles Mackenzie,' said Carla.

'This man says I cannot wear my costume because it is gold. No gold in English *Aida*. Ah! Everything blackened silver. We have recession in Egypt! Eh!'

'So what did you do?' asked Carla.

'I say nothing. I try on this dreadful costume. Well, maybe in Wagner, is OK. In Wagner, everything is ugly. I come back to the hotel. What else was there to do, *amici miei*?' Ruggiero clasped his hands firmly together, as though announcing an unpopular Papal bull. 'If I am ill, I say to myself, no one will bother me. No conductor, no designer, no producer. And it makes a little publicity.'

He scratched his nose and gave his audience the famous smile, which passed through defiance to geniality as the corners of his mouth moved slowly upwards. 'Tonight I will make a miracle recovery and meet the Queen of England.'

When he had picked the stalks clean from a bunch of grapes, Ruggiero surveyed Livia and the children, Emily, Carla and Maurizio. 'Now, my friends, I must rest.'

Livia disappeared into an adjoining room, and returned with two expressionless, square-jawed minders, their profession betrayed by their thick necks and powerful shoulders. They walked straight over to Ruggiero, took first one, then the other, dripping foot from the milk-filled pot, and rubbed them dry with a towel. Holding him under his armpits, they expertly raised him from the armchair, like trained extras removing a corpse, until the massive bulk of his body straightened to the upright position. Leaning with the weight of his arms on their shoulders, Ruggiero made a small step by step exit towards his bedroom.

*   *   *

Carla, Emily and Maurizio stood in the marble foyer of the Halcyon Hotel, waiting to collect the entry cards to their rooms. This hotel had been chosen by Emily because the staff wore Armani uniforms, the food was California light, the design was Milanese international, and the façade was so very cosy and English. They were talking sotto voce. You never knew when journalists were lurking.

'Poor Ruggiero.' Carla giggled. 'He's becoming like a *bomba di mascarpone.*'

'As long as he has regular angiograms. I'm sure he does. But think of the voice, the power of a church organ. How can we criticize him? He has merely sacrificed his body to his voice. What charisma. What spirit. What a man. He's too big for this country.'

'Then I'd be just about the right size.'

Emily decided not to show her disapproval on this occasion. They were, after all, on holiday, but she knew what Carla was thinking, as she always did. It was good for her to hear a singer like Ruggiero. It would give her an understanding of the qualities needed to dominate a huge stage: the humility, the dedication, the slogging physicality of it all.

Maurizio was outside his forbidding sapele door, fumbling with his piece of plastic, and telling himself that fear of technology was a sign of declining years.

'Singers are mysterious,' he remarked to Carla, as he retrieved his glasses from a pocket. 'From such coarseness emerges such beauty.'

'It's like seeing an elephant balance on one leg, wondering if it might fall over.'

'A circus? Perhaps that's all it is. I'm too old for circuses. If I fall asleep . . .'

'Hardly likely.'

He managed to open the door, and Carla disappeared into the adjoining, but not interconnecting, room. As he prepared for his elaborate toilette with an array of badger brushes, lotions and unguents, he wondered when they

160

might be alone together. She had promised she might visit him, but naturally her parents would not expect them to share a room. Nowadays, everyone kept to the old proprieties not because of an outmoded morality, but for the sake of tradition.

Carla telephoned from her room. She was coming. He examined himself in the mirror. The severity of evening dress made him look younger, masked his sagging neck. He felt at home with constriction.

Every time she changed, he saw a new Carla, each one different, more beautiful than the last. He wanted to contemplate at his leisure this blinding perfection, hair partly piled up and secured with a Venetian glass clip he had given her, stray locks tumbling round her face, parted expectant lips. This evening she had painted them dark magenta. Her face was paler, white like a swan through morning mist. He looked down at the shadowy form of her long legs through the sheer fabric of her dress. Did he imagine it or could he see the leaf-like shape between them?

'Anything wrong, darling?'

'No, no. I'll even sit through *Aida* as long as I can gaze at my beloved.'

A few weeks before the opening of the Opera Palace, Stasi arrived back in England. Muswell Hill had entered the August dead season. The windows of Gloria's Salt-Beef Bar were masked by tightly closed pink Venetian blinds, and a gaudily painted parrot was suspended on the door with a message in its beak: 'Even I need a holiday. The proprietor is on vacation for two weeks.' Regular patrons, however, knew that this year Gloria Wagner would be taking her vacation at Rosedene Avenue. Her daughter, Anastasia, was coming home.

At the end of *Carmen*, Stasi had sadly declined Assunta's invitation to visit her olive grove. *La famiglia.* She'd been away so long. *Carmen* had ended with tears and kisses. How fragile it was, the brief illusion they had

161

created together, nearly a hundred of them. If they had been stranded on an uninhabited island, they could have built and designed a village, harnessed the wind, created symphonies, sung, danced, trapped animals, cooked, and left a legacy worthy of humankind. Yet they had all dispersed, Assunta to her olive grove, Guido to Rimini with his boyfriend, Rico back to his wife.

She had expected scores of offers after her success, but there were none she would consider except Passattella's offer to play Liù. Had he forgotten about her? She had received neither a letter nor a phone call from Dominic Morrison. Just as she was leaving for England, she took a slug from her emergency bottle of brandy, took out his card and dialled his number in Paris, her heart pounding.

'Morrison. Who's there?' He sounded gruff.

'Anastasia.'

'Who?'

'Anastasia Wagner. You said I should call.'

'Oh, sure. I just got up. Listen, I'll make myself a coffee. Call you back. Give me the number.'

'I'm supposed to catch the train today. To England.'

There was a pause. Her hands were clenched round the receiver like a vice.

'Is that where you want to be?'

'My seat's booked.'

'You sound like you're sailing on a convict ship. Tickets can be changed. Come to Paris.'

'Now?'

'Why not? I'm preparing *Traviata*. We could see how we get on. You want to sing something for me?'

'Yes, yes. I'd love to, Mr Morrison.'

Stasi took the train from Florence to Milan, then another from Milan to Paris. To change plans at the last minute was something she had never done, for the Wagner family made plans in five year diaries, even for a holiday in Bognor Regis. If she had told him what it meant, he would have laughed. One day she would tell him, how he made her feel that the conditioning of years could be thrown off in an instant. Such was her elation, she did not consider whether he had cast *Traviata*, why he had not implored her to take the leading role. He wanted to see her, it was enough. *Strana ragazza*.

Stasi hurried up the Metro steps, clutching her suitcase, and ran down the Boulevard St Germain, past the milling students and the street vendors, barely registering that the sun had pierced through the clouds, was brightening the puddles and creating an aromatic steam from the damp leaves and the mingled smells of coffee and Gitanes drifting from the open cafés. He was staying there, above a bookshop. Was it the right one? She looked up at the tall windows, and pressed the bell.

He must have been away on some sun-soaked beach, his skin washed with a sea-breeze tan, his brown hair blond-streaked by summer, white jeans, an open-necked vivid blue shirt heightening the colour of his grey-blue eyes. Stasi struggled to distance herself from his overpowering physical presence. She felt awkward, as though he could read her thoughts. Their meeting, which she had rehearsed so many times, should have taken place in some grand foyer, she in evening dress, he running towards her to take her in his arms. And here she was, holding a suitcase, longing for a bath, fatigued with the constant rhythm of the train, wondering if she had the energy to give him the sound he was expecting.

'This isn't my apartment. I expect you can tell. It belongs to a rich American lady who thought she could make a New York loft out of a French boulevard apartment.'

Stasi was mesmerized by the space, the tall ceiling, the white grand piano, the forest of plants, the stark black furniture and bare wooden floor. Books and videos were piled into shelves, spilling over round the desk half hidden by a bright red screen. An ironing board was propped against a wall.

'Take a seat, Anastasia.'

She went over to a leather-slung chair and sat down, placing both hands over her crumpled dress. 'Where do I start?'

'Something funny. What made you laugh as a kid?'

'I thought this was meant to be an audition.'

'OK. How would you take an audition? What should I make you do?'

He made her smile. She did not mind that he was mocking her, just a little. She looked towards the white grand piano. 'Shouldn't I sing something from *Traviata*? You might not like the way I do Verdi.'

He got up and paced round the room, then suddenly stopped to face her. 'Tell you what. Think a minute. You're a big name prima donna, Miss Wagner. Why should you sing? Everyone knows what a fantastic voice you have. You know the part. Your chauffeur is waiting outside. In half an hour you have a recording session with EMI. You're difficult, temperamental, most people are frightened of you. You've sung *Traviata* all over the world. As a special favour, you'll sing for this American jerk who knows nothing from nothing. Take as long as you like. First, you'll keep me waiting. Then you're going to scare me like hell. The singing doesn't matter. I want to see this lady. Have a warm-up, and call me when you're ready. I'll be in the kitchen.'

She was right. Passattella was wrong. His type, of which there was no type, would never stoop to the casting couch. Stasi knew he would ask nothing ordinary from her. For some reason, which she found strange afterwards, with Dominic she had no fear.

'You can come in now,' she called.

He sat down in her leather chair, leaning back with total concentration, one leg dangling over the side. Stasi swept over to the white piano, opened it and placed the music on the stand. She scanned the opening bars, her hands placed one on top of the other in her lap. The piano notes were cool under her fingers as she began the introduction to the aria he would expect. 'Ah fors'è lui.' Violetta's first intimation of love. She would try not to look at him, by staring rigidly at the pages she knew by heart.

As the last chord trailed away, she removed her hands, closed the piano lid with a flourish and walked over to the tall shuttered windows, without giving Dominic another glance. Then there was silence.

He was smiling, coming over to her, right up close. 'I knew it. Thank God. What a relief.'

'What? What were you meant to know?'

'I can make you into an actress, Anastasia. Inside that tight little bud there's a great flower waiting to burst out.'

'And my singing? Was it all right?'

'Your voice is just as I remembered it. I've heard nothing like your quality. Do you need to ask me, Anastasia?'

'Yes. You might have been disappointed. And been too polite to say anything. I couldn't have stood that.'

'You think I'd have asked you to come all the way from Florence to say "thank you very much"?'

'Have you cast Violetta yet? I mean, are there others you're considering? That is, if you were thinking of me for that role. I know I haven't had a lot of experience yet, but I don't think I could sing a support role. I suppose that must sound dreadfully arrogant.'

'Of course it does. I can't offer you a huge fee, but, if you're free in October, we'll start to create Violetta Valéry together.'

She looked at him with shining eyes, and glanced quickly away. 'I've started learning the part. Dominic? Would you mind calling me Stasi?'

'Anastasia is beautiful.'

'Mum calls me that when she's cross.'

'I'll call you Anastasia when you've done something right. Agreed?'

He pronounced it Ana-stay-ja. She only wanted to hear her name on his lips. She knew so little about him, except that she had experienced a brief, blinding understanding which she had never felt before. She wanted to hear his story, his past, but Dominic was reluctant to give her more than meagre details. Everyone wants to interpret the artist in terms of personal history, he told her.

'You want to be a mystery?'

'No. But I don't want you to create me like a role. We find out from what we see.'

'Then I'll invent. And you won't like that.'

'What shall I tell you? I'm thirty-two. My father emigrated from Poland and ended up as a film editor for NBC. My mother walked out on him. She's living in Los Angeles, teaching dance therapy.'

'Why did she leave?'

'He preferred vodka to marriage. Still does. But he gave me everything. Sent me to Yale, then Oxford. After that I started working in the theatre, met this actress, lived with her for a few years.'

'And then?'

'I was crazy about her. There's something about you which reminds me of that time.'

'Is that good or bad?'

'Terrible! Don't you hate being compared to someone else?'

'Not by you.'

When they parted, he kissed her on the cheek. She felt he would be part of her future; they would form a great partnership like Joan Sutherland and Richard Bonynge, Maria Callas and Tullio Serafin. She had completely forgotten the vow she had made when Gloria left the convent for England. She would entrust her career, her love, her life, to this extraordinary man and she would sing for him as she would sing for nobody else.

Everyone in Rosedene Avenue knew that Gloria's girl had come back home. Now Stasi had to face the onslaught of friends and relatives. Did she know? Larry Cohen had got engaged to Dora Levy's girl. One shoe shop had closed, another opened. Mrs Kurtz, who lived next door to Sarah

Weintraub, her husband had run off with the au pair girl. Someone had smashed the windows at number ninety-two and taken the silver candlesticks. There was a coloured doctor in Dr Cohen's practice. No one wanted to be a doctor, not like the old days.

'It's changed, this area. Terrible,' they all said. To Stasi, nothing seemed to have changed, except the colour of Gloria's hair which was a cross between purple and russet. Raymond was still living at home. Aunt Lizzie was still knitting. Uncle Monty was still puffing at the same pipe.

'Will you be appearing at that new place?' asked Lizzie.

'Of course she will,' replied Gloria. 'When she's finished in Paris.'

'I might,' said Stasi.

'Did you get the pictures I sent you?'

'Yes, Mum.'

'We're all waiting, darling. For when your name's up there. No good being famous abroad.'

'No one knew who Dusty Springfield was when she went to America,' added Lizzie. 'Lovely singer. Such a waste.'

'Since when did Dusty Springfield sing classical?' retorted Gloria. 'Anyway, Raymond's got a ticket. His surprise. He's going to take his sister to *Aida*. Don't tell him I said.'

Stasi was sitting at her old jangly piano, thinking only of Violetta, in love with Verdi, in love with Dominic, in love with Paris, when Carla Livorno telephoned. Just looking up old friends in London; she never expected she'd be there.

'How about Julian Lieberman landing up at the Opera Palace? Isn't it just too marvellous? You didn't know?'

'Why should I?'

'Sure. I've been watching rehearsals of *Aida*. Mind-blowing. You coming to the première?'

'I'll be going later.'

'Stasi, you must. I'll see if I can get you in on Ruggiero's guest list.'

'I can't. It's Friday night. I've got to be home.'

'You kidding? What's Friday night?'

'The sabbath.'

'Jesus. You some kind of a religious nut?'

'I'm staying at home. Mum would go out of her mind if I went out.'

'Never mind, Stasi. I've decided to stay in London for a while. There's so much happening. See you soon. You got something lined up?'

'I'll be singing *Traviata* in Paris.'

'Fantastic. Just your kind of role. Who's producing?'

'Dominic Morrison.'

'Oh, well. I guess you know what you're doing.'

'Have you met him?'

'Forget it. I'm sure it'll be great. Anyway, he's supposed to be *una meraviglia* in the sack. Keep in touch.'

'And you? Anything happening?'

'Couple of interesting offers. I'll let you know, Stasi. You got somewhere to stay in Paris?'

'I'll be with a French actress called Nathalie Laroche. Friend of a schoolfriend.'

'As long as you don't shack up with Morrison.'

They were all waiting for the Queen. Gloria took the opportunity to make more tea, Uncle Monty went to the toilet again, Aunt Lizzie took off her shoes, Raymond drained his tankard of beer. For this special occasion, Gloria had removed the plastic covering on the four piece suite, bringing to light the unaccustomed brilliance of deep crimson moquette. It was after all Friday night, sacred to the family even if nowadays nothing else was sacred, and tonight she'd bend the rules so everyone could watch TV. The Friday night candles, like the Wagners, appeared to be engaged in animated conversation, flickering unpredictably this way and that.

Gloria plugged in the kettle and called upstairs. 'Stasi? Where are you? The Queen's coming any minute.'

'Drying my hair,' she shouted.

'You washed it two days ago. Takes all the oils out.'

Friday evening guilt was pervading the lounge.

'We should have gone, Monty.' Aunt Lizzie twisted her cable needle, and shook out the sweater she was making for Stasi, but which would be worn by Raymond.

'You know something? If we'd bought seats, it would have cost the same as all of us going to Italy for a month. Best we didn't.'

'Who's singing? Anyone I know?'

'We've told you a hundred times. Ruggiero Gasparini.'

'So you did. The fat one who's ill.'

Stasi came into the sitting room bearing a tea-tray covered with a doily, followed by Gloria carrying an army catering teapot in both hands. As the National Anthem sounded, Raymond adjusted the television set for no apparent reason, and was bombarded with indignation.

'Shut up everyone!' screamed Stasi. 'And stay shut up.' Then, in a normal tone. 'Please. Just this once. I'm trying to watch.'

'Think you'll learn something?'

'Raymond,' Gloria said severely, having no ear for sibling banter, 'don't be rude to your sister.'

They were bowing before the Queen, Sir Miles Mackenzie and Julian Lieberman. The camera panned over the exterior of the floodlit building, then tracked down the vinyl flooring of the artists' dressing rooms, and paused outside a door with a gold sign: Mr Ruggiero Gasparini. The conductor was walking up to the rostrum. Behind him, at the back of the arena, were two rosy-cheeked, flowing-haired nymphs supporting a banner: Ars Populis – Art for the People.

'Tell me when it starts. Must finish this row.'

'You'll hear it, Lizzie.'

Someone turned round to show her profile, a young girl, as though instinctively sensing the presence of the distant camera. She was fluttering a black lace fan. Carla Livorno with Emily and Maurizio.

Stasi bit savagely into a marshmallow and hurled it back

onto the plate. What was she doing? Hadn't Dominic told her, throw yourself into experience? Hadn't she promised herself that she would fulfil her duty and leave? What had made her stay? Sudden rage possessed her, rage at herself for sitting sullenly in front of a screen, rage that she had allowed herself to be sucked into family inertia, and rage that she had accepted the limitations they had all set themselves. The performances failed to touch her. Ruggiero Gasparini was merely going through the motions, the orchestra was too loud. All they said was wonderful, wonderful, one day you'll be singing there at a Royal Performance and we'll be dressed up in the front row, start saving up now Monty . . .

Raymond opened another can of beer, and ignored Gloria's plosive tut.

'What d'you think, Stasi?'

'Hate it. I wouldn't have anything to do with a production like that.'

How Dominic would have despised this desecration of Verdi. She would deny, if he asked, that she had seen it.

'What's up?'

Aunt Lizzie had given up watching, and had returned to her knitting. Gloria and Monty, their heads dropped on their chests, were snoozing. Raymond clapped his hands, but they failed to respond.

'Come on, Stasi. Let's give Act Four a miss and get out.'

In the Horse and Groom, Stasi made a decision. Raymond listened without interrupting.

'We've got to go our own ways, stop hanging on to the family. Get your own place, even if it's a bloody room in Hackney. You're twenty-six, Ray.'

'I get by.' Raymond tore open a packet of shrimp-flavour crisps, banned from Rosedene Avenue.

'Why are you still living at home?'

He gestured 'same again' to the barman. 'No one's offered me a two-bedroom flat where I can practise at whatever time I please, for peanuts. No one's offered me a solo recital at the Wigmore Hall. And I haven't met a girl who thinks I'm the next Yehudi Menuhin.'

'You'll end up pushing Mum in a wheelchair. Honestly, Ray, don't be such a dumb duck. Where's your pride? Where's your ambition?'

He patted her on the arm and grinned. 'I missed out on the assertiveness training course. They only take girls.'

'Ray, I've got to get out of England.'

'When?'

'Tomorrow.'

'What? You're not serious? I thought you were going next month. When did you decide? Does Mum know?'

'I'm going to pack just one case. My friend Susan has found me a place to stay. Haven't you ever wanted to go down to the station, get a train and take off, just like that? Arrive somewhere, nothing planned? Without telling anybody?'

'She'll have a heart attack.'

'Mum's immune. You know that. Anyway, I'm going. Early. Every time she goes into one room, I go into another. I can't stand her voice, I can't stand the smell of salt-beef, I can't stand her never keeping quiet for longer than a minute, I can't stand her on the telephone yakking away for hours.'

'Steady on. She's had a tough life.'

'I hate her. I'm going away until I can stop hating her.'

Raymond put his hand on his forehead. Stasi was being dramatic again, the way she was as a kid when she tripped on the carpet or broke a toy. What would he have to mend this time?

They'd all woken up by the time they returned home. Dinner had been digested long ago; now it was time for a snack. The salf-beef sandwiches were out, special Italian mustard, pickled cucumber, cold chicken.

'Where have you two been? To the pub? What's so wonderful about the pub? And I'd got in all that beer specially. Can't stay at home for more than five minutes, you two. Missed the best part. At the end we cried. Even

Uncle Monty. Have some. What do you mean, you're not hungry? Bad for you to go to bed on an empty stomach. What time you getting up tomorrow, Raymond? I want to clean your room properly before I go to work.'

Stasi set the alarm clock for six, packed a case, checked her passport at least ten times and began to worry about the journey. Like her mother, she was not a born traveller and was always imagining that the unplanned and unexpected would end in disaster. She might look like a wanted terrorist. They might have invented new laws to exclude singers from the country. She might get on the wrong train and land up in Spain instead of France. As she tore open the envelope marked by Gloria 'Only For Emergencies' Stasi was overwhelmed by guilt. Two hundred pounds, untouched for five years. How could she do it? Euphoria took over. Her fate, she was sure, would be determined from the moment she landed on Dominic Morrison's doorstep. If Gloria screamed and shouted later, she could pay her back.

As she sat trying to ignore the smell of spilt beer and reheated hamburgers in the littered bar of the cross-Channel ferry, watching a grey lifeless sea with barely a white-flecked wave, Stasi studied a map of Paris. It would be like *La Bohème*. Nathalie Laroche, a successful Parisian actress who, she'd been told by her friend Susan, could sing, dance, write poetry and speak four languages, designed her own clothes and had a string of fascinating lovers, would surely live nowhere but Montmartre.

Chapter Seven

Stasi left the Gare du Nord and hurried to find a taxi. She checked the address again. Boulevard Pereire. 'Is it near Montmartre?' she asked.

The taxi driver shook his hand and laughed. 'Near the périphérique. Not too far.'

They came to a halt some way down the long, anonymous street which stretched in an unwavering straight line into the distance. The Boulevard Pereire bore a closer resemblance to the Edgware Road than the rickety, balconied narrow backstreet she had expected.

'*Voilà*,' said the taxi driver, pointing to what appeared to be a shop across the road. It took several minutes for her to find a gap between the hurtling cars and lorries to cross to the other side. Small dusty shops, a garish supermarket, insurance offices, a pharmacy, blank windows with 'Soldes' flashed across in luminous lime green, formed the underbelly of forbidding blocks of grimy-windowed flats. There was a note on the door for Mlle Wagner: 'Ask for Marie in shoe shop downstairs.'

Stasi was handed a clutch of heavy keys, which released several locks on an iron-grilled front door, and she pushed her case over the threshold. Immediately she entered the bare hall with its peeling, yellowed walls, she decided she would only stay a day or two before moving in search of the real Paris, the Paris of *La Bohème* and Violetta Valéry. Staggering up five flights of narrow marble stairs, she arrived at another door which, in spite of being unlocked, resisted her attempts at entry and only swung open after she had heaved her shoulder against it.

When she first laid eyes on the strange assortment of

objects, she wondered if she had made a mistake. Was this the home of a famous actress? Why would she live in a junkshop? Garish pictures jostled for space on the walls, plants and flowers with voracious leaves overflowed from strange-shaped pots with missing handles. Hanging over her head was a huge brass chandelier gap-toothed with missing crystals. There were threadbare chairs of every style draped with Eastern fabrics, a worn velvet settee sagging in the centre, leather-bound books with ragged spines standing piled up in the empty marble fireplace. Every conceivable space was occupied, crammed with chipped sculpted heads, torsos, Balinese puppets with arms and legs missing, china dolls and lacquered boxes.

Stasi fingered a faded lace dress with the remnants of seed pearls spattered across the yellow-stained front, hanging unevenly from a dressmaker's dummy. On a scored, ink-stained table, there were half empty wine bottles, raddled candles keeling over in wrought iron holders, a few leaves of paper covered with hasty sketches.

After a moment's reflection, Stasi changed her mind. Nathalie Laroche must be the most incredibly creative person she had ever met. She was going to be staying with a genius. The door burst open.

'Anastasia! Good, you've come. How lucky to be so tall! Ouf! I'm sweating like a pig. The relief of Mafeking is here.'

Nathalie threw several heavy bags onto the table. In spite of the warm September day, she was dressed in a velvet waistcoat, a thick coarse striped shirt massed voluminously round her wrists, a flowered bow-tie at her neck, tight-belted gaberdine jodhpurs and bright red boots. Her hair was pulled back severely in a glossy black pony tail, and a solitary earring formed of cascades of silver bells hung down her cheek.

'Eleven o'clock last night, my friends decided to eat. Nothing left. Ouf! I'm hung over.' Nathalie loosened her bow-tie, unbuttoned her sleeves, and rolled them up her forearm.

'I'd never guess.' Stasi was unable to take her eyes away from the wide scarlet mouth, the thin sweep of the arched eyebrows. Nathalie reminded her of a fuchsia, with her constantly moving head and long thin arms, protruding from her slight, slim-waisted body like delicate stamens.

'I'll make a spritzer. You found the kitchen? Chaos. I live in chaos. But that's honest. My life is chaos, my room is chaos. I am who I am. A moment.'

She came back with two chipped crystal glasses filled to the brim. It was difficult to tell her age. She had the assurance of a mature woman, say about thirty-five, but she didn't look as old as that.

'Do you want ice? I forgot ice. I remember now, there isn't any. My fridge is always too hot. Every time my lover comes, he offers to buy me a new one. He can't understand why that makes me so cross. Do you have a lover in England? Of course you do. I always ask important questions at the beginning. Then, never again. Afterwards, we can discuss music, philosophy, cinema, anything you like. Here. Let me show you a poem. I wrote it last night when I was alone.'

She put her hand inside her shirt, and plucked a crumpled wine-stained scrap of paper from her vest. Stasi took it gingerly, asked the meaning of a few words, and read it through. Nathalie knelt on the floor and addressed the armchair with tragic intensity.

> 'You left my bed, you left again
> To catch the early morning train.
> Your socks were clean, your pants were pressed,
> My spirit, soiled. You never guessed.

Do you like it? It's just a first draft, of course. I'm very influenced by Sylvia Plath. Can you tell?'

Stasi was lost in admiration. Of course she knew of Sylvia Plath; there was a volume of her poetry, inscribed 'Gloria Wagner. Her Book' on the glass bookshelf in the lounge, but she could not admit she had refused to read it.

It did not seem to matter. 'It's very good, Nathalie.'

'Women, we are like that, aren't we? Everything secret.'

She refused to say much about the theatre where she was working, or the footling part she had taken at the insistence of her agent. How had she ended up with such a disastrous lover?

'Disastrous? But no! He's just ordinary. Monsieur Filofax. Do you like my flat? Isn't it exquisite? The proportion, I love it, I want to die here. Three bedrooms. Three bedrooms in Paris. Do you know what you would pay for this in the sixteenth *arrondissement*?'

Stasi shook her head.

'Many millions of francs. Most actresses share one room, and I have this, my Versailles, my retreat, my secret friend. Virginia Woolf, your great Virginia, she wanted only one room, good God, I have four. I am so lucky, lucky, lucky.' She loosened her pony tail with a single, deft movement, and a swathe of thick black hair fell round her face. Then she pulled off one boot after the other. 'Do you like it, my place?'

'Who couldn't? You know I do.'

'Well, it's not mine. He pays. He, Bernard, the man in the poem. He still asks me to marry him. Imagine. Nathalie Laroche married to the area manager of the Amoco oil company!' She laughed, not unkindly but as though the idea amused her. 'He's not bad. He's kind, but I tell him lies. And of course, I have different lovers. But one mustn't lie on paper. Never, never, never. And never to friends. I call it my bargain flat. Because I've made a bargain. And for this he has three nights a week when I'm not working. A meal if I feel like making it. A bottle of whisky if I've remembered. And the best cunt in Paris. It's been like this ever since I was sixteen and left home. Heavens. It's four o'clock. Help yourself to anything you like. I'm working tonight. If Bernard calls, say I'm asleep.'

Suddenly, Stasi felt famished. She sniffed the laden bags full of pâtés and encrusted cheeses and fresh-baked, uneven bread, drinking in the strong aromas of France, the pungent smells of garlic and yeast, the sun-ripened perfume of swollen tomatoes, strangely scented unrecognizable herbs with feathery leaves. After she had eaten, she tiptoed down the corridor, and found a small dark room where a single bed had been made up, covered in a tattered crocheted rug. She would sleep there, next to a tiny desk, surrounded by watercolours of the desert, dried flowers and velvet cushions.

Stasi was getting herself some breakfast the following morning when Nathalie appeared at the front door, wearing a black tracksuit and carrying a large bag. Her face was pale, unmade-up, and there were circles under her eyes.

She gave no explanation for her presence, or her absence. 'I've got to sleep now. You OK? Happy?'

Stasi smiled.

'Good. See you for lunch. I'll take you out. Did Bernard call?'

'No. A few other people did. I've written down the messages.'

La Coupole was how Stasi imagined the lounge of a 1930s ocean liner, a great space crammed with rowdy, carefree hordes who were making a festival of lunch, arguing, laughing, shouting across tables, pouring out flagons of wine, the aloof young waiters carrying out their tasks with the precision of cats walking along a fence. It was hard to imagine that they had come from work, or would return. Nathalie waltzed in, wearing her signature style, jodhpurs, boots, bow-tie, striped shirt and waistcoat, but with a man's hat tipped over her face.

'I can't see a table,' said Stasi, observing the crowd. She picked out several girls dressed as she was, in a plain, fitting black dress. The city of black dresses. Nathalie had caught the distant eye of a hurrying waiter, the slight nod. She clasped Stasi's hand and took a serpentine route to a banquette, with just space enough for two.

'What do you sing?' Nathalie picked up a few *pommes frites* from a tangled pile on her plate, taking them one by one between her expressive fingers, which seemed to move as though touching random keys. Then she rested her chin in her hands. 'Tell me everything. Where you live. What you like. Who you are.'

Afterwards, Stasi realized she had never talked for so long about herself in her life. The words came haltingly at first, then more fluently. Occasionally Nathalie interrupted. Mostly she nodded, as though acknowledging a mirror of her own experience. Every girl wanted to leave home. It was natural. Finally, she said, 'So? What do you want in Paris, Stasi?'

She seemed to be expecting some great philosophical plan of existence. Stasi laughed. 'I want to be with Dominic and sing.'

'Sing first. If I like your Dominic, he can stay. If I don't, it will be bad for all of us.'

'He's not expecting me for a few weeks. But I do need to find some work. I've no money left.'

'Of course. That is usual.'

'Could I be a secretary in Paris? I can type.'

'Type? Oh, no. Impossible.'

'And I can't practise my part unless I have a piano.'

'That's simple. I have friends who are musicians. Now let's have a pudding. You like Mont Blanc? I adore it. Do you know anything about Isabelle Eberhardt? No? A poet, an explorer, a fantasist, my heroine. I'll show you the script of my film. Everyone tries to make her story, they never succeed. I will be the first. It should be an opera. Fantastic woman.'

For three days, Stasi hardly saw Nathalie. There were meetings about her film, an audition for a Girardoux play, a day out with Bernard. One needed to empty the mind from time to time. Stasi asked more than once what part she was playing and if she could come to the theatre to see her performance, but Nathalie dismissed the idea. 'It's nothing. A piece of commercialism. I go, I do it, I come home.'

Stasi accepted the strange hours she kept. One after-noon, she opened the door to a man in a dark suit carrying a slim attaché case, with a newspaper tucked under his arm. He introduced himself briefly as Bernard, and then went straight to Nathalie's room. The panting moans and mounting staccato cries echoed down the corridor as Stasi left to take a typing test at the Agence de la Femme Moderne.

It was a beginning, a job. When she had completed the typing test, the woman in the agency, who had at first thrown lavish compliments at this well-presented English girl in a sober black dress, merely took the paper out of the machine and tore it up.

'You can come back when you've learned about lay-out,' she said tartly.

'Isn't there anything else, madame?' Stasi asked, confronted by this miniature dragon with a flame-coloured mouth who was examining her through half moon glasses.

'Your voice isn't bad,' she conceded. 'And you have a neat appearance. There might be something going in reception work. Have you done it before?'

'Certainly.'

It sounded as undemanding as standing in a bus queue, whatever 'reception work' might be. She could hear the dragon phoning somebody, in the inner office.

'Just the person for you. I've just completed an exten-sive interview. She's English but speaks French. Very good family. Intelligent, discreet, well-groomed, and she can also type. And another thing, she's passionately interested in flower arranging. Altogether an asset to your company, monsieur.'

'I've never done flower arranging. Professionally, that is.'

'Never mind. You'll learn, Mademoiselle Wagner. They'll take you on a week's probation.'

'What do I get paid?'

179

The figure mentioned was meaningless. Stasi had no idea whether it was an hourly, daily, or weekly rate and she forgot to ask.

Nathalie was unimpressed. Reception work? Where? When she heard that Stasi's first job was to receive clients at a funeral parlour, she fell into a chair with a fit of giggles. Stasi was miffed. 'It's money. Now all I need is a piano.'

The hilarity stopped abruptly. 'How much are you getting?'

When Stasi told her, she let out a hoot. 'My God. Less than the statutory minimum wage. Disgusting. Exploitation. What is this agency? What are they doing? How dare they? Who are these imbeciles? Poor Anastasia. We must denounce them immediately. Come, let's go now. Where is it?'

Nathalie's impetus was cut short by the croaking bell of the decrepit telephone. It was always difficult to pursue a conversation for more than a few minutes without interruption. After talking for almost an hour in top gear, she put down the phone with an exasperated sigh. Almost immediately, it rang again. A couple of minutes later, she had abandoned the call to the barricades to fight injustice in the workplace and was running round the flat, picking off a belt hanging on the wall here, a scarf draped round a picture there, rummaging through drawers, until she had amassed enough accessories to 'make an impression'.

'Sta-si!' she called out from the corridor. 'I think I have the solution to your life. My God, I'm late. But tonight, you can come with me. See you later.'

At nine o'clock that evening, a dark-windowed limousine was waiting outside Marie's shoe shop in the Boulevard Pereire, parked halfway up on the pavement. Nathalie was not in the mood to answer questions. She was so preoccupied that Stasi assumed she was getting into her part.

'Can you see?' she asked anxiously, once they had settled in the back seat of the car.

'What?'

Nathalie thrust her face forward. 'My spot. Shit. They always come out at night. Like lousy lovers.'

'There's nothing there. Are you nervous? I'm always nervous before a performance. Where are we going?'

'*Haut bourg*. You've heard of Neuilly?'

Stasi shook her head and looked out of the window, searching for the dotted lights and spotlit posters which would advertise the theatre district. All she could see were tall light-coloured buildings, with grandiose façades rather like those in Park Lane except they were set in landscaped gardens.

'Does the theatre in Paris always start this late?'

'Sometimes you are so serious, Stasi. So English.' Nathalie felt the contours of her cheeks and rubbed the imaginary spot with her finger. 'As a matter of fact, I work in a club. Very chic. Very exclusive. So that I can earn money to start shooting my film. The owner is very sympathetic. She's very impressed with having someone of such high quality. Naturally. I would rather be playing Hedda Gabler. Don't you think I'd be fantastic as Hedda?' She pushed her pony tail up, stretched her neck and rested both hands on her head. 'I'll introduce you to my *patronne*. Just smile and say yes. If she likes you, she might find you something.'

In Paris, there were clubs where the paparazzi congregated – Regine's, Castel's – and a very select few, where membership was invited by word of mouth, whose entrances were so discreet and unadvertised that they were known only by name even by society reporters. The intimidating entrance foyer of La Maison Blanche, disguised by a tangle of shrubbery in a residential street off the rue de Longchamps, was designed to guard the publicity shy inhabitants of the palatial apartments high above as well as the members of the club below. Snarling, crouched Chinese lions raised a rampant paw in front of black screens awash with faded water-lilies, and there was someone half hidden by iron trellis-work mounted on a slab of marble.

Two girls came in, wearing long raincoats and dark glasses. Their movements were followed by an aloof guard, his black tunic embroidered over the pockets with a purple crocus, the emblem of the club. He glanced down at a bank of monitors which relayed the sweeping gaze of the tiny cameras positioned amongst the trailing greenery. There was no need to move, he recognized one of Saffron's girls.

Nathalie signed Stasi's name in a black leather book, and pulled out an identity card. 'The people who live here could buy up the whole of Paris,' she said, as Stasi followed her behind a screen and down some steps to the basement. 'There's a back entrance to the club through the underground car park. For gold key members. What should I call you? We all have different names here.'

'How about Violetta Valéry?' said Stasi.

Nathalie unlocked a small wooden box by the side of two heavy multi-panelled doors to reveal a bank of numbers, and pressed out a code. The doors silently swung open, and Stasi felt the rush of circulating, floral-perfumed air, and blinked. In front of her was an overblown replica of the English country house – chintz-covered sofas and heavy armchairs, oil paintings of sporting scenes, tall gilded standard lamps with heavy silk shades, smaller lamps placed in the centres of low, polished wood tables. Opposite the entrance was what appeared to be a pocket-sized bandstand with carpeted steps. To one side, surrounded by tall candelabra, was a white grand piano. The room appeared to be empty, the only illumination coming from an overhead chandelier.

'Justine? Is that you?' called a voice, in impeccable English county tones.

'Yes. I've brought my friend. She's called Violetta Valéry.' Nathalie winked at Stasi. 'Good luck. Must go and change.'

Nathalie tossed her black bag over her shoulder and was gone. Stasi noticed a lofty inlaid vase overflowing with ferns, branches, lupins and delphiniums standing on the gleaming tail of the closed grand piano. The quivering flowers were being manipulated by an invisible hand. As she approached the source of the voice, a young woman appeared from behind the vase and walked towards her. There was no mistaking the owner of La Maison Blanche. She moved as though there was a vast army of servants at her back, in a ruched, plain dark red dress which betrayed its English origins, a Harrods strapless ballgown which was cut in a straight unflattering line across her breasts and fell in inadequate folds to the ground. She could have been the young headmistress of a girls' boarding school in Sussex or Hampshire, the kind who has secret affairs with the divorced fathers of her richer pupils. Her face looked younger than Stasi had expected, the blue eyes gazed straight into hers.

'I'm known by my guests and my staff as Saffron. How do you do, Miss Valéry?' She led Stasi to a chaise-longue to one side of the room. 'I understand from Justine that you are interested in seeking a position here. Do I take it you're Italian? Or are you French?'

'Um, Italian. Half Italian.'

'Is your father in banking? The name seems familiar.'

'He worked in newspapers. He died when I was five.'

'I see. Never mind. I'm so sorry.' It was unclear whether her hint of disapproval was directed at his profession, or his untimely death. She invited Stasi to stand up. 'Let me see your legs. Would you mind awfully raising your skirt a few inches? Thank you. Good. Bad legs would have disqualified you straight away. A plain face, insignificant breasts, we can do something with, bad legs, never. Forgive me for being so frank. One wishes to be fair, for both our sakes.'

Sadly, there was no vacancy for a waitress in the dining room, though one might become available. One of her girls would soon be marrying a French tycoon. Did she by any chance have an ear for music? Could she sing? Just a little, Stasi replied. At any moment, she expected to see a file of uniformed, pigtailed girls trooping into the room for inspection.

'Go to the piano and I'll fetch Muriel.'

While she was gone, Stasi opened the keyboard. A custom-built Steinway grand: what a miracle. What a waste.

Muriel was tiny, rouged and about sixty, Stasi guessed. Like Aunt Lizzie, but with hair dyed black instead of blond. She had a sheaf of ragged music under her arm.

'Muriel was a very fine concert pianist,' remarked Saffron. 'We're frightfully lucky to have her.'

'Arthritis. I don't play anything too fast.'

Muriel played a surprisingly agile arpeggio in chords up and down the piano, and then placed a music book on the piano ledge, opened it at a turned down page and began a genteel slow-paced Palm Court rendering of the opening chords of 'I've Got You Under My Skin'.

Stasi looked over her shoulder at the music. Aunt Lizzie at twenty, belting it out at Ronnie Scott's in a silver mini-dress, strawberry ice-cream lips and eye make-up like a giant panda, stuck in Gloria's photo album, still belting it out thirty years later at barmitzvahs and weddings, more Barbara Windsor than Barbra Streisand. Yes, she knew the words. Just think loud and Hollywood, she thought.

'Very good. You kept with me all the way. How about "Don't Cry for me, Argentina"? Could you manage that?'

'I'll have a go.'

'That's the spirit.'

Muriel looked questioningly at Saffron.

'Excellent. You not only sing in tune but you have a wonderfully strong voice. Most refreshing. Has anyone ever suggested you have it trained?'

Stasi smiled. 'I've had a few lessons.'

'We'll try you out tonight. Would that be agreeable?'

'Oh, yes. Of course.'

She looked Stasi up and down. 'A size ten, I imagine. Come with me to the dressing room, Violetta.'

An hour later, Stasi was fingering the snaky sequinned

dress, selected by Saffron, which clung to her buttocks, and parted when she moved to give a tantalizing glimpse of her thighs.

'For the face, I think we should aim for something a little Left Bank.'

She watched Saffron wielding a set of brushes with the aplomb of a professional make-up artist. In a curly red wig, frizzing down to her shoulders, helped by the heavy use of panstick, blusher and different coloured bands sweeping up from her mascaraed eyes, Stasi was confident that even Gloria would fail to recognize her.

Satisfied with her creation, Saffron led Stasi across the great salon, now theatrically lit in pools of light, and escorted her towards a seating area in the centre. 'Heinrich will be joining us tonight. Awfully interesting man, you'll like him. He comes from Frankfurt, but he adores Paris. One of my most regular guests.'

Stasi was greeted by a heavily built man with *cheveux en brosse* and fat, perfectly manicured hands, who immediately requested another bottle of champagne and began to air his opinions on the state of the German economy. He had just read an appalling article in *Le Monde* whose author failed to appreciate the Berlin dilemma. 'You are liking politics?' he said to Stasi.

'I know so little,' she replied nervously. She had not expected to make conversation with her audience.

'Everyone thinks they know all.'

To Stasi's amazement, Saffron appeared to be well-informed on the problems arising from the reunification of Berlin and the vulnerability of the Deutschmark. When she left them alone together, Stasi could think of nothing to say. Heinrich stroked her knee. Stasi assumed that he had drunk too much and was becoming familiar.

'You are most beautiful.'

'Thank you. This is my first time here.'

'You are nervous? Everyone, they are friends.'

Stasi gave an embarrassed smile, and looked across the room, waiting for Saffron to return. The men all seemed old to her, and many were smoking cigars. That was the worst kind of audience, apart from drunks, Aunt Lizzie always said. Like singing under a blanket. Different from a theatre, entirely different. Stasi decided they must be immensely rich, all these men lounging at their ease on the scattered sofas and armchairs, for they all had young girlfriends. It reminded her of a posh disco she had been to once, and she assumed that they would be dancing later.

It was only after her second glass of champagne, when she was becoming used to her surroundings, that she began to observe the girls. They were stunningly beautiful. Large breasted, small breasted, from black skinned to ivory skinned, they all looked similar. Then she realized they were wearing the same skin-tight strapless cocktail dress, in different colours. When their faces were not transfixed with studied smiles, they would relapse into profound, blank boredom. My God, she thought. I've been engaged to sing in a brothel.

Saffron returned to sit beside them, and caught Stasi's startled expression. 'Don't be nervous, Violetta. My guests are all civilized gentlemen. I'm sure they'll applaud your performance. Have you by any chance been to Germany?'

Stasi gulped. She need only play this strange role for an evening, then surely this well-groomed procuress would realize she had made a mistake. 'No. But I've always dreamed of going to Bayreuth.'

Saffron beamed. She prided herself on hiring intelligent, cultivated girls. This one might prove to be a valuable addition.

'Ah!' Heinrich's serious, set features relaxed into a warm smile, contradicted by his chilly, pale grey eyes. For a moment, he was almost attractive. 'Now you mention my passion. Wagner. Allow me to take you. I would be honoured to pleasure such a charming companion.'

Stasi looked confused, and turned to Saffron apprehensively.

'Violetta will have to consult her diary. But thank you for your generous offer.'

'Of course.' Heinrich kissed her fingers, and replaced his hand on her knee.

When he left the table to 'make himself fresh' as he put it, Saffron whispered in Stasi's ear. 'Heinrich comes from an eminent German family. Friends with Princess Michael. In fact, they met at Baden Baden earlier this year.'

'What does he do?'

'Do!' Saffron gave a throaty chuckle. 'You mean, what is his company's position on the Nikkei index? Second only to Bauer and Hoechst. He is pioneering a drug to retard ageing. Can you imagine the impact if he succeeds? You should buy a few shares. I'm sure it could be arranged. He likes you.'

Stasi stared at Saffron's smooth, flawless features and shuddered.

A low rhythm was faintly audible, the bandstand was suddenly bathed in light and the first act was announced. A tall blonde Amazon, with the legs and arms of a body builder, bronzed and oiled, naked except for tiny filigree cages glittering on the tips of her taut breasts and over her pubic hair, slowly mounted the steps at the back, stood for a moment in the spotlight, and then leapt lightly down to the floor.

'I've seen her in Prague,' Heinrich whispered, again sitting at Stasi's side. As though to reassure her, he added, 'This girl is not for me.'

The Amazon paraded amongst the audience, muscles rippling. She placed one bare foot on the sculpted edge of an ottoman, bent over backwards until her head touched the floor and grasped one ankle. Then she curled upwards, flexed her buttocks, jumped back onto the bandstand and raised one leg in the air until it was perpendicular.

'Are you finding this erotic?' murmured Heinrich.

'I'm not sure,' replied Stasi, her eyes riveted on the body, which was now contorting so that the blonde head was protruding, octopus-like, between two long legs.

For the finale, the Amazon balanced on one hand,

slowly spread her legs wide apart until they formed a straight line, and craned her neck forward.

'Now she is like Concorde. You have been on Concorde aeroplane?'

'I don't like flying.'

'Me neither. Not unless I am the pilot. But I do it much.'

There was another act before Stasi. The 'guests' talked throughout, occasionally turning away from their companions to glance politely at the stage. The Amazon was succeeded by another girl in a long riding habit, her face disguised in a half mask, one hand holding a whip, the other grasping the spiked collar of a shiny-coated black hunting dog, a Great Dane of a dog, which reached up to her waist. At a crack of the whip, the huge animal sat on its haunches, ears cocked, mouth open, a long red tongue heaving up and down as it panted. Directing her attention to the dog, the girl dropped her coat and rhythmically unbuttoned her shirt, then a bodice, until she was naked above the waist.

To the accompaniment of the 'Ride of the Valkyrie', the huntress lay on the ground, raised a booted leg in the air, and stroked the leather buckles. The full skirt fell back. The dog rose to its feet, and pushed its nose into her cunt, at which she leaped to her feet and cracked the whip once more. The dog slunk back to its position.

'This is very thirties Berlin,' commented Heinrich, observing Stasi staring into her champagne glass, longing to escape. 'I know how it is done.'

'Oh?' she replied, looking into his detached grey eyes.

'They put on the scent of the rabbit. On the private parts.'

'Ugh.' Her voice felt as though it was clamming up in her throat.

'I prefer it without Wagner, don't you?'

'Definitely.'

She was beginning to consider the idea of, perhaps, having dinner with this man. Nothing more, but his air of benign worldliness seemed unthreatening. When the applause began, muted but prolonged, she looked up. The girl had removed her mask and was lying naked, spreadeagled on the floor, the dog stretched across her as though guarding the kill.

Stasi put her hand over her mouth and then quickly withdrew it.

'Something is wrong?' Heinrich put a warm hand on her arm.

'I know the girl, that's all.'

'She's your friend? She has a good body. But I think yours is better. I am liking English girls. Especially in the bedroom.' He was moving his hand upwards towards her breasts, and Stasi leaped to her feet.

'I'm sorry, Heinrich, but I'm not . . .'

'Please to sit down, Violetta.'

Stasi obeyed, leaving a space between herself and Heinrich, wondering how she could avoid offending him. 'I'm just here to sing. Not for other things,' she said, hoping she sounded severe. 'You must ask one of the other girls. Don't you find them beautiful?'

'One moment, please.' Heinrich poured himself another glass of champagne. 'I'm staying at the Impériale. If I want a woman, they find me one. The reason I'm here is not to spend an evening watching movie channels. I stay in Paris for about two or three weeks. Maybe you would like to come one night to the opera with me? You like French opera? They have *Pelléas et Mélisande* at the Paris Opéra. A very fine production. After, we have dinner, and then, if you want to make love, I will give you pleasure. But only if you want. It is up to you.'

'I hate opera.'

Nathalie had disappeared from the stage, and Muriel was slinking towards the piano, like an old cat towards a favourite chair. My one night stand, Stasi thought, as she walked casually over to the Steinway. She kept her eyes on the audience, and gestured to Muriel to keep her hands off the keys. Even for one night, she had no intention of singing in front of chattering indifference. The character in the long red wig and the clinging sequinned dress raised her hand for silence. When she saw several faces turned towards her, she took a few paces over to the microphone, standing neglected in a corner, and carried it with her, walking forward amongst the first few tables.

'Tell us your name.'

She had seen this man somewhere. Or his picture. It scarcely mattered. 'My name is Violetta. And I'm going to sing "I've Got You Under My Skin".'

She nodded at Muriel, moved back to the piano. The words came into her head, Aunt Lizzie's words, and the song poured out like melted chocolate. At the end, Muriel stood up and bowed her head. It was rare to hear applause at La Maison Blanche.

'Encore,' someone called. Even the girls were smiling at her, but she came back to Heinrich, raised a glass of champagne to the audience, and sat down.

'In you, Violetta, there is something of an artist. I am so sad you do not like opera. I would like to persuade you.'

Stasi laughed.

'If you change your mind, telephone me at the Impériale. Ask for Monsieur Heinrich in room four nine six.'

Saffron came over, and congratulated her. 'Next time, you can sing some more songs. Muriel will go through a small repertoire. With some training, I might be able to give you something regular.'

'Do you mind if I think about it?'

'Of course not. Let me know tomorrow what you decide.'

Nathalie stayed to repeat her performance, but Stasi declined to keep her company. As she was waiting in the foyer for her taxi, she noticed a man leaving with a laughing black girl, swathed in grey fur, one of Saffron's girls. He was tall, dark-haired, the one she had thought she recognized, who had asked her name. The black girl left his side and came over to Stasi.

'Just wanted to tell you, you were great. My, I've never heard it sung like that. Some voice!'

Stasi shook her hand, and the man turned towards them. He registered a moment of surprise but said nothing. After they had left together, she knew he had recognized her too. At first, in the scented gardens of the rented villa above Fiesole, in the splendour of the Pitti Palace, she had admired him. Now, for some illogical reason, Stasi felt deceived. Julian Lieberman, the boy-friend of Beatrice Livorno, wealthy, handsome and charming, going off with a whore. Was that why Carla disliked him, she wondered? Did she know? Was that what she meant by 'the secret life of Saint Julian'?

And then Stasi covered her mouth in panic. He might have thought she was one of Saffron's girls. Suppose he told Carla? Remember Anastasia Wagner? Couldn't find any work so she's filling in at La Maison Blanche. You know, Saffron runs it. She'll fix you up with anything. You make your own arrangements. You could have her all night. For a price. Yes, Pa. That's where he saw her. With his own eyes. Imagine! Stasi Wagner a whore. Who'd have guessed? She was probably bedding the whole cast of *Carmen*. You know the type. Shy, sensitive, butter wouldn't melt, and fucks like a rabbit. Probably doesn't even need the cash. Her voice is ruined now. Sad.

Carla would tell everybody. All those people running the round of smart cocktail parties. Micaela in *Carmen*? Was she? Did she? Never. It's true. No one will cast her now, of course. If Maestro Passattella had known. He hates scandal. If the press got hold of it, one hates to think. They'll find out in the end.

By the time Stasi reached Nathalie's empty flat, she was trembling. In a few hours, she had wrecked her career. Why hadn't she thought? What a daughter. Why don't you think before you act? Now I suppose you'll blame me. Don't say I didn't warn you. He would get to hear. Dominic Morrison would never see her again. 'I'm so

191

sorry. I'm going to have to cancel your contract. You do understand, Stasi. My reputation is at stake.'

A faint dawn light was showing through the shutters. She must have slept for a few hours when Nathalie came bouncing in, shiny-faced, her tiny frame disguised by a voluminous, patchy velvet robe, bearing a large cup of *café au lait*. 'I've negotiated your fee with Saffron. She's agreed. Everyone liked you, Stasi. Now you can buy me a bottle of champagne! Did you like my little act? I'm still refining it, of course.' Nathalie handed her a folded note addressed to Violetta. From Heinrich. She tore it open, and threw it onto the floor.

'I can't sing there. Not in a million years. Why didn't you tell me they were all tarts?'

'Oh, là. Just because they sleep with men? They only do it if they want. Did you have a bad experience?'

'Is that what you do afterwards? Have sex with them?'

'Me? A few times only, for a lot of money. They were so rich, it was nothing for them. But I went to Algeria to research my film. Thank you, my friends! What is the difference if you go out with a man, he buys you dinner, you go to bed, he gives a little extra. This is usual, isn't it?'

'I can't help it. It's immoral. I could never do that.'

'You hurt no one.'

'That's not the point.'

Nathalie sighed. 'Oh, *les anglaises*. They make such a big thing of sex. In France, not so.'

'It's a problem for me.'

'Ah. Always *le grand problème. Pour les anglaises.*'

'I don't think like you, Nathalie.'

Nathalie laughed at her *problème*. There were artists and there were girls. Surely she realized that? Who would dare to criticize Toulouse-Lautrec because he haunted brothels? And you could hardly classify La Maison Blanche as a brothel, the kind of tatty locale you'd find near the Place de la République. Not with such a distinguished clientele. Would Nathalie Laroche have allowed herself to display her talents in a place like that? One had to be practical, no? Or would Stasi prefer to work in a funeral parlour?

Nathalie continued her analysis as she was ironing her lacy strips of underwear on the kitchen table. 'The real *problème*, is not you or me. It is *le problème de la femme*. You're curious because I strip in the Maison Blanche?' *Le striptease*, she explained to Stasi, was the expression of the unarticulated female vocabulary, unarticulated because women's voices had been silenced by men. It should be respected as the art of oppression, like lace-making. And wasn't it the same for her? Who composed the words and music of her songs? Men, naturally. Women had been dispossessed of language. Their only language was that of babies and children. 'I want to make a statement in my film about this,' Nathalie continued. 'Perhaps my heroine should begin life as a striptease artist, but I am not sure. It might be seen as exploitation. The feminist dilemma.'

Stasi was inspired by Nathalie's practical yet passionately argued logic, but she was still unsure. 'Suppose I went on singing at the club, someone might recognize me.'

'So? What is so awful?'

'Someone already has. When I was leaving, he was waiting by the door. An Englishman I met once, Julian Lieberman. I know it was him.'

'What are you worrying about? He's a very English gentleman.'

'How do you know him?' Stasi asked suspiciously.

'He's a great buddy of Saffron's. He has business in Paris, so he comes often. They go to Longchamps together, when he's not hanging out at Régine's. Mr Lieberman is the English dream, don't you think? The kind Parisians try to copy but end up looking like extras in a low budget movie. There's a character in my script like him. He's called Bertie. Is that a good English name?'

Finally Stasi was convinced that she would not be cast into obscurity by singing a few chestnuts of the jazz singer's repertory with a former concert pianist. Everyone could see it was a joke. Nathalie called it l'Opéra Jazz. Was it worse than Ruggiero Gasparini singing 'Goodbye Naples'? Or Selina Price, star at the Met., making a botch of *West Side Story*?

After a few days, the guard in the foyer gave Stasi a slight nod of recognition. One of Saffron's girls. Came in early, not like the others, but the reason seemed convincing. A hard worker, this one. Came in early to practise at the piano, she said. He checked it out with Saffron. Yes, it was allowed.

Stasi added a couple more songs to lengthen her spot at La Maison Blanche. Heinrich came to every performance, once with a tiny, diamond-encrusted watch. Having consulted Saffron, Stasi was told that a present should never be refused, but acknowledged with a gracious note of thanks, like a garter given to his beloved by a knight of old. She admitted to herself, though to no one else, that she felt a sensual thrill as she swayed her hips and stretched out her arms towards the perfumed heat of her audience. Violetta Valéry, entertaining in her salon, would move like that.

By the end of a month, Stasi had enough money to take the train to Milan. For a few days, she stayed wth Amelia Busconi.

'You are happy now, Anastasia?' she asked, as she finally packed away her score. 'I think the producer will be very, very happy. Now the notes are beautiful.'

'And Violetta? Is she real?'

'Everyone will cry. So romantic, so sad. Few modern singers can manage this role, but you convince me.'

'I have to convince Dominic Morrison, too.'

Then Signora Busconi laughed. 'That is not so important. You sing for your audience. In the old days, that was all that mattered. Now a singer has to please the producer. I hope for your sake, my dear Anastasia, that this will change.'

Chapter Eight

It wasn't long before Stasi began to look forward to her evening shift at the Maison Blanche. No one minded if she sang the same songs, as long as she changed her costume, and she no longer felt ashamed. If you didn't have a private income or a rich husband, you had to earn your living somehow. How else could she have paid Signora Busconi and made a contribution to Nathalie? Some of the girls even had degrees. One was an economist, another a tax consultant. They liked the life, they liked Saffron. The money was good, even without the late-night extras, and Saffron had offered her a rise. On that occasion, Stasi decided to tell her the truth.

Saffron was sitting at an elegant escritoire in her tiny office. In front of her was a pile of thick envelopes with a handwritten name on each one.

'I do hope I haven't missed anyone out,' she remarked, shuffling through the envelopes. 'Ah yes. Violetta. This is yours.'

Stasi put it in her bag, unopened.

'I hope you find it acceptable, my little Maison Blanche bonus. And I thought there should be an increase in your nightly rate.' She adjusted the pleats of her navy skirt and beamed. 'One likes to share in good fortune. My economy is booming. So satisfying.' Having named a respectable figure, she was surpised when Stasi looked doubtful.

'I don't know what to say. You're very generous, Saffron, but I can't accept it.'

'I could go to a little more,' she replied, mistaking Stasi's reticence for the opening gambit of a bargaining session.

'No, no. It's just that I can't stay much longer. I do like it here; it's nothing to do with that.'

'Another offer? Or have you become secretly engaged to one of my gentlemen? It's so thrilling when that happens. Strangely enough, some of them come back here even after they're married. Loyalty, I suppose.' Saffron retained an enquiring expression, as though preparing herself for either sympathy or a rebuke.

'I usually sing opera,' Stasi began. 'But you don't go around telling people that kind of thing. The trouble is, you're not meant to sing anything else. Opera's so snobby.'

'But very good for airing one's evening gowns. That's wonderful news, Violetta.'

'Anastasia, actually. Anastasia Wagner,' said Stasi, warming to her enthusiasm. 'I chose that name because I'll be singing Violetta. Have you heard of Dominic Morrison? It's a great honour, to work with him. A new production for the Salle des Arts Modernes. It's bound to be different; they only do experimental work there. Will you come?'

'Of course. I really should know, but the name of the opera escapes me.'

'*La Traviata*. But the story's French. Do you know *La Dame aux Camélias* by Dumas?'

'Ah, that one.' Saffron looked faintly disapproving, then suddenly broke into a smile. 'Just the kind of thing for my friend Julian Lieberman. He adores opera. He's awfully well-informed, but so good at not ramming it down one's thoat. Opera cognoscenti who can't sing are usually such a bore, don't you think?'

'Please, Saffron, come with someone else,' said Stasi vehemently. 'I mean, he knows lots of people in Engand. We have met, and he might . . .'

'I understand. There's no need to explain.' Saffron gave a deep, hearty laugh. She wouldn't have thought Anastasia was his type but she didn't show her surprise. Julian was so unpredictable. 'If you only knew, the girls who leave here and become famous,' she said, rising from her chair. 'I know you'll be a huge success. Do drop in to see us after you've left, won't you? Champagne on the house. Heavens. You'll be on soon.'

They hugged one another, then Stasi ran to her dressing room, joyful at having unburdened her secret.

Dominic's phone number in Paris had been written down in four separate places, including the back of Stasi's watch, in case her bag was snatched, or the flat burned down. Nathalie wanted to know everything about him but her cross-questioning yielded little more than a physical description, a detailed picture of every room in his flat, and as much of their conversation as Stasi could recall. Nathalie had heard – who hadn't – reports of his spaceship *Don Giovanni*. At last, she managed to worm out of Stasi that they hadn't gone to bed together.

'Fantastic. So it will be the first time. You're so lucky, Stasi. The first time you remember.'

'There might be someone else.'

'But of course. There is always someone else. He will like you better.'

'How do you know?'

'Because he is a genius. You are a genius. Your great love has got to be perfect,' Nathalie said. 'And since he's perfect, he's going to trust you and adore everything about you.'

'Dominic? Suppose he has a girlfriend living there?'

'Did you see any of her clothes in his flat?'

'No. Not that I noticed.'

'If there was anyone serious, you'd have seen a fluffy pink dressing gown left hanging in the bedroom, with pink slippers to match. Or ghastly pots of Clarins and Roger Gallet eau de toilette littering up the bathroom.'

Nathalie persuaded Stasi that paying the full price for a Lolita Lempicka tightly clinging tailored dress was appropriate, normal, essential. She also lent her several 'refinements', and it took a whole afternoon of devotion in front of her long mirror to determine the right combination of shoes, bag, scarf and jewellery.

'When you undress, do it slowly and carefully,' advised Nathalie. 'First, it's more sexy. And second, you don't want to look like a crumpled *femme de ménage* when you leave. Whatever you do, don't put it on a hanger, though. Very *mauvais chic*. A chair will do.' Fortunately, their meeting was fixed for the afternoon. 'Better for the eyes,' Nathalie had remarked.

'I'm not a model, I'm not an actress, I'm a singer for God's sake. That's fine. Everything's fine. I'll go like this,' Stasi eventually snapped, rapidly losing patience. The phone rang again, and she shouted, 'How can you spend so much time on all this stuff?'

But she had to admit that when she was about to leave the flat, oiled and conditioned and groomed like a prize hunter, even the fine rain dribbling down the gloomy facias opposite did nothing to quell her spirits. She felt like a beautifully bound book whose pages were, as yet, blank, waiting for the artist's brush.

Dominic kissed her on both cheeks, then stood back. It took them a moment to register a different time, a different place, and the changes in between.

'Why don't you take off your coat?'

'It doesn't take off. It's French.'

They both gave an embarrassed laugh.

'I'm overwhelmed. I feel I must call you Miss Wagner.'

'Really? Do you like my diva-look?'

'Remarkable. Where's the chauffeur?'

'I've given him the day off.' Stasi followed him into the sitting room.

'And how's the voice?'

'I had a touch of laryngitis, nothing serious. August in London, dust and the family, that's my diagnosis. But I've nearly learned the part. And I've read *La Dame aux Camélias*. Of course I cried. Every time I practise the scene with Alfredo's father, I cry. Violetta is so impossibly noble, so wonderfully romantic, isn't she? Every singer's dream. Mine, anyway.'

'Mm. You might change your mind.'

'Is that wrong, then?'

'Not wrong. A bit traditional, perhaps.' He passed her a large brown envelope balanced on a pile of books. 'We'll start with some research. See what you think of these.'

Stasi pulled out a sheaf of photographs. The first one showed an expensively dressed girl in fluttering silk, swathed in a headscarf, holding the bridle of a racehorse. In the background was a modestly turreted château. With only a quick glance at the second one, she blushed. The same girl? It seemed so. This time she was posed sitting up on a grand four-poster bed, like the one she had seen in the Palace of Versailles, her mocking eyes looking straight to camera, her long manicured fingers resting between her parted legs.

'Now look at the back.'

She turned it over. A telephone number. A name, Sophie. 'I've seen these kinds of pictures before, you know.' He had disturbed her, but not in the way he had imagined. The girl resembled one of Saffron's hostesses; she had seen that expression before. Was there some way he could have known? She pushed the photographs back into the envelope. 'What's the point of showing me these?'

'I've been trying to find today's equivalent. After all, Verdi was excited by setting the opera in his own time. That's what I'm doing. Sophie is the modern courtesan. Seen in the best places. Available for special engagements. I think she's quite cute. And she owns that castle. There was a story about her in *Paris Match*; her protector is a duke. Her speciality is visiting stars from Hollywood who get lonely in Paris.' As he took the envelope from her, he smiled. 'Now you get the point of departure.'

'What do you mean? I've got to sing Violetta naked?'

'Don't jump to conclusions, Stasi. I'm setting *La Traviata* in the present because that's what the composer intended. I want to create timelessness from the present. I want it to jump out of the nineties.'

'Oh.' Stasi was crestfallen. She had imagined their ideas matching, fusing, growing, like the blossoming of their love. 'The present? Do you think it will work?'

'I know that's the way to do it.'

'I mean, I hadn't thought of it that way,' she added tactfully.

'And then, we have the conjunction of sex and sickness, sex and death. Materialism. The parallels are so striking. It might have been written today. Just take the symptoms of consumption, the nineteenth-century euphemism for tuberculosis – they're a mirror for the AIDS-related illnesses. Both are wasting diseases, the terrible effects are the same. Shortness of breath, a dry cough, aching limbs, leaden lassitude, a dwindling of all body fat, sheets drenched in sweat. Once you have created illness inside yourself, then you must superimpose the woman for sale. Then we must work on why she falls in love. Eventually, everything must come together. Then we will have Violetta.'

After they had discussed her memories of illness, he put on a video of *Klute*. Jane Fonda had really understood the prostitute, he said. Watch her. They were sitting together like two kids on a Saturday night. She could feel his warmth next to her and it would have been natural to roll over and put her lips over his. Her body was jumping with energy and desire. If only he would make the tiniest gesture, put his arms round her shoulder. But he didn't.

'Have you ever been with a tart?' she asked, looking straight into his eyes, not knowing whether she would be pleased or not if he had.

'You mean, paid for sex?'

'Yes.'

He grinned. 'Never had to. Mind you, some guys get a hard-on the moment they hand over dollar bills. I know someone like that. Tell you what, maybe we should go visit one of the places where the hookers hang out. Maybe they'd talk.'

Stasi decided. Now or never. He made you want to take risks. 'I know somewhere. The Maison Blanche,' she said casually.

'How come you know that place?'

'I work there.'

Dominic sprang to his feet in jubilation. 'Oh, Anastasia. I love it when you surprise me. What a girl! So calm, she says. I work there. Yeh.'

'Not as a tart,' she replied primly. 'I sing a few numbers.'

'Great. Great. Can we go now? Are you on tonight? Can I come?'

'Certainly not. You're not old enough, ugly enough, famous enough or rich enough. They wouldn't let you in.'

'Shame. So make me feel I'm there. Who's in there? What are they doing? What's the decor? Come on, Stasi. Create the picture.'

He sat beside her again, listening intently as she told him about Saffron, her girls, Muriel, the white piano, Nathalie's act, the guards. And then she gave a brief portrait of Heinrich.

'You like him?'

'He's polite.'

'Would you go to bed with him?'

'No.'

'Would you kiss him?'

'Kiss him goodbye? I might.'

'Show me how.'

She looked startled. 'What do you mean?'

'Heinrich has just bought you a bottle of champagne. He's being friendly. You like him. Maybe he's bought you a little present. He's spent a lot of money on you. He leans over, like this, waiting for your lips to meet his. He knows you're pretending, he's a wise guy, but he wants to be back in his youth, when kisses meant something. He's paid for that kiss.' His breath was caressing her cheek, then his lips were against her ear.

'I can't,' she cried, drawing away. 'Don't ask me. Don't.'

He took her hand and pulled her towards him. 'It's only acting. We have to get it right. You'll see why. Don't be afraid. We can both act like fools. Trust me.'

She turned towards him, her dark brown eyes glistening. 'With you, I'd mean it.'

And then, at last, he took her in his arms, hugged her, cupped his hands round her face and thrust his tongue deep into her mouth. Stasi closed her eyes, ready for the next moment of surrender. When she opened them, he was gazing at her with a mixture of pleasure and regret. 'Darling Stasi. You mustn't fall in love with me. Mustn't. Mustn't. I know that.'

'Why not?'

'If we're lovers, everything will change. Once we truly know one another, you'll stop being you. You'll just want to please me. And then you'll think I'm taking advantage of you. And then you'll be crippled with resentment. It's happened before. And I don't want to lose you. I don't want to see you walking out. I want you to be a great singer. And you will.'

'It's too late, Dominic.'

'No, no. Listen. You must sacrifice everything for your voice. For Violetta. You're going to be the one they'll always remember. Once you sing, there'll be no other way.'

'I don't care.'

His tone changed to anger. 'Oh yes, yes, you do. Never say that.'

They strolled down the Boulevard St Germain, his arm resting on her shoulder, the lights bright against the waning sky, until they reached the Café de Flore. Dominic pointed to an old man, seated in the window with a battered fedora and a woollen scarf round his neck, reading *Le Figaro Littéraire*, and talking angrily to himself. Next to him, two students were embracing, books piled up between them. The old man registered their entrance, and gave them a yellow-toothed smile. Stasi was entranced. Picasso might have sat where she was now, doodling masterpieces on a paper napkin.

202

Dominic clasped Stasi's hand across the table. 'There's something I think you should do. I'm not forcing you. But it will help you to understand Violetta.'

If it had come from anyone else, she would have slapped him in the face, screamed abuse, taken the next plane back to England. Perhaps it was the way he explained why he had asked, searching for motives, seeking to clarify his ideas.

'We still have moral hypocrisy. Kept women. So why not show it as it is? I'm not interested in resurrecting *Traviata* like some old Garbo movie, all cloying strings and blooming flowers. I'm not turned on by the Sistine Chapel theory of opera. Look up and admire. But my way means seeking out danger. And hard work. Experiments. Mistakes. I want to see the kind of hard-bitten, pleasure-seeking glutton whom any guy in his right mind would run a mile from.'

'How can I do that?' Stasi was indignant. He was destroying all her weeks of work. 'I don't see her like that at all.'

'There are plenty of *Traviata* productions up and down Italy where you turn up a few days before, get your position for each scene. Then all you have to do is sing in tune and die gracefully. Many sopranos don't even understand the words they're singing. Or have never met the tenor they're sharing the stage with.'

'What do you expect me to do? Make myself ugly?'

'Start with the Maison Blanche. Work on the idea of what it means to sell your body. What it does to you, Stasi. When you come on stage, I want to see a girl who only gets horny when cash is thrown on the bed.'

'You want me to be a whore?'

'I didn't say that.'

'How would that improve my singing? What kind of nutty idea is this? You think I'm not able to imagine what goes on? You think I can't observe what's around me? Isn't that why I'm a singer? Do you just want to shock people, Dominic?'

'Just? Is there anything wrong in that? I'd rather shock than send them to sleep. If it sells out my productions.'

'Ah. Now I see.'

'What a brash jerk. It's written all over your face. How about giving the well-behaved English girl a break?'

'Me?'

Seeing her look of astonishment, he blew her a kiss.

'When I'm ready, Dominic. How about getting the music right first?' Stasi twisted her finger round a lock of hair, and said nothing for a while. What would it be like to turn up at La Maison Blanche, blanked out in heavy make-up, wondering who would buy her for the night? What would it be like in the morning? She found herself staring at Dominic's thighs. That would be cheating, doing it with him. 'If I fuck someone, I'll keep the money. You won't get a centime. Agreed?'

'You say fuck like it's a foreign word. I love it.'

'Would you mind if I did?'

'Don't ask me that. It's up to you. Myself, I think anything is legitimate.'

'Would I have to murder someone to play Tosca, then?'

'I wouldn't go that far.'

'Good. I like to know what the limits are.'

It was time for her to leave. She would think about what he had said. She allowed Dominic to kiss her on the cheek, and walked briskly out of the Café de Flore.

It was all very well fantasizing about the act. Who had not dreamed of picking up some divine young man in a bar, spending just one passionate night with a stranger, walking away without knowing his name? But Heinrich? Stasi was overcome with revulsion: that greyish skin, the thinly-spaced short-cut hair, his thick fingers. And he was so old, not quite as old as Maurizio but forty at least. She had never seen anybody as an object. She would have to think of him as a shadow man. If it happened quickly, in the dark, would it be so terrible? She would have to come up with vacuous things to say. Sounding sincere and saying the expected, like waiters asking you if you'd enjoyed your meal. Nathalie would give her some suggestions.

'You think too much, *voyons*.' Nathalie poured a slug of brandy into Stasi's breakfast cup and continued devouring a chocolate croissant. 'It's a part. You are not you.'

'Well, I can imagine feeling sorry for him. Perhaps I do, a little. But how can I make him pay? It's so obscene, taking money from someone because they go inside you for a few minutes.'

'Money is nothing, just a symbol. He likes you, he pays. First of all you say, "We must discuss business first." Simple, like buying a packet of Gitanes. You say the price, he agrees, *voilà*. Next day, you go shopping and spend everything.'

Heinrich sat at his usual table, having become expert at detecting the moods of the unapproachable Violetta. 'The Lady is a Tramp' suited her; her singing was punchier than usual. The pianist had taken to an unmaidenly swing from the waist as she accelerated into an up-tempo beat.

When Violetta had finished her set, he could see her whispering something to Saffron. Then she made a triumphal tour, saying a few words to the guests whose lavish spending was evident in the array of empty champagne bottles on their tables. He watched her longingly from a distance as the sequins on her dress caught the light from the glow of the lights, her red curls fanning out as she moved. She stopped and leaned over the back of an armchair and a heavy, dark-haired Greek gazed into her eyes. Heinrich recognized Michael Filandris, one of the last Greek shipping tycoons. If I was her, he reflected, I would prefer a handsome young man who has a palatial yacht with a uniformed crew sitting in the Aegean.

Saffron interrupted their conversation, and he could hear her deep, almost masculine laugh, surprising the first time you heard it, like a sparrow with the vocal cavity of a bullfrog. She was gesturing in his direction.

A moment later, Stasi slithered into the space beside him. 'Did you like my tramp?'

He kissed her hand and beamed. 'Tramp? *Ein Vagabund*?'

'No, Heinrich. A naughty lady.' She moved closer, so that their hips touched. 'I have to apologize. I didn't reply to your sweet note.'

'I was too bold.'

'We could go to the theatre, if you like.'

His look of delight was so unrestrained, she was able to overlook his fleshy jowls, his narrow chin out of proportion with his wide forehead, his small, deep-set pale grey eyes. Stasi was tempted to change her mind. Couldn't they just be friends? As she kept the smile on her face, she repeated to herself, 'It's a role. I'm learning to act.'

'We'll discuss business first, if you don't mind,' she said.

Heinrich took a gold pen from his pocket and a tiny notepad. 'Please write on here.'

Stasi betrayed her surprise. 'What should I write?'

'Your fee.'

'Of course.'

'You take credit card?'

Stasi thought for a moment. 'Cash.'

As she was leaving, Stasi was quaking with fear. Now she would have to go through with it. And there were minor but niggling problems which she had forgotten to ask Nathalie. Should she wear her red wig? Suppose it fell off in bed? Would she provide the obligatory *capots* or would he? Would she be expected to undress him? Would they do it with the lights on or off? She was opening the door to the underground car park, a route she took to avoid the brilliantly lit foyer, when she heard running steps behind her.

'Violetta.' It was Saffron. A large crested Bentley with darkened windows was slowly descending the ramp. 'Would you mind using the front entrance tonight? British royalty is so awfully paranoid these days.' She took Stasi's arm. 'Heinrich is a very good choice for you. I've had no complaints.'

'What do you mean?'

'No arguments about fees. Such a good idea to have things in writing, I always think.'

The play which Heinrich had chosen was a boulevard farce acted at such incomprehensible, breakneck speed that Stasi could only take her cue from the audience, and giggle when they did. Heinrich occasionally let out a dry 'Ha, ha', and halfway through he clasped her hand in a firm grip as though she might run away under cover of darkness. If only she had just turned up at his hotel, performed the billed-for act, and made her escape. But at least, during the vapid spectacle, there was no need to make conversation. She wondered what they talked about, the favoured Saffron-girls.

Only once before in her life had she talked to anyone she knew was a prostitute. She had been given a lift outside King's Cross station during a rainstorm by a girl who had taken her to Muswell Hill, refusing payment with a cackling laugh. 'Think I'd take money from girls? Never. Tell your mum you had a ride with a tart. Bet you never sat next to a tart before. Ta-ra and good luck.'

Stasi had never forgotten her face, white complexion, greasy, peroxide-thinned yellow-white hair, purple lip-stick, her expression hovering between amusement and contempt, and the chipped varnish which failed to hide the chewed nails of her stubby fingers.

By the time they reached the Hotel Impériale, Stasi's nervousness had been superseded by hunger. Would he feed her? Heinrich led her into his room, neither grand nor intimate, with a bed which looked like a sale reduction at Maples, wide enough for a family of four. As he switched on the bedside lights, Stasi picked up the room service menu.

'You have hunger?' he asked, as though anxious to prolong the evening.

'Starving.'

'Then we have something. One moment, I call.'

The waiter covered a table in a white cloth, set out some

heavy silver cutlery and a series of platters, lit a candle and left. It had never entered Stasi's head that you could eat in a hotel bedroom, nor that she would eat raw meat, but she watched Heinrich as he swirled an egg yolk onto his steak tartare, and spooned out some capers.

'You, too?'

She nodded, drank half a glass of wine at one gulp, and cautiously took a forkful of meat. Heinrich glanced sideways to study her image in the angled cheval mirror at the side of the bed.

'So graceful. The last girl I had, she made a noise when she ate. I was not liking this.'

Stasi dabbed at her lips, wriggled one shoulder so that her silk blouse gaped open and pushed forward her breasts. Then she, too, looked in the mirror. Heinrich moved his chair closer to hers, and suddenly put his hand down her blouse. It came as a shock. She had expected some introduction, but then she realized that if you had bought something, you were entitled to feel it. Stasi Wagner, a returnable purchase. She tried to think of herself as a shop-window dummy, being handled for display. It was troubling, his silence.

'It's funny,' she began. 'You never know what other girls do. But I suppose we all do the same things.'

Heinrich kept his hand on her breast, squeezing it like Dr Cohen checking for cancerous lumps. 'Sometimes they say, "Oh, Heinrich, your penis is so big." I do not find this interesting. Or sometimes, they are making me come over their chest, all the time groaning. English girls are doing much biting, like a cat. This I don't understand.'

Stroking the back of his neck, Stasi whispered in his ear. 'What do you like? You must tell me what you want.'

'With you, I'm not ordering from the menu. Violetta, you are not like the others.'

Stasi smiled, and spooned a mouthful of steak into his mouth. 'Of course I am.' She waited until he had laid his knife and fork precisely parallel on the plate. 'Heinrich, it's getting late. Won't you come to bed?'

Didn't he understand? That it was a job? That all you thought about was the money afterwards, counting the notes again one by one in private, stuffing them into your bag, lining up the shops to visit, filling up the gaping hole of existence until it had emptied again, and you had tired of the jewels, the silk underwear, the frilled blouses and tight skirts, the soft leather shoes, driven by an unstoppable urge to replace them all?

'May I kiss you, Violetta?'

'I don't do that,' she replied.

Nathalie had told her that you never kissed on a 'paying date'. There had to be something left to give to people you cared about. You could surrender your cunt, but not your lips. The lips, she had remarked, are the mouthpiece of the soul.

Heinrich hid his disappointment by producing a large portable stereo from a cupboard, and Stasi began to fret. He would become hard, enter, come. What if the tension in her body communicated and the juices refused to flow? Was there some secret she should have known?

'Listen to this. Even if it means nothing, you will pretend to like it?'

Stasi kept a smile on her face and nodded.

'This girl who sings, her name is like yours. So I can think of you.'

He must have picked it up at the airport, some cheap recording. Stasi listened to a few bars of an unsteady voice singing 'È strano' from *La Traviata*. She was about to ask him who it was, then stopped herself. Someone who hated opera wouldn't ask who was singing. But it sounded just like Carla Livorno: the same pure high notes, and the weak lower register. For a moment, she panicked, as though Carla was in the room, laughing at her, seeing what she would do next. And then the idea came to her. She would imagine herself as Carla. Carla laughing, Carla tossing her hair, Carla putting one leg over another, high up on her thigh, Carla stretched out on her side, on the floor, Carla dreaming of hot nights and female fingers sliding up her cunt. Carla, with the body of a whore, the face of a whore. The daughter of Paolo Livorno as one of Saffron's girls. It was as though Carla had entered inside her, and was showing her the way. Carla would be her secret model for Violetta, the Violetta of today which Dominic wanted. The character of Carla and the voice of Anastasia. Stasi felt light-headed. Nathalie was right. To every *problème*, there was always *une solution*.

Heinrich was sitting on the bed, listening to that inadequate voice as though it was Maria Callas.

'Come on, Heinrich, darling. Cash up front. Let's have some fun.'

'My wallet. In my briefcase over there.'

She brought it to him and sat at his feet, sitting on her heels.

'Take what is required.'

They were crisp and clean, in a Deutsche Bank envelope. Deutsche Bank francs. She folded them neatly and put them in her pocket. It helped that she did not find him attractive; it made the transaction neutral. Stasi took her shoes off, unhooked her stockings, unzipped her dress. Carla and Rico. She would imagine them leaning against some dark wall, performing highlights from the Livorno repertoire. First, she must undress him, then she would let him remove her bra and pants. It was difficult, pulling the shirt out of his trousers while he lay stiffly on his back.

'I like big men. You're a big man, Heinrich.' Her face was against his cock. It was still soft. When she had unfastened his belt, and was beginning to pull down his zip, he pushed her hand away.

'Violetta, I don't want this.'

Stasi stroked his chest. She began to feel sorry for him. Perhaps he was as nervous as she was. 'Relax, Heinrich.' She was about to kiss him, before she remembered, and wondered if he could sense that she had no idea what to do. Carla had told her that what men liked best was being sucked off. If she had to do that, she'd be sick.

Heinrich pulled up his zip, reached over to the bedside

table and took out a packet of cigarettes. 'You mind? Because of the voice?'

'It's good for the low notes, so they say. People always smoke in clubs. I'm used to it.'

'In opera, Violetta, this is not allowed.'

'Really?'

He had changed his mind. Or would he wait until later? What did Saffron say was the all-night rate? Could he ask for his money back, if they didn't have sex?

'For opera, you must go to Germany.' Heinrich inhaled deeply. The aria selection coming from the speakers of his stereo stopped abruptly. Her Micaela piece wasn't bad. She'd put some work in on that. There was no clapping; Carla must have recorded them in some studio. Perhaps her own.

'Violetta? I ask you to remove your undergarments. Then please to stand against the curtain.'

'You want to see me naked?' Stasi looked at him seductively, and he nodded.

'Just so.'

She unclipped her bra, slipped one side off to reveal a breast, then the other (that was how Nathalie did it), tossed it aside and stretched down from the unyielding bed until her feet touched the ground.

'Over there. And now turn. Good. And raise your arms, like so, over your head. Now the head backwards, to look at the ceiling. Beautiful, so beautiful. No, no, you must not look at me. Like so.'

Stasi stood immobile until her arms began to ache. Nathalie knew where she was, if she failed to return. She had promised to ring her at midnight, from the Maison Blanche.

'Can I move now?'

'Yes. You can move.'

She relaxed her head, and saw him staring steadily at her, leaning against the pillows. 'Did you come? Did you feel good, Heinrich?'

'Now I must tell you something.'

Stasi gave a nervous smile. 'Is there something you want me to do?'

'No. I am in love with a girl.'

'Why didn't you say? You tried to be unfaithful and found you couldn't? There's no need to feel bad about it. I think you should be proud. Lucky girl, whoever she is.'

Stasi briskly gathered up her clothes. It must count, going through with it, even without penetration. If he had insisted, she would have allowed it. What was the difference? In retrospect, it was no worse than Saffron judging her legs, except that there were those crisp, Deutsche Bank notes in her pocket.

'Please to sit down. You are not understanding.' Heinrich clasped his hands tightly and cleared his throat. 'From the first night I saw you, there was no one else in the room for me. Only you. Every night in my bed, I see this beautiful girl, with blackberry-coloured hair, autumn colour, pale English skin, the long limbs of a dancer, the voice which is reminding me of La Divina who to you means nothing. Then I think, maybe she is not one of Miss Saffron's girls. But what good if she is not? For a man to be rich and ugly, life is sad. The girls, they see my face and they think, "Such a man will always pay."'

'How can you say that? You have such an interesting face.'

Heinrich smiled at her for the first time. 'Very interesting when all is dark.'

He confessed that his love was so strong, he would give her anything she wanted, if only she would live with him in Germany. In Hamburg, in Frankfurt, there were many beautiful nightclubs where she could sing. She could have an apartment, an allowance if she wished, there would be no need to do these dreadful things for money.

'I bet you say that to all the girls,' said Stasi, tossing her head.

'You don't believe me,' he replied, looking at her mournfully. 'Let me prove it. Let me, Violetta.'

'Dear Heinrich, you're such a decent man. But girls will

always let you down. Especially ones like me.'

'Not you. I can tell.'

Stasi took her bag, and made it clear she was about to leave. 'I don't know why you think I'm any different. I'm going now. Thank you for a nice evening.'

Heinrich rushed towards her, took her hand and kissed it fervently. 'I made up my mind, one minute after I saw you. I will dream about you always. Can you understand this?'

'No,' she replied quickly. 'No.'

'I must say goodbye? For ever?'

'You can see me at the Maison Blanche.'

'Your eyes are saying something different, Violetta.'

Stasi forced herself to smile brightly, and kissed him on the cheek. He escorted her out of the hotel, and stood by the entrance, holding open the door of a taxi.

'I knew you would not accept, but your beauty is in my heart for ever. Each time I come to Paris, I will ask for this room. The tragedy is mine, not yours. If you change your mind in ten, twenty years, I will be the same.'

Back at Nathalie's flat, Stasi began a letter to Heinrich. Tears came to her eyes. She imagined herself writing the letter to Armand's father, renouncing the man who loved her. If she asked Dominic to advance some of her fee, she could leave the Maison Blanche. Soon, when rehearsals began in earnest, she would need to preserve her energy. Poor Heinrich.

'Thank you for taking me to the theatre. I enjoyed the play. I won't be singing at the Maison Blanche any more, as I have another engagement' – she paused and wrote – 'in England.' Before she sealed the envelope, she took out the Deutsche Bank francs and folded them inside the letter. Then she pulled off her red wig, and looked in the mirror. Even if he did come to see *La Traviata*, which was unlikely, he would never recognize her.

By the time she had sent the letter, she felt overwhelmed by guilt. What must he think of her? How could she have been so heartless? Nathalie was impatient. 'You must be a realist, like me. He has paid only once to dream about you for the rest of his life. Such generosity, for such fantasy. Would he fall in love if he'd seen you this morning with no make-up buying pasta in the supermarket? Ouf! Typical German. Love in the head and angst in the belly. Tell me, Stasi, did he drink champagne from your shoe?'

'No. Why should he?'

'You charge extra for that.'

Nathalie decided that she, too, would shortly be leaving the Maison Blanche to devote herself to her art. By the end of the month, she would have saved enough money to shoot five minutes of her film, half the test reel. An American producer was very interested. Ninety-nine per cent sure. He wanted to cast an American actress as Isabelle Eberhardt.

'The imbecile! But I said nothing. Could you see me giving in to the crapulous taste, the philistine, whorish commercialism of Hollywood?' With each expression of contempt, she threw an armful of dirty laundry to add to the pile in the hall. 'We must think about important things.'

On Stasi's last night at the Maison Blanche, Saffron organized an early champagne breakfast for her girls. She had an announcement to make.

'I've taken quite a batty decision. I'm going to open another Maison Blanche in London. But it's such a gorgeous place, I couldn't resist it. One should have a presence in London, don't you think?' Then she turned to Stasi. 'You know you can always sing for us. With a decent pianist, naturally.'

'Thank you.' Stasi gave a broad smile. 'Where will I find you, Saffron?'

'Mayfair. Where else? I'm just an old-fashioned gel who likes a good address.'

'You must find me a rich Englishman to finance my film,' said Nathalie.

They left in one of Saffron's limousines, weighed down with two enormous bouquets of flowers.

'She's so kind and pretty. I wonder why she isn't married?'

'Saffron can have anyone she wants. And buy her own diamonds. Why should she? Can you see her in an apron cooking English bacon for a husband? She will be in my film. One of those colonial French ladies who scandalized the bourgeoisie of Algiers. Can't you imagine? And, I have been thinking. You will be an incredible Isabelle. You will play the part for me?'

'Of course I will.'

Nathalie shook her head. 'No. Soon you will be too grand for my little film. Your agent will say no thank you Miss Laroche.'

'Then I'll fire him.'

It was sometimes traumatic, living with Isabelle Eberhardt and Violetta Valéry in the same flat. The two women, Nathalie decided, would have hated one another, and besides, Dominic's intense rehearsals were having an intolerable effect on her flatmate. My God, what was happening? The character of Violetta had taken over her home, like a stray cat. Violetta was either tra-laing over the washing-up, which she didn't mind, or feigning faintness every time they went shopping, which she did mind.

'You don't have to be Violetta to answer the phone,' she snapped one day. 'My God. Act normal. You're bugging me, Stasi.'

'See what happens if you ever get a big part,' Stasi shouted back. 'You'll be just the same.'

To her shame, the impulsive jibe struck home. Nathalie retired to her room, banging the door. Big parts had always passed her by and landed in the laps of actresses who didn't deserve them. The ones who were always in work anyway. And the American producer was now refusing to return her faxes.

When Stasi arrived at Dominic's flat, he was rehearsing with Philippe, the French tenor who would play Armand. She wanted him to herself. She wanted to tell him everything, to let him know how he had inspired her; she didn't want to hear this man taking up his time. While they continued their discussion, Stasi sat in silence. Philippe was shorter than she was, and agreed with everything Dominic said. Something about him, the hair cut high above the large ears perhaps, reminded her of Larry Cohen. When he had gone, Dominic sat on the edge of his desk, his head bowed in thought.

'Can we start?' said Stasi.

'In a minute. I'm working something out.'

Stasi went over to the pianist, and turned the pages of his score. 'There,' she said, pointing to the place. Then she took a deep breath, threw back her head and attacked the brilliant tempo of her aria in praise of pleasure, the restless life of the senses – and freedom. 'Sempre libera.' She threw herself defiantly towards the high C, and swam down the falling cascades of coloratura notes, rising again like a series of orgasmic cries, lengthening into long held sighs, until the sustained final note of completion. Then she leaned over the pianist, closed the score and turned to face Dominic. 'That's how I'm going to sing it,' she said defiantly.

He came over to her and took her hands. 'Stasi, darling. It was electrifying. If you can keep up that intensity for three acts . . .'

'I did what you suggested. I won't always, but I did this time.'

'Whatever happened, the result was spectacular. Fantastic.'

'Good. You liked it.'

He smiled at the triumphant expression on her face. 'Don't get me wrong. I never give compliments.'

'He was called Heinrich and he paid me money.' She paused, scrutinizing his face to see whether a tiny flicker might betray his concern, but she could see none. 'I sent it all back.'

'Quite right. She would have done that. Violetta is foolishly generous.'

'Heinrich is in love with me. He must think I'm a bitch

like the rest. I was the one who was acting, but he wasn't.'

'Stasi, don't take it so seriously. He must pick up girls in clubs all the time.'

'I took my clothes off.'

'And?'

'I had to stand there while he looked at me. Just looked, with his little piggy eyes.'

'Did you mind that?'

'That was the only part I didn't mind, if you want to know.'

'Because you're a performer, Stasi.'

Her eyes filled with tears and she hid her face. 'I'm a person, for Christ's sake. How can you be such a shit?'

Dominic disappeared into the kitchen and came back with a tray laden with éclairs bulging with cream, glazed berry tarts and filigree *tuiles*.

'I can't eat that,' she said, ogling her favourites.

'They're for you. I bought them specially.' He took an éclair and inserted it into her mouth. 'I may be an impossible bastard, but I'm not a shit. Believe me.'

Stasi smiled. 'Today, I'll believe you.'

The best time to phone Gloria, who expected a call once a week but yes, it was too much to ask, was in the middle of a wave of euphoria, when no amount of searching questions could persuade her that deep down there was some unhappiness crying out for a mother's love.

'Is it so hard to pick up the phone? Reverse charge, and still it's difficult.' Gloria paused to let the weight of her accusation sink in. 'You still in Paris? I can hear you so well.'

'Mum, you know I am.'

'There was no need to leave like that.'

'Do we have to go over that again?'

'Not even a note to tell me you'd gone. If it hadn't been for Raymond, I'd have called the police.'

Stasi had caught her at the wrong moment and her heart sank. She could tell from that voice, the voice of constant drizzle, bad business and getting fed up with Raymond.

'I suppose you're studying *La Traviata*. I got your card. Five days from Paris it took.'

'Yes, Mum. Violetta is a great part.'

'Still studying? You need all that time?'

'And Dominic Morrison is a marvellous producer, fantastic to work with.'

'Oh?' Gloria sounded suspicious. 'He can't be Jewish, not with a name like that. Mind you, I knew a Morrison once, changed it from Morrewski. Friend of your father's, but you'd be too young to remember Nathan. Had a good education and then goes and sells insurance door to door. Terrible thing.'

Before Gloria could bring up more examples of life's tragedies, Stasi cut in brightly: 'Listen, Nathalie says you can stay here when you come over for my first night. You can have her room. She'll stay with her boyfriend. And we'll meet you at the station, so you can't get lost . . .' She heard a drawn out sniff. 'You got a cold, Mum?'

'Cold? Since when do the Wagners get colds? No, I've got something to tell you. How could I be so stupid? Over a year ago, she told me, and I put it in that nice five year diary you gave me. And then what? I forget. Until she bumps into me in Nu-Clean.'

'Who does?'

'Mrs Cohen.'

'So?'

'Sandra Cohen, Larry's mother. Still fond of you, Stasi. Always asks. Anyway, I promised last year I'd cater the barmitzvah and I can't let her down. Smoked salmon sandwiches for two hundred. All I need. He's a nice boy, David, but nothing like his brother Larry. Still, with that red hair, what can you do?'

'You must tell her you can't. Get someone else to make the sandwiches,' Stasi said, with a trace of irritation, expecting to be reminded of the error of her ways. Broken engagements were never forgotten in Muswell Hill.

'How was I to know David was having his barmitzvah on your first night?'

'So you can't come?' Ashamed to find that she felt relief at the prospect, Stasi added quickly, 'Never mind. I'll get you seats for later.' There was silence from Gloria's end for several ominous seconds.

'Monty's got dry rot in the kitchen. Nearly a thousand pounds to put it right. Terrible.' Finally, she said it. 'I wouldn't come to Paris, not on my own.'

'Couldn't Raymond drive?' suggested Stasi.

'Raymond? I wouldn't let Raymond drive me to Sainsbury's. Mind you, I don't go to Sainsbury's.'

Stasi could feel the beginning of a headache. Her temples throbbed. 'Why can't you say that you don't want to come? You're still angry.'

'Me? Angry? Now you don't believe me?'

'It's the most exciting thing I've done, and you'd rather make sandwiches for Sandra Cohen.'

'Have it your way. See if I care.'

At that moment, Nathalie kicked open the front door and gave Stasi an excuse to put down the phone.

At the end of the first performance of *La Traviata* in the Salle des Arts Modernes, a large, functional space intended for experimental work, Nathalie turned to Bernard, as the clapping and cheering echoed around them, and shouted in his ear, 'She is a phenomenon. I am living with a phenomenon.'

Early next morning, Stasi awoke with a start. Where was she? Rosedene Avenue? Florence? Paris? She closed her eyes again, and felt her forehead. It was cool, there was no fever, she was not delirious. For the moment, all she wanted to do was to relive her triumph.

'I, Anastasia Wagner, am a singer.' She need never say it again. How could she have deserved it? She could still hear the pounding feet, the sharp percussive beats of clapping hands held high as the audience rose to their feet. They called her back, time after time. Her face was streaked

219

with unexpected tears, her white dress covered in blood. Violetta Valéry was dead. She put her hand in his, pulled Dominic onto the stage. He bowed shyly, accepting the tributes of success. Then her bleak dressing room was crammed with strangers who threatened to stifle her.

'You awake, Stasi?'

The man she loved to distraction was spreadeagled beside her, his arm resting across her breasts, one leg lying heavily across hers. He kissed her until she opened her eyes, then swung across her body and leaped to his feet.

'What's wrong?' Stasi murmured, yawning.

'Stay there. I'll be right back.'

She drifted back into sleep, then heard him coming back, the aroma of coffee stealing out of the kitchen. Suddenly there was a whoop of delight and he came bounding into the bedroom clutching a pile of news-papers.

'Listen to this!'

'The reviews! I'd forgotten!'

'"Mademoiselle Wagner's debut in Paris . . . powerful portrayal of debauchery redeemed . . . a startling modern re-interpretation of this withered flower, *La Dame aux Camélias* . . . gained strength after Act One . . . a heart-rending performance which the occasional harsh phrase did nothing to lessen. This young singer left us all spellbound."'

Stasi sat up and took the newspaper from him, scarcely believing what she had heard. 'Do they say anything about you? What do the others say?'

'No matter, Stasi.'

'Are they dreadful?'

'Appalling. Send this English girl back to London.'

'No? Who wrote that?' Then she laughed. 'Come on. What do they say about you?'

Dominic changed his voice and looked down his nose. '"Dominic Morrison, the man who paints a moustache on the Mona Lisa. Like Marcel Duchamp, he shocks us, taunts us, and gives profane new meaning to our cultural icons."' He threw the papers on the floor. 'Bullshit. Still, this kind of stuff keeps us in work.'

Stasi could not keep her eyes from him. As yet, she had not seen him naked, only sensed his body as it left its imprint on hers. They had made love drunk with fatigue, his hands stroking her body as if he had made a joyous discovery. She had wanted to cry out, yet did not want to betray her passion, instead pressing his hand against her mouth. He did not seem changed, but she felt transformed, possessed, fragile, vulnerable, newly born. All she wanted was for him to give her a sign, the smallest hint that she was special to him. Anything, however banal. She wished he had said something.

After they had taken a leisurely walk in the Luxembourg Gardens, he stopped outside his flat in the Boulevard St Germain.

'Hadn't you better go home and rest? The word will have gotten around. We'll have a full house again.'

She let go of his hand.

'Don't worry. You'll be OK, Stasi. You can do it again. I'll be there every night.' He hailed her a taxi, and gave a cheerful wave as he ran inside his building.

Nathalie was at a loss. All those roses and lilies and carnations she had carefully arranged in vases and tins and bottles, the letters of congratulation sent on from the Salle spilling over on the table, reviews which would send her straight into the arms of the top opera houses in the world, and there was Stasi, lying on her bed, her head cradled in her arms, refusing to speak.

'Can you imagine? I never cry. I was like a watering-can, make-up running down my face. Bernard was sniffing, but he thought I didn't notice.'

'I spent last night with Dominic. He doesn't love me.'

'You know that?'

'He didn't say a word.'

'Oh là. What a monster. Don't cry, please. Did you tell him?'

'What?'

'You loved him?'

'Why should I?'

'Perhaps he doesn't know.'

Stasi sniffed and wiped her eyes.

'But he likes you.'

'I suppose so.'

'There is someone else?'

'I don't know.'

'So, you can be friends. You find yourself another lover, you work hard, you become very famous, then he'll come running after you. But you'll be off with some rich gorgeous man who'll worship you. *Voilà*.'

The ripples of Stasi's success were beginning to spread beyond the stage door of the Salle des Arts Modernes. Oscar Broderick was faxing, telexing, telephoning, sending flowers and screaming abuse at his assistant because Anastasia Wagner had failed to respond. He had spent valuable time travelling to Paris, seen her just on a rumour and a few hysterical press cuttings. Nobody behaved like this with a top agent, nobody unless they were a nobody. He was about to advise Sir Miles Mackenzie, with whom he kept in regular contact as he did with all opera supremos, that he had the soprano to make the Palace world class.

'Is she greedy or stupid or has Mathew Gotfarb got there first?' he wondered as he received his confirmation for the George V Hotel, and prepared to fly out to Paris for the second time that week. Then he reflected. 'Do we have one on our books who isn't? Do pigs have wings?'

Oscar was ingenious, when pushed. He obtained Dominic Morrison's home number and justified his second trip. He talked himself through his dialogue. Music first. How many Traviatas had he seen? Must be at least a hundred. Saw Callas at Covent Garden. They hated to be compared but it gave you parameters, like comparing a dancer with Nureyev. He'd seen the best, and his father had seen Gigli and Tetrazzini.

They listened, both of them. He thought he was doing a good pitch, not too pushy, sympathetic. She was nodding. Then Morrison came out with it straight. He didn't approve of agents, monopolizing the opera houses, tying up multi-broadcast deals, taking away the artists' freedom, shooting them down the obvious tracks.

'I hear what you're saying, Mr Morrison.'

'You haven't persuaded me,' Stasi interjected. 'I think Dominic's right. I don't think I need an agent for a while. I'll be singing in Dominic's next production. And maybe the one after that.'

'Fair enough.' Oscar had crunched his way through a bowl of crisps, which was now empty. The pot of tea was cold. 'I meant to ask you something, Miss Wagner. The other day I was called up by a young Italian soprano who wants to change her agent now she's in London. Looking down her CV, I notice you had the same teacher. Amelia Busconi. Wonderful woman, the best. Do you know Carla Livorno? Of course you do. If I remember rightly, weren't you sharing roles in the Passattella *Carmen*, back in the summer?'

Dominic glanced at Stasi. 'Yes, Stasi sang Micaela. But she should never have run second.'

Oscar turned to address Stasi. 'Do you think she's got staying power? From the professional point of view?'

'I'd bet on that.' Then Stasi blushed. 'Oh yes. I mean, she's good.'

'That means a lot to me, Miss Wagner. I always trust one singer about another. I'd have preferred to take you on, because this year I decided to take on just one soprano, but I suppose I might do worse than Carla Livorno. Similar repertoire but not quite in your class yet.'

'Carla has different qualities. I think she'd be marvellous in comedy,' Stasi said.

'You're a very generous person. That's rare. I'm sure you'll do well.' Oscar Broderick rose to his feet, making it clear that there was nothing more to say.

Chapter Nine

Every Sunday evening, Emily Johnson-Livorno had open house, an informal soirée, she called it. Anyone could drop in, or at least that was her assertion, but her friends knew exactly the kind of people she wished to come: those who could enliven the evening with witty, informed conversation, those who were well-connected socially, or those whose beauty and elegance made further attributes unnecessary. Some of Eduardo's more tedious companions who indulged in lengthy comparisons of wine vintages were discouraged after a first visit, as were a couple of Beatrice's shy, unattractive musician friends whose destiny lay at the back of an orchestra, and not at Emily's glittering table. Emily's soirées were well-attended not only for the splendour of the food and wines, but because they provided a palatable disguise for career advancement. When they were in Milan, Carla, Beatrice and Eduardo were expected to be on parade, for Sunday evening was also a celebration of the family. The Livorno family.

Carla's stay in London had been far less permanent than she had hoped. She had met Julian's friend Saffron briefly, but all she would talk about was Colefax and Fowler wallpaper, country house auctions and structural beams. (The London Maison Blanche would only open when her astrologer had selected the propitious date.) The Scottish National Opera had talked vaguely of a small part in the future. It was nearly a year since her debut in *Carmen*, and no one would gasp at her achievements. The *Tales of Hoffmann* in Trieste, *Die Fledermaus* in Naples, which Stefano Montini had dismissed in a few lines, a recital with Beatrice, and a recording of a few arias for some obscure label they sold in supermarkets which was scarcely good enough for a demo tape. Oscar Broderick, who had at last decided to take her on his books, was sure she'd eventually make it in England, had made a few phone calls – *e basta*.

'In Italy, agents are for getting work. What are you for?' Carla had screamed at him.

Stefano Montini, who was now regarded as the only opera critic of consequence in Italy, extracted a silver toothpick from his top pocket and began to eliminate the lingering remainders of his dinner. The four-act menu would have been appreciated by Rossini, one of those rarities, an Italian gourmet.

'Congratulations, my dear Emily.'

Emily gave the broad hostess-smile. 'Oh, I just slung a few things together. It was a simple Sunday supper.'

'You're the only person I know who treats beef with respect.'

Paolo Livorno pushed away the empty plate in front of him, and leaned forward. 'So you think I should accept?'

Carla stopped chattering to Beatrice, Eduardo put down his glass. They had an instinctive understanding of when to listen, when the conversation was about to change gear. Stefano removed the fragment of beef which had been worrying his back tooth, and took a sip of wine. 'Excellent, Eduardo.'

Emily stopped stacking up the plates and sat down at table.

'There's no denying that the Opera Palace has made an extraordinary impact.'

'Thanks to Ruggiero.'

'And, as I wrote in my review, dear Emily, the production of *Aida* was nothing less than what the British expect from Italian opera. Loud voices and animals.'

'No animals in *Butterfly*. Just a Japanese geisha. I guess the Brits think that's the same thing,' retorted Emily.

'I make no predictions. It's far too early. But I think the

will and the enthusiasm – and possibly the finance – is there.'

'Finance? In Britain? They can't even support one opera house properly.'

'I have discovered, Paolo, that when they set their minds on something, they often accomplish the impossible. Even if they don't know what to do with it afterwards.'

'This Miles Mackenzie, is he serious?'

Stefano considered for a moment, aware of the weight carried by his opinions. As a critic, he felt responsible for Paolo's career. 'It would appear so. When I interviewed him, he was very clear about his objectives. "They accuse me of being grossly popular," he said – you may have read it – "but only in order to become boldly experimental when the time is right."'

'Same old crap. That's what they said in Chicago. Experiment my arse.'

Emily was watching her husband. It would mean long weeks of staying in London, transporting all the essentials of decent Italian living, finding somewhere to stay, something to occupy the dark London days.

'You've had an offer, Pa? Why didn't you say? I say, let's go.'

Paolo ignored Carla, waiting for an outcome to Stefano's concentrated deliberation.

'For one production, why not? I think you can handle the artistic director, who's entirely under Mackenzie's thumb. And the musical director is, I would say, respectable.'

'But is the fee?'

The two men laughed, but Emily cut in sharply. 'If they're cleaned out after Ruggiero, they'll want you cut price, darling. No way. I know these people. The Brits always trade bargain basement.' She resumed clearing the table, while Stefano put his napkin on the table and stood up.

'May I use your telephone?'

'Sure. It's over there.'

Carla had to wait until Stefano Montini had made his phone call, paid more compliments, taken up his cane, and finally departed, having said several times, 'My dear friends, I really must be on my way.'

'Pa, I told you, I met Sir Miles. He's a great guy. Don't you remember me telling you? He came to Fiesole specially to see me.'

'Yes. Vaguely.'

'So will you do *Butterfly*? Will we go to England?'

Paolo looked anxiously at Emily. He hated committing himself and would have preferred conducting a small chamber orchestra, trying out his own compositions, leading a quiet, industrious life. But a quiet industrious life would not support a luxury apartment in Milan, a seaside villa and the demands of Carla, Beatrice, Eduardo and Emily.

'I think this time we'll go on our own. You can all come over for a weekend.' Emily came behind Paolo and put her arm round his neck. 'Pa and I would like a little time to ourselves. Wouldn't we?'

'There's a Japanese garden in London, with a waterfall. Somewhere, I believe. In a park?'

'We'll find it, Paolo,' said Emily.

Carla said nothing until Beatrice and Eduardo had retired to their rooms, Paolo to the music room. Last thing at night, she usually left her father and mother to enjoy a glass of brandy on their own, savouring brief moments away from the family. Emily was surpised to see her still sitting at the table.

'Ma. You know I could do that part. Can't you persuade Pa? I mean, he only has to ask, to get me an audition. Look.' Carla put her fingers on her cheekbones and pulled them outwards. 'Me Cio-Cio-San from Nagasaki.'

Emily smiled sympathetically. 'Over there it's different. Pa doesn't have that kind of influence yet.'

'He could try, why not?'

'"I won't conduct unless my daughter plays Cio-Cio-

227

San"? Is that what you want him to say? Come on, Carla. It's England we're dealing with.'

'Ruggiero could say something. They'd listen to him.'

'I don't think Ruggiero had a happy time at the Opera Palace. Anyway, you know he only helps tenors.'

'Julian Lieberman could put in a word.'

'What could he do, for Christ's sake? He has no artistic control. Anyway, I thought you hated each other's guts.'

'Never! I just don't get his English sense of humour – you know, putting down girls every second in case I think he's sissy.'

'Sissy?'

'A guy who likes arse.'

Emily laughed. Only her daughter understood her sense of humour. They were more like sisters, she would tell her friends proudly. The plastic surgeon in Rome had performed marvels in lessening the age gap even though dear Paolo hadn't noticed any difference. If you stayed around long enough, men rarely did.

'Julian's so fond of Pa, he'd do anything.'

'I hadn't noticed.'

'They can talk, can't they?' persisted Carla.

'I'm not meant to say anything, darling, but maybe I should say it now.'

'Say what?'

'Stefano told me they're going for that English soprano, the girl you were friendly with, Anastasia Wagner.'

Carla banged her fist on the table. 'Shit. Shit. Shit. Just because she got hyped for that crap production of *Traviata*. Anyhow, she's too tall for Cio-Cio-San. Crazy idea. What the hell's Oscar up to? He should have put me up for it. Maybe I should go straight to Sir Miles.'

'Carla, darling. Listen. Haven't you forgotten something? Even if you did get the part, you wouldn't be able to take it. I don't think Maurizio would consider changing the date of the wedding again.'

'Fuck. You're right. I'd stand a better chance as the Marchesa della Robbia. They really dig aristos over there.'

'Sweetheart, do you mind? Quit swearing so much. They don't "dig" that too much in England. And neither does Maurizio.'

'Sure.'

'When we're over in London, I'll lay down a few tracks. Take it easy. Until we see what kind of a guy runs this outfit.'

Carla knew Emily well enough to understand the motherly brush-off. Early next morning, she put in an urgent call to Oscar Broderick. She was geared up for combat, and there was little time. If she landed *Butterfly*, that would take care of September to November. The wedding was set for December and afterwards she would have to spend a few months at least in the Villa degli Spiriti. The marchese deserved a few months of her presence, she conceded.

It was tough being surrounded by talent. Stasi Wagner didn't know how lucky she was, starting from nothing. In the Livorno circle, you either made it young or got the hell out. Carla refused to take her place with Eduardo as the second failure of the family. Being the Marchesa della Robbia was a plus, Emily was right. You could give interviews for the society columns.

'Carla, the charming wife of the Marchese della Robbia, told me that she fully intended to return to her brilliant career as one of Italy's most promising young opera singers, as soon as she had completed the refurbishment of the house.'

They liked writing stuff like that in *Hello* magazine.

Oscar Broderick, as she had suspected he would be, was out of the country. His secretary gave her the standard, clipped response. Undaunted, Carla called again an hour later, disguised her voice, announced herself as Cecilia Bartoli's secretary, and was able to track him down to a hotel in Stockholm. Although it was one in the morning, Oscar did not complain.

'Broderick. Who is it?'

'Carla Livorno.'

He clicked into action, dropping his voice to a warmer tone. It was almost possible to hear his self-censorship mechanism. 'So sorry I didn't manage to catch up with you in Trieste. Are you well?'

'Listen. How come I'm the last to know Stasi Wagner is doing *Butterfly*?'

'Why call me at this hour to ask me this, Carla?'

'Because you should have put me up for it. I'd be much better than her for this role.'

'When I last saw Sir Miles, he was considering several sopranos. I mentioned your name.'

'Big deal. I'm amazed you remembered it.'

'I was under the impression that the Opera Palace was considering several singers.'

'But not me.'

'Carla. Allow me to be frank. You're not in a position yet where I can use my muscle. Be patient. You're doing the right thing, getting good experience. In another five years, it will be a different story.'

'You mean, you're pushing someone else. Don't give me that. I haven't even had a decent recording contract. And the jobs I did get, I got myself. Is that called being an agent?'

'I'll be stopping over in Milan on my way back. Why don't I give you a call then, and we can meet.'

Carla was about to object, then changed her mind. 'I'd really love that. Will you come over to dinner? Pa keeps saying he'd like to meet you.'

'How kind. I'll do my best. See you in Milan.'

Carla put down the phone and muttered 'Like fuck you will,' as she began to dial another number. She left a message on Stefano Montini's answerphone saying she would be in Paris, and was really keen to see her dear friend Stasi Wagner. Ages since they'd had a good gossip. Did he by any chance have her phone number? She'd managed to lose it.

It was no surprise to those who knew Stasi, that her second

production with Dominic Morrison at the Salle des Arts Modernes was to be Massenet's *Manon*. Everyone was comparing her interpretations of the two most famous courtesans in opera, Massenet's Manon and Verdi's Violetta, but by now not even Stefano Montini compared her with anybody else. Although not quite a *phénomène*, Anastasia Wagner had attracted adoration which extended far beyond the limited circle of opera fanatics.

As she came out of the stage door, they pressed round her, jostling her, thrusting programmes into her face, demanding that she write her name. She learned to keep a smile on her face, to write Anastasia with a flourish in a sweeping hand. Little by little, warming to the nightly sea of young faces gazing at her with adoring eyes, she began the metamorphosis from promising singer to emerging opera star. Instead of pulling on a shirt and jeans after the performance, she would prepare herself for stage door adulation, remaking her face after removing the heavy cake make-up and the strong lines needed to project her features to the farthest row, changing into simple, un-patterned, dramatic clothes, pinning on a piece of chunky jewellery, often from Nathalie's collection. Her move-ments were more studied, more gracious. Walking out through the artists' door was no less a performance than making her first entrance on stage. She was preserving the illusion for her audience.

Many of the cast from *La Traviata* had returned to work with Dominic again. They had formed friendships, could weather minor storms wrapped in their shared experience, seeing the outside world as though through a clouded window where faces loomed and faded away. That peculiar group intimacy had become Stasi's lifeblood, and she did not want it to end: her calmness and ability to work depended on it. If her intimacy with Dominic waxed and waned, when he was by her side all her fears and disappointments melted away. They spent much of every week together, but Stasi was still wary. He would make love passionately, assume she would stay the night, and then the next time they met put her in a taxi, saying he had to work, or had to see someone. She felt he was keeping her at a distance. Was the intensity of their love too much for him? Or was his passion not as strong as hers?

'I just want to be alone sometimes,' he had said, but she had not understood his need for solitude.

One evening, as she was applying the final brushstrokes to her mouth, after she had spent two precious nights and three days in Dominic's company, she wrote in lipstick on her dressing room mirror: Happiness. Paris. Anastasia Wagner. And that night she gave one of those faultless performances which are rare even for great artists, where the audience almost stops breathing, unable to believe such perfection, such power, such beauty.

Sir Miles Mackenzie was in the audience, seated on a cushion thoughtfully provided by the wife of the British ambassador. After Manon had given her final, shuddering gasp, as the lights dimmed over the bare landscape and the prostrate figure of her lover, illuminating only her waxen face, Sir Miles gave a short sneeze, allowing him to extract a handkerchief and wipe the dampness from his eyes. It was the first time he had ever cried in public. Calling by the stage door, he left Stasi a hastily scrawled note, expressing formal appreciation and a request for her to contact him.

'Stasi. Just pick up the phone.' Dominic threw her nightgown onto the bed, reached over and put the receiver in her hand.

'I don't feel like talking.' She often behaved like a petulant child until he placed the warm *café au lait* between her hands. 'What am I going to say?'

'Listen to him. And if he wants to engage you, say you'll think about it for a day or so.'

'You don't want to work with me any more? You want me to leave?'

Dominic sighed. He didn't feel like giving the reassurance she needed, not now. 'Of course not,' he replied, a little wearily.

'Do you mean it? You don't mind me meeting him?'

He dialled the Crillon hotel, and asked for Sir Miles Mackenzie. 'Over to you,' he said, as he left the bedroom.

Stasi arrived deliberately late at La Coupole for coffee (her choice of rendezvous), but only half an hour late. The mark of a diva was to dispense with punctuality. Or rather, Carla was always late and gained more attention than those who arrived on time. When Stasi met Sir Miles, she regretted her calculated decision. He was warmly courteous, appreciative, understanding, gentle. Taken unawares, she found herself discussing the role.

'You don't think I'm too tall for Cio-Cio-San?'

'Not with the right tenor. There are plenty of tall tenors around nowadays. Your voice is right. That's all that concerns me.'

'And acting? Does that concern you?' she asked gently.

Sir Miles shifted on the bar stool. 'You're thinking of Ruggiero Gasparini in *Aida*, no doubt?' He had a gleam in his eye, waiting for her response. Stasi laughed. Before long, she had forgotten where she was, whether she might, as she did when nervous, blurt out some tactless remark. The way he talked, occasionally searching for the correct word, in long considered sentences, captured her attention. Soon she was unaware of his gaunt looks, his small eyes and gangling body. His sympathy and dry humour made him almost attractive. Or was it because he was the director of the Opera Palace?

Stasi was beginning to consider the idea of working in England. He talked about young British singers who became famous abroad but were unknown in their native country, forcing them to abandon their roots, their family, their friends, and the remark struck home.

'I don't want to influence you,' he said. 'Do you think Paris will give you the opportunities you deserve? The Parisians are fickle. They have a talent for giving adulation one moment, and transferring their enthusiasm elsewhere the next.'

'You've talked about me, but you've said nothing about the production,' said Stasi.

Sir Miles gave a toothy laugh. 'Have we all day?'

'Did you like it?'

'When young Morrison gains more assurance, he will make a fine director. I always prefer to see too many ideas, even if they don't always gel, than too few.'

'I think he's brilliant.'

'I know. Don't think I don't understand. You're very lucky that you have this, this . . .'

'Working partnership. Isn't that what they say?' They both laughed. 'You should get Dominic to direct for you, Sir Miles.'

'Then you'd come to the Opera Palace? I'm afraid I'm not keen on making the package, as they say in Italy. I don't like strings.'

Stasi flushed with anger. 'I didn't mean I wouldn't come without Dominic. I don't work like that. I never will.'

Sir Miles drained his small espresso. 'Whatever you decide, you'll make a marvellous Butterfly. By the way, if you came, we could pay a fee which would be the envy of the Met.'

'That isn't important.'

He looked relieved. 'I wish others thought like you. With many singers, I have to bargain like a carpet salesman.' He smiled apologetically. 'Anastasia, will you think it over? Could you let me know within a couple of days?'

After they had parted, Stasi left La Coupole more disturbed, less composed than when she had entered. She rang Signora Busconi in Milan. What should she do? Without hesitation, her singing teacher told her to accept. At this stage in her career, she needed to work with different producers. After all, she had only worked with Passattella and Morrison. They all said the Opera Palace would be setting the style for opera in the next decade.

'You'll make a beautiful Cio-Cio-San. We can do a little work together. I would love that. Say yes,' she urged.

'And afterwards, Mr Morrison will want you even more. You can always return.'

It was impossible to judge from the state of Nathalie's flat whether she was in residence or not. Stasi returned to the usual chaos of cups and glasses, abandoned clothes, newspapers and magazines hastily read, dropped and forgotten when the phone rang. There were more empty bottles than usual. In the small kitchen, Stasi found a note pegged to the piece of string which served as a washing line, next to the lacy, crumpled pants and bras impregnated with the comforting smell of pasta sauce and garlic.

'Stasi! I am away finding locations. We shoot a scene next week!!! Everything *fantastique*. You too? *A bientôt*. N.'

Her first impulse was to pick up the phone, to ring Sir Miles at his hotel and tell him that she would accept his offer. If they were paying her well, she could fly out to see Dominic whenever she was free. He would understand. She would work with him again as soon as she could.

The phone had been buzzing with activity, its messages channelled into the unreliable machine which Nathalie refused to change, saying it had been part of her life for too many years. *Le throwaway* was yet another symptom of Uncle Sam's depravity. Stasi flung herself on a moth-eaten chaise-longue, revelling in the stillness, the friendly junkstall debris of Nathalie's existence, anticipating a day to herself, when she caught a tinny American twang coming from the answerphone. Even distorted through the tiny speaker, there was only one person whose 'Hi' plunged caressingly down the scale like that, a summons to a long lost friend. Carla. Remember? The first feeling was guilt. She had not written, not even a note. (After all I've done for you. Not even a postcard.)

Stasi stood up and looked at herself in the black-speckled mirror over the fireplace with the half burned wood left from days ago. Scrutinizing her image, her long hair expertly cut to fan out down her back, the simple lines of a well-cut shirt, the Parisian sleekness she had absorbed from the style around her, she had to remind herself that everything was different. Anastasia Wagner had arrived. In France, at least. She had been invited to a party at the British embassy, had dined with the Minister of Culture and sung an aria at a reception in the Elysée Palace, been asked to model clothes for *Elle*, featured in the weekend *Figaro*, 'Les jeunes qui arrivent'. How could you forget your own success? As yet it was sitting lightly on her shoulders, as though it could blow away and settle elsewhere, and she had to remind herself that life had changed, even though her voice, her expressions, her recurring thoughts, had not.

No one in France had heard of Carla Livorno. For the first time, there would be no need to bask in the reflected Livorno glory, there would be no threat, no discomfort, no niggling discrepancy between the Girl Who Had and the Girl Who Had Not. They could be equal, with Carla's money, her family, balanced by Stasi's new status. Stasi could invite her to Chez Marthe, where she was known. If she ate little and pretended she was dieting, she could just afford it. 'My favourite little place. Dominic and I discovered it. Oh yes, they insisted on putting my signed photograph on the wall.' Stasi ran over to the phone.

They both arrived at the same time outside the restaurant. Carla flung her arms round Stasi, kissed her on both cheeks, and took a step back.

'Stasi! Great to see you. Hey, what chic! Fantastic dress! You met someone? Who's the lucky guy?'

Carla had changed appearance again, her curls streaked lighter blond, barely touched by make-up, a long, full, silky sweater hanging over tight-cut jeans, a jungle printed fur (fake this time) hanging from her shoulders. For a moment, Stasi regretted her choice. She must look overdressed, like Gloria wearing a hat to go 'up west'. Then she stiffened her back and took a deep breath. Anastasia Wagner was treating her friend to lunch today. The door opened noiselessly, and the manager greeted

Stasi with effusion, barely glancing at her companion.

'This is my great friend. Carla Livorno.'

Her usual table was set aside. Carla threw her coat into the arms of a waiter and slid into a chair.

'Here. Take a look.' Stasi handed her the menu, but she shook her head

'I pigged myself last night, Stasi. Just get me a salad. And a diet coke.'

'Are you sure?'

'Yeh. I can't get over it. Stasi Wagner, *style français*.'

Stasi gave the order, but her appetite, which never failed when she and Dominic were here together (Carla was sitting in his place), instantly subsided and she regretted ordering *rognons de veau*.

'What are you doing in Paris, Carla? You singing here?'

'Christ, no. No time for that. I'm having pins stuck in my arse at the atelier Lacroix. They're doing their best to make me look like a virgin.' She giggled, and held up her hand, twisting round the sparkling engagement ring. 'I can't decide whether I should wear a wedding band. Who needs to advertise a husband? Things won't be any different. What d'you think, Stasi?'

'It's really happening? You're getting married? Seriously?'

Carla shrugged, cupped her chin in her hands and leaned on the table. The waiter stood by, waiting until she changed position so that he could set down the elaborate bowl of salad. 'It's decision time. Wedding in December, the full works in Maurizio's church in Roccagrande. I wanted to do it in Mexico, no boring relatives, much more fun, but he was against it. So now it's marriage first, career second. I told you it was on the cards.'

Stasi looked at her, incredulous.

'December the eighth. Can you come? Will you be free? You don't believe me? Please come. I'd feel so much better if you were there. Maurizio's friends are all so geriatric. Sorry, I shouldn't complain. It's just, well, it hits home sometimes.' She gave a fleeting smile which faded into an expression of sadness.

'Age doesn't matter,' said Stasi. 'But Carla, you must go on singing. You'll go crazy. How will you stand it? Never seeing a stage again? Don't you think you'll regret it?' She glanced at the waiter, and Carla sat back in her chair, stretched out her legs and looked at Stasi defiantly.

'I'll go through with it. Why not? I can be singing again in a couple of months, you can bet your life. Then I'll get going on that jerk Broderick. My so-called agent. Who's your agent, Stasi? Any good?'

'Oh, Dominic looks after . . .'

'Dominic? Dominic Morrison? You let your producer handle your affairs?'

Stasi blushed, and looked down for a moment.

'Here. Have some salad.' Today Carla's eyes looked almost grey, fringed with black, staring into her face, forcing her innermost thoughts to the surface. 'Jesus, Stasi. You screwing Dominic Morrison? Is he your guy? It's true what they say? Fantastic. Congratulations. Fancy you nailing him!'

'I love him!' Stasi burst out angrily. 'It does happen.'

Carla pushed a bundle of frisée into her mouth. Eating oily dressed salad inhibited the quick response; better to have chosen bite-sized hors d'oeuvres. 'Sorry, Stasi.' Carla swallowed the mouthful, and dabbed her lips. 'I'm happy for you, really. And a bit jealous, maybe. When my girlfriends fall in love, they fade away. It's hard to stay close. But I'll work on it, Stasi. You're special to me.' She speared a miniature radish and held it on her fork. 'If the sonofabitch treats you badly, I'll come over and give him hell.'

It was only now that Stasi ventured to ask if Carla had found work since *Carmen*.

'Oh, couple of boring things in Italy, nobody noticed. Few auditions. That was a smart move, getting in with Morrison. At least he gets press coverage. What's he like?'

Stasi found herself talking about Dominic, the way he

238

worked, how he surprised her, how he was thinking about his next production, consulting her, even basing his choice of opera round a role which would suit her. If you found someone who sparked you, made you reach out, made you do things you'd never suspected you could do, always asked your opinion and cared for you as a person – how often did that happen?

'I'm longing to meet him,' said Carla, having listened thoughtfully for over five minutes without interruption. 'What's he doing after *Manon*? You'll be staying in Paris, I guess. Still, takes no time to fly over from Milan. What does it feel like being European? You look quite different, Stasi. Paris and love. He's lucky. I hope he deserves you.'

Stasi was silent, forcing down a mouthful of meat which she found difficulty in swallowing. 'I don't know what to do, Carla. I want to stay with him so much, but . . .'

'There's loads of other guys out there. Every time it happens, you ask yourself, "Is this the right one?" I know. If he's like you say, he'll stick by you. He'd be crazy to pull out. You're the one who's making his name, don't forget. I saw the reviews. Most of them about you.'

'But everything might change. I've had an offer from London. The Opera Palace wants me to do *Butterfly*.'

'No kidding!'

'Signora Busconi told me I should accept. And I'd love to do some Puccini. But I feel awful about Dominic.'

'You told him?'

'Of course. He's not pressuring me.'

'Jesus! That's tricky. If you say yes, you'll be miserable. If you say no, you'll be miserable.' Carla raised her eyebrows and laughed. 'Maybe you'll just be miserable for a time.'

'You mean, my normal state!'

'Not any more, kid. I tell you one thing. From what I've heard, you'd be crazy to take on *Butterfly* at the Opera Palace. Pa's going to conduct it. He's had meetings with the guys over there – the music director, the artistic director. Hopeless. All of them. Miles Mackenzie is a real schmuck. Everyone's giving the place two years at most. Hopeless management, everyone unhappy, half empty houses. You know how desperate they are? They're paying Julian Lieberman to try and get them out of the shit. Remember Julian Lieberman?'

Stasi was staring at Carla, wide-eyed. 'Oh, yes.'

'He's gotten himself on the board. Imagine! But he doesn't spend much time there. Still the same. I never know where he is.'

'Coffee?' suggested Stasi.

'Not for me. I've given it up. Bad for my throat. As if it mattered.' She smiled, and glanced at her watch. 'Pa's only going to conduct for the Palace so he can pay for my wedding. Isn't that sweet?'

Ever since her conversation with Sir Miles, Stasi had begun little by little to imagine herself back in England. She was even thinking that she could afford to buy a small flat. Stasi Wagner, with homes in Paris and London. Dominic could come over, her mother would meet him . . . Now Carla had saved her from making a tragic mistake. At this stage in her career, one failure could have dragged her down for years. 'I never knew it was that bad at the Opera Palace. I'd better say no, then.'

'Unless you want a trip back home to see your folks. It won't make you in England, Stasi. You're happy here. They love you. Why not stay? Maybe in a few years the Opera Palace will sort out. Who knows? Jesus, I nearly forgot!' Suddenly Carla dived into her capacious bag, and deposited a boxed bottle of Veuve Cliquot on the table. 'From Eduardo. Always asks after you. There's a card somewhere. Here.'

While Stasi was deciphering the affectionate Italian message, Carla stood up. 'Listen. I've got to go – seen an amazing tapestry in rue Montaigne, perfect for the main staircase in the villa. Must rush – I said I'd be there at three. I'm coming to see your Manon tonight to chuck flowers at you. Hey, thanks for lunch.'

*   *   *

After two seasons, the Opera Palace was in trouble. What did everyone expect? How could you launch a new venture without being massively in the red for the first two years at least? Sir Miles Mackenzie was looking over a press release, surrounded by the trappings of managerial royalty: wood-panelled walls, pale Wilton carpet, stiffly arranged flowers, with the obligatory busts of composers, international opera magazines and opera programmes arranged on a series of mahogany shelves.

Decisive, immediate action was required. Sven Larsen was unable to come to the rescue, and was pulling his investment out of Britain. The gutter press had decided to take against anything associated with the Opera Palace. Hacks had been seen skulking round the wardrobe department, buttonholing members of the chorus as they left. For some reason, everyone wanted the Opera Palace to fail. The only thing which could reverse the tide of disapproval was financial stability. Sir Miles, raised in more morally explicit times, regretted Britain's fall from grace, but kept it to himself. Jeremiahs were unfashionable, and an opera house, like every other institution, was subject to fashion.

He forced himself to adjust to the modern practice of open management and financial revelation, whilst still voicing his distaste. Was it really necessary to publish such a detailed cost breakdown? Would a Harley Street consultant itemize every phone call, every strip of bandage? Did the public really wish to know the cost of the chorus, the musicians, the sets, the stage-crew, the artists, the accommodation, costume and wardrobe, electrical and plumbing overheads, secretariat expenses, cleaning bills? Would it make them feel better about paying over one hundred pounds for a seat? He doubted it. Was the greatest concern of the grand art of opera to be reduced to the purchase of recycled paper? Would a red red rose with a price tag have inspired Robert Burns's immortal lines? Why should opera be subjected to the bloody knife of unwarranted dissection?

It was not that he was against careful economies, for that was how he had been educated, but he objected to the targets which had been agreed upon. He had been told by the accountants that he could no longer give Monday night and matinee seat-reductions to the new public he was attempting to woo away from the debilitating diet of multi-channel television. The bars, video stalls and computer games were producing more per capita income than the seats themselves. There was talk of having pop groups performing in the foyer. And there was even a plan to develop part of the car park as a 'virtual reality arcade' where you could fly with the Valkyrie and plunge down from the battlements with Tosca. Why have an opera house in the first place?

At least the Matsuhishi corporation was sponsoring *Butterfly* and there would be no towering pyramids and elephants to bump up the budget. Although regrettable, it was fortunate, in a way, that Anastasia Wagner had rejected his offer. Now he could have the Japanese soprano they had charmingly hinted would be available. Her engagement was politically and artistically correct, even though Malcolm Fuerstein, the music director, doubted if her voice would reach to the back of the auditorium. The acoustic engineer disagreed. With the right sound equipment, it would do so perfectly. Boosting was an art which Fuerstein couldn't possibly understand. They didn't teach it at Cambridge.

Julian Lieberman had said little during the meeting, except to make it clear that his instinct was against issuing such a press release. Public sympathy would not be gained by cries of woe.

'I'm here to talk about solutions, Sir Miles.'

'Oh?'

'Long term.'

'Ah.'

Sir Miles braced himself. He would listen.

'In my opinion,' began Julian, leaning against the boardroom table, 'we don't need to resort to baring financial breasts, or adopting vulgarian tactics. I think we should aim to be independent of the whim of corporate generosity, unreliable at best.'

The subject had been aired too often. Sir Miles gave a sigh. 'It would help if we had a government grant, however small. Then we might be able to attract steady finance. I'm afraid I've had a bleak response. Andrew Broughton seems totally uninterested. He spends all his time shoring up Covent Garden.'

'Andrew Broughton?'

'Minister for the Arts.'

Julian wrote his name on a pad. 'If I could have your full approval and mandate for pursuing other avenues, I might be able to set the Opera Palace on its feet for a while.'

'You mean, there might be possible backers?'

The conversation was continued in the Garrick Club of which both Julian and Sir Miles were members. Julian, it turned out, was also a name at Lloyd's and a member of the Hurlingham Club and the Royal Yacht Club. His particular interest, which he described so amusingly, was collecting Russian icons. Would Sir Miles object if he sent him one? Not everyone appreciated them. He picked them up on his travels – Russian markets had always been underestimated. 'I'm merely a merchant adventurer with a passion for opera.' That was what he said to Sir Miles, during a brief moment of self-revelation. His hero was Lawrence of Arabia; loved the desert. The Bedu – men at peace with themselves. He'd even been up the Amazon, seeking out some rare medicinal chemical concealed in the bark of a tree. Extraordinary that this good-looking, soberly dressed young chap had faced up to such hardship. Admirable.

Julian Lieberman did not bluster and push himself like the older members of the board. Foreign office type: that terse, economical way of speaking leavened by unexpected bursts of frankness. No waffle. Sort you could trust. Who'd get on with the job. Rare nowadays.

Sir Miles left the Garrick to pick up his vintage Alvis, a

trifle uneasy. It took him a while to realize why. Julian had not mentioned his wife. Or girlfriend for that matter. Sir Miles had known homosexuals during his career but preferred not to associate with them. Untrustworthy and fickle. On the other hand, City men were rarely pederasts. Perhaps it was his suit. A little two well-cut. Something a little brutal about the jaw perhaps? Overdoing the Penhaligon eau de toilette? Still, one should never confuse the man with the job, unless it was a security risk. His private life was his own affair. His social standing was beyond dispute, and if anybody could set his ship in order and launch the Opera Palace into calm waters, what surer captain than Julian Lieberman?

Julian's next appointment was in Mayfair. While he was abroad, Saffron had established the London Maison Blanche. Its presence was unnoted, except in the diaries of those wealthy and distinguished enough to appear on her introductory guest list. The property she had chosen, off Berkeley Square, was one of those stately but not offputtingly imposing residences which are often occupied by the ambassadorial community. The English upper classes adore anything which resembles a house, Saffron had observed, preferably one familiar since childhood. She had researched the drinking clubs springing up in the capital, where you announced your presence into a speaker placed beside a homely front door, and entered by dingy, steep, thinly carpeted stairs going either upwards or downwards. You then found yourself in a series of tattily furnished small rooms with rag-rolled walls and second-hand furnishings, a selection of eccentric objects like warming pans, broken-springed settees, bouquets of dusty dried flowers, inlaid pianos with candle-holders and notes missing, even the odd pair of mud-spattered wellington boots, which gave the impression that at any minute a family of grown-ups, children and dogs would come bounding in to resume the weekend houseparty. The secret of success lay in taking the germ of an idea and turning it on its head. Saffron had another kind of houseparty in mind.

When asked by wealthy admiring friends who were unable to put up a pair of curtains without an interior decorator, she said it was just a small talent, like being able to set a pretty table or making a delicious picnic. She would never admit to the hours she had spent combing East End markets, the days haunting auction rooms and country house sales, the weeks it took to order exact copies of fabrics and wallpapers she had admired in stately homes, seeking out old craftsmen who could reproduce a French chair or an English settle and give them the authentic marks of wear in the appropriate places.

There were thoughtful touches everywhere. Like the soundproof telephone booths concealed behind curtains in every room, the 'Office' where a half-clad secretary would run off a letter or take dictation, the 'Games Room' with a special billiard table whose transparent surface could be observed from below. In the entrance, on a marble plinth, stood a specially made dolls' house where every room, including the 'Nursery', the 'Headmaster's Study' and the 'Tuck Shop', could be inspected in miniature.

The only room not on view was Saffron's office, which she referred to as the 'Ops Room'. Having shown Julian round the facilities, she unlocked the door and ushered him in. There he handed her a small brown-wrapped present. He always bought her something on his travels.

'Julian, how stunning. An icon. How adorable. It can go in the Chapel Room. You are a darling.' Saffron carefully examined the Byzantine face of a sullen, swollen-cheeked virgin while Julian gave her a light kiss on the nape of her neck.

'It's authenticated. Here.' He handed her a thin scrap of paper covered in cyrillic script. 'For anyone who reads Russian.'

'Of course. I knew it would be. So you like *ma petite Maison Blanche*?'

'Absolutely gorgeous.'

'Let me give you the *Menu du jour*.'

Julian scanned down the card, illuminated like a mediaeval manuscript but with erotic figures peering behind the antique script.

'I would suggest Catherine, if you want a recommendation. I think she would suit you. Only on Tuesdays and Thursdays,' Saffron said, walking over to a fearsome safe, concealed in a locked cupboard. She tapped out a long combination until the door was released. Inside was a heavy leather book whose neatly handwritten information would never reach a computer nor the long hand of the investigative journalist. Names, titles, brief physical descriptions, addresses, telephone numbers, business companies, names and descriptions of wives, credit card numbers, everything necessary to ensure the privacy of her guests and to avoid embarrassing confrontations.

'You can read my writing?'

'Even in code.'

'Are you looking for anybody in particular?'

'Not really,' Julian replied. 'Just curious. And to make sure you don't have visitors of whom I disapprove.' Before he put down the book, he pointed out one name. 'Andrew Broughton? Isn't he the Minister for the Arts?'

'I wasn't sure about him, but he was introduced by Lord Singleton. You know, the kind of man who takes a girl to the Hilton for cocktails and wears a tie on Sundays. Awfully dreary, and, so they tell me, completely ineffective as Minister for the Arts.'

'That's the best kind to have. I need to bump into him. Here.'

Saffron took the book and replaced it in the safe.

'May I sample the *Délice de la maison*?'

Saffron unlocked the office door, escorted Julian out, and triple locked it behind her. 'Catherine, then. She'll be in the Chapel Room in about fifteen minutes. A glass of the Maison Blanche champagne first, perhaps?'

Julian opened the arched door of the Chapel Room and

found Catherine sitting upright in a bishop's chair, wearing the costume of a nun. Her age looked about right, sixteen or seventeen, he would guess. Behind her was a small altar, covered with an embroidered cloth, some silver cups, tall wax candles and a silver crucified Christ. His icon had already been fixed to the wall in a prominent position. At precisely the right volume, loud enough to recognize, soft enough not to intrude, he could hear the music of Bellini's *Norma*. Joan Sutherland. A heavy perfume, musk-based, with sandalwood overtones, was mingling with the burning incense. Saffron's flair was evident in every detail; even the uneven stone floor was convincing.

Julian could see at a glance that her proportions were right, even in the long habit. Hair the colour of unripe sweetcorn. Slim. High-waisted. She looked young, the face bereft of experience like that of a masked Japanese dancer, but she was probably older than she seemed. The eyes were too knowing.

By reserving sex to the confines of a brothel (it was convenient to have an Italian girlfriend who was expected to remain a virgin until, at the very least, she was engaged) Julian managed to keep his strange desire within bounds, but sometimes he wondered if other men felt this way.

'Good evening, Julian. I don't believe we've met.' A soft, well-modulated, cool voice, just a hint of the Essex vowels. 'Would you like me to say a Hail Mary? Lying naked on the altar?'

'I haven't the time,' he replied. 'Just stand with your back to me. Let me see your arse.'

Catherine lifted up her skirt. Tanned, firm buttocks. He preferred them white.

'Have you washed recently?'

Catherine had accumulated enough experience during her stay in Paris not to be fazed by unexpected questions. Men in brothels liked to give free reign to their madness. She knew that it didn't mean they were always like that. He sounded like her teacher checking whether she had nits in her hair. Without moving, she answered, ''Course I did, Julian. Just before I changed.'

'An antiseptic douche? Or does your cunt stink like all the others?'

She dropped her skirt, and slowly turned to face him. For a brief moment, she looked at him with hatred, then she gave a saucy smile. 'If you'd like someone else, it can be arranged. No problem.'

'You'll do,' he answered. Then he came up to her, pushed her against the altar, unzipped his trousers and threw the long skirt of her habit over her head. While she was leaning over, he extracted a condom and pulled it over his cock, stroking it meticulously until every wrinkle had disappeared. She had begun to pull back the lips of her vagina, but he pushed her hand away. Like a skilled worker on a production line, he checked the position of his tool, created the required opening, and thrust it home.

'There's no need to move,' he said, just before he ejaculated into the rubber container, as though donating his seed to a sperm-bank. Then he withdrew abruptly, and the lank condom hung down limply against his thigh. 'I've finished. Where's the bathroom?'

Catherine pulled down the skirt from over her head and pointed to an arched door marked 'Vestments'. 'Through there.'

He began to walk away, first pulling off the condom and throwing it onto the stone floor.

'You didn't have to do that!' exclaimed Catherine, still young enough to be provoked. 'Why didn't you jerk off on your own in a public lavatory? Far cheaper.'

He turned round, registered her look of contempt and gave a broad smile. 'I like spirit in a whore. Goodbye, Caroline.'

'Catherine, actually.'

'I won't kiss you, I never do.'

'Neither do I,' she replied. 'It's unhygienic.'

Some men he knew performed this function on the office floor with their secretaries or in aeroplane lavatories, the kind of men who never looked at labels on wine bottles, but he came from a different species. One had to stoop to their porcine level occasionally. As he signed himself out of the Maison Blanche, he could sense Saffron behind him.

'I hope I see you again soon,' she said, as she picked off an ailing flower from the arrangement on the reception desk.

'That depends on Broughton's diary,' he replied.

'You didn't stay long with Catherine. Was she disappointing?'

'Not at all. Perfect service.'

Saffron looked surprised and a little apprehensive. 'Did she say anything?'

'Nothing in particular. Her body reminded me of my Italian girlfriend, Beatrice Livorno. When she was younger.'

'I thought you said she was only eighteen now.'

'Nineteen. She's getting rather old for me. Shame they grow up. The female body, unlike the male's, is unsuited to maturity, like cats. In my opinion.'

Saffron lowered her gaze seductively, and it didn't escape her attention that his trousers were just a fraction too tightly cut for a real gentleman. 'It depends on the male. And whether you worship cats.'

As he was leaving, Julian gave the kind of intimate, reluctant smile ten-year-old boys give to their mothers when they have exeats from their private schools and are asked for an account of their activities. 'By the way, do you remember a girl called Anastasia Wagner?'

'Naturally. I remember all my girls. Tall, dark, most striking. Wasn't she on the last time you visited me in Paris?'

'I believe so.'

'One of my clients was in love with her. It happens, very occasionally. Quite a good voice. I wanted her to stay. Is she involved in some scandal I should know about?'

'Unfortunately not. She's become a professional opera

singer. Sir Miles wanted her to play Madam Butterfly but she turned him down. I thought it might amuse you.'

'I only hire talented girls,' retorted Saffron. 'I knew she had a voice the moment she came in. She could have made enough money to live decently. I saw her not long ago in some tatty show in a dreadful Parisian barracks. Some opera about what I believe they used to call a fallen woman. Frightfully sentimental I thought. Showing her tits for peanuts. Stagestruck, I suppose.'

Julian waited until a Burberry-clad man with a turned-up collar signed in the leather book on the reception desk and passed through the door into the Library before patting her behind, scarcely discernible under a loose-cut gaberdine skirt. They behaved like two people who lusted after one another but would never go to bed. People made the mistake of thinking they were lovers, but Saffron had never considered the idea. She had known from the first day they met at the Maison Blanche in Neuilly that Julian was obsessed with a rather eccentric ideal of femininity, the pubescent child. Like his love of opera, it was something she was unable to understand. Had he had sex with her raven-haired chanteuse? She had assumed so, at the time. It would not have been from physical attraction, even though she was undeniably beautiful.

'Was she a good Violetta? Unfortunately, I couldn't get to see her.'

'Wonderful on stage. I couldn't take my eyes off her. But I hear she's in love with her producer,' said Saffron, escorting Julian to the front door. After he had kissed her lightly on the lips, she watched him crossing the street, turning his head to look up at the windows of neighbouring houses, observing the cars drawing up, taking in every detail around him.

Chapter Ten

Maurizio had a quiet wedding in mind, suited to retirement and declining years. They had both agreed to that, but Carla had rejected his suggestion of the Hotel Cipriani in Venice for the winter honeymoon. Why did young girls always dream of hot sandy beaches and coconut palms, in places with insignificant architecture and bad service? Then, quite fortuitously, a friend had lent him a house hidden away high above Castres on the lushly tropical island of St Lucia. A week should suffice. He could sit in the shade while she cavorted down the beach. He sometimes forgot the energy and curiosity of youth. She was quite right to remind him that sometimes he must give way to her desires, that withdrawing into selfishness was a vice of old age which should be resisted.

Close family only would attend the simple ceremony in the church dominating the Piazza della Pace, resting place for generations of the della Robbia family. Carla would bring in extra chairs and sofas for the reception at the villa, as those amongst Maurizio's friends who were still able to travel were long past the days of standing without support. She phoned him every day to report her progress – seeking his advice on the minutest details, the type of lettering for the invitation, the colour of the chairs, the variety of flowers, the uniforms of the staff – closeted in the music room in the Livorno apartment, which she had commandeered as an office, assisted by a social secretary. It was no more arduous, she assured him, than organizing a dinner party. He admired her energy, her persistence, her optimism.

'I am constantly surprised how well we get on together,'

he confessed to Umberto, one of his oldest friends. 'But Carla has such a sweet nature. It has nothing to do with the attraction of age for youth, which vulgar minds assume.'

If only he didn't feel so tired, so lethargic. The gardener at the Villa degli Spiriti, who was well-versed in the philosophy of folklore, assured him that the great events of life took their toll, on the young as well as the old. It would take time to adjust to the shock of happiness after years of grief, years of adjusting to solitude after the marchesa's death. If you cut back a mature tree, after a brief period of inaction, the leaves thrust through with the vigour of youth. After the honeymoon, the gardener promised him, he would be reborn, like the old, spent fig tree in the orchard which had unexpectedly yielded a heavy crop.

Apart from Eduardo, whom she rarely saw, Carla was alone in the Livorno apartment. Emily and Paolo were in London. Sir Miles had spoken warmly over the phone. They had already cast the Japanese soprano, but after the autumn season he would gladly find time to see her. Carla didn't mention that his Madam Butterfly had been in her singing class. Keiko could just about manage Cio-Cio-San, she thought, but what else could she sing? Sweet girl, pretty smile, she'd wow them in Tokyo. Carla called up Stasi in Paris and told her she was right to take her advice and stick with Morrison. Emily had told her that the production looked to be as exciting as those gluey Japanese rice-balls with seaweed. Soon the Opera Palace would be looking for a production where the audience could stay awake till the end.

Emily Livorno left Paolo to find his feet in London and returned reluctantly to Milan. At least she had paved the way, by installing her husband in that darling little place in South Kensington, renewing his wardrobe to conform with the casual style of the British, entertaining Sir Miles and Julian for dinner, and meeting everyone who mattered at the Opera Palace. They were all so utterly charming. Such a wonderful rapport between the cast, and Paolo had really hit it off with the little Japanese girl.

She had always found it easier to fulfil the duties of a wife than those of a mother. Paolo lived for his music, as she had known when she married him, and he couldn't possibly understand the complex emotions she was going through now. (Italians had a disregard for motivation and analysis she tolerated but found difficult to accept. Dr Reuben Mainz attributed their neglect of Freud to their preference for living in a permanent regressive childhood, fixated at the oral stage. Americans ate steak, Italians sucked ice-cream. That said it all.)

When she had asked Paolo why he was so distant with Carla, and showed far more affection to Eduardo and Beatrice, he had looked at her in bewildered amazement. 'You talk to her, Emily,' he would say, whenever Carla presented a challenge. There was no way Emily could discuss what was weighing on her mind, least of all with Carla.

However long she had lived in Italy, Emily had clung to certain American values. Even if he thought her brash and interfering, there was a delicate question she had to raise with Maurizio. In Europe, she realized, it would never be posed directly. It would not have been too delicate for her folks back home, the ones who had remained in Iowa and resisted the urban migration to New York. Through living in Italy and meeting with cultivated minds, Emily had been sharp enough to pick up the nuances of refined sensibility, to appreciate European subtlety, but there was no etiquette procedure she had come across which would guide her on this occasion. Goddamnit, how did you discuss those kinds of things with a marchese? They had never talked of intimate matters together. How on earth did you open the conversation? How the hell could you act the mother when your daughter's fiancé, your future son-in-law, was almost twenty years older than you?

When Emily, dressed in a trim, long-skirted suit, came face to face with Maurizio, her courage failed her. It would seem an obscenity. He was leaning against the bookcase of his library, and you could see how handsome he must have

253

been, slightly built like Fred Astaire, tangoing across some pre-war ritzy dancefloor. Only an Italian marchese could have given that kind of greeting, so sincerely warm, but then his family had been schooled in good breeding for several hundred years. Emily, although herself unschooled in good breeding, could identify it in dogs, horses, furniture, people, even voices. It was a quality she esteemed above all others, even though she knew she could never quite master its complexities. She hoped, with time, that Carla would acquire the finesse of Maurizio, and start behaving like a proper marchesa.

Emily apologized for Paolo's absence, and explained that she had come to go over a few business matters. Then Maurizio handed her a glass of sherry and addressed her as though he had prepared a speech, but it sounded so natural, so elegant. None of the young kids could speak it now, that sonorous, old-fashioned Italian. He thanked Emily for giving away her most precious gift. In the daughter, he recognized the mother. The same vital spirit, the same beauty, the same intelligence.

'May I call you Emily now?' he requested. Even the maids called her Emily, but she couldn't tell him that. 'I would like to set your mind at rest,' he announced, as he opened the drawer of a document chest. 'I am quite realistic, Emily. Have no fear. If I am given even ten years of happiness, I will consider myself the most fortunate man on earth. After that, I would like to be the benefactor of your daughter's future.'

'That's truly noble,' replied Emily. 'Thank you.' (Such a discreet way, she thought, of raising the subject of a settlement.)

'My lawyer has drawn up a will. Perhaps you would cast an eye over the contents. The language is not one I admire, but nevertheless I hope you will appreciate its intent.' He handed Emily a heavy sheaf of papers, headed with the della Robbia seal, handwritten in perfect calligraphy.

'There's no need to go into detail, Maurizio, I'll be here till suppertime trying to make this out.'

'Let me tell you what I intend,' he began, summarizing the document.

Some benefaction, thought Emily. The house, the land, a couple of farms, tenure of the village, share income. She had never guessed that Carla would be set up for life. Comfortable, yes. Substantially comfortable, no. In Italy you never knew. They didn't spell out the terms of security like they did back home where even strangers knew the dollar-power of the rich. This was old money, and none the worse for that.

'It's real kind. You know, I was raised to count every cent. My family was poor and I only became a singer because a rich sponsor paid for me to go to college. It's easy for me to appreciate the generous gift you're offering, Maurizio. As for my daughter Carla, well, how can I say . . .'

The marchese lowered himself carefully into an armchair. 'The young think that money falls like ripe peaches at the prompting of appetite.'

'Precisely. You put it so well. Carla has been spoiled, I don't deny. But she knows about discipline, I made sure of that. While she was studying, I only gave her three hundred dollars a week. And she managed, I will say that. But you need to explain. Set out the limits and she'll respect it.'

He leaned towards Emily. The strain of catching the unfamiliar American accent, the unfamiliar sentiments, was beginning to tell.

'She's a bright kid, Maurizio. She'll understand. You won't have a Nancy Reagan on your hands, believe me.'

The late autumn sun was beaming into the marchese's eyes. He rose to close the shutters as the butler brought in coffee and macaroons. She'll need to have someone nearer her own age around, Emily decided. Young staff to brighten up the place. Preferably young and plain to avoid temptation.

'I've seen a splendid Boesendorfer pianoforte,' remarked the marchese. 'I thought it might mark the occasion. Or would dear Carla prefer something more frivolous? It's many years since I bought such a present for a young lady.'

'That would do just fine. She'd be thrilled.'

'Would jewellery be more appropriate? There are some family heirlooms, a ruby necklace, a diamond bracelet, a rather fine emerald ring, I believe. I can't quite remember.'

Emily gave a comforting smile. 'You could always give something for the wedding anniversary. I know she'd appreciate that, Maurizio.'

A cloud crossed his face, and for a moment he betrayed his years. Emily caught sight of a small, silver-framed photograph hanging over the chest. The former marchesa, a fifties beauty in a white satin dress clinging to her slender hips, was studio-posed by Karsh of Ottawa (with the authentic signature, she observed) in dramatic black and white, inclining towards the young Maurizio on an ottoman. She was wearing some fine pieces. Those drop earrings with matching choker would soon be glinting against Carla's neck. She would take her place in history, wearing the mark of the della Robbia family. Then Emily caught Maurizio's look of anguish, the anguish of recalling other times, other anniversaries. It reminded her of Grandpa Johnson, young and vigorous one moment, a fearful old man living in the past the next. Old age was never predictable, not until the limbs finally gave way.

The question had to be asked. Emily cleared her throat, and nervously fingered her pearls. 'Has Carla talked to you about her singing career, Maurizio?'

'My dear Emily, she knows my feelings. I will never stand in her way. But the life of an opera singer is distasteful to her. She is wearied by it, she has said so many times.'

'She has?'

'Carla longs for nothing more than to be my wife.'

Emily was dismayed by the calm, confident reply. Although she had encouraged the marriage, she now began to wonder if she had made the right decision. Carla would run rings around him and Emily had no wish to see the bitter lines of disillusion etching into his face day by day, month by month. Ought she to have chosen a tougher opponent, an older version of Julian Lieberman? How could Maurizio understand the brutal, competitive world in which she had grown up, in which her daughter was burning to make her name? She turned away, unable to face him, looking out of the window at the long row of cypresses marking the drive. 'It's so beautiful here. Peaceful.'

'Carla is planning a rose garden, an English rose garden,' he replied with pride.

'There's just one thing I must bring up, Maurizio. Forgive me, but . . . well, as a mother . . .'

'Please,' said Maurizio, opening his hands in a welcoming gesture. 'Anything, Emily.'

'As a mother, you think naturally of the future. The joy of watching over your daughter's first child.'

'And I hope to share your joy. There is no impediment, if that is what you fear. You can't imagine how I long to be a father again.'

'But I have to ask,' Emily cut in, 'whether you would mind consulting your doctor. In the States, every couple, no matter what age, likes to have a check before they marry.'

'A check? What kind of check?'

'You know, a medical check.'

'My health?' He laughed. 'I've never had a serious illness in all of my seventy-one years. And the della Robbias are long-lived. I have an aunt who lived to be over a hundred. Do you imagine I would be entering matrimony as a dying man?'

'You know how we Americans are.' Emily gave a nervous laugh. 'We like to think of everything, particularly nowadays. What I had in mind was just a straightforward kind of test. Paolo agreed to it before we married. He saw the logic. Forgive me. To put it crudely, I mean a sperm count, Maurizio. To make sure the child will be healthy. They can tell that kind of thing nowadays. I mean, I don't think Carla could cope if anything went wrong.'

The marchese looked at Emily with astonishment. 'The della Robbia family has existed since the sixteenth century. Need I say more?'

'My husband's specialist is a wonderful doctor, Maurizio. He'd give you peace of mind.'

'There's no need for such concern, Emily, although, naturally, I can understand it.' He gave Emily a bemused smile. That American obsession with health, which had turned robust young Italians, even his nephews, into jogging-suited fools and faddish diners, never ceased to amaze him. 'To please you, Emily, I will arrange a visit to my doctor.'

'Thank you, Maurizio. It was hard for me to ask, believe me.'

By the time she left the Villa degli Spiriti, Emily felt the recurrence of a prickling rash creeping up her neck. Driving back to Milan, she was stopped by the traffic cops for speeding and was shaking just as she did before she went in for facial restructuring. The moment she got home, she went straight to her bedroom, tried to meditate without success and telephoned Dr Reuben Mainz in New York.

Weddings put everyone in a state of high anxiety, especially the mother, who took on the burden of the future. Dr Mainz, whom she had consulted throughout her career, specialized in the artistic temperament. He talked her through the whole thing over the phone. Carla was taking a positive step. Having been neglected by her father, she was now transferring her rejected feelings of love towards a fatherly role-model. Such relationships, in his experience, were usually highly successful.

'I guess she does love him,' Emily conceded.

When Carla made her vows, her clear voice ringing round the beautiful flower-decked church in Roccagrande, Maurizio staring straight at the priest with such pride, the stained glass windows taking fire from the winter sun, Emily was unable to watch her and lowered her head. She felt she was intruding on a private moment between her daughter and the Lord above. Such dignity, such joy. How she had changed, in just a few weeks.

Emily clutched the handkerchief in her pocket, ready for the tears she anticipated, but her eyes were dry. For the first time, she felt able to glance at the imposing strangers around her, most of whom were swathed in shawls and furs. It was only when Maurizio pulled back Carla's veil that Emily realized that her daughter's choice of wedding dress – tailored white satin, tightly waisted with a peplum, beaded plunging neckline – bore a striking similarity to the dress worn by the first marchesa in that silver-framed photograph. Men always preferred the styles that were around when they were young, Carla had said, as she rejected the high-necked Victor Edelstein layered guipure lace dress favoured by Emily. She was right. It would bring back happy memories.

The triumphal march from *Aida*, in a recording with the La Scala orchestra conducted by Maestro Paolo Livorno (later presented to guests as a leaving present), echoed round the church as the couple paraded slowly down the aisle.

'Look at his face. Maurizio looks twenty years younger,' Emily whispered to Paolo, who squeezed her hand.

Outside the church, a small crowd of villagers aimed confetti at the new marchesa, but the wind blew it back and covered them in paper snowflakes. The bells pealed out in uneven, clanging cascades. Then they turned their heads as a black landau, emblazoned with the della Robbia crest, drawn by two high-stepping, beribboned white horses with clusters of bells jingling round their necks, wheeled into the square and stopped at the bottom of the church steps. The new marchesa blew kisses to the crowd, pulled up her dress above her knees, flashing two silver garters, and swung herself into the carriage. Then she extended her hand to the marchese, pulled him up beside her and shouted '*Andiamo, andiamo!*' to the groom. The horses leaned against the traces, moving away in unison. As they broke into a trot, Carla leaned out of the carriage window, flinging flowers from her bouquet into the narrow street leading out of the village square towards the villa. Before the guests had finished filing out of the church, they were gone.

As they drew up to the Villa degli Spiriti, the cook, the housekeeper, the butler and the gardener, all of whom had served the first marchesa, were lined up on the steps outside the main door. The butler stepped forward and bowed. 'May God bless you and may you both have long years of happiness,' he said. Then he handed Carla the keys. 'We welcome you, marchesa, as guardian of the house. Pray, open the door.'

As Carla inserted the heavy key into the lock, Maurizio put his arm round her shoulder. 'An old della Robbia tradition.'

'May you enter with joy,' said the housekeeper as the door opened.

Once inside, the staff stood to attention and Carla looked from one to the other, wondering how she was expected to respond. 'What should I say now?' she whispered to Maurizio. 'You didn't tell me about this.'

He smiled, took her hand and made a short, formal address. 'I thank you for your gracious welcome and I promise to protect this house and all who serve in it.'

The men bowed, the housekeeper curtsied.

'You may go now. Is everything prepared?'

'Yes, marchese. The extra staff will be arriving in a couple of hours.'

Maurizio, still holding Carla's hand, walked up the main staircase.

'It's so tiring, being formal,' sighed Carla, as she began to remove her satin shoes in the flower-strewn bedroom. 'Shame I won't be able to wear this dress again. It's so cute, I can't bear to take it off. Can we get married again another day?'

Maurizio was seated on the edge of the bed, clutching a champagne bottle swathed in a white napkin, struggling to obtain some movement, to twist round the cork.

'Hey, let me do that. Why don't you go put on your robe? You kept saying how uncomfortable that suit was.'

'Let me do this first. Some bottles are difficult.' He was trying to draw strength from his frail shoulders, but it made him breathless. 'Or perhaps I'm a little tired, too.'

Carla took the bottle from him, gave a determined twist, and the cork leaped into the air. 'Oh, say, it's going all over the bed.' She leaned back her head, and poured the bubbling foam down her throat. 'Here. Your turn.'

Maurizio brought over two fine-stemmed glasses which had been placed in a bowl of crushed ice, and took the bottle from her. 'A toast, darling. To my wife, the glorious marchesa.'

She gulped and said, 'I don't feel like a wife yet. I'd rather think of you as my lover. It's more sexy, don't you think? Come, why don't we get into bed?'

'Sweet Carla. You don't mind if we rest?'

'Of course. I should have realized. It's been exhausting for you.'

'I'm sure I'll manage to please you later. Wait till we arrive in St Lucia. There's a private terrace where the sun can kiss your body and then we can watch it setting over the sea. It will be a place of rebirth. If nature approves, perhaps the seed will take root . . .'

'Seed?' Carla looked startled. 'What are you saying, Maurizio?'

'Our child, of course.'

'Really? But we never talked about that.'

'Don't you long to have a child? Our child, my darling? Last month I paid a visit to a medical specialist. There is no reason to prevent you from giving birth to a healthy baby. My baby. If the answer had been negative, I would have called off the wedding.'

'But why? I love you! What about love? Or doesn't that count?'

261

He pushed aside the tight satin covering her breasts, and kissed her nipple. Then he leaned back, and soon Carla heard him snoring softly beside her. For a moment the gentle growl stopped and he murmured, '*Mia carissima Eugenia.*'

Poor old man. His mind was wandering back over the years, back to his first wife. It had all been rather too much for him. Three hours till the reception. She'd wake him up in good time, give him a shot of brandy.

'Signore Domenico Morri-son and Signorina Anastasia Wagner.'

They had been announced, but it was impossible to take more than a few steps into the packed Salotto. Around the edges, on cushioned sofas, an array of wizened faces glanced curiously at the new arrivals, jewels glittering on aged necks and shrunken wrists.

'Stasi! Carla said you were coming. How wonderful to see you.'

Stasi turned round to find herself looking into the soft, grey-green eyes of Eduardo.

'Are you still in Paris?'

'I'm living there.' She turned with a shy smile to Dominic. 'That is, we're living there. Eduardo, this is Dominic.'

As Eduardo took in the tall figure, he inclined his head slightly. 'I'm delighted to meet you. Stasi is a great friend of the Livorno family. We're all very fond of her. Are you a musician? I suppose you are.'

'He's a well-known opera producer,' Stasi said, a little too indignantly.

'I know nothing about music. Remember?' Eduardo gave a candid smile. 'Are you two getting married?'

Dominic laughed. 'We work together.'

'Carla said you were. Come and say hello. She's over there, see? Follow me.'

Through the bodies, Stasi saw a splash of brilliant daffodil-yellow, and the glint of emerald earrings, swinging from side to side as Carla turned her attention from one to another of the guests surrounding her.

'Where's her husband?' asked Dominic. The scene fascinated him. He was taking and storing every detail, noting the stiff postures of the Italian aristocracy, the slight smiles as they acknowledged one another, the turn of the head as they ignored someone who was clearly a stranger, like the man in the green silk jacket with a floral cravat whom he vaguely recognized. Oscar Broderick, the agent. Stasi, too, had seen him.

'There's that awful pushy man,' she whispered. 'I'm surprised she invited him. She won't be needing him now.'

'He probably invited himself,' said Dominic. 'Oscar wouldn't be deterred by not having an invitation.'

They had nearly crossed the room. Carla was smiling.

'I can't see Maurizio,' said Dominic.

'There he is.'

'Where?'

'Sitting next to her.'

'Him? That old guy? You serious?'

Carla raised and lowered her eyes, looking at Dominic just long enough for him to register her look of approval, then she held out her hand.

'My dearest Anastasia, I'm so glad to see you,' she said in Italian, with a trace of affectation, as though she had already lived long enough with the marchese to absorb his speech mannerisms. Then she laughed. 'Great you could make it, Stasi. Hey, Maurizio? You remember my friend? She came once to the villa with Eduardo.'

Stasi glanced at Dominic. She could not tell whether he was disturbed by this reference to her past. The marchese's eyes were a little glazed, as though he, too, was reluctant to bring up former memories.

'Anastasia,' he repeated. 'Anastasia. Yes.'

'You having a break after Manon, Stasi?'

Carla had reverted to English. The marchese was

greeting an elderly woman whose figure was indistinguishable under a sparkling tier of flounces.

'Yes. We're driving around Italy for a while. Just going wherever we please.'

Stasi looked round for Dominic but he had walked away. She wondered if he had guessed that Eduardo had been her lover. It was a long time ago. She wanted to tell him that, to reassure him that when you left home and came abroad, it was easy to be mistaken, that she hadn't loved him really. He knew all about Carla, but she had never mentioned Eduardo. Now that they had met him, her brief obsession could shrink back into a memory. Wasn't it like that? When you loved or hated with passion, and met the person who had eaten away your heart months or years later, only to find that you wondered why you'd cared?

She was still unable to take her eyes from Carla. Even if Stasi had never met her before, she would have had the same effect, like the great mistresses of history: Helen of Troy, La Pompadour, Diane de Poitiers. It was easy to imagine that when you were in their presence you just wanted to stare, and felt gauche and ill-favoured confronted with the splendour of such beauty, like a monkey gazing up at a queen, or the hunchbacked jester in *Rigoletto* wondering at the perfection of his daughter. Stasi was tongue-tied. She could think of nothing to say.

'Stasi. Don't worry, we'll have fun later.' Carla gathered up her long primrose skirt and came to stand by her side. 'When you get married, make it quiet. Can't tell you what it took to get this lot together. Maurizio thinks it happened by itself. After this, I could take on Aida, camels and all.' She gave her coquettish smile, and Stasi recognized the Carla she knew. 'We'll find a moment to get together later. All those boring toasts to come. But we're having a big surprise. Just wait. Prince Niccolò de Ferrara is going to make a speech first. Really, I never knew my quiet little Maurizio was so well-connected. I don't think some of them approve.' She tossed back her curls and touched the wide gold band on her left hand. 'But they can't take this away, so who the fuck cares?'

'I've never seen you look so happy, Carla.'

'I'm onstage. That's when I'm at my best. Haven't you noticed? Will you come and see me in my little retreat?'

Maurizio was looking anxiously in her direction and she lowered her voice.

'I've got to do something with that place. God, how I hate it. Dark as Aida's tomb. But he'll never sell it. Goes with the job, I guess.'

'I'll swop places, then. I know how you feel, going to live in someone else's place. Dominic's flat is fantastic, but it's nothing to do with me. I just get a wardrobe and cupboard.'

'Stasi! Why didn't you say? You living with him? Great news.'

'You knew that.'

'I wasn't sure. But my agent did say something. Oscar's such a gossip.'

'Can't think why he was so interested.'

'Don't be so dumb. Everyone's interested. Don't give me that shit. Doesn't it feel good, being famous?'

'Only when they clap and throw flowers. And the critics say nice things.'

Stasi found Dominic again, talking to Emily and Paolo. Emily kissed Stasi warmly.

'Carla hasn't put a foot wrong. I'm real proud. It's quite a thing for a young girl, going through all this. But there'll be compensations.' Emily winked at Stasi. 'There'd better be. I can't wait to have a baby in my arms again. Isn't that crazy?'

'Will you be producing another opera in France, Dominic?' Paolo asked.

'Well, Stasi and I were thinking about *Wozzeck*. She'd like to try something quite outside her experience.'

'Do you like Alban Berg, Paolo?' Stasi asked.

'Let's say he impresses me.'

265

As Paolo and Dominic moved away to meet Stefano Montini, Emily put her arm round Stasi.

'He's some guy, your Dominic.'

'Mine? I can't say he's mine.'

''Course he is. Think I didn't see the way he looks at you? Just you keep an eye on him. Every time Paolo went away, except when the children were babies, I'd turn up wherever he was. Just for a coupla days. So everyone knew the score. You two gonna marry?'

'I can't say. I don't think about it. Just being with him is enough. It's all I want.'

Emily laughed. 'No harm in being in love for a while. The best part's when you've gotten to be fond of one another. Your ma met him yet?'

'No.'

The 'no' was so final that Emily wondered whether to continue. 'Is there a problem?'

'No. Let's say she's not my best friend at the moment.'

'Stasi, that's awful sad. But I know how you feel. Carla and I have terrible rows, too. Then I go off and see wonderful Dr Mainz, and we re-enact the whole damn thing. Shame he's in New York, but I'm sure he knows a good shrink in London. They all know each other, you know. The good ones.'

'I don't want to discuss it, Emily.'

'Family matter, darling. You just make it up otherwise they'll catch you out, like they did with Callas. They'll find out your mother is living in poverty when you're buying your third home. It doesn't look good, Stasi.'

'If they want to bitch about me, they'll find something. I'm not going to change how I am.'

Emily meant well, but Paolo had survived as a top conductor without giving interveiws, without hiring a publicity agent, without making saccharine remarks about his family, without compromising his standards or flaunting his wealth or – if he had any – his mistresses. Stasi would do the same.

The people in the room began to regroup, as though

some invisible director had given them new positions. Those seated turned their heads towards the dark portrait of a della Robbia general fingering his sword, giving a haughty sideways glance from his position over the marble fireplace. Those who were standing began to form expectant lines.

A shrunken man, with a strong, hooked nose and thick grey hair, mounted a small podium which had been placed in front of the portrait. The marriage of the Marchese della Robbia had been blessed by God. Now it would be blessed by the Principe di Ferrara. He recalled the friendship of their mighty families, their continuing role in history, their importance in the fragmented democracy of their beloved country.

'What's he saying exactly?' asked Dominic, pressing his lips close to Stasi's ear. 'I can't catch it all.'

'Just how marvellous they all are. How Italy would collapse into the dark ages without them.'

At the end of his speech everyone clapped, and Carla turned towards Maurizio, head held high, as though she had been personally responsible for the dynasty whose name she would now bear. Her husband rose to his feet, and a microphone was thrust in front of him.

'Let's have one glass of champagne, then we can go,' whispered Stasi.

'Sure.'

At first, as they were waiting for their glasses to be filled, she failed to recognize the slurred voice behind her.

'For wedding champagne, it's passable, don't you think? Eduardo's choice, no doubt. You look even more splendid than the last time I saw you. Did you know I'd opened in London? Julian told me to ex-pand. Funny word. Everyone tells me to ex-pand. The only thing I know which expands is a suitcase from British Home Stores. I believe the word was used once to describe ourreconomy. But I'm far, far too young to remember. Violetta? Hello.'

'Are you enjoying the wedding? We're laying bets on who the first lover will be.'

267

'I have to say,' said Saffron, stifling a hiccup, 'that we're slighty over the limit. Drink-wise, darling.'

Julian looked balefully at Stasi, then took her hand. 'I'm jealous. And I think this handsome creature must have persuaded you to say no to Sir Miles. A very foolish move, I'm afraid. Don't confuse success in the sack with success on the stage. A common mistake with singers. How is the voice, by the way? Is it gainfully employed?'

'Stasi, darling,' Dominic said soothingly, trying to avoid confrontation. 'He's drunk. Tomorrow he's going to regret it. He barely recognizes who you are. Let's go.'

Everything seemed to go still, as though the brilliant candelabra glittering above her were about to dim. Stasi threw out her arm, wrenched the glass from Julian's hand, and hurled the contents over his face. He blinked, smoothed back his hair and smiled.

'I was teasing. Can't you tell? I really shouldn't be here. Look at them all. Nothing wrong with being bought for an hour. But Carla has been bought for life. And I'm here to celebrate the purchase. I'd rather drink with a whore.'

He was calmly taking another glass from a passing waiter when a young girl, dressed as if for her first ball in a pale blue taffeta dress, came up to Julian.

'But her sister would never marry an old man. True, Beatrice?'

She appeared not to recognize Stasi and took hold of Julian's arm. 'You said you wouldn't drink any more. And you've got champagne all over your shirt. It's disgusting.'

Julian removed her hand and smiled at Saffron. 'One always drinks too much at happy events. Have you met my mother? She has the unlikely name of Saffron. But I call her Mummy. Are you having a wild time? Any old men you fancy?'

Stasi gestured to Dominic and began to retreat. As she turned away from him, Julian gave her the ingratiating, twitching smile of the drunk.

'Come back to England,' he called out. 'Then I'll know I'm forgiven.'

'We meet at last,' said Saffron, leering at Beatrice. 'I've heard so . . . so little about you.'

'I don't know who you are. Julian, why are you being so ghastly?'

'Because I'm drunk. And I am ghastly. Aren't I, Mummy?'

Moving over to stand in front of Saffron, Beatrice pulled Julian away. 'Do you have to be so hateful? You didn't have to come.'

Attempting to restore her spirits with a peck on the cheek, but caught off balance, Julian swayed uncertainly and clung on to her shoulders. 'I'm, I'm sorry. Are you going to play piano for us? The "Pathétique" would go down a treat. Have you managed to learn it yet?'

'You're a pig, Julian,' said Beatrice, shaking him off, her voice rising in a crescendo. 'And you never come to my concerts.'

'If you will play in Tokyo . . .'

'You don't care about me any more, I know that. Why can't you say? Who is that beastly woman anyhow? Where did you pick her up? She's much too young to be your mother. Is she your mistress?'

'Only sometimes. No, no. I am lying. Never.'

'There is someone else, isn't there?'

Julian collapsed onto a nearby chair, took out his handkerchief and attempted to dry his shirt. 'One should never be emotional at weddings. Bad form.'

'You used to like me but you don't now.'

Julian leaned forward. All he could see was a blurred face with two pale pink lips pursed tightly together like a boxer anticipating a punch. 'Beatrice, you should never get involved with old men. They always have trouble with their waterworks. I need a piss.' He staggered to his feet and lurched off in the vague direction of the terrace.

The hired car was rattling towards Milan. Every now and again Dominic cursed as the unwilling engine failed to respond. Stasi was leaning back beside him in resentful silence.

'Forget about it, Stasi.'

'That bastard made me lose my temper. I'm not meant to do that any more.'

'Why ever not?'

'I thought you would have hit him.'

'No need. You did a grand job, darling.' He put his hand behind her neck. It took so little, he only had to say a few words, touch her, and she was restored. Nobody had ever understood that.

'Why do people need to get drunk?' she asked. 'I hate it.'

'It's one way they can find out who they are . . . and who other people are. Provoke them far enough, and they might reveal something.'

'What did Julian reveal?'

'Nothing.'

'It's not true, then.'

'He won't ever reveal anything. Not even when he's dead. He's that type of guy. Saffron's easier. I've met her kind. They run Hollywood agencies, but always pick up the tab when they take you to Ma Maison. Once they decide you're bankable.'

'And Carla?'

'Want me to tell you?'

'Yes, yes.'

'If I was a kid, I'd put her picture on my wall.'

'Do you love me?'

Dominic gave a dramatic sigh. 'I guess I do.'

At the Villa degli Spiriti, the last morsels of wild boar, quail, pheasant, salmon and beef had been carried off to the kitchen. Several of the elderly guests began to grip the sides of their chairs, preparing to leave, when a buzz ran through the room. The guest of honour had arrived.

'He's come!' shrieked Carla and Maurizio grasped her arm to restrain her as she leaped up. She rearranged the voluminous folds of her yellow gown and slowly sat down again. Ruggiero Gasparini walked majestically, ponderously, throwing out his arms with all the confidence of a man who had managed to lose three stone and regain the power of movement. Only the younger guests, Carla's friends, were able to appreciate the honour. The others were asking one another in whispers whether he was a relative. On her side, one would assume.

Taking Ruggiero's great hand in hers, Carla led him to the microphone. As they stood side by side, she beckoned for the photographers to come forward. Ruggiero kissed her hand. They both smiled, keeping their eyes wide and unblinking for the battery of flashes. Then Carla gestured for them to leave.

'My dear friends,' she began. 'At the request of my husband –' she gave a giggle, 'I'm allowed to say that now – I'm going to sing a little duet with Ruggiero Gasparini who has been a dear friend of the Livorno family since before I was born. Some of you may know that I intended to make a career as an opera singer.' Carla gave a long, adoring smile towards Maurizio. 'But once I had met Maurizio, I discovered that love was more important to me than applause. I dedicate this song to the dearest man in the world.'

As the clapping died away, Ruggiero picked up a guitar and began to pluck the strings. Emily clutched Paolo, the emotion she had restrained throughout the day bursting out in an avalanche of tears. It was her daughter's swansong. She had even remembered to clasp her hands simply in front of her. That little Neapolitan love song they had sung so beautifully together. It would be the last time she would coach her daughter. Beginnings and endings, sorrow and joy.

The last chords whispered round the room and the applause had begun to gather momentum when there was a shriek. Except for those standing to either side of Maurizio, no one had heard the soft thud as his legs crumpled and he slid from his seat, unconscious. Carla had watched him for a second in disbelief before crying out. A knot of people gathered round. Someone took a cushion and propped up his head, but his eyes were closely shut, his face pallid, his mouth slightly gaping.

'*Un medico. C'è un medico qui?*'

'Move away, move away,' cried Emily, pushing her way forwards.

Carla, on her knees at his side, looked up terror-stricken at her mother. 'Ma, do something, please do something. He's not dead? He's not dead? I can't bear it. Maurizio, darling, open your eyes, open your eyes.'

She bent over his pale face, and scarcely noticed when one of the guests, a retired doctor, grasped his pulse. Carla was already seeing herself dressed in black, veiled, lost in grief by a marble tombstone. Then, suddenly, his eyes opened wide and he murmured, 'Sleep overcame me. How foolish.'

Carla kissed him on his brow and took his hand.

'We've called for an ambulance,' said Emily, at which Maurizio immediately attempted to rise to his feet.

'Carla, you can call my doctor if you wish. But he won't be pleased at being called out to an old man who has fallen asleep.'

'But you must be examined!' urged Emily.

'He can use my helicopter,' said Ruggiero, who was standing tactfully at a distance. 'I shall stay here.'

'Let's get him to bed,' suggested Paolo, helping Maurizio to his feet.

Early the following morning, Carla was awakened by the rustle of paper. She had fallen asleep on the bedroom couch. In spite of Emily's protestations, Maurizio had refused to be taken into intensive care. If the first nuptial night had been a disappointment, Carla would keep to herself that she had sat up reading Burkhardt's *Civilization of the Renaissance in Italy*, the only book with pictures she had found in the pile at the bedside. Emily and Paolo had stayed overnight, Ruggiero had reluctantly agreed to depart in his helicopter, although he was quite prepared to cancel his television appearance the following day.

'Are you awake?' asked Maurizio, hearing a grunt from the couch and putting down his newspaper.

'What time is it?'

'My usual waking time. Seven o'clock or thereabouts.'

'So early.' Carla yawned, came over to him, and slipped off her négligé. This was marriage, she thought. He had returned to reading his paper, propped against the heavy, carved ebony bedhead, apparently failing to notice that she was naked.

'Come next to me,' he said, without moving. 'The financial report is disappointing. Remind me to ring my broker before we leave.'

'We're leaving?' Carla exclaimed. 'But we can't go away now. You have to see your doctor. How are you feeling?'

'As I always feel, only better. I thought you looked so beautiful in your yellow dress. Did I tell you? I do notice your clothes, but I don't always remark on them.'

'How about noticing when I don't have any on?'

He allowed one hand to wander over her breasts, and Carla waited for it to move downwards, but he took it away and continued reading. 'I think we should make love in the evening,' he remarked. 'I have never felt roused in the morning, not even when young.'

Carla slipped into bed beside him and lay on her back, wondering what colour to paint the ceiling.

There was a rap on the door.

'Come in, Roberto,' called out Maurizio. The elderly butler entered, averting his gaze from Carla, set down a tray with a silver English teapot and matching jug, and quickly left. She fell asleep again, imagining the warm smooth limbs of a young man entwined round hers, his cock pushing up against her belly. What was his name, that baritone in *Carmen*? No matter – she could remember his eyes, his tongue, his strong, hairy thighs.

When she came down to the breakfast room, a couple of hours later, Carla heard shouts of laughter.

273

'Come over here, my dear. Meet my doctor and friend, Dr Filippo Cairoli. He doesn't believe in hospitals, either.'

A congenial man with a paunch and wild, tangled hair kissed her hand. 'I've told your husband that if he doesn't go on his honeymoon, I'll go instead. You must come to dinner when you get back. One of the benefits of retirement is that I now have time to entertain. Maurizio tells me you sing. Wonderful! I'll arrange a meeting of my amateur musical society. They're not bad, are they, my friend?'

'Especially the cellist,' said Maurizio.

'Steady on. You're married now,' replied the doctor with a wink.

Carla forced a smile. Every morning, she would have to feign the kind of cheerfulness which Maurizio clearly expected at breakfast. Grandpa Johnson was always perky around this time; up with the lark, whatever that sounded like. Old people didn't realize that the morning was either for sleeping or fucking. Goodbye to late nights and lying in bed till she could decide where she would take lunch. It wouldn't last for ever.

Chapter Eleven

No one was expecting the Marchese della Robbia to leave this world with such indecent haste, least of all Carla. During their honeymoon in St Lucia, he had seemed more like an old man of fifty than an ancient seventy-one-year-old. It had taken little persuasion for him to expose his wrinkled belly to the sun. Enjoying the anonymity of a tropical island, he took to wearing shorts patterned with orange palm trees, and a floppy straw hat. The locals had grown used to the early morning sight of Carla leading Maurizio by the hand down the winding path which led from the wooden house surrounded by tangled vegetation towards Castries and the white, palm-fringed beach. Still hand in hand, the young girl encouraged the spindly legs of the old man to perform a gentle jog. Or he would float in the sea on a gaily striped water bed, Carla splashing, diving under him, pulling him along, lying on her back, breasts bared. In the hot December sun of this fertile island, age counted for nothing. Day by day, Maurizio was recovering his strength. 'Today?' he would ask eagerly.

'Let's see. Perhaps tomorrow, darling.'

Dawn was breaking as he crept down from his bed and crossed the divide to where Carla was sleeping a few feet away. He knew now that he could conquer her, assert the power of the della Robbia male; that nothing would stop him from taking her. The sun had melted away his fatigue and restored his youth. Her legs were slightly apart, as though she was expecting him, her hands resting on her thighs. He replaced her arms by her side, then climbed onto her bed and crouched over her, his shrunken balls resting on her downy pubic hairs. Like a cat stroked in sleep, she arched her back, pushing her hips outwards until he could see the pink tips, the rosebud folds nestling under the lambsdown curls. Her furry fanny, she called it.

This morning it would be easy, easy as it used to be. He looked down. His cock was rising up, shedding its wrinkles, the tip glistening. Leaning with his hands on the bed, at first he refrained from touching her. He did not want her fully awake. Then he crept over her body, lifted up her buttocks, lifted her upwards, pushed, pushed again until he felt the tight, velvet sides of the vagina, the sucking hold, once more, further. He prayed that she would not move. He wanted to make sure it would reach its destination, the hidden source of fertility. Carla was still, as though she realized that this was no random coupling, no thoughtless satisfaction of a chance desire.

'Now, my angel!'

'The life was streaming out of him, pulsing into her. Maurizio shuddered, his knees gave way, and he lay flat along her body, panting through smiling lips. Maurizio della Robbia, he thought, has become a man once more. And without calling upon the feminine skills of arousal, he had made a victorious entry. This achievement would set him beside his ancestors. How proud they would be, how they would salute his vigour. Her arms were around him now, pressing him to her, suffering his weight on her slender body.

'There, darling,' murmured Carla. 'You were like a lion. I told you it would be like this, but you didn't believe me.'

'One day you can tell our son that his father became young again for one night in St Lucia.'

'What do I say if it's a girl?'

'Would you like that?'

'It makes no difference to me,' said Carla. 'As long as whichever it is looks like you. You know how people are. If they can't see a resemblance, they start saying awful things. Are you feeling tired? Shall I get you something?'

'No, darling.'

'Maybe we'll leave out the walk today.'

Maurizio lay on his back, his mind fixed on a future date. He would see his child beginning to walk. That was all he wanted, to survive long enough to see him becoming a della Robbia, to watch the baby features give way to the first intimations of manhood.

Carla waited until Maurizio was settled on the verandah, pen in hand, bowed over a sheaf of papers. Then she took her jewellery box from a drawer and released the hidden compartment. When she had swallowed the tiny pill (ninety-nine per cent certain, they said, and she could afford to ignore the one per cent with a man that old) she cleared her throat and opened it wide in front of the mirror. She might have chosen a profession which didn't make her look so ugly. Screaming or singing? Soundless, you couldn't tell. Quietly she began to sing a scale. Five notes up, five notes down, and again. What the hell, she thought, and began again, singing more loudly. The voice still sounded under strength. She hadn't sung on stage since October.

'I hear you singing,' called Maurizio. 'My little cricket.'

'It's because I'm so happy,' she trilled.

While he was having his afternoon sleep, Carla put on a poppy-coloured sarong and pushed a red flower into her curls. At her favourite bar in Castries she ordered a fruit-laden sundae dripping with golden cream, sucked at a rum and coke and shifted this way and that on the wicker chair. She knew she was being watched and that he was built like Othello, with the muscled arms and powerful legs of a baseball player. The moment she was alone, they seemed to appear from nowhere, the tall young men with rippling black skins, wet from the sea, their cocks barely contained in taunting pouches. How did this one know that she had just had enough of a man to set her on fire for more? Could he tell from her face that her body was crying out for satisfaction, that her throbbing cunt, moist from a previous encounter, was driving her insane?

She did not intend to do more than accept his offer of

another rum and coke, but oh, how she needed to rub herself against firm young skin, to have a man who could hurl her in the air, fuck her with insolent pleasure, pierce her deeply, send her into rippling shudders, one wave succeeding another, until she cried for him to stop. Ignoring her cries, he would take her again, so that a new orgasm would rise up from her spent body, then another and another until she subsided into darkness, sinking down into a black hole, the non-being of spent passion, fucked into oblivion.

They had done it in one of the changing rooms by the pool, but she couldn't see him again. There was no harm in letting him walk alongside her on the beach. He had thrown her up in the air, over his shoulders, until she had screamed for him to put her down, kissed her savagely as she leaned back on the soft sand, and then she had run up the hill, suddenly slowing to a walk. She had almost forgotten she was the Marchesa della Robbia.

Maurizio, elated by the return of youth, had awakened early. Sitting on the warm terrace, following the bright wings of jewel-coloured birds with his binoculars, he had caught sight of her poppy-red sarong, the black skin next to hers, two moving dots on the dazzling beach far below. He zoomed in on his white teeth, her laughing eyes. It took him a while to compose himself. Maurizio della Robbia a cuckold? Only peasants made the sign with two fingers, the sign of the horn. There was a burning pain in his chest, the bile rose in his throat, but he put on his straw hat, his cotton jacket, while composing a way of hiding his disgrace.

As he walked slowly down the path, Carla greeted him. 'Hi! I just went for a walk. Where you going, darling?'

'Just to post a few cards,' he said pleasantly. After half an hour, he managed to get through to Avvocato Mugnoni, the family lawyer. Just a few minor adjustments to his will. He would dictate them to the charming secretary.

Only when they returned home to the Villa degli Spiriti

did the newlyweds engage in their first argument. It was difficult to avoid raising the question of age and Carla blurted out that the butler, Roberto, was far too old to be carrying out his duties. When Maurizio objected, saying that he was only a few years younger than himself, she accused him of being cruel.

'I'm sure you'd prefer to have a handsome young man bringing in the breakfast tray,' he remarked acidly. 'But I refuse to indulge you in that respect.'

'How dare you?' cried Carla. 'You know I never look at other men. If I wanted to do that, I'd hardly be staying here. Are you accusing me, Maurizio? In my house, we treat servants properly.'

'This is your house now, Carla.'

'My house? Everything here is yours. Your taste, your style. I mean, it's fine. But don't you ever think I might like to alter some things, just brighten up a few rooms?'

'Brighten up? Like a cafeteria? Or a Jolly hotel? I wouldn't like that. No one has ever complained. Except you.'

'No need to get so grumpy. Anyhow, it would give me something to do, wouldn't it?' Carla twined her arms around him, and fondled the mossy white hairs on the base of his neck.

'You could decorate the nursery, Carla. That might be an idea.'

'Isn't it a tiny bit soon for that, darling?'

'As you wish.'

Emily had no need to ask when the happy event would take place, so certain was she that Carla would wish to give the news herself. She knew when to stand back. Her daughter's decision to begin a programme of song therapy for disabled children in a nearby residential home showed that she was nurturing feelings of motherhood. It would also provide her with a worthwhile objective, bring a positive attitude into the marriage. Giving unfortunate children the benefit of her gift was far more valuable than exhibiting herself in an opera house.

The Marchesa della Robbia swiftly acquired a reputation for taking charity work seriously, unlike some ladies who spent all their energy in organizing fund-raising balls for the pot-bellied waifs of Africa whom they never met, merely to show off their latest couturier gowns and family jewels. The sad children of the residential home, with their wasted limbs and lolling heads, swayed and stared and giggled when the fairytale princess sang her magic songs. And Carla would tell them stories about wicked Spanish witches, evil kings, and maidens who died for love. The sisters gathered round the piano, even when she was practising scales. They had never heard such a pretty voice, been so close to it, felt its vibration. It was like hearing echoes from heaven.

The only person who shared Carla's secret was Signora Busconi, whom she visited for weekly singing lessons in Milan, on the pretext of meeting her mother.

'My husband is kind and good,' she told her. Then she sighed. 'How can I explain? You know how it is when you're first married. Even when I go off to be with my poor dear children, just a few kilometres away, he wants to know when I'm getting back. Often, he asks me where I'm going and then he calls to find out if I've arrived.' Carla gave a proud smile, as though she was flattered by his attention. 'I guess it's traditional, for a husband to keep tabs on his wife. And Maurizio – well, you know how the aristocracy clings to tradition.'

Signora Busconi nodded in sympathy. She had always suspected that Carla Livorno would change when settled in the stability of marriage. This dignified young woman, in a light grey coat-dress with a neat white collar, one gold chain round her neck, bore little resemblance to the fledgeling prima donna who used to throw her fur coat on the floor. If she worked hard, she might yet make a serious career.

'There has never been an artist in the della Robbia family. How can he understand what it means? But I'm sure he'll change. He loves to hear me practising. Maybe I should start with a concert recital?'

'We could work up a programme.'

'I'd just love that. Then, when I'm ready, I could hire some place . . .'

Signora Busconi looked at her sternly. 'When you reach a standard we both accept, that won't be necessary.'

'I'll do anything,' Carla said fervently. 'Anything you say; so long as I don't offend dear Maurizio.'

'I'm sure he'll come to understand,' replied Signora Busconi, hugging her affectionately.

Carla began to attend Dr Filippo Cairoli's fortnightly musical evenings. Maurizio spent much of the time after dinner disguising yawns behind his handkerchief, sometimes dropping off to sleep, but he was in good company. If the quartet and trio suffered lapses, or the second violin took to playing one bar ahead of the other musicians, no one would criticize, least of all Carla. After a few amiable soirées, when she had talked of the moving experience of introducing music to the unfortunate children of the Casa di Sant'Agata, Carla was prevailed upon to give them a little song, just one. Soon afterwards, she gave a private recital at the prompting of Dr Cairoli, in the salotto of the Villa degli Spiriti.

'You know, Maurizio,' said the doctor, 'that wife of yours should be giving joy to the public. In my opinion, her voice is good enough for her to sing professionally.'

'She wouldn't hear of it,' the marchese replied firmly. 'And neither would I. Performing in public? For money?' He laughed. 'There is no need to stoop to that.'

'It isn't considered a disgrace, not today. Even the British royal family are not ashamed to accept payment for their artistic endeavours.'

'I hadn't heard,' Maurizio said abstractedly, as though such behaviour was beneath contempt. 'And you are suggesting she should sing for people who are unknown, who come off the street and buy a ticket? Besides, can you imagine? Singing for those wretched children? How much happiness it gives my wife?'

The doctor patted Maurizio on the back and chuckled.

'My dear friend, I was merely giving you my opinion, expressing idle thoughts. Isn't that what doctors are for?'

Dr Cairoli would remember that conversation. He knew why the marchese had betrayed such indignation; the pain behind his words. He could not bring himself to tell Maurizio that it was unlikely his wife would ever bear his child, but he must have known. That last conversation with a dear friend acquired an importance in retrospect which it should never have borne; it came to sum up a lifetime of friendship. Should he have said more? Should they have confronted the issue together?

Hadn't he suggested, on several occasions, that it was time for a medical check-up? On the other hand, there was something to be said for Maurizio's bland disregard for the failings of the body. Didn't he offer further tests, which needed to take place in hospital? And hadn't Maurizio refused? Even Carla had been unable to persuade him. There was a remote possibility of diabetes mellitus, he had told him, which would mean a slight change of diet, a few pills every day.

'Diabetes mellitus? Why do you talk to me in Latin? Latin is the language of Horace,' was all he said, and changed the subject.

Maurizio, Dr Cairoli consoled himself, would have chosen to leave this world in such a manner, lying in his great bed, overlooked by golden cherubs, his chilling fingers slipping away from those of his beautiful wife.

That day, Maurizio had driven into Milan to see his stockbroker, followed by lunch with his lawyer. Carla would come to know his every movement, the time he left the offices of Avvocato Federico Mugnoni, the route taken by the driver to the quiet restaurant in Via Manzoni, what he had eaten, at what time he had arrived back at the Villa degli Spiriti. She would also have to recall how she spent each hour, each minute of that time, even whether they had breakfasted together.

The interview with the coroner had lasted longer than she expected, given that Dr Cairoli had certified the cause of death as heart failure. The sharp-nosed man with ruffled eyebrows was a stickler for detail. Probably a former Communist, Carla decided, trying to overcome his dislike of inherited wealth. Only a former Communist could show such lack of sympathy. No, she had no idea whether her husband had made a will. Their partnership was based on love, respect and a mutual passion for music – she was a keen amateur singer, a regular visitor to the musical evenings for which Dr Cairoli was famous. It made her cry just to recall the intimate happiness – he must forgive her, just a moment, she would control herself . . .

'So you spent the afternoon and evening at the Casa di Sant'Agata? All evening?'

'Yes. I had organized a small charity benefit.'

'To which your husband was not invited?'

'We discussed it, and he decided that he would be too tired to attend after his appointments in Milan.'

'Naturally. The marchese was an old man.'

'But very vigorous for his years.'

The coroner twitched, and looked down at his notes. 'You were unaware that his state of health might be less than appropriate for a man of his years? Did he never complain of ill health?'

'The marchese never complained.' Carla clutched her hands tightly, and bowed her head. 'He would take a rest, often in the afternoon.'

'Did he, on that day, take a rest when he returned from the Via Manzoni?'

Carla frowned. 'I assume he must have done.'

'The staff at the villa, signora. Were they in attendance?' (Did he need to indicate his hostility so crudely by ignoring her title?)

'Yes.'

'They had no reason to enter his bedroom, they knew his habits? He would have called them if he had needed anything?'

'Quite. That is what servants are for.' Carla shivered, and pulled her coat round her shoulders.

'Are you cold, signora?'

'It's cool in here. I've been walking in the sun.' She countered his stare with a smile. 'I needed to buy a few things.'

He continued writing. The picture in her mind was clear. The butler, still in employment, was down in the wine cellar, checking his inventory, taking the odd sample to establish which bottles had reached maturity. The housekeeper was cleaning silver in the kitchen, as she did every Monday, taking at least two hours. The gardener was out, visiting a nursery. He had taken the truck.

When she had returned that afternoon, to collect a piece of music she had forgotten and to change her shoes, no one had seen her. In any case, no one would have known that she had gone to their bedroom.

At first, she had almost fainted with the shock. Maurizio was on the bed, his head hanging over the side, his glasses on the floor. Although his face was pale, she thought he was breathing. She had seen her grandfather, Paolo's father, lying on his deathbed. Maurizio had not looked like that. He did not have the parchment features of a departed spirit. There was little time; she had to get on. It did cross her mind, as she took her route back to the Casa di Sant'Agata, that there was something disturbing about his appearance, but she was unused to illness. Who would have believed her? Who would have understood that she saw no reason to call Dr Cairoli? She could not be absolutely sure that he was dying. He was asleep. Very still. Just asleep. They said he must have died at about seven o'clock, when she was singing the first bars of 'Un bel dì' which, had he heard it, would in itself have been sufficient cause for a heart attack.

The coroner asked a few more questions and then told her that she would be relieved to hear that a post mortem would not be necessary. He looked up at her, raising those bushy eyebrows, his small eyes glued to her face like pigeon-droppings on a windscreen, waiting for her to say something.

'So,' Carla began hesitantly, 'will it be . . . may I . . . ?'

'Yes, signora?'

She breathed in and composed herself. 'Make arrangements for the funeral?'

'You may.' He led her to the door. 'My sympathies,' he added, drily.

The rose bushes, planted just after the December honeymoon, were unfurling their petals of salmon pink, yellow and white, reaching towards the hot May sun. Carla clipped a few tight buds and carried them off to a guest room she had transformed into a nursery. Refusing Emily's offer to be with her in this traumatic period, she had shut herself in the only room which did not breathe his presence, which did not have scattered reminders of the first marchesa, her sons' toys saved from childhood, the presence of generations of della Robbias. Emily understood. She had arrived shortly after Maurizio's death with a removal van containing a few things from Carla's childhood, her piano and her favourite books, to make the nursery into a homely place. It would help take her mind off it all, to make a little nest for herself. Then she could face up to the funeral.

Her daughter was pale, her eyes shadowed. She had not even bothered to dress, wandering listlessly round the room in the peach négligé they had chosen together in Via Montenapoleone. Emily took her in her arms and kissed the matted curls.

'My poor girl. You cry, darling. It's better to cry. I want you to lean on me. Be a little girl, if you want. You sure you don't want to come home? Stay in bed for a while?'

'I've got to be here, Ma.'

'Then I'll stay.'

'No need. How's Pa?'

'Don't worry, he'll fly back from Chicago.'

'I want to get away. I can't bear all his things around. What do I do about the clothes? Could I give them to a

285

charity shop, Ma? There's cupboards full of suits and stuff.'

'My poor girl.' Emily found herself staring at the lace-frilled cot in the corner, and then she rushed over to the window. Mastering her tears, she turned round to face Carla. 'I think we should take that out of here, don't you?'

'Oh, the cot.' Carla sniffed and put a handkerchief to her nose. 'I'm giving that to the children's home. Someone's coming to collect it. I forgot.'

'You shouldn't have to think of these things, Carla.'

'His sons came over to pay a visit. Make sure I do everything right. You know what? They've got some idea he wanted to be embalmed. Isn't that creepy? So everyone can pass by the coffin and say, oh yeh, that's the marchese, he really is dead. Jesus, it's sick. Then they'll stick him in the family vault until the next one comes along. Well, I tell you, Ma, it won't be me.'

'When you marry nobility,' Emily said solemnly, 'you take on their culture. I guess you'll have to go along with it for a while. It's no different from those guys in California who have themselves frozen. Shall we take a walk? Why don't you put on some clothes, show me the garden? Then I should go. But I'll stay if you like.'

'I'm fine, Ma. Maybe I should go take a shower. Wash my hair.'

'That's right. Don't you neglect yourself, darling. He wouldn't have wanted that.'

In his study, Maurizio's desk was just as he had left it, correspondence neatly piled up under a paperweight waiting for his attention, the financial daily *24 Ore* still in its folds, unread. Carla swept everything off into the waste basket and extracted the wedding guest list which she had kept in his bottom drawer. Some of the names had small ticks, the ones whose wedding presents he had acknowledged, his friends. Her friends were on a separate page. She would know whom to ask and whom not to ask. What better way of delivering a snub than to cross a few off the invitation list? She hadn't forgotten those relics of grand families who had made their disapproval clear at the wedding reception, barely acknowledging her.

Then she changed her mind. They would all come. Everybody would come, her friends from Milan, the poor dear children who would gargle and shriek during the priest's oration. Even Rico. Black would become him. Why not invite him to sing? Something by Puccini. Then, afterwards, she would take off the grey Krizia dress, not the black Versace – black was for cocktails – and she would let him fuck her until stars danced in her eyes. In that great, unyielding, cold marriage bed, the sheets would be slippery with sweat and come, and when they awoke, she would summon Roberto for some chilled champagne. Wasn't it fashionable to turn funerals into a celebration of life?

Ettore, Alessandro and Claudio della Robbia refused to give any sign of the outrage choking their throats as their beloved father went to his rest surrounded by cacophonous mayhem. As Carla stepped into the landau, they gave her a cursory bow, saluted their father for the last time and drove off in the opposite direction. They would only need to meet this disgraceful woman, who had seduced their father in his dotage, on one more occasion. Avvocato Federico Mugnoni had assured them that there was no cause for disappointment and that the honour of the family would be preserved.

'Maurizio has been as generous as I thought he would be,' was the only opinion Carla voiced when the lawyer had finished enumerating the paragraphs and subparagraphs of the many-paged document legitimized as his final will. She assured the family that she would take good care of the villa and the gardens, and would continue to live in the modest style to which she and Maurizio had been accustomed. They shook hands frostily, their only consolation being that after Carla's death, the inheritance would revert to its rightful owners.

The Marchesa della Robbia would retain her title, the

villa, and lands comprising the residential estate. She would retain the jewels given her by her husband. However, in the event that his death should take place without issue (if issue there was, it would be verified as a della Robbia by medical tests), certain conditions would prevail. The executors of the will, Alessandro, Ettore and Claudio della Robbia, the marchese's sons by his first marriage, would be responsible for the upkeep and maintenance of the farms, vineyards and agricultural lands still remaining. A monthly allowance would be paid to the present marchesa during her lifetime. However, in the event of her re-marriage, she would forfeit any claims.

Carla shut herself in the nursery to gather her thoughts. The allowance he had made her was scarcely sufficient for a pair of gloves. Living on the budget of a schoolteacher? It was unthinkable. And who would feel pity for a marchesa down on her luck, joining the rest of the moaning, impoverished aristocracy? Who would want to marry a girl with nothing except a house his children would never inherit?

'You mean, shitty old bastard!' she said aloud, as she knocked back a second bottle of vintage champagne she had unearthed from the cellar.

The following day, Carla paid a last visit to the della Robbia resting place in the vaults beneath the Chiesa di San Pietro. Through the glass, she could see Maurizio resting in his drawer, waxily peaceful, his eyes for ever open, gazing up at her through the glass, dressed in his wedding suit. Even the red carnation in his lapel was preserved.

'You just wait, darling,' she whispered. 'Sleep well.'

Before he died, he had left her no words of love or hate, nothing except that lifeless remnant of the embalmer's art.

Carla found herself a table in the sun at the café on the corner of the square, tilting her face to receive its warmth. (Maurizio always sat in the shade.) The owner of the café greeted her with a pitying smile, and hastened to put up the umbrella, but she waved him aside. The young mothers, the old men sitting around her, stared with a mixture of curiosity and disapproval, as they stared at rich tourists. She felt like a stranger who would never be accepted. However long she stayed, however many times they saw her crossing the square, they would be waiting for her to leave, the upstart foreigner who had trapped their marchese. Maurizio must have known that she would never stay. She could still hear his courteous, dry voice. 'Carla darling. You are free now to do as you please.'

On her return to the villa, Carla informed the butler, the cook and the gardener that she was taking a world cruise, to get over the pain, the sorrow of losing her husband. Regrettably, she would have to dismiss them, for she had no idea when she would return. When the butler asked if he could stay, even unpaid, she shook her head. It was impossible. The builders would be coming in. There was much to do; the place hadn't been touched for years. The gossip spread round the village. Pino, the local taxi driver who had taken the grief-stricken trio to the station, held court at the bar. Hadn't everyone suspected she was rotten through and through? Sending them off with only a month's wages, which hadn't gone up for twenty years? And they'd seen her on the very day of the funeral, laughing over dinner with that actor who sings in the olive oil commercial. And he'd never even set foot in the guest room, either.

Carla called in an emergency locksmith from Milan, to bolt and bar every window, every door, in the villa. The garden would grow wild, the shape of the flower-beds and the rockery would be lost in a tangle of weeds, the paint would peel, the roof would leak. And no one could stop her.

'I'm selling a little jewellery. We've had so many break-ins they won't insure it,' Carla told the dumb-struck assistant in Mauro Bruccoli's antique shop. And she would only take cash. 'I'm sure you're used to it. We all have to sell our treasures now. It's to mend the roof. You know what contractors are. So tremendously greedy. Do take my card.'

The grey Krizia ensemble, the flashing jewels about her person, were identity enough. They studied the settings, then took the diamonds, rubies and emeralds into a safe, and placed the notes discreetly in her Gucci briefcase at the back of the shop.

The last phone call Carla made was to her mother. She decided against telling Emily that Maurizio had changed his will. She would want to know why.

'At least you're provided for, darling. Now you'll be able to transform that gloomy old place. It'll be the finest home in Italy. You really must keep yourself busy.'

'I know, Ma.' She paused for a moment. 'That's why I've decided to take a break in London. Julian's been so kind, he says I can stay. And he's away so often, it'll be like having a place of my own.'

'That's not a good idea, darling,' said Emily. 'You know he's not welcome any more, not after the way he behaved to Beatrice.'

Forgetting to maintain the subdued tones of mourning, Carla jumped to Julian's defence. 'Jesus. What about the way she behaved? He only had to look at another girl and she went ape-shit. It's her fault for being so possessive. Julian's a fun guy. She should grow up.'

'She is growing up,' replied Emily tartly. 'If Julian wishes to see my husband, fine, but I don't want him hanging around my daughters.'

'He's not that bad really,' said Carla, twisting the ancient, knotted flex of Maurizio's telephone round her finger. No one on the board of the Opera Palace with a roomy apartment in London could be that bad.

'It would be so much better to stay in a hotel, especially so soon after the funeral.' Emily realized she might be overplaying the omnipotent mother-role. Dr Mainz had warned her. She lowered her voice to a warmer tone. 'You know how people gossip, darling. Don't forget, you have a position to maintain. And the British do expect decorum.'

'Sure. But I'm still in a state of shock, Ma. I'm hardly likely to party all night.'

'I know, darling.' Emily was beginning to sound more reasonable, so Carla began to expand her imaginary itinerary.

'I just want to walk around the streets, visit those amazing markets, take in a few galleries, do quiet, normal things. See a couple of friends, maybe.'

'How long will you be away? The children will miss you.'

Carla held the receiver under her chin, pushed up her skirt, and proceeded to examine her thighs. Too much cellulite. That's what happened, once you stopped clubbing and having a good time. She'd diet in England; easy with that godawful bread and pastry pies they ate all the time. 'The children?'

'At the home.'

'Oh yes, the children. I haven't forgotten. Isn't it called Hamley, that toyshop in Regent Street? I'll be away maybe a couple of weeks. Give you a call from London.'

Julian Lieberman had moved from Kensington to Docklands when everyone else was escaping in the opposite direction. It was not where she had expected him to live, not in this dark street in an industrial neighbourhood, unless it had suddenly become fashionable to be within a stone's throw of Tower Bridge. She could not imagine why. How ugly, she thought as she pressed the small bell and peered through the glass at the bare foyer in Concordia Wharf.

'I'm here. What shall I do with the car?'

'Wait. I'm coming.'

Julian looked in amazement at the hulking grey Bentley, now dusty and dented, packed with cases and boxes. 'Where did you get this old thing?'

'It was Maurizio's. I like to be reminded of him. He used to sit in the back and tap Peppe on the shoulder to make him drive more slowly. Do help me unload.'

291

'Where's the manservant?' he asked. 'Doesn't he come with the luggage?'

'Too old, poor dear. He had to stay behind.'

'I'm glad to see you're not too mournful,' said Julian as he pushed open the door. 'Was it absolutely dreadful? Are you aching inside? Do cry on my shoulder, but not over dinner, if you don't mind. Saffron's cooking Japanese tonight. Or rather she's reheating something chilled from Marks & Spencer.'

Carla dropped a case at Julian's feet, more violently than she intended. 'Is Saffron living here?'

Julian grinned. 'So to speak.' He glanced at the back seat and the open boot of Carla's Bentley, still crammed with luggage. 'What have you got in there? The della Robbia silver? Pocket fold-up missiles? Never mind, I'll find a trolley from the porter. Go up, I'm on the sixth floor.'

Carla was impressed. You didn't expect Englishmen to understand about decor, but Julian's place had the kind of style which could have come from Milan. An expanse of wooden floor, white screens, black lacquered furniture, a small fountain bubbling into a pool where pink-tinged water-lilies floated, low white calico beds, rounded porcelain pots and a panorama of windows edged with trailing leafy tendrils. Below, the inky waves of the surging tide swept past the shining mud-flats of the bank.

Carla subsided onto a large, down-filled cushion, pulled off her shoes and waited for Julian to reappear.

'Well, Carla? Does it pass the design test? Saffron's ideas, not mine. The set from *Butterfly* came in useful, too. What's the point in paying for storage space?'

Carla shifted onto her side as he came and sprawled across a silk rug. 'Tell me about you and Saffron,' she said.

'How about a drink?'

Carla grinned. He hadn't changed much. Whenever Julian was questioned about his emotions, he either briskly changed the subject or gravitated towards the nearest bottle. 'Later. Listen, I just wanted to say I never thought you and Beatrice were right together.'

Julian was reluctant to pursue the topic, but as Carla said nothing more and appeared to expect a comment, he relented. 'One is always ashamed when one behaves badly. How is the dear girl? I do hope she's found someone more suitable.'

'Oh, she finds plenty of guys to hang out with,' replied Carla. 'She moped around for a while but now she's OK. Doing a recital tour some place.'

'Shame you missed *Butterfly*.' Julian rose to his feet and headed towards a glass table laden with various bottles. 'Gin and tonic? Ice and lemon?'

Carla nodded enthusiastically. 'I do so love England. Do you think I could pick up something here? Just to get back? You know how it is when you haven't sung for a while.'

'One can imagine,' he said, coming to her side with a large glass. 'By the way, Sir Miles will be dropping in for supper later on.'

'Oh, Julian, that's fantastic. You are a darling. Do you think I could mention that I'm singing again?'

'I wouldn't,' he replied tersely. 'Sir Miles won't give you a part. He's still intent on buying Stasi Wagner for the next season. But once he sees you're serious, I'm sure he'll give you a few introductions.'

Carla leaped to her feet. 'I'd better change.' She looked down sulkily at her crumpled shirt and jeans. 'I've only brought boring clothes. Maurizio wouldn't let me buy anything. He didn't even notice . . .' Her anguished lament drew no response from Julian, who was sucking at the lemon he had removed from his glass.

'Have a look in the wardrobe in my bedroom. Second door on the right through there,' he said, pointing to a black lacquered door at the end of the room. 'I'm sure you'll find an amusing something.'

A few minutes later, Carla danced barefooted down the

corridor in a short multicoloured kimono. 'How about this? Do you think he'll like it?'

'Inordinately sexy.'

'You don't think it'll put him off? I don't want to be too outfront. I know it's different over here.'

'Not that different,' replied Julian.

'He-ll-o,' sang out Saffron. 'Has the gorgeous marchesa arrived?' She came breathlessly into the room, laden with Marks & Spencer bags.

'Hi, Saffron.'

'Darling Carla. We'll make absolutely sure you're not lonely and sad. How terrible for you. But you do look gorgeous. I always said you needed tits to wear a kimono.'

'I've just driven from Italy.'

'With bare feet, I hope.' Saffron gave her a welcoming hug. 'We're so pleased to have you here. We're eating Japanese. I do hope you don't mind. Julian, you're good at reading instructions. Give Carla something to drink and come to the kitchen.'

A sheaf of salad leaves was hurled into the sink, and Saffron lined up a row of unusual oils and flavoured vinegars. Green salads, the unvarying beginning to a meal, were her speciality and, besides, they cleansed the system. On a blackboard hanging over the stainless steel burner range, she wrote down a plan of campaign, according to the requirements of each dish: oven temperature, shelf position, and timing. Although her principle skill lay in making a superb emulsion for the salad, Saffron understood the principles of cooking, even though she did not cook. Her neatness, planning and organization would have been the envy of a professional kitchen.

'I'll have to think of someone for Carla,' she said, as she pounded a thick bud of garlic in a mortar. 'It's the best way to get over a funeral. Poor thing. She couldn't have had much fun with that old stick. Didn't he collapse at the wedding or something? I was so drunk, I can't even remember what I wore. I do remember Anastasia's little tantrum, though.'

'You'll be pleased to hear I wrote her a grovelling letter afterwards. Fairly grovelling, anyway.' Julian scraped the garlic carefully into a bowl, and began to dry the salad leaves in a towel, one by one. 'Carla could do with a break. Emily pushed her into that marriage. Anything to stop her going on stage.'

'Doesn't she want her daughter to succeed? Most unusual for an American mother.'

'Emily Johnson was once a fairly well-known opera singer. In America, at least.'

'Ah, rivalry,' said Saffron, pulling out the china plates. 'Isn't it absolutely dreadful when mothers are jealous of their daughters?'

'Worse than that,' said Julian. 'Emily Johnson was playing in Philadelphia once and they booed her off the stage. She never recovered. When she met Paolo Livorno, she turned her shame into a tragedy. She told him she'd lost her voice overnight and would never sing again.'

'How do you know?'

'It's the kind of gossip you pick up. If you're interested in opera.'

Saffron began to measure out her various oils with the precision of an industrial chemist, prolonging the task until Julian volunteered more information. She suspected that he had some kind of plan for Carla. Why else would he have invited her to stay?

'I've been thinking,' he began, at which point Saffron looked up to give him her attention. 'I thought Carla's particular talent might fit in rather well at the Maison Blanche. Useful to have around.'

'A little too much weight on the thighs, I would guess,' Saffron remarked, as she set about beating the oil. 'But we can change that.'

Julian shrugged. A minor detail. 'We could introduce her to a few people first. Andrew Broughton, for example. I'd like him to take a more positive attitude to the Opera Palace. A small government grant would give us the prestige we need at the moment.'

'And Sir Miles?' Saffron said, with a meaningful smile.

'I doubt if she'd have much success with him.' Julian held up some packets of daikon, shirataki and wakame. 'What do we do now?'

'Open them. Shall we have nasturtium flowers in the salad?'

'Charming idea.'

'Taste this.'

Julian swirled the thick dressing around his tongue, and licked his lips. 'Mm. A little lemon?'

'Lemon? Honestly! We're not having fish and chips.'

As Saffron piled the cutlery and plates neatly on a tray, she remembered something she ought, really, to ask. 'What's her voice like?'

'I've never heard her,' he replied, as she handed over the tray.

Sir Miles had not yet reached the stage where he dared go sufficiently native to sit cross-legged on a floor cushion, but he had taken off his shoes and was lying on his side on the calico couch. Being without shoes for dinner gave him an extraordinary feeling of liberation.

'Do take off your jacket,' suggested Carla, crouching on the floor in Julian's short silk kimono, pouring out fragrant tea into tiny, translucent cups. He was looking down at her smooth, brown legs, her delicate feet with their tiny silver-painted toenails. 'If you'd feel more comfortable, that is.' She handed him a scented towel.

'Coming here is so wonderfully civilized,' he said, looking into her comforting, grey-green eyes. 'Especially when I've had to spend most of the day worrying about the type of carpet in the star dressing rooms. They took a little piece of it off for fibre analysis. Can you believe it? One of the singers complained that it provoked an allergy. He's trying to sue.'

'The only thing which used to bother me was dust,' began Carla, but Julian gave her a warning glance.

'Have you been singing in Italy since we last met?' Sir Miles enquired, politely.

He remembered every minute of their brief meeting in Milan. Still a pretty little thing, but much quieter now. Easier to cope with. Then she was trying too hard, nervous. He might possibly have auditioned her for *Butterfly*. He would bear her in mind for the future, watch her progress. She might do well in some light-hearted Christmas show.

'Carla has become awfully grand,' Julian said, with the slight drawl he affected when indicating the opinion of the masses. 'She's the Marchesa della Robbia. But she adores England – especially London.'

'My best friends are here,' added Carla, smiling at Saffron.

'And do you still see that rather good English singer – wasn't she a friend of yours? You know who I mean.'

'Anastasia?' Carla kept the remnant of her smile and continued, unconsciously adopting Saffron's accent. 'I believe she's singing in France. Our lives are rather different now. It's so difficult to keep in touch. I know I shouldn't say this, but I do get bored only talking about opera. And that's all singers talk about, as though no other world existed.'

'Does your husband like opera?'

'We go to La Scala occasionally,' replied Carla dismissively. She had found herself using the present tense out of habit. On reflection, the marchese might be more valuable alive than dead. Julian hadn't interrupted; perhaps he was thinking the same. Talking of your late husband was acceptable for old ladies. To mention it now would be like bringing up the subject of famine in the third world over dinner at Le Gavroche.

Sir Miles accepted a thimbleful of saké, which seemed more potent than he remembered it during his stays in Tokyo and Osaka. Saffron took over the conversation, surprised to find that he had never been proposed as a member of the Maison Blanche, had never been invited there by anyone, and had never heard of it.

'What happens there exactly?' he asked. 'Is it something like a modern version of the Garrick?'

'There are some similarities. But it's much smaller, more intimate. I've tried to recreate a vivid feeling of the past. One hasn't the advantage of that wonderful staircase.'

'Saffron tells me that Andrew Broughton has recently joined. It might be useful for you to drop in. Meet in a friendly atmosphere.'

'You're welcome at any time,' smiled Saffron. 'Just let Julian know when you're coming.'

'Can one dine there?' he enquired.

'Sandwiches at the bar, that's all, I'm afraid. But there's a thought! The Maison Blanche Dining Club.' She looked first at Sir Miles, then at Julian. 'What a super idea. How clever of you to think of it.'

'Judging by this dinner – better than I had in Japan, by the way – I would be the first to attend.'

It was difficult to take his eyes off Carla. Her kimono had slipped open and she seemed unaware of her spreading cleavage. He was confused, and began to imagine her breasts encased in a tight bodice, one with sticky rubber buttons like Moira's. Julian and Saffron were rocking with laughter, inventing Rabelaisian feasts, contorting themselves recalling shared memories so that he felt like an intruder. Julian must have been a hero at school. You could see it: that square-jawed face, the wide cheeks, that determined mouth, the mop of dark hair; you could imagine him charging into the fray on the rugby pitch, making the boys laugh in the changing rooms, clever, witty Lieberman, good at sports, good with girls, top marks without being a swot, getting away with everything, chosen to read his essay in class, knowing the answers. Big shot Lieberman. Moira would have taken him into her bed. Like a shot. Mackenzie, you're a quiet one. 'Come on, Bumbles, open up your tuck box. Let's see what you're hiding in there, you mean Scottish geek.

Come on then, sock it to us, or we'll tape your cock up to your arse.'

'I'd better get back. Could you call a cab?'

Carla rose to her feet. 'Do you have to go? Don't forget your shoes.'

'Cabs take for ever round here,' said Julian. 'I'm sure Carla can drop you home. As long as you show her how to get to Marylebone.'

'Oh, I know that, Julian. I have been in London before.'

Before Sir Miles could object, Carla ran to her room, found a silk quilted jacket and a pair of satin pumps, and presented herself at the front door. 'You ready, Sir Miles?'

'Are you quite sure? That's most kind.'

During the drive from SE1 to W1, the realization dawned on Carla that this serious man sitting beside her presented a greater challenge than she had given him credit for. It intrigued her that he never looked into her eyes for longer than a second, that he spoke as though addressing a distant audience, that he was so self-contained. She could not imagine him as a child. He was like Julian. How did the British manage it, this aloof, impenetrable layer with which they distanced themselves from women? She wanted to prise his secret out of him. Would he suddenly fling himself upon her, rip off her clothes in the safety of his home? Would it be a slow seduction with dimmed lights and low music, a whispered suggestion to retire to the bedroom? For once, she had no idea.

He pointed out a block of red-brick flats with an ungracious entrance. 'You can drop me here.'

Carla slowly applied the brakes of her Bentley. 'Would it be awful of me to ask if I could have a cup of coffee? Only I did drive from France and it's beginning to hit me. This big old car is so exhausting, you wouldn't believe.'

When she was sitting in his small flat with her knees together like a bright-eyed bird waiting for a crumb, she tried to find a clue to penetrate his reserve. There were

framed opera posters and stage designs, unpeopled landscapes in oil, two leather Chesterfield sofas, two
armchairs, all neatly placed, an unstained mushroom
carpet and a photograph of schoolboys in uniform. The
only thing which enlivened the stuffy, overheated room
was a large tropical fish tank, brightly lit, with bubbles
breaking on the surface. Between waving fronds, tropical
fish with strange heads and filmy tails darted and posed.
One of those English hobbies, she supposed.

She didn't mind what he did, even if he did nothing.
She wanted to see his clothes lying in a disordered heap on
the ground, she wanted to grasp his thighs and feel his
cock between her breasts, she wanted him naked, like
stripping a picture from its frame. That was all. Then she
would be the envy of every opera singer who had shone on
that great stage. It was not simple desire, which gathered
energy, roared up and died away, running the predictable
slow-fast-slow like Rico's lunges, the straightforward
thirst-quenching Italian lust she knew so well. This was
something far more challenging.

He was standing awkwardly in front of her, wondering
whether he had any coffee left. When he came over to her,
she barely reached his shoulder.

'Ah. You've found my fish tank. Beautiful. Or perhaps
you think keeping living creatures in a confined space is
cruel. Many people do.'

'Oh no. You can see those fish are happy.' She smiled
and tapped the glass.

He did not move, bewildered and embarrassed, as
though he had come in late and the overture had already
begun. Was he determined to deny that he found her
attractive? Was he going to stand there all night?

'Miles. Won't you sit down?'

'Where?' he asked in a startled voice.

Carla pointed at the buttoned, leather Chesterfield sofa.
'There.'

'Won't Julian mind?'

Carla let out a peal of laughter. 'Julian? We've known

each other so long, I can't see what girls see in him. Just good chums. Isn't that how they say it here?'

'I'm not used to this,' he said, as he attempted to lean against the hard back. 'I'm not much good at it, you see. I don't want to disappoint you. One out of ten, I'm afraid.'

'Why are you afraid?' Carla stroked his face, nestling against him. He cleared his throat, and took her hand.

'It only needs a girl to tell you once that you're not up to scratch. And one fails to rise to the occasion.'

'I don't give scores,' she said. 'Kiss me.'

She felt his tight lips parting a little, unwilling. She pushed her tongue onto his, but he drew away his face, mouth closed like a vice.

'Open, come on, good boy, open.' She teased open his mouth and he suddenly thrust his tongue around hers, then pushed it down her throat, leaving her breathless.

'My God, that was wonderful. How did it happen?' he murmured, reeling back. Carla adjusted her kimono. He had not even realized he was pressing against her bare flesh. She picked up her jacket from the floor.

'If you're nice to me, we can do it again,' she said, sucking at her aching jaw.

'I'll always be nice to you.'

'Carla. Say it, Miles.'

'Carla.'

'Oh, you make me feel so grand when you say it. Now say I'm beautiful, that you'll dream about me all night. You must see so many fantastic girls.'

'Not really.'

'Longing to get you into bed. All those great singers. Thinking themselves lucky they even got to see you.'

'I hope I don't abuse my position. I try not to.'

'But you get tempted. Any man gets tempted.'

'I suppose I do.'

'Do you know what every singer dreams of, who comes to your office, waiting for the door to open, trembling like crazy when the secretary says, "Sir Miles is ready to see you."?'

He thought for a moment, then moved his lips slightly. He rarely smiled. 'I've no idea. That I'll choose her, I suppose. That I'll go down on my knees and say, "You're the next Maria Callas."'

'Miles. You're impossible.'

'What was I meant to say?'

Carla ran her fingers down his thighs and whispered, 'She won't admit it. She'll bend her head, like this, so you won't see her looking down. She'll be dreaming that you'll come down her throat.'

He stared at her, mesmerized by the glistening grey-green eyes, the half open lips parted over small, even teeth.

'You can still go down on your knees but you don't have to say I'm the next Maria Callas.'

Carla allowed him to pull the kimono off her shoulders. He buried his face in her breasts and abandoned himself to the caresses of her silky hand. She clutched his cock and, on hearing her unexpected command, he came when she ordered it, spilling over between her lips, heaving with shame. Then he got up from the floor with an effort.

'I don't normally do this. I was overcome.'

'Get dressed. There's no need to say anything. Oh, Miles, I feel just like someone's taken me to the moon.'

'Really?'

'You think I do this with everyone?'

'Indeed I don't. I can't think what happened.'

She began to button up his shirt, licked round the aperture of his ear, then whispered, 'I don't even let my husband do that.'

He put on his jacket, and replaced his tie. 'I'd appreciate it if . . . I don't want to sound pernickety . . .'

She was holding the door handle, about to go.

'. . . you didn't mention it to anybody.'

Carla laughed. 'Of course not.' She kissed his cheek then looked up at him. 'Anyway, we didn't even fuck.'

'Will I see you again?' he called towards the lift, but the doors had already closed.

Chapter Twelve

It had been nearly eighteen months since Sir Miles had sat uncomfortably at the Salle des Arts Modernes, informed by Julian Lieberman that the young soprano, that unforgettable Micaela, was stunning Paris audiences in *La Traviata*.

Seeing her for a second time, in *Manon* confirmed his first impression. She had an hauteur, her movements were both unexpected and graceful, and she had the kind of voice which you could hear in your head months later. He could not remember other singers with the clarity with which he could summon up Anastasia Wagner. When he thought of all the productions, all the singers he had seen that year, in Europe, America, even Australia, there was no one with that strange, dazzling voice, not the conventional bel canto in which she had been trained, but something more expressive, more daring. You never quite knew what she might do next.

When Anastasia turned down his offer to sing in *Madam Butterfly*, he had been surprised and hurt. He wondered why every girl he had longed for had turned her back on him. At his first charity ball in Edinburgh, a girl with dark flashing eyes and a pale green taffeta dress, who had been dancing all evening with unflagging energy in the arms of what he considered to be unsuitable partners, turned to him and said, 'Terribly sorry. I'm too tired.' Anastasia had the same expressions: arrogance one moment, uncertainty the next. He had thought about this tall, enigmatic girl more than he would admit, least of all to Carla.

Throughout his life, intimacy had led to nothing but disaster. The close attentions of women quickly turned to contempt. His fiancée ran away with his best friend a week before the wedding. The flaming Highland sunsets, their rhapsodies of love, had counted for nothing. Perhaps a girl like Carla was all he deserved.

But he still dreamed of being alone with Anastasia on some remote Scottish island, hearing the crash of the sea and the shrieking gulls. Anastasia was timeless, unaffected by the transient moods of fashion. He would have written her passionate letters, thrown himself on his knees in front of her, braving her ridicule, just to confess his adoration. It was allowed at sixteen, laughable at forty-two. Nobody was likely to penetrate the turbulence which lay behind his deep-set intelligent eyes, and he considered himself fortunate in having a face in which feeling was so successfully masked.

Not even the sharp Lieberman, who could detect an imminent change of mind, a change of heart in the space of half a syllable, could fathom the drift of his emotions. Yet it was he who had set his heart racing again. One morning, he had placed a German opera magazine on his desk, with two pages clipped together and a note: 'Thought this might be of interest.'

He read the German text with disgust. Some opera critic inflating his ego with a messianic portrait of a director he would never dream of employing. Sheer idolatry. As though Dominic Morrison could possibly be the new Piscator, the new Visconti, the new Peter Brook, this American who stripped opera to the bone and re-dressed it in the lurid garments of sensationalism. There were other ways of attracting large audiences, he could prove it.

He had put on two 'spellbindingly original productions', Delibes' *Lakmé* in Paris, *Sadko* in Amsterdam. Morrison confessed to pursuing the *'magischer realismus'* a new and exciting direction in his operatic career. Ambitious directors, came the sour thought, liked making their name by pumping up obscure operas into 'rediscoveries'.

Then, later in the article, he saw her name, underlined.

A quote. 'No, why should he be a Svengali? I've never thought of him like that. It just so happens that we think the same way about important things. People are surprised that we can work together all the time. How can I put it? I believe he is like someone creating a mirage in the desert. That's what opera is for me: a shimmering mirage in the desert.'

Swiftly skimming through, he found what he was looking for. 'When she returns to Paris, Anastasia Wagner will be spending a couple of months at their home for a well-deserved rest before commencing Gluck's *Orfeo*, in a new hitherto unknown version which Morrison will produce later this year.'

Taking out his diary, he made a note to contact her. Was it this week that he had been invited to Saffron's new dining club? No, the following one, pencilled in, in case of a crisis. Carla, fortunately, had landed herself a part in some musical and was taking it all very seriously. Dancing lessons, voice lessons, even trying to lose her American accent. Her voice was developing well, but she still had some way to go before he would even consider giving her a part like Mařenka in *The Bartered Bride*. No, not even Musetta. In spite of her pleading and tantrums, he refused to give way.

Taking her to bed (or had she taken him?) had changed everything. Why did he continue? She was married. Irate husbands had a habit of turning up at inconvenient moments, though Carla assured him it would never happen. She and the marchese respected one another, but led separate lives. Divorce, she said, was such a terrible drama in Italy. She had her freedom, so what did it matter?

The freedom to discover the filthy black mud lying beneath the clear waters of his calm exterior? Only one other person had dived down to those fetid depths. Willoughby. Even at fourteen, he had understood too much, had found a way of forcing him to do his Latin homework.

He had never thought it would last more than a few weeks. There was too much about her which jarred: her continuous chatter, the way she bullied him and distracted him from important matters. But he had grown used to her, as you did with mistresses. Carla reminded him sometimes of the tart he used to visit off Windmill Street, a French girl from the Pyrenees. Same hair, same smile, similar perfume. The only girl who could make him lose his mind in bed, who could recapture the wild excitement of boyhood, the delirious and illicit desire unleashed by Moira, the round-breasted, flaming-haired matron at his public school.

Carla was beginning to take him for granted. He didn't like her staying overnight and leaving her corset, suspenders, filmy black stockings, and toys in his underwear drawer where the cleaning woman could find them. They were now meeting about twice a week. She might even think he was getting serious. What if she was the deliciously pretty daughter of Paolo Livorno, and a reasonably talented singer? He could never fall in love with a girl who reminded him of a tart. If only Anastasia had given him some encouragement instead of throwing herself at that American. He would try again.

'Where were we? Barcelona. Yes, Spain. Pesetas. We're going back to Paris. Are we up yet? Look, my magazine's fallen on the floor. I can't find my diary. I can't breathe. I feel sick.'

Stasi averted her eyes from the window as the ground careered out of reach below her, and clutched at Dominic's hand. She had lost count of the fearful take-offs and landings when, eyes tightly shut, she waited to be shattered in fragments should the plane either fail to rise or fall like a dead duck out of the sky. Did Daddy fall down screaming? As they bumped down at Orly airport, she sat tightly strapped, and the secondary fear took over – that the plane would overshoot the runway and burst into flames. As the plane taxied to a halt, she wanted to thank

God for delivering her safely, like the Italian peasants who crossed themselves and clapped with every landing. At last, there would be a few weeks of rest and no airports. Since *Manon,* she had sung in Lyons, Brussels, Amsterdam and Barcelona.

Working with Dominic was a constant challenge. He had edged her into the abyss of personal discovery. Through him, she learned to acquire the layers of understanding culled from Jung, Freud, mystic poets, surreal painters. He unblocked her mind, opened her senses. She no longer felt stupid. She now knew that she deserved the adulation, night upon night of faces illumined by what she had given them, roaring out their thanks. She had come to accept it as her due. The opera houses of Europe had welcomed them, but she was still dissatisfied.

When they reached Paris, she opened a letter from Sir Miles.

'He wants to see me, Dominic.'

'Why not?'

'We won't work at the Opera Palace unless everything's changed. And you must have artistic control.'

Sir Miles arrived at the flat in the Boulevard St Germain promptly at twelve thirty. Anastasia had sounded welcoming and confident on the telephone, and she had insisted on making him lunch. He noticed the worn carpet, the large room in need of redecoration, and the pictures round the walls which would have no place in a Bond Street gallery. There was no sign here of the fabled opulence of the top class singer. He had yet to meet one who failed to display her success on the walls, on her body. She was wearing tight black jeans and a full, flowing white shirt, a wide belt clutching at her diminutive waist, dark hair pinned back showing the fine line of her chin, that long neck like an Etruscan queen.

He directed his attention at Dominic, only occasionally looking into her dark, languid eyes in case, for an instant, he might give way with some softness inappropriate to the occasion. Together, she and Morrison had that easy intimacy which he couldn't help noticing: the way she touched his shoulder as she went to fetch something. It was as if he had stolen her from him and was flaunting it, but he had no right to think like that. Two men and one woman, two women and one man, it was the stuff of opera. She might eventually tire of this obsessive American. The plot could always move on.

They had finished lunch. He had listened to them both, contributing little.

'We're rather out of touch with England,' began Dominic. 'But you've probably heard the gossip. Some of it's true. Did you see that piece in *The Times* a week ago?'

Stasi shook her head.

'The government is seriously thinking of withdrawing sponsorship from Covent Garden.'

'And are they selling Buckingham Palace and the Tower of London as well?' Stasi said indignantly. 'I'm glad I didn't pin my hopes on making it in England. Terrible. And the Opera Palace? What's going to happen there? What are they doing to you?'

'Fortunately, we've been able to attract substantial private finance. Some say we've drained it away from Covent Garden, but that's untrue. I think it's because we're run properly. May I be immodest?'

'Why not?' said Dominic. 'I keep telling Stasi it's not a sin to be positive.'

'I need to brush up my self-image,' replied Stasi, with a mocking smile at Sir Miles, who saw no reason for her to brush up anything.

'We've both read about the great things you're doing, Sir Miles,' continued Dominic, 'but we've been working so hard in Europe, we haven't had time to come over.'

Sir Miles was doing his best to control his loathing of this younger, unlined, easy-mannered American. He didn't need his praise. There was one consolation. Singers always performed better when they were happy. He cleared his throat.

'For our next season, we've decided to be more adventurous, so apart from the Verdi spectacular in the summer there'll be no Verdi and no Puccini next year.'

'You're so right. I couldn't live with those kinds of constraints,' said Dominic. 'I think we should perform operas which speak to us. Then the public follows.'

'I agree,' said Stasi. 'Why do singers always start by building a standard repertoire? It just perpetuates the same old warhorses. Do we really want another *Aida*, another *Bohème*? Do I just want to be remembered as a great Violetta? I respect my public too much for that.'

'Let's be honest,' said Dominic. 'In Europe, they'll come to see Stasi in anything. Packed houses. I guess you get spoilt. But we'd both love to face the challenge of a new audience.'

'Dominic's never been to England,' said Stasi, glancing at him affectionately.

Sir Miles put his hand over his mouth and lowered his head, aware of the difficulties he faced. It was a situation he had confronted before, the opera star who believed that only one man in the world held the key to unlock her talent. Unfortunately, Dominic Morrison was a director. It would have been easier if he had been her business manager, the more usual situation.

'In England, audiences are unpredictable. I never thought, for example, that *Zaïde* would be such a success.'

'*Zaïde*? At the Opera Palace? Why did you do it there?'

He neglected to tell her that this early Mozart opera had been a concert performance in the experimental hall of the Palace, which seated a mere two hundred.

'Do you object to Mozart? Or do you think this minor work should not have been attempted?'

'Of course not,' she replied.

'But you don't think of yourself as a Mozartean singer.'

She looked at Dominic. 'With the right production.'

'I was wondering if you might consider *Così fan tutte*.'

Sir Miles stayed another half hour, and apologized for

leaving with such haste, but the scenery for *Boris Godunov* had failed to arrive from St Petersburg, and the Russians were due to open the following week. He had no intention of having *Così fan tutte* performed in a spaceship, or whatever ludicrous location took Morrison's fancy. There was little chance she would accept.

As soon as Dominic heard the lift beginning its descent, he rushed over to Stasi. 'You know what this was all about? He needs you. My guess is, the Palace is in some kind of trouble. He thinks he'll pull back audiences with your name. He hasn't had one production which breaks new ground.'

'So why did you say that guff about a new challenge?' she retorted.

'Because I know you want to sing in England. You want the folks in your home town to adore you. Why not?'

Did she want to sing in *Così fan tutte*? If Dominic had suggested it as his next production she would have said yes. She longed for the cool clarity, the rippling cadences beginning and ending in elegant focus. Singing created its own appetite. Sometimes you wanted a disordered banquet, a feast of colour, and then you longed for an omelette and a glass of wine.

For the first time since she had been living with Dominic, Stasi began to think seriously of working on her own. It was difficult to know where his thoughts ended and hers began. They had become so used to constant interchange that Stasi sometimes wondered whether, if they were apart, her opinions might be different. When they argued over interpretation, he usually won. She had grown used to believing that he was right. If only Sir Miles had asked him to direct.

'Would you mind terribly if I accepted?' she asked later that afternoon.

'Mind? Why does "mind" come into it? If you want to sing Mozart, why not say so? We can talk about it. Just because it's not where I'm at right now, doesn't mean I'm not open to thinking about it. What's the problem?'

'You believe I could do it, though?'

'Who's the most versatile singer in the world?'

They laughed, but Stasi soon returned to the subject.

'Raymond keeps writing to say I should make up with Mum. I feel bad. Going to London would mean I could see her. Why does she still make me feel so awful?'

'Is that new, darling?'

'And we could do with the cash. Wouldn't it be nice to have somewhere, some little farmhouse in the hills? Or a new car?'

'Miss Wagner conquers the Philistines and seeks fame and fortune in her native land. Right?'

'No!'

'A little bit.'

'I can still do *Orfeo* in Hamburg first.'

'How long will *Così* take? Three months? Maybe it's not a bad idea.'

'You think we should be separated for a while?'

'Did I say that? If I thought we were getting on each other's nerves, and needed a break, I'd tell you. I'm being quite selfish. Once you've done a Palace Mozart, you'll come flying back to me. *Please, Dominic, I want to work properly again.*'

'Will you come over?'

'Of course. And I'll meet with your ma.'

'Never. If girls get like their mothers, you'll never want to see me again.'

How many opera houses could boast of engaging Paolo Livorno, Ruggiero Gasparini and the most exciting new soprano since Callas? Julian was jubilant when he heard of Sir Miles's coup, and even his tone-deaf partners in the Domination and Control Corporation couldn't fail to be impressed. He phoned Eddie in Las Vegas, told him that Stasi Wagner would be bigger than Streisand and that he had to come over to England to hear her.

'Great news, Jules. But you'd better get her over here. You know how it is. No one goes on vacation in Europe no more. Has she got stage-appeal? If she has, I can fly her out, arrange a spot in a charity gala.'

'She'd really love that. I'll mention it.'

'You coming out next month? Few things to tie up.'

'See you soon, Eddie.'

The only person who was likely to greet the news in sullen silence was Carla. She had refused to accept that the Palace had no plans to engage her, and she might take it badly. It would have been better if Anastasia was just a name to her, better if they had never met. In the end, he decided to bring it up casually, after Sunday lunch at home.

He had settled into the everyday life of a ménage à trois with Carla and Saffron. Or that's what the occasional dinner guest would assume. Sometimes Saffron invited him into their bedroom; it excited Carla when he watched them writhing together. He pretended to be aroused, but he felt nothing except curiosity as to what they would do next. All he did was to spray perfume on their bodies to mask the smell of rising female excitement he found so repulsive.

In other respects, the arrangement suited him perfectly. Relieved of the duties of the bedroom, there was no reason why the warring sexes should not live in friendly harmony. He was fortunate. How many men could fly first class round the world on business trips, weep at the opera and come home to two amusing, beautiful and undemanding girls? It had just happened, the arrangement which most men dreamed of as they gloated over page three lovelies in litter-ridden laundromats and take-away chippies. He came and went without complaints or recriminations, the fridge was always stocked, his dry-cleaning and laundry collected, his mail piled up neatly on his desk. Why did other men feel the need to poke at home?

He did bring it up, casually.

'Why didn't you tell me earlier? That my friend Stasi was coming to England? Mind you, I don't see her in Mozart. *Così fan tutte*? She's far too serious for Fiordiligi. Who's playing Dorabella?'

312

'Coffee, anyone?'

'You haven't told me, Julian,' said Carla petulantly. 'Who's playing Dorabella?'

'I think they've decided on Grace Walker,' he replied.

'Grace? Jesus. I was in class with her.'

'Sir Miles saw her in Sydney.'

'But there's hundreds of girls as good as her. And she isn't even British.'

Julian smiled. 'Sir Miles likes to support the Commonwealth. Haven't you noticed? Is there some coffee left?'

He collapsed onto a pile of cushions to finish reading the Sunday papers while Saffron went to the kitchen.

'Julian? Don't you ever help your friends?'

He replied to Carla's question without looking up. 'All the time.'

'What does that make me, then?'

'I respect you enormously, my dear.'

She was away for several hours, but Saffron knew she would come back. It was the one evening in the week which they kept for themselves, with no social engagements, no rehearsals and no telephone calls. She didn't ask her where she had been. Carla threw off her clothes and lay on Saffron's bed, leaning on her elbows, staring gloomily at the massed pillows. Saffron had had experience of Italian girls. They were spoilt, glutted with attention like the miniature poodles they dragged down the Via Veneto. All they needed was a little common sense and understanding.

'I'm not in the mood,' Carla mumbled.

'You must be in the mood for something. Would you rather I sucked? Or do you feel like Big Johnnie?' said Saffron cheerily. 'Or is it just Sunday blues?'

'I don't need a sex therapist. Cut it out, Saffron. Leave me alone.'

'What do you need, then?'

'Jesus! You know. Stop acting like a waitress in a Tex

Mex diner. Sit down and talk to me. Julian's a fucking arsehole.'

'What do you want me to do, darling?'

'You could have said something.'

Saffron sat beside her and stroked her hair. Carla hadn't got the message that Julian was uninterested in taking too much effort to promote her career.

'What if you do get a part in some boring opera at the Palace? Then you'll want something else. You've got a starring role in a West End musical which most girls would kill for.'

'I've only had one drippy profile. What d'you have to do in this country? In Italy, I'd be famous by now.'

'I think I've done rather well for you. Considering you arrived here a year ago as the Marchesa di Nowhere, darling. That didn't get you to dinner with the Duke of Westminster.'

'I said talk to me. Not lecture me. I wish you took me more seriously. I know I'm better than all those crappy English singers.'

'I know, darling. But that's not how they see it, those ghastly men on the board of the Opera Palace. Sad to say.'

'So how do I get to be big time?'

'By creating an opportunity to seize.'

Saffron covered her hands in perfumed oil, then worked her fingers down Carla's back, lingering down the parting of her buttocks. Usually she behaved like the golden retriever Saffron had cuddled as a child – as soon as she was touched, she would lean back her head and stretch out her neck, expecting endless caresses. This time she pushed away Saffron's hands.

'Come on. There must be some way of making Sir Miles see me differently. Couldn't you find out?'

'Isn't that precisely what you manage to do, Carla? Give him what he wants?'

'Maybe I shouldn't, then. Think I should go on strike?'

'Withdraw your labour? Heavens, no. Awfully non-productive.'

'OK. So what's productive?'

'I'm thinking.' Saffron gazed up at the ceiling, as though she was puzzling out some faded mural. 'One hesitates to suggest it. It sounds so awfully . . .' She paused, wondering what it was awfully. 'Guttery.'

'Guttery? What's that?'

'Absolutely a last resort, of course. But I suppose having a title, of some description, does make it more acceptable. We need to make you irresistible to people of taste and breeding and people with none. The right kind of publicity. I believe they call it blanket publicity.'

'Oh, yes?' Carla jumped out of bed and surveyed herself in the mirror. She knew exactly what Saffron meant. 'If I lose a few pounds, I could do it. I know a great photographer in New York. They banned his pictures. Opera pics in the nude? That kind of stuff?'

'Been done,' said Saffron. 'And, besides, you have to be intellectually stimulating. There's no point in being in the *Sun* if you don't appear in what Sir Miles reads over breakfast.'

'So what's the idea? What do I do?'

'The idea is to convince the Opera Palace that hiring a gorgeous girl with enough pulling power to fill every seat is a better idea than hiring an Australian girl with a face like a kangaroo.'

'What about Stasi Wagner? They've bought her pulling power. Isn't that why they've got her?'

'She's well-known in, where was it? Hamburg, I think Julian said.'

Saffron was so clever. Carla could feel the tingling prelude to sex rippling up and down her body. She faded the light to a crepuscular glow, and slipped her hands over her thighs.

The role of Eurydice, which she sang in Hamburg, would not be included in the authorized biography of Anastasia Wagner. She could only later define why she had been unhappy with Dominic's production, which had been the subject of lengthy interpretations in the German press. The German energy, the ordered traffic, the cleanliness, the hard-edged modern buildings, had made her uneasy, as much as she saw from the back of a Mercedes which transported them from the hotel to the theatre, from the theatre to the hotel. The opera singers, directors and critics she met at receptions wanted to devour her, asking her intricate questions which she was unable to answer. Had they really liked her? The audiences had been restrained, she thought, before she had learned that the rhythmic beating of hands, if continued, was a mark of generous appreciation.

At first hesitant, she came to accept Dominic's idea of setting the Greek myth in an Indian landscape, the nearest contemporary culture, he explained, which preserved the mythic celebration of life and death forgotten by the West. *Orfeo*, after all, was precisely that. She learned the snaky movements of the Indian dancer, but was unable to acquire the stark, angular purity of voice which Dominic demanded. Above all, she was unhappy with the singer he had chosen for Orfeo. Through an Indian poet, a friend of his, he had tracked down an Indian castrato from an outcast group south of Delhi. Rajit had a woman's beauty, and an extraordinary power of mimicry. She resented his unerring ability to draw attention to himself. He was half-way between a clown and a striptease artist, halfway between a woman and a man. Without understanding the music of Gluck, he could reproduce the emotion, tear the heartstrings with the unique timbre which no other singer could acquire. One night, her voice faltered and she took a clumsy breath in the wrong place.

'It's difficult for me,' she said emphatically, when Dominic asked what was wrong. 'Those long held notes – it's fine for you. You just listen. I wish you'd been a singer, then you'd understand. And the conductor takes the tempi too slow. You're expecting too much.'

'What's the real reason, Stasi?' he asked, taking hold of her hand, which she pulled away.

'I'm telling you.'

'What other reasons?'

'I think Orfeo should have been sung by a contralto. It upsets the balance. I'm sure in Gluck's time, when all those poor castrati were prancing around like pet idols, it was perfectly acceptable. But now? Imagine. The audience are wondering about this strange monster, what's he like down there, instead of thinking about the music.'

'You mean, he's had more attention than you. Is that what's bothering you?'

'Sometimes, Dominic, you talk utter rubbish. I'm talking about the musical effect. Do you think I care about some Indian peasant whose head's been turned by a load of Germans? What's he going to do after this? Go back to his village and say he's a big star in Germany? What happens when the money runs out? Have you thought of that?'

Dominic refused to be drawn.

'All right,' she cried. 'I haven't had the attention I deserve. I'm a leading singer now. All everyone is talking about is your production. And Rajit. At last, the era of Guadagni has returned. Dominic Morrison brings Gluck back to life. What about me? What about the work I've put in? What is this doing for me?' A second later, Stasi was in tears. 'I didn't mean that. I'm tired. I don't like Hamburg. I want to be back in Paris.'

'Darling,' he whispered, taking her in his arms, 'tell me what you want to do after *Così*. We'll do it.'

'That's not an answer.'

'What do you want, then?'

She was unable to tell him. Lying in the bath, watching the steam rising in a cloud, then subside as the water turned lukewarm around her, she could only think of her longed-for debut in Mozart. Anastasia Wagner comes to the Opera Palace. They would speak her language. They would love her. The second soprano, who would sing Dorabella, had a fine voice. Dear old Grace, Australian Grace, with the gawky frame and the pudgy face, she hadn't seen her since the early days in Milan.

With the best opera productions, Stasi could sense right from the beginning that everything would come right. The smallest signs, like the cast welcoming one another in the rehearsal breaks, a sympathetic répétiteur whom the singers liked, everyone arriving on time, coming to rehearsal knowing the basic mechanics, the words and music, of their parts. She already felt optimistic about *Così fan tutte*. She was impressed by Sir Miles Mackenzie.

Once again, she had stayed with Signora Busconi in Milan. There were times when a singer needed to reinvigorate her technique. Although Stasi was leaping forward in her dramatic interpretation, she needed pulling back vocally. Lightness, lightness, my dear. The maestra encouraged her to bring out the agility in her voice. She had an instinct for Mozart. Remember the audition pieces they had rehearsed in class? And how happy she was that two of her former students would be singing together, in that wonderful new opera house she had yet to see. Signora Busconi gave Stasi her blessing. She would try to come to London, if her troublesome hip allowed.

She had found her way again. Stasi left Milan and flew first class to London, a luxury which, if offered, she and Dominic rejected on principle. It was some weeks before she would begin rehearsals, but she wanted to see London in June, to step back slowly into the country she had left for so long. And she wanted to walk quietly down Rosedene Avenue before they knew, the press who would hound her and seek out her secrets.

Sir Miles came in person to greet her, bringing a great bouquet of flowers to the VIP lounge.

'You look magnificent,' he said, as he grasped her hand, having allowed himself to glance at her mulberry pink tailleur from Chanel, which had only elicited tepid approval from Dominic, taken aback at her unusual extravagance. She had barely time to register that this was London, leaning back in Sir Miles's grey chauffeured limousine, sealed off from the dreary entrance to the city, following a route which was strange to her.

'I thought you'd prefer to stay somewhere intimate and personal, rather than somewhere like the Savoy or Claridges. I do hope this suits you,' said Sir Miles, as he left her in the country-house splendour of the Capital Hotel. Flowers and champagne awaited her in her suite. Stasi jumped on the four-poster bed, nibbled at the glistening bunch of grapes the size of small plums, undressed and wrapped herself in a soft towelling robe. She could imagine the conversation with Gloria. 'You're staying where? Never heard of it. What kind of meanness is this? My daughter's famous. She should be staying at the Ritz.' That could wait until tomorrow.

It took a while before Stasi picked up the remote control. Any station she wanted. Quiz shows, horror movies, minute by minute news, cartoons, even football. Joyfully she flicked the button as the fancy took her. Now she didn't have to watch significant old movies. Or read books on Indian mythology. Or compare different record-ings. Or watch opera videos. She could be stupid Stasi Wagner, doing what all singers did in hotel rooms, although few of them would have a room like this. She would empty all the sachets of perfumed oil at one go into a pool-deep bath. Wash her hair, with enough foam to neutralize an oil-spillage. She could even ask room service for the first thing which came into her head.

'I'd like a peanut butter sandwich with fresh straw-berries on top.'

'Certainly, madam. Anything else?'

'Not for the moment.'

When she summoned someone to open the champagne, she would ask for a cream bun. And someone else could iron her dinner dress. Or even clean her shoes. A totally female, personal orgy, just for a few hours. If only Dominic knew. She had been longing to do this for months.

While Stasi was channel-hopping, drying her hair, finishing the wild strawberries nestling in a vineleaf, she half thought that she had seen a familiar face in a commercial. Being away from England, it was easy to imagine things which belonged elsewhere. Going from country to country, memories of people and places became detached from their environment. If she had seen Maestro Passattella or Signora Busconi walking out of the lift at the Capital, for a moment she would not have recognized them.

Her mind was drifting in a no man's land of odd memories coming in and out of focus: standing with Gloria at windswept bus-stops stamping her feet with cold; singing scales in the damp living room heated by the wheezing gas-fire; wistfully eyeing the Italian ice-cream van outside the park; Raymond crashing his motor-bike into a lamp-post; the dim lights of Covent Garden viewed from the gods; the first day of Abroad seen from a convent window. Then she came closer to the screen. Was that the wife of Maurizio della Robbia on British television? Riding a white horse in a jeans commercial?

She smiled to herself. Carla looked beautiful. She always had. If she had not been a Livorno, she would have drifted into modelling earlier. It was the kind of fame she really wanted, flashing onto a screen for a few seconds, enough for them to stop her in the street and say, 'I saw you on TV.'

Waiting in the foyer for her car to arrive, her eye was caught by a red and black poster behind the reception desk. *The Reluctant Virgin*, a musical comedy starring Carla Livorno as the girl who could never say yes. 'See this, and your sex life will never be the same' (*Daily Mirror*), 'An erotic cocktail of sex, lies and greasepaint' (*Sunday Times*). Stasi smiled to herself. She might even go to see her, if she had time. There was no need to be snobbish about it, no need to say that she was singing in *Così fan tutte*, though Carla was sure to ask. 'If I had your body,' she imagined herself saying, 'I'd do the same.' Now they could swan around the designer shops together, giggling the way they used to, trying on the expensive clothes which she could now afford, jumping into taxis clutching piles of bags advertising their extravagance.

Stasi made a note in her diary of the theatre, and she saw an accusing entry she had made earlier. Phone Mum. If she made it Friday night, there was less chance of a row. It was an appropriate time for the prodigal daughter to stand on the doorstep of 12 Rosedene Avenue. She hoped the telephonist would not be listening in, as they did at some hotels.

'Who's that? It can't be. You, darling? My daughter? What daughter? Where are you phoning from? America? What's happened? You ill? You're ill so you remember you have a mother? I'm not talking. All that time and you expect me to talk, as though you'd written me letters, kept in touch? I'm not coming running. Not any more. I've changed. Time to be selfish, Gloria, I told myself. If life hasn't turned out for the best, at least I'll be selfish. No more worrying about children and husbands. And no one to criticize my dress sense. It's a relief. And I'm making jewellery in evening class, very good they think I am. Primitive talent. You never guessed I'd be artistic, did you? Not diamonds, but semi-precious stones and I only use real silver. See what your mother does on her own.'

'Mum? Can I say something?'

'Am I stopping you?'

'I'm only here for two days. I'd like to take you out for a meal, somewhere nice.'

'I don't eat out. Waste of money.'

'I'll pay. Or maybe you'd like to see a show?'

'I don't care if you're rich, I don't care if you're poor. See what you've done to me? I knew you were alive, your brother told me. Famous, he said. Over there. France, isn't it? What good is that to me? You staying somewhere? The Ritz, I suppose.'

'A little place in Knightsbridge.'

'So far out?'

'I'm going to be singing at the Opera Palace in the autumn. I want you to come.'

There was a sniff from the other end of the phone. 'I might. If it's not my jewellery evening. Tuesdays and Thursdays. And on Fridays it's Twentieth Century Revolutionary Politics with Professor Dixon. You married?'

'Of course not.'

'Thought you might have run off and married a goy. There had to be an explanation. But even if you had, it's not a reason to shun your mother. Is it?'

'No, Mum. How are you? Are you well?'

'I've got more modern, you'd be surprised.'

'Great.'

'And I suppose you'll be seeing that friend of yours. An Italian comes to England, and everyone's heard of her. Anastasia Wagner? Where's your name? She's always on the telly. Raymond's type, he says. Anyone's his type except nice girls from Muswell Hill. Lovely smile, mind you.'

'Friday night. I'll come round on Friday night.'

'I'll be in, darling. It's Friday night. Raymond and Monty and Lizzie, we never miss. Where you staying? You can stay at home, you know that. I nearly forgot. We've got central heating in. Eight radiators for the price of four. Friend of a friend of Raymond's did a lovely job . . .'

Stasi saw herself drawing up in a car which would be longer than the frontage of 12 Rosedene Avenue. Being rich, or appearing so (the suit, the proper accessories which looked new, not slung together from oddments in a drawer, the shining car), was one way of putting a blank page between her and the past. She could show them that money didn't make you unhappy, she could survive without them, even without their approval.

Raymond had grown a beard, Uncle Monty was nearly bald, Aunt Lizzie had taken to wearing rouge. Stasi saw them lifting up the pink net curtains ruched across the bay window, waving as she drew up. It was raining. Whenever

322

she came home it was raining. The house was shouting its presence among the drab, murky-bricked neighbours of Rosedene Avenue, the woodwork painted bright ochre-yellow like a buttercup in a clump of nettles.

Gloria was on the doorstep, waiting till Stasi lifted the latch of the curlicued wrought iron gate and came up the few feet of the crazy-paved path. She had grown plumper, her skirts tighter, wrinkled over her curving stomach, her feet still bulging through the thin straps of her high-heeled sandals. Stasi leaned down and her mother's arms were tight round her neck, like a wrestler's lock, immovable in a look-what-you've-put-me-through squeeze.

That was the only indication she gave that her daughter had been away. After the hugs and kisses, Stasi's cheeks were covered with red Valentine imprints. Gloria licked a corner of her handkerchief, with which she had surreptitiously dabbed her eyes, wiped off the marks and ran into the steaming kitchen where she gave herself away with the sound of clattering pots, the violent clunk as she heaved open the oven door and the volcanic crash of cutlery on a tray.

Aunt Lizzie was already seated at the dining table, best linen cloth, silver-plate newly shined, cut glass bowls, white napkins in plastic rings.

'My tummy's rumbling. Can you hear it?'

'What did you say?'

Uncle Monty opened the drop-down cocktail cabinet. 'Not yet, Lizzie. We're all having a sherry.'

'Nearly ready. I don't want any help. I know I've forgotten something,' said Gloria, running into the room, pausing distractedly, then running out again, oven-gloves in the shape of crouching cats dangling from her arm on a string.

The candles were burning. Monty gabbled the blessing, Gloria ladled out the soup, Lizzie licked her lips, and Raymond said, 'Only a little, Mum.'

'You don't like my soup?'

Stasi took a sip of the honey-coloured liquid gleaming

with bubbles of chicken fat, lukewarm as it always was, mustn't hurt the throat. She gave a good-to-be-home smile to Gloria. The heavy atmosphere, the recriminations she had been expecting, were absent. Perhaps it was enough that she had come back.

'My Stasti's been so busy,' Gloria said to Monty, as though she had not spoken of her every day. 'They work her too hard. Not even time to write us all a letter.' Then she looked accusingly at Lizzie. 'You can't expect it, not when you're travelling around all the time. But she always kept in touch, didn't she, Raymond? Postcards saying where she was, not that you can say much on a postcard.'

Monty was shaking his head from side to side, which he did when business was bad. He was used to Gloria's fibs. What was the point of dwelling on the truth when all it did was to drive her to anti-depressants? Hadn't there been enough suffering in the Wagner family without making more?

'Did Raymond write you his news?' Aunt Lizzie burst in cheerfully. 'He's got an audition for the orchestra in Covent Garden.'

'I'm on trial for a week,' said Raymond. 'Third desk of the second violins.'

'Never mind,' Lizzie continued. 'Next time it'll be leader of the orchestra, just you see. I've got this feeling.' She patted her stomach and glanced at Gloria as though to seek her approval. It was so delicate, knowing what to bring up, when to keep quiet. 'I'm just dying to ask, Stasi. Raymond told us you're living with this wonderful man in Paris. He sounds just my type. Artistic.'

'Don't be so nosy, Lizzie. Stasi will let us know when she wants to.' Gloria got up, which she had done several times during dinner, and looked out of the window.

'Sit down, for God's sake,' said Uncle Monty, yet again.

'Stasi's car's still outside. You've got a driver who waits?'

'I'm being spoiled rotten.'

Perching herself sideways on a chair, Gloria beamed at

her daughter. 'It's what you deserve. Shall I ask him in? Give him some chicken? There's a leg left. He won't mind it cold.'

'He's all right. He's got some sandwiches.'

'Remember, Monty, when Sam was working nights? They always gave him a car and driver. And he always came in for a nightcap. Still, I suppose it's different now we're living in post-revolutionary times. No one's equal any more.'

'I'm equal,' said Lizzie indignantly.

'We're not arguing tonight,' countered Gloria firmly. 'Stasi has hardly got a word in. What opera did you say, darling?'

'*Così fan tutte*.'

'Lovely.'

'That's Mozart,' exclaimed Lizzie with pride.

They all sat silently as Stasi told them the stories of the operas she had performed, her impressions of the cities she had visited, her life in Paris, but their interest, she felt, was skin-deep. How could she expect otherwise? They had covered her absence with a lie and were trying to hide from themselves that anything had changed. The great warm homecoming was a tepid affair. Stasi found herself wanting to be back in the turmoil of emotion in which she was a part. Instead she felt like a foreign guest having bed and breakfast in an English home selected by the Tourist Board. She took a deep breath.

'I'm living in Paris with an American producer, Dominic Morrison.'

'I guessed!' said Gloria triumphantly. 'Didn't I guess?'

'I told you Stasi had met Mr Wonderful. She went on for pages,' replied Raymond, but she ignored him.

'Have you got a picture?' asked Lizzie. Stasi drew a crumpled photograph from her bag, Dominic sitting at his desk, looking up at her.

'Just like Kevin Costner. That's what I call a handsome young man. Not that Larry Cohen didn't have his good points.'

Gloria snatched the photograph from her and scrutinized it, as though searching out tell-tale signs of character weakness. 'Nothing like him. Funny how you can tell that he's American. Different facial characteristics. All those mixed races.'

'Like us,' added Raymond, peering over her shoulder. 'Looks a nice chap, Stasi.'

'There's fruit salad, pear flan, and chocolate mousse. Who wants what?' asked Gloria.

'All three,' said Lizzie.

'I found this new recipe,' Gloria began, but Stasi was no longer listening, wondering how soon she could escape.

'I still love you,' Gloria confided later, standing at the gate. 'But it's not the life I would have chosen for you. What kind of stability is that? I know you. Stability is what you need. Nice, regular routine. And you won't get that from an American, always wanting to go here there and everywhere. You should have stayed in England. You happy, Stasi?'

'Can't you see, Mum?'

'Well, as long as one of us is.'

'Next time, when I come back, we'll have a big night out.'

'You don't have to. I don't need it, Stasi.'

'Aren't you pleased? Didn't you always want me to do well?'

Gloria kissed her. ''Course I'm pleased.' Then she added, as an afterthought, 'Depends what you mean by doing well.'

The car door was being opened for Miss Wagner. Gloria was about to say something more, but changed her mind, gave a vigorous wave and clacked rapidly down the stone path, clutching at her newly bubble-curled hair to ward off the rain.

For the next twenty-four hours, Stasi spent all her time in the company of Sir Miles. Over dinner he told her stories of great singers she had only read about. He made her feel part of centuries of history. He threw everything aside, showed her the stage, the dressing rooms, introduced her to everybody he could find. Everyone wanted her to be part of the family, the great Opera Palace family which drew singers from all over the world.

She agreed to be photographed hand in hand with Sir Miles, alone on the vast stage, and sitting in the flower-decked dressing room which would soon be hers. When Stasi returned to her hotel, she rushed to the phone. If only she could see the expression of pride on Dominic's face as she described it all. His brief acknowledgement was all she needed, until they would work together again. Anastasia Wagner was about to reach the heights of her profession.

Chapter Thirteen

Outside the Aldwych Theatre, almost the last coach parties were shuffling bemused through the doors. Across the beckoning banners – 'Will set your foot tapping and your pulse racing', 'An amusing romp', 'Geography will never be the same', 'I give these schoolgirls top marks' – a notice in red proclaimed: 'Positively the last two weeks. Book now!' After several weeks of half empty houses, all references to sexual titillation had been removed by the management. Without one word being changed it had become a show for all the family.

Carla's debut on the London stage had gone smoothly and uneventfully, the sure sign of obscurity. The music, she complained to Saffron, was as thrilling as a trip to EuroDisney. The leading man, with whom she could have spent one, maybe two nights, had only eyes for the oiled pectorals of the stage carpenter, who spent every afternoon trying to fix the door in the Act Three gymnasium. Every night without fail, it managed to swing open with an alarming creak, distracting the audience when Carla was singing her best solo number, straddled over the vaulting horse, with a chorus of schoolgirls in bottle green gym knickers and airtex shirts performing acrobatics suspended from ropes. Carla's artistry was politely applauded but mostly lost on the audience, who spent the evening rustling chocolate papers, fanning their programmes and turning their tightly permed, thinning grey heads like neurotic budgerigars.

On the first night, Sir Miles had walked out after the second act, protesting that he had to meet some singer from the airport, and he never saw the gymnasium or

Carla in green knickers. Worst of all, by the time she had removed her make-up and caught a taxi to Marylebone, he was in bed and probably asleep. Carla refused to accept defeat, even though she soon realized that playing principal girl in a dated musical about an exclusive girls' school in Somerset was not guaranteed to make her an object of wonder and desire at Saffron's exclusive Maison Blanche dinner parties, most of which she was unable to attend. Julian thought the addition of a Mafioso Italian tutor or a couple of serial child molesters might have given *The Reluctant Virgin* a better chance, but that was of little comfort.

'Come up with something, for Christ's sake. This could be a really good show. Just needs a few sassy ideas.'

Julian looked pityingly at Saffron. 'Play Fiona Marchmont-Wetherall as a boy,' he suggested on one occasion.

'That would spoil the plot, stupid.'

'Plot? Did I miss something?'

'Very cute, Julian. Any other bright ideas?'

'Take your clothes off, then,' he replied wearily.

'It's not that kind of show. Very original. Really helpful.'

Saffron glanced at Julian. 'One should always go out with a bang, don't you think?'

A few selected members of the press had been primed and they knew that a husky phone call from Saffron (who thought her voice was unrecognizable) would at least be worthy of page two. She sometimes told them overheard indiscretions of minor royalty who had run up exorbitant unpaid bills at the Maison Blanche. There could be something in it.

For the last night of *The Reluctant Virgin*, there was an inexplicably full house and the Absolutely No Photographs in the Auditorium notice had been surreptitiously removed. After the performance, the holders of free tickets, Saffron's special guests, were invited to hear a statement to be issued the following day by Carla Livorno,

Marchesa della Robbia, in the Library of the Maison Blanche. It would be the only occasion when outsiders were allowed through her doors, but they would only see the well-upholstered interior of a typical London club-room.

Saffron sat by Carla's side, in a severe, mandarin-collared cocktail suit of dark green ribbed silk, with a simple emerald brooch on one lapel. She had selected Carla's dress herself, a gunmetal-grey half-shouldered creation by Prince Ladislav. All Carla had to do was to give the occasional smile, remember not to fidget and to keep her legs closely parallel, whilst saying what they had rehearsed.

'You,' Saffron said, pointing to a long-haired man with folds under his bleary eyes.

'Why are we here? Is this a publicity stunt to give a kick up the arse to an ailing show?'

'Very good. Mr?'

'Jones.'

'Jones. Should I know you?'

'Well, is it? What I said?'

'Is it, Carla? Would you like to answer this delicate gentleman?'

Carla began to speak, slowly adapting her tongue to the articulations of the English accent, moving her lips round vowels, carefully accentuating the consonants, occasionally managing to slip in a charming faulty lisping r of Milanese inspiration, looking to the end of the room, past the stony faces in front of her.

'Look them right in the eyes,' whispered Saffron.

Next day, Andrew Broughton, Minister for the Arts, rang to give a congratulatory message. Dame Mary Whitehouse wrote a letter to the *Telegraph* deploring the fact that a girl needed to be naked nowadays in order to be heard. And a rising drama historian from Leicester University tapped out ten paragraphs for the *Independent* noting the re-emergence of the Comedic Reversal and unearthing the subtext of *The Reluctant Virgin*.

It had all been so easy. Saffron, who had just applied the usual principles of forethought and organization to the event, which any secretary could have done, was taken aback at the furore caused by Carla. When you knew how often someone washed their hair, which body lotion they preferred, and had seen them with half-shut eyes nursing an overdose of Veuve Cliquot, it came as a shock to find that this familiar person was the object of fascinated scrutiny by the nation's media.

The picture of Carla lying on the vaulting horse, pert buttocks inviting attention, a bowed ribbon encircling her head, her neck held high enough to reveal the nipple of one breast, dazzling with a Madonna smile of unselfconscious glee, had been reproduced throughout the press the following day, in large and small format, in colour and monochrome. Carla Livorno did not approve of 'gratuitous nakedness' (Saffron's phrase) and had been driven to take this step only to draw attention to the new entertainment tax which was crippling the theatre (Julian's idea), forcing talented actors to take permanent rest, and closing down decent family shows which were the mainstay of London's West End. *The Reluctant Virgin* was the latest of the many victims of the Chancellor's savagery.

The combination of physical titillation and intellectual sincerity (hadn't a famous nubile newsreader once slit her skirt up to her thighs and complained of 'body fascism'?) was a perfect recipe. Carla had merely gone one step further and removed the skirt. She also showed a surprising ability to expound the nub of an argument without understanding it. By picking up phrases from others and repeating them with energetic emphasis (it could be a consequence of being a foreigner) she convinced even self-proclaimed intellectuals and academic pundits that she had a mind of consequence, and they discussed the implications of her statements as though she had just given the Dimbleby lecture.

The influence of Sir Miles, Saffron thought to herself,

was very noticeable. She was beginning to lose the harshness of that Black and Decker voice. There were few girls who had the double advantage of a superb body and the appearance of an intriguing mind. Why she wanted so desperately to make her name as an opera singer was as inexplicable to Saffron as the desire of her beautiful younger sister to keep bees in Epping Forest, but there was no reason now why she shouldn't. Fame cast a remarkably seductive veil over the failings of talent.

Overnight fame, however, could be sustained for a week, rarely for a month. Having put Carla on the first rung of the ladder, Saffron wished to see her rise with rapidity. Everybody now knew who she was, but did they know she could sing? Her affair with Sir Miles, which should, at the very least, have produced a minor role of some significance, had as yet achieved nothing. Dear Julian, who failed to understand that a favour in bed should be recompensed with a favour out of it, was not exactly indifferent to Carla's frustration, just unhelpful.

Saffron kept thinking of a riveting exhibition she had been to with Julian at the Hayward Gallery: 'The Sex Object Rebels'. Pauline Fudge was an unlikely name for a rising artist of the twentieth century, but no more unlikely than Francis Bacon. The most striking picture in the exhibition had been a modern interpretation of Salome, a young girl hacking off the head of a gaunt black man in a suburban kitchen. Fudge would make an ideal designer for *Salome*, an opera Saffron did not know, but which, she learned, possessed the same combination of eroticism and violence exhibited in the works of Fudge. It also had one of the few decent leading roles in the operatic repertoire, Carla told her, which any girl with guts should get under her fanny. Sir Miles's horizons would first need to be broadened, and then gathered into the convenient and controllable circumference of an intimate circle.

Carla found a clue as to how she might make herself more invaluable to Sir Miles in some pornographic photographs hidden in his underwear drawer, a treasure-chest for the foibles of man. With Saffron's help, she tracked down an obliging source in West Hampstead which supplied stock ensembles. One of Saffron's girls, red-headed Eileen who was a specialist in such matters, told Carla that it was all perfectly routine, happened every day. Very much in demand, she said, safe sex was all the rage. Easy to do, piece of cake. She suggested a few lines of dialogue and Carla tried out a few scenarios which had gone down well in the Games Room.

'We hate bad boys. We get rid of them in the loony van. Bumbles? Why have we been bad?'

Carla put one stilettoed heel then the other on the cross-bar of the high wooden stool and looked down fiercely through heavy, clear-lensed horn-rimmed glasses, allowing the black scholar's gown to part over her golden bush.

'I don't know, miss,' answered the man sitting cross-legged on the floor, biting his nails.

'You'd better think, then. I'll count to ten. One, two three . . .'

'I forgot to polish your shoes.'

'Shoes, my arse. I have servants to polish shoes. Bumbles doesn't polish shoes. What day is it today?'

'Um. June the tenth.' He looked at his watch and began to uncross his legs.

'Stay there, idiot. It's the eleventh. I'll tell you when you can go.'

'I'm supposed to meet . . .'

'You're staying behind in detention. Or have you forgotten that too?'

'Really, I can't. I'll be late. I'm never late.'

'Didn't you promise something else? Are you a liar, Bumbles?'

'I almost remembered, really. Yesterday I remembered.'

'Weren't we going to buy her a present? Did we ask her what she wanted? Did we think of going out at dinnertime to find her something? No. We did not. Bumbles is a horrid, selfish, moronic, fat pig. I think I'll have to call the loony van.'

'No! No!' the man squealed, rolling onto his back and kicking his legs in the air. 'Please, please, please, don't. I'll go to the shop tomorrow, tomorrow.'

Carla gave him a look of contempt, marched over and jabbed his thigh with her steel-tipped stiletto heel. He let out a yell and nursed the stinging bruise.

'Get up,' she ordered. 'And stand by my desk.'

'Shall I . . .' he began excitedly, getting to his feet.

'In there. Go on, move, Bumbles. I haven't got all day. Belt,' she said, as he leaned over the desk. 'Trousers down. Quickly.'

Then she grasped his boxer shorts and wrenched them past his buttocks, catching his cock in the elastic of the waist. 'Yaaah,' he yelled again, but by this time Carla had gone over to the glass bookcase, unlocked it, and extracted a thin, black wooden case from amongst several others piled behind the neatly ranged volumes.

'What's written on the box? Isn't that cute? Sir Thomas Beecham. Fancy you having that.' She drew out a long, slim conductor's baton. 'One wave, and boom! Beethoven's Fifth.'

'Not that one,' he whimpered. 'There's Furtwängler's. Or even Toscanini's you can take.'

'It's only a stick. What do we do with sticks?'

He rubbed his eyes, trousers and pants round his ankles, his bottom twitching with anticipation, looking at her mournfully. 'We beat naughty boys.'

'Clever Bumbles. He's got it right. I say super-jolly-good. Turn to the wall immediately.'

At last they came, the stinging arrows of pain, as Carla gripped the baton, described a few beats in the air and brought it down again and again on the clenched cheeks of his buttocks.

'Stop. Enough.'

She did stop, and he slowly uncurled and turned to face her.

334

'Now, now. Please. I can't wait any more.'

Instead of sucking his palpitating cock as she usually did, Carla threw the gown to the floor, put one net-stockinged leg onto the chair, took the baton between her fingers like a flute, and gently inserted it up her cunt.

'That's for your Tommy Beecham,' she said. 'And all conductors who think singers are dumb.'

'Carla! For God's sake. Take it out. It's the most valuable one in my collection.'

'Did I ask you to speak?' she shouted angrily. 'Stay there.'

He watched as she twisted the baton round like a kid making a hole in the sand. Then she withdrew the slim wand, sucked at its tip and threw it onto the floor, on top of her gown. 'OK, Bumbles. Get on with your homework. Five minutes then you can go.'

He took her as she stood there, as he had taken Moira leaning against the damp, painted brick walls of the murkily lit corridor, his legs apart to firm his balance, lifting her up against him, pile-driving into the soft flesh. He closed his eyes and saw Moira's freckled face, her gap-toothed smile and snub nose and the smell came back, her armpits, like damp socks left in a basket. Then he took a towel from a drawer, and wiped away the evidence. He would never approach godliness, but at least 'Bumbles' Mackenzie would be clean.

'If you're in, you can see me on the BBC 2 Arts show tonight,' said Carla, as she touched up her smudged lips. 'A live discussion with Andrew Broughton on Opera – Crisis or Rebirth?'

'Oh?' Sir Miles wondered why he had not been invited to take part. Broughton must have refused to appear with him. Slimy chap. 'I'll be halfway to Stuttgart. I told you.'

'So you did. I'll tape it.'

'Must rush back to the office. Julian's expecting me.'

Carla smoothed back his hair and straightened his tie. 'No playing with yourself in Stuttgart. Else I'll be awfully cross.' She came out of the bedroom, and stood by the fish tank. 'Poor things. Shall I feed them? Won't you miss them?'

'The cleaning lady does that. My car's waiting downstairs. Take it on to wherever you're going.'

'Thank you, darling,' replied Carla, instantly planning her route. She would end up in a silver-painted house in Fulham, owned by a young man in commodities whose ejaculatory brio and power of lubrication excelled even that of Rico. Her voice was returning to its former liquid beauty, she decided. A chat-show producer had agreed to her singing a shortened aria from *Così fan tutte* on television, which she told him she had sung at La Scala two years before. Who would bother to check? It was all so easy in England, just as Saffron had told her. Dress right and smile to camera. And if she was challenged, she could always say, 'Sure I sang it at La Scala. I did a great audition.' That would make them laugh. If you made them laugh, the Brits would forgive anything, even a prison sentence.

Carla was getting to grips with England. Once you realized that Gentlemen Inglesi leaped into action once they were given the right signal, like eighteen-year-old Battle of Britain pilots jumping heedlessly into their Spitfires at the chance of a raid, it was easy. If they pulled out the throttle too fast and too soon, it was less tiring, and in any case she preferred to prolong the refinements of love with Saffron who needed no introductory lecture as to the siting and potential of the clitoris or the technique of holding back an orgasm.

The oil painting of Carla Livorno as Fiona Marchmont-Wetherall in *The Reluctant Virgin*, leaning vertiginously across a vaulting horse in distorted perspective, signed Pauline Fudge in swirling letters, was a striking addition to the etchings and icons hanging on the white wall in Concordia Wharf. Julian was away on business, or rather 'seeing to a couple of things', and Saffron was putting in an appearance at the Maison Blanche in Paris, so Carla had taken the opportunity for some private entertaining.

Andrew Broughton, the high profile Minister for the Arts, was wrapped in an embroidered kimono which reached just below Julian's thighs, but skirted the knees of this confident, ill-proportioned man with the long body and short, beetle legs. He was admiring everything within sight in this boldly designed riverside loft.

'I always knew Pauline Fudge would go far. We sponsored an exhibition at the Whitechapel. My idea, actually.'

Carla tipped a small glass of warmed saké down his throat, before he had time to enquire as to the nature of the beverage.

'Your flat is so totally you, Carla. Does that sound silly?' (As Minister for the Arts, he was loathe to use the vocabulary of aesthetic appreciation, particularly with girls.) 'Do you mind if I say something?'

'Go ahead, Andrew.'

'You're very wonderful.'

Carla slid to the floor. 'I'm not. I've been a real bitch. I feel so awful.'

'I don't regret it. That we went all the way. You mustn't feel bad. Anyway, Jean isn't the possessive type. Not that I indulge frequently,' he answered, in soothing tones whose flattened vowels Carla was unable to identify. When she had confessed to him how terrible she felt about betraying Sir Miles, the man she thought she loved until this moment, he had looked taken aback, but quickly rallied. 'Anything in my power. Anything I can do. I'm putty in your hands.'

By two o'clock in the morning, Andrew Broughton understood. He must put aside his prejudice, and take a more indulgent view of the Opera Palace. The trouble was, Sir Miles took such a bloody independent line. It didn't go down well. She wouldn't understand, but it was difficult not to be influenced by the pro-Covent Garden faction, powerful chaps in industry putting in big oars. He would lobby the House Arts Committee to take a more positive view of Palace activities. Covent Garden, after all, was a milestone in history, a legacy of the past. A government committed to conservation was bound to shore up the crumbling edifices of former glory, and he had set his signature to the policy. But, on reflection, the time had come to hammer out new objectives and thrust forward into the future.

Why had Carla been refused? Just because she was Italian? Outrageous. If La Scala had seen her Despina, why should the Opera Palace turn her down? How dare Sir Miles be so narrowly chauvinistic, so petty, so mean-minded, so pompous, not that he was surprised, as to try to damn up the flowing river of her talent? The politics of opera sickened him, he assured Carla. If all else failed, would she consider singing at Covent Garden?

'They couldn't afford me,' she replied wistfully. 'My agent wouldn't allow it. Oscar says once you accept low fees, everyone thinks they can get you cheap.'

'Precisely. He has a point. That's the trouble with England. Everyone thinks they can get us cheap.'

He never thought he would go into the bedroom for a second time, but the mating call was overcoming the desire for sleep.

'It's so exciting to find a girl who really likes sex,' he exclaimed, after he had jumped on top of Carla and given her a juicy kiss, stirring his tongue round the gorgeous cavern of her mouth. 'Are you ready?'

The way she smiled, he knew she was. He needn't have asked. 'You're so much better in bed than Miles,' she murmured.

Shortly afterwards, following a friendly meeting at the Maison Blanche between Sir Miles Mackenzie and Andrew Broughton, Carla Livorno was contracted to sing Despina in ten performances of Così fan tutte at the Opera Palace.

They'd be in the same show. She wondered how Stasi would take it. Julian had told her she'd paid an earlier visit to London; Carla was glad they hadn't met then. She could hardly deny that she was appearing in a godawful musical, it was advertised all over town. How could she have asked Anastasia Wagner to come and see her in *The Reluctant Virgin*? You didn't parade failures, least of all to Stasi. She would not have been unkind, but she would have expressed by a word, a look, that Carla was only doing what she had expected. It was that English way she had of dismissing the activity of someone she disapproved of, without actually saying so. Carla's marriage, for example. She hadn't even stayed to the end of the party. That said it all.

It would be different when they were working together. Stasi was getting the top billing, she had the better part, she had her guy. They could be friends again. More than anything, Carla wanted Stasi's respect, wanted to hear her say that Carla's voice had improved, her acting was right, she had lost her mannerisms (with the help of Signora Busconi). Not that she would, but one slight glance of admiration would be enough, one glance which said, 'Carla. It's amazing, you're so much better now.' She did not feel that about the opinions of anyone else – her mother, her father, Maestro Passattella, Julian, or even her teacher. Stasi had a way of reaching down inside you, just as she reached down inside her audience. She made you want something better.

There are some opera houses where singers are left to their own devices, where they arrive for rehearsal as though turning up at an office. Sir Miles was determined that the Opera Palace should retain the trappings of the great days when singers were stars and conductors remained in the pit. Since Julian was in Paris on business, he asked him if he would see Anastasia. It had been sprung on her, Carla singing in *Così*. One never knew with singers. Past history, that kind of thing. You had to care for them like delicate tropical fish. The slightest change in emotional temperature could freeze them into deadening hostility. They could take the same plane, and fly back together.

During the brief journey from Paris to London, Julian

showed the right degree of flattery and frankness, concern and attention. Stasi regretted not keeping in touch with Carla, but it was so difficult to keep friendships alive. She seemed distressed when she heard of Carla's tragedy and could quite understand that Sir Miles had agreed to give her a break. It was hard for any singer to lose her husband just when she was starting to make her name.

'I liked Maurizio,' she remarked, remembering only a happy day spent at his splendid villa, sitting by the fountain in the sun with Carla. 'It's good that Carla has a decent part. It'll help her to forget.'

'Personally, I can think of better singers, but Carla needs the money,' said Julian. 'He left her hardly enough to survive.'

'Maurizio! But I thought he was loaded.'

'So did everyone else. Badly managed stocks and shares, I imagine. Typically Italian. No liquid assets.'

'How has she managed? Poor Carla. That explains why she was in a jeans commercial when I was last here. No wonder. I can't imagine her hard up. Is she still in that musical?'

'Oh, no. That came off weeks ago. So she's broke again. Anyhow, living with me and Saffron saves on the living expenses.'

'Saffron?' Her face dropped. She had put their friendship out of her mind.

'Didn't you have fun in Paris? I thought all opera singers longed to swing and wiggle their bums.'

'You came to the Maison Blanche, didn't you? You saw me.'

He smiled at her. 'I liked the red wig.'

'If you don't mind, I'd rather not tell the world what I did to pay the rent.'

'Being a nightclub singer at the most exclusive club in Paris? I enjoyed your performance. Do I detect a hint of cultural *snobisme*, Miss Wagner?'

'My family would disown me.'

'In some cases, that might be an advantage.'

It was impossible to take offence at Julian's dry comments – equally difficult to imagine that he had a family, or had suffered from one.

'So is Saffron your new girlfriend?'

'She's hardly new. Saffron has never been new.' He smiled with closed lips – Julian used the minimum of expression, as though it might mar his broad, amiable face. 'Strictly what they used to call platonic. Good chums. It makes life for the travelling man so much easier. Anyway, pretty little Beatrice has deserted me. I don't think I quite came up to scratch.'

Then it dawned on her, but she wanted him to confirm it. She sounded disapproving, in spite of herself. 'You're having an affair with Carla, then?'

He leaned back and looked at her through half-closed eyes. Suddenly she realized that she found him compellingly attractive, and she blushed.

'I don't have a death-wish, Stasi,' he murmured. 'Only when I'm drunk.'

Stasi laughed. She could barely recognize the man she had insulted at Carla's wedding.

'She's dying to see you. Will you come over tonight?'

'Of course I will.'

'I've got to see a couple of bankers. If I don't get back in time, I'll see you at the Opera Palace.'

She looked at Julian as he pulled out a sheaf of documents covered in figures, remembering him as she had first seen him in the Livorno villa, stoking the barbecue, seeking her out in the warm, scented garden, leaping into the air to lob a tennis ball. Instead of this equable, charming man, she had chosen to live with an unpredictable, moody American called Morrison who never knew from month to month how he would survive, almost always wore jeans and didn't even have a Jewish grandmother. If she knew, Gloria would think she was meshuga. Utterly crazy.

When Stasi arrived at Concordia Wharf, wondering at the vast space, everything arranged so perfectly, the lightness of the Japanese decor, the books, the paintings, the September sun streaming through the windows, she immediately thought how Dominic would have admired it. Those lofty, shabby rooms in Boulevard St Germain – with some of her fee she could make them beautiful, like this dream of a place.

'Oh, Stasi. It's so good to see you. Together in England at last. Why's it taken so long?'

Carla was a little plumper than she remembered, her hair shorter, curls descending over her eyes, her figure hidden under a man's sweater hitched over her hips with a belt, necklaces jangling from her neck.

'Saffron!' she called. 'Where are you? Stasi's arrived.'

A distant voice came from the corridor. 'Washing my hair.'

Carla giggled. 'We keep losing each other. This place is so goddamned big. Like it?'

'Amazing.'

'You can stay here if you like. Loads of room. And a jacuzzi. Julian adores having bubbles up his arse.'

When Saffron came in with her hair wrapped in a huge towel, Carla ran off to find a dryer. Then the three of them sat together, sprawled across the white cushions, Carla running her fingers through Saffron's hair, teasing out the fine strands. Occasionally, Stasi thought she saw a shadow of anxiety come over Carla's bright face as they laughed about the past, the dreadful *Carmen*, the good times they had spent at the villa. She did not say what she had done after the death of Maurizio. Not to mention him was strange, Stasi thought, but Carla had always been squeamish, superstitious even, when it came to illness and death. It was understandable, so soon afterwards, to want to be with a girl. They seemed comfortable together, and Stasi was undisturbed by a physical intimacy she herself would have found repulsive.

'You seem happy. I'm so glad,' Stasi said, when Saffron left the room.

'Saffron's great for making you forget. And you should

342

see her wonderful new club in Mayfair! Don't you adore London? I couldn't believe we'd be working together, Stasi. I've got some wonderful ideas for you and me in Act Two. Isn't Despina just made for me? And Fiordiligi for you? Grace, too. She'll be OK once she's in costume. Brilliant casting. Wow! Know anything about the producer?'

'Ian Davies? Not much.'

'Don't worry. I've heard he's a walkover. Lets singers get on with it, not like some.'

'Well, that's not always . . .'

Carla stopped her, putting her hand to her lips. 'You're not going to mention Dominic Morrison. Verboten. This is England, kid.'

Stasi was given what she had requested, a suite at the Savoy, with a piano in the adjoining room. Sir Miles, she told Dominic, was paying her every attention. She could ring him whenever she liked, even at home. The strict discipline would begin the moment she arrived – rest times, rehearsal times, time to grasp hold of the flighty character she was to play. The letters waiting for her, requesting interviews, reminded her that she could be as great a sensation in London as she had been in Paris.

It was only after a week that she finally admitted to Dominic during her nightly phone calls that her first impressions were mistaken. Ian Davies, the producer, was a dolt. She would have liked to throw him into the river. She began to come in to rehearsals thinking only of containing her anger, and refused to sing full voice.

'He's so vague about everything. Everything I suggest he says, "Mm. That's a possibility." All he's concerned about is getting the "Mozartean feel". Doesn't have a clue about Mozart. He gives me nothing,' she complained. 'And he had the nerve to suggest I change the phrasing in "Come scoglio immoto resta". No wonder British opera is so uninspiring. I should never have come.'

Dominic had suspected as much. 'What about the conductor?'

343

'Gottfried Kellerman hasn't arrived yet. Malcolm Fuerstein is taking the music rehearsals. He seems OK.'

'Work on the music. Play it safe and static, if that's what he wants. Don't give in. Show them beauty. Don't worry about acting. Just be yourself.'

Then, one day, she snapped on stage. Ian Davies had ventured to comment on her performance.

'Your Fiordiligi is not flirty enough, Anastasia. Couldn't you do something with your fan? Sort of Merry Widow idea? It's all getting a bit serious.'

She ran across the stage, pulling up her rehearsal skirt, closed her fan and playfully slapped Ian Davies on the cheek, harder than she intended. 'Like that, you mean?'

Carla roared with laughter, but the giggles of the cast, eyes fixed on his irate face, soon subsided into silence.

'Is that your idea of a joke, Miss Wagner?' he asked through clenched teeth, holding his cheek.

'No. I meant it,' she bellowed. 'When they give me a producer, I'll come back.' Flinging two fingers in his face, Miss Wagner made her exit.

Next day, Stasi was refusing to take calls, locked in her suite. The head of costume was screaming that the dress for Fiordiligi would not be finished in time unless she came for a fitting. Ian Davies marched into Sir Miles's office demanding a replacement for Anastasia. He refused to waste time indulging tantrums, it wasn't fair on the cast. Andrew Broughton telephoned, saying that he had a day available to watch the rehearsal of *Così*, and would be taking up Sir Miles's invitation. *Vogue* had booked a studio for Miss Wagner and were pressing for a time. The tenor playing Ferrando had a cold. London Electricity would be cutting off the supply for a couple of hours for essential maintenance, blacking out the theatre for the rehearsal of Act Two, scenes four, five and six. The accountant was calling a halt to the expenditure occasioned by the designer who was asking for changes and additions after every rehearsal. The musicians in the orchestra wanted parity with Covent Garden, which had just negotiated a crippling rise, and were threatening to work to rule. And an unidentified throat virus was creeping its way through the Opera Palace offices, forcing feverish secretaries to abandon their posts and head for home, creating a wave of panic amongst the artists. Sir Miles was on his feet all day.

Stasi was unaware of all this clinker dampening the fire of creation. Lying in a darkened room, she was going through torments none would guess except Dominic. It was he who had taught her to work only from her feelings, first sensing the intention of the composer, then breathing life into the librettist's words with something unique to herself, even to be prepared to sacrifice the requirements of technique to emotional truth, her emotional truth. If only they had chosen another Mozart opera. Ian Davies could not understand her difficulties with the part. Too much fuss had been made about the black cynicism of *Così*, he thought. It was just Mozart having fun, a jolly pantomime, a Whitehall farce, silly ladies shown up by masquerading men. Who cared about fidelity nowadays? The whole premise was a joke, Mozart poking fun at the opposite sex.

And he had told her that on the day when she felt her interpretation had finally fallen into place, when she had explored within herself and painfully dredged up what she had feared to confront. Wasn't *Così* about the fragility of love? That however deeply a woman was suffused with love for a man, given the opportunity, that love could be taken back and handed to another? She was beginning to doubt that love could be eternal. Away from Dominic, could she survive the test? Would they be together in years to come? Had she merely imagined the uniqueness of their passion? Would she be any different from Fiordiligi, saying tearful goodbyes to her lover Ferrando in the morning, and accepting a proposal from a fiery Turkish stranger in the evening?

Stasi began to hate the creature who was taking root inside her, growing distinct features like a developing

345

foetus. The creature had begun to talk with Carla's voice. When she had looked into the eyes of Ferrando in disguise as a Turk, she had seen Julian Lieberman. Carla was laughing. 'Sure you fancy him. Why not? Who doesn't? Give yourself a break, Stasi. I told you, he's keen.' If Julian paid court to her, she feared she would succumb. If he knocked on her door, she would tell him to enter and fall into his arms.

When someone did knock, much later, she jumped up immediately and opened the door, forgetting her determination to refuse any caller. Sir Miles was standing there, clutching a small bunch of roses.

'I'm sorry. I didn't want to disturb you, Anastasia.'

She looked at him with bewilderment, then realized that she was greeting him wearing nothing but pants and a faded T-shirt.

'Come in,' she said hastily. 'I was having a rest.' He handed her the flowers. 'I should be giving these to you, Miles. I'm not ready for a peace offering yet, though.'

He stood near the door, as though fearing to intrude, and she gestured to a couch.

'Do sit down.'

They sat facing one another, Sir Miles gazing at his feet, averting his eyes from Stasi's bare feet and willowy legs, unable to think how he would broach the subject he had come to discuss, wishing he could bring himself to say what went through his head whenever he was alone.

'I never meant it to be like this,' he began quietly.

'You engaged the producer. You must have known what he was like.' Stasi flung one bare leg over the other and clasped her knee.

'He has an excellent reputation.'

Stasi sniffed. 'Really? In England, perhaps. The reason I lost my temper is because I'm not used to working with unmusical idiots. Not because I wish to see my name in the gossip columns.'

'Ian Davies did a splendid *Butterfly* for us. It was a great success.'

'You mean Paolo Livorno made it a great success.'

'Not only.' He sighed. 'I don't want to argue. I know these things happen, but we have many problems at the moment. Everyone is under a lot of stress.'

'It must be catching,' replied Stasi acidly. 'Because for some reason, I'm not singing.' She threw over a couple of newspapers which landed at his feet. 'Someone has done a fine job, inventing a character I don't have, putting words in my mouth, as well as using a photograph which is four years out of date. Still, maybe you're used to that kind of crap. Is that how you get your audiences, Sir Miles?'

He stood up and paced round the room, then leaned against the piano, on which rested a closed copy of *Così fan tutte*.

'How could we improve the situation, Anastasia?'

'Simple. A decent director. That would be a good start.'

'Dominic Morrison, I presume.'

Stasi flushed and pushed back her hair. 'I do work with other producers. Good ones, of course.'

A moment later, she regretted her outburst. Why hadn't she leaped to Dominic's defence, insisted that he came over? He was free, he would do it, but it was too late.

'I'll have a word with Julian Lieberman.'

'Julian Lieberman? Is he artistic director now?'

Sir Miles coughed. 'No. But I trust his judgement. He has given us invaluable guidance. We might be able to put Ian Davies on to another production, and bring in someone else. We wouldn't normally, you understand.'

'Oh?'

'We do have many international stars here, and we usually manage to iron out difficulties. I know it's your first time here, and I want to do everything I can . . .'

Stasi interrupted him. 'Listen, Sir Miles. There's only one thing I want, and if I can't get it, I might as well go back to Paris. If I can't sing this part as I feel it, as I've worked on it for several months, I'd rather someone else took over. You think it's easy for me to tell you this?'

'No, no.'

347

'I want to sing Fiordiligi. I want to sing it here. I want the production to be outstanding. The other singers are superb and with Gottfried Kellerman conducting, why ruin everything with a man who's not worthy of their talent?'

'I take your point.'

'Good.' Stasi rose from her chair and faced Sir Miles. Her voice suddenly dropped to a quiet mezzo. 'Do you believe in me?'

He looked away. She was making him feel like the evil Baron Scarpia in *Tosca* when he was yearning to be Captain Rhadames enfolding Aida in his arms.

'More than I can say. I'll do everything I can to find a solution.'

She began to walk towards the interconnecting door, and before he left he stretched out his arm, then changed his mind and kissed her hand, like someone who was unused to the gesture.

A new director was appointed, Timothy Routledge, an earnest young man, only three years down from Cambridge where he had obtained a first. He listened and made careful notes of the briefing given by Julian and Sir Miles. From now on, they would not be concerned with new interpretations, or drastic changes. All he had to do was to bring the production to harmonious fruition.

'How's it going?' whispered Julian, coming up to Carla and Stasi who were sitting with their feet up in the front row of the auditorium, waiting for their next call.

'Stasi is happy. Grace is happy. I'm happy. Our scenes are great.'

'And Carla's promised she won't get up to any unexpected business.' Stasi laughed. 'Or only on the last night, in which case we'll fight it out!'

'Is she getting better?' asked Julian, nodding at Carla. 'Because she's been working so hard even I know every note of her part. If she falls sick . . .'

'Shh, Julian.'

348

'I could always sing it,' he concluded. Then he looked at Stasi. 'Sir Miles is very impressed by what he's seen. Rather pleased, he told me. That's high praise.'

'He's so sweet and sincere,' Carla replied, in her almost-in-the-bedroom voice. 'I love it.' She gave Julian a penetrating glance, which he did not acknowledge. She was never quite sure if he knew of her secret meetings with Sir Miles.

'Stasi, if you're up to it, we could have dinner at the Maison Blanche. Saffron keeps asking when you're coming.'

Stasi looked at Julian, then at Carla. 'Yes. Why not? What about Carla, though?'

'I've got a business engagement,' she replied, sounding satisfied. 'But I might come on later.'

The Dining Club of the Maison Blanche was held in a private room off the main sitting room on the ground floor. There was a smell of cigar smoke, the rustle of newspapers, and the sound of low conversation. A blonde waitress, in a long skirt and a transparent organza shirt, was serving a tray of whisky. Stasi thought she recognized the girl from Paris but Julian swept her past and led her to the corner table of a magnificent dining room, lit by tall candles and papered in rich paisley, with huge gilded French mirrors.

The men rose to salute her and she smiled at Sir Miles. It was impossible to be angry with him. Julian introduced her to Pauline Fudge, a new member who might be persuaded to donate one of her provocative paintings. She leaned across and raised the black spangled veil which covered her face to give Stasi a kiss. Gottfried Kellerman, who would be taking over the orchestra the next day, bowed; Andrew Broughton shook her hand. Oscar Broderick, international impresario, acknowledged her with a bow. The women gave admiring smiles. They were all looking at her, as though she was giving a performance.

'You can always have something else,' Julian said,

watching her reading with dismay through the menu, placed between the arms of an Art Nouveau nymph balancing on a silver log. 'A boiled egg, if you like.'

Stasi swallowed. Her head throbbed. Overcome with nausea, she clutched her stomach. 'I think I'll have to leave,' she said.

'Is Anastasia not feeling well?' Sir Miles threw aside his napkin, and came over.

'Get her home,' shouted Oscar Broderick. 'She should be resting.'

'My car's outside. I'll take her.'

'Does she suffer from ill health?' asked Gottfried Kellerman, twisting on his chair. 'This is not good.'

'Bound to be the curse. What don't I know about the cramps!' cried Pauline Fudge in a shrill Cockney voice. 'Leave it out. She'll go if she wants to.'

Saffron, standing at a neighbouring table, walked quickly across to Julian. 'Take her back to the flat. She looks dreadfully pale. And call Dr Morton.'

'It's tiredness.' Stasi pushed aside offers of help and got to her feet. 'Please don't make a fuss. I'll take a taxi to my hotel.'

Julian wouldn't hear of it. His driver was waiting outside. Stasi noticed the darkened windows and got into his car.

'If one's not in the mood, it's best to leave. Are you recovering?'

'I'm spoiling your evening.'

'No need to be upset, Stasi.'

'They were all waiting for me to do something outrageous, I could feel it. Who will I hit this time?' She took out a small bottle of pills and swallowed several in quick succession.

'Singers' remedy?'

'B6 deficiency. Sometimes the vitamin–mineral ratio gets imbalanced. Then the lung muscles contract too much.'

'Really? Most extraordinary. I never knew that.'

'You don't believe it?'

'Stasi, darling. How could I not believe anything that comes from those exquisite lips?'

'For God's sake, don't tell Saffron, don't tell anyone I take vitamin pills. I couldn't cope with being called a drug addict and a temperamental bitch. You don't believe what they say about me, do you?'

'I think you're lovely, irresistible and far too good for any man.'

Suddenly Stasi's qualms melted away.

Returned to the Savoy, Stasi came to the door of her bedroom in a velvet robe which trailed behind her, open over a sheer silk nightdress. Julian was where she had left him, reading one of her books and picking at a bunch of grapes in the adjoining sitting room.

'How awful! I haven't offered you anything.'

'There's no need. Florence Nightingale never ate on duty.'

'I'm feeling better.'

'Shall I go?'

'No, no. Not yet. Isn't it strange? It's the first time we've been alone.'

'Let me tuck you up in bed. I'll even read you a story. How is Dominic? He's a good chap. Do give him my regards when he calls. Does he call every day?'

'Usually when I'm in the bath,' replied Stasi, moving back towards the bedroom. 'You can come in,' she called.

Julian went over to the bed, picked up Rabbit, lying on a pillow, and hopped him onto Stasi's bare shoulder.

'I'm a lucky rabbit. Look at me, sleeping every night with Anastasia. But I'm very well-behaved. I stay to my side of the bed and I do everything I'm told.'

'He isn't jealous, he likes you. You can come on the bed with me.'

'Don't throw anything this time.'

'I promise.' She wanted to touch him, but drew back. 'It was hard, meeting you with Dominic.'

'Was it?'

351

'You don't mind me being honest? When I first saw you, I wished I was in your bed instead of Beatrice. Isn't that terrible? Then I thought I didn't deserve you. I wasn't Italian with a famous Pappa.'

'I didn't imagine you were interested. But that didn't stop me hearing your voice in my dreams. I hoped, I still hope, that it's the last thing I'll hear on this earth.'

'You felt the same? Kiss me, Julian.'

He pressed his lips against hers. They were cooler than she expected. 'You'll hate me, Stasi.'

'No, no.'

'Dominic loves you and you feel the same. Why spoil it? Such a good chap.'

'You said that before. Suppose I found out I loved you more?'

'Dear Stasi, I'm no good for you. I wouldn't ring you up every day, I'd forget your birthday, I wouldn't be there to read your wonderful reviews. And I prefer sleeping alone.'

'I wish I didn't want you so much.'

Julian pulled the sheet up around her shoulders. 'I don't need to put my cock up you to prove that I adore you, worship you.'

'I wish we had met when I was sixteen.'

'So do I.' He leaned over her, and pressed her shoulders back on the pillow. 'You must sleep now. *Bella Fiordiligi*.'

'If we had been engaged, would you have trusted me to keep faithful? Do you think Mozart is right, that all women give way at the first opportunity?'

'Only if you believe that women are stupid.'

'And you don't?'

'There are exceptions.' He kissed Stasi on the forehead, and she smelled the aroma of a subtle French eau de toilette, felt his smooth, boyish skin, and then he left her side. If Carla had been in her place, she thought, he would have crawled into the bed and run his hands down her thighs, and within seconds they would have been thrashing with the joy of sex. Heinrich, too, wanted to gaze, in awe. She longed to know what Carla knew, to flit

352

from man to man with a toss of her head. It would all end soon, when Fiordiligi's costume had been packed away. The telephone began to ring and she buried her head under the sheets.

Two days later, just when everything seemed to be progressing as he had hoped, a pile of newspapers were placed on Sir Miles's desk, with the relevant sections circled in red. He came to the office at eight o'clock, and for an hour he fumed in silence. It allowed him to collect his thoughts, waiting for the adjacent offices to come to life.

'Opera Palace in new drama'.

He skimmed through the article. Fortunately, the first three performances were sold out, but the rumour that a lead singer had been taken ill could mean falling attendances, demands for ticket returns. He had just tossed the papers aside when Campton-Fausey knocked at the open door and walked in with a long face.

'Isn't it terribly annoying? No one mentioned that she rehearsed all day yesterday. Would she have done that if she was sick?'

Sir Miles was not in the mood to accompany Campton-Fausey through the swings and roundabouts of his thought processes. 'I've decided what to do,' he said, since a decision had suggested itself instantly, a characteristic which meant that Sir Miles, and not Campton-Fausey, was heading the Opera Palace. 'Our company doctor will examine Anastasia and will find that she has had a mild attack of food poisoning but is now fully recovered. Make them print that.'

'Poisoned by rival soprano?' Campton-Fausey twitched, catching Sir Miles's expression of contempt, and changed his smile to an earnest expression. 'Who could have told them? Any idea, Sir Miles?'

'Does it matter?'

'No, of course not.'

'If you like, you can circulate a memo to the company about not talking to the press.'

'Straight away, Sir Miles.'

The first night of *Così fan tutte* was attended by three thousand people, including two dukes, three earls, five ministers, several actresses, three rock stars, many of Saffron's girls, one cricket hero, one housewife from Barnsley who had won the *Mirror* competition for a night with the stars, and Gloria Wagner.

Gloria Wagner's party, which occupied six seats in the third row, was proving a trial for the scanning cameras trying to focus on the stars and nobles sitting behind and in front of her. Every shot seemed to contain a Wagner, and Gloria Wagner was destined to be a local heroine in Muswell Hill, Golders Green, and even as far as Stanmore. Aunt Lizzie, Uncle Monty and cousins Jeannie and Michael were dressed up in what they had worn to Raymond's barmitzvah fourteen years ago, special timeless garments proliferating bows, tucks and frills. Louis Goldbaum, who supplied the salt-beef, arranged Gloria's mink stole around her shoulders.

'We're ready. Where's the conductor?'

'Shh, Lizzie.'

They clapped after each of Stasi's arias, and several of Carla's, but at the end of Act One they clapped until their hands were red and stinging.

'That's what I call Mozart,' said Monty.

Aunt Lizzie wiped her glasses. 'I'm speechless. I can't believe it's our Stasi up there. Lucky she's a tall girl, stands out from all the rest. And every note so clear. Wonderful in such a large place. Mind you, I always hated a large stage.'

Gloria just sat there, while the rest of the row struggled past her, tears running down her face. All she could say was 'My daughter. My daughter,' between sobs.

'It's a good show,' remarked Mr Goldbaum. 'Very well done. Lovely costumes.'

Her performance was over. Stasi sat in her dressing room, staring at the mirror, blinking, then she buried her damp face in a towel. All those curtain calls. Sir Miles, Andrew Broughton, Julian, and a crowd she barely knew were clustered round her, but she did not see them. Their voices were ebbing and flowing without meaning.

'Stasi.'

She swung round, uncovered her face, and Dominic lifted her up in an embrace.

'Was I good, darling?'

He pushed back the hair screening her face. 'The best I've heard.'

'Really?' Then she added, breathlessly, 'What did you think of Carla?'

'Her Despina had its moments. Look. There's a woman going crazy back there.'

Gloria, having pushed her way past the admirers standing outside the dressing room, was waving and shouting, jumping up and down. Catching sight of her mother's bobbing head, Stasi took a red rose from a bouquet and flung it towards her. Sir Miles edged round Dominic to offer his congratulations. 'Come to my office and have some champagne. When the crowds have gone, we can go quietly to dinner.'

Stasi followed him, sleep-walking down the long corridors, Dominic's arm heavy on her shoulder.

The photographers and cameramen were crushed against one another outside the stage door. An Opera Palace attendant was screaming at the crowds to keep back. When would she come out? Would she come out this way? No one was going to cheat them of this moment, when they could see the star in front of them, drink in the magic of the goddess come down in human form, touch her, fling programmes and autograph books in her face, boast later of the precious sign of their close encounter. A great white Rolls-Royce drew up, and inched forward as they pressed round.

Then the chant began. 'Car-la. Car-la. Car-la.'

On the arm of Oscar Broderick, with Saffron just behind her, Carla Livorno, in dark glasses, lips newly glossed, diamonds swinging from her ears, an ankle-length blond mink coat round her shoulders, made her brief appearance. As she scrawled her name, she looked up towards the cameras. When the three climbed into the white Rolls, a man in a badly fitting dinner jacket straining across his stomach stepped in behind them.

'Where would Miss Livorno like to do the interview?' he asked, once the car door was closed.

'Here will be fine,' replied Oscar. 'We can give you half an hour.'

'Did you talk to the people I mentioned?' asked Saffron. 'I do hope they were helpful.'

'Quite helpful,' answered the stranger, taking out his tape-recorder.

Chapter Fourteen

Over the splendour of the Savoy breakfast, Dominic and Stasi had done nothing but argue. He could not understand why she was screaming when the music critics had hailed her as the new Elisabeth Schwarzkopf, as a singer who, they predicted, would set the yardstick for performances of Mozart. They had lavished such praise on her that he teasingly asked whether she had taken them all to bed.

'I've better things to do. And I don't care about critics.'

'Yes, you do. Suppose they'd given you terrible reviews?'

'I'd get Sir Miles to ban them from the opera house.'

He was laughing at her again.

'I mean it,' she said indignantly.

'I'm glad you're not in politics. You'd be worse than Stalin.'

Stasi was studying two pages of a tabloid newspaper as though she was learning a part, reading them over again and again. 'Can't you do something?'

'What do you want me to do, darling? Sue? Challenge Carla to a duel?'

'Yes. No. It isn't true. Any of it. And I don't get my underwear from Christian Dior. Why do they want to crucify me? What have I done except sing? This bastard can't even write.'

Dominic took her hand, but she pulled it away. The untouched bacon, eggs and mushrooms were congealing on her plate.

'If you want to give your fee to lawyers, it's up to you.'

'Ever since I got here, they've been writing this shit.

Someone must have put her up to it. Why would she invent all this rant? It won't get her better notices.'

'Forget it, Stasi. In a week, no one will remember.'

'I will. All that hypocritical stuff about being my friend. I thought she was making a good stab at the part. It's not as though she's embarrassing. Why does she bother?'

'Why don't you ask her what the fuck she's doing?'

'She'd deny it. I want her to apologize.'

'Why wait? Confront her, Stasi.'

'You think I should?'

'Didn't you stand up to Ian Davies?'

'He's a man.'

'Hey! What's the difference?'

'I don't fight women. It's not right.'

'Tell that to your mom.'

'All right. You win.' Stasi broke into a smile for the first time that morning, and thought of their long, warm, tender night. 'Tell the waiter I'd like another plate of scrambled egg with lots of cream and bacon and some hot coffee, and two croissants and some toast. Have you time?'

'Sure.'

'Do you have to do that play in New York? Is it so important?'

'It's a good script.'

'Not that good.'

'See if I can still do it.'

'Of course you can.'

'Can I decide that, Stasi?'

'Sorry. Everything builds up when we're apart. I can't help it.'

'Look, if we're together half the year, that isn't bad. And you wouldn't have me trailing around, like some guys do, pretending it's a full time job being your manager, doing fuck all else.'

'Sometimes I think, what's wrong with domestic bliss – coming home and making you supper every night, fixing up the flat, doing ordinary things all day? But I know I'd hate it.'

'Unless you had a luxury home with a few staff, maybe.'

'We could, one day. Why not?'

Dominic shrugged. 'You think I'm that kind of guy? Could you see me worrying about leaves mucking up the pool and wondering what to do when the maid's off sick? If you want that kind of life . . .'

'I don't.'

He stroked her knee under the table. 'I know you don't.'

Dominic jumped into a taxi outside the Savoy. If only she had been leaving for New York in his place. It was always easier to be the person leaving. Seven more performances, alone and abandoned. And she couldn't help resenting that he had chosen this moment to direct a play about a failing international boxing champion.

Later that day, before the second performance, Sir Miles called together the whole company in the auditorium. Anastasia would not believe him when he said it happened all the time, that she had not been betrayed, that she was not hated by all the cast. She wanted a public apology from Carla Livorno, otherwise she would fly back to Paris.

'Is everyone here?' asked Thomas Campton-Fausey, looking at his watch. Two members of the chorus were missing. 'And has anyone seen Miss Livorno?'

'Perhaps she's in her dressing room,' called a voice. 'I saw her car.'

'Or she could be in wardrobe,' suggested someone else. 'She said her costume needed taking in.'

After fifteen minutes, Campton-Fausey went in search of Carla. The wardrobe mistress, Gwen Compton, passed him in the corridor.

'Have you seen Carla?' he asked.

'Miss Livorno is here,' she replied coldly. 'Somewhere, I believe.'

'If you see her, tell her we're waiting for her.'

'I'm not surprised. We've all read it, you know. Someone should tell her how to behave.'

'That's what we're attempting to do, Gwen.'

'Well, you can tell her from me we all think she's a cow. And we've seen some around here, believe me. Stasi Wagner isn't one of them.'

Carla had foreseen that she would have to make a speech, and had been trying out a few woebegone expressions in the mirror while her costume was being pinned. And then she had been running down one of the corridors when she had hurtled into John Llewelyn. As yet, she had found no one for the role so ardently filled by Rico, but she had noticed the beefy Welshman, throwing his musket from one hand to the other as though he meant it.

'Hi, John.'

John, with rosy cheeks and short-cut raven-black hair, who had taken lead roles in small touring companies and was hoping to rise from the chorus of the Opera Palace, stopped dead in his tracks. She knew his name.

'Hello, Miss Livorno. You going to the meeting?'

'There's no hurry.' She walked by his side, past the costume stores. Someone had left a key in one of the locks. 'Why don't we take a look?' Carla pushed the door open.

Leading John down the rails of silken cloaks, encrusted doublets, heavy linen robes and embossed leather straps which hung from the waists of Egyptian soldiers, she took him to a voluminous red silk tunic covered with gold embroidery.

'Guess who wore that?' she said.

'It's familiar, like. Aren't these the *Aida* costumes? Should I know?'

Carla pressed the red silk against her face and gave a long, ecstatic sniff and thought of a name to impress. 'Ruggiero Gasparini.'

'His costume?' John's mouth dropped open.

'Why don't you try it?' suggested Carla. 'Go on. See if it fits. I bet we could both get in there.' She placed one hand under his buttocks, pushed him towards the voluminous folds, and lifted up the hem.

Campton-Fausey was alone on stage, making notes, when Carla appeared.

'Sorry I couldn't make it earlier. I've had trouble with my costume.'

'Sir Miles will have a word after the performance.'

'Of course he will,' replied Carla, giving him an ironic smile. 'He always does.'

That night, Stasi and Carla managed to sing together without once looking into each other's eyes. The libretto had not changed, nor had the music, but both were glossed with a new interpretation which would have intrigued Mozart. Grace was forced to make subtle changes to her interpretation of Dorabella, since her sister Fiordiligi brazenly ignored the presence of their maid Despina whenever she came onstage, as though she had just been fired for some unspeakable misdemeanour and was working out her notice. The hatred between the servant and her mistress went far beyond Fiordiligi's disapproval of Despina's gleeful cynicism. When they took their bows, Stasi refused to take Carla's hand as rehearsed. For the next six performances, Stasi forced herself to ignore the wheezing coughs covering her high notes, the rose petals raining on Carla from the same group of admirers, the forced clapping she received from her claque on one side of the theatre on each occasion. Stasi refused to talk to the press, refused to talk to Carla, and avoided the cast, convinced that everyone was conspiring against her. She would be a silent martyr for her art.

'You know her. It would be better coming from you. I've done all I can.'

Julian gave Sir Miles a reassuring grin. 'If it was me, I'd give Carla a kick up the ass.'

'Andrew Broughton thought she was excellent, by the way. He was raving about her. I thought it was a lively performance.'

'Did you?'

361

'Of course, not in the same league as Anastasia.'

'We really must get the little minx to apologize.'

'Of course. But the publicity. Marvellous.'

'Is that the only consideration, Miles?'

'No, no. I wasn't saying that.'

'So you want me to speak to her?'

'Probably more effective. She's a tricky girl.' Sir Miles shuffled some papers on his desk. 'Andrew thinks he'll be able to get us fifty thousand. Isn't that good news? I know it's not much, but it'll start the ball rolling.'

'Is Carla Livorno part of the deal?'

'Good heavens, no. What made you think that?'

'At the rehearsal, Andrew couldn't take his eyes off her. I thought perhaps . . .'

'A man like him? She wouldn't even take a second look. But she has that effect on everyone. Haven't you noticed?' His fingers were drumming on the desk.

'Don't worry, Miles. I'll talk to Carla and think of a way of getting her and Stasi together.'

It was predictable they would both be late. Exactly at the time arranged, four o'clock in Fortnum and Mason's Piccadilly tea-room, Stasi was inexplicably detained in Hatchard's bookshop, thumbing through the music section. Carla, having sought out a small bar ideal for a quiet rendezvous in the nearby Meridien Hotel, was enquiring the price of a room.

Forty-five minutes later, they bumped into one another in the food hall, both looking equally startled.

'Hi, Stasi. I got held up.'

'So did I.'

'Isn't this a great place? How about this?' Carla had picked up a jar of crystallized fruits and was ogling the syrupy contents. 'You like these? I adore them.'

'Sometimes,' said Stasi tersely.

'I'm going to buy two jars. One for you. One for me.'

'Then I'll find a table.'

362

'My favourite shop. Ma gets a hamper at Christmas. She adores that pudding. Ever had one?'

'Of course I haven't.'

'Jesus, I forgot you don't have Christmas.'

Carla arranged herself at the table, and glanced quickly at the ladies in camel coats and Hermes scarves seated around them, thinking how much sexier they would be in the Italian version of the English look, Prince of Wales check jacket, neat black skirt, silk foulard carelessly round the neck, which she had chosen.

'Strawberry jam and scones and cakes. I want the lot. How about you?'

Stasi pushed the menu aside. 'I'll just have a pot of tea. I had a big breakfast.'

Carla giggled. 'And we all know what that means. How long's he staying?'

'Dominic? He's gone to New York to direct a new play.'

Carla swung round in her chair as the waitress approached, and suddenly caught sight of someone she knew. 'Christ! It's Leonora and Giorgio. They never told me they were coming to London. I'm sure it's them.'

Bounding off, she left Stasi to order. Out of the corner of her eye, Stasi observed the hugs and kisses, heard the extravagant adulation – they had evidently seen the first night of *Così*. The pot of tea was stewed, the scones untouched by the time she returned. Stasi folded up the newspaper she had brought with her and put it by Carla's plate.

'Oh, Stasi. Sorry about that. Something wrong? You in a hurry?'

'No.'

'You're not cross about that ridiculous article, are you? It was a joke. I made it all up, but I never thought they'd print it.'

Stasi put both her trembling hands round her cup. 'You made it up? That I punched Ian Davies? That I couldn't take direction? That I always got ill before first nights? That I was having trouble with "technical problems"? That I refused to talk to the cast and only sang half voice at rehearsals? That on one occasion the orchestra walked out because I asked for extra time? That my fee was the highest ever offered, and you were getting only half? That I was behaving like a diva before her time? That I spent all my evenings in the exclusive Maison Blanche? That I only wore silk underwear from Christian Dior? Congratulations, Carla.'

Carla poured herself some tea from the unwieldy china pot in a slow stream, watching it attentively. 'Did it say all that? I only skimmed it.'

'You needn't apologize,' Stasi continued. 'Just tell me why.'

'I'm truly sorry you're upset, Stasi. Things like that never bother me. You know me, I just didn't think. I did say you liked silk stuff from Christian Dior. Maybe I went on a bit. You have to say something when a reporter calls you up. This guy was hanging around the rehearsal room, taking down phone numbers. What was I meant to do? Stop him asking questions from people who wanted to talk?'

'Who wanted to talk?'

'Does it matter? How do I know? Some of the chorus, stage hands, maybe some of the orchestra, guys like that I suppose.'

'Why did you have to bring Saffron into it?'

'I must have mentioned the Maison Blanche. How was I to know some jerk would ring her up there? Julian could have said something.'

'Are you serious?'

'I wouldn't put it past him. If he was feeling bored.'

'He'd never do anything like that.'

'Really? How do you know? You live with the guy? Hey, have one of these.' Carla pushed a plate of scones towards Stasi with a sympathetic smile. 'Your reviews were fantastic, Stasi. Why worry about some arsehole reporter? Who cares?'

'I do. He made me sound like a spoiled bitch from Golders Green.'

'Oh? Where's that? Should I know?'

'Listen, Carla . . .'

'I'm listening. But I have to go meet my friends soon, they're only here a few hours longer.' Carla flipped away the crumbs from her mouth. 'Come and meet them. She's a designer in Milan. You'd like her. Let's get the check.'

'Sit there a moment.'

'OK, OK. I apologized, didn't I?'

'Why did you do it? Because I'm in the way? Because you want to grab all the attention for yourself?'

'Oh, that. I don't have any trouble in that direction.'

'You didn't hate me in rehearsals. What happened?'

Carla changed her tone, and began examining the hallmark on a silver spoon. 'I'm not getting the opportunities I should. I should be singing lead roles by now. Always the fucking bridesmaid.'

'You will. The right parts . . .'

'What right parts? I can sing any role I choose, you know that.'

Stasi looked round, and waved at an elderly waitress in the distance. For this production there was nothing she could do. They must never appear together again.

'Stasi? Well? Can't you say something? You think I'm good?'

'You know I do,' Stasi replied.

'You never mentioned it. How much better I'd gotten since *Carmen*.' She stopped fiddling with her spoon, and stared straight at Stasi. 'But not as good as you.'

'Different.'

'Different like Maria Callas and Renata Tebaldi? Who remembers Renata Tebaldi?'

'You can't compare yourself with . . .'

'Like hell I can. You're so goddamned superior, Stasi. Oscar Broderick thinks I've got what it takes. And he should know.'

Stasi took a deep breath, trying to stop herself saying

what she wanted to say. 'What's so wrong with being a commercial success? I'm sure you will be. You'll have everything you want.'

'Oh yes? What do you know about what I want?' Carla pulled at the wedding ring on her finger, and lowered her eyes. 'What I wanted has gone,' she said sadly.

'I know it must be hard, Carla. Without Maurizio.'

'He was so good to me. I'd gotten real fond of him.'

'So you find it easier, being here in England?'

'Yes. I want to stay. You can't imagine what it's like, being in a place where they don't say, "Gee! You any relation of Paolo?"'

Stasi smiled, and began to regret her outburst. 'We should have swopped places. Try having a mum like Gloria, then you'd really tear your hair.'

'You really want to know? I wish I didn't like you. I wish I hated your guts.'

'Why? I'll be going back to Europe soon. I'll be out of your way and you can talk to anyone you like. Didn't you say once there was room for all of us? All those opera houses, all those productions? Remember? After Signora Busconi's class that time?'

Carla laughed and handed over the newspaper. 'It was a silly joke. Now we can forget it.'

'You might.'

'I thought you'd have realized by now. Everyone wants singers to hate each other. Wow! They love it. Bet you all the performances are sold out. No one cares as long as you sing most of the notes. I've done you a favour. If you're sharp, you'll phone up that reporter and tell him what a bitch I am. Then there'll be another story. Singer fights back. How about it?' Carla took the bill, and Stasi stood up to leave. 'Say, you're not really cross, are you? OK. So I made a boob. Nothing's changed.'

'Yes, Carla. It has,' said Stasi, walking away.

Wrapped in Calvin Klein, Stasi left England determined never to return. They begged her to come back, Sir Miles, the conductor Gottfried Kellerman, the music director Malcolm Fuerstein, Julian Lieberman, everyone at the Opera Palace, and she gave an encouraging smile, but said nothing.

'I can't sing in England,' she told her mother. 'They don't understand me.'

On the plane, she sat next to the window and found herself able to watch the ground receding, until the outskirts of London became an unfocused pattern seen through the gaps in the clouds. The stewardess adjusted the stream of air blowing into her face, handed her a glass of iced mineral water, and asked her if she would mind signing her copy of *Vogue*. She looked again at the photograph of herself, taken against the glassy sweep of the Opera Palace, hair flying in the wind, one leg elegantly forward, eyes wide open, intense, the mouth subtly reshaped into a more sensuous line, and thought she was almost beautiful. The photograph on the next page, where she was giving a haughty smile, looked nothing like her. Next time, they would have to seek her approval for every picture.

She wrote Anastasia over the photograph she liked and the stewardess walked down the aisle holding the magazine flat over her hands as though she was about to have it framed and was guarding against the slightest crease.

A week later, Oscar Broderick phoned Stasi up in Paris, to tell her that she was being considered the following year for one of the great dramatic roles in the only place it counted, New York. How did it feel being part of history, drawing part of the line which stretched back to Caruso, Toscanini, Flagstad, Sutherland, Pavarotti?

'I want to be myself,' Stasi replied curtly, but she agreed to see him. If Dominic's career took off in New York, they could be together.

She still disliked Oscar's jowly face, the beard which needed encouragement, his way of touching her on the arm, but over lunch at the Crillon he paraded his knowledge of opera, and convinced her that no one had her interests more at heart than he. Hadn't he told the Met. she was the only choice for Lady Macbeth? They were desperate, just desperate to take on a top calibre artist. He'd seen her in Paris and cried, and he only cried for genius. Anastasia Wagner was going to be diva assoluta.

'Did you say that to Carla Livorno too? Don't you handle her?'

'Listen, Anastasia. Carla is a good girl, she'll get work, but if I was to say she was a great singer, I wouldn't be where I am.'

'I won't ever be on stage with her again. And I won't talk about it. To anyone. It's a personal matter, nothing to do with the garbage in the papers. Can you handle the press?'

Oscar gave an avuncular smile. 'You do the singing. I do the rest. From now on, let me assure you, it's roses.'

'I'll sign a contract with you when you get me the part,' said Stasi, pushing away his pen.

'Good girl. That's how it's going to be,' he replied, nodding with admiration. 'Believe me, you'll make it, Anastasia.'

During the months while she was learning the part of Lady Macbeth, Stasi gave several recitals in Paris, signed up with a record company, recorded *La Traviata* and *Orfeo* for television, made several appearances on French and Italian chat shows, took to wearing dark glasses and a headscarf in the street. She also knitted Dominic a sweater and learned to make home-made pasta. It was a few weeks before the subject surfaced which she dared not contemplate. Dominic was lying on the carpet, covered in paint.

'You didn't have to do the bedroom,' Stasi said, taking her afternoon break. 'I could have got someone to fix it.'

'Of course you could, Stasi.'

'What did you get for supper?'

'Fish.'

'Nathalie loves fish. Isn't it fantastic that she's got her

368

film together? At last! I'm dying to hear about Algeria.'

'Did anyone ring when I was out?'

'I'd have told you.'

'You might not have heard, if you were practising.' Dominic took a file and began to scrape the paint from under his nails. 'As long as I don't get a lecture on the régime. Nathalie always talks as though she's telling a bunch of infants how to spell cat.'

'It's just her manner.'

'Sure.'

Stasi extracted the file from between his fingers, and rubbed his shoulders. 'Still stiff?'

'Not stiff. Just totally seized up. Brain and body.'

'We could go out with Nathalie. I'm sure she wouldn't mind. You don't have to cook.'

'I don't have to do anything. Not that there's anything to do at the moment.'

Two productions which Dominic had been promised had fallen through. The play he had directed in New York had come off after two weeks. If he had had something planned in Europe, she convinced herself, she would have turned down Lady Macbeth. There would be no joy in discovering New York together; for him it was the city of failure. All her friends in Paris were working on something, acting in something, singing in something, except Dominic.

'It won't last long. We could go away for the weekend, Dominic. I can stop for two days.'

'You mean Lady Macbeth can go on vacation? Where will it be?'

'Wherever you like.'

'It makes no difference, Stasi. If you want to go away, we'll go away.'

He was trying to hide from her what it meant to have whatever he wanted from the Stasi Wagner fund. She could have been mean or generous, it would have made little difference. How much longer could he take it? he thought, every time he put on the Gaultier jacket she'd bought him, sat behind the wheel of her limited edition coupé, and went to parties where everyone was bright and shiny with success.

'Hi! I'm Dominic Morrison, Stasi's live-in guy. Dominic Morrison, controversial, talented, out of work producer. You've heard of me? Great.'

'We don't have to,' Stasi said. 'We could see . . .' She tailed off. There was no point in going to the theatre. It would remind him that someone was in work. How did Nathalie cope? Waiting five years to make her first film? It must help being French. They put a brave, arrogant face on everything. Americans were more sensitive. 'Does it upset you very much that things are going well for me at the moment?'

'Stupid thing to say. Do you think I feel my male psyche is under attack because you're firing away?'

'No. But I'm frightened that . . .'

'I'll leave?'

'No, no. You read about it all the time. One person does well, the other doesn't for a while, everyone feels sorry for the one who doesn't. It's like two horses pulling a carriage. One gets lame, and the other one goes off in another direction.'

Dominic laughed. 'So I'm a lame horse, am I?'

'Of course not. I couldn't do anything without you.'

'I can't help thinking maybe I've stopped being flavour of the month. There was nothing wrong with the play I did. With a good lead actor, it would have succeeded.'

'I know, I know.'

'Maybe I should start my memoirs. Else they'll start saying, "Dominic Morrison? Remember that *Traviata*? Did you see his *Don Giovanni*? Where is he now, I wonder?"'

'Honestly! You've only had no work for a few months. It's just like being an actor. Then suddenly up comes a starring role.'

'Stop consoling me, Stasi. It's not self-pity, it's frustration. I want to be out there.'

'Where I am?'

'For Chrissake! In the Met? In that towering inferno of a place?'

'You think I shouldn't have accepted? Why didn't you say?'

'Stasi, I can't stop you being a great singer. Let's wait till after *Macbeth*. See if you want to do a low budget production with me.'

'That's all I want to do. Honestly. But will you come to New York? Please? I'm sure something might happen there.'

'Right now, I can't say. Don't you think it's best you should be on your own for a while?'

'If you're not there, something dreadful will happen. I know it. One of the stage hands committed suicide the last time they played *Macbeth*.'

'Maybe the production was lousy.'

Stasi laughed, stood up and stretched out her arms. 'I'll make you king.'

'*Fatal mia donna*.'

'I wish I were. But I do love you, Dominic.'

'Better than my Gaultier jacket?'

'Pig!'

Then they made love, rolling and kissing and laughing, and she was on top of him until tears came and she lay back on the floor, gasping, calling his name, praying that it would always be like this.

Not even Dominic had prepared Stasi for the onslaught of New York. The first time she gazed at the tall façade of the Metropolitan Opera House, openly displaying its interior through an uneven net of black-framed panes subdividing the cathedral-high windows, the spotlit Chagalls with sweeping figures swirling against ochre-yellow and fiery red, the chandeliers like petrified jasmine, she wanted to run back down the stone steps. Even the Opera Palace would have been dwarfed by its towering opulence. She could imagine a whole army marching up the poinsettia-red

371

carpet of the wide central staircase. When she was taken onstage and looked out at the auditorium, with its sea of gold half moons suspended on three sides around her, she felt as though her breath was being sucked out of her, that she could never fill her lungs again.

'Will they hear me?' she asked the general manager.

'All four thousand of them,' he replied.

It was everything she had dreamed of as a child, the massive splendour of grand opera which engulfed cast and audience alike in fear, exhilaration and wonder. Years later, Staşi could recall the rapture of the opening scene, when she first heard the distant whine of a piper cutting across the tearing of the wind, and looked up towards the dark purple clouds stretched in jagged flags across the sky; the moment when the drawbridge of a towering, granite-grey castle eased down across a watery moat, and the massing clouds darkened to a thunder hue, until suddenly a bolt of laser lightning shot down onto the heaving grass.

She could almost feel the rocks under her feet as she drew her heavy velvet cloak around her. Her hair was hanging wild and wet about her face, a thonged band round her forehead, hunks of gold clasped round her arms. She stood summoning the rage, the driving force which would carry her through three acts. Love and ambition. Now she could embrace them both. Bred from stone and heather, white-faced, barely illuminated, she took one step forward, then another, then another until she was swamped in torchlight. Without turning her head, she glanced at the conductor's baton.

Several times, they applauded when she did not expect it. As though splashed by a wave, she waited until it subsided and gathered her strength. She felt her voice flowing out of her, pure, unhindered, as if escaping from every pore in her body in a golden haze.

At the end of the opera, she was borne aloft wrapped in a white nightshirt, and they carried her down towards the audience, Macbeth at her side. The rest of the cast moved slowly across the battlements in single file. Then they all froze, the stage darkened and the wind began to howl.

She heard her name, Ana-stasia, Ana-stasia, the stamping of feet, and came forward. Now she looked into their faces as they hurled out their expressions of joy. Flowers landed at her feet, showers of paper rained down on the stage, the cacophonous roar of shouted cries, whistles and hoots, assaulted her ears. Twenty minutes went by before the producer led her away.

Oscar Broderick moved slowly down the great stairs as though he had difficulty in walking. This allowed him enough time to eavesdrop. A series of long gowns swished past him. The beginning of the season, and an opera based on Shakespeare, which would account for the presence of Jane, Elizabeth, Jackie, Ivana, and Margaret. He could tell, the way they wore those continuous smiles which the British had never mastered, that rapture was in the air. Occasionally he nodded as an ancient opera star whom his father had represented raised her head fractionally to acknowledge his presence. This was why he was in the business, he told himself. It was like discovering penicillin: you knew the world would never be the same afterwards.

'The pasta's a dream!'

Stasi drew in a forkful of melting linguine mixed with slivers of truffle. She wanted to eat and eat, to quell the racing adrenalin still electrifying her after the performance. At her table in Le Cirque were Dominic, Oscar and his wife Amy. Stasi kept her eyes on Dominic. He had come to New York for no other reason than to see her, and he was laughing, which he only did when he was at ease.

'If you dropped a bomb on this place, there'd be no more movies,' said Oscar, casting his eye round the crowded tables.

Stasi giggled. 'I daren't look in case I don't recognize them. Is this the smartest place in New York?'

'Smart enough,' said Oscar. 'But now you don't need to recognize anyone. They're going to recognize you.'

She heard Amy asking Dominic whether they would be going back to Paris at the end of the run.

'I guess so. Looks like I'll be doing a TV show.'

'Dominic! You didn't tell me!' Stasi sounded a little too surprised and delighted.

He shrugged. 'Nothing spectacular.'

'It must be pretty important,' she said to Oscar. 'That's what I like about Dominic. He never shouts about things. But he gives out more in five minutes than other people do in five hours.'

Oscar recognized the signs. She had only sipped the heady drink; she didn't realize yet what it would mean to be known from Tokyo to Tucson. She clearly liked the guy, but give her another year and she'd want someone quite different. Dominic was a nice enough kid, perhaps he even had talent, but she had enough of her own; she didn't need his. When they'd developed a closer relationship, they'd be able to talk about her personal life. It was all part of it. Being a top agent was like having lots of families all crying for attention. Soon she'd be ringing him at three in the morning, like the others, except he'd take her call. Any time.

'May I join you?'

'Julian!'

'Do forgive me for being improperly dressed, but I've just come from a business meeting in Budapest.' He kissed Stasi on both cheeks. 'Superb, dearest girl.'

'You saw me?'

'Naturally.'

Stasi turned to Dominic. 'Julian's so crazy about opera. Some Englishmen are, you know. Remember? You met him at Carla's wedding.'

'And I haven't misbehaved since. I'm glad you're looking after Stasi,' said Julian, returning Dominic's glance. 'We want her to come back to us one day.'

He sat down next to Oscar, and Stasi noticed Dominic watching him.

'It's you he came to see,' Dominic said under his breath.

'Julian only likes singers when they're on stage,' she answered. 'Can't you see how disappointed he is? Lady Macbeth stuffing pasta into her mouth. How disgusting! Why don't you talk to him?'

'I'm sure he's more interested in listening to your agent. Later.'

'Once you two get talking he'll never stop. I know he likes you, Dominic. I can see it in his eyes.'

'I can't say I noticed his eyes, Stasi. But I noticed yours.'

'He was kind to me at the Opera Palace. That's all.'

'You're beautiful. That's what I meant.'

Stasi threw her arms round his neck and whispered, 'We can go. Isn't it wonderful? That I can leave whenever I like? You should see the suite they've given me, darling.' She put down her fork, and looked round the table. Her performance was finished; there was nothing more to say. The admiration was spent, and the conversation had veered onto discussion of the economy of the Eastern bloc.

'Dominic, darling, let's go.'

'OK. In a minute.'

'Now. Please.' She stood up, came round behind him and kissed his cheek, then tapped Oscar on the shoulder. 'Will they send my flowers round to the Plaza Athenée?'

'They'd fill a field. How about I give some to a hospital?'

'Can you arrange that?'

'Of course. No problem.'

She took Dominic by the hand, and as they crossed the restaurant the manager pressed a small sheaf of hand-written notes into her hand.

'Miss Wagner, small tokens of appreciation from our guests. Do come again, with our compliments. They tell me the Met. will never be the same again.'

She looked at him shyly. 'I'm sure that's an exaggeration.'

'Everything here is exaggeration. But we mean it.'

Oscar followed them out of the restaurant, observing

the glossy heads turning to watch her go, the expressions of satisfied curiosity. Yes, that was the girl who'd sung Lady Macbeth. Anastasia Wagner. From London. They didn't recognize the man with her, nor did they register his features.

Oscar returned to sit beside Julian. He excused himself to the ladies, and turned his back. The men would be talking business the next day; no harm in setting the agenda.

'Will Sir Miles be coming over?' he asked.

Julian smiled, and sipped at his brandy. 'It's an order, Oscar.'

'Next thing, Anastasia will be booked up for five years. That's America for you. What a debut. Even I didn't guess . . .'

'I know Sir Miles wants her to sing Tosca for the Palace. He's talking about it for next year. I'd say she's up to it, wouldn't you?'

Oscar lit up a cigar and leaned back in his chair. 'She had a bad experience in *Così*. It's going to be tough, Julian.' He was already treading the delicate path of negotiation.

'But not beyond your ingenuity, Oscar. We're both aware of the obstacle. Couldn't you find Carla Livorno something in Italy?'

'She won't hear of it. I've tried. But she might listen to you. Or Sir Miles. If he said there was nothing suitable for her voice, for example. Not for a couple of years, anyway.'

Julian brought out a packet of cigarettes, and peeled back the cellophane.

'You taken to the weed?'

'Only amongst friends. And when I reach a roadblock. We've got to find a way out. Sir Miles understands the situation, but his hands are tied. So to speak.'

'Meaning?'

'I don't think he appreciates Carla for her voice.'

Oscar's voice dropped to a whisper. 'Sir Miles? Are you saying what I think you're saying? Him and Carla

Livorno? I don't believe it.' Then he grasped Julian's hand. 'He wouldn't be so crazy as to have her sing Tosca? Don't tell me.'

'It's only a hunch on my part. I do know Carla a little, as she stays at my flat when there's nothing better to do. I'm a friend of the Livorno family, used to go out with her sister Beatrice. Sweet girl.'

'I see the situation.' Oscar crunched some Amaretti. 'We'll talk tomorrow.'

Within a day, tickets for *Macbeth* were being touted for several hundred dollars. Miss Anastasia Wagner had a pile of invitations and, having no idea which to accept and which to reject, decided at the last moment what to do. Within a very short time, she had found out where she should be seen. New York hostesses overwhelmed her with advice, with introductions to their favourite designers, specialist doctors, beauty therapists, and health clubs. They didn't mind that she wanted to go to the top of the Empire State Building without looking at the view, that she lingered in Tiffany's and Macy's and Bergdorf's and Saks, taking several hours to choose something they would not have bought, presents for Gloria and Lizzie and Raymond and Monty and Nathalie and Signora Busconi. And she never complained. Stasi Wagner made them feel proud of their city and they took her to their hearts. She was unique: the highest praise they could bestow.

Dominic stayed as long as he could bear it. She couldn't understand why he wanted to leave.

'Can't you see?' she said. 'I'm doing everything I've never been allowed to do. Don't you like me spending money? Isn't that what people do in New York?'

First, they stopped lunching together. Then he began to turn down the odd invitation. Then he refused to give an opinion on a piece of jewellery, a dress she had bought.

'I left the States not to be part of all that,' he said when she complained.

'I'm not part of all that. Just for now.'

'OK. Just for now.'

He almost wanted her to be unhappy, so he could take her in his arms and watch her mouth slowly curl into a smile, the spring come back into her step, her sad brown eyes regain a vivacious sparkle. Instead she was like a gladiator storming into the ring. Little by little, he began to think of losing her. Fearing the emptiness of her absence, he found himself longing for the day when someone else would pass sentence, when he could stop shoring up the pain with an acquiescent, distant smile.

Their first Sunday together, Oscar Broderick chose to ring early in the morning.

'Stasi? I have to disturb you. You well? You resting? Asleep?'

'Of course I'm not asleep.'

'Everything happy?'

'I love New York. Last night, another twenty minute ovation. I can't believe it.'

'Marvellous, marvellous. And Dominic?'

'He's fine.'

'Listen. Now you're going to love London. I've finally got you a deal. Weeks it's taken me. I've lost four pounds. It's the first time it's happened, Stasi. You've been offered a three-year contract at the Opera Palace.'

Stasi put her hand over the mouthpiece. 'Did you hear that, Dominic?' She stroked his back but he didn't move. 'Oscar, I can't possibly take it.'

'Will you let me explain?'

'No, I won't.'

'Then I'm coming right over. Just listen.'

'I've listened long enough, Oscar. When I've finished here, I'm going back to Paris.'

'Who says you can't go back to Paris? I didn't say you had to live in London.'

'What about me and Dominic? We have plans. I told you that.'

'I'm not coming between you and him, Stasi. Is he there? Shall I talk?'

Stasi put her hand over the receiver again. 'Dominic? Are you awake?' He grunted and rolled over on his side. 'It's Oscar. A three-year contract at the Opera Palace. Tell him I won't do it. He's waiting to speak to you.'

'Say you'll ring back later.'

That night, Stasi did not sleep clinging round his body, but hung over the far side of the bed, clutching the pillow, listening to the whirr of the hot air which was like blotting paper sucking up the moisture in her throat, that dry heat, enemy of the voice. She tried to open the window without success, and picked up the phone.

'Get someone to turn off the heating. Now. I can't sleep. I won't be able to sing. Why don't the windows open? I can't bear it. I can't bear the noise. And there's no mineral water.'

She felt a movement the other side of the bed, then a click. 'Can't you turn a switch, Stasi. What's gotten into you? It's off. Now go to sleep.'

'I can't.'

Dominic got back into bed, and pulled her round to face him. 'You're overtired.'

'Don't tell me what I am. I'm angry, not tired.'

'Why?'

'You know why. Why didn't you tell me not to take that contract? Don't you care? I thought we were going to do a production together. Have you gone off the idea? Tell me.'

'Stasi. You chose to have an agent. It's not my decision.'

'Of course it is. Oscar will do what I tell him.'

'Now you can do anything you want. You don't need me, Stasi. Not to make that kind of decision.'

'I do, I do. All right, I don't. I won't take it. Are you pleased now?'

'I'm pleased you're a great Lady Macbeth.'

'You think so? Really?'

'You know.'

'I don't. I want you to say turn it down. I don't need the Opera Palace. Why can't you say what you feel?'

'I love you. Don't ask me to plan your career. You've

379

got me on a hook. Whatever I say, you can blame me later. "Dominic wouldn't let me." Oh, Christ, Stasi. You know where I'll be. But I won't be forced into being a driving instructor. You're behind the wheel, so for Christ's sake learn to drive.'

'Why can't we be like we were?'

Convinced that Dominic was distancing himself from her because he no longer loved her, Stasi began to make arrangements on her own. She left her diary open on the table so that he would know where she was. He returned to Paris earlier than planned, and although he had not told her it was the end she read it in his strained face, the small lines which showed round his eyes. She tried not to think of their months together, the flat in Paris, the old piano which constantly needed tuning, the temperamental cooker jammed with boiled-over dishes they had neglected whilst lying in bed, the times she leaned over his shoulder to stop him working into the night, the times he used to come into the spare bedroom where she practised, helping her over a difficult passage. And she tried to put out of her mind that soon there would surely be another girl, packing away her clothes, admiring the freshly painted room, finding her tights at the bottom of his wardrobe, leaning over his shoulder. She heard the voices saying, 'Of course, now she's where she is, he couldn't take it,'; others saying, 'Who can blame her? Now she can have anyone she wants.'

Unable to accompany Dominic to the airport – she had promised to attend a lunch party given by Ivana Trump – she hung on to his neck in the foyer of the Plaza Athenée and wept tears down his collar.

'See you in Paris, darling,' he said, as he pulled her gently away, but she knew he didn't mean it.

At the end of the run, she had the choice of staying in the Hamptons with the De Veres, going for a short cruise with the Marningfords or visiting the Mississippi mansion of a former star of the Met. It was hard to think of going anywhere without Dominic, even harder to throw off the character whose mantle she had worn for three weeks. Her sadness at his leaving was changing into fury at herself. If she insisted, they could be working together again. He had set her shooting into the sky, now she could do the same for him. Then he would love her again.

Oscar put his foot down.

'Stasi,' he began patiently. 'It's a very generous thing. But no one has that kind of power. Can you imagine, dictating to the Met. or La Scala or the Opera Palace that you'll only sing with the guy who shares your bed? Even movie stars can't do that.'

'I thought you said anything was possible.'

'I'm not his agent, I'm yours. One day, you'll have enough money to put on your own shows, then you can have him. Right now, he's no good for you.'

'All right, so you don't like him. He's not big time. I don't care what you think. Are you going to tell me who I should go out with? Did I miss something in the small print?'

'Stasi. The last thing I'd do is interfere. If Dominic loves you, he'll let you alone for a while.'

'He's doing that all right.' Her voice choked. There was no one else she could tell. 'I wanted him here so much.'

'Something happened? Tell me.'

'I think it's over. Us.'

'Are you sure? Aren't you just tired? Always happens, Stasi. After a big success, you come down, nothing seems to mean anything for a while. It won't last, I promise. But I do have to give Sir Miles an answer.'

'Ah. So this is a business call. Miss Wagner isn't in the mood for business.'

'What did Dominic think?'

'I don't give a damn what he thinks. Not any more.'

Oscar heard her sobs escalating into a wail, then waited for more choking sobs. 'Anastasia? Are you listening to me?'

There was silence, as she bit into her handkerchief.

'Everybody loves you. I love you. Dominic loves you. The audience loves you. Have faith.'

'He's left me. It's my fault. I should never have sung Lady Macbeth. It's bad luck. Everyone says it's bad luck. I'm cursed, Oscar. What can I do?'

'No one who sings like you gets cursed. Don't be meshuga.'

'What?'

'I said don't be meshuga.' He heard a slight giggle.

'Funny. You don't look Jewish.'

'That's my girl.'

Stasi took hold of Rabbit, put down the phone and buried her wet face in Dominic's pillow.

Chapter Fifteen

Oscar was thundering down the phone, reminding Julian irresistibly of Beethoven's Fifth. Even though Julian was just about to leave New York, to tie up a couple of things in Los Angeles before he took off for Las Vegas, he let the agent talk. How could they both stand by and see a great singer hurling herself on the rocks? He begged Julian to help. She might swallow pills, lose her voice, throw herself out of the window. Would he be ringing if it wasn't a crisis? This was a nuclear alert. They'd spoken last night, then he'd rung again this morning. Thank God she was conscious. This was a potential disaster. And what brought disaster? Need he ask? The boyfriend, some boyfriend. He'd walked out, just when she'd really hit it big.

'Has she agreed to the contract?'

'Contract, contract?' Oscar screamed. 'You expect a girl in that state to think contracts? With a broken heart, would you talk contracts? She needs love and affection right now. You're in New York. You can save her.'

It was an irresistible appeal. Stasi was facing one of the first sacrifices on the altar of her sacred art. Sir Miles would do anything to have her in London again. Only Julian Lieberman could bring her back. It would be his mission, to return with her signature, no more difficult than tracking down the leaves of the bula-bula tree in the presence of hostile Amazonian tribes. And then it suddenly came to him. Oscar had got it wrong. Wasn't it more likely that she could rescue him? The more he thought about it, the more the idea fired him. Stasi Wagner, with the voice of an angel, would deliver him from his torment.

Hadn't she shown, in her hotel bedroom, that she wanted to save him? There would be a day when they made love, it was destined to happen, and as he took her in his arms the Wagnerian trumpets would herald his rebirth.

'Listen, Julian. I'm begging you. Even if you lose a deal, what's money?'

'Calm down, Oscar. I'll stay a couple more days, take in her last night. I'll look after her.'

'Julian,' said Oscar, his voice cracking, 'history will thank you.'

Following Julian's phone call, Stasi refused all her invitations, bought a couple of extra suitcases, had a massage and a beauty treatment, and spent a few thousand dollars with Calvin Klein. As she left the Plaza Athenée, she was presented with a forest of flowers. The stretch limousine with black windows was waiting for her. She would fly to Los Angeles in a private plane.

'I've never heard of an opera house with its own jet.' Stasi walked round the luxurious cabin, a champagne glass in her hand. Julian was sprawled across a scarlet settee like a liver-fed cat.

'I lend it to them. For special people. Do you like the red seats? Saffron doesn't approve. She thinks they're very British Rail.'

'Is the Opera Palace making that much money?'

'There are many people like me, who would rather create art than curse their stockbrokers. Getty created a museum of art. I prefer live opera houses.'

'The strange thing is, I've never seen you work.'

'I don't have to practise scales. Nothing like that.'

'Are you rolling in money? Should I have heard of your dad? I wonder what it feels like, being really rich.'

Julian laughed. 'It makes it easier to throw things away. I'm a self-made man from an averagely boring family who happens to have gone to a minor public school. Everyone hates it, of course. They'd rather you came from Balham or Oldham and worked your way up from selling whelks on a market stall. I think it's quite fun, being in trade. Intellectually stimulating.'

'What kind of trade?' she persisted.

'All trade is buying and selling. That's what I do. But I spend more time in banks than on street corners.'

'You're a banker?'

He grinned. 'In a sense. Fancy watching a movie?'

'What movie?'

'My favourite ever.'

As the opening titles of *Death in Venice* came up on the screen, Stasi came and sat beside Julian, leaning against his shoulder. Soon she was steeped in the music of Mahler, spellbound by the haunted face of Dirk Bogarde, weeping tears of sadness at his fate, tears of joy that she was going away on holiday with the man she must have loved all along, the man she should have met when she was sixteen.

They were like two larks wheeling upwards in the sky who would only descend when the sun went red and night fell. She couldn't remember when she had been so carefree, so little concerned when one day ended and the next began. She felt like Alice in Wonderland who had stepped through a movie screen, passing through into half familiar landscapes, half remembered scenes from the Radio Rentals monster which Gloria kept in the living room. The images passed by the panoramic windows of the air-conditioned Cadillac: lanky palm trees, distant hills, long avenues, sirens which battered her ears, a high shimmering sun which lost its harshness in a veil of dust and haze.

Julian was curious, amiable, good-humoured, and didn't mind taking her on the tourist route to the gaudy memorials of Hollywood's past: Valentino's grave in the Memorial Park, the tomb of Jean Harlow in Forest Lawn, the shabby footprints outside Mann's Chinese theatre. And then he showed her the people who would have no memorial, the mad inhabitants who put stickers on car windows saying 'La Vida Loco', who advertised their services with crudely painted signs saying 'Quick Divorce.

Bankruptcy', who hovered in junk-filled shops called 'Whacko' and 'Mania', and ate low-cal salads in 'Pazzia'.

'Stick a wide-angle lens over your eyes, Stasi,' he told her, 'and be a crazy Angelino.'

There were no rules, not for them. They could pick an hibiscus from a bright-turfed garden, take what pleased them without enquiring the cost, cross on Don't Walk, stroll down hot deserted avenues, accost people in shopping malls and bars for no reason except a smile, a jaunty hat, a child who took their fancy.

Julian never told her where they were going, as though he held the secret of a plot he refused to reveal. 'You should never give away the story. It spoils things.' If she asked, he gave so little information – 'Somewhere in the hills'; 'I'm trying to remember a place I went to once'; 'I think I was invited to a party tonight around here' – that she gave up asking questions. In the end, he agreed to give her clues. What was the point in having four suitcases packed with gorgeous clothes hiding in tissue paper? Julian evolved a game, a code which became part of their private language.

'Red dress', he might say, and Stasi knew that it would be a casual evening in someone's home. 'Blue dress': something for the beach. 'Green dress': early evening cocktail in a smart bar; 'gold dress': pull out all the stops. It was all she needed to know. He would always find some hotel, book a room for a couple of hours while she metamorphosed into the spirit of the moment.

She still had little idea of the sprawling city, but made notes for her memoirs – Julian's suggestion – to help her future biographer. After a week, she had learned the limited geography of the rich, had penetrated the barricaded mansions of Beverly Hills, driven down Laurel Canyon, had barbecues round countless azure pools. She could recite the litany. They always asked her where she had been, what she was doing, whom she had met. It was quite acceptable, Julian told her, to talk about yourself for half an hour without pausing for breath. If you stopped talking, they might think you were depressed, or had made a bad career move, or had financial problems. No one could be depressed in sunshine heaven; a little unhappy if your health was bad.

Stasi was doing just fine. She no longer showed surprise when budding film actresses acted girly and showed her the pistol they carried in their purses, or said, 'Am I dizzy, or is this an earthquake?' She was acting the star so successfully that she was often asked about her latest movie.

'*Così fan tutte.*'

'Of course. I adore foreign movies.'

'Is it on release? Video out? Don't worry, I'll catch up on it.'

She had been to the right places at the right time – cocktails in the Polo Lounge or in the designer-doodle bars on Venice beach, parties in Beverly Hills, in the Canyons, quick visits to the crammed antique shops down Melrose – and she had been recognized dining in Spago's, Citrus, and Ma Maison. 'Hi, Stasi, how you doing?' she heard from diet-shrunk, peepy voices as she was hunting out couture in Rodeo Drive or whacky originals in La Cienega.

'I'm just fine,' she said, giving a generous, toothsome smile, her eyes hidden, like theirs, behind a shaded mask.

One morning, Julian abandoned the code.

'Fancy a weekend by the seaside, Stasi? What'll it be? Brighton? Bournemouth? Or Frinton?'

They had moved from the Beverly Wilshire to the Château Marmont hotel, which Julian preferred. It was part of the Gothic Hollywood he loved, the old Hollywood, before they discovered the bland facias of 'style', when they went for broke with rickety imitations of anything which caught their fancy, from Scottish baronial to Moorish kitsch.

'I'm not going back to England, Julian. Can't you stay longer?'

He grinned. 'I'll force myself. Right. We'll go to Malibu.'
'Can I swim?'

'In the sea? Certainly not. There are sharks and sting-rays and giant octopuses and man-eating whales . . .'

'And mermaids?'

'The mermaids have taken jobs as waitresses, thinking they'll get into movies. "Really, Mr Spielberg, I can have my tail removed. I'm right for the part, I know I am."'

The driver pulled into a beachside café, where they were playing Tammy Wynette at shuddering volume. Stasi stood at the entrance of the plastic-timbered room, juke-boxes flashing, waitresses in shorts and drawstring blouses running from order to order. 'We're not going in here?'

'I'm having a coke,' said Julian. 'And a double portion of French fries and something which has come from the sea. Fish, I believe. And then I'll summon up something simply dreadful from the juke-box. Preferably the Righteous Brothers.'

A waitress greeted him with a giant-sized smile. 'Hi, Giulio. Great to see you back. Who's your friend?'

'She sings occasionally.'

The waitress laughed as she passed. 'Don't we all?'

Stasi sat staring at the ocean, having rejected a pink, cloying milk-shake after the first sip.

'Why did she call you Giulio? Does she know you?'

'Of course she knows me. It's her job. She knows everyone. Sometimes she makes a mistake with a name, but who cares?'

'So it's a sin not to know someone? This place is dreadful. Why are we here? Can't we find somewhere else?'

'I like it. Real America. People who sweat under the armpits and would rather eat half a kilo of steak than undressed salad and Perrier.'

'You're kidding me.'

'And they'd go for Gloria Wagner's salt-beef if the portions were twice as big and it was called pastrami and came with a Caesar salad and fries.'

'Don't remind me. I've come here to forget all that. And now I can. I want to go. Please.'

'In a minute, Stasi.'

Julian left the scallop-shaped table at which they were standing and wandered over to the bar. A fat, florid-faced man in a white polo-necked shirt and a houndstooth jacket slapped him on the back. Julian pulled out a notepad and wrote something down. The man gestured, as though wanting to buy him a drink, but Julian shook his head.

'Who was that?' asked Stasi, when he came back.

'An opera lover. He has one of the best collections of archive recordings in the country. Let's go.'

'Here? What on earth's he doing here?'

'He likes the shrimps,' replied Julian, taking her by the hand.

They left the driver to meet them later and Stasi ran along the fine sandy beach. In the shallow waters, a long way out, a few figures were balanced on rocks, carrying woven bags on their shoulders, bent double. Long-legged dogs bounded along, zigzagging across the space, coats glistening, but there were no deck-chairs, no ice-cream booths, no promenade, just a beach with the occasional shell, and giant gulls and sandpipers wheeling round aimlessly across an expanse which stretched to the horizon like the avenues which ended in another country.

Then the first wooden houses appeared, at first sight like shacks belonging to a tribal chief who'd abandoned a grass hut for something more regal, standing on criss-crossed stilts, cracked and weather-bleached, the wood-stressed, faux naif houses despised by the poor, prized by the rich. Stasi looked up, and saw a black-eyed, brown-skinned girl with two long plaits, naked except for a sarong round her waist, staring at her from a window. A man in cowboy boots, blue denim and a Mexican sombrero hat was spraying a flame-coloured plant on his balcony.

'Is this where the Puerto Ricans live?' she asked, thinking of the dispirited bus queue, at least an hour and a half away. 'What a state the houses are in.'

'If you sell a million discs, you might just be able to afford one,' said Julian. 'This is country living, American style. Movie stars getting back to their primitive roots. Getting their toes wet in the early morning, pretending they're in the backwoods about to kill for their supper. Seaside rustic. One of the houses here crashed to the ground in a storm. The ones who don't want to live so dangerously take a place in the hills. Up there, behind us, you can take the San Francisco freeway, escape the tedium of nature, and get back to art.'

He pointed to a long low house with a wattle-fenced balcony where a tangle of trailing creepers waved in the breeze like a sea-borne octopus. 'I think we'll take that one, don't you?'

'We're staying here? Who does it belong to?'

'An Italian film producer, friend of the Livornos.'

Stasi laughed. 'I might have guessed. And next you'll tell me that Carla stays here regularly.'

'Not that I know. But Marlon Brando used to shack up next door before he discovered Tahiti.'

As the sky darkened and a red sun plopped into the ocean, Stasi was impressed again. There were no sounds except for the gulls and the intermittent creaking of the wattle fence. The owner of the house must have been to Mexico; the floors and walls were covered in bright rugs, there were earth-red pots, silver-shuttered mirrors and masks with mouths hanging open, turquoise and silver necklaces hanging round the white walls, and multi-coloured tapestries covered in cavorting animals. The driver took the cases two by two up the steps.

'Thanks, Ben. Have a good time in LA. We'll be leaving Monday morning. Eight o'clock OK?'

'OK by me. Shall I get them to deliver the boxes of chocolates on Sunday, then?'

'Ring first. And make sure they're packaged right.'

'Trust me.'

Stasi overheard them as she stood on the balcony.

'I thought you were meant to be on holiday, Julian,' she called.

'Isn't this holiday?'

'Don't you ever stop? Why are you selling chocolates anyway?'

'Why not? Americans like them. Haven't you heard of chocolate futures? Dear Stasi. You should read the *Wall Street Journal*. Everyone's into chocolate nowadays. Finest quality rich dark smooth bars of profit. Want to unpack? One pair of jeans and some T-shirts is what I advise. I might even make you a marguerita.'

'Does Ben work for you all the time?'

'Yes. He likes travel. Anyone who comes from Birmingham would like travel, don't you think? And this is better than driving a long distance truck.'

Stasi followed Julian into a bedroom. He placed his cases on the one giant bed, then hers.

'Are you sleeping here too?' She was grateful that he had always booked her a separate room. He understood without asking that the loss of passion had to be mourned.

'The only other bedroom contains a cot and a bunk suitable for juvenile midgets.'

'I can sleep in the other room. I don't mind.'

'You mean you want me to.'

'No, of course I don't.'

'I told you it would be primitive. And there's only one shower room. Anyway, you decide.'

Julian opened a case, pulled out some jeans and a sweatshirt, tore off his travelling clothes as though she was not in the room and aimed them at a chair. She wanted to look away, but he was so unselfconscious she was ashamed of being coy. When you had lived with one man for so long, even looking at another's nearly naked body seemed like a betrayal. While he was removing his shoes and socks, she studied his wide back. Then he turned, and, as though he had guessed her embarrassment, he stood up to face her.

'I want your opinion, Miss Wagner. Should I lose some

391

more weight? Would you have me in the chorus as a naked slave? Would I pass the test? I fear not.'

Now that she was free, the prospect of having another man was awesome. The moment had passed, the moment in the anonymous luxury of her hotel when she had longed for his arms to crush her, longed to close her eyes, to open herself out, slowly spread her legs. Now that she was free to desire him, desire had flown. If he entered her now, everything would change, she was sure. Desire had given way to friendship. She loved watching his handsome face, the chestnut eyes which she had seen change from amused interest to the determined gaze of someone who was driven by an energy she shared, but which he reserved for her audience. He was forever seeking what lay round corners, perpetually stalking an unknown quarry, constantly confronting her with the unexpected. At times, she detected a hardness in his expression, belied by a lazy smile and the dimple in his chin. There was a mystery in their relationship and she did not want to discover his secrets in case the tension of unfulfilled desire was replaced by disappointment. She did not want to compare him with Dominic.

'I know you think of him every day,' he said, catching the dreamy, wistful smile which was clearly not intended for him. She lowered her head and for a moment admired his well-muscled thighs, the thighs of a man who would stride up a mountain. Then, having had a quick glimpse of his cock stiffening under the thin covering of his briefs, she looked at him again. He seemed changed. Suddenly she saw him as someone who wanted her, someone she need do nothing for, who would accept her without challenge. 'But I can't understand how he could have walked out on you.'

'He didn't. It wasn't as simple as that.'

'I thought it was. Still, I've yet to meet an American who knows how to appreciate women.'

'You think he didn't appreciate me? How can you say that?'

'If he did, you wouldn't be thinking about him. You'd be walking down the beach at Malibu hand in hand. Or he'd have taken you off to some flower-strewn villa in the Med. He should have given you a good time, Stasi.'

'You're wrong, Julian. Just because he couldn't afford . . .'

'Ah, yes. I do forget sometimes. Or rather I want to forget. Perhaps that explains why I detest *La Bohème*. I've never found poverty romantic. But unlike poets, painters and composers, your genius can be rewarded. Do you know how I felt, the first time I heard your voice?'

'Whatever you say, I won't believe it.'

'Why?'

'I've been in America too long.'

'You convinced me I had a soul. Nothing to do with God. I thought that everything I did, buying and selling, dealing with the petty things people grub for themselves, had a meaning. I don't care what I do as long as you remind me of my soul from time to time.'

'That's the first time you've been serious, Julian.'

'It does help. Being almost naked. Everyone should be naked when they go to church. If only the mean bastards heated them properly.'

Stasi came up to him and ran her hand over his shoulder, stroking his arm. 'Why don't you ever touch me, Julian?'

'Because you wouldn't make love to me in the way I want anyway. And I wouldn't ask you. What beautiful eyes you have, Stasi. Some cats don't like being touched, but they still purr.'

After she had changed, she found Julian lifting boxes out of the deep-freeze. All she could see in the kitchen was a microwave oven and a rotisserie embedded in the wall. Dominic would have brought out just ripe cheeses. There would have been crusty, uneven French sticks, Normandy butter, dewy wet salad leaves and a *tarte aux pommes*, overleaved with the finest slices of glazed, crunchy apple. She could not understand why Julian did not share her passion for food, why he was unable to appreciate the intimate connection between voice and stomach, music and the earth, how, being familiar with the best restaurants in the world, he could serve out a reheated glutinous hodge-podge labelled 'Sea-food fantasy in a velouté sauce' without apology.

'Shall we see who's on the beach?' he said, after Stasi had scraped most of the contents of her plate into the waste bin.

'But it's dark.'

He was dressed in a white track suit, headphones over his ears. 'How about a little *nachtmusik*?'

Outside, the moon beamed down a tenuous pool of light in the sea, the rush of air stirred the debris of twigs littering the beach. Stasi stood by the steps which led up to the glass front door, warm salty air rushing past her cheeks, watching him as he jogged into the distance, lifting up his feet to the beat of something she could not hear but which must have had a measured, regular rhythm, judging from his slow-motion movements. Then he turned, a white dot like a distant sailing boat, and came tacking back towards her.

'I'm short of breath,' he said, as he came up to her.

She took off his headphones and put them round his neck.

'Isn't it enough? The sound of the waves? The wind? Why do you need those? Shutting yourself off like a teenage kid.'

'Just enhancing nature. You don't think I can take it raw, do you?'

'What about Brazil? I bet you didn't walk through the jungle with headphones.'

'Certainly not. One doesn't want to provoke the natives. They think anything they can't understand is a weapon.'

Then he ran, leaped into the air, grasped hold of one of the beams supporting the house, and swung from it, raising his legs to a parallel position, before dropping down onto the sand.

'I'd never have guessed you were a fitness freak, Julian.'

He smiled. 'I'm not. But I like the idea of being ready for anything. I never know when I might have to jump a wall. Or fend off an assailant to protect your honour, Miss Wagner.'

'I can look after my honour, thank you.'

'Didn't you know? You're in dangerous territory. Let me be your knight in armour. Can I wear your favour in my helmet?'

'I don't like armour.'

That evening, she heard the creaking of the boards as Julian went into the bedroom. He had not said good night, as though he expected her to follow, but she curled up on one of the wicker settees, wrapped a rug round her waist, and tried to lull herself into sleep. Leaves toughened by wind and salt tapped intermittently against the glass and the distant reverberation of the sea began to irritate her. She had become accustomed to being enclosed in air-conditioned suites, with the objects she had collected around her: Nathalie's pot, Assunta's crucifix, an old lace fan which Dominic had given her, her music books.

This house belonged to a stranger who had not been there to receive them, and here she was with a man whom she was unable to fathom. It was like learning a part and never getting past the first rehearsal. As you continued, you expected things to change, to acquire layers of meaning. She couldn't imagine what lay beneath the well-tempered surface of this man. Did he never scream with frustration, or jump for joy instead of testing his muscles? What was it which drew him to the emotional heat of opera? She could not understand him. David Bowie in *The Man who Came Down to Earth*. He was like that.

Eventually she got up and walked quietly into the bedroom, half expecting to find that he had disappeared. But he was lying on his back, his eyes closed. A candle was guttering by the bedside.

'Were you reading? I came to bed. I always get tired when I'm not travelling. When I opened my eyes, there was my dream, gliding into the room. Come and be warm.'

'Would you like me to?'

'I was waiting for you.'

'You didn't say anything.'

'Dear Stasi, don't you know me by now?'

'No. What am I expected to know?'

'Come to bed and I'll tell you.'

She waited until he lay on his back again, and took off her clothes hurriedly, in a far, dark corner of the room. Then she lifted the light cover, and when he felt her next to him he blew out the candle, and put his arms round her waist. Her breasts were pressing against his chest.

'I love your body, I love your hair, your eyes, your voice. I love being with you, I love seeing your face.'

Stasi smiled. 'You sound as though you're making excuses. Why don't you kiss me?'

He pressed his lips on hers, then he turned her onto her side, still clasping her waist, and she could feel his cock hard against her buttocks.

'Let me see you, Julian.'

He was still behind her. One arm left her waist, and she knew he was holding himself, edging his soft tip down the divide. Then he was inside, just. At that moment, she thought of nothing but her desire to be penetrated. She had stopped thinking of who he was, what would happen, whether she should have, shouldn't have. He was there and she wanted him, wanted the aching gap to be filled, wanted to come and shriek into the night, to forget the man who had walked away. Julian put one finger on her flaming clitoris and she gave a great shudder. Then lights danced behind her closed eyes as he thrust ferociously upwards, making no sound. She was being fucked by a stranger, falling into an unknown chasm, crossing rivers, being hurled into the sky, heaving, panting, until she sank slowly towards the earth, floating downwards feather-light until she came to rest.

When she opened her eyes, he was lying still, his dark

eyes open like a sleep-walker. She stretched out her hand to stroke his head.

'Julian! Why?'

He took off the headphones, and she heard them clatter onto the bedside table.

'I was hearing you sing. Do you mind?'

'What was it?'

'"Casta diva."'

'So that's all I am to you. A voice. You could have done it with any girl. After what you said, I thought it might have meant something. How do you think I feel?'

'Don't be so upset. Didn't you enjoy it, Stasi darling? I thought you did.'

'Did you listen to my voice while you fucked with Carla? With Saffron? And how many others?' Stasi pulled his arms away.

'Stasi. We're friends. Take me for what I am. For God's sake don't end up like one of those girls who thinks that men have to be changed. I couldn't bear it.'

'I'm going to take a shower.'

'Don't be angry.'

'I wish you hadn't touched me. I wish I hadn't come,' she shouted. 'I wish I'd stayed in the other room.'

He heard her slamming the door, and knew she wouldn't come back to lie beside him. The shower was turned full on, the torrenting water bringing back memories of the jungle, thick leaves bending under the rage of angry skies, drenched clothes, a longed-for baptism.

It had been a failure. His redeemer had turned down the role. Hearing her voice had temporarily banished those other voices, but she must have sensed them instinctively, like some dogs who walked away in fear from a welcoming stranger. If only he had lived in Guadagni's time, when the castrato had a vocation. What would they do now? Measure out his life in mind-numbing pills and give him therapy? He had been with a tart once who said, 'That'd do the trick. How could you fuck with that?' She knew

397

someone who'd had it done, never had a woman since. How could he? Somewhere in his address book, under E for Emergency Services, he had her phone number.

Next morning, Julian found her curled in a ball on the wicker settee.

'Coffee?'

She stirred. 'I'd rather have tea.'

'I'm going to Las Vegas. I'll take you to the airport first, if you'd prefer. But I thought you'd like to see the grown-up Disneyland.'

'I'll think about it.'

Stasi looked at the relaxed face, the skin fresh as though he'd just dipped into the sea. For some reason, he had chosen to dress up as an eccentric Englishman, in long khaki shorts, with a jacket and tie, and knee-length white socks.

'Are you going to sort out a flare-up with the natives?'

'I'm going crab-hunting. See you later.'

'Where's the silly round hat?'

Julian laughed, and picked up his briefcase. 'Have you seen a carrier bag anywhere? To put the crabs in?'

'In the cupboard under the kitchen sink.'

The moment she heard Julian running down the steps, Stasi rushed over to the phone. She couldn't think what she would say, but she had to talk to him. They hadn't quarrelled. She could say she was staying with friends. No, he would know she was lying. She'd wait until he asked. 'I'm with Julian Lieberman. He's looking after me in the States. Nothing more. We're just friends.' Or would she blurt out that she hadn't meant to, she had done it just once, it hadn't meant anything, she felt terrible? No. A few minutes of pleasure which she would forget. That was honest. She wanted to confess to him. Well, not confess, just share what she had been going through. Make him realize that she had to experience things in her own way for a while. Hadn't he suggested that?

She was about to call, when she stopped. It would be

three o'clock in the morning in Paris. Dominic might be in bed with somebody else. Would he say anything? She would be able to tell, by the tone of his voice. The thought of someone else began to choke her. Another singer, perhaps, lying where she had lain all those nights, waking to steaming coffee and warm croissants, a tender kiss on the lips. The interloper had the face of Carla Livorno, although it would not be Carla, blond curls, sparkling eyes, naked breasts. As Stasi fought back her rage at the imaginary stranger, she told herself, 'I have to know.' Then she calmed down and thought that no one could ever be to him what they had been to one another. And could be again.

She heard the long ringing tone, could imagine him slowly coming to in the bright, freshly painted room, reaching across half asleep, his hair across his eyes. But there was no answer, not even a recorded message. Perhaps he was away working. She pressed the repeat button and slammed down the receiver when she heard the hollow hiss of the recorder. There was not even a message. Perhaps he'd forgotten to leave one; he sometimes did. She would try every day. One day he would answer. Every day he didn't answer would heighten the pleasure of hearing his voice when he eventually did.

Julian came back a couple of hours later, opened his briefcase, put the carrier bag on the floor and lifted out a large, beady-eyed crab the colour of well-baked brick which was languidly waving its claws.

'Take it away, Julian. For God's sake, put it back in the sea.' The briefcase was lying open and Stasi was horrified to see six unopened packets of cigarettes. 'What are you doing with all those? Don't tell me you've started to smoke?'

'All right. I'll confess. I couldn't find any crabs big enough to take home, so I found a native to barter with. Six packs for one crab. Always carry something which is prized by the local peasantry, preferably cigarettes. Cigarettes are useful currency, I find; much more reliable than a fluctuating dollar. A good deal, most satisfying.'

'You should try beads. They don't cause cancer.'

'They don't sell beads at airports, unfortunately.'

'What's wrong with paying for something?'

'Don't you find bartering more satisfying? Isn't he a handsome brute? You'd have to go a couple of miles out to find them this size. I would have thought you, of all people, would approve of bartering.'

'And I suppose you think all Jews are moneylenders. Julian, I give up on you.'

He held the crab up close to his face, just avoiding the lunging claws. "How would you like him? Hot or cold? I'd like him with Hellmann's, myself.'

'Ugh. It's hateful, killing something like that. I don't know how you can think of it. Take something out of the deep-freeze, if you're hungry. Please.'

'Live crab is better than dead cow,' he said, as he carried it off to the kitchen. He came back into the room a few minutes later. 'By the way, I made a reservation at the Desert Inn in Las Vegas.'

Stasi frowned.

'Your own room, naturally. But since there's always a convention there, I thought I'd make sure. If the idea appals you, I'll cancel and take you to the airport tomorrow. I'll only be staying a couple of days, enough to indulge myself. Then back to England. What are your plans, Stasi?'

'I'll probably spend a couple of weeks in Paris.' He looked curious. 'With Nathalie.'

'Ah yes. The film director.'

'How did you know?'

'You must have told me. Isn't she a close friend of yours?'

Las Vegas, Stasi decided, was Julian's kind of place. It suited his perversity, all those buildings constructed by wilful child architects, hotels with façades like ogres' castles from stand-up story-books. It was like what

400

everyone wanted Oxford Street to be at Christmas time, Blackpool to be in the summer, a fantasy town in which you could walk all day in the sunshine and never find yourself in grubby suburbs. It was as though someone had bought up a job lot of all the pillars, arches, battlements, gables and turrets from the sets of a hundred different operas and set them down at random.

They left the air-conditioned Cadillac and stepped into one of the streets intersecting the Strip, knocked back by the dry desert heat, passing pornshops and pawnshops with similar facias. Stasi bought a teapot which sang when the lid was lifted – Lizzie would be amused – a tea-towel with the portrait of one of the founding fathers of Las Vegas, Meyer Lanksy, to prove to Gloria that in America they had Jewish gangsters, and cufflinks shaped like violins for Raymond's concert shirt.

Julian disappeared inside the Golden Nugget. She took one step inside, smelled the mixture of powerful deodorant, unwashed hair, rolled tobacco and spilled Coke, and was assaulted by the jangling racket of banks of hungry, bulimic machines, flashing red and purple and yellow, being fed and vomiting out coins, being fed again. She saw a spinning wheel in the distance, and the shape of Julian's dark head outlined by the low hanging light.

'Did you win?' she asked, having retreated to the back seat of the Cadillac, thinking it was the heat which had emptied the streets.

'Fifty dollars. I'll show you where to play for high stakes. This is just an appetizer. Now I'll stay awake for forty-eight hours, like everyone else.'

For a while she followed Julian as he went from hotel to hotel, giving her a quick tour before he settled into serious gambling. In Caesar's Palace several men greeted him. Some sounded foreign; one was English. Unlike the shirt-sleeved sweating gamblers gripping the flickering machines, they wore suits. She assumed these were the ones who had fortunes to lose, the ones who talked in riddles.

'He rolled over on his back and shunted five from New York to LA,' she heard Julian say.

'Mickey's getting tight with the boeuf stroganoff. Maybe he should try goulash.'

'Give him a ten. Then try a twenty if he comes up.'

A grey-faced man in a check jacket and over-polished shoes gripped Julian by the hand. 'You looking for Eddie? Good to see you around, Juan. Did it rain in Barcelona?'

'A few showers. But the barometer's rising nicely.'

He nodded at Stasi, turned on his heels and disappeared into the crowd milling round the tables.

'Juan? Why Juan? Have you become a Spanish waiter with a passion for weather forecasts?'

Julian turned his head, as though searching for someone in the darkened hall with the cotton-wool air. 'He gets confused. He thinks I look like a guy he knows from northern Spain.'

'Everyone seems to think you look like someone else.'

Eddie turned up. He too had the pallor of a cinema usher, hair well-greased back, a dark blue silk suit.

'Glad to see ya.'

'Busy?'

'A guy dropped half a mill last night. Left twenty-five thou in tips. And he's meant to be bankrupt!'

Stasi was learning to identify a restructured nose. This one was a fraction small for the heavy chin.

'My friend, Stasi Wagner.'

'I know the face. You been here before?'

'Anastasia Wagner. She sings opera.'

''Course, you told me. You're the girl they made all that fuss over at the Met. Am I right?'

Stasi gave a surprised smile.

'You want tickets tonight for the benefit? Two?'

'Thanks, Eddie.'

'She's beautiful. Better than on TV. Lots of them aren't.'

Eddie took Julian by the arm, half turning to mutter something in his ear.

'Eddie wants to know if you'd take a spot. It's a concert to raise money for an AIDS hospital, Stasi. People like Barbra Streisand, Tom Jones and Grace Bumbry dropping in. All casual, like talent night at the local . . .'

'I can't appear with them, don't be crazy. I'm not prepared. I can't, Julian.'

'Eddie can get you a pianist, a rehearsal hall, steam room, masseur, beautician – anything you want. If you insist, he'll fly in a laryngologist. Starts at nine. That gives you ten hours.'

'What about a costume?'

'The gold dress? Let's take a look at the stage.'

'What should I sing?'

'Something from *La Bohème*, maybe. "They call me Mimi" should get them going.'

Stasi groaned.

'The Italians can sing along with you. There's quite a few out here. Mostly Eddie's cousins, so he says.'

While Stasi was sitting at the white and gold grand piano, easing into her voice, she thought how she would make the tense-faced men and women forget the neon lights, the sweet, decaying odours of beer and coke, the coins splattering and pinging like hailstones on a tin roof, the cards held in tiger-grips, the falling dice, the bored eyes of the croupiers. She would transport them far away from the wilting, transplanted palm trees, the pulsing neon lights, the steamy saunas in deserted pools.

They were joking and laughing in the dressing rooms. Grace Bumbry – taught by Lotte Lehmann, one of the great Lady Macbeths, and, rarest of all, someone who had sung Carmen and Micaela with equal ease – popped her head round the door and grinned, saying she missed her in New York but would catch her next time. For a moment, Stasi was overawed, and wished she had not chosen to expose herself with such a hackneyed aria; then she realized that more than anything she wanted to sing in public. Only another singer could understand that intense longing to feel the power of her voice furling out in the darkness towards the heat of an audience, the delirium she experienced from thunderous applause.

It was the first and only time that Stasi would sing Mimi in front of a gushing waterfall, a spangled weeping willow tree, and a cascading spray of coloured lights. The audience, primped and glittering, was almost quiet. She conquered Vegas as far as anyone could conquer a place where the highest praise was reserved for the biggest win.

'You sang real good. I can't remember the last time we had a British singer. But I'll sure remember this time,' said Eddie afterwards, when he had given his fifteen-minute speech of thanks. Four hundred and niney-eight thousand dollars in an evening. He'd make it up to five hundred. That kind of generosity made it all worth while. 'Take home good memories, baby. We're a hard-working crowd here, and I'm proud of this town. Tell them back in England that behind the high rollers, there's heart. Real heart. People forget that. Anastasia, just you come back soon.'

Stasi gave him a quizzical glance, then quickly smiled. Pompous creep, she thought, but she could never say it, not even to Julian. For some inexplicable reason, he appeared to like him.

Limp from the exhaustion of performing before a strange audience, it was only now that she began to miss England, not as a cloudy green respite from the glaring desert sun, but because it was the only place where she could say what she thought.

When I'm not on stage, who am I? she asked herself as she prepared to leave, unable to decide whether she would put her hair up or down, a stack of jewellery in front of her, a pile of clothes lying on the bed which could trans-form her into whatever she wanted to be. Soon she would be driving back to Los Angeles, flying direct to London, stopping overnight with Julian, then flying on to Paris. April in Paris. Cool showers, bursts of hot sun, fresh green leaves against grey buildings with filigree balconies.

Nathalie would bring her back to herself, with her she would breathe again, safe in that anonymous street far from the Boulevard St Germain. Stasi pulled on a clinging black dress, her Paris uniform, piled up her hair, inserted a pair of chunky gold earrings inspired by ancient Egypt and painted her lips bright, fiery red.

'I can't tell whether you've won or lost,' she said, as Ben drove them back in the dark towards Los Angeles.

'I've no idea. Look in my pockets.'

He switched on the reading light and threw across his linen jacket. Stasi felt about in the silk lining, and pulled out a thick bundle.

'How could you not know? You did win!'

'I may have done. After a while, you forget.'

They sat back in silence, listening to the gentle elegance of a Mozart quartet. Stasi thought Julian had fallen asleep until he suddenly spoke.

'Have you decided, Stasi?'

'About what?'

'Staying in England. I believe someone has offered you a contract. Are you going to join us?'

'I might. I haven't thought about it, really.'

The music came to an end, and a simpering DJ broke the spell. Julian leaned towards the intercom. 'Find something else, Ben.' Then he turned to Stasi. 'You know how much we want you. I want you. Sir Miles wants you. Malcolm Fuerstein wants you. Everyone who cares about music in England wants you. But we can't have you without your signature. What's stopping you?'

She flushed, unwilling to elaborate.

'If you're worried about Carla, I believe she's planning a film career.'

'If she's staying in your place . . .'

'Not any more. Actually, I've no idea where she is.'

A large banner outside the Opera Palace was bellying outwards, filled by the squally April wind. 'Welcome to the Kingdom of Song'. Dazed by her flight, Stasi followed

Julian through the thronging foyer, where a juggler was throwing silver balls into the air in time to the overture of *The Marriage of Figaro*, children were sliding down a giant dragon, a clown in a patchwork suit was cranking up a street organ and the elongated figure of Sir Miles was announcing future attractions from a giant screen.

As they left the lift to enter the glass dome where Sir Miles had his office, Julian took her arm.

'You promise it'll be different now?' she said, as she passed the familiar posters framed along the walls.

'Just wait. Even the Met. is jealous, Stasi. We can do anything we want. Fantastic costumes, stunning sets, the best people in the world. Open this door. There are some people waiting for you.'

'*Cara Anastasia. Mi hanno detto tante belle cose di Lei.*' Ruggiero was standing against a sweep of window, arms outspread, beaming at her approach. 'What a marvellous surprise! What pleasure! How lovely to see you!' he said as he embraced her, showering her with wet kisses. He gave a booming laugh. 'We are singing together. Two big stars who love each other. The press will go mad, but first I tell my wife. She will like you, I know that. And I? I will like your voice. *Che bellezza.*' He winked at Sir Miles, who kissed Stasi's hand.

'Ruggiero has just agreed to sing Cavaradossi. But only if you sing Tosca.'

The part she had longed above all others to play, with the most splendid tenor she had ever heard. All she could do was giggle.

'I'm sorry. I'm just surprised. I can't believe it.'

'Of course Paolo will be conducting,' Ruggiero added. 'The opera *in famiglia. Che bello.* I will eat rosbif with you when I return. Yes?'

Stasi was seated in Sir Miles's high-backed leather chair. The first thing she saw on his wall was a framed photograph of herself, sleep-walking as Lady Macbeth. He came forward and embraced her on both cheeks.

'We're going to have a fantastic three years together,

Stasi. People will look back and say, "Those were the golden years of opera."'

Oscar Broderick pressed a document into her hand. 'Read it. Never mind the small print, I'll take care of that.'

Stasi flicked through the pages, and stood up.

'Is there any objection?' asked Sir Miles, glancing at Oscar. Stasi observed them for a moment, Julian, Oscar, Sir Miles and Ruggiero, all attempting to hide their concern.

'Have you a pen?'

As Sir Miles handed her his, she smiled and said, 'As long as I don't have to wear a red dress. That belongs to Maria Callas.' She moved gracefully into a chair, read the contract quickly from end to end and scrawled her name.

Chapter Sixteen

Saffron had just returned from Paris. While she had been away, Carla had settled into the attic rooms at the top of the Maison Blanche. The long drive from Julian's flat to Mayfair took up so much time, so much smog smothering the throat. More flexible sleeping arrangements suited them both, and Carla could keep an eye on Saffron's deputy, who was a young divorcée, daughter of a west country landowner with impeccable social graces, but a habit, Saffron suspected, of helping herself to things which did not belong to her, a common consequence of an unsatisfactory divorce settlement. Saffron showed her sympathy, and held back some of her pay each month to compensate for the straying bottles of champagne and perfume. Business was booming and Edwina had a delightful way with customers.

A prison wardress pushed open the bamboo door of the Jungle Room, clad in a tight-buttoned belted tunic, official cap, clumpy shoes and thick black tights. Her lower garb would have been rejected by Her Majesty's Prisons, as it consisted of a pair of silver chainmail knickers and lacked the customary knee-length skirt.

'Champagne and a Bloody Mary?'

'Thank you, Melanie. Leave the tray down there.'

Carla had descended from her attic flat, nursing a temple-throbbing hangover: some ghastly stuff called port which she'd been given by Andrew Broughton.

'I feel like shit,' she announced, flinging herself on the grassy carpet which had replaced the original parquet.

'What do you think so far?' asked Saffron. 'I would like

something more arboreal. Does that monkey puzzle tree look jungly enough?'

'How would I know? Ask Julian. He's the expert.'

'Splendid idea. And he's got a chum at Kew, I seem to remember. One has to get these things right.' Saffron dropped a swatch of fabric at Carla's feet. 'Jungle print for the curtains. Does it go with the faux grass? I've found a darling little stuffed monkey. We could have him hanging from the tree. Over the hammock. It's coming together, don't you think?' She mounted a ladder and adjusted a spotlight picking out the open jaws of a garishly painted tiger. 'Did I tell you, Julian was in with Andrew earlier?'

'Next time you see him, tell him to pay for the crates of wine Eduardo sent over. Mean sod. He hasn't called me for ages.'

'Only because he hasn't had time. He and Andrew are in on some exciting business deal together, I gather. It must be property. I wonder if Andrew's thinking of selling off Covent Garden? Such a marvellous position.'

'Why should he? The Gilbert and Sullivan season did OK. And next they're putting on a classic musicals season.'

'And which starring role will be taken by Miss Livorno?'

Carla snorted. 'I'll never do another boring musical. And it's not my ambition to sing "Hello Dolly" to a bunch of wankers. Jesus, do I need that drink.' She gulped down the thick tomato juice and spluttered. 'That's fucking strong.'

'You've been in England too long. This is how it should be,' said Saffron, as she climbed down the ladder. She picked up a beaded African whip from a pile of props, placed it against the wall, and then searched for a hammer in her tool-box. 'Things are going awfully well for Julian. He's opening up in America.'

'Opening up what?'

'One doesn't ask. Hotels, I imagine. Apparently his

enterprise is showing unexpected dividends. And guess who went with him to Los Angeles?'

'How should I know? I don't get to look in his diary.' Carla groaned as the gentle hammer-taps seemed about to demolish her scull. The hammering stopped, and Saffron came to sit beside her.

'Your friend Stasi Wagner.'

'What about her?'

'Julian took her along. The great romance with that American is over. Isn't it sad?'

Carla let out a screech, and clutched at her head. 'She's nuts. Fancy letting him get into her pants. She's just as dumb as my sister. But he is meant to be a friend and I thought they taught loyalty in those goddamned private schools . . .'

'Public schools, Carla.'

'He's not her type, anyhow. She must have been desperate.'

'Stop being so horribly bad-tempered.' Saffron leaned over Carla, pulled back her curls and stroked her face. 'Cheer up. I doubt if Julian was in it for the sex.'

Carla swung round to look at her. 'I wasn't thinking about sex.'

'How disappointing.'

Carla began to pick at the grassy matting under her legs, pulling out green strands and tossing them aside.

'For heaven's sake, Carla, do something useful or keep still. Or go and have a sauna and sweat it out.'

'I know why he went away with Stasi,' she continued, ignoring Saffron's outburst. 'Sir Miles wants her to come back to the Opera Palace so he sends out his pet arse-licker. It's obvious. Be Mr Nice Guy and then she'll sign up again. Why is this business so fucking corrupt? I can't stand it.'

Opening a box in the corner of the room, Saffron pulled out a succession of ropes. 'I want your opinion, Carla. Which one to hang from the tree? Thick and hairy or thin and silky?'

'Silky. It unties better.'

'Quite right. One has to be so careful. Are you seeing Sir Miles this week?'

'I doubt it. He's at some arts festival somewhere. Talent spotting. Maybe he'll find the next Stasi Wagner, who knows? Then she'll get a surprise.'

'Only I was planning a special dinner party for the end of the month. Pauline Fudge has come up with some wonderful ideas. She's so creative. Could you persuade him to come?'

'It'll have to wait till I'm back from Italy. I'm off on Monday.'

'Something exciting?'

'A little business to catch up on.'

'Who is it? Anyone I know? Is it a girl?'

Carla smiled at Saffron's casual interest. 'Are you jealous?'

'I just like knowing where you've been. All right. I do hope it's no one special, if that puts you in a better mood.'

'I need to check out my estates, if you want to know. Then maybe I'll go see my singing coach.'

A beeper sounded from Saffron's pocket, summoning her to the duties of the day.

'Heavens. Five o'clock. I must be off. I've got someone coming in later who likes having a naked girl covered with pancakes so he can squeeze lemon all over her. Then I have to find one of my girls who hates spiders for the Spider Man. Are you in later?'

'I've got an audition.'

'Super. Good luck. Something nice?'

'Yummy, darling.'

It was not exactly an audition, more of a performance, even if it did last only twenty seconds. Had the Wolverhampton-based manufacturers of Rigoletto ice-cream known that the Marchesa della Robbia was soon to take part in a new opera about the slave trade, given added poignancy by several near-naked arias, they might have

411

withdrawn their offer, since their commercial was targeted at peak-time family viewing. However, fortunately for Carla, the dates did not conflict. By the time *White Slave, Black Country* by Edward Fawcett, winner of the Andrew Broughton New Opera award, had had its première, half the population of Britain and most of the population of Italy (there would be two versions) would have seen her stepping out of her carriage, the same carriage in which she had arrived for her wedding, to buy an ice-cream from a lowly vendor.

Carla went out to Italy accompanied by Elgin Beaston, the commercials director, the only name she cared to remember, together with the designer, the casting director, the animal trainer, the lighting cameraman, the head of sound, the head of wardrobe, the head of publicity, a go-for driver and a girl called something like Sippy or Sappy who always went on foreign shoots because she had long legs, was good with telephones and spoke essential phrases in a few languages. They would wait for two days, during which time Carla would spend the night with Emily, Paolo and Eduardo, see a few friends and buy a few things, and they would research Italian ambience in the haunts of the aristocracy, mostly bars and restaurants suggested by Carla.

Before opening the great gates of the Villa degli Spiriti for the members of Pyramid (International) Productions, there was someone she had to see, someone who was waiting to meet her. He would always be there, waiting to meet her, no matter how late she arrived. Carla parked her hired Mercedes in the square and walked over to the café. Pino the taxi driver was seated in his usual corner with a few voluble cronies.

'Marchesa.' He kissed her hand. 'You've come home at last. Like a bird who comes back to her nest.'

'Only for a weekend,' she replied loftily.

'There has been a lot of trouble.'

'How awful. What kind of trouble?' Carla replied, opening her eyes wide in astonishment.

She had tried to forget about the existence of Maurizio's disagreeable sons Ettore, Claudio and Alessandro. Now, Pino told her, they were starting to interfere, trying to arrange for the villa to be leased by the state. The decaying, neglected mansion had been featured in the local newspaper headlined 'Villa of Shame', and their honour was at stake. Although they could not take it over under the terms of Maurizio's will, there was now a case for state intervention. The historic villa would be fully repaired and opened to tourists in the holiday season. There was no plan to evict the marchesa. She could live there as long as she wished to, but who wanted more tourists? Weren't there enough already, making the village into a cattle market?

Carla kept her eyes on the church across the square, and maintained a numb serenity. 'I suppose I have to accept it. As long as I could come when I wanted to and it was renovated properly. Poor Maurizio. God rest his soul. He didn't realize what a state it was in.' She let out a sigh and refused the glass of brandy offered by Pino. 'When you're first married, you don't think about houses.'

'Of course you don't. A lot of the locals are disgusted,' said Pino, lowering his tobacco-cracked voice. 'But as I keep saying, we don't want interfering idiots from Milan around here. Next thing, they'll be checking up on us. So what if the villa needs a coat of paint? Unfortunately, you know how it is with traditional families. They shouldn't have lawyers, always creating trouble.'

Carla smiled sadly, then picked up her bag. 'I think I'll ask Maurizio what I should do.'

Pino and his friends watched her cross the square to enter the church, nodding approvingly and flinging out comments only delivered in male company.

'Nice piece of stuff.'

'Shame we can't see more of the legs.'

'She's the only della Robbia I wouldn't want to see in hell.'

'Eh.'

The priest unlocked the vault, and left the marchesa alone with her prayers. Carla unlocked the long drawer with a small key she carried in her purse, gave a heave and pulled it towards her.

'Hi, Maurizio. You're keeping well, I see.'

There was the waxen face gazing out of the glass with ever open eyes, the carnation in his wedding suit looked freshly picked, the blue striped suit uncreased, the atheist hand still grasping a wooden, silver-edged crucifix.

'Thought I'd let you know what's happening. You must feel so awfully cut off, locked up in there. Since you and I left, I've been having a good time with bad guys. Oh, and girls, too. You'd have liked that, Maurizio. And I've done things we never did at all. You jealous?' She tapped a long fingernail on the glass. 'Wakey, wakey, old boy. Your Carla is doing fine. Shall I sing you something from *Butterfly*? Would you like that? No. I've changed my mind. How about this? Imagine this opera house, bigger than the villa and all its grounds, that's where I'll be. Just me centre stage. The huge orchestra waiting. The roll of the drums. The conductor pauses, waiting till I'm ready. Everyone's hushed, paralysed with expectation. You ready? You're not allowed to drop off. Listen to this.'

She straightened her back, opened her throat, ran up and down the scale a few times, then began to scream out the ascending phrases of the part she was determined to sing. Carla Livorno as Salome was rejoicing in the discordant chromatic sounds of madness echoing round the vault, the notes bouncing off the walls like tracer bullets. Then she stretched out her arms, leaning her head back to address the cracked stones of the low ceiling, and swooped towards the high notes with abandon, spitting out Salome's venom.

She began to quaver at the last high A flat, and clutched at her throat. 'Fuck. Poor Maurizio. You can't give me my treatment any more. Never mind. Just needs more practice. I've been working on an earlier scene. How about a preview of Salome's dance?'

414

The priest, hearing the strange, leering sounds of the devil, came running down the steps. Then he let out an agonized cry and crossed himself. He saw the waving head, the undulating body of a half-naked woman, casting off her clothes, scattering them over the stone floor of the crypt, barely visible under the faint overhead light. Unable to believe that what he had seen was human, he averted his eyes and ran gibbering and ashen-faced into the square. Pino saw him taking a few steps one way, then another, as though trying to escape from a swarm of bees.

'Father, Father! Çalm down. I'm coming.'

'Desecration, desecration! The dead are about to rise!' he cried. 'Satan is calling them.'

Then he fell to the ground. Pino ran back for a tumbler of grappa, the owners of shops round the square stood outside, asking each other the reason for the commotion. Father Antonio had seen a vision. Father Antonio had had an epileptic fit. Father Antonio had eaten some poisoned fungi. He was helped to his feet, and staggered into the café. Shortly afterwards, Pino fetched his ageing Fiat and helped him into the back seat. At the *clinico* they would give him *calmanti*. 'It's a neurological crisis. Don't worry, Father. In Milan, they have them every day.'

Carla picked up her clothes, dressed, adjusted her hair, said some more comforting words to her late husband, made her exit from the back door of the church and called a couple of friends from her portable phone, leaning against a piously carved stone angel in the graveyard. One or two people noticed a woman in dark glasses wearing a scarlet coat and high patent leather shoes stopping at the small supermarket next to the bar, but hardly gave her a second glance. *Turista da Milano.* She bought a bar of thickly encrusted nougat, a couple of postcards, and strolled across to her car.

Elgin, too, was waiting for her. Four cars were parked haphazardly by the entrance of the Villa degli Spiriti. Carla accelerated to within an inch of the rusting, wrought iron gates, jumped out waving a bunch of keys, and gestured to the film crew to follow her. With a splatter of stones, they roared up to the façade.

'Is it Palladio?' asked Sappy, who had boned up on the architecture of northern Italy.

'It could be one of his,' replied Carla. 'But I told you it was in a dreadful state. God knows what we'll find inside. I just couldn't live here after my husband died.'

'We won't need to go in there, marchesa. I wouldn't dream of asking you.' Elgin took her arm. 'But that façade will be perfect. I can just see you coming up in a sweeping tracking shot, then the little ice-cream man dressed as a clown on his bicycle dings his bell and you get out – oh, it's all there. Fantastic.'

There was a brief consultation with the other decision makers in the crew, whilst Carla examined the thin-stalked roses which had lost their lustre and, choked with weeds, had reverted to a puny ancestor.

'Marchesa.' Elgin stood at a respectful distance. 'Can I tell you what we'd like to do? Then you can say, absolutely not, how ghastly, go home and I never want to see you again.'

'Sure,' replied Carla, noting his tight leather trousers with anticipation.

'The thing is . . .'

'Feel free, Elgin.'

'As we're pushing the Pistachio Pagliacci ice-cream we feel the best way of conveying the essence, the romance, the excitement, the escapist desire, the longing . . .'

'Yes?'

'It's a fantasy. A dream. Hot nights, the shock of soft coolness against the tongue, this mysterious woman who sacrifices everything for the one thing she desires above all else. She can hear the sound of the violins striking up from inside the house, the ball is about to begin, and then . . . this little man pedalling his ice-cream cart wheels into shot, smiling sadly, sound mix to that lovely "Vesti la giubba", then we cut to you, inside the carriage, then . . .'

'Fine. Sounds great. But what is it you want to do, Elgin?'

'Could we possibly paint the exterior?'

'Why not?'

'The designer wants to have it pistachio green. All green, a beautiful almondy green wash. Walls, shutters, green vines. Flowers. A kind of delicate Matissey, Gauguiny green. Subtle yet sensuous. A cool icebergy colour with overtones of earthy sensuality. That's how we see it, marchesa.'

Elgin put his hand on his mouth, as though expecting it to be slapped. Carla tilted her head back, contemplating his request, the villa, barred, shuttered, and rampant with weeds spread before her.

'So it would mean painting the lot, I guess.'

'Afterwards, of course, we'd restore the façade to any colour you thought appropriate.'

'OK, Elgin. Just one point.'

'Yes?'

'When you've finished, I want your guy to paint the shutters and the door a special shade of pink. That's all. You know that kind of pink on old ladies' false teeth?'

'Don't worry. We'll get it exactly as you want.'

'My late husband adored that colour.'

Elgin mastered his surprise and handed her a form fastened to a clipboard. 'Could you sign your consent, marchesa?'

'With pleasure.'

After three days of intense work, interspersed with anguished viewing of the rushes in a caravan brought from Milan, Carla quickly learned which camera filter suited her face best, how to avoid three-quarter profile, how to Vaseline her lips and hold her mouth a fraction open, and how she could nonchalantly hitch her long wedding dress higher than one would in real life as she came out of the carriage.

'And you've never made a proper movie before? You're a natural, Carla.'

Elgin reserved his anger for the poor clown who looked more like a San Remo waiter than an angst-ridden Pagliaccio. For Carla's performance, he had nothing but praise.

'In the next commercial, why don't you have me singing?'

'Great thought.'

Carla rested her hand on his thigh, keeping her eyes on the screen. 'When your guys have gone, care to join me for a drink at the Principe?'

The last cables had been coiled away, and the deep salmon pink paint was still wet on the doorway and shutters. Carla took a small brush to add a final touch.

'In blessed memory of my beloved Maurizio,' she wrote in Italian, sprawling pink graffiti across an expanse of green wall. To fix the image of ghastliness, she took a photograph just as the sun was setting, turning the pink a blood red. She would have one copy framed for herself – it could hang over the bidet – and the remaining copies would be sent to Ettore, Claudio and Alessandro della Robbia, care of the della Robbia family lawyer, Avvocato Mugnoni.

Before leaving Italy, she planned to call in on Avvocato Mugnoni at his office. She had been away for over a year, and she toyed with the idea of taking the cheque for her allowance and tearing it up bit by bit in front of him. Then, remembering the Pauline Fudge designer dinner party, she decided she would rather spend it on something outrageous in leather from Vivienne Westwood. Sir Miles was gradually discovering the uplifting potency of leather.

For once, Carla arrived on time at Sir Miles's flat in Marylebone.

'Bumbles!' she called out. 'Where are you?'

'In the bath,' a muffled voice called back. She flung open the door, and a wave of steam surged into the dark hall.

'It's bad for my voice. I'll put in some cold water.'

'How was Italy?' he asked, as a cold current swirled round his feet and crept up his legs. 'I'll get out.'

'No. Stay there.'

'But it's getting icy, Carla.' He reached for the tap, and she smacked his hand.

'You've been indulging yourself while I've been away.' As she spoke, she took a block of pumice stone and rubbed it harshly down his back. Next she poured some shampoo over his hair, rubbed it vigorously, and pushed his head down under the water. The suds lingered over the surface of the cold water, and he took hold of the side of the bath.

'I'm getting out. I can't play around, Carla, not today. Life is even more hectic than usual. I've got three meetings tonight.'

'Excuses,' she said, playfully pushing his hand away. 'Who is she? Anyone I know? Would I like her?'

'I told you, I haven't time for that kind of thing,' he said, pushing her away irritably. 'This is our biggest ever production, and I want to avoid mistakes. Major mistakes, anyway. When it's over, I'll be able to relax.'

'What's the production?'

'I can't tell you for the moment. Not until everything's under way. Come, I must get dressed.'

'We haven't finished, Bumbles,' she said, plunging her hand down into the water and gently pulling the foreskin of his cowering cock.

'No!' he said, with firmness. 'Leave it.'

'And your stomach. What's happened? Not enough exercise, Bumbles. Look at this! Been stuffing yourself. You'll end up all fat and puffy rushing off to the cardiologist.'

He pushed her aside, and got out of the bath.

'Let me guess. Which is it? Which of the four Ts? *Turandot, Tosca, Traviata* or *Trovatore*? No, you've done half of those. I know. It's got to be *Carmen*. It must be so hard finding an Engish girl to act vampish. They should teach them that in high school instead of hockey.'

As he vigorously pulled the towel from side to side he smiled at her, admiring her persistence. If she did well in this new little opera which Broughton was putting on, he might find something suitable, something light and frothy for Christmas.

'You're not going to tell me.'

'Bad girl. No, not yet I'm not. I'm saying nothing.' He took his razor from the essential supplies placed in order of urgency in the bathroom cabinet. When he was dressed, he found her poring over a large folder in his sitting room.

'What is it?'

'Lithographs by Pauline Fudge. Remember? You met her at the Maison Blanche. She's got an exhibition at the Albemarle Gallery. Fantastic reviews. Sold nearly everything on the opening night. I do so love her work. Did you know she adores opera?'

'No,' he replied, tightening his tie.

'Have you had the invitation to her dinner party?'

'I believe so.'

'You should have got her to design *Tosca*. She'd be fantastic. Is Stasi singing in Italian? I do hope not. It's so awful, Italian with an English accent.'

He should have guessed. It was never worth the effort, trying to keep things secret from Carla. 'I suppose your father told you. But I don't want you talking to the press. Understand?'

'Wouldn't dream of it. Here. Have a look at these pictures.'

'Only for a minute. Then I must go.'

He sat down to examine them and Carla laid herself across his lap. The heady waft of her perfume, and the erotic female figures in front of him, stirred him. When he was with her, he found her difficult to resist. He had only to slide to the ground and her writhing limbs would entangle with his. There was just time. He began to unbuckle his belt.

'You'll be late, Bumbles.'

'Quickly.' He pulled out his cock. 'Carla, I beg of you, suck me, suck me now.'

Carla looked at the incongruous pink organ starting up from his striped trousers and slowly lowered her face to lick the upstart into submission.

'In your mouth, in your mouth, dear.'

She drew back her face, smiled, and pressed her fingers round the base of his cock. 'Open your eyes, Bumbles.' A sudden jet of liquid hurtled into the air, and splashed down on his trousers. 'Naughty boy. Go and get changed immediately.'

Carla could see that Sir Miles was now in a more receptive mood. The trouble with absence, her absence, was that the habit of desire was dulled. He was all too easily distracted by appointments, lengthy phone calls and committee meetings, which drove him to file away the priorities of the flesh and submerge himself in the momentum of work. Men supposedly thought about sex twenty times an hour. If he did, he kept it to himself. Whereas Carla was constantly fired by the urgency of sex, and her singing was an expression of this urgency, he seemed to need a perpetual reminder.

'Get out your diary,' she said, when he had replaced his suit with another and stood before her with his briefcase, as though reflecting on a speech he was about to make.

'Why?'

'I want to make sure that you haven't planned anything which conflicts with Pauline's dinner party.'

'I'll come. It's written in.'

'Of course. Have you thought about your costume?'

'Costume?'

'Didn't you read the invitation? It's fancy dress. Julian's going as the Marquis de Sade. And he's trying to persuade Andrew Broughton to come as a cardinal.'

'Really? I never wear fancy dress.'

Carla pulled at the waistcoat of his suit, the dark blue

chalk-striped double of the previous one. 'Of course you don't. Leave it to me.'

Andrew Broughton climbed up the back staircase of the Maison Blanche with a spring in his step. Since returning from his cultural mission to Russia, Poland, Hungary and Estonia, he had achieved precisely what was closest to the Prime Minister's heart. His energetic diplomacy would result in cultural exchanges in Budapest and Warsaw, exhibitions in Moscow and St Petersburg, a Russo–British factory planned in the Urals, another factory on a superb site just by Tallin docks, and a month's retrospective of the best in British contemporary art. And Julian Lieberman had introduced him to just the kind of people he wished to meet – co-operative entrepreneurs who understood the relationship between raw materials, labour costs and financial returns. Flushed with pride, having achieved the marriage of culture and trade which he had expounded so eloquently at the last Brighton conference, he was longing to present himself before his golden girl.

He was surprised at the time and effort needed to effect a transformation. Four hours having his hair cut, or rather sculpted, by Benino in Knightsbridge, two hours of 'facial resurrection' at Don's Studio in Park Street, a morning spent in Effetti, being accessorized for the suits he had ordered from Frank and Sydney in Brixton, where all the young Turks flocked, according to *GQ, Vogue Men* and *Vanity Fair*, which now appeared regularly at his office. Once you acquired the knack of colourizing, mixing the right textures, finding your style – Julian had introduced him to a super girl who seemed to know what was required – it was easy. Now he viewed the baggy saggy appearance of his colleagues at the House with new eyes. It just wasn't necessary to look like that. Why be the laughing stock of those well-groomed buggers in Europe?

He hadn't expected Carla to start removing his clothes with what he considered to be indecent haste.

'Just a moment. I want your opinion,' he said proudly, as she was removing his foulard.

'On what, darling?'

'The look. My look.'

'Unbelievably attractive, Andrew. Love the suit.'

'And the hair? Do you like the wavy bit over my eyes? It does get in the way a bit. But when I've got my glasses on. Here. See my new glasses.'

'Andrew. This is serious style.'

'Oh, good. It cost me over two thousand pounds.'

'How wildly extravagant. What did your wife say?'

'She only noticed my hair. Said it wasn't me.'

'Stupid.' She began to unbutton his silk shirt. 'What's happened, has someone left you a huge inheritance?'

'Gracious, no. Careful. Don't just throw my shirt on the floor.' Andrew smirked. 'Our little business ventures got the green light. Julian says I worry too much. I suppose that's why I've got where I am. Do you think it's awful to worry?'

'I think it's awful to stand there in your shoes.'

'Feel them. They're not real crocodile of course. We're against the crocodile trade. Ersatz is acceptable. I told the V and A they could have my clothes for their collection of contemporary fashion. They were really excited.' He suddenly observed that he was lying on a rug which looked suspiciously like leopardskin. 'I say. That's not the real thing, is it, Carla?'

She giggled. ''Course not. You think Saffron would have anything real in here? Come on.'

'Can I fuck you now? You don't mind me saying fuck? I don't normally.'

'Screw my arse off!'

'Indeed I will,' he replied ecstatically, as he grasped her generous breasts and threw himself on top of her.

After he had left, and Carla was on her knees straightening the rug, she caught sight of something which must have fallen out of his pocket and slipped under the settee. A full packet of Winchester cigarettes. She had never noticed that Andrew smoked. Perhaps he did, the odd one when he was alone. You don't light up with a singer in the room. Next time, she would tell him she didn't mind the odd one. For her next role, she would be smoking a reefer, after all, and that would be the least shocking scene.

When Pauline Fudge made her appearance at the Maison Blanche, bearing a kestrel on one leather-laced arm and followed by two security men bearing vast canvases, only one of Saffron's girls passed comment.

'Who has asked for this bird?' said Carmen, the seventeen-year-old Brazilian girl from Sao Paolo who was learning how to extract a handsome tip from Julian Lieberman. 'Can someone else do it? I'll do spiders, but not birds. In my country, we have them not in the house.'

'That's Pauline Fudge, the artist,' explained Saffron. 'No one touches that kestrel, I assure you. She's rather batty, in a nice way.'

'Bat-ti? What means it?' Carmen had not mastered Saffron's vocabulary.

'A little mad.'

The slightly mad Pauline wanted everything slightly Dada. The usual Fudge approach was to take a typical Victorian pictorial favourite and give it an unexpected twist, though she would not describe it so simply. For example, a grand piano draped in a chenille covering had human legs ending in stiletto heels. Saffron's favourite had been commissioned by Carla. In a homely Victorian kitchen, a long-aproned curly-haired siren in a frilled gingham dress (with a remarkable resemblance to Carla) was embellishing a severed human head with bunches of parsley. It was entitled 'Salome in the Kitchen'.

Having pondered the effect of her *mise en scène*, Pauline sat down cross-legged with her kestrel, who also appeared to be hatching an opinion, his head darting in sudden movements to left and right.

'I've been thinking. You know my painting, *Ophelia in Bloomers*?'

Saffron nodded. She had admired the languorous face of

the bare-breasted girl lying on her back with arms outspread and legs together as though she was floating in a pool.

Pauline spoke slowly. Her Cockney accent waxed and waned according to the solemnity or frivolity of the concept struggling to assert itself. 'Be good to have a dining table like that.'

'Like what?'

'That shape. The furniture's got to be integrated in the concept. Otherwise the conflicting messages will nullify what I'm trying to achieve.'

'Quite,' said Saffron, waiting for a moment of clarity.

'So the guests . . . um.'

'Yes?'

'The appearance, I mean. Ought to be time specific. Now-time. And now-person kind of thing. If they're in costume, it downgrades the originating nexus.'

'Do I take you to mean that you've gone off the idea of fancy dress?'

'Not exactly.'

'Slightly.'

'Yes. Slightly. Kind of smart but not-smart contemporary.'

At the end of the conceptualizing session, Saffron phoned as many of the guests as she could muster and advised them that the artist, Pauline Fudge, would prefer more relaxed dining attire in order to emphasize her carefully calculated gastro-pictorial dinner. No fancy dress.

Nothing would induce Carla to discard the carefully engineered strapless leather evening dress with perspex breast enhancer and perspex viewing windows precisely situated over her spangled pubic hair and lower buttocks. She arrived at Sir Miles's flat, and threw open her cloak. He gasped, touched her as though she was on fire, was lost for words, and stuttered, 'I'm dreadfully sorry. I haven't had time to find anything original.'

Carla frowned, eyeing the chalk-striped suit, of which

he had a dozen replicas, with disapproval. His only concession was a bright yellow shirt with a velvet bow-tie. 'Never mind,' she said. 'We'll think of something.'

His expression brightened. 'A scarlet opera cloak and a cane, perhaps?'

Sir Miles tried to forget that evening, and hoped that the consumption of several crates of vintage wines, with the addition of champagne, port and brandy, would dull the memories of anyone else who happened to be present. He could only recall Andrew Broughton, Saffron, Carla of course, Pauline Fudge,. Julian, someone who apparently resided in Las Vegas, and a tiresome Texan who kept telling him he had financed twenty-three operas and only made a loss twice. There were several gloriously beautiful girls who said little, but smiled a lot. He did remember signing his name on a table which, in his inebriated state, he imagined to be in the shape of a naked woman. And he remembered saying to Pauline Fudge, following something which had happened, that the event was positively Bunuelesque.

The beginning of the dinner party had been unsensational. Realizing that Carla and Sir Miles would inevitably be late, Saffron had guided her guests away from the works of art, and brought on trays of caviar and oysters, and little succulent won-ton parcels with delicate, creamy fillings, urging her guests to begin the feast.

The conversation was earnest, if loud, the linen napkins still neatly unfolded on their laps, and everyone was observing the proper protocol of formal dining – talk to your right, talk to your left. Pauline Fudge was attempting to feed her kestrel with a spoonful of caviar, but otherwise Saffron's dinner could have taken place at any private dining room in one of London's fashionable restaurants without exciting comment.

'I say,' shouted one of the shining girls, who happened to be glancing towards the latticed door.

'Is it who I think it is?' whispered Andrew Broughton, leaning across to Julian. 'Oh, my goodness.'

Saffron, who was on her feet, directing one of the waitresses, had enough time to say quietly, 'Don't show surprise. Act normally. It's all part of the event. Do carry on eating.'

Carla, in a leather mask and a long tight leather dress, moved forward carefully, brandishing a long-tailed whip in one hand. In her other hand she was clasping a long chain. The chain was attached to a diamante collar, placed round the neck of a man who was crawling into the room on all fours, dressed in a Savile Row suit, but with bare feet. As his face was directed towards his shuffling knees, he was unable to see more than a collection of trousered and untrousered legs between the metal chair legs spaced round the strangely shaped dining table.

'Good boy, good boy,' said Carla, leading him foot by foot towards the table. She sat herself in a vacant chair and gave her order. 'Now sit. And don't move.' She turned to the company around her. 'I'd like to feed my dog. Is there anything left?'

'Here. Have this.' Entering into the heightened-environment factor which Carla was introducing, Pauline pushed forward a small bowl. 'The bird wouldn't eat it.'

'Thank you.' Carla looked down at the creature leaning on his hands below her. 'Now beg. Good boy. You can have all of that. Just ignore Bumbles, everyone. He's very well-behaved. Aren't you?'

He began to arch his back.

'Down, down. Stay there until we've finished. Mind you don't make a mess, else you'll have to sit outside.' Carla parked her whip by her chair, shortened the chain, wound it round her wrist, and began to join in the conversation in between spoonfuls of caviar. 'Just ignore him,' she said, noticing a few perturbed faces. 'Too much attention is bad for animals.'

'Shall we give him a cracker?' asked Saffron brightly, as though the sight of a man in a pin-striped suit on his hands and knees, his head hanging down between his arms, was a necessary adjunct to a successful dinner party.

'Later. If he deserves it,' said Carla.

'I could start painting men,' remarked Pauline Fudge. 'Funny. I've never got round to it.'

Andrew Broughton had suddenly lost his appetite. Turbulent emotions were causing his cheeks to burn, and he had developed an irritation in his ears which he was longing to alleviate by digging round with his finger. Things had gone a bit far for a fun evening, and his playmate siren was taking on the appearance of a hornet. You couldn't help feeling sorry for him, but perhaps that was the idea. No one was glancing in his direction, or even commenting. He had seen someone take his clothes off on the District Line once. Same thing. No one raised an eyebrow. But Sir Miles Mackenzie on a lead, that was a different matter.

'I assume this is a private occasion,' he muttered to Saffron, as a plate of monkfish en croûte landed in front of him.

'Everything here is private,' she replied, cutting through the pastry-sculpted body of the fish with a silver knife.

'I'm surprised Miles came along with Carla.' He hesitated. 'I didn't know she went in for, well, that kind of thing. Are they, as you might say, together?'

'Good heavens no! Merely dinner partners.'

By the time the meat course came, a blood-red rib of beef, he had changed places with Julian to be by Carla's side.

'Is he going to stay down there for the whole meal? I mean, we've all got the joke by now.'

Carla jerked on the chain. 'Say hello to Andrew, Bumbles.'

'Woof.'

'Now sit down again. I'll take you walkies later on.'

Andrew cleared his throat, and scratched vigorously at one ear, waiting for a similar opportunity, when no one was looking in his direction, to do the same with the other one. 'How's the autumn season coming along, Julian?' he asked, trying to retreat to safer ground. When they had last met, there hadn't been time to discuss artistic matters. Russians were exhausting in business. It was like being in a ten-act play by Chekhov set in a vodka distillery, but Julian definitely had the patience and the flair. Clever chap.

'We're thrilled. The jewel in the crown will be *Tosca*, of course. Two world-class singers in one production is quite a coup.'

'Is that English singer all she's cracked up to be?'

'Anastasia Wagner? She's going to be phenomenal. She's the kind of singer you get once in a century.'

Carla abruptly stopped finding so much in common with the Texan banker. 'She doesn't stand a chance with Ruggiero Gasparini. I feel sorry for her. Imagine sharing the stage with the world's greatest tenor. No way. And darling Ruggiero just has to dominate. Still, you can't blame him. It's what the public wants.'

'I disagree,' said Julian. 'Because, unlike most so-pranos, she's got the looks as well as the voice.'

'Woof, woof.'

'Are you suggesting I don't have the voice?' retorted Carla, giving a tug at the chain.

'Of course not. We all thought you coped with Despina terribly well. Delightful performance. But we weren't so thrilled by your performance with the press.'

Carla smiled at Andrew. 'Julian hates publicity. He's so old-fashioned. He thinks it degrades opera. But audiences are far more interested in which club I go to, where I get my shoes from and what I take for a sore throat than whether my phrasing is accurate.'

'Couldn't agree more,' said Andrew, noticing the hostile glance Carla had thrown in Julian's direction. He added hastily, 'But I'm sure your phrasing is always accurate.'

'You bet. Anyway, I've decided to leave Mozart for a while. And I know what I want to do after *White Slave*. Maybe next year.'

'*The Sound of Music?*' Julian suggested.

'Oh no,' said Andrew. 'Can I tell him, Carla?'

'Sure. Why not?'

'It's an opera I don't personally know. *Salome* by Richard Strauss.'

Julian sipped at his glass of wine and carefully replaced it on the rosily painted knee of the table. 'I hear they like Strauss in Australia. But then they like anything loud over there.'

'She's been practising the part. And I think she should do it at the Palace,' persisted Andrew. 'Fantastic story. And Pauline Fudge is dying to do the design. How about it?'

Several woofs were heard from under the table. Carla gave a kick.

'Unfortunately, we've got next year already planned.'

'Sir Miles is very keen on the idea,' remarked Carla, giving a further kick under the table.

'In that case,' concluded Andrew, 'perhaps we should all have a chat about it.'

'Certainly.'

Julian's powers of diplomacy were about to meet another challenge. Andrew's support was more valuable than he knew. The small government grant he had obtained for the Opera Palace would just about cover a couple of the star costumes. His position as director of one of DCCI's tributary companies was far more crucial for its survival.

Andrew was tucking into toffee pudding, swirling the gooey creamy caramel round his mouth. 'Carla dear,' he whispered. 'I think Sir Miles must have had enough by now.'

'No need to whisper. Don't be such a spoilsport.'

Sir Miles was biding his time. If you came into the room as a dog, under the mistaken apprehension that you would be met by similarly wild flights of fancy masking human guise, it was inappropriate to make an apology, rise to your feet, and sit down to dinner. Nor would it be acceptable to show that he had been fooled by Carla into enacting a role, albeit exaggerated, with which he was familiar.

'Woof bloody woof,' he muttered, waiting for the stiletto heels under his nose to edge out of vision. His knees were beginning to ache. At least in a rugby scrum there were other chaps to lean on. Then he heard Carla's name being called, Saffron summoning her for some jape or other, by the sound of it. His lead dropped slackly to the floor, and the coast was clear.

'Are you all right, old chap?' asked Andrew, as Sir Miles eased himself into Carla's empty chair.

'Just entering into the spirit of things,' he replied. 'I've only been a donkey before. Bottom in *A Midsummer Night's Dream* at school. I was rather good.'

'Well, fancy that. We did that at our place, too.' Andrew gave a complicit grin, remembering his own debut as a bewigged Titania. Good fun, school plays. 'Do you want to keep that thing on?' he added, noticing that the diamante collar was still in place.

'Why not?' Sir Miles replied with bravado, turning it round his neck. This gave him a few moments to think up some further explanation of his behaviour. 'Carla bet me I wouldn't do it. No point in losing at the last minute.'

'Well done, well done. Shame you missed out on the food. Shall I get you something?'

'I had some dog-biscuits before I came. But I wouldn't mind a drink.'

Julian reached across and filled up his glass. Both men were smiling. Andrew was looking at him with admiration. They hadn't looked at him like that at school. He should have acted the fool, just occasionally. Difficult when you're tall, but John Cleese made people laugh.

There was no sign of Carla, nor had she appeared when Saffron clapped her hands to call for attention.

'I hope it's charades,' shouted Andrew, trying to force his way through the rising volume of conversation, but he was to be disappointed. Since her gesture was ignored,

Saffron tapped a wineglass with her spoon, and managed to subdue the chatterers.

'For the finale of our little meal, we have something inspired by the Japanese. When they are about to enter a business relationship, so Julian tells me, they have a traditional way of proving the worthiness of their partners. A little test of character. We thought it would amuse you to see how it's done. All you have to do is to continue drinking your coffee and brandy and talking to one another, just as you are now.'

'How is that a test?' asked Andrew.

Saffron chuckled. 'You'll see. But whatever happens, you are not allowed to show surprise.'

'I think we've all done jolly well so far,' he replied, thinking of the way everyone had ignored the extraordinary behaviour of the man under the table.

'Close your eyes. I'll count to ten, and then just carry on as before.'

The guests, ears trained, caught the noise of shuffling, and, on cue, opened their eyes, looking at one another in silence. At that moment, the kestrel sitting on Pauline's shoulder shook out its wings.

'He can't be hungry. I fed him before I came.'

She chose this moment to give a detailed description of his diet, including the fieldmice she bred to make him a happy bird and her experiments to discover the quickest and cleanest way to despatch them. During this account, two of the guests let out a gasp.

'Leave the table,' commanded Saffron. 'I'm afraid you're out.' As two panting men, one supporting the other, collapsed onto chairs handed to them by one of Saffron's girls, Julian embarked on the gossip of Las Vegas.

'No, no. Ah, ah!' came a high-pitched squeal.

Soon Julian, Andrew and a Kuwaiti prince were the only men left. Of the women, only one had left the table, demanding to be taken home. A German baroness of uncertain age stared stonily at Pauline Fudge. The victors were given bottles of champagne by Saffron, those still present receiving consoling boxes of chocolates. The evening had come to a close, and Saffron summoned her girls to encourage the lingering guests to make a shaky exit down the servants' stairs.

Sir Miles found himself alone with Andrew, who was examining the table, shifting the debris to find the approximate position of the part of the female anatomy he wished to observe.

'I wouldn't mind taking this home. Shame the wife doesn't appreciate modern stuff,' he said. 'B-b-buttons, Miles, buttons,' he added drunkenly, noticing that Sir Miles had forgotten to take remedial action and was displaying a pair of old-fashioned Y-fronts.

'How did you manage it?' asked Sir Miles, leaning on his shoulder with one hand, attempting to button his trousers with the other.

'By trying to remember who won the Turner prize last year,' he answered smugly. 'Couldn't. Not for the life of me. Good way of stopping premature, premature . . .'

'Ejaculation. Come on. Bedtime, Andrew.'

'Bedtime,' he repeated, as they jointly attempted to negotiate the vertiginous downward slope of the back stairs.

'Poor thing. You must be exhausted. What did you do with your doggie?' asked Saffron, as she waltzed into Carla's bedroom bearing hot chocolate laced with brandy.

'Andrew must have taken him home. Anyway, Pauline was thrilled. She wants to do it again. And she's going to paint a portrait of Sir Miles. For free.'

'On a lead?'

'She wouldn't do that. This is official, for the Opera Palace,' said Carla, rather pompously Saffron thought.

'How kind. How are you feeling, darling, after all that exercise?'

Carla stifled a yawn, stroking her mouth. 'There were two of us. Anyway, it's only the same as one guy coming several times. Did you know it's the best way to sing Rossini? I might do that one day. Hey! You got the video? I'm dying to see.'

They lay back on Carla's bed as the screen above flickered into a fuzzy replica of the dinner party.

'I'm sure I knocked that little microphone under the table. Oh well. Who needs sound? Where was the camera, Saffron?'

'One was inside one of the gold cupids around the chandelier, and the other one was underneath the table. Alan was so clever, even Pauline didn't guess.'

Carla ran the video fast then slow and giggled over the freeze frames, but Saffron had little taste for the endless shots of sucking mouths and hairy balls.

'How ugly they are,' she exclaimed. 'Like bathroom fittings in MFI. I can't imagine how you could do it.'

'Show me a man's cock and I'll tell you who he is. I get it right most times. Come on, let's see it again. There's one guy I can't guess.'

'No. I'll lock it in the safe and then I'm going to bed. If you go to the *News of the World*, or anyone else for that matter, you'll never sing again, my dear. This is purely for my personal records department. And, besides, it could destroy Andrew's career.'

'Christ, Saffron. I'd never do a thing like that. I owe everything to that guy.'

'Forward planning, darling. Something you're not awfully good at.'

It was like having a bad grade in school, but that was just Saffron's way. She could get away with it, being superior, looking at you as though you'd got lipstick on your teeth.

'Know something? You ought to be running this crazy country,' remarked Carla.

'I am. In a way,' she said, as she removed the video-cassette from the player and snapped shut her bag.

Chapter Seventeen

Gloria Wagner had bought herself a second-hand electric typewriter in a car-boot sale to keep up with her correspondence. To tell the truth, she said to everyone, fame appeared to have come all at once, but really it had been creeping up on her. It started when *Hot Gossip* magazine had featured Gloria's sandwich bar, and the caption read 'Opera star Anastasia Wagner making one of her regular visits to see her mother'. Of course she hadn't, they'd done technical things with the picture, but if a little fib changed your life, who was complaining?

The Long and Short of It hairdressing boutique had a photograph of her and Stasi hanging askew in the window. Gloria's mantelpiece was littered with invitations to cocktail parties given by people with obscure surnames, distant relations suddenly claiming kinship. She was invited to give teatime talks at the Jewish Women's Culture Group and the *Muswell Hill Echo* ran a whole page on 'My daughter – the mother of international opera star Anastasia Wagner gives an exclusive interview'. And there were over fifty letters a week to answer, asking for details of the method she advocated for bringing up a child prodigy.

'One thing about being a celebrity,' she confessed to Lizzie, 'you can't go out of the house and collect milk bottles in a housecoat. But I suppose you have to make a sacrifice.'

Lizzie, who was to be seen in a selection of Gloria's last season's cast-offs and had taken to wearing a hat, was also enjoying the fruits of Gloria's spectacular rise to fame. She often heard passers-by remark, 'That's Gloria Wagner's sister. Did you know she was a singer, too? Such a talented family.'

And another thing. The wife of the kosher butcher who had been supplying the salt-beef all those years suddenly passed away. Louis Goldbaum, after a decent interval of widowhood, asked Gloria to go with him to a show up west. After he had asked her the second time, she agreed. There was no need for her to tell her boy that she'd been asked out. After all, Raymond had moved away. (He'd found a little place in Cricklewood, which she couldn't understand – why rent when you can live for free, but that was Raymond through and through – when he could have been saving what little he earned playing violin in Covent Garden.) All those years, she'd never had a man back to the house. You couldn't, not with children.

He wasn't what you'd call a handsome man, not like Sam. Shorter, too, but he had qualities. He only booked front-row stalls, pre-ordered martinis for the interval, picked her up in plenty of time, and always wore a tie. The Honda was spotless, no Kleenex on the back window or sweet wrappings screwed up in ashtrays, and she'd seen photographs of his two grown-up daughters, serious and brainy girls studying at Manchester University. His three-bedroomed house in Finchley had well-polished furniture and he read the *Independent*. As if that wasn't enough, he was thoughtful.

If Louis hadn't suggested it, Gloria would have never thought of sitting down with the bank manager and raising a loan to buy the floor above the shop to make into a sit-down area, and getting a licence to sell Israeli wine. And now Gloria's sandwich bar, with added Kosher Bistro Dining Room facility, not only had a clientele who came from Stanmore, Golders Green, Hampstead, and even as far as Regent's Park, but it had entered the *Good Food Guide* Gourmet Bargain section. Being well-off, which is how Gloria saw herself, was better than scraping a living, although she would never confess to her new status. 'I manage,' she'd say with a resigned smile. But the new affluence did bring headaches. 'Better a headache than an empty stomach' was a motto she had cut out and pasted on the fridge.

'I want to talk about Louis,' she announced at a family conference. 'We've been going out for three months and two weeks. I think he's serious.'

'Wonderful!' exclaimed Lizzie. 'Has he talked of buying you a ring?'

Gloria snorted. 'Ring? No one wears engagement rings. Not at my age. I've still got the one Sam gave me, anyway. Who wants two? But I want you to tell me. Honestly.'

'I like Louis,' said Monty. 'And if he makes you happy . . .'

'That's not the point,' said Gloria.

'He's got a nice business. Lovely clean meat he has,' added Lizzie.

'Neither here nor there. Well, he wouldn't be a nudnik, would he? I'm worried.'

'Gloria, do sit down, for God's sake.'

For once, Gloria took Monty's advice, stopped folding linen napkins into swan shapes, and threw herself on the settee with an anguished sigh. 'I'm worried.'

'We gathered that, Gloria. Who wouldn't worry, what with Stasi coming back to live in England? It'll come as a shock. You've got to face it.'

Lizzie held up her knitting under the fringed shade of the white gilded standard lamp. Her eyes were going. 'Why a shock? What is he? Some kind of a monster?'

'He'll be the first butcher in the Wagner family,' Monty said, thinking his way through the family tree.

'So? What's wrong with making an honest living?'

'Nothing, nothing.'

'If you want to know, I'm worried that he's going out with me just because I'm well-known. It bothers me. Sometimes I can't sleep nights thinking about it.'

'Maybe you should ask,' suggested Monty. 'Be frank. Nothing wrong with being frank.'

'He's very different from Sam. What would he think,

my Gloria marrying a butcher? And he working for the *Financial Times*.'

'Only in the advertising department. It wasn't as though he owned it,' said Lizzie. Gloria gave her a stony glare and threw her over a napkin.

'Stop knitting and make yourself useful.'

Monty put down his pipe. 'Why don't you wait till Stasi comes to England? See what she thinks.'

'Mind you, I wouldn't expect her to call him Daddy. Not like Ruth Fischer when she married second time around. What do you think, Raymond? You've been very quiet.'

'What am I supposed to say? He's OK. Good for you to have a man around the house again.'

'Even at my age, Raymond, there is something called romance and intellectual compatibility. Louis buys me flowers and we have long discussions about all kinds of subjects. He has very interesting views.'

'Wait and see, Gloria. No hurry.' Monty relit his pipe and turned on the news, his way of signalling that the agenda was exhausted.

Shortly after Stasi had settled into her suite at the Savoy, and had found rooms on the same floor for her music consultant, her publicity organizer and her hairdresser/secretary, she retired to bed. Having sung in six countries in eleven months, she was not only tired, but her throat was showing the first signs of fatigue. Even stepping from her limousine into the hotel, in spite of the silk scarf wrapped round her mouth, she had been hit by the fumes and the dank, droplet-laden air of London. England, country of chills, phlegm, hacking coughs and sudden fevers. She could feel her resistance lowering, and the first signs of laryngitis were prickling in her throat.

For two days Stasi spoke to no one, writing notes to Barbara, Mike and Herbie, who always travelled with her. Two days to learn her moves was enough; she had already sung the role in Monte Carlo. She would need every ounce of her strength to make Floria Tosca a pulsing reality for ten thousand people. Only five performances, but would her resilience stand the test?

Having inherited the strong physique of the Wagners, until recently she had assumed that her body would continue indefinitely functioning on all cylinders, like Monty's Volvo. Supposing it failed? Supposing the virus-ridden city infected her voice, brought fever to her chest? What if she had to stop singing for a while? How could she support her team, the furnished flat in Paris, the holiday villa she shared with Nathalie? It could happen so quickly. They used to say it took three generations to emerge from nothing and go back to nothing. Now it could happen in a year, six months.

Stasi wanted to be a child again, to have the bedclothes tucked up tight around her, to have a cup of something warm pressed against her lips, to hear the soothing words of comfort: nothing is going to hurt you. She broke her code of silence and telephoned Gloria.

'It's me. I'm in England.'

Gloria let out a whoop. 'Darling! At last. I've been counting every day. So much to tell you. You long distance? Faint it sounds.'

'Saving my voice, Mother.'

'You're calling me Mother? We've got formal all of a sudden?'

'I can't call you Mum. It sounds ridiculous.'

'Well, whatever you call me, I'm the same only different. Wait till you see Rosedene Avenue. You won't recognize it. And the front garden has been landscaped by a man who landscapes.'

Stasi laughed. 'You sound cheerful, anyway.'

'Cheerful? I've always been cheerful. My daughter comes back home, of course I'm cheerful. How's your health? How's abroad?'

'Would you ask Dr Cohen to call in on me at the Savoy? Tomorrow, if possible?'

'What's wrong? Something wrong?'

'Not really. I just want a check-up.'

'Stasi, I can't ask him to do that. He's still on the National. He won't even do East Finchley, not nowadays.'

'I'll pay him, don't worry. I need a doctor I can trust.'

Stasi remained in her suite, refusing to stray into the malevolent atmosphere of London's autumn. Apart from a very slight rise in blood pressure, Dr Cohen pronounced her fit enough to take on the world, but she still behaved as though she was fading away in a five star hospice.

The newest reporter at the *Daily Mail*, Sophie Wormington-Jones, who was assigned to 'celebs', sucked at her Mont Blanc pen, mentally cancelling out the first fifteen minutes of her interview. She'd have to get something more original on Anastasia Wagner, who wasn't yet a grade A celeb, the kind who only replied to prearranged questions, even though she clearly thought she was. Anastasia Wagner could say nothing about *Tosca* which would be of interest to her readers.

'What are your views on *White Slave, Black Country*, the new opera by Edward Fawcett?' Sophie began, placing an elegantly ringed hand on her tiny black tape-recorder.

'I don't know the work of Edward Fawcett.' Stasi spoke in a whisper and smiled, waiting for the next question. This girl might even know the difference between *Tosca* and *Turandot*.

'It's caused a sensation here. I just wondered if you might be seeing it.'

'Would you recommend that I should? I'm afraid I haven't heard of the composer.' Without waiting for Sophie's reply, she turned to Herbie, who was sitting behind her. 'Has that man from *Vanity Fair* turned up yet?'

'He's waiting downstairs,' he replied.

Sophie continued. 'In Fawcett's opera, there's an Italian girl with an American accent singing the part of a girl from Devon, but I suppose you get used to that kind of thing. When I interviewed Sir Miles Mackenzie . . . just a minute, I've got it here . . .' She flipped back the pages of her notebook. '"Given twenty years, *White Slave, Black Country* might well find a place in the repertoire of the Opera Palace. Fawcett is a talent to watch."'

'I can't keep up with every new opera.' Stasi gave a glacial smile. 'But if I have time, I'll make an effort to go.' Herbie coughed, to remind Sophie that she was exceeding her brief.

'The singer who's playing the lead in *White Slave* is Carla Livorno. I believe you've sung together here at the Opera Palace. *Così fan tutte*.'

Stasi stood up, opened one of the bottles placed round the room and poured some more mineral water noisily into a glass. She could feel the blood surging round her neck. Taking the glass, she paced round the room, hoping to be beyond the reach of Sophie's recorder.

'Is it true that you've refused to sing if she's even in the same building?'

Stasi glanced at Herbie, who was shaking his head. 'Absolutely not.'

'So the row you had during *Così fan tutte* is forgotten?'

'What row? There was never any row. Would you mind keeping to the subject? I agreed to discuss *Tosca*, and how I prepare for the role. Do forgive me, but my doctor has ordered me to say as little as possible.'

'Carla Livorno said recently that she was looking forward to meeting you in England, and that you had made it up.'

'I'm always glad to see Carla. We've sung together many times. Why do you have to invent these things? The life of a singer means hard work and little else.'

'Thank you, Miss Wagner.'

'You have three more minutes,' said Herbie but Sophie had put her recorder away, and was making for the door.

'I thought you handled that beautifully, Stasi. Can I tell the man from *Vanity Fair* to come up?'

'No. Send him away,' she said, rushing into her bedroom

and slamming the door. 'And get me some information on Edward Fawcett.'

She had thought like that once, of making herself known for singing in modern opera. But there was no one, in her view, who could hold a candle to the great masters. Why spend hours working on a production which would never be repeated? Yet what if Fawcett became the new Benjamin Britten? What if Carla had committed herself to the artistic rewards of an important new opera? What if she had received artistic acclaim? Dear old Stasi. Yet another production of *Tosca*, yet another mega-star throwing away her talent, prostituting herself in front of thousands, accepting vast fees instead of working for the future of opera.

For three more years, she would be a slave, a slave to the commercial values she despised. Even after months of giving staggering performances, Carla Livorno still had the power to turn her again into the doubting girl, the trembling singer who was pushed onstage by Assunta Melati. Worst of all, Carla had the power to make her hate herself, the hate which paralysed and dammed up the flowing strength of her voice. She put some eye-drops in her eyes, creamed down her face, pinned up her straggling hair and then attacked her nails, filing them with vicious sweeps.

She forced herself to rest, trying to rekindle her enthusiasm, trying to forget Carla, determined not to be broken by the physical and mental demands of a role which had defeated many a hardy singer. If only they knew, all those avid to penetrate the secrets of the famous diva, that she was spending most of her time curled up on her bed, trying to banish an all-devouring, humiliating emotion, watching the same television programmes they watched, having the same inconsequential telephone conversations with friends she rarely saw, reading one magazine after another, hoping for a white-out in her mind which would obliterate the sharp surges of loathing.

*　　*　　*

The mighty Opera Palace production of *Tosca – The Spectacle* had already been in preparation for several months. The vast sets, including half a cathedral, were being constructed in the hangars of a disused airfield in East Anglia. Over a thousand costumes were being assembled by outworkers in Hungary and Bulgaria. The lighting and sound rig would need twenty lorries to take the equipment to its destination. The revolving stage, technically the most advanced of its kind, would be transported from Las Vegas. A chorus of over a hundred and fifty dancers would be painstakingly trained. Even with a budget of three million pounds, the Opera Palace could not afford to pay Ruggiero Gasparini and Anastasia Wagner to feel their way into their roles.

The producer of this megaton production had been culled from Hollywood by Julian Lieberman. Mel Donitz had mounted shows, amongst others, for Madonna, Liza Minnelli and Michael Jackson. There was nothing Mel didn't know about giving ten thousand spectators a historic entertainment. Sir Miles had come round to defending the lavish spectacle he had initially derided. It was what the people wanted. Opera was now competing with film and rock shows, so why not admit it?

Tosca would have the biggest budget of any opera ever staged in Britain. And Julian had managed to tie up some impressive sponsorship. There were those who objected to the participation of tobacco companies, but Sir Miles swept their objections aside. Would the principled minority have preferred them to have opened another cigarette factory, rather than support a purely artistic venture? In any case, this was low profile participation. Winchester Tobacco's discreet lettering and tiny logo in the programme would be identified by those who cared to make the connection, but people rarely made connections, as Julian reminded him.

In a site forming part of the industrial wasteland of St Petersburg, the part which lined the brown polluted waters of the Neva entrance with rusting relics of Communist industry, abandoned trucks, roofless warehouses, soaring piles of rusting iron and rows of cranes with long arms hanging down dejectedly, a shining royal blue and silver aluminium shed stood out against the surrounding debris. Tall red neon letters spelled out Iskra along the roofline. The name had been Julian's idea, a mocking reference to Lenin's revolutionary paper. *Iskra*, the Spark. A speedboat roared past an ailing, smoke-belching cruise liner, and came to a halt against an ancient wooden jetty with enough planks remaining to form a precarious foothold to the shore.

'Grigor! Good trip?'

Julian nodded. Piotr, he noticed, was wearing a Western trilby which made him look like a street extra from *The Godfather*. 'Are they here?' he asked in Russian.

'In one, maybe two hours.'

They walked past the stacked cases of tobacco, and Julian stopped by the blending silos, watching the sandwich of leaves building up like autumn mulch.

'Good aroma. Hope it's not too good.'

Piotr grinned, showing two gold teeth, like the trilby hat a mark of his new-found prosperity.

'We make Russian grade smell like Virginia. Very clever machine.'

In another shed, thousands of cut cigarettes trundled round rollers and dropped into trays. Julian picked one out, turned it in his fingers, and examined the lettering at the top. 'The W looks right now,' he remarked. 'Now let's see the packs.'

Piotr took Julian into his tiny office and showed him a few samples. Under a magnifying glass, there was no fault that he could detect. Taking a packet of Winchester cigarettes from his pocket, he put the two packets side by side for comparison.

'Well? Which is ours?'

'Both same,' replied Piotr.

'They'd better be.'

Piotr went over to a rusty filing cabinet and handed Julian a pile of used document-sized brown envelopes, swathed in sellotape. The system worked on trust. By now, he wouldn't need to count the well-handled, grubby dollars. He put the envelopes in his briefcase, and was escorted back to the waiting speedboat, whose twin engines were still idling. Eight hundred thousand dollars in cash. Next day, it would be banked in Amsterdam. According to Julian's calculations, five thousand was missing, but for the moment he said nothing.

The Russian operation never ran smoothly – even if the smart boys refused to handle anything but dollars, a few of them went missing, the occasional lorry broke down and the cargo was 'lost', or simply disappeared over the border. But they were learning. A five per cent 'spillage' was acceptable. More than that, and 'Grigor' might decide to pull out. Two hundred workers would be jobless, and the empty factory would be yet another advertisement for the Russian inability to cope with the demands of capitalism.

Alexandr, one of the city's entrepreneurial interpreters, whose sister worked in the Iskra cigarette factory, had attached himself to a visiting British film crew. The service in the heavily curtained, bare-boarded bar in the Nevsky Prospekt was lethargic. He saw his opportunity to open an ideological discussion with his employer, a reporter from British news television, who was determined to seek out as many examples of the twists and turns of the black market as he could find. His bosses must have sent him to do that and it made Alexandr sick that they only looked for bad things. 'Nikolai, you don't understand.'

Nick Morgan took a stale piece of toast spread thinly with rancid fish paste and looked in desperation towards the bar, but Alexandr tapped his arm.

'Listen, please. If Western countries, they invest, then slowly slowly we can learn. For us, your idea of working is new. Under Communism, everyone is thinking the opposite. How not to work. My sister Irena is young, she begins to understand. Now she is employed in a very good factory. They make these. Here. American. Very good.' He handed round a packet of cigarettes.

'These aren't American.'

'But yes.'

The crew took a few puffs.

'Worse than Russian ones.'

'No! No! Here, we pay five dollars for one packet. Best quality cigarettes.'

Nick winked at the cameraman. 'Sounds like we've got another scam. Alexandr, why don't you bring your sister along?' He suddenly began to show an interest in the Iskra factory. A direct lead would be useful.

The foreman of the factory had been unwilling to let in strangers, but Nick expected that. His contact in Moscow could find a girl who would work there for a few months and report back for an additional fee. Preferably a curvy blonde who used to report to the KGB. There were still plenty around.

There were so many names to follow up, that Nick put the Iskra factory in the MAYBE section of his pocket computer. The crew were restlessly waiting for two hot-shot operators to come across and were discovering a taste for flavoured vodka. Alexandr's suggestions usually met with 'OK, tomorrow', but he managed to convince them that it was impossible to leave St Petersburg without the heady experience of the Kirov Opera. Like the Bolshoi, only better, he said. And they would see *The Golden Cockerel*, very popular in Russia. He had been several times, but his sister Irena had been only once. 'It is for rich people,' he said.

'Just like England,' replied Nick tactfully, as he handed over a few dollars for each seat in the front-row stalls.

The crew were losing their tolerance for Russian culture, so Nick ordered Georgian champagne in the interval to revive their interest. The spacious bar was peopled by foreigners, the idea of alcohol between acts being still alien to the native audience. The few tables pushed to the perimeter of the threadbare carpet were occupied.

'I don't know about that. I wouldn't mind trying out a couple of their singers.'

Nick slowly turned his head. The sound of the upper-class English drawl, cutting through the conversation of evening-gowned Americans discussing the shortcomings of their tour guides, was rare in St Petersburg. When he passed Irena a glass of lukewarm, fizzing champagne, he noticed her staring at two Englishmen, the only men in formal dress. It was unusual for Russian girls to stare.

'Someone you know?' he asked. The handsome square-cut face of the man who was speaking reminded him of a British actor. Or perhaps he was a visiting director.

'It's Grigor,' Irena said in a whisper. 'He comes to the factory. His English is very good.'

A voice announced the end of the interval. The Englishman's companion rose to his feet. Nick touched the cameraman on the arm. 'Know that face?'

'Wait a sec. Begins with B. Politician. I shot him for the arts show on BBC 2. That's it. He was going on about Covent Garden. Broughton, that's the name. Stupid cunt.'

'I thought it was him.'

Julian caught his flight from Amsterdam, and a few hours later he was picked up from Heathrow airport by Ben and taken to temporary offices in a vacant block in the City owned by DCCI. Whenever he saw the unlighted building, it reminded him of a bad deal.

They were preparing a progress report for *Tosca – The Spectacle*, which would take place in a ten thousand seater stadium, part of a new shopping and hotel complex nearing completion north of Luton for which DCCI had contributed some investment. Given a few years, and a free bus service, there was every chance that it would rival Birmingham as a cultural and business centre. And Sir Miles had been attracted by the idea of a new, underprivileged audience who would see opera for the first time in productions which would be the envy of London. When he saw the huge trucks leaving his Thames-side site, their sides luminously painted with 'The Opera Palace comes to Luton', he knew that he was going in the right direction. As soon as he had a moment, he would visit the site.

The bubbling bowl of cona coffee had long since lost its aroma. Phil was chain-smoking small cigars. Howard had changed shirts three times. Val and Bella were knocking back tumblers of whisky as though they were assisting at an Irish wake.

'Hi, Jules.'

'How's it going?'

'Bloody marvellous. They haven't finished the sets. Dennis wants the colour changed. One of the horses has gone lame. The children need homework time and they have to leave by ten. The fire regs man is kicking up stink. And I'm slaughtered.'

Julian sat on the edge of a desk, reached across to pull Phil's Manikin cigar from his mouth, stubbed it out in an ashtray and pushed away some empty polystyrene beakers, leaving a trail of coffee stains.

'Do you have to work in a nuclear waste dump? Why do you think I employed you? This isn't some half-arsed rehash touring in the stix. This is opera. Maybe you haven't realized. Phil, get down to Norwich. I want to see those sets tomorrow.'

'There won't be anyone in the place.'

'Get those lazy bastards working. I said get down there. Now. For one night, you can do without being screwed up the arse, can't you? Where's Mel Donitz?'

'He's over with Anastasia.'

'Val, why did we run out of brochures?'

'You only said to print five thousand.'

'Use your perfectly formed pea-sized brain. What have you been doing all this time? Topping up your sun-tan? I want to see fifty thousand. In here. Rapido. Where did you say you worked before? If you have a deafness problem, I should go back to being a Norland Nanny.

Always better if you can't hear them scream.'

Howard attempted to stem Julian's bilious flow. 'She's just lost a baby.'

'This isn't a lost property office. Did I tell you? We're working to a budget. You're being paid to make this happen. In three days' time, Ruggiero Gasparini and Anastasia Wagner will be on that stage. That's all that matters. Do you think they'll have sleepless nights wondering if you're behind with the mortgage? Mel has been sweating his guts out to make this happen. You want him to fly back to LA? Right now? Well do you? Will you kindly inform ten thousand people that we couldn't make it? And perhaps you'd care to repay three million pounds. I'll give you the account number.'

Phil doodled on a pad. 'The kids are tired, Jules.'

'I'll call an ambulance. Maybe that's what I should do. Give them all a blood transfusion.'

'Want some good news?' asked Howard. 'The chorus are all singing the same words now. And that's some achievement. And the dancers for Act Two are managing to avoid falling down the steps.'

'Val. Costumes arrived?'

'Half of them have. At least they've arrived in France.'

'Where's the other half?'

'They'll be coming soon.' She gave an anxious look at Howard.

'French customs are being a pain in the arse. We'll probably have to fork out some readies.'

'Will I by chance see *Tosca* costumes in the street markets of Sofiya? I'd hate to do that, Howard. Or hanging in the tourist shops of Calais.'

'OK if I get our man out there to pay them off, then?'

'Like hell.'

'What do you expect me to do, Jules?'

'Phone the French cultural attaché and tell him to extract his digit from his bum. Any other problems to make my evening?'

449

'Just a word.' Phil followed Julian into the corridor outside. 'No one's been paid for six weeks. The accountant keeps saying the cheques are in the post.'

'You saying my accountant's a liar? I thought everyone around here loved opera. I sometimes wonder. Ring me on the mobile at eight o'clock tomorrow morning. If I get some action from this twilight home up here, I might consider paying for it.'

As Julian walked smartly down the corridor, Phil contorted his face and mouthed a silent reproach. 'Fucking animal.'

They met for lunch at the River Café, the only place, Julian said, where the pasta would meet with her approval. This time, he had greeted her with a long-held kiss on the lips. After all these months, she had forgotten how attractive he was. He seemed less formal, more exuberant, and had discarded his formal suit for an open-necked shirt and a gaily patterned pullover.

'You look very Hollywood, Julian.'

He laughed. 'Do I? It must be the liberated Russian sun.'

'Did you have a good time?'

'I went observing wildlife round a lake outside St Petersburg instead. Charming place, dreadful mosquitoes. How's the precious voice?'

'Fingers crossed.'

'Have you seen the marchesa yet? She's appearing in something they call an opera.'

'I know. I haven't seen it. Should I?'

'White girl taken hostage by black revolutionaries falls in love with guerilla leader. I think it's about revenge and humiliation. But what isn't in opera? The rape is offstage, but the undressing is onstage.'

Stasi grinned. 'And the music?'

'There was a lot of drumming. By the way, don't be surprised if Carla drops in to rehearsals with Sir Miles. *White Slave* ends tomorrow.'

450

Stasi gulped. 'I might have expected it, with Daddy conducting.'

'Carla has decided that Miles needs evening classes in musical appreciation. *Educating Rita*, only he's Rita. He is discovering a passion for obscure, neglected or unperformable works. Unfortunately, his passion is costly. He wants me to raise a few million pounds for a production of *Salome*.'

Stasi fingered her heavy silver bracelet and allowed the waiter to remove the plates. For a moment, she wondered whether she could attempt the part. Technically, it would be possible, but how could she get inside the skin of a Salome, a creature who stood by in exultation while soldiers butchered the man she most desired in the world?

'That's not my kind of role. I must talk to him. If I was a Wagnerian singer, I might take it on. But he must recognize my limitations. Doesn't he understand? Hasn't he discussed it with Malcolm Fuerstein?'

'He's thinking of bringing in another singer. One Carla Livorno, his bonking partner.'

Stasi stared at Julian in disbelief, then she laughed. 'Miles Mackenzie? With Carla? Don't tell me he's in love with her?'

Julian looked mystified. 'Perhaps he likes travelling down well-trodden roads.'

'You can't let him be such a fool. Carla couldn't do that role in a million years. No one would ever take the Opera Palace seriously again. I wouldn't sing there. Neither would Ruggiero. You wouldn't allow him to do that? Would you?'

'I think the board will support me if I say that the Opera Palace would be bankrupted.'

'If she got her way,' said Stasi, 'where would that leave me?'

'Looking for another opera house. Being paid off. You'd be swimming in cash, though.'

'You think I'd leave, because of her?'

Julian leaned towards her, a gently cynical smile curling

451

his lips. 'I wonder why I prefer angry women? It's the fighting instinct. I find it very erotic.'

Stasi smiled, and touched his hand. 'I'm only angry when I have to be.'

'But if someone tried to stop you singing?'

'I'd kill them.'

'No need to go that far. I think you'd get bored in solitary confinement. The room service is atrocious.'

'Julian, you do care, you will do something, won't you?'

'I wouldn't be here if I didn't. I'll do my best. A dilettante will sacrifice everything for his art.'

When Stasi returned to her suite, she noticed several more vases overflowing with flowers vivid with autumnal colours: dahlias, deep-hued roses, daisies, and orchids. She read the cards propped up against each one. A pile of opened letters, with written comments pinned to each one, waited for her attention. There was a note from Carla, which she tore carefully into shreds.

Stasi arrived early, before her rehearsal call, and stood at the back of the stadium. Great chunks of set were lumbering upwards and swaying into position. Batteries of lights were fading up, fading down, booming bells echoing from the speakers. The stage rumbled round, and a prison courtyard replaced the cathedral, tiny-windowed cells rising up in gaunt rows. She tried to imagine being part of them, the audience of thousands, who would wait all night if need be to hear just a few notes from Anastasia Wagner. The fear which she thought she had mastered began to return, and she was trembling. In Verona they had called her back countless times. She had stood at the end with her head bowed, her costume clinging to her panting, sweating body, while they had roared and stamped and rained flowers on the stage. Could she capture this new, untried audience whose only subliminal acquaintance with opera had been gained from an ice-cream commercial?

Paolo Livorno was a distant figure, like a jet at the end of a runway. With only his face illuminated by a low-angled light, he resembled the bust of a craggy Roman emperor. The orchestra was barely visible. She had to resist the need to have someone close to her. On this stretch of stage, even a duet had to be sung at a distance. Julian would catch her last performance; he had left her a note saying he had had to leave the country again. If she had even caught sight of him briefly, she would have been consoled by his presence. Now she had to unpeople the space around her, divorce herself from the knocking, the hammering, the cursing, the thundering footsteps. She put her hands over her ears, and surveyed the huge area where, for those at the back, she would appear like a tiny, featureless marionette.

She could see Mel Donitz standing at the side of the stage, microphone in hand, next to the designer, screaming instructions. The terror began to take hold. The voice might crack. The lower register, so vital in *Tosca*, might let her down. The microphone might cease to function, so that they would only see a singer mouthing words, a distant puppet dwarfed by great pillars, statues of the saints towering mockingly above her. She could imagine the tittering crowd. And then she remembered a famous singer whose aria had been silenced by a mocking chorus of 'Brava Callas'. The ghosts of singers past were always there, daring you to follow in their footsteps.

She was halfway through the first act when she stopped. Paolo put down his baton. Mel Donitz rushed over. Ruggiero whispered, *'Cos'è?'*

'It's so cold in here. Can we have some heating?'

'Sure, sure. I'll see to it.' Mel turned to the designer. 'You got a coat around?'

'If I turn, like this, when Ruggiero takes my arm, I'll have my back to one side of the audience for several minutes.'

'You want to be centre stage, Stasi, that's OK by me.'

'That's not what I'm saying. I'm trying to get the move so it feels right. I need to walk up here. There's that great block of pillar in the way. Paolo, would you mind taking this part a little slower?'

Paolo nodded and Stasi paced round the stage.

Howard was working out the cost of Stasi reworking her move. Five minutes. He ground his overchewed gum to a tasteless, stringy ball. The equivalent of two symphony orchestras was eating up the budget. Twenty sheep were penned up outside, two sheepdogs. A chorus of a hundred and twenty would be getting made-up. All the ballerinas would be complaining about their shoes by now. Just when he thought everything would grind to a halt, she started to sing, and the weary crew stiffened as though they had received a thousand-volt charge. Paolo continued, even though they were clapping. No one ever clapped at a rehearsal. Then, suddenly, she stopped again, for no reason. She was in character, as though Scarpia had been standing there, but he hadn't arrived yet.

'I don't want any strangers here.'

'There's no strangers.'

She walked away, past the pillars, and came face to face with Sir Miles, observing at the side.

'I said I didn't want anyone here. Not even the head of the Opera Palace.'

'Stasi, I've only come to have a quick word with Mel,' said Sir Miles hastily. 'Then I'm leaving.'

As she continued the rehearsal, she noticed something disturbing out of the corner of her eye. One of the wardrobe girls, wearing something bright, a forbidden colour, deep, intense, throbbing violet. When she came offstage, she found it was Carla, sitting on Scarpia's stool, reading a magazine.

'Hi, Stasi. You don't mind? Ruggiero invited me,' she said, without looking up. Stasi stiffened. 'Funny how things pan out. Me in a whacky experimental piece, you doing Ben Hur. Pa says they haven't given him enough rehearsal time. Don't worry. He'd grumble if they gave him a year.'

'I'm not worrying,' Stasi replied, giving her a radiant smile.

On the second day of rehearsal, the Hungarian baritone, Laszlo, who was playing Scarpia, betrayed his curiosity. He and Ruggiero had barely talked, never having worked together before. Laszlo nodded in the direction of Carla.

'This lady is in love with me? Or you? Every time she is sitting there. I think to know the face.'

'Famous singer. Daughter of Paolo Livorno. All the Livornos I know very well. My wonderful friends.'

'Of course. Everyone is your friend, Ruggiero.'

In the dressing room, Gwen, the head of wardrobe, was supervising the addition of some pearl-studded lace to Stasi's neckline.

'Everyone's noticed. But I told them to ignore her. She just sits there reading all the time, even when you come on. But you can see she's watching you all the time, looking up when she thinks no one's noticing. I told Mel he should ask her to leave. But he won't. We all know why.'

Stasi was folding the brim of her wide hat in different directions, attempting to find a shape which would reveal her face. 'Oh?'

'You'd have thought Sir Miles would have got tired of her by now. Poking her nose into everything, giving her opinion. And I'll tell you something else. She was up to no good in one of my store rooms, with . . .' Gwen caught Stasi's look of disapproval and stopped. 'If you asked, Stasi, Mel would send her away.'

'At least I know where she is.'

'We all admire you, not making a fuss. One of the ballerinas – you know, that little dark one from Naples – she said she's got evil powers. Well, never mind. Just gossip.'

Stasi grinned and fingered the silver crucifix round her neck. 'Do you believe in that kind of nonsense?'

'Heavens no! We don't get hocus pocus in the valleys, where I come from. There. You like that better?'

Stasi stood up, and turned from side to side, attempting to swing the weight of the long, velvet folds to follow her movements. The heavy costume was like another character to be mastered. She would have to make sure the long train was well behind her when she ran up the steps, when she leaped forward to take Scarpia's knife, that Laszlo avoided treading on the hem when he clasped her neck.

'How is it?' Gwen stood with her hands on her hips, watching Stasi anxiously.

'It's beginning to live,' replied Stasi, gathering up the train and taking small steps backwards.

'Miss Wagner for Act Two,' came the crackling voice.

Whatever triumphs would mount up in Stasi's list of achievements, Gloria Wagner would always say that *Tosca* at the stadium was her favourite. When your daughter had reached the top, in front of ten thousand cheering spectators, with an ovation which lasted eighteen minutes and ten seconds (Monty timed it) you never wanted anything else again. It was all worth it, being a mother. It no longer mattered that Monty had never made it to Peat Marwick, that Raymond had never progressed beyond the second violin section, that Lizzie's blazing career had ended in a one-room flat in a converted semi. They had all come into their prime, emerging from the shell of obscurity, dancing in Stasi's waves, able to prove at last that a Wagner, their Wagner, had grasped the fame and fortune which God had held back, waiting for the right recipient of His glory.

'My apo-gee,' remarked Gloria, as she was driven off in a car which could seat eight in comfort. There had been a reception in London, at the Garrick Club, and she had met Emily Livorno (lovely outfit she had), Pauline Fudge (never did like birds), a Rothschild (not even Jewish), Jilly Cooper (asked me if I was on the stage!), and Monty had pointed out Melvyn and Clive from the telly.

'It makes me think of the Kennedy family,' she remarked, as the trees of Muswell Hill flashed past. 'Talent and money. And now we've got it. But we mustn't let it go to our heads.'

'If I won the pools, I wouldn't move,' added Lizzie, struggling to keep her eyes open.

'Quite right. Money isn't everything. It's hard work which counts.'

As the car came to a halt outside 12 Rosedene Avenue, Gloria was thinking about a nice house in Hampstead, one of those big ones near the Heath. Stasi needed a house, even if she wasn't married yet. Please God.

Sir Miles came to visit Stasi in the afternoon following the first night, laden with messages of congratulation. 'Everyone said last night, it was a definitive performance. Breathtaking, Anastasia!'

Stasi smiled weakly. The huge energy she had spent, the gargantuan effort, had left her reactions dulled.

'Ruggiero said he would return, just to sing with you. I doubt if he has ever said that before.' Sir Miles waited for a small sign of encouragement from Stasi, but she sank back on the couch where she was sitting and stretched herself out, her hands behind her head. 'Mel is over the moon,' he continued. 'Did you know he saw you in a charity performance in Las Vegas? Julian told me about it. If you wanted to take time out, now that you're so big in the States, we'd have no objection. I'm sure the Met. will want you again.'

'I'm sure they will,' Stasi said, with a sigh.

'You don't sound keen.'

'I'm tired, that's all.' Sir Miles would never understand, no matter how often he came to rehearsals.

'It wouldn't alter anything you do for the Opera Palace,' he persisted. 'Perhaps we could come to some arrangement.'

'Perhaps we could.'

'Do you want to rest now? I'll go if you like.'

He sounded as though he was avoiding a child in a bad mood. Couldn't he tell that her slightly clipped voice, which could sound abrupt, came from a throat which had given him Tosca? That the day afterwards, she would rather he'd talked about anything but her future performances?

Stasi found herself staring at his tie, bright yellow and blue circles chasing across a black background. His hair was longer, and he was wearing tinted glasses. Carla's work, she supposed. If she had wanted him to look like a Las Vegas impresario, she was succeeding.

'Would you like some tea?'

'A scotch would be welcome.'

Stasi picked up the phone and gave an order.

'Mel loved working with you. And Paolo, too. It may seem uphill sometimes, but they respect someone who sticks out for what they want, as you do.'

It was not that his tone was obsequious, but he seemed to be filling in time, waiting for her to say something. Her irritation began to gain the upper hand.

'Has Carla decided what my next production will be?'

'Carla? She's nothing to do with the Opera Palace.'

'Really? Judging by her constant presence, I imagined she was.'

'She gives me her opinion, that's all,' said Sir Miles, as though it was of little consequence. 'She's so proud of her father. I was sure you wouldn't mind her being around.'

'Who said I minded?'

'You are still friends? I know she behaved badly over *Così*, but she is terribly thoughtless.'

'I'm surprised.'

He looked startled. 'At what, Stasi?'

'At you and her. That's all.' Stasi subsided into a chair, without inviting him to sit down.

'I know she arouses hostility. But Americans often do, you know. They approach everything so differently. But I'm not here to talk about Carla. How is your delightful mother?'

'Fine.'

Sir Miles looked towards the tray, which had been silently placed on a table.

'Shall I help myself?'

'Do.'

'Have you heard from Dominic? Are you still in touch? I hear he's trying to raise money for his own company. I always like to hear what he's doing. One needs people like him to wave the flag of experiment. It keeps the rest of us on our toes.'

'I'm sure he'd like to hear that,' said Stasi. Then her face relaxed and she gave a slight smile. 'He sends me cards every now and again. It's difficult, when your lives change and you can't share the same jokes. Still, staying together was impossible. I wanted too much.'

There was something Stasi could not put her finger on. His slightly cavernous face now looked puffier, his cheerfulness sounded assumed. She wondered if he had taken to drinking more.

'There is an opera I've been considering,' she said deliberately. 'Not immediately, of course, because it would be too great a strain. But it's the first step towards Wagner. I've been thinking about *Salome*. What do you think?'

He laughed, almost with a sense of relief. 'There's nothing I'd like to put on more. We have talked about it. But that's some way in the future. We'll have to be thinking of something less taxing. Taxing in terms of the audience, I mean.' He paused, scrutinizing her face. 'Did Julian tell you?'

'He did mention that you were keen on the idea.'

'Did he say that Carla wanted to play the role?'

Stasi took a deep breath, but remained silent, as he lowered himself cautiously onto the edge of a stool. 'It would be out of the question,' he said, in his boardroom voice. 'I may not be the most knowledgeable person about opera, but I have some idea of singers' capabilities.'

Before leaving, he kissed her hand. Stasi felt sorry for him. He seemed like a man who had been reconstituted by somebody else. None of the parts fitted, like an incorrectly assembled jigsaw with the pieces forced into place.

For three more performances, Stasi became used to

seeing the flash of violet at the side of the stage. A few times, she thought she heard the sound of a smothered, hacking cough coming from the wings, or it could have been from someone near the front. Audiences always coughed in England.

Rumours ran round the orchestra, the chorus, that Carla Livorno was responsible. Exactly what she had done, no one was sure. Sitting there spewing away into her handkerchief was bad enough. Someone had heard Ruggiero telling her to go home. A tickle in the throat, incense always did that, she said. You couldn't infect someone, not from that distance. Evil eye, whispered the dancers. Only once did they meet in the dressing room corridor.

'Great idea to have that picture in the church looking like me, Stasi. Whose idea was that? But why the blue eyes?'

'Blond hair and blue eyes. It's in the stage directions. And in the plot.'

'Really! I never knew that.'

Stasi gave a strained smile and hurried away.

It was during the fourth performance that Stasi detected the first signs of a malaise, like seeing an enemy in the distance whose identity was as yet uncertain. In the intervals between acts, she stroked her throat, searching in the mirror for signs of anything unusual. At first, she wondered whether the lace round her collar was making her neck so hot and flushed. While she was singing, there had been moments when her throat had seemed unwilling to open out, as though someone had placed an obstacle in the cavities. She knew that some of the notes had been forced, underpowered. By the end of the second act, it was as though a fight was taking place in her larynx, the vocal chords quivering in expection of the next blow. The terror of losing her voice, of fading out in mid-performance, made her start to shake. She could barely swallow.

Mel and Paolo met in her dressing room to discuss her last appearance in *Tosca*. Paolo put his arm round her shoulder. 'No, Stasi, no, absolutely no. You do not sing. I could see you were in pain. Only I could notice, don't worry.'

Stasi chose her words carefully, every one a whisper. 'Tomorrow morning. Let's see. Don't tell anyone.'

'Look, it's no problem,' said Mel. 'Been done loads of times before. Voice trouble doesn't mean backing out. I know how you feel. How can you disappoint the fans? I've got your voice tape. We'll go mime. One thing about a big venue, you can never tell mime. OK?'

Stasi croaked with fury. 'No, Mel. No.'

'Sh. Sh. Go easy.'

'Some singers, they don't mime,' said Paolo.

'Sure, sure. But this ain't the Met. Different kind of show, Paolo.'

'You must not ask her to do it. You do not ask a lame athlete to make marathon.'

'Will you cancel?' croaked Stasi.

'I think Eva is free, Mel. She is a good friend.'

'Good thought. Anyhow, have the specialist come. Maybe tomorrow she'll be on top of the world.'

Sir Miles was in his shirt sleeves. He had been talking for two hours.

'I wish they'd leave us alone. Can't they see I'm running an opera house? Why does it take me a whole morning to convince the press that Stasi has tracheitis?'

Julian doodled a succession of interlocking triangles on a press release someone had left behind. 'Can I suggest something?'

'Certainly.'

'I'm the last person to give you advice. But if I were you . . .'

'I've done everything in my power for Stasi. If she needs rest, she can rest. I talked to her earlier this morning. What the press concocts is irrelevant. The public will still come to her next performance, and if at first it's from morbid curiosity, they might come to discover the artist. Isn't that the whole idea, why we're in business?'

'Indeed,' said Julian. 'But I was thinking of Carla.'

'That's my affair. She didn't talk to anyone, if that's what you mean. You can't blame her on this occasion.'

'Are you sure?'

'I know Carla. She's come to terms with how she feels about Stasi. We've discussed it very frankly. And I'll find the right moment to tell her I don't think she's ready for Salome. Do you agree?'

Julian nodded in approval. He was accustomed to others taking his opinions as their own. 'As long as I don't have to call her Lady Mackenzie.'

'Good heavens no. In any case, there's no chance of her divorcing the marchese.'

Julian betrayed a moment of surprise, then suddenly realized that Carla would find a husband more useful alive than dead, until the right candidate appeared for serious consideration. Sir Miles would not comprehend her desire for extravagance, let alone have the means to support it.

'Carla's a good chum,' he said emphatically, mistaking Julian's silence for disapproval of his liaison with a married woman. 'You don't love someone you lark around with. You take it too seriously, Julian. I'm a straightforward bloke, like all the rest. I expect I'll find some decent girl to settle down with when the time comes.'

'I'll be your best man.'

'I'd be honoured. Will you be around later on?'

''Fraid not. Some financial matters to attend to.'

'Is everything all right?'

'Couldn't be better.'

Sir Miles walked round to the back of Julian's chair, and put his hand on his shoulder. 'I sometimes think how unfair it is. The Palace couldn't exist without you, and yet I get all the kudos.'

Julian grinned. 'Two things I've never lusted after. Fame and immortality. Why should I? I'm neither poor nor a genius.'

Julian's cheerfulness was not entirely due to sell-out performances of *Tosca*, or his relief that he would not be pulled into financing *Salome* with Carla Livorno. The number listed for Donna under Emergency Services had been taken over by Mary-Lou, but it had only taken a day to track Donna down to a housing estate in Leicester. She gave him the address he wanted, just mention her name, the doctor would do him a lovely job, cash up front, mind. Very clean he was, took the right precautions and gave you a cup of tea afterwards.

His operation had been successful. The pain and bleeding of the initiation rite (that's how he thought of it) had stopped after a remarkably short time. He had considered displaying the fruits of his trip to Birmingham in the Turkish baths at Cliveden, then changed his mind. There had to be a trial period, when he could gauge the success of his experiment in familiar surroundings, rather like assessing your will to diet in a favourite restaurant by ordering consommé instead of foie gras.

Chapter Eighteen

At two in the morning, the Maison Blanche exuded the warm comfortable odour of cigar smoke and the last vestiges of mingled perfumes. Andrew Broughton, Sir Miles and Julian had just torn themselves away from the yielding sofas and low lights of the Library. Saffron liked this particular hour, when appetites had been satisfied, and the night had reached a calm, replete conclusion. Two of her guests were asleep, their heads lying in the laps of two of her feathered and corseted girls who were staring vacantly at the disappearing bubbles in their champagne glasses, having consumed the last of the day's ration of cocaine. Saffron turned a blind eye. She didn't expect well-educated, sensitive girls to last out without some assistance.

'Bedtime,' she sang out. There were grunts and snorts as the two men staggered to their feet. 'Time to go home, gentlemen.'

Each of her girls came to say good night, she insisted on that. If they wished to, they could spend half an hour with her every Monday, bring up things on their minds, chat, giggle, discuss guests, family problems, children.

Saffron was sitting there, quietly listening to Julio Iglesias, when she heard screams and sobs outside the door. She rose to her feet, fearing that a fight had erupted. That was the only problem with Latin American girls, they were so volatile. 'What is it?' she called. 'What's all this noise?'

A stunning Mexican girl with damson eyes pulled at her hand. 'Come quick. Awful thing happen.'

The studded oak door of the Chapel Room was ajar.

Saffron entered, and immediately put her hand to her mouth. The heavy sickly smell of Jasmine incense was mixed with that of a backstreet butcher's shop: drying blood. Carmen, only seventeen but a jewel, was lying on the white cloth covering the altar, eyes closed, mouth gaping open. Someone had tossed her nun's habit over one shoulder, leaving her legs to dangle awkwardly apart, like a puppet pulled upwards from the knee. A rivulet of blood was splashing to the floor, staining her frilly white suspender belt and white stockings with random blots.

Saffron felt her pulse, while the girls looked from one to the other in horror.

'She's alive. I'll get an ambulance. Now get out of here,' ordered Saffron. 'Take taxis home. And don't say anything. When I find out what's happened I'll tell you.'

The ambulance from the private clinic had been a few times before. Sometimes guests had minor heart attacks, or seized muscles; others suffered from more obscure illnesses noted on their membership files. Without their medical history, they would not be admitted. No one would be able to accuse the Maison Blanche of not being well-run, *bien organisé*.

Saffron laid Carmen flat, staunched the blood with a towel, then raised her legs. It was what she dreaded most, an unseemly crisis. There was a retired police chief who came regularly to the Maison Blanche, but she could hardly consult him. Neither could she summon anyone from the local station. The Maison Blanche was a law unto itself, a small island in Mayfair, a secret service immune from the forces of law and order.

'Someone has gone too far,' whispered Saffron, as a tall, bearded man in a white coat leaned over Carmen. 'A new member, doubtless. We've never had any trouble before.'

The tiny body in the grey nun's habit was lifted carefully onto a stretcher and Carmen started to regain consciousness, her large brown eyes, encircled like the markings on a peacock butterfly, moving from Saffron to the ambulance men and back to Saffron.

'We're going to look after you.' Saffron pulled the blanket up over her frail, bony shoulders, and kissed her forehead.

Dr Aziz, the doctor on duty, left Saffron in an overbright, chintz-curtained waiting room. It was over an hour before he returned.

'She'll have to stay here for at least a week,' he began, adjusting his gold-rimmed, polarized glasses. 'The internal injuries are quite appalling. Severe laceration and haemorrhaging. We'll have to wait to see the full extent of the damage. It's possible she will be unable to bear children. Though, in her situation, I suppose that would be unlikely.'

'Not at all,' replied Saffron, riled at his assumption. 'Many of my girls have children. It gives them an incentive.'

'Of course. Now, I must ascertain some details from you. This young girl . . .'

'Carmen is her name,' interrupted Saffron.

'. . . has been subjected to penetration by a particularly unpleasant instrument. There are wounds which would suggest some kind of gouging apparatus.'

'What on earth do you mean?'

'The walls of the vagina have been ripped to shreds.'

'My God! How ghastly!'

Dr Aziz continued in the flat voice of a police coroner weighing up the defects of a corpse, so that Saffron was unsure whether he was making a moral judgement or disguising his sympathy in case she dissolved into tears, a situation, she imagined, with which he was ill-equipped to cope.

'The instrument would appear to have been metal rather than wood. Often we find a common kitchen implement has been employed in these cases. Not being a cook, I'm unable to imagine exactly what. I know that some of your clients have unusual tastes. All I could think of myself was some kind of metal sexual aid. Do you have such things?'

Saffron clasped her hands tightly over her knees. 'I never allow anything which might hurt my girls, you know that. No guns or knives. One of my many house rules. Let me know when Carmen is well enough for me to talk to her.' She stood up and belted her camel coat tightly, adjusted her scarf and shook Dr Aziz by the hand. 'I'm shocked. Carmen had such hopes, that she would marry here, have children, a little place of her own. Why don't people know how to behave any more?'

By the time she arrived back at the Maison Blanche, dawn was breaking. The back gardens of Mayfair, crammed with bare cherry trees, Michaelmas daisies, bobbing fuchsias, spiky broom and the glowing bonfire-red of virginia creeper, were hosting the autumn birds. It all looked so domestic, so cosy, so small in comparison with Paris. The worst events, Saffron thought, happened in the most unlikely places. Why should anyone wish to defile the Maison Blanche? She knew all the sadists, and they knew the rules. There was an alarm button in every room. Why hadn't Carmen pressed the one under the altar? According to her records, the last person to have booked with Carmen was Baron von Liebnitz. She summoned up his details on her computer. He was an out of town member who came rarely, lived in Switzerland, never said anything but how could he? Cancer of the throat, poor man. She could recall his face, thick glasses, greased-back greying hair, always muffled in a scarf, suffered from arthritis. He even had difficulty climbing the stairs. The idea was preposterous.

She decided to clean the Chapel Room herself, before the domestics arrived. It was true what Mummy had said when she had gashed her knee as a child, falling over on the stone terrace: bloodstains were frightfully hard to remove, and the smell of bleach made her retch.

She stood in the centre of the arched room, wondering whether she was staring at something which could have been turned into a weapon. The silver crucifix was far too large, the hanging containers supporting single lilies too small. The beeswax candles surrounding the beautiful icon Julian had presented to her were in their usual position. Taking out her keys, she gingerly unlocked the ecclesiastical cupboard, dreading to find some blood-stained kitchen utensil. There were a couple of riding crops, a bishop's silver-coated plastic orb, a couple of wooden crucifixes, a silver-plated chalice, a tin of communion wafers, all the usual items.

At the back, she noticed a long box, slightly larger than the kind carried in school satchels to hold pens and pencils. It was marked JL. The lid slid open easily, and inside was a clean, pink, smooth, suitably veined replica of the male organ in full arousal. Julian's toy. She breathed a sigh of relief.

For a couple of days, the Chapel Room was out of bounds. The bloodstained altar cloth she wrapped in a plastic bag and deposited in the Cleaner London dog-excrement receptacles provided by Westminster council at convenient intervals. One of the clients had got carried away, she told her girls, but it would never happen again.

Eddie looked round the empty foyer of the Royal Horseguards Hotel in Whitehall, and wondered why Julian had refused to meet him in Joe Allen's. This wasn't a business trip. Once a year he left Las Vegas and brought himself and the wife to London, more often if the pound was weak against the dollar. They sat drinking coffee and orange juice.

'You do business around here?' he asked, downing his second orange juice of the morning.

'It's a short walk to Parliament Square.'

Eddie scratched his neck. 'What's the problem, Jules?'

'I've had to pull down the shutters on the blini factory. Somebody informed Winchester that we wouldn't pass the quality test.'

'One of our boys got a complaint?'

'No. Why should they? They're getting the black

market rate, and converting it into by-products. Kalash-nikovs, I believe.'

'So how'd it get out?'

'Customer complaint, so they say. It took them a couple of months to track down the source, but one of our drivers opted for a Christmas bonus and volunteered his opinion. So a couple of the Winchester boys came over for an inspection. They weren't too keen on the design of our packet, then they took some tobacco for analysis. They twigged that it was a mix of Russian and Winchester reject which hadn't reached the recycling plant.'

'Shit.'

'Rather than have them on our tail, I took the decision immediately.'

'That's one hell of an operation thrown away, Jules. Could we start up in Moscow?'

'I think you'll find they've figured that one out. So Piotr tells me. They've woken up to the market potential.'

'Fucking wankers. What we do? Step up the Turkish operation?'

'It makes sense, Eddie.'

'At least they don't speak Russian. You reckon it's stable enough out there?'

'Then we can move on to Hong Kong.'

'Too much competition.'

Julian laughed. 'Wouldn't you like to have the Chinese buy us out and discover the joys of lung cancer all on their own? It'll keep the acupuncturists in business. You can cure anything with needles, Eddie.'

'You serious?'

'I wouldn't recommend it.'

'The Chinese are good gamblers. They deserve a healthy economy, you're right.'

'How long are you here, Eddie?'

'Four days. So the wife can buy out a few stores.'

Julian grinned and drew out a large laminated brochure from his briefcase. 'Take a look at this. Remember Anastasia Wagner?'

'Sure I remember. Some singer, Jules, a real belter. High notes like Liza Minnelli.' Eddie licked his finger and drew back the pages. 'Great presentation. Your show?'

'That's right. She sang Tosca for me, in the new stadium.'

'That's what I call opera. A hit in every aria. You came out in profit?'

Julian gave a slight smile. 'For once. Winchester handed over a sponsorship package.'

'You're kidding?'

'Why do you think I'm in this game?'

'Ask me. But you sure know how to pump at both ends.'

Julian left Eddie working out the below the line cost on the personnel, and made a quick call to the Maison Blanche. He had a friend over who'd appreciate some sophistication while his wife was doing late-night shopping.

When Julian joined him later for an early evening drink in the Library, he only attracted brief glances from the few girls leaning against the bar. They were secretly mourning, but since they were not allowed to communicate their sadness, except in the privacy of the dressing rooms, silence was their only refuge. At first, Saffron told them that Carmen had returned to Brazil, but they refused to believe her. No one as poor as Carmen went back home for medical treatment, they knew that. Blood poisoning, Saffron eventually admitted. Carmen had been given a transfusion, but it hadn't saved her. She had been conscious only for a few minutes, unable to speak. They would give her a proper funeral, and a service in the Brompton Oratory.

'Having a jolly time?' Julian said, as he approached them.

Catherine turned round. 'Oh, it's you.'

'Don't I even get a smile? And where's the lovely Saffron?'

They looked at one another and shrugged.

'You are in a dreary mood tonight, girls. It's like Sunday afternoon in Harrogate in here. This is my friend Eddie. He likes buying champagne. Take care of him.'

'Great lookers,' remarked Eddie, settling himself on a stool.

As Julian crossed the room, peering round screened sofas for signs of animation, he came across Edwina, Saffron's deputy, talking earnestly to an Indian.

'Do excuse me,' she said. 'Julian? Could I have a word?' She got up, and stood far enough away not to be overheard. 'Did you by chance drop by last Monday?'

'Monday? No. Why should I? Monday's my poker night. I have to devote one evening to vice,' he said, with a conciliatory smile.

One of the straps of her black cocktail dress was slipping down her arm.

'Here. Allow me,' he said, pulling it up onto her shoulder. Since she had acknowledged neither his smile nor his gesture, he took her hand. 'Is anything wrong?'

'Oh, just something went missing. We're asking our guests if they noticed anything or anyone unusual.'

'Sorry I can't help.'

The 'haw haw haw' of Sir Miles was unmistakable. Julian found him in an alcove leaning over a table spread with thick sheets of white paper, anchored by a decanter of whisky. Pauline Fudge was drawing sweeping lines with a felt pen, and his arm was round her waist.

'Julsie darling,' she shouted. 'We're brainstorming, me and Miles. Do join in.'

'Another time.'

'Julian doesn't approve of, of . . .' Sir Miles tailed off, drunkenly sloshing round for a word he was unable to grasp.

'But Andrew's awfully keen, you know.'

'I've got Salome's first entrance all worked out. Filmy dress, bird on a leather studded arm, and a pinlight in his eyes. That's all you'll see, these great eyes . . .'

Sir Miles gave an embarrassed smile, which ended in a

chortle, and he looked round for Julian, but he had disappeared amongst the thick-fronded plants and screens arranged by Saffron for the privacy of her guests.

How could he expect a man like Julian to appreciate his dilemma? That he was unable to bring himself to destroy Carla's hopes? Once she had set her heart on something, she seemed to be able to dissolve away doubts, merely by the strength of her wanting. She had started mentioning it in public, at Saffron's dinner parties.

'I am reconstructing the whole role and function of the singer,' he heard her say to an admiring Andrew Broughton. 'And in *Salome* I will be incarnating the hidden desires of today's woman, the desire for beauty, strength and power.'

He had tried to bring up the subject on many occasions, but without pursuing it. Carla hated men who said no: the mean-minded brigade of barbarians, she called them. One day, he would find the right moment. Perhaps tonight, their night.

Once he had torn himself away from the fascinating Pauline, he went home and didn't fill his tumbler of whisky until he had consumed several cups of black coffee. He unlocked the chest in his bedroom and examined his ritual wardrobe. Everything was neatly folded, and she had made him sew his nametape with an unwieldy needle onto every item – B. Mackenzie – so that his fingers bled. His school uniform was neatly folded: blazer, grey shorts, tie, cap. There was a coarse flax robe, plus rope belt. A pair of dungarees. A soiled white tennis outfit. A pair of striped pyjamas. Canes and chains and ropes at the bottom. His collection of conductors' batons lay untouched, like books he had read once, whose covers he still admired.

Soon, she would be standing in front of the gas-flaming coal fire, transformed. Every time it was different, every time she inflamed him with a desire which would only abate when the clothes and props were locked away again, and he lay exhausted at her feet. Tonight he would have to disappoint her. It was Pauline's fault. He had meant to attack his pile of correspondence, finish a report, but ideas had flowed, cascading from Pauline's unpredictable imagination. How could he run a Palace of Opera without this vital juice?

This time Carla arrived unexpectedly early.

'Just been seeing Pa off to the airport. Can't stay long.'

'Never mind. I'm rather busy. Did your father see Stasi before he left?'

'Sure. She's OK. Exhausted, of course. Was it your idea to make her do all those performances? I'm meant to be the slave-driver, Bumbles.'

Carla took up her usual position, on the rug in front of the fire, the curve of her thigh outlined by chalk-striped trousers, tightly hugging the mound of her crotch. Schedules could be rearranged. He could finish the report next morning, dawdling through the traffic.

'Pauline's got some drawings to show me. So exciting. And Pa says he's getting around to the idea.'

'What idea?'

'Conducting Strauss, dumbo.'

'Carla . . .'

This might be the right moment. He could say it now. He was thinking how he would begin. She might laugh at him. You could never say anything straight out to women. How would Julian have put it? And she did look so splendid, in those clinging trousers and plunging top, eyes gleaming brightly as Navy buttons, hair ruffled round her face. Could he bear to see the pretty mouth turn down? She might even cry. That would be intolerable. Now his wave of lust was betrayed, there was nothing he could do.

'You'll have to waste that hard-on, Bumbles. 'Cause my mind is someplace else.'

'Could we? Just quickly?'

'What do you think I am? A two-bit whore?'

'No, no. I didn't mean that.'

'Do you ever think of anything else? I'm going through such a creative phase, Miles. So thrilling. It's like being on fire with ideas. Can you imagine? It's like being fucked in the head.'

'Shakespeare must have felt like that.'

It was what he had always dreamed of, being so close to the creative process. All those young men at the BBC, throwing their hearts and minds into strips of filmstock.

'There's almost too much going on. Playing Isabelle for Nathalie, Salome for you. Two characters are enough to hold in my head. It takes months, you know, to make them come right. Never mind. I don't expect you to understand, sweetheart. Just get me a drink. Then I might just decide to put my mouth around something hard.'

If Julian had not telephoned, he might never have told her. It gave him the excuse he had longed for. Thankfully, the uncontrollable urgency of sex had passed.

'Carla. I was discussing *Salome* with the board. If we do it, and we're not sure it's right for us, it won't be our next major production.'

'Who says?'

'Julian is right, I'm afraid. If we did something like *Salome*, we'd end up with no budget for anything else. And I can hardly go against the man who is keeping us afloat. I know you'll be disappointed, but I don't want to let you down. It might be an idea to try Germany. Oscar thinks they'd be keen.'

Carla got up and stood with her back to the fire, her eyes unblinking. She appeared to be appraising him from different angles, like an abstract sculpture, trying to determine her response.

'I'm sorry,' he added.

He heard the distant wail of police sirens coming near, screaming down below outside the window, gradually muffled as they speeded into the distance. Then there was silence. Carla was staring at a purple guppy, lazily fanning the scarlet fronds of its tail in the illuminated tank. A wide-eyed black swordtail was flitting up to the surface.

'They're cute, your fish. Sure they're not hungry? How often do you feed them?'

She seemed unlikely to rush off. Sir Miles began to ease out the cork of a bottle of Barolo, a present from Carla.

'They get fed by my housekeeper once a day.'

'I went with Julian to a restaurant once where you pointed to a fish in a tank, then they cooked it. I nearly threw up. Would you eat one of those, if you were starving?'

'That's like asking if you would eat your best friend if your plane crashed in the Arctic. It's not something I think about.'

'Do they all get names?'

He handed her a long-stemmed glass. 'Have you time to try this? Perfect for drinking now.'

'Sure.'

'I suppose you find it strange, the need to have something living around the house. I have fish because I couldn't keep a dog. One needs contact with the natural world. Even I have to escape the artifice of opera and the demands of singers from time to time.'

Carla pointed to the fan-tailed guppy. 'What's that one called?'

'Mélisande. The long tail reminds me of her hair.'

'And that black one?'

'Figaro, he's called. He's always darting about.'

'Jesus. This wine is smoky.' Carla leaned over the side of the leather armchair in which Sir Miles was sitting, dipped her finger in the dark wine, and ran it round his lips. 'I thought you said your little pets were to make you forget all those dreadful singers.'

'The names suit them. They've all got different characters. You'd be surprised. Some are coy, some are greedy, some are always hiding, some like to show off.'

'Which one's like me?'

He laughed. 'The kissing gourami, the one with the white transparent fins and the pale pink stripe. Very good at sucking.'

Carla let out a throaty growl, and slipped over the armchair into his lap.

'I wish you wouldn't. Not when you're going.'

'Want me to stay?'

He squeezed her full breasts, Moira's breasts. He loved releasing them, little by little, feeling the soft contours springing back under his hands.

'Give me the key to the chest, Bumbles. I'll choose something special. Eyes closed.'

He heard her unlocking the chest, then the heavy lid thumped down. It was like hiding in the back stair cupboard during Postman's Knock, fearing that you would pee with excitement, longing for the moment when a grown-up hand would reach out into the darkness.

Afterwards, Carla declined his offer of dinner, and hurried back to the Maison Blanche to enter into the part which really mattered. Isabelle. She could identify with this outlandish girl who dressed as a man and shocked the quaking bourgeois of Algiers, had Arabs up the arse, wrote insipid poetry, and became a spy for a sexy French general. The film would be fun, but the kind of thing they showed in late-night art houses. Nathalie was too intellectual, too hooked on the male/female dichotomy which didn't sell movies. *Salome* with Mel Donitz, that made sense, career-wise, but as long as Stasi Wagner was under contract there wasn't a hope in hell.

The thought came to her while she was discussing her part with Nathalie. After they had discussed Isabelle for over an hour on the phone, she directed the conversation towards their mutual friend. She had told Nathalie how close they were.

'She should have a *grand amour*,' said Nathalie. 'But I think she always loves Dominic. *Une tragédie*. They were so good together. Ouf! Sensational.'

'She never mentions him. What happened?' asked Carla.

'Foolish man. Without her, who is interested? Now he makes some production in Sicily. A little thing here, a little thing there. He will never have a singer like her.'

'You think he'd like her back?'

Nathalie sighed. 'Who knows? If only they would have him at the Palace. It broke her heart. The English, so protectionist.'

Carla thought a moment. 'Maybe I could help. It's a long shot, but I've got to see someone in Rome. Easy to take in Sicily while I'm over there. Where did you say he is?'

'At the Palermo Opera House, they will know.'

'If I saw him, I could tell him, as a friend, that Stasi still cares. Then I can find out if he does, too. You think that's an idea? He can only tell me to get lost.'

'That would be fantastic. Only a woman can think like this,' said Nathalie. 'Men are idiots. They throw away everything.'

The heat in Palermo was stifling. Dominic was avoiding patches of melted tar as he strode along the Via Roma, passing the dark, crumbling doorways, the broken balconies which needed the softer light of early spring to reveal their poetry. When he had received Carla's message at the Opera House, the artistic director had been present. Ah yes, the Marchesa della Robbia. Paolo's daughter. She had sung there once before, he remembered, not bad, not bad. Here, he told Dominic, my audience is old-fashioned. They come for the music.

She was waiting for him by a marble statue in the great foyer of the Grand Hotel Palme, dressed all in white, a white chiffon scarf draped round the décolletage of her neck, and he followed her to the narrow bar.

'I was very sad to hear about Maurizio. Stasi told me,' he began. 'But I heard you were singing again, in a modern British opera. I'm sorry, I forgot the name.'

'Oh, it was nothing important. But it helped me forget, for a while.'

'Are you hoping to work in Italy now?'

'Maybe. But I need a rest, even though my agent keeps pleading with me. One thing I don't intend is to end up with a voice in tatters when I'm thirty. Like Stasi, for example.'

'What do you mean?'

'You heard about *Tosca*? By the fifth performance, she couldn't sing a note. Of course, they said it was laryngitis. But I heard from Sir Miles Mackenzie what's really going on back there. He's a very good friend.'

'Like Stasi, you mean?'

Carla giggled. 'Not quite.'

'I read she had tracheitis. It happens.'

'I wish Stasi wouldn't get so hysterical. Still, you lived with her. You know.'

Dominic looked at her suspiciously. 'What do you want from me, Carla?'

'I just thought you might want to know.'

'Know what, for God's sake?'

'Still, she's out of your life now, I don't suppose you care.'

'Of course I do, Carla.'

She leaned one elbow on the bar, and sat side-saddle on the stool, slowly placing one leg over the other.

'I've known Stasi a long time. She was going to be the greatest, everyone in class knew that. Of course, we were jealous, but only because we knew we'd never end up where she was going. Now she's gotten so big she won't listen to anyone. But I thought maybe she'd listen to you. That's all.'

Dominic looked round the bar, to avoid the hypnotic eyes which were searching his. 'What do you want me to tell her?'

'I believe she needs you. Do you still love her, Dominic?'

He glanced at her warily, then smiled. She sounded like a wife asking her husband the truth about his mistress, prepared to sacrifice her marriage if he admitted his passion. 'Why the sudden concern? Has she stolen one of your boyfriends?'

She slipped down from the stool and picked up her bag. 'I was trying to be a friend. Maybe you don't know what that means. Maybe you just think of her as good in the sack. Like all the others.'

'Carla. I'm sorry. That was impolite and I made a mistake.'

When she had finished talking, she stretched out her ring-laden fingers for him to kiss, but instead he grasped her hand.

'Goodbye, Carla. And thanks.'

In spite of his distrust, some of her words had hit home, like repeated bars which could not be cut.

'Stasi Wagner will be used to keep the Palace on its feet.'

'A sacrificial offering for the great British public.'

'A voice in tatters.'

If any of it was true, he could go over to England, advise her as a friend, painful though it would be. Then he realized it would be too difficult. Theirs was not a passion which could mellow into friendly concern. If she was driving herself like a demon, it was her destiny. Perhaps it was the only way she could live. There were some performers who could not be held back, who would sacrifice their lives rather than dampen down the blaze of their talent. For several months, he tried to put her out of his mind.

Stasi was almost ready for her house-warming party. The bleak November rain lashed against the tall windows. There were no curtains except in the bedroom. Gloria was having them made by a little man. What did it matter? She was now enshrined in privacy, a garden thick with bushes and trees hiding her away in a peaceful conservation street in Highgate.

The central heating was turned up, augmented by the glow of coal fires in open grates; there was the sound of a distant piano being tuned, the repeated notes echoing into the hall. She could take the joys of fame, give herself for a few brief hours, and retire to her walled fortress. That's what everyone did. You went from one fortress to another, visiting the select few who had been marked out for fame. Pauline Fudge was a neighbour, an acre away. They understood the need to isolate yourself from remarks from strangers, blatant stares, autograph books pushed in your face. You made yourself public property, and then went to ground. If you could no longer walk along any but neighbouring streets, visit only the odd local shop where they only noted your presence after you had left, it was a lack of freedom to be expected. If you went for a walk, it was in the grounds of someone's private estate. Stasi rarely went out. In similar fortresses around London, she met those whose existence was similar to her own. From her windows, she could see only bushes and trees, leaves quivering as squirrels jumped from branch to branch.

Stasi was unable to keep still, pacing from one room to the other of the four-storey house, finding nothing to do except remove a vase of flowers from one place and put it in another. All she thought of was that he wanted to see her. At home, not in a restaurant, not in a hotel. He had written to her; only a small group of friends knew her telephone number. Could they spend some time together?

He was walking up the drive, looking around him, in a leather jacket and jeans, but she could only see the top of his head. That long-legged gait – she had forgotten he took such long strides. Her heart was pounding, she could not think what she would say. Lady Macbeth in New York was years ago. Fourteen months. A lifetime for a singer.

The manservant let him in. Unlike some of her friends, she refused to insist that he wear a uniform. She disliked the formality of wealth, and was surprised when everyone talked openly about servants. She had no servants, just people who helped in the house, refugees to whom she had given a home, talented students who cleaned and cooked for the pleasure of being near her. It never entered her head that she might open the door to him, for she opened the door to no one.

'You'll find Miss Wagner in the first-floor drawing room. She's expecting you. First door on the right up the stairs, Mr Morrison.'

She stood near the door, listening, wondering if his

voice had changed, but she heard only the creak of the stairs.

He kissed her on both cheeks, the standard greeting. Then they stood back and looked at one another, smiling awkwardly.

'Good to see you.'

He glanced round the bare room. There were two chairs and a settee she had bought hurriedly at an auction.

'When do I get to see the set?'

'I've just moved in. I'm having a house-warming party in a couple of days. There's so much to do. When the designer is free. Pauline Fudge. Have you heard of her?'

'Great name. Love the fire. Shall we sit down on the rug?'

'I'll be changing it. Something temporary to put on the floor. Do you like my house?'

'Sure.'

'You can stay. I've plenty of room. Of course, I don't know how long you'll be here. But I've arranged a dinner party with a few friends. We'll be camping in the kitchen, but it'll be fun.'

Stasi sat cross-legged in front of him. It was like an audition. She no longer auditioned, but she clasped her hands in her lap as though he was about to propose a new role. Sir Miles had allowed her to take time out. Would it be possible to work together again?

'I suppose you expected to see a monster. Most people do. I've grown used to it. That's why I shut myself up here. Somewhere to work in peace, that's all I need. Want to see round my cage?' He followed her up the twisting staircase, whose wrought iron baluster would be repainted. She paused outside her bedroom. 'I don't usually show people in here. It's ghastly at the moment.'

'Come on, Stasi. What is this? Some kind of a hotel?' He pushed open the door, went over to sit on the edge of the ornate, four-poster bed, the only furniture in the room, and took her hand. 'It's wonderful. You always wanted a house, Stasi.'

'But I loved your flat in Paris.'

'Not bad for a two-bit director.' He laughed, that warm laugh she remembered, and she flung her arms round his neck, tossing off her shoes, and they rolled back onto the bed. They made love, as they had made love then, their rhythms coinciding, waning, rising, waning again, preserved in a time capsule. He didn't ask who shared her bed, and she, likewise, refrained from asking him. It was enough to recapture their passion. She was reconciled to the gradual fade to reality, when the harsh light of the present would send their moments of love receding once again into the distance.

'Is this why you've come? For love in the afternoon?' she said, smiling into his eyes, as his hands stroked her hips, rediscovering the curves and inclinations, the familiar sweep downwards to her long ankles, the slender feet which used to curl when he touched them.

'Someone like you needs a guardian angel. You're racing downhill and you can't see the trees. I can't stand by and see you crash. Even though you left me.'

'Me? Leave you? Who let me sign the contract? You could have stopped me. One word.'

'You wanted to go, Stasi. You didn't have to say it. Those big brown eyes, reproaching me. I couldn't stop you going where you belong. You wouldn't have drifted round Europe with me. I'm a hobo, the kind your ma wouldn't give houseroom for a night. But it doesn't bother me. I'm not in a hurry. Right things happen at right times.'

'I didn't want you to possess me. Couldn't you see?'

'Dear Stasi. You see the cage door open, and stick on your perch. Strange girl.'

When he began to tell her about Carla's visit to Palermo, back in the summer, Stasi fell silent.

'Don't you want to know what she said?'

'Before or after she got into bed with you? Honestly, Dominic! I don't need gossip. Or Carla Livorno. I don't care any more. Either I sing well or not so well. I thought you might have come because you wanted to see me.'

Dominic gave a playful tug at a strand of her hair. 'We both kept our clothes on. Isn't that a miracle?'

'Because you're keeping faithful to someone, is that why?'

'Nope.'

'You're impossible. I must know. Are you living with someone?'

'A cat called Fred with four legs and a tail.'

'Now you're meant to ask me. Go on.'

'I heard you were marrying Julian Lieberman.'

Stasi let out a hoot. 'I said that to get the press off my back. One has to do that kind of garbage.'

'One does. Was it an invention of the press that you're singing yourself out? Or is that from Miss Livorno's book of quotations?'

'Utter junk. Do I look like a wreck?'

'Just as I remember you. Full of sound and fury, Stasi.'

She pressed her face against his. 'I still love you.' She waited a moment, then stared at him.

'What, Stasi?'

'Dominic. Just say it. And if you don't mean it, you can tell me afterwards.'

'I loved you when I first saw you. I loved you afterwards. I love you now.'

Tears welled up, and then she burst out angrily, 'Why couldn't you say? I told you I never wanted another man but you.'

'Didn't you know? Did it ever seem like I didn't love you? What was I meant to do? Go down on my knees every day and recite it like a Hail Mary? Anyhow, I knew you were going to make it. There've been enough Hollywood stars throwing out struggling actors to exchange them for a glitzier model when the going got good. I couldn't face that. They'd come along like wasps round a honey pot. Guys like Julian Lieberman.'

Stasi sniffed. 'I only did it once. If it's confession time, you can tell me now. Or will it take all night?'

'I go for girls with long dark hair who used to live in Rosedene Avenue.'

'You remember!'

'Most things. Do they have custard buns in, where are we, High-gate?' He jumped out of bed, and lifted up her lacy woollen dress, lying in a heap on the bare boards. 'You got anything you hang around in when there's no one here? Any old stuff?'

Stasi rummaged in a case and pulled out a pair of crumpled black jeans. 'Here. I've still got them. My Paris uniform. Hope they fit. I'm meant to be losing weight.'

They ran down the stairs, and into the spacious kitchen. Her fine black hair was tangled, her face still flushed, the carefully applied make-up washed away. No one would ever see her like this except him. It was the private face of Stasi Wagner.

'So what are you dying to tell me about the Opera Palace?' asked Stasi, stuffing a large portion of Gloria's seedcake into her mouth.

'They're saying . . .'

'Carla's saying.'

'I spoke to Oscar, darling. The rumour is that Julian Lieberman is in financial trouble and may be resigning from the board. Without his support, the whole place will start to crack. If he pulls out, no one will be queuing up to part with millions to keep the show going.'

'Opera houses are always in crisis. But they always keep going. If things are difficult, they should put on smaller productions. I wouldn't mind. Maybe people would pay more attention to the singing, instead of gawping at towers and animals.'

'Sir Miles plans to do the opposite. He wants you to do a major world tour with *Tosca*.'

'I won't do that. It's unthinkable. I'd end up a croaking wreck.'

'He'll have you singing major dramatic roles, and then touring to recoup the costs. He sees you as keeping the Palace on its feet, Stasi. Roll up roll up and see the greatest actress singer in the world. In the flesh. I gather he's keen on *Salome*. In between, there'll be rock shows, musicals, who knows, maybe the odd medium or evangelist packing them in.'

'My voice would be dead in two years, he must know that.'

'You'll be the sacrificial offering, Stasi. For the great British public. Check it out.'

Sir Miles was evasive at first, indignant that Stasi should have made such suggestions. Then he admitted there had been an adjustment to previous policy. He had to think long term, the economic climate dictated artistic decisions more than was healthy. It was a passing phase. Every opera house had its lean periods. He would rather find commercial solutions than see his great enterprise become a conference centre.

'How flattering. I've never thought of myself as a commercial solution before.' Stasi glared at him across his desk.

'I wasn't referring to you, Anastasia. I was only trying to explain what I have to contend with.'

'I made a mistake. I thought you were interested in my development as a singer. I wouldn't dream of touring *Tosca*.'

'With a microphone, there would be no need to strain your voice. It's your acting people want to see. That's your precious gift, surely. Or would you rather spend your time in recording studios and concert halls?'

'I don't need your advice. We're wasting each other's time.'

'We'll try and find a compromise.'

'For me, there's no such thing. That's where we differ, Sir Miles.'

He showed her to the door. 'I admire you more than you can ever imagine. We must keep talking.'

'If I have a voice left to talk with.' She tilted forward her large felt hat, adjusted her dark glasses, and strode down the corridor, ignoring the people who greeted her.

* * *

When Carla came back to England, having been persuaded to appear in a further series of Rigoletto ice-cream commercials, she saw the headlines she had been waiting for. 'Top Singer Breaks Contract'. As yet there were few details; no one was talking. Anastasia Wagner, torn between her career and the man she loved, had chosen love. That was the real story they all wished to hear. The photographers waited with their long lenses all night and all day on either side of the iron gate of her house in Highgate until they had the proof. There she was, a moment before she noticed them, the great singer, hair flying in the wind, a laughing smile she never volunteered to strangers, holding the hand of Dominic Morrison, the handsome man who had seduced her away from the bright lights of fame.

It was rare for Sir Miles to abandon the veneer of democracy, but, on this occasion, he decided to present Julian with a fait accompli.

'I've been re-thinking *Salome*.'

'Really?' Julian looked drawn, as though his faculties had been jet-lagged into submission. His eyes were puffy and his hair, usually neatly edged round his neck, was straggling over his collar. 'Going out with a bang? Or rather, a severed head. Is that the idea? What's made you change your mind? Or rather who? I suppose there's no need to ask. Do you think Carla is up to it vocally? But, now that Anastasia's gone, the Palace needs pulling power. Is that your thinking?'

'Even if it's a failure, it will be a compelling failure. There's a large section of the audience which longs for opera to collapse in ridicule. After all, there are comedians who've made a spectacular living out of operatic parody. I see nothing wrong in that. What's wrong with laughter? It's just another way of introducing audiences to opera.'

'Is that a serious suggestion?'

'We need controversy, Julian. Excitement. A change from the respectably received productions we've been

486

importing. And *Salome* speaks to our age. Lust, venality, decadence, murderous butchery. It's all there. The bloodshot skies of a fading century. Warped desires wielding the knives of satanic retribution. If Samson hadn't pulled down the temple, he would have had no place in history. It's here, here within our grasp.'

'Except for the right Salome.'

'The costumes are sensational. The fabrics will be hand-woven in China. The colours! The world dissolving into a rainbow. Absolutely magical. The gore and splendour of the palace, I see it all, rising up, huge pillars, thunderous clouds hurtling across the sky. Carla entering in a dress made of gold silk strands, a kestrel on her arm, heavy gold across her brows, crimson bangles piercing her arms, soft bare feet crossing black marble, winding herself round green malachite pillars. Shedding her diaphanous coverings seven times, like a snake sloughing off its patterned skin.'

Julian wondered whether he had been attacking the whisky bottle in his cupboard. 'What are you trying to do, Miles?'

'I'll recreate Babylon. If we go up in flames, we will be remembered.'

'Just because Anastasia has decided to abandon us, it doesn't mean the Palace is finished. There are other singers. Miles. Listen!'

Unaware of Julian's presence, he was staring motionless out of the window, like a heron waiting for a fish to rise, his hands in his pockets.

'You must try to keep her out of the courts, Miles. Breach of contract cases are always messy.'

'What is lawful? What is unlawful? I'm going to bring her back. After this production, she'll come back. The bugles call. Can you hear them?'

'Miles. We haven't the money. We're in the red.'

'Red, pillars of red. You don't like green? I'll suggest it.'

'I'm tired, too. Come to my place, have a rest.'

'Why are you looking at me like that? I can't come. I've got a meeting tonight.'

Julian went and stood by the array of framed photographs behind Sir Miles's desk, straightened the picture of Anastasia plunging a knife into the back of Baron Scarpia.

'I suppose all opera is madness,' he said, as he picked up his briefcase.

Chapter Nineteen

The wave of euphoria which Carla had experienced at Stasi's departure was rapidly dying away. Pauline Fudge had started work on another project and had deserted the Maison Blanche for the Chelsea Arts Club, where she could have a decent noisy discussion about the decadence of post-modernism without suffering Saffron's little sniffs of bourgeois disapproval. Even Andrew Broughton was beginning to lose interest.

'What do you expect me to do?' he said. 'If Sir Miles has said no, that's it. Why get so upset? I offered you *The Merry Widow*.'

'He wants it to happen. Julian's stopping him, I know that. Why's he so influenced by him? Anyone would think they were having it off together.'

'Really?' Andrew looked at her in surprise.

'Oh, Jesus! Look, Julian's never wanted me to succeed. That's the reason.'

'I've never got that impression.'

'And he knows fuck all about opera. He just wants power.'

'Nothing wrong in that,' replied Andrew.

Everyone had let her down. Didn't they have any guts, these pathetic men digging down like worms in a drought? Pretending that everything they did was so damned significant? Preening themselves because they managed to get it up once a week, wanking off in the dark, lording it in the daylight? There was one more chance. Sir Miles's secretary told her he was in London, but his diary was full for a month. He was unable to see her.

Carla heaved her Bentley into the kerb, then splashed

half a bottle of Fendi over her throat. She let herself into Sir Miles's flat in order to plan her special performance. It would be better in near-darkness, she decided as she turned off all the lights in the living room, so that the only illumination came from the bubbling fish tank and the flickering gas-flames. Now everything she hated was dimmed into obscurity, the rows of operatic silhouettes dragooned into straight lines across the walls, the still-life oils of unappetizing fruit and stiff flowers, the dreary carpet, the colour of yellowing trodden-down grass, the sickly orange and green floral upholstery, the heavy bookcase, the dark tables. Everything looked as though it had formed part of a large family inheritance, worse than the Villa degli Spiriti. Not even valuable. Just old, dark and ugly.

She was looking for something. In the kitchen, she opened one cupboard after another. Pâté paperium, peanut butter, marmite, gentleman's relish, whisky marmalade and muesli. A set of piled-up bone china with fading flowers, flower vases. Digestive biscuits and fish meal, dusty beans in a jar, lumpy sugar, empty salt drum, discoloured remnant of wine vinegar. Little inspiration there. There might be something in the bottom cupboard, by the sink. In the end she found what she wanted in a narrow broom cupboard which she had missed. She heard the crunching of the double locks and Sir Miles's heavy tread as he walked down the corridor.

'How was your day, sweetheart?' she called out.

'Is that you, Carla? What are you doing here?'

'I was passing.' She took his bulky overcoat and went towards the bedroom.

'I shouldn't be meeting you tonight. Far too busy. We're not doing anything naughty.'

Carla fetched him a tumbler of whisky. 'I've put out your favourites. Come on, Bumbles.'

Everything he needed was arranged on the bed. She began to release his tie, then his shirt.

'We'll have to be quick. Lots to do.'

'There you go. Now button up the blazer. That's better. You've forgotten something. What have you forgotten?'

'My cap. I couldn't find it.'

'Well, you'd better. Hadn't you, Bumbles?'

'Drink first.'

'What did I say?'

He rummaged in the chest, found a crumpled purple and grey cap which he pushed down over his forehead, and stood for inspection in the doorway of the living room.

Carla moved a high-backed wooden chair away from the dining table and placed it in the middle of the room. 'Sit down there and don't move.' She took a thin rope and fastened his hands loosely together, then covered his eyes and ears with a scarf and knotted it.

'Don't be cross with me. Please don't.'

'I'm not cross. It's for your own good. When it's all over, you can go play.'

'What did you say?'

Carla repeated herself, shouting. 'Take off your shoes and socks. Come on, I haven't got all day.'

He lifted up his legs, struggled to find the laces of his shiny black walking shoes, untied them with fumbling fingers and pulled them off his feet. 'Are you going to beat me?' The rope jerked viciously tight, cutting into his wrists.

Either he was unable to hear because of the thick scarf over his ears, or Carla was refusing to reply. He felt her hands unclipping his snake belt, worming it out from the tabs, then releasing one button after another. His cock began to strain against the airtex Y-fronts and he was wriggling in anticipation. He was panting into the woolly scarf, hot and damp against his mouth, his cap pressing down over his head. Soon, when his suppressed gasps turned to cries, she would tear off his gag, then stand, hands on hips, watching while his sperm rose up, spurting over his legs, albumen blobs marking his trousers, the carpet, milky drops of disgrace, Onan spilling his seed to taunt the Lord. Once, they had competed, the boys standing in the shower room, holding their dicks. Who could get it over the line? Templeton-Smith. It was the only subject in which Templeton-Smith excelled.

Suddenly, the scarf was wrenched away, sooner than he had expected, before he had come. His hands were still tied and there was no light except for the greeny glow from the fish tank. He stared at it, bewildered. There seemed to be some alien predator in the tank. The water was heaving up into waves, the fish were quivering, convulsing, rushing from one side to another, rising frantically to the surface, sinking down. Figaro was trying to bury himself under a small pebble, Mélisande was knocking her head against the side, thrashing her tail. He could see their mouths opening, closing, opening again as they pressed against the glass.

Tears ran down his face as he writhed and strained and clenched his buttocks, unable to free himself, and then he shuddered uncontrollably, stopped struggling. A clear, high unbroken voice in his head urged him on.

'I say, come on, Bumbles. You can jerk off faster than that.'

He closed his eyes. He was like a rutting elephant charging through the forest. Then it came in a torrent and he threw his head back against the chair with a strangled cry of pleasure.

By the time he had managed to release his hands, the water in the tank was still except for the soft bubbling of the aeration. On the surface of the water, small corpses rocked, pale bellies upward, touched each other, then drifted apart, like wads of mould on long-forgotten milk. When he lifted off the covering of the tank, the stench of hydrogen peroxide stung his nostrils.

'Carla,' he called, whimpering. 'You've killed all my fish. That's not fair. I loved my fish. It's not fair.'

She was nowhere to be found. Beside the tank, he found an empty bottle of bleach, the one Mrs Thompson, his daily, kept in the broom cupboard. The fumes penetrated his nostrils, the exhalation from long dark corridors, urinal walls and white-tiled kitchens. The whole school reeked of it on the first day of the new term, the pungent cleanser of grime and defaecation, annihilator of the stink of urine-soaked sheets, the rancidity of the sick-bed, killer of virulent germs lurking in uncleaned orifices. Dirty little boys.

He found a rusty sieve in the kitchen, and lifted out his dead heroes and heroines, their bright colours faded to sickly pink and grey, eyes covered in a filmy glaze. Then he washed them, and wrapped them in a silk handkerchief. When he was a child, his father had buried his dead hedgehog under a rose bush. There was a bay tree in a pot standing on his balcony. He would place them there, under the sweet-smelling leaves.

The blazer, the cap, the short trousers, the tie, he pushed into the chest without folding them. The chest took up too much room. He could put the contents in bags and leave them for the dustmen, and his secretary could arrange for the chest to be sent down to his cottage in Hampshire.

In the great scheme of world events, or even on his passion-ridden stage, Carla's act would hardly be worthy of notice. Children played games which ended in tragedy. The boy who had tied Jeremy Deakin naked to a tree in winter (he had been in the sick bay with pneumonia for two weeks) was popular in class, always cheerful, liked the odd prank. Girls were different. They always went too far, couldn't distinguish between spitefulness and high spirits. When they pulled your hair, they meant it.

Carla had gone too far. The games you played in private had rules; he had imagined she understood that. On second thoughts, why should she? Italians, he sometimes forgot, behaved like children in one of those progressive schools. No discipline, no rules. Without rules, there could be no moderation. Moderation in all things. Knowing when to stop. Drawing boundaries. How else could you prevent cruelty and anarchy? But once someone had gone too far, they had no part in your life.

There would be no need for a scene. Once his telephone

number had been changed, and he had ordered his secretary in no circumstances to take calls from Carla Livorno, she would divert her attention elsewhere. If the weakness began to return, he would take up squash again. Good game, squash.

He retired to his bedroom, drained the bottle of whisky, thought of replacing his fish, and began to make notes in his diary for the following day. Stasi Wagner had promised to see him when she returned from somewhere in Cornwall. Decent girl. It would be easier now. He opened all the windows. That smell lingered as long as Carla's perfume.

He was just slipping into bed when the phone rang.

'I didn't mean to. Are you mad at me? I only wanted to see what would happen. What did happen, Bumbles?'

'You're disgusting.'

'I'm an opera singer.'

'A murderer, Carla.'

'Only on the stage. Or can't you tell the difference?'

'I won't see you any more.'

'But you can come to rehearsals. I don't mind.'

'No. Julian is right. Wrong thing. Budgets. That's the word.'

'Drunk is the word, Bumbles.'

'Production not on. Tell Oscar.'

'How sad, sweetheart. I really didn't want to tell anyone about us. But they're all dying to know. I won't mention the fish, of course. But if someone asks me about a certain dining club or what's in your bedroom chest, I must tell the truth. Anyhow, what's wrong with having people know? I agree with Pauline. Why keep everything under the table?' He heard her trying to contain a giggle, muffling her mouth.

'Do what you like. I'm going to sleep.'

Sir Miles cancelled the morning's appointments from his car phone, called Henry, who fortunately was not in court that day, and told the chauffeur to take him to Lincoln's Inn Fields. The legal profession was the last bastion the press was unable to storm, especially an old-established firm like Markson Taylor who specialized in representing the landed aristocracy, newspaper tycoons, royalty and litigious writers.

He gave Henry brief details of his spot of bother, trying not to betray his nervousness. Henry was short, with dark hair pulled over his balding patch, beetling eyebrows, and an air of impatience calculated to elicit facts in the shortest possible time. He had to seek points of clarification. Sir Miles, usually lucid, kept straying from the subject.

'The girl. Not English, is she?'

'No. Italian. American mother.'

'Singer?'

'Yes.'

'Is she on drugs? A lot of them are, I believe.'

'Not as far as I know. She's a classical singer.'

Henry grunted, which he frequently did when gathering information.

'I have been in a compromising situation.'

'How compromising?'

'Compromising. During a private dinner party at the Maison Blanche.'

'Hm. Saffron's place. I went once. Were you with the girl you mentioned?'

'Not exactly.'

'Well, who then?'

Sir Miles took a deep breath, and attempted to adopt the same neutral tone as Henry. 'There were several things which happened at the dinner party. Somewhat embarrassing. I was wearing a dog collar, on all fours. Carla was holding my lead. She told me it was that kind of party, so I thought I'd go along with it.'

'Mmm.'

'Then. Certain things happened under the table.'

Henry gave another neutral grunt, and made some notes in tiny handwriting. 'Who else was there?'

'Saffron, of course. Andrew Broughton, Julian Lieberman, member of the Opera Palace Board. A painter,

495

Pauline Fudge. Lots of rather attractive girls, a few others I don't remember. Saffron often gives dinner parties. This was the first one in fancy dress. At least, that's what I was told. Turned out I made a fool of myself.'

He wished Henry would keep still. The lawyer had an annoying habit of swinging from side to side like a pendulum in his swivel chair.

'Happens all the time,' he commented. 'Especially at country house parties. I was at one in Wiltshire the other weekend. We were having coffee and liqueurs before bedtime – usual distinguished gathering – and this gorgeous girl said, "Honestly. Won't anyone beat me? You are a dreary lot."'

'That isn't very consoling,' said Sir Miles. 'What do you suggest I do?'

'My usual advice in these circumstances is to do nothing. Let's get down to business. What's the name of your counterpart at Covent Garden? Hampshire, is it?'

'Lord Hampshire, yes.'

'Isn't he a buddy of Rupert Murdoch?'

'Conrad Black, actually. Lady Hampshire is a fellow Canadian.'

'Hampshire would be quite pleased to see you in the mud, I suppose.'

'He and Andrew Broughton don't see eye to eye. That might cause problems. Andrew transferred his support to us, which left Covent Garden somewhat doddery.'

'Andrew Broughton? Minister for the Arts? That one?' Henry prided himself on being well-informed, and kept up with thespians, sportsmen, academics, businessmen, even bishops.

'The same. It was Broughton who forced Covent Garden to go downmarket in an economy move.'

'Meaning?'

'Gilbert and Sullivan. Lehar. Easy listening for the Radio Two brigade. Why are we going into this?'

Henry scribbled a few rapid notes and looked up over his half-glasses. 'Tricky one. You and Broughton together makes it rather too interesting for the raincoat brigade. If the girl tells all, your little dinner party would become an orgy – I believe that's the word favoured by these suburban twits – which might mean humiliation for you and Broughton out of a job.'

'Might? Of course it would.'

'Can't you give this girl some kind of a part?'

'Certainly not. She wants to sing one of the most difficult roles in the entire repertoire. Salome. Marvellous vehicle. But not for her. And it would cost at least two million pounds to stage it properly. It would clean us out. I don't know how we're going to manage next year as it is.'

Henry twiddled his pen and reflected. At five hundred an hour, it paid to reflect. 'How about a cheap production? Experimental. Isn't that what they call it? What was that thing called the girl was in, *Black Slave*, something or other? Not a decent set in it.'

'You saw it? *White Slave, Black Country*?'

'I was taken by a client. Good body, I see the attraction. Well? Quarter the budget, put on the show, she'll get the publicity. Isn't that why she's doing it? Singers are all the same, like actresses.'

'Not all, Henry.' Sir Miles looked morose. He was beginning to wonder whether he had done the right thing.

'No point in taking it to heart, Miles. It'll get her off your back. And if we can get her to sign a legal document guaranteeing up to a million in damages if anything surfaces about the dinner – bingo, you're home and dry. It's not a bad deal. She gets her show, you get her off your back.'

'You think it's that simple?'

'Can't do any harm. If it doesn't work, we'll have to go another route.'

'Oh?'

'Immigration can be very helpful. A few packets of heroin, that's all. And then . . .' he clapped his hands. 'Back she goes to Sole Mio country.'

Sir Miles finished his coffee and shook his hand. 'Jolly helpful, Henry. As ever.'

'Don't lose any sleep over this, my dear fellow. Happens all the time.'

Henry was right. Girls were always trying to make fools of you. You didn't need to be there to imagine what went on. Whispering intimacies to bitching hair-stylists in glassy designer parlours, allowing the waiters to eavesdrop over giggling lunches, betraying personal secrets in the changing rooms of Bond Street, comparing lovers pedalling away side by side in those over-heated gyms, sweating out their grudges in the sauna. However hard you tried to do without them, there were times when you had to give in. Temporarily. They tried to drive you mad, that was the aim. To make you lose the logical processes of reason they so despised. Vile-mouthed Bacchantes with suffocating breasts in Chanel suits.

Had he sufficient time to make his mark? Could he keep his great glass edifice blazing out into the sky? Or would someone take his place and act as surrogate father to his baby if the authorities declared him unfit? What would he leave behind when he had gone? A few review copies of books on music, a pile of magazines, a stack of computer discs, music discs, video discs. Publicity posters, several photographs of Anastasia Wagner, and one of Carla outside the Villa degli Spiriti, getting out of a carriage. A collage of framed reviews, costume designs. Would he be worth a full page obituary in *The Times*? Sir Miles unlocked his cupboard and reached for a bottle of Glenmorangie.

Stefano Montini, voted Music Critic of the Year, sat in his usual stalls seat at La Scala and furiously scribbled a succession of adjectives on his programme. It was what every music critic waited for, and never expected to see or hear. He had witnessed almost every role she had performed, but this was superlative. By now, he knew her voice better than that of his mother, and he had been the first to tell his public of Anastasia's return to the home of opera. Hadn't he been sitting with the director of the opera house hours after it was announced that, having sung the definitive *Tosca*, she had turned her back on England in disgust? La Scala had rearranged its programme, and were taking an unscheduled production. Dominic Morrison had been asked to revive *La Traviata*, the Parisian triumph which, just a few years ago, would have seemed inconceivable in Milan.

'How quickly the climate changes,' he wrote, tapping out his words on an IBM computer reserved for his use alone in a niche of the opera house building, so that he could breathe the exalted air of this temple of music. 'But La Scala grows with the times, marking each era of achievement with rings on the great tree of artistic progress. Anastasia Wagner, descendant of the fiery Richard, has brought tears flooding from our eyes. What can I say about this miracle of grace, presence, perfect tone and exquisite artistry? She has never sung better. It is after an evening such as this, that I wish to lay down my pen.'

'Do you believe this one? Shall we frame it?' asked Dominic, showing Stasi the review of reviews. She took the page from him, and kissed it.

'Suppose Richard Wagner was a distant cousin,' she said. 'He might well be. They say we're all related in the end.'

She wondered if Signora Busconi had seen it. She wanted to tell her that everything they said was true. Only when you had triumphed at La Scala were you written into history. She had expected Amelia to come backstage, but, when she had phoned, she was informed by someone she didn't recognize that the maestra was having a little trouble with her health and was staying at home. Dominic had asked to meet her several times, but Stasi had refused. She could not explain why. Either she wished to keep their special intimacy to herself, or she feared Amelia might disapprove of him. At last she relented. They would pay a short visit.

Stasi took Dominic past the convent where she had stayed, the café opposite where she had counted her lire to buy a creamy custard doughnut. The passers-by stopped, shouted, crowded round, touched her in awe, until they had to take refuge in a passing taxi. 'Via delle Stelle.'

They wound round the backstreets, and Stasi hung out of the window, breathing in the smells she remembered, gazing longingly at the places she could no longer enter without being besieged by admirers, the pasticcerie, the cafés, the museums and galleries which had once been her refuge. Then she rang at the bell, her heart beating.

'Is Signora Busconi there?'

'Where else?' replied a haughty Milanese voice. 'Who is it?'

'Anastasia.'

'I'll enquire if she wishes to see anyone.'

The room was little changed since she had last visited, but to Stasi it seemed like another era. Five roles ago. 'Amelia. Dear Amelia.'

A shrunken figure was sitting upright in a wheelchair, cushioned in position. And then she smiled, the sweet smile struggling to recall the past. Stasi took her hand and kissed the taut fingers.

'This is Dominic. My fiancé.'

'You are getting married?'

'Yes. We only decided a few days ago.'

'Stasi decided.'

'Not true. You asked me if I thought it was a good idea and I said yes.'

They both laughed and Amelia gave a wry smile.

'Dominic. I'm so pleased.' Her voice was faint, but the words were enunciated clearly.

'I'm singing *Traviata* at La Scala, Amelia.'

'Of course I knew that. You've come home to us. You must stay here. To come to my funeral. Will you sing? Will you tell them how I wouldn't let you get away with anything?'

Stasi continued holding the spent hand in hers. 'I'd rather sing for you now.'

The sunken eyes brightened.

Dominic went over to the polished piano, and Stasi whispered some instructions in his ear. As she began 'Vissi d'arte, vissi d'amore' Amelia Busconi closed her eyes. At the end, she murmured, 'It will never be sung like that again.'

The uniformed nurse came into the room. 'I think you had better leave. Signora Busconi is tired.'

They both kissed her hand again. She looked up at Dominic. 'Keep her well. Singers are easily destroyed. I have known great singers. But Anastasia? I would sacrifice them all to her.'

Outside in the street, Stasi stood looking up at the curtained window, tears slipping down her cheeks. Dominic took her arm, and gently pulled her away. A few days later, Stefano Montini called her to say that Amelia Busconi had died. As she took her final, ecstatic curtain calls from La Scala that night, Stasi walked forward in front of the swinging velvet drapes and lifted her arm. She wanted them all to remember the woman in the Via delle Stelle who had given her enough inspiration for a lifetime. Amelia Busconi. The audience gazed at the grand diva, standing proudly before them, her head bowed from the neck, newly risen from the lingering deathbed of Violetta Valéry, and with her they mourned in silence.

As soon as Stasi had given her last performance, Dominic took her back to his old flat in Paris. The spring sun was pouring through the dusty windows, the leather chairs were cracked and sagging, books spilling over from the shelves onto the floor, the plants were gone and the black furniture, which she had once admired, looked ready for retirement.

'I don't believe in facelifts. It was Violetta's birthplace, after all.'

'A few flowers and a new rug or two. That's all we want.

God, Dominic. How embarrassing I must have been. Remember when you first started trying to make me act?'

There was a huge pile of mail on the table. Dominic picked out two long white envelopes, marked with the Gothic gold lettering of the Opera Palace, forwarded from La Scala.

'What is it?' she asked. 'Sir Miles begging me to come back again?'

'Another screed from the lawyers. This one's more serious.'

'I don't care. Throw it in the waste basket. I refuse to answer them until I get an apology. If they want me back, it will be on my terms.'

'Now they're threatening to sue.'

'Let them. Julian won't allow them to bankrupt me. And if I have to stand up in court, I can let the world know how I've been betrayed. At least no one will have to invent what I say.'

Stasi extracted an envelope postmarked Paris. Nathalie had written her a long letter which opened with a series of exclamations. 'I have a movie!!! It has taken me the same time as to give birth to an elephant!!! Come and see my baby!!! We will say *merde* to our success.'

There were a few more paintings crammed edge to edge on the cluttered walls of the 'bargain' apartment in the Boulevard Pereire. Stasi admired some heavy amber necklaces and silver Arab pots clustered round the fireplace, but Nathalie quickly dragged her off to the kitchen. *Voilà, mon trésor*. A new fridge, very modern, self-defrosting, freezing compartment, dispenser for cold drinks. She had given way at last. Now Bernard was wondering when they might get married, but she refused to name a date. Suppose *The Secret Life of Isabelle* was a big success? If she was forced to live in Hollywood, what would he do, poor thing?

Nathalie cleared a space on her rickety table and poured out some thick, black coffee. Squawking sounds came from one of the bedrooms, now transformed into an editing suite. Only Stasi, amongst her friends, had been allowed to see the rough cut.

'Now you tell me really what you think of my film. Will it be successful? Artistically?'

'It's extraordinary, wonderful. I would hardly have recognized her.'

Nathalie grinned. 'I know. You saw only Carla in a black wig, nothing else.'

'No, no.'

'Very good in my film because she is so bad. I capture this badness-goodness. Today, to be a *phénomène*, you paint yourself with mediocrity. Then, everyone says, I can be like that. That is Carla's genius. False genius, Stasi. She is Antichrist to your Christ.'

'Why does she still have that power? When I am where I am? When I'm with the man I'm crazy about?'

Nathalie took the last puff of her cigarette and stubbed it out in the cracked, overflowing ashtray.

'Every role for you is a test, but you can conquer it. No one has written the role of Carla Livorno except you. Now you must conquer this role.'

When the coffee had been drained, Nathalie got up. 'Are you cross because I chose Carla for my film?'

Stasi shook her head and smiled.

'Now this foolish girl is preparing *Salome* in London. It's like Tin Tin playing at the Comédie Française. One day you will sing this, much better.'

'Never.'

Julian rarely came to the offices of the Opera Palace. Business commitments abroad had reached the delicate stage where his presence was necessary. And if there was one excrescence he wished to have nothing to do with, it was *Salome*. In spite of his reasoned argument, Sir Miles had stubbornly refused to listen.

'It's not opera. It's a wailing screech. It's an obsolete period piece. For Christ's sake, Miles, can't you leave that ghoulish stuff to the Krauts? If you want your piece of stuff to make a balls-up at my expense, we may have to part company.'

'Carla has a fine voice. Your personal antagonism to Strauss does you no credit, Julian. Mel Donitz has guaranteed it will be a triumph.'

'I don't like the figures.'

'Then you shouldn't be involved with opera. You're behaving like a dwarf. I want giants.'

'You'd better put on the Ring.'

Julian picked up his briefcase, gave a contemptuous glance at Sir Miles, and walked out. Sir Miles had lost his marbles. And his hobby was getting to be like an expensive mistress: the outlay wasn't justifying the return. Going through the great glass doors no longer gave him that buoyant rush of anticipation. He could sit in his flat, in his car, and hear Anastasia's perfection pouring out of his speakers. Without her, the Palace was an empty shell.

When he returned to Concordia Wharf they were waiting. He had forgotten that he had agreed to give a short piece to camera on private sponsorship. Usually, he refused to appear on television, leaving that kind of inanity to Sir Miles, but he could no longer be trusted. While the crew was setting up the first shot, he changed into an open-necked shirt, and the woollen patterned pullover which Stasi had admired.

Nick Morgan, the reporter, looked as though he would be more at home interviewing football hooligans than discussing art. Tough little face, close-cropped hair, that dogged look of the working class boy made good.

'I'd rather you didn't zoom in. Not with no make-up. A chap has his pride,' Julian interjected casually, noticing the cameraman's forefinger pressing on the zoom button. 'I've said all I need to say.'

'Just a couple more brief questions, Mr Lieberman.'

'Brief, then. I have to get to the airport.'

Nick moistened his lips. 'I noticed that Winchester Tobacco was a sponsor of the Palace *Tosca*. Do you have any objections to funding opera through the sale of nicotine?'

Why did they persist in asking the same questions, knowing the answers in advance?

'I'm an investment broker,' he replied wearily. 'You'd better ask the tobacco companies. It's their province, not mine. Sir Miles has never hidden the fact, anyway.'

'Does the name Iskra mean anything to you?'

'Nothing.' He noticed that Nick was rummaging in a scruffy satchel. 'Next question? That's right, why don't you consult your notes? I'm sure there's a next question.'

'Take a look at this.' Nick handed him a sheaf of photocopied pages, headed with the familiar lettering of Winchester Tobacco. Julian read the first page and handed them back.

'Very interesting. That kind of fraud is rather outside my area of expertise, I'm afraid. But I'm told it's becoming quite common.'

'If you read on, you'll see they've collected evidence to show that, under different names, you've been recycling substandard tobacco, marketing it under the name of Winchester Tobacco with counterfeit packaging and pushing it out via a series of agents in Russia and Eastern Europe.'

'I wish I was that clever. Fortunately, I've been successful in the kind of straightforward business activity which makes for very boring television programmes. Have I said enough? Or do we need more on the morality of sponsorship?'

As the cameraman moved to change his angle, Julian turned his head to look into the lens. 'Fine piece of gear, that. Unusual these days,' he said with a grin.

'What interested Winchester,' continued Nick, 'was how the operation was funded. They had to wait until Eddie Focaccia was seized in Las Vegas in Operation Permafrost before they could establish the link. It was just a question of shifting money from a Colombian cartel from one drug to another. Heroin to tobacco. I presume the singer under contract to the Palace, Anastasia Wagner, knew nothing of this when she sang for one of Focaccia's charity benefits in Las Vegas.'

'She wasn't under contract then. Is this a sample of your reporting technique? Or perhaps she doesn't remember. Singers have frequent lapses of memory.' Julian moved from his position by the wall and came over to Nick. 'You're a hardworking lad, and I'm sure your programmes are excellent. But you won't make your name by inventing allegations. Or by talking to singers. They are notorious for being unable to distinguish between fact and the pulp fiction they read between entrances.'

'You know my information doesn't come from there.'

'Oh? That's where I would have begun. If I wanted to invent something outrageous enough to go on air.' Julian smiled, took a small card from his trouser pocket and presented it to Nick. 'Here's the name of my lawyer. He'll explain how libel works in this country. You can send him a transcript of my interview, when you've rearranged it to suit the artistic requirements of your programme. I'm awfully sorry I haven't time to offer you a drink. Goodbye, everyone. Don't forget to take the camera with you.'

After he had jotted down Nick's office number – the 354 code confirmed what he might have guessed, an address in lefty Islington – he escorted the crew through the door and then called Saffron.

'Hello, darling girl. Could you make an appointment with that excellent office cleaning service? I need to have some premises made over like new.'

Julian's office search yielded nothing except a few files on Russian black marketeers and transcripts of past programmes on subjects of parochial interest. It was likely that Nick Morgan kept the hard stuff at home, if he had that much sense. And even if Winchester Tobacco had supplied him with a few documents, who would be interested except the trainer-wearing, lentil-eating, pallid members of the anti-smoking lobby who thought trading in tobacco was worse than dealing in arms?

And who in Britain would be interested in a respected Las Vegas financier who spent much of his time raising funds for charity and happened to fall in with the wrong people? Neither the police nor the inland revenue would be prepared to spend millions funding an investigation into DCCI unless pressed to do so in the public interest. It was what kept the City alive, and everyone accepted that the injection of foreign funds could do nothing but help a terminal economy. Even if Nick Morgan's little show found late-night airspace on some minority channel, no one would pick it up.

Although remote, there was an unpleasant possibility that Nick Morgan had established the connection between Andrew Broughton and the DCCI trading company based in the Cayman Islands. If it hadn't been for his friendship with Sir Miles, he would never have taken Broughton on board. There was always one bad move, one bad shuffle of the pack.

Julian packed one case of essentials, gave Saffron Nick Morgan's office number, asking her to find out when the programme on sponsorship was being transmitted, told his driver to go back to his minicab firm for a while, and took a taxi to the airport. There was a pretty hilltop village outside Larnaca which he fancied as a retreat, and Cyprus was a good base for the routes to Turkey, Syria, the Lebanon; even Saudi Arabia with hefty long-distance trucks.

It was the first time Andrew Broughton had visited Sir Miles in his flat. His surroundings were so modest, not a decent piece of furniture in the place. A man who lived for art, whose dreams only came to life in the Opera Palace. Even the fish tank was empty, the glass dusty.

'I want to tell you everything, Miles. Better that way. I've been a dreadful idiot.'

Sir Miles listened stiff-necked while Andrew described what he had seen. Some reporter he'd never heard of had made a film about the Opera Palace. Forty-five minutes of far-fetched allegations, but there was a grain of truth in it. Instead of reviewing the highly praised productions, the film had zeroed in on part of Julian Lieberman's commodity empire. Chap had done his homework, part of it was true. They had engaged in a little business together, setting up a few factories, tobacco factories, to help the cash flow of the Eastern bloc. But it was merely a sideline, a way of showing good will. Over there, it was a choice of tobacco, hamburgers or guns – moral niceties were, after all, a feature of advanced capitalism. They needed to generate capital. And if it put food in starving bellies, why not? And besides, their venture, and others no doubt, had sustained Britain's finest opera house.

'You are involved in the tobacco business?' shouted Sir Miles.

'It could have been anything. It happened to be tobacco. Sadly, it's the one product which has a universal market. In the old days, it would have been salt. Or sugar. Or spices.'

Sir Miles sniffed. 'I suppose I'm to congratulate you that it wasn't cocaine or heroin. Or contaminated baby food.'

Andrew shifted his position on the upright winged chair, and wondered when he might be offered a drink. 'Anyhow, the PM has decided the programme won't go out. Detrimental to public confidence. Etcetera.'

Sir Miles put his hands across his face, then slowly pulled them away, dragging down his cheeks.

'I want to see Lieberman. Where the hell is he?'

'Actually, I've no idea.'

'The impact on the public. Appalling, appalling. What will I say to the board?'

'Nothing. You knew nothing, Miles.'

'Like Himmler, you mean?'

'You didn't kill anybody.'

'Oh, no. Not directly.'

'And you didn't mind that Winchester helped to sponsor *Tosca*.'

'That was different, and anyway it was a reluctant decision. Do you think I'd have entertained the idea of running an entire opera house on the back of the tobacco industry? I do attempt to maintain some principles, Andrew. From time to time.'

'We built our empire on slave labour, Miles. Does that mean empires should never have been created?'

At last, Sir Miles brought out a couple of bottles, and their minds became more lucid, their sentences shorter, as the evening passed the dining hour. Andrew moved from his chair to sit beside his host. At one point, he found himself with his arm round his shoulder.

'You're a good chum, Andrew.'

'Wish I was.'

'You realize the Palace is finished. Pop groups or porn shows, you get money for that. Just a few big decibel concerts in aid of world famine. No point in pretending. No one feels guilty enough about art. Not when you can rent the video.'

'Couldn't you make it smaller, hive off some for offices?'

'Offices? The whole city's full of empty filing cabinets.'

'Make a good hotel. Take the money and run.'

'I've never run in my life. Not even at school.'

Andrew struggled to his feet. 'Must get back to the wife. Want to stay with me? Shouldn't be alone.'

'Face the music. Apt. In this case.'

Outside, in the narrow hallway, Andrew leaned with one hand against the lift, holding the door open. Before he lurched inside, they hugged one another. Then Sir Miles returned to his room, switched on his player and put on highlights from *Tosca*. Puccini, like amyl nitrate, swelled the blood-vessels. Dear, incomparable Anastasia.

Mel wanted the oily sweaty look to express sexual aftermath. Salome, the Liebestod, love in death. This theme was elaborated by spraying bubbles of glue onto the red surfaces of the set (putrefying meat colour was

Pauline's instruction to the scene painter). From the middle of the auditorium, the swirling form could be made out, if you knew what to look for. The main stage area, which resembled a cave from Hollywood space fiction circa 1930, was in the shape of the female vagina, the pink hills in the distance were breasts. Jokanaan the prophet would emerge from dungeon-steps approximating to the position of the anus. A programme note, written by Pauline, explained the Focal Modi of visualization, Uber-sattigun (over-satiation) conceptualized from a psychotic Weltanschauung.

Carla was painting her nipples gold. Lying on her make-up shelf was a replica of Jokanaan's head, with wide open eyes, mouth gaping in horror. She was expecting some-one else to come knocking on her dressing room door.

'Ready, honey,' she called. Then she saw Mel's rotund figure in the mirror.

'Hi. Like it?'

'Sensational.'

'Let me show you something.' She stood up, and inched off the seventh veil which was tied round her hips, hanging down between her legs. Fitted neatly over her pubic hair was a halo of golden spikes, like a sea-urchin.

'Pauline's a genius. Feel. It's plastic.'

'Can you stop a moment? Put on a robe, if you like.'

Carla moistened her lips and pouted at the mirror. 'Another pep talk?'

'I know it's a tough role. But we've had four weeks of rehearsal, Carla.'

'Really? Feels like only a day.' She put her hands behind her head, and rested her gold-painted toes on the make-up shelf.

'I'm still not happy. With the music.'

'I hit some of the notes some of the time. What more do you want? Have you seen my picture in the programme? Pauline says it'll get seized by the vice squad.' She giggled, and stroked her leg.

'We haven't much time left, Carla.'

As soon as he had left, Carla locked the door and examined her gold-streaked face in the mirror. How was she to know it would be this bad? Better to lose your voice overnight, like Ma, than be subjected to hoots of derision. She had heard those English audiences expressing their disapproval in echoing silence, the odd faint-hearted clap. The critics, the worst in the world, would slaughter her with sneering praise.

Stasi was giving a dinner party. Carla could hear the clattering of plates, the laughter, Dominic's interjections in the background.

'Why the hell are you calling?'

'Stasi, thank Christ you're there. Please listen. This production is a complete fuck-up. No one's giving me any support. I should never have agreed to do this goddamned part. Sir Miles doesn't even come to rehearsals. The conductor's a heap of shit. You were so right to walk out. But they asked me to do it. I needed this part. God, Stasi, I feel so bad.'

'Carla, I can't talk at the moment. I've got friends round.'

'I wouldn't have called, but I'm desperate. No one understands what I'm going through. The cast won't even talk to me. Everyone avoids me, except Pauline, and she's only hooked on her set. I've just made the biggest mistake of my life. I even thought of taking pills. That bad.' She sounded distraught; her voice was a cracked monotone. Stasi had never heard her in such despair.

'Do you want to come over here?'

'I don't want to spoil things.'

'You won't.'

'Stasi. Will you do something for me? Come to rehearsal? Tell me what I should do? I'm sure you'd have some ideas. Anything, anything. It would make me so happy.'

'But I don't know the role, Carla.'

'It doesn't matter. Know something? You're the only real friend I ever had. The only honest one.'

The next day, Stasi installed herself at the side of the Opera Palace arena. When the lights went up on the red-encrusted set, she could only think of a body opened by the surgeon's knife. It took a moment for her to realize that part of the swirling structure, a vaginal tunnel curving upwards centre stage, was pulsing, and the breast-like hills were also moving fractionally, like tethered balloons. Herod's court erupted into life. Listening with rapt attention to the rich firm tones of the Hungarian tenor playing Narraboth, she was taken by surprise by Carla's entrance. She was running down the tunnel, every bump and curve of her body outlined by a scarlet skin-tight structure from which sprouted fine fluorescent tentacles. Two black slaves were tethered to each wrist, running with her. The kestrel had escaped and was veering round the set in panicked confusion, before settling on one of the bosomy hills.

Carla was staggering through. It would not be the first time an underpowered singer had been supported by the strength of those around her. But then she suddenly stopped, came right downstage, and spoke to the conductor. She had forgotten that her microphone was on, and her voice boomed round the auditorium. The conductor screamed.

'There is only one tempo. My tempo, Miss Livorno.' Confronted by her abuse, he began to splutter. 'This is the worst set I have ever seen. And the singer matches the set.'

The string sections tapped their music stands, the horns let out a couple of fart-like bursts. Mel leaped from his seat and attempted to restore order. A shaky compromise was reached, the conductor continued at the same tempo. Before long, another row broke out. Thomas Campton-Fausey was beside himself.

'This is too terrible,' he said to Mel. 'For God's sake, get her to do the dance. That's all they'll come to see.'

The stage went completely dark. Only Carla was lit. Stasi thought back to the Maison Blanche in Paris.

Nathalie knew how it should be done. Carla was bumping and grinding like a housewife in a belly-dancing class. The orchestra grew louder, swamping her with sound. At the end of her dance, she stopped.

'We continue,' shouted the conductor.

Sweat was pouring down Carla's face. Her voice came out in a thin metallic stream, the notes flat. Then, throwing herself this way and that, she waltzed defiantly round the stage, mouthing her words. The conductor put down his baton.

'Mel,' he called. 'Either she goes or I go.'

'Let's just get to the end,' the producer said.

Carla stood with her arms folded and tapped her foot. 'If I go,' she squawked, 'there's no Salome. If you go, who'd notice?'

The conductor turned on his podium, bowed, handed his baton to Mel and walked out of the auditorium. Then there was a rustle followed by a clatter, as one by one the orchestra left their seats and disappeared.

Stasi clasped her throat. It was all too easy to imagine, the abuse of the irreplaceable human instrument, the effort, the choking, the unattainable notes, the agony of vocal chords which throbbed with exhaustion. She could tell Carla's voice had been ruined. After this, she would be banished from the stage. It was what Stasi had been waiting for. Now she could admit to herself that she had willed this scene, as though Carla Livorno had been responsible for the death of her father, the terraced house in Rosedene Avenue, generations of Wagner failure and the accident of birth which had denied her blond curls and an impish smile.

The stage had emptied. Stasi went up the steps towards Carla who was sitting leaning against the throne. She wrenched off her wig and put it on John the Baptist's head.

'Hi, Stasi. What a bitch. I'm exhausted.'

Stasi sat down beside her. 'Why did you do it?'

'It's my part. It's always been my part. Always will be.

Better than the victim roles. They're yours. I couldn't do them.'

'Carla. I wouldn't take it away from you. But back out, for Christ's sake, back out. You're killing your voice.'

'You mind?'

'Of course I do.'

'No one else does.'

'There's nothing I can say. Can't you tell them you're ill? That your doctor won't allow it? If it was me, I'd leave right now.'

Carla went to retrieve one of her veils, and wiped away the sweat still dripping down her neck.

'I've decided to go through with it. Carla Livorno in *Salome*. Biggest disaster in town. No one likes success. Failure. That's really big. I realized. That's my talent. Ma was right. If you've got talent, use it. I'm going to be such a towering failure, when I'm dead they'll make a movie about me. Like Isadora Duncan.'

They walked out to the car park together, both swathed in furs to protect them against the sharp February air. Carla's Bentley was parked by the artists' entrance, next to Stasi's Rolls. They kissed one another, then parted.

Dominic was waiting. 'What was it like?'

'She's not going to make it.'

Dominic touched Stasi's arm. 'The production, Stasi.'

'No one deserves that. Not even Carla.'

Chapter Twenty

When he was alone, Sir Miles put the whisky bottle to his lips, drained the last drop and locked the empty bottle in his cupboard. The report he had made, with the accountants' appendices, was still lying on his desk. He knew every word by heart. The agents of liquidation had walked round, mouthing into pocket recorders, passing the local youths still playing the video games in the foyer, the old ladies spending an hour or two with a cup of tepid tea in the deserted Aria Café, a couple of students flipping through the marked down books in the Words and Music shop.

He had observed them, each assessing his speciality – the carpet, the chandeliers, the velvet-covered chairs, the cherubic trumpeting angels. He had walked beside them to the auditorium where the stripped-bare set of *Salome* still stood upright in position. They could see no use for that. What was it exactly? Not even suitable for a shopping arcade. Then they had fingered the costumes lined up in the wardrobe stores, joking about what the wife would say if they came home in that get-up. The computerized lighting rig, that must be worth something. Good seating, but too much of it. It could be split into lots. Best thing was to have an auction, get rid of it all in one go. If there were a few little things he wanted for himself, no one would mind.

On the day of the auction, they were spilling outside the front entrance, pushing against one another, waving catalogues in the air, fighting their way into the foyer. Sir Miles was there. It was unforgivable to miss the last act. And he wanted to be present, to confront the smooth-faced rapacious brigade who scoured the country picking over the remnants of bankrupt stock, digging in cold, dusty attics to unearth the relics of the dead like looting barbarians treading a civilization into the mud. There was only one thing he wanted to take away.

He was half expecting to see her there. Following the direction of the auctioneer's shifting gaze, he looked behind him. Three photographers were aiming their lenses towards the central row of canvas chairs reserved for serious bidders. Even in dark glasses and a wide-brimmed hat, he could recognize the swift turn of her head, the blond curls clustering round her neck, and he was aware of a woody sweet wave of her dense perfume. She was pushing a hot-dog into her mouth with one hand, raising one jewelled finger of the other as though summoning a waiter, clear grey-green eyes directed at the lenses without bothering to see if her instruction had been heeded.

The other bidders for item six-nine-two dropped away. The price was ballooning far beyond his reach, and then the hammer came down. Sold to the lady in the big hat. His collar was damp, his shirt clinging to his jacket. He sat for a while chewing at his lip, waited until the wide-brimmed hat had disappeared, and then passed unnoticed through the crowd to find his car.

He was halfway to Marylebone before he noticed the high bonnet of her Bentley behind him. Accelerating, he changed his route and headed towards Regent's Park.

As he was walking briskly towards the rose garden, she caught up with him.

'Well, Carla? What do you want now?'

'Nothing. How could they let it happen? Why didn't those arseholes on the board do something to save you? And Andrew? How about him?'

'He did his best. But the Opera Palace is hardly in the forefront of priorities. And *Salome* didn't do a lot to gain the sympathies of those who might have done something. Couldn't you at least have chosen something by a British composer?'

She sniffed the damp air and fingered a heavy, rain-laden rose, its pink petals browning at the edges. 'The production was great. The publicity was great. And that German soprano who took over from me wasn't half bad. Everyone came.'

'Julian was against it from the start. He thinks *Salome* is overrated.'

'Come on, Miles. Why couldn't you see? Julian got bored and moved on. I know him, he always does that. Same with girls. I bet he was trying to find an excuse to back out. With his kind of money, he doesn't need to be serious. Did you really think he'd stick around for years, supporting a crackpot place like an opera house? Only nuts do that.'

'That wasn't my impression. But I don't need to discuss it with you.'

'If he'd looked like the stoat he is, you'd never have had him around.'

'Nothing to do with it.'

'No?' Carla sat down on a bench, removed her glasses and extracted a large stapled box from an Aspreys carrier bag. 'Thought you'd like a memento. To remind you of the good times.'

He shook his head, and she tore open the lid.

'Whatever it is, you keep it, Carla.'

'Recognize this? Stasi's Tosca costume. Isn't it a great colour?' she said, pulling out a braided sleeve from the box. 'I wasn't bidding for myself. You can keep it, or give it to her. Either way.'

'My dear Carla. What prompted this? Or is there a quid pro quo?'

'Whatever that is, I hope you'll accept the dress. From the Marchesa della Robbia to her dear friend Sir Miles Mackenzie.'

He fingered the peacock-blue velvet, replaced the sleeve in the box, took it gingerly from her, and tucked it under his arm. 'Decent of you, Carla. But you paid far too much. Or is the marchese footing the bill?'

'Maurizio? Unfortunately not.' She tilted her head to one side, and gave a regretful smile. 'I know I should have told you, but you were out of the country at the time. He passed away.'

Sir Miles lowered his head, and tried to avoid looking at the rise of her breasts showing at the open neck of her shiny black raincoat. At this moment he was feeling a mixture of guilt and desire. He had, he confessed to himself, treated her badly, taking no account of her private anguish, as though all that mattered was her career.

'I'm so sorry,' he said weakly. He started to rise to his feet. 'I really must be off, Carla.'

'Wait, Miles, just listen. Every singer does something awful once and I did it. My Salome stank. Think I didn't know that? But the learning experience was fantastic. So what if I end up doing Lloyd Webber instead of Wagner? It's no big deal. Without you, I'd never have stretched myself to the limit, realized who I am. I'll never forget what you did for me, Miles.'

He gave her a wry smile. It was the last time he would be looking into those sparkling eyes, wondering when her lips would part.

'I'm so pleased to have contributed to your learning experience. Even though you threatened me with blackmail, slaughtered my fish, hounded out my best singer and lost me the Opera Palace, I'll be eternally grateful. At least the public won't have to waste money watching a singer who can't sing.'

As he strode away, Carla screamed after him, 'You never did understand artists.'

The *Nessun Dorma* was a convenient mobile home for someone who was accustomed to luxury and unable to live without an office, a gym and satellite communications. The thirty-metre yacht could sometimes be seen harbouring for the night in Port Said or Alexandria but was more often at sea, plying the Eastern Mediterranean where it was taken for a cruise liner with a remarkable turn of speed. The crew uniforms, of royal blue and gold, were inspired by the packet livery of Winchester Tobacco, one of Julian's whims. The name of the yacht, too, was appropriate for a man who stayed awake while others slept.

Living at sea had its drawbacks. There was only so much Julian could take of the ebb and flow of the tides, the capricious turnings of the wind, the open, unhindered skies and occasional stops in ports where one had to entertain pompous harbourmasters and fellow yachtsmen – arms dealers or Texan oilmen whose talk consisted of either uninterrupted boasting or detailed discussion of minor nautical mishaps.

He showed them pictures in English newspapers of the stripped Opera Palace, but it meant nothing to them. They preferred to hear about cigarette factories and where you could get a good screw in London. Julian played his discs at full volume, even through the night, drowning out the sounds of the gulls and distant fog-horns. Behind his back, the crew called him the Fliegende Engländer, the Flying Englishman who hated lying at anchor and moved from place to place as though he was driven by the devil, pushing his boat through fair weather and foul.

The only person who knew approximately where he might be at any given time was Saffron. She refused to believe the appalling lies in that ghastly television programme, which could only have been made by a Communist. One of her guests who had seen a rough version at a private showing had told her all about it, and she had immediately sent him an urgent fax.

'Do stay away for a while. Even though I'm assured there's no question of it being shown.'

The sea-salt gave him an unbecoming, ruddy complexion and roughened his hair. As Julian was trimming his black beard in the long tinted mirror of his bathroom, he thought of 'Grouchy' Peters, his tailor in Old Burlington Street. Grouchy, who disapproved of beards except during the shooting season, had begun to make him a couple of suits before he left London, and they had still to be collected. And then he thought longingly of Saffron's inviting house, the gossip whispered in corners, the heady scent of freshly showered, glowing young skin, the musky incense of the Chapel Room. This time he would avoid getting undressed – that had been his mistake. If Carmen had been able to master her revulsion, he would not have punished her. But there was no reason to stay away, and he would avoid passing by the empty glass box of the Opera Palace.

The first name which came into his mind when choosing a name for his new passport was Peters. Captain John Peters had the right kind of ring, and Grouchy would have approved of Julian's well-cut, elegant naval uniform. A naval man could still command the right kind of respect, though the army had long since lost its cachet. Although he could have slipped quietly into Heathrow in the private jet at his disposal, Julian chose to travel by a scheduled flight, rather as one might choose, on occasion, to kerb-crawl in the King's Cross area instead of being chauffeured to Mayfair.

Saffron was almost taken in. Captain Peters? She tried to place the member of the Maison Blanche with horn-rimmed glasses, naval cap and well-trimmed black beard. She gave his beard a sharp tug – it was real – and then she sniffed his neck. She could always tell a man by his eau de toilette.

'Julian! I told you not to come! Haven't you any sense?'

'A brief visit. I was missing you.'

She took him into her office and locked the door. There were some photographs lying on her desk of new applicants aspiring to a post. Julian picked one out.

'She isn't bad.'

'Julian, listen. A dreadful little man in an anorak called round here this morning. Nick Morgan, the one with the grudge against you. Now he's trying to blacken my name, too. Can you imagine? He wanted me to confirm that you, Sir Miles and Andrew Broughton were members. "When I wish to open my private dining club to the public," I told him, "I'll let you know." Why is he being so nosy? What's he got against you? Why has he picked on me?'

'I can't imagine.'

'Do you think he's spying? He could be hiding in the mews.'

'He'll get cold.'

'How can you be so calm? Supposing I was forced to close? I've created this place, and I'm proud of it. It may not seem much to you, but I put my soul into every room. If I was Pauline Fudge, they'd invite me to the Tate.'

'Darling Saffron, why are you worrying? You're doing nothing illegal. No one will close you down. I wouldn't let them.'

She smiled with relief. Julian had the extraordinary ability to convince one that the world was in order, that nothing unexpected could happen in his presence.

As they entered the Library, Julian listened to the rippling notes of a sonata being played on a harpsichord.

'A new girl,' said Saffron. 'An American music student.'

Julian glanced at the bowed pigtails hanging down her bare back.

'Like the hair. Did you know that Alessandro Scarlatti wrote over seventy operas?' he remarked.

'No, but I'm sure she does,' replied Saffron.

It was still early, not yet ten o'clock. Most of her guests would still be at dinner. Julian made a quick survey of the girls sprawled on the couches. One or two had sat up and smiled as he entered; several had their heads bowed over embroidery frames.

'How long are you staying?' enquired Saffron

'I'll be leaving after I've called in on my tailor. And paid a visit to the Chapel Room. Anyone you'd like to recommend?'

Saffron pursed her lips and considered. Since the incident in the Chapel Room, she had restricted entry to gentlemen of an advanced age who would only observe, even though some of them could barely see. She refused to bend the rules, it was unfair to make an exception.

'I'm afraid the Chapel Room is out of bounds. It's fully booked,' she replied with a regretful smile. 'It's so popular. How about the Games Room?'

'Does nothing for me, Saffron darling, I've been looking forward to this for months. Tossing around in my little lonely cabin. Come on, be a sport. I'll pay ten times the price. I'm sure one of your lovely young things would like some overtime.' He pulled a wad of dollars from his pocket.

'How awfully generous. Are you sure you can afford it?'

'Five thousand do?'

Saffron quickly opened her bag, but before she shut it she said, 'Julian, I must tell you something before you decide. One of my girls was viciously attacked in the Chapel. I had to have video cameras installed in every room. One can't afford to take risks.'

'You didn't tell me. How absolutely appalling. Who was the attacker? One of your foreign gentlemen?'

'I think he was German. Have you heard of Baron von Liebnitz?'

'Sounds vaguely familiar,' replied Julian. 'One of Heinrich's friends, is he?'

Saffron shook her head. 'Most puzzling. I tried to contact him, but no one had heard of him. He's probably hiding out in a Schloss somewhere.'

'Which girl was it?'

'Carmen. The Brazilian girl.'

'I don't remember a Carmen.'

Saffron took his hand, and stroked the delicate, manicured fingers. 'The beard is sexy, but you wouldn't pass for a naval man.'

'Only women look at hands,' he replied. 'I've made my choice. The little dark girl in red silk with antelope eyes, sitting by the screen.'

'That's Elza. She doesn't work the Chapel Room, except for a very large bonus.'

Julian began to pull out another sheaf of notes clipped into a silver holder. 'Why not?'

'Elza is Carmen's younger sister.' Saffron hesitated, then said quickly, 'Carmen was so badly injured, atrocious wounds. She never recovered. We were all terribly shocked.'

'My dear Saffron, so upsetting. You should have told me.'

'Such a kind girl, too. If she hadn't sent most of her money back to Sao Paulo, her family would have starved. Of course, when they begged me to take her sister, I agreed instantly. Even if Elza had been ugly, I would have found something.'

'Dreadful, dreadful,' murmured Julian, as he extracted a few hundred pounds from the holder. 'Will this do? It should buy a few baubles.'

How could you deny one of your best customers? Saffron gave a beaming smile, and pushed his outstretched hand back towards his pocket.

'Give it to her yourself. She'll be so pleased.'

Saffron beckoned to Elza, who fixed her expressionless dark eyes on Julian, and slowly rose to her feet. Having waited for Saffron to complete her whispered instructions, Julian followed Elza's swaying hips through a curtained door, and up the stairs.

The view on the video screen was blurred, but enough to see the distorted forms of two people. The man took off his jacket, tie and shirt. The girl in the nun's robe ran her fingers over his face, and put her hand on the catch of his trousers, but he pushed it away and went over to the Bishop's Chair. Saffron saw the glint of the silver holder as he took the notes from his pocket and handed them to her, Elza's shy smile as she placed them carefully under a candlestick. Then Saffron watched her slowly rise to her feet, lifting her skirt as she turned round in front of him, displaying the two half peaches of her buttocks. He lunged towards her, but she pushed him back against the altar, ran her hands down his chest and slipped them beneath his trousers. With Elza's back towards her, Saffron could only see Julian's expression. He was staring into her face with a triumphant smile. Strange, how men thought of an erection as such an achievement when a fake substitute could provide the same effect – and it was not as though he was one of her elderly clients. To her surprise, Julian did nothing, just remained there, leaning against the altar as though he was waiting for the barman to take his order. But some men were like that, showing what they were capable of without wanting to do anything about it. Elza moved away, as though he had said something, insulted her perhaps, but she hadn't seen his lips move. They were very touchy, Brazilian girls.

The session appeared to have ended. Julian leaned over to pick up his shirt and jacket, then straightened, dressed himself meticulously, smoothing down his shirt, adjusting his tie, and finally looked towards her. Elza was beckoning him. Poor girl, thought Saffron, she must learn to smile more with clients, and hide her distaste. Surely Julian was expecting a little more than this? He had paid, after all.

Panning the camera slightly, Saffron could see why Elza had made the gesture. She had climbed on to the altar, and was pouring out some wine from a decanter into two of the silver cups. She made the sign of the cross and took a sip from one cup, then Julian turned round, put the other to his lips, and threw back the contents. It was obvious, from the expression of distaste she was unable to hide, that such an act of sacrilege repelled the girl. She leaned back to lie full length on the altar, like a marble effigy. It was then that Julian attempted to remove her robe, but she slid off, clutching her breasts, screaming and laughing as she scampered round the chapel like an overexcited child.

There were two figures chasing one another, blurring past the camera, intermittently disappearing. Then they ceased to reappear. The altar was in the centre of the frame, the chair to one side, the tall candles flickering, the door marked 'Vestments' in the background.

Saffron changed the angle of the camera. There was no sign of Elza. Julian was lying face downwards on the stone floor, in a bare corner. She pressed her emergency bell to summon Sam, her security specialist, and ran from her office without stopping to lock the door.

She tried to breathe back life into Julian's gaping mouth while Sam thumped his chest.

'Good heavens! He can't be dead.'

'He went happy. Heart attack, I suppose,' said Sam.

'So embarrassing. He's not meant to be in the country. I can't possibly inform the police. They'll start digging around, and I can't have that.'

'Remember the Spanish geezer we took back home to his bed? How was we to know he wasn't plastered?'

'What on earth does one do?'

'Same as with drunks. Carry them out. Take 'em for a drive and a bit of fresh air.'

While Sam went in search of a large golf bag – there was one in the Games Room, he remembered – Saffron looked around for Elza. She found her weeping over a basin in the adjoining bathroom.

'I killed him, I killed him,' she repeated.

'Don't be so silly, Elza. It's not your fault. How could you have known that he was a sick man? We've done everything possible, darling.' Saffron took a towel and dabbed away her tears.

'I can stay here?'

'You want to?'

'Please, please.'

'Then you will. Would you like to go over to the Maison Blanche in Paris for a while?'

The girl threw her arms round Saffron, and kissed her neck with fervour. Then she started to wash the communion cups, the termination of her duty in the Chapel Room.

'You go home to bed. Take a taxi. Don't bother with that.'

'No, no. It's better I do something, Miss Saffron.'

It was as though he had just gone away. Saffron refused to believe that Julian was dead, then she consulted her astrologer. Just as she had suspected, he had undertaken a voyage at a time of malevolence. Typical of the man, to take such risks. Even if she had told him, he would have laughed at her. He always laughed at fear. Gamblers were like that. Saffron would not have been surprised to see him walking through the door, taking a weekend break from heaven. One of her girls swore she had seen a man with a black beard gazing up at an icon in the Chapel Room. Drug-induced hallucinations were common at the Maison Blanche.

A few days later, a body was recovered from the Thames, bobbing against the tufts of grass overspilling from the heron-haunted riverbank near Teddington Lock. It might have been logged as yet another of the anonymous suicidal corpses regularly retrieved from the murky waters, identity unknown, except for one characteristic which strained the credulity of the pathologist. The traces of curare, which a sympathetic nurse at a Sao Paulo hospital had hidden in a crucifix and sent to Elza, had long since leached out into the Thames. The flesh was partly crumbled away from the bones, like an over-boiled chicken, but the male organ was relatively intact. It appeared to be riveted in bars forming a gold cage, rooted in the scrotum with a series of studs running down each side. Fine gold spikes sprayed out from the bars, some dotted with tiny precious stones. Just below the tip, the penis was pierced horizontally by a thicker gold bar protruding on either side, with a ring at each end.

Until now, the only two people to have seen Julian's barbarous mutilation were Carmen and the man with dubious medical qualifications who had performed the operation. Elza, who had merely felt the harsh spikes and studs between her fingers as she performed her duty in the Chapel Room, had no need to view the atrocity. The evidence of touch was enough to convince her that she had found the man who had savaged her sister. Carmen's death had been avenged.

The corpse, covered in a plastic sheet, became an object of curiosity, like a baby with two heads, and 'Charlie's Organ' would gain a place in the police museum. It was a superb example of an elaborate 'Prince Albert' or 'dressing ring', originally intended to disguise the disfiguring bulge of male genitals in tight Victorian trousers. By piercing through the urethra and inserting a bar attached to a ring, the offending organ could be tied back to the leg to give the hermaphroditic form favoured by Queen Victoria's consort.

Called in to join the investigation team, a specialist in tattooing and body piercing revealed that the practice had been recently revived. For connoisseurs of such skills, there was no mistaking the work of a Birmingham piercer with a worldwide reputation. Although no one came forward to identify the body, the owner of 'Charlie's Organ' was traced without difficulty, but details of his aberration could not be disclosed since there was talk of making the operation illegal.

The view taken by outside commentators was that the spectacular collapse of the Opera Palace and the derision heaped on its last production had led Julian Lieberman to take his life. Saffron volunteered to sustain their opinion. As a member of the artistic circle of the exclusive Maison Blanche dining club, he had made his obsession plain. It was all he would talk about. Only his tragic death had prevented him from becoming one of the greatest patrons in the world, the Diaghilev of opera.

She was the only one to know of his close friendship with the great singer Anastasia Wagner. Her marriage to opera producer Dominic Morrison had shattered all his hopes and driven him to despair. After this rejection, he had heedlessly poured his fortune into the Opera Palace, and had seen it swept away by the unpredictable tide of critical opinion. The critics, in her view, should bear the responsibility for destroying him, for destroying the Opera

Palace, and for destroying the career of her dear friend Carla Livorno, another great singer now living quietly at her mansion in Italy.

Nick Morgan pieced together the fragments one by one. As a leading exponent of the post-feminist erotocentric analysis of late twentieth-century patriarchism, Pauline Fudge was driven by her sense of duty to set the record straight. In a long interview, reclining on one of her artefacts, she expounded the tragedy. The Opera Palace had foundered on the capricious desires of three men: Julian Lieberman, a bored playboy with cavalier charm; Andrew Broughton who used the talent of others for political preferment; and Sir Miles Mackenzie, a sad figure who should have been quietly ruminating in some professorial post. Carla Livorno had taken both of them as lovers, Andrew Broughton and Sir Miles, hoping to further her career by the traditional route, acting out a dated role-model, the indicator of female oppression.

She handed over to Nick Morgan a few stills she had taken of the dinner party, for her personal records.

'That will give you an idea of my work. I was rather proud of the dining table. Do give them back to me, won't you? Saffron doesn't know I took them. She's rather fussy about things like that.'

Stasi was in London for a few days before returning to La Scala. She had read of the collapse of the Opera Palace, and had written to Sir Miles expressing her sadness, but he had not replied. The great glass building had faded away in her memory, so that she could barely remember her dressing room. She would never sing *Tosca* again. When Nick Morgan asked her if she would be interviewed for her comments, she declined. He rang her several times, until finally she agreed to spend an hour checking his programme for musical inaccuracies. His earnestness won her over.

Nick came to her house, but refused to sit down, holding his satchel tightly to his chest. 'Hardly anyone's seen it yet,' he said, as he slipped the video-cassette into the machine in the music room. Stasi noticed that his hands were trembling. 'It's still a rough version. I might be forced to take out certain things. You never know. It's very warm in here. Do you mind if I take off my jacket?'

'Of course I don't. Don't worry, Nick.'

'You won't tell anyone you've seen it?' He heard voices outside the door. 'We'll be alone? No one else is coming in?'

'No. We won't be disturbed.'

After the first minute, Stasi froze. 'Why didn't anyone tell me? Julian Lieberman? I can't believe it.'

'Wait, wait.'

There it was, the first production. *Aida*. Sir Miles being congratulated by Princess Margaret. Ruggiero, kissing her hand. A short excerpt from *Così fan tutte*. Anastasia Wagner and Carla Livorno. Did he have to rake that up? Sir Miles, talking about his hopes. Then the three men, standing in the foyer at a first night. The outside of the Maison Blanche, a blurred figure going through the back entrance. Saffron, getting out of Julian's Maserati. One of Saffron's dinner parties, shown in a series of stills. Pauline Fudge, two gloved hands covering Andrew Broughton's eyes. Julian, his arm round Saffron's waist, whispering something in her ear. The Maison Blanche, London's most exclusive brothel. Now the film began to follow Julian. His flat in Concordia Wharf, from the outside. Julian talking, in that intimate, confident voice, then fading out as Nick took over.

'Andrew Broughton's lifestyle began to change soon after he became involved in the business interests of Julian Lieberman, who used the aliases of Giulio, Juan, Grigor, and doubtless others. Julian Lieberman, who made his first fortune from liquidating the assets of recession victims, began to broaden his horizons. An accomplished gambler, and regular visitor to Las Vegas, he teamed up with one of that city's most notorious characters, Eddie Focaccia. Eddie is presently being investigated by the FBI for a suspected connection with a worldwide drug laundering operation. Using illicit funds, Lieberman was able to successfully mount a secondary and highly profitable cash operation, manufacturing cigarettes from cheap dumped tobacco, reproducing the familiar Winchester packet, and distributing them via street traders in various former Iron Curtain cities at the inflated price such a brand commands. Recently, he diversified into Turkey . . .'

At the end of the programme, Stasi sat stunned, staring at the blank screen. 'It can't be true. Julian was a close friend of the Livorno family.'

Nick ejected the tape and shut it in his satchel. 'I got an interview with Carla Livorno. Absolutely useless. She had nothing to say. She kept on about her affair with Sir Miles, how he wanted to marry her, but how her career came first. Said she hardly knew Julian. He couldn't have been that close a friend. I'm sure you knew him better than Carla.'

'Not really.'

'But you used to see a lot of him. I've a load of press cuttings, you and he together. I don't want to fish around your private life, but if there was anything you can think of that I should say . . .'

Her first impulse was to tell him everything, then she hesitated.

'You haven't said the most important thing about Julian.'

'What's that?'

'The only reason he might have killed himself was if he had gone deaf. I've never known anybody who isn't a singer who was so passionate about opera. When he was listening, he looked like someone who had seen a vision. Transformed.'

Nick looked doubtful. 'I don't think it was suicide. But I've no way of proving it.'

'If he was a criminal, he never behaved like one.' Stasi pushed back the long hair covering her cheeks and looked straight at Nick. 'He was good to me.'

530

'You think it's OK then?' asked Nick hesitantly.

'Brilliant piece of work. Congratulations.'

'I'll never get to do a story as good.'

'Could I just say one thing, Nick?'

His expression became tense again. 'Have I got something wrong?'

'The part near the beginning, with me and Carla Livorno. It doesn't really have to be in, does it?'

'But it's what people remember about the Opera Palace.'

'It was never even true, that story. Someone invented it.'

'If it wasn't true, then I'll take it out.'

Nick Morgan's concern with 'The Nicotine Palace' had been to build up his story, brick by brick, until it turned into an unassailable bastion. With minor changes, his programme was eventually transmitted in a late-night slot devoted to issues considered too ponderous to air during the day. He would later be given a special award for services to investigative journalism. Following in his footsteps, the press and television jumped to the assault, finding byways which Nick had deemed of little consequence to his investigation.

One of Saffron's girls decided to tell her story and 'High Jinks at Mayfair Brothel' became a six-part series. There was no alternative but to close the doors of the Maison Blanche. One Sunday, a removal firm took away the more unusual furnishings. Anyone wishing to view the Mayfair residence immaculately decorated in traditional style, suitable either as a family home or for formal entertaining, was welcome to do so by making an appointment with Hampton's estate agency. From the Maison Blanche in Paris, Saffron began to prepare her libel case.

Since Sir Miles Mackenzie was refusing to answer questions, and had retreated to his family estate in Scotland, Andrew Broughton stood alone in the firing line. It was generally agreed that he behaved honourably. Few men in his position would have had the courage to admit such misguided behaviour. Not only did he offer his wife a divorce, but he tendered his resignation to the Prime Minister. Only the latter was accepted, in view of his unfortunate business partnership, but it would not prevent him being offered another post in the future.

Five years later, Anastasia Wagner came home. She stood on the steps of Covent Garden, side by side with Dominic Morrison. The new artistic director had already created controversy by insisting that her husband should direct two new productions a year. It would take several more years before her success was acknowledged. Occasionally she performed, to rekindle the fires of applause, to confirm that she was the queen of the operatic firmament. She was still nervous, still insisted that Dominic stood in the wings, refused to sing if he wasn't there. There had been times when she thought she saw a splash of violet in the darkness, when she caught sight of a face in the audience with those tangled curls, the bright mouth standing out like a red buoy in a mist-ridden sea.

The authorized biography of Anastasia Wagner omitted any reference to the Opera Palace, which had been divided into small workshops surrounding a lofty exhibition centre for the new tourist craft initiative. There was no reference to Carla Livorno amongst the students of Signora Busconi, only one reference to Paolo Livorno, the distinguished Italian opera conductor. The story of Anastasia Wagner's rise to fame centred on the loving support of her teacher, her mother Gloria, her uncle Monty, her aunt Lizzie, her talented brother Raymond and her wonderful agent, Oscar Broderick. Most of the book was devoted to the years she had spent with Dominic, their stormy beginnings which resolved into respect and harmony. There were long quotations of delirious praise from her favourite critics, descriptions of how she identified with every role she played, the occasional vocal problems with which she battled, and the impossibility of being an artist without the inspiration of love.

Stasi liked to audition every potential singer herself, even the members of the chorus. Over twenty singers had stood before her, aspiring to a contract at Covent Garden. Most of the singers she had heard came from the British Isles, but there was one from Italy who had flown over especially to see her.

The rehearsal room was empty. Only Dominic and her assistant were sitting beside her.

'Where is Lucia Pavese?'

'She's supposed to be coming.'

'Never mind. Margaret Finch has tremendous potential. Dominic, what do you think?'

'We should hear her again later on,' he replied.

They ran down the list again. There was one other close contender. Just as they were about to leave, a girl came running through the door.

'I'm so sorry I'm late,' she gasped. 'Traffic in London, *impossibile*. In five minutes, I am ready. *Momento, prego, signori.*'

Stasi took in the small figure, the blond curls, the pert nose, the fur coat slung over the shoulder, the long smooth legs, the high polished boots.

'I'm afraid the auditions are over. Could you come tomorrow?'

'No, no. Tomorrow I must depart. Please, maestra. If I do not sing to you, I kill myself.'

The pleading eyes looking into hers were not quite green, not quite brown. Thick gold chains encircled her slim neck, rings glinted on every finger. Dominic glanced quickly towards Stasi.

'OK, Lucia. We'll hear a few minutes. Go ahead . . .'

The young singer turned towards Dominic, tossed back her curls and thrust out her breasts, giving him a look which she had not given Stasi, the look which she must have given to many men before, even though she was only twenty-two. Then she opened her mouth and threw back her head, clasping her hands to her cheeks. The pure heartfelt tones of 'Ah, fors'è lui' from *La Traviata* reached to the back of the room. Then, suddenly, halfway through the aria, Stasi raised her hand and the pianist stopped.

'Lucia,' she said firmly. 'Only I sing Violetta.'

Lucia Pavese ran from the room, tears streaming down her face.

'She was by far the best we've heard today,' said Dominic. 'Why did you stop her?'

'I didn't like her middle register,' replied Stasi. 'And, besides, she didn't look right.'

She said it with such passion that Dominic looked up from the notes he had been making.

'Stasi, she's nothing like her. She can sing.'

Epilogue

Gloria craned round from her seat in the front-row stalls, scanning the packed, murmuring audience, but all she could see were the shaded lamps, red glow-worms following the sweep of the auditorium, and the occasional flash of diamonds as heads turned, signalling impatience.

'What's happening now? Where is she? I can't see her any more. She can't have gone home already. A speech, you expect a speech.'

Louis extracted a pair of spectacles from Gloria's handbag. 'Wear these. Then you can see. Look, up there.'

'I don't need those, only for reading.'

It was better now they'd put the lights on properly, now she could see her again, leaning out of a box in a low-cut dress.

'Still beautiful, my daughter. Looks younger than I did at her age. Marvellous what they can do nowadays. You'd never guess,' she said as she leaned back her head and waved towards Stasi, seeing only the vague shape of a familiar face, long neck, dark piled-up hair, and a shimmering dress.

There were two fewer Wagners than there used to be, and two more who had entered the immediate family. Raymond had married Irma, a cellist, half Jewish on the mother's side, just as well it was the right side, better late than never, and Gloria had married Louis Goldbaum the butcher, only he'd retired long ago, taken up wood-carving, lovely hobby. Monty and Lizzie, if only they could have been there. Gloria would be going soon. 'What do you expect?' she told everyone. 'At seventy-four, you know you won't last for ever, even if some of us do look ten years younger.'

Stasi had been invited to Buckingham Palace. She had had some cards printed, with the name embossed in gold. Dame Anastasia Wagner. The stage was heaped with flowers in her honour, special arrangements in tall silver vases on pillars, beautifully done like a wedding.

At fifty, Stasi had decided to retire and it was the last time she would be seen in public. The strength of her voice was still as sure as ever, its purity as unfaltering, but she wished to make her exit in her prime. Young singers she had helped to form lined up on the stage. Lucia Pavese, now a world-renowned soprano, stepped forward and blew kisses towards the box where Stasi was sitting with Dominic.

The audience clapped and stamped and shouted. She could hear them as she left the box and walked down the corridor, towards the stage. Her speech would be short. She had always hated speaking in public. People in the audience tittered when she least expected it, as though they, too, were nervous. Dominic could make them laugh, but after all this time he had been unable to teach her. If they insisted, if they refused to let her go, she might sing.

Yes, she would sing. Putting out of her mind that she would never again feel that stage beneath her feet, never again look out into the warm expectancy of an audience who knew her, loved her – some had been coming to see her for over twenty years – she clasped her hands and looked up towards Dominic, leaning forwards out of the box, smiling at her. Even now, she felt a surge of energy in the presence of the man whose grey hair she scarcely registered. She was back in his Paris apartment, remembering the first, torrential release of passion. *Fors'è lui*.

Afterwards, they would argue. Even with a slight loss of power, Anastasia Wagner was incomparable. Those who had been present at *La Traviata* in the Salle des Arts Modernes insisted that her performance then had been a turning point. Hearing her now was like resurrecting a memory. Singers nowadays would never recreate that electrifying sound. But Stasi was oblivious of the voice of criticism. She was there just to remind them. I, Anastasia Wagner, am a singer.

At the end of the aria, she bowed her head, fought back the tears, looked round the brilliantly lit auditorium and opened her arms to the audience. Lucia Pavese ran on stage and placed a simple bouquet of country flowers at her feet. Then Stasi took her by the hand and led her downstage. Unclasping her tiny silver crucifix, she placed it round Lucia's slender neck, pushing up the blond curls framing her face.

'I've worn it onstage ever since my first performance,' she said. 'Not for luck. But to remind myself not to be nervous. Even if you don't need it, I'd like you to have it.'

The lights dimmed long enough for Stasi to make her exit. When they came up again, the audience remained seated, staring at the empty stage, unable to believe that she had gone.

Ruggiero Gasparini and a host of friends were the first to appear in the foyer. The doorman still recognized him, though his voice had been silent for many years, and hurried to open the door. He was carefully lowering himself into his limousine when a woman tapped him on the back.

'*Ruggiero! Dammi un bacio.*'

So many people to greet, at an occasion like this. All the old faces lighting up, coming close, recognizing one another, exchanging reassurances that they would meet again in the future. Ruggiero had begun to smile before he was able to put a name to the face. Presenting his cheek, he waited for a kiss, having glimpsed enough of the features through the carefully shaded make-up to realize that she was of a certain age, wearing a long fur coat which looked as though it had shared much of her life. One of the many women from his past, *senz'altro*. He would always be gallant.

537

'Lovely to see you, *cara*,' he replied.

The woman prevented the chauffeur from closing the door. 'You've forgotten who I am, Ruggiero,' she said teasingly. 'Or you're pretending. Carla Livorno, Marchesa della Robbia.'

'My God! Of course. Daughter of my dear friend Paolo. May he rest in peace. Forgive me. I am overcome with emotion. Wasn't she spectacular? Dear Anastasia. What a joy, that voice, still so wonderful. You are coming to the party?'

'Of course I am,' Carla replied instantly.

She had known there must be a reception, somewhere. Unfortunately she had no idea where it would be. Carla glanced behind her as though looking for someone. 'Shall we go together? My chauffeur hasn't arrived.'

Ruggiero was doubtful. There were six people already crammed into the back of the car. Then he smiled again. 'We all squeeze up. Come, everybody. My dear friend Carla.'

She pushed herself in beside Ruggiero. A young man with the impassive face of a Californian surfer, and eyes of a crystalline blue, came forward and stood awkwardly.

'Where do I sit, Carla?'

'In the front, next to the driver. Ruggiero, this is Duane.'

'What a beautiful young man. Like his mother!'

As they drove towards Highgate, Carla attempted to redraw the dark line round her lips with a scarlet pencil, peering in a small mirror.

'I don't know how I'm going to tell her, Ruggiero, but Duane lost the tickets and they wouldn't let us in. All I heard was the clapping. What did she sing?'

'Violetta. "Ah fors'è lui", what else? And she was like a young girl of twenty. A moment of history. My dear Carla, it's disgraceful. Why didn't I know you were in England? You should have come to my box.'

Carla folded up the mirror and replaced it with the lip-pencil in a bag which was unfashionably large and worn at

538

the edges. 'She'd be so upset to think I'd missed out on her last appearance. Still, I won't say anything.'

The house in Highgate was full of Stasi's friends, but Carla recognized none of them. Once, she would have been on smiling terms with all the leading names in the tight-knit world of opera. Even Dominic, who stared for a moment, failed to recognize her.

'This meant to be a party?' said Duane, stuffing down something which looked suspiciously like home-made grandma food. 'Where's the beat? Don't I get to dance?'

Carla scowled. 'This is a formal occasion. Isn't this house so English? Perfect taste. I expect she had someone fix it up.'

'Better than your place.'

'Different style, but you wouldn't understand. Didn't I tell you that the English worship Palladio, ignorant boy? Let's go find her. Don't say anything about the tickets.'

'Never mind. I got a good price for them, so now we can stay somewhere decent,' said Duane with a smirk.

A voice from Sydney Australia hurled itself in Carla's direction. 'Hey, blow me if it isn't Carla!'

Grace was still singing. She'd gone over to Wagner and stayed there. Carla was not in a mood to answer questions.

'I appear now and then, but only with the right producer,' she replied loftily when Grace enquired if she, too, had stayed the course.

'I'm so glad Stasi asked you to come, really I am. We're nearly all here, class of Amelia Busconi. How about that?'

Duane ambled up to Carla's side. Resigning himself to another evening on duty, he adopted his usual pose, his hands stuck in the pockets of his studded jeans, legs slightly apart.

'And I see you've brought your son. Quite a dish. He should meet my daughter.'

'I wish she'd cut it out,' Duane remarked grumpily, as Carla guided him in the direction of the group surrounding Stasi.

'She's only jealous. With a face like a pudding, who can

blame her?' replied Carla, craning her neck to try and catch Stasi's eye. It was over an hour before they met.

'Stasi, you were wonderful, just wonderful. I came over specially. You didn't think I'd miss the old girls' reunion?' Carla glanced over her shoulder at a life-sized painting of Stasi reclining on a littered, bloodstained deathbed. 'I guess that's what they were all expecting, Violetta. I had to see you sing that again.'

'Oh?' Stasi was trying not to cast a critical eye over Carla's unfashionable figure-hugging dress, the over-heavy antique jewels laden round her throat, her wrists, her fingers, the puckering around the cleavage of her breasts. 'You never came to Paris, when I sang it there.'

'Didn't I? I must have done. I wouldn't have missed that for the world. Just because I couldn't come back-stage . . .'

'But you saw me in every performance of *Tosca*. Except you weren't needed. Eva Marton took over, if I remember.' Stasi stopped herself abruptly. 'We shouldn't talk about the past. Even though I didn't invite you, it's good that you came. Now we can just think back on the good times.'

'You're not like me. You forgive. I can see you do.'

'I can hate too.'

'But not for long. You never had a talent for it. Always far too soft with Baron Scarpia. Tosca wasn't your best role.'

'I don't understand why you came, Carla. To make me feel guilty I didn't invite you?'

'Just to say how much I've always admired you.'

'You said that once before. Envied my voice, you mean.'

'The same, almost the same. If you admire something enough, you ache to possess it. Call it envy, if you like.'

'If you love someone, you let them be. My voice is me, it isn't a thing.'

'Sorry, Stasi. Wrong libretto. I never did understand love and sacrifice. That's your department.' Carla looked round distractedly, noticed Duane in the distance and beckoned to him. 'Remember the Villa degli Spiriti? I'm still there. With my boy.'

'And married again, I imagine,' Stasi said, not unkindly.

'Jesus, once was enough. Duane, come meet Stasi.'

Duane stood to attention and kissed her hand, then, looking straight into her eyes, he flashed a brilliant smile which vanished as soon as Stasi turned to Carla.

'One thing I do envy you, having had a son. I was always too frightened that having a child would change my voice, even though they say it doesn't. And I wanted Dominic to myself. Isn't that terrible?'

Carla pushed back a wave of hair which was hanging over Duane's face. 'Same colour. He could be my son. But take a look at those gorgeous blue eyes. Not Livorno eyes.'

'House-boy,' said Duane, shaking back his hair to its original position over his eyes. 'Isn't that what they say?'

'You say. I don't.' Carla gave him a frosty look and turned her attention to Stasi. The remnant of a previous row was apparent in her resentful tone. 'He hasn't grown up enough to be grateful.'

'One hell of a mean bitch is Carla,' said Duane, as though appealing to Stasi. 'Know something? It was her idea. There were all these guys waiting outside the opera house, waving money at us. She made me sell the tickets for your farewell show so we could stay some place with room service. Even though I know she's really loaded.'

Before Stasi could register her disbelief, Carla waved him aside.

'Kids are so thoughtless. Someone offered him ten times the price, and the silly monkey sold them behind my back.'

'She's lying through her teeth. And they're not even hers.'

'Duane! I don't want to see you again. Get your arse out of here.' He turned on his heel, and began to stride off towards the hall. 'I didn't mean it! Come back.'

Stasi looked at her with horror. 'Carla, let him go. Why did you bring him? Who is he?'

She was attempting an impish smile, but it looked forced, as though she was trying to hide her pain. 'Duane's in a bad mood – hates England because they don't have beaches like Santa Monica. But he'll change his mind when we're in the sack. At least he keeps me young.'

Stasi looked round anxiously, but Duane was still in the room, leaning against the door jamb, staring moodily at the floor.

'Don't worry, Stasi, he won't insult your guests. Only me. He thinks it's cute. You know what kids are like.'

Taking her firmly by the arm, Stasi led her past Duane. 'Let's go into one of the other rooms.'

The only empty space Stasi could find was in her studio, which no one had dared enter. Carla fingered a music stand, and edged round the Boesendorfer piano (hers, the present from Maurizio, had been sold long ago).

'Remember Pa's studio in Milan? Half the size of this. And I thought it was enormous.'

Stasi grinned. 'So did I.' She watched Carla moving round the room, peering at the busts of composers, the trophies from foreign tours, costumes hanging behind glass, as though she was worshipping at a shrine. Then she went over to a bank of gold-framed photographs covering one wall. She recognized some of the familiar faces, the ones who'd been friends of Emily and Paolo; others she didn't know. Then she gave a delighted squeal.

'Say! There's us two larking around in Fiesole. I remember that picture. Rico took it, at rehearsals. Didn't we have a great time? Isn't that Assunta Melati in the background there? Don't we look cute? You don't look so different, even now.' Carla's face lit up, her grey-green eyes danced with mischief, as they had then. 'Are you really retiring, Stasi? So young?'

'I've been a professional singer for over twenty-five years. Don't you think that's enough?'

'You're just about ready for Wagner now. Jesus, I forgot.'

'I don't sing Wagner,' they said in unison, and then they collapsed into giggles.

'And you?' said Stasi, as their laughter died away and they stood looking at one another. 'We'll have to wait a few years before your final performance. Am I right?'

Carla pushed back her head and struck a dramatic pose, one arm resting on her breast, the other pointing upwards, fingers outstretched. 'I've decided to make way for the young ones. They say I look just like Lucia Pavese.' Suddenly she dropped her arms by her side, and screwed up her eyes. 'Say, is there a bathroom around here? I keep having this goddamned pain in the gut.'

'Come with me. Don't worry.'

'The journey was terrible, Stasi. It's late. I'm not usually out this late, you know, living in the country. I'd better find Duane. It was true about the tickets – I told him not to say anything. Only I found myself . . . you know . . . London's got so expensive. But I wanted to hear you, Stasi. And say hi. And then I met Ruggiero, haven't seen him for years, and he said I could come along. He was always so generous. Hope you don't mind . . .'

Stasi offered Carla her car and driver, but she refused.

'When you're next in Italy, you will drop by? Stay maybe? There's lots of room at the villa. It's only half an hour from Milan, remember? You don't have to call up first – I won't be far away. Or you can always send a card – tell me what you're up to.'

Gloria was waiting to leave at the front door, Louis was bringing the car round, just as Stasi was kissing goodbye to someone, knew the face, used to be on the telly years ago. 'Ice-cream commercial,' she whispered loudly to Raymond, standing by her side. 'You know the one. What's the name? Italian girl. Friend of Stasi's.'

'Don't ask me.'

'Dreadful. My memory. Bound to be someone famous.

543

I never forget a face. Come on, you must know, Raymond.'

Raymond watched the woman with the stiff curls and ancient fur coat strutting down the drive, followed at a distance by a young man with his thumbs stuck in the pockets of what appeared to be jeans.

'Didn't she do the catering?' he said.

'Catering? You call that catering? No, no, that's not her. Never mind, I'll ask later.' Gloria tapped Stasi on the shoulder. 'Come on, darling, say goodbye to your mother. We're going home. Such a wonderful evening.'

Early the following morning, when Dominic was still asleep, Stasi crept down to the music room, and searched for a score. Bartok, Beethoven, Bellini, Berg, Berlioz, Bizet. *Carmen* – Opéra Comique by Georges Bizet. It had remained unopened all that time, the pages brown-speckled and yellowing, the faded ink on the frontispiece just discernible: Mary Garden.

Then she took down the photograph which Carla had admired, pulled it out of the frame and wrote on the back: 'For Carla with love from Stasi. Happiness. Fiesole.' She left the score and the photograph on the desk for her secretary. When she arrived, Stasi would ask her to find the full address. The Marchesa della Robbia, Villa degli Spiriti. Somewhere in the Franciacorte region, not far from Bergamo.

THE END